PRAISE FOR **ADVENTURES OF V**

With a few brush strokes, Reid creates a whole world. It's like magic –
the reader is sucked into that world, instantaneously. V swirls us into an
extravaganza, a detailed, delightful, dystopic, alien, familiar future – primal,
ferocious, and gratifying.
– Susan S. Senstad, author of *Milk and Venom* and *Music for the Third Ear*

Vivacious, vampish, victorious, voluptuous, vibrant, villainous … An
eternal 19-year-old, gorgeous vampire, monster-vixen named "V" – a pagan
Goddess, reborn as a super-heroine beauty who lives off the blood of the
bad, to rescue the souls of the good. Irresistible hijinks!
– Ed Cowen, producer, impresario

A wild ride into adventure, fantasy, and chills, V gifted me with glimpses of
arcane current and historical knowledge. Not for years have novels been as
much fun and enlightening.
– Chuck Shamata, actor

Utterly engrossing, rich, dark, and deep, Gilbert Reid creates worlds within
worlds of vivid, bold adventure.
– Bernice Landry, artist

Gilbert Reid's prose is so sensuous and evocative! When he takes you down
unfamiliar paths, and into situations that excite suspension of disbelief, you
follow him because the energy of V' s personality is so witty and alluring,
she charms you into the universe the author has created. Vivid, complex,
wildly imaginative.
– Diana Leblanc, actor, director

PRAISE FOR OTHER BOOKS BY GILBERT REID

PRAISE FOR OTHER BOOKS BY GILBERT REID

PRAISE FOR *LAVA AND OTHER STORIES*

Very powerful, poetic and nasty and tough.
– Anna Porter, novelist, author, journalist

The writing is terrific. The characters are glamorous, decayed, old, young, loved, unloved. Reid inhabits each one. His raw, elegant prose, his vivid and sensuous images leave one breathless, with recognition and terror.
– Diana Leblanc, actor, director

The women, how they speak, what they confide, and omit, what they expose about each other! It's as if only sexuality happened that summer.
– Susan S. Senstad, author of *Milk and Venom* and *Music for the Third Ear*

PRAISE FOR SO *THIS IS LOVE: LOLLIPOP AND OTHER STORIES*

Reid's stories are in the great traditions of Alice Munro or Mavis Gallant.
– Margaret Macmillan, historian, author

Powerfully rendered and suspenseful.
– Joyce Carol Oates, author of *Night. Sleep. Death. The Stars*

An unerring and compelling examination of aggression and compassion.
– *The Vancouver Sun*

One of the 100 best books of the year.
– *The Globe & Mail*

VAMPIRE
CLONE

ADVENTURES OF V: VOLUME 2
"The Goddess is back. Her hour has come."
– Jules Cashford

VAMPIRE CLONE

by
GILBERT REID

TWIN RIVERS
PRODUCTIONS

Issued in print and electronic formats
ISBN 978-0-9953108-8-9: *Vampire Clone:* Paperback
ISBN 978-0-9953108-9-6: *Vampire Clone:* EPUB
ISBN 978-1-9994790-0-8: *Vampire Clone:* Kindle
ISBN 978-1-7773141-1-8: *Vampire Clone:* Amazon paperback

Cover and text design by Counterpunch Inc. / Linda Gustafson
Illustrations by Niki9door

Published by
Twin Rivers Productions
20 Bloor Street East
PO Box 75070
Toronto, Ontario, M4W 3T3

To receive a free book or novella, sign up at:
https://gilbertreid.com

This book is dedicated to my parents:
Jean Thyrza Reid, and James Waddington Reid

If you wrestle with monsters, take care! You too may become a monster.

   – FRIEDRICH NIETZSCHE

CONTENTS

CAST OF CHARACTERS

Aimi Hosokawa – Japanese microbiologist, Sabrina Jacob's lover

Alexandra Anders – German-Swedish actress, mother of Sabrina Jacobs

Alex Wolf – American microbiologist, once married to Judy

Avatar – V's double, her soul, to be evoked in emergencies

Big Boy – Nightclub owner with Little Boy, rapist, sadist, murderer

Claire – non-scientific name for the 14-year-old female Clone

Clone – 14-year-old girl, created by Sabrina Jacobs from V's DNA

Crystal – mechanism left on earth, the World-Destroyer

David Stanford Adams III – sleuth, working for Sabrina Jacobs

Dmitry Pavlov – Russian Oligarch, CEO of Bio-Prom

Duncan – Captain of the research ship Andromeda

Geoffrey James – high UK security official, possibly Home Office

Helen of Troy – ex-lawyer, stripper, real name Helen Guerrera

Ian – Chief Engineer of the research ship Andromeda

Jean-Pierre Emmanuel François Saint-Poix Junior – A Parisian clochard

Jed Baker – Cambridge UK criminologist, friend of Sabrina Jacobs

Joseph Rothschild – Chief Financial Officer of Andromeda Corp

Juan Rodriguez Alvarez – Mexican drug lord, targeted by V

Little Boy – Nightclub owner with Big Boy, rapist, sadist, murderer

Marcus – V's mentor, father & controller, from the Andromeda galaxy

Old Bess – cook for Sir Alfred Jacobs and Alexandra Anders

Ralph – watchman at the Holy Beatitude Storage Warehouse

Sabrina Jacobs – British molecular biologist, CEO of Andromeda Corp

Sally Blake – Psychologist, monitoring the Clone for Sabrina

Sergei Pavlov – Russian Oligarch, brother of Dmitry Pavlov

Sir Alfred Jacobs – Nobel Laureate geneticist, father of Sabrina Jacobs

Sonia – A Russian scientist, works for Dmitry Pavlov

Tania – Russian, skipper of the *Zeus*, an Andromeda Corp launch

Toni Anderson – Scientist, working for Andromeda Corporation

V – Ancient Phoenician, vampire superheroine, shield of humanity

PART ONE – THE BEAST

CHAPTER 1 – CRUCIFIXION

Christ! They'd crucified the woman!

It was midnight, July 11, 2059, in southern California. A thick, sultry sea-borne fog pressed against the windows of Andromeda Corporation's giant Boeing 777 Super Cargo.

When he entered the cavernous hold of the aircraft, Freddy Bokhari's face glistened, wet from mist and rain. Shaking drops off his windbreaker, he rushed to a window, pressed his fingers against the glass, and peered out. It was like an old-fashioned black-and-white film set! The tarmac shone black and silver. Security people were running every which way. Floodlights had been set up. Armored cars and two tanks stood on guard where the prisoner's cage had been unloaded. The atmosphere was electric. Wow! He would never forget this moment. Freddy Bokhari was seventeen years old.

The pilot's business-like voice announced over the intercom, "Buckle up, ready for takeoff." Freddy sat down, his back to the wall, locked the seat belt, put his pistol in his lap.

Then, finally, he dared steal a glance at the prisoner. She was in the metal cage on the opposite side of the hold. She hung, suspended, her ankles, wrists, and neck manacled, from a wall of steel.

Yeah, they'd totally crucified the woman!

The engines revved up. Instructions were given. The aircraft began to move. But Security Guard Second Class Freddy Bokhari – on the first real summer job of his life – just stared, hypnotized, at the sight across from him. It was like an old painting by ... by ... he couldn't remember the guy's name ...

A guy who crucified people in paint ...

People in cages, bodies, bits, fragments of flesh, carved into slabs of meat ...

Bacon, Francis Bacon ...

Inside the massive, steel-barred cage, lit by floodlights and pinned to the wall of steel, the prisoner was spread-eagled – a butterfly on a corkboard – an anatomical specimen, vivisected, splayed out, displayed, on a wall of glass in a museum.

Her mouth was jammed open with a steel-and-rubber ball gag. She was stretched tight – every muscle straining – against the steel, her wrists, ankles, and neck locked in place by those thick gleaming steel manacles.

The woman's skintight black wetsuit, streaked with drying mud, sculpted her breasts and ribcage, belly and thighs, with the anatomical clarity of a Renaissance crucifixion scene, or one of those 3-D recreations of sculptures by Bernini or Michelangelo: every lineament, every line …

Might as well have been naked.

Freddy swallowed; he licked his lips.

Patterned in black-and-green camouflage, the woman's face shone with the savage beauty of a wild beast. The eyes searched, searched, searched, desperately searched. Against the matte war paint, the whites of her eyes glowed, wild and frantic. Freddy thought of a poem his teacher, Ms. Keller, had made him memorize.

Tiger, tiger, burning bright
In the forests of the night,
What immortal hand or eye
Could frame thy fearful symmetry?

In what distant deeps or skies
Burnt the fire of thine eyes?
On what wings dare he aspire?
What the hand dare seize the fire?

Saliva drooled from a corner of the gagged mouth. It gleamed – bright silver in the floodlights, the glittering string dripping to her collarbone, painting a smeared, glossy sheen on her breasts. Freddy blinked. The whole thing was sadistic – erotic, awesome, orgasmic! He took a deep breath. What was she feeling? What was she thinking, this demonic dream? It was as if she had arisen out of one of his midnight fantasies – out of a video game dungeon – out of a sadomasochistic scenario from some torrid, sweaty night, flicking through porno on the Net.

Within minutes, the plane was in the air.

Freddy relaxed.

He had not been told much, except that the woman was a very special prisoner – and extremely dangerous.

As he sat there, he flipped through an electronic *Maxim* magazine, but he kept his pistol ready, cradled in his lap. He was directly opposite the cage, so he could keep a close eye on the woman. She was much sexier – in an unsettling way – than any centerfold from those antique hard copy men's magazines he collected.

The other guards, the professionals, using multiple camera links, were watching the woman from the forward cabin, where the seats were comfortable.

"Guards are redundant," Freddy's boss Dave De Blasio said. "We're frills. There's no way that woman can escape. Sit back and enjoy the show, Freddy!"

The flight plan would take them from the southern California airbase just outside San Diego to the Virginia Headquarters of Sabrina Jacob's giant bio-technology firm, Andromeda Corp. The plane had been reserved just for this one lady prisoner.

Freddy stole a glance at the woman. Underneath the camouflage makeup, her face, even distorted by the gag, was perfect – classy, symmetrical, and, somehow, friendly. A stunner! The eyes were large, soulful. And, as for the body, well, in Freddy's opinion, this lady was a knockout, really stacked. *Wow!* She had, as they used to say, *a body to die for.*

Freddy was super successful with the girls at school. He was a charmer, and he knew it – in fact, he knew, from experience, he was irresistible. And he really liked girls – as people – so, naturally, he wondered what this beauty had done – or what she *was* – that made Sabrina Jacobs and Andromeda Corp want her so bad.

Ten minutes after takeoff, Freddy's curiosity got the better of him. He tried to catch the prisoner's eye. He waved at her timidly.

She was gagged, of course, and couldn't talk. But her eyes instantly focused. She blinked, staring directly at him. Her eyes, pools of darkness, *bored* into his soul – and he *heard* her say – *heard* was the only word for it – he *heard* her say, *inside* his head: "*I'm awfully sorry, Freddy, but I'm not feeling especially friendly right now.*"

Awfully sorry …

He *heard* her speak – in his head.

And with a classy British accent, or so it seemed to Freddy.

Awfully sorry … Awfully sorry, Freddy …

Freddy … How the hell did she know his name?

That had been 15 minutes ago.

Doctor Toni Anderson, an Andromeda Corporation molecular biologist, came into the hold. She was a real pretty lady, cute, pert, friendly. She had short blond hair and the bluest eyes. She paced back and forth in front of the cage, staring at the woman. She turned to Freddy. "Amazing, isn't it, really amazing!"

"Amazing?" Freddy stared. What was amazing?

"She's not human. But look at her – so real, so beautiful, and so seemingly human!"

"Yeah, yeah, I see." Freddy didn't see at all. Beautiful, yeah; but *not human* – what did that mean? She sure looked human – 150% human!

A few minutes later, Tom Riley sauntered into the hold. Riley, in Freddy's humble opinion, was a total jerk. He started teasing – no, *torturing* – the prisoner. Riley was one of the Andromeda Corp so-called psychologists. But he was a bully, an asshole. He called Freddy "kid," twisting the word into a taunting sneer. He told off one of the junior guys in a really nasty way – in front of everybody. How this idiot could be a *psychologist* – for Christ's sake! Why he was allowed to work for a classy company like Andromeda Corp, Freddy for the life of him couldn't figure out.

Riley scraped a metal cup along bars of the cage. *Clack, clack, clack!* The idiot was taunting the woman.

"You're an animal!"

"Just a total animal!"

"A she-devil, that's what you are!"

"The beast, the beast!" Riley laughed and clattered the cup: *clack, clack, clack …*

Freddy blinked at the man. Was Riley drunk?

"Stop that, Tom!" Toni laid her hand on Riley's arm.

Riley shook her off. "You're a sniveling idiot, Toni. You're a stupid dreamer. This beast will be a real happy camper when I give her an injection of this little silver bullet," he said. He held up a needle. "Silver nitrate! Triple dose! She won't even be able to whimper!"

"Cut it out, Tom!"

"It's a *thing*, not a person!"

"Tom!"

"Did you ever work with the thing's Clone? I mean, talk about animal! The Clone's a pure raging animal, an obscenity, no mind at all."

"That's not true, Tom, the Clone was brilliant – it's just that –"

"It's a mindless savage beast, a killing machine, like its mother here! Hey, you! Hey *Thing! You Thing*, hey!" He smashed the cup against the bars.

WHAM!

"Come on, Tom, for Christ's sake! She does have a mind, you know."

"You are a softie, Toni. You'd cuddle a rattlesnake! When I give the little beastie a shot of this, she'll be a rubber doll, unable to think her way out of a paper bag! Isn't that right, *Thing*?"

"God damn it, Tom!"

Riley edged close to the cage. He grinned and held up the *needle*, squirting it to see that there were no air bubbles ... and that was when ...

That was when ...

That was when ... Freddy was really mad. Why the hell would even an asshole like Riley tease somebody who was *helpless*, particularly a *woman*?

... and that was when he saw a sort of blur in the cage ... and ...

That was when ...

The "woman" turned into a sort of ... *reptile* ... a she-demon, a *thing*.

Christ!

"Hey!" Freddy dropped *Maxim*, gripped his pistol, and jumped out of his seat.

WHAM!

Metal flew everywhere.

The *thing* burst out of the manacles. It rushed straight at him, like a bolt of lightning, through – *through* – the bars of the cage. The bars disintegrated, pieces went flying. Bits careened like shrapnel, cutting chunks out of the fuselage.

Air whooshed out.

One of the bars, Freddy saw out of the corner of his eye, cut Doctor Anderson in half – Jesus! Her body went flying, in two pieces!

The *thing* twisted Tom Riley's neck right around – it was a blur – Riley must have been dead before he knew what hit him.

Wind roared. Pressure plunged.

Freddy had his arm up to shoot, but the *thing* swept his arm aside, snapping his bones. The pistol went off.

"*Sorry*," the *thing* said, in Freddy's mind. It was still wearing the gag, but somehow ... it spoke ....

Sorry!

Other guards came rushing in from the second hold. One of them had a submachine gun. He let fly with a burst of fire ... He missed.

She was above him, on the ceiling – then … she *swooped* …

His head was gone – an explosion of blood and bone.

Another guy went flying, and smashed against the roof. It looked like the guy's neck was broken. And the last guy, Dave De Blasio, Freddy's boss, nice guy too, a friend of Freddy's dad, the guy who'd arranged for Freddy to have this "cushy" job, well, she took a swipe at him with her claws, and his head was gone, in a geyser of blood. *Jesus Christ Almighty!*

Not even a single bullet got near her – the *thing*.

Freddy saw all this like it was in slow-motion; the pain from his broken arm began to penetrate his consciousness.

Freddy tried to get the pistol into his left hand; the woman – or *thing*, or whatever she was, was suddenly in front of him. She gazed at him, this reptile creature – and she snapped that arm too and threw the pistol away.

"*Sorry, Freddy,*" she said, projecting the words directly into his head, her head tilted to one side, looking sad somehow.

The plane was trembling and jerking.

The *thing* – the *She-Devil* – whatever it was – went forward, toward the cockpit. Freddy collapsed back into his chair. The pain was excruciating. He tried to buckle in – he couldn't. His arms hung useless, his hands were paralyzed, didn't belong to him anymore.

After what seemed like an hour of agony – or was it an instant – the reptile woman – the *thing* – was back.

Freddy shrank into his seat. Now this *thing* – this woman – was going to kill him.

"I'd help you, Freddy," she said, straight into his mind, "but there's no time. I'm sorry."

I'm sorry – Jesus! God, the pain was awful!

The engines screamed, a weird, whining shriek. The plane was headed down. It was bucking, vibrating, trembling. Freddy flew out of his seat and, as he tumbled down the hold, in a fog of pain and terror, he screamed, "Christ, we're going to crash; we're going to die!"

The *thing* smashed her claw against a door. The door popped out and disappeared. Air whooshed. The *thing* looked back at Freddy, sprawled, helpless, against the bulkhead. Yeah, it was true: She was beautiful – shimmering green, turquoise, and gold. The light gleamed on her claws. She nodded and jumped! She jumped from the fucking airplane!

How high were they?

Sprawled in a tangle against the side of the hold, Freddy wondered if, with both arms broken, he could get on a parachute and jump, if there was time enough and he could …

The *thing* had said there was no time.

And there wasn't – *there was no time.*

Four minutes later, the Boeing plowed into the desert full tilt, nose first, at about a thirty-five-degree angle, and at almost 500 miles per hour.

The desert was lit up by a gigantic thunderous flash – pieces flew, scattered over a half a mile – the boom echoed for perhaps twenty-five miles. Fires burned here and there, for a time; and then all was again darkness, and silence.

"We'll give it a couple of more passes – expand the radius."

"Roger, expand the radius."

"Could anybody have survived the crash?"

"You kidding? No, of course not."

It was four hours after the crash. Sunrise was an hour away. Three helicopters skimmed low over the desert. Their sensors – visual, infrared, and bio-detectors – scanned the sand, the pebbles, and the scrub. The drones – twelve of them – had spread out below, but they were already heading back to base. Floodlights under the copters lit up the desert floor. But there was, apparently, nothing to see down there – no sign of human life, or anything resembling human life.

If – and it was a huge *if* – the prisoner had survived the crash, where would she have headed, in which direction? There were no bio-signatures or thermal or morphological abnormalities that would indicate the prisoner's presence.

As daylight spread over the desert, the helicopters again swooped low over the scrub and sand and pebbles, looking for a visual sighting – a lone woman, or a reptilian creature the size of a woman, anywhere within a fifteen-mile radius of the crash site.

There was nothing. The sun beat down, the heat rose; it was soon over 100 degrees. The lead pilot, an ex-military man, Jimmy Hawks, clicked on the mike. "Let's go back in. The big boss is coming tonight. She'll decide what to do. We'll send out ground teams later. But, personally, I figure there's nothing out there."

It was dark, twenty-three hours after the crash, approaching midnight. Andromeda Corp CEO's helicopter hovered over the crash site. Floodlights, set up on the ground, lit up the biggest hunks of wreckage. A temporary laboratory had been set up, with tents and trucks and tractor-trailers. From above, it looked like an army base – or maybe a giant film set.

"Sabrina, nobody could survive that." Henry Rothschild's face was ashen. He stared at the scattered bits of aircraft. Chief Financial Officer of Andromeda Corporation, Henry was a distinguished, pale, tall, gray-haired Scotsman in his mid-70s, a pillar of the New York and London and Shanghai financial establishments.

"So, you think the creature is dead." Sabrina glanced at Henry. The day had begun so well! Just hours ago in New York City, 8-year-old Alice Kelly had woken up, her eyes clear, her skin already gaining color, and able to breathe. A cure for cystic fibrosis had at last been discovered. Sabrina was ticking them off, one by one, her victories over human weakness, over human suffering, over human disease. In the end, Sabrina Jacobs would conquer death itself. Humans would become immortal. She would make them so.

But now this – a disaster, an utter disaster! Her face reflected darkly in the helicopter window, she scanned the wreckage. Already a Nobel Prize Laureate, Sabrina was thirty-four years old, and looked twenty-five. Her blond hair was cut short. She had a perfect tan, and an intelligence that was – as she well knew – too sharp and too quick for her own good. "Well, I for one am sure she's still alive," she murmured. She slammed her fist on her thigh. "Damn it! I *know* she's alive. I *feel* it! I don't know how she did it, or where she is, but the damned thing is alive."

"I doubt it, Sabrina."

"Destroy a whole airplane! How did she do it? A Boeing 777 for Christ's sake!"

"God knows!"

"Fuck! Fuck! Fuck!" Sabrina twisted her lips. "I needed the beast alive! Our work with the Clone is a horrendous fiasco. I need the prototype, the original."

"She's a woman of infinite resource."

"Woman! *Woman!* God damn it, Henry. She's a monster, a freak, a deadly beast, not a woman, Henry, she is not human; she's a shape-changer, an animal, a dangerous, deadly animal; she's not even an animal, she's … a reptile … she's a … a … a … *thing!* She's a … a …"

Sabrina took a deep breath. To have the greatest resource – the greatest source of genetic material on the planet – a unique combination of *human and alien* – and then to have it escape, or be destroyed! It was, as some Frenchman said about something Napoleon did, "Worse than a crime; it was a mistake."

"She's a what, Sabrina?"

"Alien. She's an alien. Her DNA is alien – literally not of this world."

"Half her DNA is alien."

"Yes, her father's."

"But her mother was human."

"Sure, human! Her mother was human – thousands of years ago! And, Henry, there's another thing – the modifications. The human side of her DNA – her mother's DNA – had been radically modified, certainly by the aliens. Her mother was no longer human. So the human side counts for little; it's a mask, a disguise, a facade, a trick. She's a Trojan Horse, an invader."

"Yes, the modifications …" Henry sighed. "But we know all this; why rehearse it?"

"Because, Henry, you – gentle idealistic soul that you are – you want to *talk* to her. You want to look *deep* into her beautiful eyes, and *reason* with her – no, with *it!* You are a fool, my dear Henry, a wonderful, generous fool, but a fool: there is *nothing* in those eyes. You might as well reason with a cobra."

"Well …"

"Admit it! You are *fascinated* by the creature; you talk about it as if it were …"

"Are you jealous?" Henry raised an eyebrow and tilted his head, allowing himself a sly smile.

Sabrina paused, then laughed and punched him on the shoulder. She leaned over and kissed him on the cheek. "Dear Uncle Henry, I've killed people for saying less!"

Their helicopter landed, throwing up a cloud of dust.

"Doctor Jacobs, there's another sandstorm coming in," said the pilot, a 45-year-old black ex-fighter pilot, hard lean muscles, and close-cropped curly gray hair; and, behind his goggles, sensitive brown eyes. "We should get out of here in an hour, not more."

"Right!" Sabrina was unbuckling. "Thanks!"

As Sabrina and Henry came to the door, they saw, through the swirling downdraft of the rotor blades, team members on the ground running toward the helicopter, shouting, "Hello, there, hello!"

Climbing out of the helicopter, Sabrina ducked from the spinning rotors and shielded her eyes from the swirling dust. Henry, distinguished as always in a dark blue pinstripe Savile Row suit, thanked the pilot, and followed Sabrina, raising one hand to cover his eyes from the glare of the floodlights.

Set up around the central crash site, the lights made the whole place garish and unreal, a stage set for a video game.

The lead investigator ran over, protecting his eyes from the glare and from the dust that rose from the helicopter's slowing rotors. Sabrina and Henry shook his hand. He was a tanned, lean, tough-looking man with a broken nose; he had narrow blue eyes, a trimmed white mustache and close-cropped white hair under his baseball cap. His name tag said, "Alan Carr."

"Well?"

"We've found fragments of twelve bodies so far – eight men and four women." Carr paused. "It's not easy. The bodies were blown apart by the crash. Some of the bodies may have been ripped apart before the crash."

Sabrina glanced at Henry. He could see her thinking: So she's human, huh? You're going to talk to her, huh? You're going to reason with her, huh?

"And the women, have you got identities?"

"Yes, we've got DNA matches: Andrea and Toni – and a flight attendant, Sally Sachs, and Joy Shanthini, an Andromeda Corporation paleontologist, who had hitched a ride back to Virginia."

Sabrina turned to Henry; she bit lip. "Henry, I'm sorry. But there you go! Toni Anderson was your favorites."

"Yes," Henry nodded.

Sabrina held his gaze. Henry looked paler than usual; though it might be the glare and the dust. Maybe the reality of the situation – death, the Grim Reaper, in the form of the monster alien – was finally getting to him.

"And I think Toni had a crush on you. You were a father figure for her, a mentor."

"Maybe."

"So, are you going to tell her parents – or shall I?"

"I'll do it, Sabrina, I'll do it."

Sabrina stared at him. "And you'll tell them that the brightest star of the family, the little girl who could, the little girl who graduated from

Princeton, Moscow, and London, the brightest young molecular biologist, the prettiest –"

"Enough, Sabrina, enough!"

"You are right! I'm an idiot! I'm sorry, Henry." Sabrina turned away, rubbed her eyes. "I'm really ranting at myself, Henry, not at you. This disaster is my fault. I'm the one that insisted we capture the creature, that we transport it, that … I'm an idiot. But I get so angry when I stop to think that you think we can reason with … that … that … *thing*!"

"Enough, Sabrina, enough!"

Sabrina knew she was high-tempered, used to getting her own way. Once she started on a rant, it was difficult to stop. Henry was clearly heartbroken. She leaned up and kissed him on the cheek. "You're right. I'm sorry, Henry, I'm sorry."

Alan Carr had been waiting patiently through all of this, in the dusty glare of the lights. "What would you like to see? You've come all this way."

"Yes. We've come all this way to see for ourselves, haven't we, Henry?"

"Yes, we have. The bodies, let's see the bodies."

"It's not pretty," Carr said, "really not pretty; but – follow me!"

CHAPTER 2 – LONELY ROAD

When Alex Wolf first noticed the hitchhiker, he thought the guy was a *cactus* – a tall thin cactus, white with desert dust.

Alex blinked at the fast-approaching cactus – or whatever the thing was. It was dark. Alex had been driving for five hours non-stop – fueled by nerves and a thermos of strong black coffee. Now, he was in the middle of nowhere, or, more precisely, in the middle of the night in a scorpion and rattlesnake infested desert that seemed somehow much worse than the middle of nowhere.

"Our world is falling apart!" Alex grimaced and tapped the steering wheel with one finger. "Damned well falling apart!"

The radio stations had gone off the air and been replaced by static. Maybe power had failed – again – in Los Angeles and many of the coastal cities. People were ceasing to care. Generators broke down. Or there was some other emergency; or atmospheric interference, solar flares, and a breakup of the ionosphere; the atmosphere had gone haywire, with super electric storms, and no rain. This was the twenty-third year of non-stop drought in California and the Southwest, and gasoline and other fuels cost so much that there were few cars on the road.

Alex was depressed, bored, and exhausted.

He'd run out of antique CDs, and his iPod was empty.

He was telling himself, for the thousandth time, that *it wasn't his fault Judy died* …

Running it over in his mind …

Judy, his wife, his partner, the love of his life – Judy, gone up in flames …

He was in the midst of these mournful thoughts when he saw the *cactus* – no, the *hitchhiker*.

Alex never picked up hitchhikers, and this particular hitchhiker was doubly suspicious since the guy was standing in the middle of nowhere in one of the deadliest driest deserts on the planet.

It was funny that Alex thought at first the guy was a cactus – *I guess I'm beginning to hallucinate* – just a dusty white ghost – an upright white slash in the glare of the headlights. Then he saw it was a person.

Yes, stop.

No, don't stop! Don't risk it.

There were serial killers of course, and the roads were full of so-called road pirates, wandering gangs who kidnapped you or killed you and took your car and everything in it and left you lying dead or wounded, fodder for the vultures, in the dust on the side of the road.

Lonely stretches were particularly dangerous, and a lot of stretches of road were lonely now that people had less money and traveled less. The police had given up policing many areas of the country – 'High-Risk No-Go Zones' – HR-NOGZ for short, though it wasn't any shorter, really.

On the other hand, the guy was in the middle of nowhere – maybe he needed help. Help – didn't everybody need help?

Help ...

Alex could see it even now: Andrea, their office manager, running up the stairs, shouting, "Help, Help!"

And Judy – of course – came riding to the rescue! Judy always wanted to help people no matter who they were or what the situation was. If Judy saw an old lady staggering along with a walker, she'd stop her car, park, and rush to help. If somebody had too many parcels and had spilled something, Judy would run up and kneel on the sidewalk to pick up the scattered oranges, bananas, and milk cartons. And she contributed to all the charity drives.

Blond, with a wide unabashed smile that made her look like a kid and wide-set thoughtful dark almond eyes and rimless glasses, a penchant for plaid working shirts and corduroy trousers that made her look extra intellectual and extra-naive – both of which she was, and talented, so talented ... so ... *hopeful* ...

Alex could hear her voice: Be charitable, Alex, pick the guy up ...

Alex's fingers played with the steering wheel: *yes, no, yes, no, yes* ...

Then he saw that the hitchhiker was a *woman*, and she was half-naked.

Suddenly, coming into focus, the image was as clear as a cartoon. Stark white skin, bruised in places, short-cut jet-black hair, and what looked like the remnants of clothes – black – a tattered work suit, or catsuit, or some sort of military getup …

A woman …

Alone – apparently alone – on the side of the only highway, almost totally untraveled, that cut like a straight-razor across the desert.

She was holding out her thumb, and she'd raised her other hand to shield her eyes from the glare of his headlights, which were on high.

No bags, no backpack, no suitcase that he could see.

He was already past her.

Okay, okay, okay, he thought – just this once!

He signaled and pulled over.

Then he remembered the radio warnings he'd heard just before the radio gave out, warnings about a dangerous fugitive, a *woman*, who was on the loose, considered extremely dangerous, and …

But it was too late now.

Damnation!

Squinting into the rearview mirror, he backed up. The rear lights lit up the shoulder of the road – white sand and pebbles, one or two cactus, like ghosts or phantom humans.

I will almost certainly regret this. He could see the woman running to catch up with him; she had a limp, one leg dragging slightly.

He sighed. Maybe, in fact, this was a crazy opportunity to begin his new life. He had decided to make a clean break, to start his life again, with a clean slate.

Everything he owned was in the car.

He was leaving his old life behind; and, now, maybe, he was leaving life itself behind …

Leaving life itself behind …

The California he'd abandoned was on fire. In the rearview mirror, he could still see the red glow in the sky. The fires had progressed down from the mountains into the outskirts of Los Angeles and San Francisco. Every-thing was as dry as dust, as arid as kindling. The air stank of burnt flesh and ashes. The most recent drought had lasted more than two decades; the Napa Valley had dried up, and the wine business had gone bust, and with long-term unemployment between 20 and 30 percent, law-and-order was a thing of the past. Localities taxed travelers, stopping cars and trucks and extracting a toll – it was worse than the Middle Ages. Road pirates and Mexican drug gangs and corrupt cops ruled the roads. The country was breaking up.

So much for progress!

You fuck with Mother Nature, and Mother Nature fucks you back!

So, what with the sequels of the Super-Quake, the Big One, of 2047, still present almost a decade later, the Californian dream was a thing of the past.

The Great Republic was adrift.

The frontier society had come bump up against the Pacific Ocean.

When dreams end, ugliness begins.

He had finally understood the horror when …

… when Andrea rushed up the stairs to their office, shouting, "Help! Help!"

And so it happened: Judy ran downstairs – leaping two or three steps at a time – to rescue George Alanis. George was a harmless homeless guy, in his fifties maybe. He was in his usual place, there, outside the offices of *Ultra Nano-Tech*, Alex and Judy's high-tech company, a marriage of nanotechnology and biological engineering, building biological and bio-mechanical entities with Bio Bricks, bits and pieces of DNA, specifically engineered to solve precise problems: creating new forms of life, by recipe. It was a cutting-edge, but small company, not like, say, the giant Andromeda Corp, run by that mad beautiful genius Sabrina Jacobs.

"Hi, George, hi," that's the way the morning usually began.

"Hi, Doctor Wolf; and how are you today?"

George camped on the sidewalk in the covered strip mall walkway, sheltered from the dust and the sun. He had a handsome, strong-featured face, the face of a Biblical prophet, or perhaps a Greek philosopher, mournful brown eyes, and a long tangled gray beard.

The company was on the second floor of the ruined half-abandoned strip mall that sat at one end of a derelict industrial park – Pacific Coast neo-rustbelt.

Judy often brought George coffee from the company espresso machine. And Andrea, the office manager, if it wasn`t Judy or Alex himself, would take George one of the box lunches they prepared in the company kitchen – a boiled egg, some tuna sandwiches, a couple of slices of red pepper, cucumber, lettuce.

George was harmless, not quite right in the head. Though how do you judge that, Alex wondered. George was probably wiser than most of us, and he was a philosopher or mystic in his own way. Sometimes, Alex would stop and shoot the breeze with George, and George would open wide his very own doors of mystical insight. *"See the morning sunshine all bright and warm on that silver-colored garbage can over there, Doctor Wolf? That's reality. That's the luminous and the numinous all in one. It's a door to another realm. It's a threshold. It's the Gate to Eternity. You stare at that garbage can long enough, Doctor Wolf, and you'll know what I mean. One day you'll step through it, Doctor Wolf, you'll step through that gate, and you'll find yourself on the other side, beyond the veil, beyond the pale, beyond the shimmering curtain of maya. Maybe you'll come back; maybe you won't. All this stuff we call reality is merely a disguise, the mundane quotidian illusion of the real – in fact, it's mostly a phantom, mostly empty space. Doctor Wolf. Let the dead bury the dead: each dawn heralds a new universe."*

Each dawn heralds a new universe …

That particular day, from dawn on, it had been hot and windy, over 115 degrees, blustery, with a dust storm moving through town.

And, like the wind, a vigilante mob was moving through town. It had been stirred up by a radio talk show host who had told the people to clean out "undesirables" and "parasites." "You know what to do!" the demagogue shouted. The mob was carried along like whirling newspapers in a hot wind, carried on gusts of anger, fear, and ignorance. It was a mixed rabble of recently or long-term unemployed, some Whites, some Hispanics, a few Blacks. The leaders were some white guys with shaved heads and leather jackets and tattoos – homegrown amateur Fascists.

They began to taunt George.

He was sitting in his usual place.

When George didn't give the right answers and didn't show the right degree of respect, it quickly got ugly.

Andrea came running up the stairs, breathless, saying there was a mob and they were going to kill George. Alex looked up and waved his hand, meaning he would come in a few minutes (he hoped); he was in the middle of a vital conference call: negotiations over a new contract that could make or break their company.

Judy rushed down, followed by Andrea.

One of the leaders, a big-bellied guy with tattoos and piercings and lots of big metal rings dangling everywhere, was pouring gasoline from a pink plastic jerry-can onto George – as the closed-circuit TV established – and then set him alight. The guy stood for a moment, savoring the suspense, the lit match brightly hovering, and then he dropped it – *Whoosh!*

Whoosh! George was a pillar of flame.

Judy tried to stop them, and then she tried to put the fire out. Alex came down just in time to see Judy engulfed in flame as one of the bastards – a white guy with his gray hair in a ponytail and a red-and-white polka dot bandana masking his face – threw an improvised Molotov cocktail that exploded on Judy's shoulders, coating her in liquid flame.

Whoosh!

Alex fought through the crowd – he broke two noses and one arm – to get to her, and he fought to extinguish the flames. The crowd was rejoicing – *fire, fire, fire, the witch is on fire!*

Judy, his love, his life, was a dying ember in his arms.

Fire, fire, fire, the witch is on fire!

She lost consciousness and never regained it.

Fire, fire, fire, the witch is on fire!

It took her five days to *really* die.

Fire, fire, fire, the witch is on fire!

By the time the police arrived, George was dead, a smoldering charcoal mummy; he was still sitting in his usual position, something like the Buddha's lotus pose, smoke rising from his carbonized flesh, but his face was turned upward in agony, and his mouth wide open in a scream that nobody alive would ever hear again.

Alex heard it though.

He heard George's scream. He still heard it, even now.

Fire, fire, fire, the witch is on fire!

Andrea was also doused with gasoline. Half of her body would be scarred for life, not her face, which was lucky, but the pain would probably never go away, not entirely.

Alex got burns on his hands and legs – nothing that wouldn't be gone, essentially, in six months; in fact, all traces of the burns were already gone – a little redness, that was all.

The fire and smoke and water from the fire department – when it finally got there – badly damaged all the equipment in the building, effectively destroying what was left of Ultra Nano-Tech's physical capital.

The insurance wouldn't cover anything because, as the Insurance Company's lawyers said, they were not hurt or killed *while working*. Trying to save a fellow human being did not count as work. And the fire had been caused because Judy had provoked the crowd, thus causing the guy to throw a Molotov cocktail at her; thus, the damage to the company was self-inflicted; this made no sense, but never mind. Some of the guys whom Alex had punched were suing him for assault, and the police – cowed by the mobs – threatened to bring charges against him. The insurance company lawyers threatened to denounce Alex as a fraud for trying to pull an insurance scam. "Burning down your own business to collect insurance is a felony," the lawyer said. Alex wanted to bash the guy's face in. His own lawyer had to hold him back. "Back off, Alex, back off," he kept saying. Alex no longer cared. And what was left of the company didn't, of course, get the key contract, because as the client said, "You are distracted by grief, Alex; we can't take a chance on somebody who isn't on this project 100%."

Alex made sure Andrea was looked after financially. He settled as much as he could on the employees he had to let go, which was everybody – some of the best scientists and engineers in the country.

It emptied his own bank account – though he still had a – comfortable – income from various patents he'd been granted over the years.

Now, he was just driving – away, away, away …

Fuck California!

Fuck the future!

Fuck the people!

Just seeing the flash of images, just thinking back on it, made Alex grip the steering wheel so hard his knuckles turned white. He was furious, furious at everything, furious, above all, at his own impotence – he hadn't been able to save anybody or anything.

Fire, fire, fire, the witch is on fire!

He braked the car to a full stop, the red lights throwing an inferno-like glare into the cloud of dust, the sort of flame-filled, dusty whirlwind out of which it is said demons rise. The door opened, and the woman slid in – bringing with her the heat. It was almost midnight, but the temperature outside was still 95 degrees. Into the cool air-conditioned interior wafted a smell of dust and desert and sunbaked asphalt.

"Thanks, awfully," she said, "You really are a good Samaritan."

She had a British accent, or so it seemed.

"You are *very* welcome," Alex had recently developed an excessively polite facade – a shield against other people, and against his own smoldering rage. He turned to look at her. "Buckle up," he said. Again, looking at her, the impression was vivid – like a cartoon. Maybe because he was so tired.

Bruises: She was badly bruised. *Clothes*: Her clothes – some sort of sexy, black, tight-fitting military-type outfit – thin synthetic bio-armor it looked like – were in tatters. *Camouflage*: She had what looked like traces of camouflage on her face.

Beauty: She was extraordinarily beautiful – flawless skin, aside from the scratches, bruises, streaks of camouflage paint, and dust. She had high cheekbones, full lips, marvelous teeth in a wide, thankful smile, huge, dark welcoming eyes – very dark – no reflections in there, no reflections at all – a high forehead and fine raven-black hair streaked with dust; her body – which was clearly visible through the tatters of her clothes – was, Alex thought, *a body to die for*.

She was so beautiful, she didn't look real.

Alex signaled and pulled back into the infinite stretch of dark empty road. "What in the world …?"

"… was I doing all alone in tatters and covered in dust in such a god-forsaken place? That's a very good question and a very long story."

"Do you want to tell it?"

"Maybe later. Right now, I'm, well, I'm exhausted. I doubt if I'd make much sense."

"That's okay. I understand. Try to get some sleep."

"Thank you. You are very understanding, Alex. I apologize for not being more sociable."

Alex felt relieved. She seemed normal, even educated and polite, not at all a monster, not at all the extraordinarily dangerous female escapee the radio had mentioned before it conked out – then it struck him: *She had used his name!* He didn't remember telling her his name; in fact, he didn't know *her* name, and he was *sure* he had not told her his name.

A shivery feeling shot up Alex's spine. He glanced over at her – her eyes were closed; she seemed to be asleep. Well, let her sleep!

Alex drove on. The minutes and hours went by. He blinked, beginning to feel drowsy. The road raced into the headlights. All he saw was sand, an occasional cactus, and the hypnotic flicker – white, dark; white, dark; white, dark – of the broken white line brightly streaming into his eyes, racing out of the silky hallucinatory blackness. He really did want to fall asleep. Maybe he should put on one of those old 20th Century CDs, things he and Judy had collected.

No, that might wake up his passenger. He sighed. What in the world was she doing there, in the middle of the desert? How had she ended up, beaten up, her uniform or whatever it was in rags, covered in dust and dirt, a beautiful girl, with leaden circles under her eyes, in the middle of nowhere – her thumb out, begging for a lift?

Maybe it was some sort of clandestine military operation; maybe it was a drug deal gone wrong and she was an addict. Maybe she'd been tossed out by her boyfriend after a punch up and fight. Maybe she'd …

Alex yawned and put his hand up to his mouth. Well, I'll ask her when she wakes up, and she'll tell me if she wants to tell me.

Alex was drowsing, beginning to drowse when …

When …

There was a luminous fluttering from the passenger seat, something Alex just caught, an impression, out of the corner of his eye, and a popping and a ripping sound – her uniform, what was left of it, tearing apart.

Luminous fluttering …

Tearing apart …

Alex glanced at the woman. His mouth opened wide. His eyes stared. A scream died in his throat. He almost choked. He jerked the steering wheel to the left – as if he were trying to drive away – *away* – from what he'd just seen – and the car swerved to the middle of the highway and across and almost into the opposite ditch.

The tires screamed.

Alex grabbed the wheel, swung it back wildly, careening across the road, tires squealing, almost plunging into the other ditch. The car skidded in the dust. Alex saw a cactus, ghostly white in the headlights, surge up and flash by. With the car careening on two wheels, he finally pulled it back to the center of the road.

"If you drive like that, you'll get us both killed, Alex," his passenger said, dreamily, with her calm, rather tony British voice – and perhaps a hint of a lisp.

Alex glanced at her. It must be an illusion or a hallucination. Where there had been a woman, there was now a reptile with scales, fangs, claws!

Maybe it was an effect of the lights on the dashboard, reflecting on her skin. Maybe he was in some sort of hypnotic stupor, from staring at the road for hours, from too much caffeine, from worry and sleepless nights, from having his life turned upside down, from …

Alex concentrated; he narrowed his eyes; he focused: No, this was no illusion; this was real – unless he'd gone stark raving mad.

Sitting next to him, slouched back in the passenger seat, correctly buckled in, was a *reptile*, not a woman, a sort of, a sort of – what? – Yeah, a *demon*.

"What the hell are you?" he said.

"What? Whatever do you mean?" She yawned and shook her head, dazed, as if she'd just woken from a dream. Yes, she had a very slight lisp, a slight slurring of the words: maybe it was the fangs; maybe it was the *long forked tongue* – flickering out of her mouth – My God!

Fangs!

Forked tongue!

Jesus Christ!

"Look at yourself! What the hell are you?" Alex gripped the steering wheel hard; his knuckles turned white. Sweat streamed down his back and from his forehead; an abyss of fear opened in the pit of his stomach.

The steering wheel was slippery.

Maybe she exuded slime, Alex thought, but, no, it's just sweat, my sweat, the sweat of fear. And maybe it was not such a good idea to rile her up, or to rile *it* – this *thing* – up, by asking questions. Maybe he should have just kept quiet. Maybe he should just have waited for her to evaporate – like the hallucination from a bad drug trip or the incubus generated by an extra-painful hangover.

But he couldn't resist. "Look at yourself!"

"Oh!" She looked down at her hands – and Alex saw in detail this time that they were not really hands: they were claws, claws of green and turquoise scales with long pointed golden nails. Her head and her stunning body – it seemed even more voluptuous than before – and her long shapely legs – shining through the tatters of her uniform – were covered in green and turquoise scales, glowing with an inner light.

She was iridescent.

"Oh, God!" she said, turning her reptilian face toward him. The eyes gleamed; the two long white fangs sparkled. "I must really be tired. I must

PART ONE – THE BEAST

really be losing it. This has never happened before – not for centuries, not for millennia. I'm awfully sorry. I really am."

"*What* has never happened before?" Alex was calculating how fast he could get the Beretta out of the glove compartment. And he was thinking, too, that reaching for the pistol was probably a really bad idea since she looked like she could tear him – or anybody else – into shreds in a split second.

But ... But at least she was talking like a human being. She hadn't just made a grab for him, eaten him on the spot. God! It was like being in a car with a high I.Q. alligator. He'd seen old horror films with girls turning into monstrous reptiles, snakes, or vampires; usually, they didn't stop for chit-chat, they just tore you to pieces and gobbled you up.

"I've never morphed like this. It's something I control. Something I choose to do."

"Really? Something you choose to do!"

"Yes. I'm sorry. I must look frightful."

"You could say that."

"And, yes, Alex, you are right: I do agree. It would be a really *bad* idea to reach for the Beretta in the glove compartment."

"What?"

"Don't reach for the Beretta; your instincts are right; it would indeed be a *very bad* idea."

"You read thoughts?"

"Yes. Intermittently – it can be a useful talent, on occasion. I do apologize for eavesdropping on your mind. It's very impolite of me. And I apologize too for startling you in this way – it really is awfully embarrassing." She reached for the rearview mirror. "Do you mind?" She was looking at herself in the mirror, like a woman checking her makeup, tilting her face this way and that.

"No. Go ahead. There's nobody out here on this road but us," Alex said, and immediately regretted it: reminding her – or *it* – that they were alone was not maybe such a bright idea. Could it be that she was some sort of bio-weapon developed by the Pentagon? When she'd been human, she had been wearing the remains what looked like some sort of special ops-type uniform, night-fighting gear, with traces of camouflage makeup, maybe amphibious, a wet suit and armor all in one. Alex had done some work in weaponry and advanced genetic redesign, and he wondered. Was *she some new form of hybrid warrior?* He'd heard rumors that Sabrina Jacobs at Andromeda Corp was trying to develop such creatures, and, in Russia, Dmitry Pavlov's

Bio-Prom had some very advanced programs of bottom-up nano redesign of biological entities and …

"Yes. Okay." She considered the image, and murmured. "Not too bad. The damage isn't too bad." She put the mirror back in position. "Thank you," she said.

She turned to look at him, and, keeping half an eye on the road, Alex glanced at her. It was recognizably her, recognizably the woman he had picked up forty minutes before; except that she was now reptilian, covered in scales, with two curved fangs, very prominent fangs, a curving smile of the reptilian mouth (at least it looked like a smile; he hoped it was a smile), and the eyes, the eyes were very large and slanted upwards toward the temples, but they were the eyes of a reptile, of a serpent, not of a human.

"You're very attractive, I guess." Alex swallowed, "for, I mean, for what you are …"

"You like it? That's amazing! You are indeed a cool chap, Doctor Alex Wolf, and rather gutsy, I must say! Most people, you know, would be a quivering mass of jelly by now." She grinned – it looked like a grin – and smiled a sweet reptilian smile, her head – its scales glittering in the reflected light – tilted coquettishly to one side. "Well, I'm morphing back to human. You may not want to watch."

Alex turned his attention to the road.

The broken white line raced out of the dark silken ribbon of asphalt. Again, it was hypnotic.

When had he last seen a car?

He was aware of a fluttery blur beside him.

And then she said, "Oh, boy!"

"Oh, boy?" Alex muttered, "What: *Oh, boy?*"

"What a dreadful mess! That was definitely the last straw for my clothes – what remained of my clothes – I'm very sorry to say."

Alex glanced at her and had to grin. She was human again, very human, very female, and, yes, not much was left of what she'd been wearing – just fluttery shreds here and there; she was effectively naked. "You can borrow some of mine," Alex said.

"Thank you. You are a true gentleman, Alex Wolf."

"We'd better stop."

"Oh."

"The suitcase is in the trunk."

"Oh, oh."

Alex slowed down, signaled, and pulled over onto the dusty white shoulder. Darkness was all around them, and empty desert, not another being or vehicle in sight.

Suddenly it was silent. She didn't move; she just sat there.

"Well?" he said.

She still didn't move. He pushed a button, and the trunk popped open.

"Now, Alex, you wouldn't be thinking of trying that old trick on me, would you?" Her voice was positively silken. She was almost purring. Alex thought of the fangs – and the claws.

"Dare I ask what old trick?" He grinned innocently, wondering, am I that transparent? God, yes, of course! She can read thoughts!

She was gazing flirtatiously at him from under her eyebrows; her eyelashes flapped a few times. Her skin was chalk-white; her eyes were exceptionally dark, glowing with dark fire. "You may certainly dare ask what trick, Alex Wolf. It's that old trick, my dear Alex, where I innocently get out of the car, saying, in a grateful, high-pitched, breathless, little-girl, Marilyn Monroe voice, '*Oh, Thank you, dear Alex, You are so, so sweet*,' and go around to the trunk, and you gun the motor – Screech! – and take off, leaving me startled like an innocent doe, buck-naked and helpless in a cloud of flying pebbles and dust on the side of the road, and seeing, through my blinking, tearful, deeply betrayed eyes, only your taillights – disappearing, fading away, *going, going, gone,* leaving me, and in some ways I'm just a girl in spite of appearances, leaving me alone with the rattlesnakes." She paused. "That trick is the one I mean." She smiled prettily.

"Leaving you alone with your brothers."

"You mean the rattlesnakes?"

"Yes."

"That's a low blow, Alex, but yes, of course, they are my brothers – the rattlesnakes. Genetically, you know, every life form on the planet is – "

"I know – related."

"DNA ... But you know all about this, Alex, since I seem to detect – from eavesdropping on your thoughts – that you are one of the leading molecular biologists on the planet."

"Whew! You can't resist, can you? Reading thoughts again?"

"Yes. As I said, it's a useful talent, and as for that little trick you were going to –"

"Now you don't believe I would have been contemplating pulling such a low-down, dastardly, ungentlemanly, contemptible little trick like that, do you?"

"I most certainly do believe it, Alex. In fact, I am virtually certain of it. After all, as you know, I do read thoughts, and, you think, quite rightly in fact, that I'm a monstrous *thing* – perhaps a weapon of some kind – and *very* dangerous: Think claws, think fangs, think forked tongue, think the warnings you heard on the radio! I wouldn't blame you."

"Look. Here are the keys. I'm going to get out and have a pee. You look in the trunk. Choose what you like. I won't get back into the car until you're back in the car. Okay?"

"It's a deal, Alex."

She took the keys, and they both got out of the car.

Alex walked back a few yards beyond the trunk, faced toward the infinite blackness of the desert, spread his legs, unzipped, and began a nice leisurely pee. The only sound was his pee hissing and splashing on the sand and pebbles. It was a familiar sound, and felt magnificently normal. Other than the sound of pee and the sound of the creature messing about in the trunk of his car, all was silence, vast, flat, infinite desert silence. The stars above shimmered in a clear dry night sky – hundreds of thousands of stars. The constellations were like scatterings of diamonds. It was a hot, extremely hot, night, but the air was dry, full of vague desert perfumes. Life was beautiful, after all; and he didn't want to die – not just yet.

Then he thought: Of course, now she has the keys! She could jump in the car and leave me in the desert. Somehow he didn't care. He was beyond caring. Maybe I should just walk away into the desert and let her take the car. No, that's not a good idea: she might not like that. And what the hell would I do in the desert? He had tumbled into a science fiction novel or a horror story without even realizing it. Never pick up hitchhikers! And he thought the night was going to be boring! He finished peeing, zipped up, and turned around. He wanted to make a clean start – well, maybe this was it, the clean start.

She was standing, stark naked, backlit by the light from the trunk, holding out some samples. She smiled at him, her old friend Alex. "What do you think? Would I look best in baggy khaki shorts – with all the pockets – and a Hawaiian shirt, or in these tight elastic jogging pants, and a T-shirt?"

Alex looked her up and down. She was holding the clothes in front of her, like a model, trying stuff out, or a woman in a store showing her booty to her husband.

"Tight elastic jogging pants and the T-shirt," he said.

She pulled them on. "Well, what do you think now?"

"The T-shirt's a bit big, but the way it drapes over … ah, the way it drapes over you is very … attractive. I'd fall for you."

"Good. You are *so* kind, Alex! That's grand!"

"You are welcome."

"This baseball cap?"

"Yes, it looks great, a bit big too, but that adds to the androgynous charm."

"Do you mind if I borrow these hiking boots and some athletic socks too?"

"No, go ahead, what's mine is yours!"

She lifted the boots out of the trunk and two pairs of athletic socks, and checked that everything was in order, and handed him the keys. "You're a darling, Alex. I wouldn't have blamed you at all if you'd run off and left me in the desert." She closed his suitcase, closed the trunk, and they both got into the car.

"By the way, my name is V," she said. "Pronounced Vee."

She didn't put the hiking boots or athletic socks on; she just placed them carefully on the floor under the passenger seat.

She sat, without buckling up, and somehow managed, with her heels up on the seat, her arms locked around her shins, her knees under her chin, to crouch there – like an elastic-limbed teenager, or like a dancer. She was quiet and didn't say anything for a long while. Her profile, Alex mused, was startlingly beautiful – a goddess.

He wondered how old she was – 19, 20, 22?

Demon or goddess or both? Alex frowned.

They drove in silence. The only sounds were the car engine, the wheels on the pavement, the hushed sound of a car going over a smooth absolutely empty road, and the whispering sound of the wind against the windshield.

"So do you mind me asking – Just what are you, V?"

"You're a scientist; you won't believe it."

"Try me. After what I saw, I'll believe anything."

"Well, I am – how shall I put this delicately, Alex, I am many things, but one thing which I certainly am, is I am a vampire."

"I see," Alex said evenly, "A vampire!"

"I knew it – you're not taking me seriously!"

"No, I am certainly taking you seriously!"

"All right, Alex Wolf, you're taking me seriously. Say: 'I believe, I truly believe, that you, V, are a vampire.'"

"I truly believe that you, V, are a vampire. I swear!"

"You see, to survive, I must drink human blood."

"It's a limited diet, I guess."

"Yes, it is." She paused. "And, if I may say so, more interestingly from the genetic point of view (your specialty), I'm also an alien, I mean half-alien, I mean not from this planet, I'm a hybrid, half my DNA, the paternal half, is not terrestrial, but that is sort of a state secret, very hush-hush, Alex, so I'd be very grateful if you didn't mention it to anybody."

"Of course," Alex swallowed: an *alien* … "I won't mention it to anybody."

"Thank you."

"Don't mention it."

Alex squinted at the road, and then glanced at the creature crouched on the seat beside him, and then back at the road which rushed endlessly toward them. She was silent and still, and for perhaps half an hour didn't say another word – then …

"Well, Alex, I must confess. I have a problem; well, I have a couple of problems."

"You have a couple of problems."

"Yes, I'm hungry, starving, in fact. I haven't fed for almost two weeks, and I have to feed, ideally before the night is over."

"Feed. Okay." Alex glanced over at her. "Are you thinking of me as your midnight snack?"

"No, I've excluded you."

"That's mighty nice of you."

"Don't mention it." She gave him a most charming smile. "Second, Alex, I need a place to sleep during the day. I was kidnapped, and for the moment, I have no money, no credit cards, and no identity."

"It seems to me that that is a whole posse of problems, V: one, two, three, four, five, six …"

"You are right. I also have enemies – people who want to kill me – or worse."

"I imagine you do, have enemies, I mean."

"Yes, well, yes, you're right – lots of enemies."

"I see."

"I'm in a mess, really; I'm in a right old pickle."

"Right old pickle? Where did you learn English? You have traces of an accent; it's not just English."

"I learned English first in England, in London, to be exact."

"When?"

"A little over four hundred years ago: Will Shakespeare, Ben Jonson, those chaps."

"Four hundred years ago." Alex felt he'd seen and heard enough. He had truly entered into the twilight zone. "Well, I can lend you some money. And I can rent us a hotel or motel room for tonight and for the day tomorrow. I was going to sleep through the day anyway."

"Excellent! Alex, you are a dear; you really are."

"As for feeding …"

"I'll do that myself, Alex. Don't worry about it. I'm quite inventive, usually, in that regard."

The motel Garden of Eden Oasis was a two-story clapboard structure with a wrought-iron open balcony up front onto which the doors to all the rooms and suites opened.

And, strangely, for it seemed redundant, the motel also had ramshackle metal fire escapes out back, for each suite – which, V thought, was ideal for slipping in and out, surreptitiously, on hunting and feeding expeditions.

Entering and exiting through windows was so much more alluring and glamorous than going in and out through the front door, at least, such was V's taste for intrigue, refined over the centuries, that she preferred it that way. Even when not necessary, the surreptitious and indirect was for her usually preferable to the open and direct route.

Besides, on returning from a hunt, she was often in rags and coated in blood and gore, not yet having been able to shower, so it was advisable to be discreet – even invisible, if possible.

The motel was in the red-light district, such as it was, of the little town that was really just one long strip of dilapidated neon-topped shacks fronted by parking lots, and motels, strip joints, hamburger joints, pizza parlors, body rub salons, gas stations, and taco bars – that stretched along the highway, with a number of side streets of run-down apartment buildings and tawdry little bungalows boasting broken or dirt-splattered windows and whose lawns had withered and whose gardens had long since been blown away into dust and tumbleweed. The town made its meager living as a stop-over and base for bandits, reprobates, road pirates, Mexican gangs, and outlaws of various kinds, and it had a substantial population of drifters and transients.

It all smelled of creosote and wood rot and decades gone by.

The Garden of Eden Oasis was about as seedy a motel as you could possibly find – which was just what V had insisted upon.

Alex signed in for both of them. Very romantic and illicit, he thought, signing in with a vampire he was not married to, a reptile, a demon, an alien, or whatever the hell she was – and utterly charming too.

What sort of genetic mechanism would allow such a transformation?

How could the whole morphology mutate in an instant?

Assuming, that is, that the whole thing was not a dream or a hallucination.

And if she was a hybrid, and part alien, as she claimed, then how had she been created and when and by whom and for what reason?

The desk clerk, a thin-faced, unshaven, bald guy – with black warts on his skull – and with his gray, sparse, coarse hair that had once been black, slicked back in thick greasy strands over his ears, and with scrawny pale pimply arms and wearing a brown leather vest over a black, short-sleeved T-shirt, and who seemed either drunk or drugged or both, and who looked up at Alex with dark dazed eyes, "*Hi Bud,*" and didn't object to one signature and one set of documents. "Your partner can clear it up in the morning," he said with a lazy drawl, and went back to sleep.

My partner …

Alex wondered if, when he went up to the landing, there would be no partner.

Just an illusion …

Incipient insanity …

But no, she was there, on the balcony-landing, waiting for him to bring the keys, show her which room they would occupy, and open the door.

She had carried the bags, all the bags, and the hiking boots and socks, up the staircase, and stood there, on the second-floor walkway, looking like a kid bellhop with an oversized T-shirt, floppy baseball cap, skintight silver shorts and bare feet – a beautiful pale kid of indeterminate sex with a black eye and a few bruises.

Alex unlocked and opened the door.

"After you," he bowed.

"Excellent!" V said, taking in the ratty red-and-yellow knit rug, the big flat bed, the plastic flowers, the blinds and curtains, the tiny frilly bedside lamp, and the paintings of a castle on some mountain top in Old World Europe, maybe in Transylvania.

"Vampire country?" Alex said, raising an eyebrow, and nodding at the paintings.

"Absolutely! Just like home sweet home, though I'm originally from North Africa, actually." She smiled at him and put down the bags; and, then, in what seemed like one smooth dance-like motion, so quick he hardly saw it happen, she stepped out of the clothes she was wearing and turned, naked, to Alex and said, "Do you mind awfully if I use the shower first?"

"No, not at all," said Alex, trying to concentrate on looking at her face.

"Just to get rid of the dust," she said, "and mud and sweat and rattlesnake dung I picked up in the desert."

"Of course," said Alex, "the rattlesnake dung."

"My brothers," she said, disappearing behind the bathroom door.

While she was in the shower, Alex lay down on the bed and closed his eyes: he was exhausted. Then, listening to the shower, he opened his eyes, sat up, and pulled a book out of his suitcase, thinking he'd better stay awake, if she got hungry, and he was the only morsel around ...

V came out of the shower covered in golden beads of water, and stood looking down at Alex. Then she stretched, arms up in the air, crossed at the wrists, turned around, doing a neat quick ballet-like pirouette, saying, "Oh, that felt *so* good, so absolutely divine!" and she toweled herself vigorously, standing in front of him.

And then she pulled on Alex's T-shirt, elastic jogging shorts, athletic socks, and hiking boots. "Well, does this look okay?"

Alex who was lying on the bed trying to read his book (something on new frontiers in genetic engineering) kept looking up, watching her: She didn't seem to mind his fascinated, objectifying, alienating, and reifying male gaze; in fact, she rather seemed to like it.

"Perfect," Alex said, "You look perfect."

"Don't tell anybody about me, Alex." She put on the baseball cap and tugged it sideways to a rakish angle. "It would be extremely dangerous."

"I won't," said Alex, thinking he'd be plunked in an insane asylum if he talked about any of this, or shot by the Pentagon, and thinking – Am I the luckiest guy in the world, or the unluckiest? Am I dead, or am I alive?

"I'm going, but I'll be back," she said and gave him a quick kiss on the cheek.

She seemed to exude a perfume, a sort of heady, spicy, exotic mix.

It didn't come from the shampoo or toothpaste – of that he was certain.

She climbed out the window and onto the fire escape.

Alex got up and stood at the window. He watched her. She paused on the fire escape for a moment, looking out over the town; then, she glanced back at him, puckered her lips in a mimed kiss, blew it toward him, turned away, and was gone.

The sky glowed red from neon and from dust and maybe from the distant reflections of the California forest fires. It was a vision from Dante's inferno, Alex thought, and into that Inferno, his beautiful demon had disappeared.

He pulled the blinds down and undressed and got into the shower thinking that perhaps a really hot shower – if there was any hot water left – would sober him up, and he would come out of the shower to find no trace of her, and no sign that anybody had ever been in the room but himself.

Just an illusion …

CHAPTER 3 – CLONE

Sabrina Jacobs swiveled around in the high-backed synthetic black leather executive chair, and glanced at the bank of monitors across from her desk in her office on the Andromeda Corporation's Research Ship *Andromeda*.

Monitor One showed, in medium shot, *Clone-1*, the *Clone*, or the *Thing – The Thing Junior*. The Clone was sitting huddled in the corner of its glass cage, watching television, or at least, watching patterns and movement on the huge multi-screen wall of her cage, 20 screens in all, and all of the screens were on, buzzing with activity.

The Clone was a product of *the Thing* – otherwise known as V. It was a product of the monster's DNA, suitably modified.

Officially known as "C-1" – the Clone was blond, blue-eyed, lithe and slender; and, yes, it was stunningly beautiful, fourteen years old, female, and to all appearances human.

The Clone was staring at a myriad of images that streamed rapidly by in ultra-fast-forward on the giant multi-screen wall of its cage. Its pose looked, at first glance, something like the Buddha's lotus position, graceful and serene.

Sabrina glanced at Monitor Two to check what the Clone was watching on all those screens: Some sort of nature show on one screen; a soap opera – no, it was a feature film – on another; then some text of something – words – on the third; and, on the fourth screen, something with lots of paintings flashing by – Renoir, maybe, Cezanne, Picasso, Mark Rothko maybe, it was hard to tell, everything was moving so fast. And then there were the other screens, of course, one showing what looked like the Berlin Philharmonic playing something. Everything was moving ultra-fast – in fast-forward. It was a senseless kaleidoscope, a mishmash – chaotic colors and patterns and movement. The Clone always set things to ultra-fast-forward; content didn't matter – just action and noise.

Full of sound and fury and signifying nothing ...

Sabrina bit her lip and turned back to Monitor One, saying, "Zoom in on the face."

Obediently, the image zoomed in on the Clone's face. The Clone's mouth was slack; its eyes were empty and unfocussed; drool dribbled from its chin.

Each time, Sabrina hoped to see some sign of intelligence. But – nothing, nothing, nothing! "Damn, damn, damn!"

That such a promising beginning, a child that had been so bright – a child that had, in fact, been a genius, unique on the planet, a blend of alien and human – had ended up turning into a mindless driveling idiot – what a failure, what a mockery!

Hubris, Nemesis – and thus – Nothing: zilch, zero, null, rien, nada!

God! How depressing! Sabrina closed her eyes and swiveled away from the monitors. She mustn't let it get her down. Maybe she was feeling particularly negative because of the crash and the long trip back to *Andromeda*. She leaned back in the chair and closed her eyes. At least the little girl in New York, Alice Kelly, was now alive – and seemed to have been cured. All the reports continued positive, at least one life saved, and one deadly condition almost certainly conquered. But, flying back to Los Angeles and then onwards to the *Andromeda* had been exhausting.

Andromeda was southwest of Hawaii and heading toward the Philippines, where Sabrina had a personal research project on the coral reefs in the Sulu Sea. A couple of weeks scuba-diving, combined with underwater research, would be a perfect way to relax, to empty her mind, to get rid of the ghost of failure – the horror that was V, the monster.

On the way back from Los Angeles, in her private cabin aboard her executive jet, Sabrina hadn't slept. She had tossed and turned and then given up and tried to read a book; she couldn't concentrate: she was furious with herself; it was her fault people had died; she had totally – fatally – underestimated the strength and cunning of the creature, the Thing – the Thing that was origin of the Clone.

V – The mysterious, alien, deadly V.

To create the Clone, Sabrina had used the V's DNA, modified to obtain a few changes – eye and hair color – and to try to reduce aggressiveness and, hopefully, to reduce the thirst for human blood. The Clone was meant to be superhuman, not a monster.

The Clone would have been the *prototype*, the first of a new super race. She would have been the salvation, the rebirth of humanity, a fusion of human and alien, with the best of both – a new Genesis.

Instead, tragically, they had created what Doctor Andrew Starr, Andromeda Corp's former chief psychologist, called "a being without any mind at all to speak of."

"I'm sorry, Sabrina," Doctor Starr stared at Sabrina over his old-fashioned bifocals, "but she's merely a collection of habitual actions, of automatic reflexes, without even the intelligence of a lower ape or a rather backward dog."

And yet – the Clone, the girl, was beautiful, extraordinary in fact: a stunningly beautiful fourteen-year-old girl – with an appearance that was entirely, divinely, human.

And this beautiful creature was an empty shell!

Sabrina opened her eyes and glanced one last time at the Clone. She turned off the monitors, stood up, went to a porthole, and looked out at the Pacific, the vast ocean, waves catching the moonlight, ribbons of silver. She hugged herself. People had lost their lives because of her, because of her ambition, her arrogance, her overreach. She stared at her reflection, a dark sketchy shape in the porthole window. "Well, the next time, dear self, I won't underestimate this evil creature, this V, this *thing!* I will build a cage, a chemical cage, so perfect the monster will never escape."

V, I am coming to get you! And get you, I will!

So much death, so much carnage had already been caused.

Sabrina closed her eyes; she shivered – suddenly, her stateroom seemed cold, freezing cold. She was back in the desert, at the scene of the wreckage.

"It's this way," Alan Carr was saying, "It's this way."

Sabrina followed him, about to go from the stifling heat into the refrigerated tent – where it was cold, cold, cold.

Thinking of it, even now, she shivered, still shivered, even now.

Alan Carr had put his hand on her arm.

He put his hand on her arm; hardly anyone dared do that!

Alan Carr opened the zippered flap of the main refrigeration tent. His hand was still on her arm. "Doctor Jacobs, Mr. Rothschild, I'll lead the way!"

It was a large tent, the size of a tennis court, maybe two.

Inside, the lights were brutally bright; the generators made a humming noise that filled the space.

It was cold. Sabrina hugged herself. She was trembling – *goddamn it!* She could not control the trembling! She felt a tear, just one tear, forming at the edge of her eye; she wiped it away. No one must ever see any trace of weakness, any lack of resolve, any hesitation, not ever: not even Henry must see that she ... that ... that she *felt*, that she felt the suffering.

Sabrina Jacobs is a woman of steel – she must be a woman of steel!

Sabrina Jacobs cannot show any sign of weakness, ever!

Her father's voice: You must be perfect, Sabrina!

It was hard to look at. The ragged bits and pieces of flesh were laid out in rough anatomical order and did not seem human. It was a frigid slaughterhouse.

At that moment, Sabrina swore to herself: I'm going to turn this *Thing*, this V, into what she really is – a mere machine, a soulless killing machine, a robot. I'll push a button, and she'll do what I want her to do, and only what I want her to do, and then I push a button, and I shut her down. She will stand there, empty-eyed, a puppet. I'll use a *neuro-blocking genetic modification* – she will have no willpower, no free-will; she will do what I say, and only what I say.

"These are the remains of Toni Anderson," Alan Carr was saying. "I can use her as an example of what happened to the bodies. The body fragments are badly burnt. The burning almost certainly occurred after the crash, during the explosions and fire. But it also looks like Toni was cut in half, and that probably happened before the crash."

"Cut in half before the crash?"

"Yes."

Sabrina glanced at Henry; he had put his hand over his eyes.

"What's left of the fuselage?"

"Bits and pieces. The biggest section is over there, outside. I'll have them light it up for you."

They went back outside, into the torrid heat – stepping from a freezer into an oven. Sweat pearled on Sabrina's forehead and ran down her back; they went inside the biggest section of the fuselage, a big round thing, like the cut-off section of a giant pipe. The steel cage was still there; the steel wall and the manacles were still there; but ...

"My God!" Henry stared at the manacles and at the bars of the cage.

Sabrina put her hand on his arm. She wanted to hammer the point home:

The creature is a killer, a deadly killer. "My, my," she said, "This V even more versatile and valuable than I thought!" She hated herself. She knew she was being cruel, needlessly cruel.

Alan Carr used a pointer. "You can see that the creature that was being kept in this cage broke the manacles. The metal manacles have been twisted outwards, away from the steel wall, and all snapped in the same direction. The same thing happened to the cage. It's as if a shell hit the bars of the cage, a shell, or a wave, coming from within the cage. The velocity and force, for an instant, must have been tremendous; the bars are all twisted and broken. Some large fragments flew away, that might explain the young woman – Toni Anderson – being cut in half. We're checking for blood and DNA on some of the bar fragments, those we've found at least. This all means that a single body, something about the size of a human body, hit the bars with one impact and flew straight through them. The acceleration alone must have been utterly fantastic. In fact, it might have been a shock wave that broke the bars, not the body itself. It seems impossible, but …" Carr shrugged.

Henry again shielded his eyes.

"So she broke out," Sabrina said, kneeling over one of the bar fragments, "and the plane crashed. Have we got a timeline? I mean, how long after she broke out did it crash?"

"We can't tell, not yet."

"The radio signals? Recordings?"

"Well, we got a few – total panic and confusion. The pilot was either wounded or dead, pretty early on, I think. We're trying to piece his body together. The co-pilot was probably still alive when it crashed, but the controls were damaged, that's what we think at least. There was a lot of shooting, and it's probable the controls were damaged so they could no longer control the plane."

"So, the crash may have been an accident."

"It's possible, even probable. What we do know, is that when the plane went down, it went down very fast. Somebody tried to level it out and bring it back into flight only a few minutes before the impact – maybe a wounded crew member, but it didn't work, and in any case, it was too late. But the prints on the pilot's controls … I hesitate to say this …."

"Go ahead, say it."

"The last prints on the pilot's controls seem to be … Well, they seem to be claws."

"I see."

"So the prisoner might have tried to ..." Henry let the possibility hang in the air.

"... she might have tried to save the plane," Sabrina said, though she wondered at herself in saying it.

"It's possible." Alan Carr nodded, "But ..."

"Could somebody have gotten out?"

"By parachute, you mean?"

"Yes."

"All the parachutes are accounted for. No, nobody got out with a parachute."

So that was that. She and Henry left the crash site and got back into the helicopter and flew toward a small airport and got a plane for L.A. and then another plane for Hawaii and then a helicopter to join the *Andromeda*.

Outside the porthole, the Pacific was silver and black, rippling under the moon, stretching away to a star-speckled horizon. Sabrina crossed her arms over her chest and hugged herself. It felt as if she was still shivering, even now. She turned away from the porthole, walked across the stateroom, and lay down on her bed and closed her eyes. Maybe the Thing had died in the crash.

Or maybe ...

Maybe she had survived ...

Yes, she *had* survived. She must have morphed into her reptile form – the claw prints on the pilot's controls – and somehow, she had survived.

Yes, she *was* alive, somewhere, alive.

Sabrina had a feeling, and it was only a feeling, but it was a definite feeling, a gut feeling, that the Thing was still alive. So, if the Thing survived, she either jumped out of the aircraft and somehow got to ground without smashing herself into bits and pieces, or she hit the ground with the aircraft, at almost 500 miles an hour, and survived explosion and fire, and just walked out of there.

Sabrina had photographs of V, taken immediately after her capture. She opened her eyes, got up, and sat on the edge of her bed. She took the photographs out of the folder. V was in a black wet suit, her face a mask of camouflage paint and bright, startled eyes ...

"You are very desirable, my love," Sabrina stared at the photograph, "very desirable indeed, luscious, and beautiful, too beautiful. You and I are connected; and I am going to get you, my dear, I am going to get you and I am going to make you mine! And I know – even if nobody else does – I know, I really know, that you are still alive."

Sabrina spoke to the bedside computer, "Get me Roberto Curry at our Virginia Headquarters, please," and when Roberto answered, she said, "Roberto, sorry to bother you at this hour, but let's start a low-level search for the Thing – for V – I think she's alive. Let's say I have a hunch. We can go into high gear if it's confirmed she's alive, or we can call it off without too much fuss if it's confirmed she's dead. Okay? I'd suggest a ground search on the desert – maybe twenty miles either side of the flight path of the plane, and some detective work on the ground on the nearest highways leading out of the desert, and nearby towns. Okay, thanks, good! Goodbye, Roberto."

CHAPTER 4 – FODDER

Standing on the motel fire escape, V took a deep breath, and glanced back at the window. Alex, dear fellow, was standing there watching over her.

She was *starving*.

She needed to find a meal, and fast – it wasn't always easy.

The night sky was blood-red from a sandstorm that was blowing up in the desert – that's what the giant screens hovering over a street corner were saying – and the thick sultry air was red, too, from reflected neon signs – *girls, girls, girls, strip, strip, strip; lap dancing, go-go, hamburgers, hamburgers, Esso, Taco, Pizza, girls, lap dancing …*

V turned to Alex and blew him a kiss, and started down the metal steps. The fire escape echoed – a hollow metallic vibration. It made her think of tenements in vast desolate cities she had known, cities with wailing sirens, bombs falling, and murderous thugs wandering the streets.

This is no time for nostalgia, V!

Tend to the present!

She figured she had about an hour before she would faint from weakness and she was not sure her improvised outfit was the best one for seducing the right sort of food – an oversized baseball cap which said "Nano-Tech," a big black T-shirt with a lightning bolt logo, and silver jogging shorts that were skin-tight but still too large at the waist, and with wrinkles in all the wrong places.

If real disaster struck, they might fall down around her ankles!

No – they were too tight for that!

Not counting the oversized hiking boots and two pairs of ankle-high white athletic socks that she needed to keep the boots from chaffing.

At least she still had the bruises that make her look like a battered woman!

And she looked like a waif, a battered waif – in other words, she looked like *bait*.

The night tingled with electricity, the unresolved electricity that can work its way up into a tremendous storm. The heat and the haze smelled of French fries and onions and grease and booze with a rippling undercurrent of musk and sex and death.

It took her about ten minutes to find what looked like the right place.

The *Exotic Dancer's Oasis Club* had a pink neon sign that blinked and was missing the last "C" of exotic.

A video screen above the entrance showed a blond stripper in a G-string doing a solo pole dance. The images were pitted, flickering. Part of the screen was black: the pixels were burnt out.

The sidewalk was pockmarked with a bad case of sidewalk acne. Rotten garbage was piled against the walls. Squalor – squalor was good.

Along one side of the club was a dark alley with large waste bins on wheels and not much in the way of lighting and no video surveillance that V could see. Rats were scurrying up and down the alleyway and crouching jealously on top of the waste bins eyeing her with their beady black little eyes. Some of the waste bins had been turned over and spilled out and the rats were nosing in the rubbish. One large rat looked up at her with an inquiring gaze – *predator, or prey, or just part of the decor?* It then lost interest and turned back to the chicken bone it was gnawing. At the end of the alley was a large mobile incinerator. It was working, a pale column of smoke drifting from the chimney, pale and rose against the inflamed night sky. Ah, that was interesting: a handy incinerator could be very useful. The alley and the empty lot behind the club looked like an excellent killing ground.

The *Exotic Dancer's Oasis Club* had no doorman and no visible bouncer, so V went straight in. She walked along a narrow wooden corridor with old faded yellowed photographs of naked girls displaying their wares and who must be grandmothers or dead by now. She pushed through a heavy, greasy, musty-smelling brown leather curtain, pushed aside a tinkling wall of red glass beads on strings, and she was inside.

It was a big, high-ceilinged room with wooden rafters. All the old guys and a couple of young guys turned to look at her as she entered. It was a gloomy, barn-like space, half full, with little round tables, spaced widely apart, and lonely men sitting alone at them nursing their solitary drinks.

The U-shaped bar had a couple of poles and a string of light bulbs overhead. Three girls were twisting themselves around the silver and gold poles; the runway formed the top of the bar, so the dancers were dancing between the bartender and the customers, their stilettos weaving, in some places, between beer cans, beer bottles, whiskey tumblers, and long-drink glasses.

In the general gloom, the lighting gave a bit of twinkling spurious glitz and a suffused gold-red tinged hue to the bar and stage; and, even though the joint was cheap and in the middle of nowhere on the edge of a desert, the girls had that burnished, buff, highly-toned look that good strippers had almost everywhere.

V adored strip clubs: they were ideal hunting grounds.

V felt all the eyes were on her, but they quickly switched back to the strippers on stage.

Sitting alone, on one of the stools at the bar, was an extraordinarily beautiful blonde in a low-cut spaghetti-strap white dress. She looked like she was by herself. V wondered what a classy dame like that was doing in a joint like this. She must be one of the strippers. The woman had a classic profile and perfect skin and what looked like a perfect body. V considered herself a connoisseur of human bodies – male and female.

She decided this woman was her first target, her contact – she would sit next to her.

And so she did, sliding onto a stool and tilting back the baseball cap at what she thought was a rakish angle – and also to give her potential fodder – whoever he or she might be – a better look at her face.

The bartender came over and looked at V doubtfully. He was a guy with thick, tousled, blond graying hair, sagging face muscles, and ragged, watery blue eyes that seemed lined with mascara or eyeliner. His skin was blotched and worn-out and sun-bleached. All the melanin factories had shut down. He looked like once he'd been a surfer, about 100 years ago: all those salty waves rolling in, V thought, all that sunshine, all the joints smoked, all the tequilas drunk, all the golden boys and golden lasses, and now all gone, now all turned to old age, wrinkles, dyspepsia, and to ashes.

V knew what the guy was thinking: Is this creature under age? Is she a very pretty boy? Or is she a girl in drag? Is he or she *trouble*? V had big circles under her eyes and what looked like a bruise under her left eye.

I look like a waif, thought V, focusing on the guy's view of her – a drug addict, alcoholic waif who's been beaten by her man and who had to borrow clothes and who probably doesn't have the money to pay for the drinks.

Before coming into the club she hadn't thought that she looked like a boy, but, then, hey, you can't think of everything, not all at once! Now, catching the mental vibrations from the bartender, she thought, *Oh, that's a different angle!* Nobody's taken me for a boy for at least sixty or seventy years – a man yes, if I'm in drag, but not a boy! Let's see, the last time was …

She put down one of the fifties Alex had lent her and boldly said, "A double whiskey, Black Label preferably, no rocks, with water on the side."

The guy looked at the money, and looked at V, and said, "Hard night, kid, huh?"

"You might say that."

"That bruise …"

"Yeah?"

"Who gave you that bruise?"

"Thank you for asking, but it's not something I wish to talk about."

"Right! Private life! It's nobody's business but yours."

"That's right." She gave the guy her most radiant smile. "Nobody's business but mine."

V thought, this guy is either being genuinely nice and concerned, or he's bored, or he's creepy and scouting for vulnerabilities. It was, her mind-radar told her, the latter: the guy was asking himself, *is this creature fodder for the boss?* V's attention perked up: *The boss* … Now *the boss* might turn out to be *the evening meal!*

The bartender went away, poured the shot, and came back with the double shot and the water on the side.

The blonde took a sip from her drink.

V drank a sip straight and then added water. She turned to the blonde and said, "Cheers!"

The blonde, without turning toward her, said, "And cheers to you too, young chap!"

One of the strippers, a sharp-featured, vixen-faced, golden-skinned girl – nice cheekbones, naughty almond-shaped, up-slanting eyes, black, neatly arched eyebrows – sidled over, like Salomé, and began dancing right in front of V and the blonde.

The girl seemed to be dancing for the blonde alone. There was something taunting, teasing and cruel in the way she danced, offering herself, beckoning with her eyes and hands, opening her legs, knees apart, lowering herself down, her breasts heavy like ripe fruit, her tummy flat, her waist narrow, her minuscule gold G-string glittering: *Here, baby, take me, I'm right here, the heart of me, take me, baby, take me.*

Then she winked at the blonde, licked her lips slowly, and, letting the tip of her tongue hang out, glanced at V, ran her tongue slowly along her upper lip, rolled her eyes as if in despair, and straightened up and went back to one of the poles and started to swivel around and shimmy up and down – now in another world, eyes dreamy, thoughts far away, her long black silken hair, when she leaned back, hanging straight down like a veil. *Yummy*, thought V, *definitely yummy.*

"Do you work here?" she asked the blonde.

"Me? I used to. I still do, sometimes. That used to be me, up there." She motioned with her whiskey tumbler toward one of the G-string clad go-go dancers.

"Oh, yeah? You were one of the dancers, huh," V said, just to say something.

The blonde turned toward V.

V's eyes opened wide.

Half the blonde's perfect face was a grotesque purple and red mask; her right eye was a clot of veined and bloody scar tissue, her skin was like a seared and twisted barbecued steak; half her mouth was wrenched up in a scarred, paralyzed, clownish, red-lipped snarl, baring teeth and gums and a glimmer of bone.

"Like it?"

"I'm sorry!"

"No need to be sorry, darling. Acid – acid did it; and oil, and a straight razor. I'm supposed to sit here every night as an example. Sometimes Big Boy orders me to do my old act, stand up there, twirl around a pole, take off my bra, flex down and bend my knees out, stick out my pelvis and beg the jerks to fold a bill into my hot little G-string, and then get down and crawl around and take off the G-string too and wallow naked. I have to keep at it until he tells me to stop. I'm a warning to the other girls."

"Who did this?"

"See those guys over there, the big one with the shaved head, he's the boss, he goes by the name Big Boy. I was his woman, not by choice I might add, and the little guy with the gray ponytail and the denim jacket, he's the executioner, the enforcer, the pal, the court clown, the inventor of refined tortures, Little Boy."

"Big Boy and Little Boy, huh?" V's nostrils quivered – *Blood!*

"Little Boy's the one who applied the acid. They wanted it exact – exactly one half of my face, so people could compare: *before and after*, you know, like in the ads for soap or acne remover. It was a work of art. Half my face, they protected with hot wax and the other half – well, Little Boy applied the acid with a brush and a sponge and even a dropper – drip, drip, drip. He was really having fun. I was tied down, and my head was in a vice, so I couldn't even squirm. Then they did a little knife work with the straight-razor – quick surgery without anesthetic – and *voila! The thing, the monster, the circus freak!*"

"Don't they mind you telling me? I mean, they see us talking."

"Mind? No, they love it! Spread the word!"

"Spread the word?"

"Yes, indeed! They boast about it. The law around here is dead as far as women are concerned. It looks the other way. Or, if you go and complain, they turn you over to the guys who raped you or beat you up. This has become Bible-thumping country. You know the Bible says women are responsible for the woes of man. Eve got everybody kicked out of Paradise; after Eve, we had to have sex, birth, old age, death, and work; so we girls get to pay for it in eternity. These guys drink their beer, thump their Bibles, and beat their women. They and the Mexican drug gangs are the only game in town."

"Big and Little, huh!"

"Big Boy and Little Boy work together. They kill together; they torture together."

"But doesn't somebody …?"

"No. There is *no* somebody." The blonde favored V with the twisted, grotesque grin, the blood-clotted parody of an eye. "They run this part of town. Nobody touches them. They have a deal with the Mexican gangs – though there's trouble coming, I think; they crossed one of the Mexicans the other day, kicked him out of the club. So anytime now there will be hell to pay – tonight, tomorrow, soon. The Mexicans will burn the joint down and skin Big Boy and Little Boy alive. But Big Boy and Little Boy are too stupid and arrogant to know their game is up. Anyway, Big Boy and Little Boy love it when I tell my little sob story. I'm an advertisement for how tough they are."

"Real sadists," said V, taking a sip of whiskey, and thinking: *Now I know where tonight's dinner is coming from. Yum, yum, yum.*

"Real sadists, yes, they are: I used to be the star; you know, the higher you go, the harder you fall. Hubris, nemesis – and Hell. They like me as I am – the new me, the circus freak, the ugliest girl in town. But I'm alive, so I shouldn't complain! *¡Salud!* "

"*¡Salud!* Is there a shower out back? I might need to take a shower."

"A shower? What the hell are you talking about? Yeah, there's a change room and a shower."

"I want to get to know your pals, Big Boy and Little Boy."

"Are you crazy?"

"Sure – I'm crazy!"

"What are you going to do?"

"I'm going to ask for a job."

"You *are* crazy! But you look like" – the blonde considered V carefully, looking her up and down – "You look like just what they will want to play with. You look like somebody beat you up; you look like a fucking masochist; you look like you're asking, begging, to get beaten up again, and abused, and abused, and abused."

"That's me," V grinned, taking a sip of the whiskey; thinking, *Oh, my love, if you only knew!*

"And you're good raw material." She took V's chin between her fingers. "Perfect bone structure. Wonderful skin. If you didn't look like shit, you'd look like runway perfection. You've got great eyes, sort of mysterious: so deep it looks like you have no soul, or a soul buried so far in there that only a real determined explorer, a true lover, some obsessed, infatuated idiot, would go deep enough to find it. And, yes, great skin too, ignoring the bruises, though it's hard to tell." She released V's chin.

"Thanks," said V, tipping back some whiskey.

"And, darling, let me tell you this: I can't figure out if you're really intelligent or the stupidest bit of tail that's ever set foot in this hellhole."

"We'll see. I think maybe we'll see."

"I hope for your sake, it doesn't cost you … too much."

"What's your name?"

"Helen. They call me Helen of Troy; it's their little joke."

"I'm V."

"V? V for what?"

"Just V."

"Cute."

"Is there a back entrance?"

"Yes, there is the *Artists' Entrance* – I love the expression, *Artists' Entrance* – in the alleyway, between the garbage cans. There's no lock. Nobody would dare to bother or rob the girls. The Boys see to that."

"I want to get to know Big Boy in particular."

"Why Big Boy?"

"Because he's the big juicy one."

"I don't know about juicy, but, honey, I'm pretty sure he'll like the look of you, the bruises and all, and those circles under your eyes, why, that looks positively perverse, in that outfit – where the hell did you get it – you look like a boy, androgynous, and he likes that too, boy and girl all in one, so you'll be a success. If he likes you, he'll fuck you every which way, and then he'll beat the shit out of you just for the fun of it. Then he'll fuck you again, all styles, all positions, all openings, and beat you again. If you are real lucky, you get the two of them at once."

"I'd like to try that," said V, but she was thinking, Two at once is one too many; I'm not sure I'm strong enough right now to handle two at once. But I need to feed – and soon!

"Are you really crazy?" Helen of Troy's one blue eye blinked at her.

"Yes, I'm really crazy."

"Well, your little boy look won't hurt; it might buy you some time."

"Are you going to be around later?"

"Why, you want a date? Are you one of those with a thing for scars, a fetish? Is that your kink – date the freak? Helen took another swallow of whiskey. Her one good eye looked hurt.

"No, not really, but I might have something for you."

"Something for me … You're a mysterious girl, huh?"

"Yeah, sort of … What did you do before you did the stripping and go-go dancing?"

"Believe it or not, I was a lawyer, a good one too. My mistake was I agreed to represent a gang; it was the wrong gang. They compromised me, framed me, and blackmailed me, whatever way you want to say it. Then they sold me to Big Boy. Big Boy thought I was snotty so he raped me and beat the shit out of me and told me he would kill me and my family – my sister has two kids – if I left him, so I became his whore and stayed, and then I tried to get away, and now I am what I am, and even Big Boy doesn't want me anymore – which is a blessing. I'm damaged goods, as they say. ¡Salud!"

Alex was starving. He dressed, went downstairs, and walked along the dusty hot street lit by flickering neon, giant screens, and dim street lamps until he came to a hot pizza automatic vending machine. He put in some money – not wanting to use his identity – and waited for his pizza. While he was waiting, he watched the Spanish news-and-advertising screen overhead. It showed floods in Europe and fires in California, crop failures in China, forest fires in Russia, and sea levels rising everywhere, and it urged people, locally, to be on the lookout for a dangerous female fugitive but, strangely enough, it didn't give a description or provide a picture of the dangerous female fugitive.

Alex had a sneaking suspicion that he knew who the dangerous female fugitive might be. Part of him was tempted to phone in and report that he was living in the same motel room with a woman who was really a vampire or dragon or a part-alien from outer space.

He even took out his mobile and stared at it, but then he thought that she was right, the girl-demon, was right, that reporting her would be even more dangerous than not reporting her.

And, if he admitted the truth, he rather liked the dragon-girl or reptile-lady or whatever she was. And, as a geneticist, and bio-engineer, he was more than curious as to what she was, who or what had created her, and why, and how in the world she could function – since she seemed to operate in violation of almost all the known laws of biology, not to mention physics. Maybe, just maybe, this would be the beginning of something interesting, possibly of an extraordinary adventure.

The pizza slid out of the slot. Alex picked it up, sprayed on a few condiments that were provided – red and black pepper – and slipped it into the package, and then, half opening the package, he ate the pizza as he walked back through the steamy, blood-red night.

He didn't want to stink up the hotel room with the smell of pizza – that would not be very romantic or polite – so he intended to finish the pizza before he got back to the motel, even if it meant lingering in the street – a desolate nowhere nondescript sort of street – really a highway pretending to be a street – and so he strolled slowly, looking at nothing in particular. Bits of paper and dust were blowing in the hot wind that came out of the desert and that probably presaged a dust storm.

The world humans inhabited was slowly dying in a whirlwind of rubbish, plastic bags, tin cans, chemicals, CO_2, methane, nitrates, nitrous oxide, poisons and pollution of all kinds.

Perhaps his new friend V was right to *cull* the human race, to kill off the baddies, if that's what she was doing.

Alex finished his pizza and walked back to the motel.

Two cats were making love and screeching and screaming and hissing on the balcony, close to his room. The male, a black-and-white tom, was clamped down astride the female, with the ruff of her neck between his teeth. Both hissed at him when he stepped over them, but, locked in amorous embrace, they didn't interrupt the ritual of copulation.

"No shame," Alex muttered, "Have you no shame!"

When he got back into the room, Alex pulled the curtains shut and pulled down the blinds, and the room was plunged into darkness.

The cats screamed, hissed, and then there was a great clattering to-do and banging with claws and screeching and scrambling as they – Alex presumed – changed positions or stopped and started again and inspired the envy and lust of other cats who caterwauled in chorus from below the balcony.

Do cats read the *Kama Sutra*?

Alex lay down on the bed and had a brief moment of doubt, frowning in the dark at his own temerity and foolishness. He was in cahoots – and maybe even infatuated with – a creature that, however alluring she might be and however good she might seem, was, by her own admission, a very ancient half-alien creature who was also a mass murderer.

Over the centuries, she had fed on humans.

Alex had made a rough calculation of how many she must have killed and arrived at an appalling result. She had told him she fed once about every two weeks.

"It keeps me slim, you see," she had said, "I'm joking, Alex, I'm joking, but that *is* the statistic. It is best, dear Alex, that you know who – and *what* – you are dealing with."

Let's see, if she needed to "feed" once every two weeks, on average, that meant at least two kills a month, that meant 26 kills, at least, a year, and that meant in a decade she killed 260 people, and in a century, 2,600 … Then there was collateral damage, some innocents, or bystanders, would be lost in some of her hunting excursions. So, let's say 3,000-4,000 in a century.

"I try to kill *bad* people," she had said, "but of course … It doesn't always end up that way. Sometimes I make mistakes – my fault, *mea culpa, mea maxima culpa.*"

Alex closed his eyes. Well, small change, I guess, when you compare that to the slaughter humans inflict on each other; but it was still substantial, still substantial ...

V sidled slowly over to the two playful slobs, Little Boy and Big Boy, shuffling in the hiking boots like she was a truant ragamuffin urchin reluctantly headed, minus satchel, in the chill mist of an unwelcoming winter morning, toward school, and a schoolmarm's sadistic rod.

Her stomach was growling. Her blood sugar was low. She must feed. Hunger drove her on. She had to go to ridiculous lengths, she thought, to obtain fodder; sometimes, she found it very annoying. It would be simpler just to order a hamburger.

The room wavered, and the lights trembled. Oh, my God! She might faint from hunger. If she did, she would be done for, doomed. She wouldn't even have the energy to feed.

She should have just taken up Alex's polite suggestion and fed on him: this was her little private joke; she liked Alex; she would *never* use him as fodder.

Never ...

"Hi guys, want to dance?"

"Who the fuck are you?" Big Boy had big slobbery lips and crooked teeth; but physical beauty, V mused, was not a pre-requisite for being added to the menu.

"Just a girl feeling lonely."

Big Boy looked at Little Boy, and then he again considered V, carefully this time, letting his gaze slide, like slimy drippy glutinous ooze, slowly up and down what was visible of her body. "Maybe you want work?" He stroked his chin, and cleared his throat. "You want work? You see yourself stark naked, twirling your twat around that pole up there, or down on your fucking grubby knees flashing your tits and begging the slobs for nickels and dimes?"

V blinked at him and grinned.

"No way we can tell if a girl's got talent unless we try her out," said Little Boy, eyes twinkling, and licking his lips.

V took a closer look: Big Boy was maybe 270 pounds of beef, with bulging muscles and a big bald shaved head where you could see the wrinkles in the skin and where the suture between frontal and parietal plates of the skull was visible as a crease mark, and it again occurred to V that he'd be full of first-rate high-pressure blood, full of iron and vitamins and energized corpuscles, white and red, just like she liked them. Her saliva began to flow; she licked it back and swallowed. Anticipation gave her a burst of energy. The tattoo on his shaved skull said, "The Will of God." On his arms were tattoos of dragons spitting fire, and V thought: I should show him my dragon.

She pointed at the dragon and said, "That sort of looks like me."

Little Boy, the skinny runt, chuckled, "Sister, you look like a car wreck, not a dragon."

"It's been a bad week."

"So you want to strip." Big Boy frowned. "You look like a kid."

"I know. It's the clothes."

Little Boy pulled at the oversized T-shirt: "You got any tits? You got any ass? You gotta show us what you've got. And the bruises – bruises are nice – personally, I like bruises, personally, I adore bruises – all black and blue is fine with me – but bruises are bad for business, you gotta get rid of those bruises."

Big Boy gave her a playful little punch. "You deserve those bruises, sister?"

"You annoy your lord and master?" Little Boy slapped her gently on the cheek.

"You disobey the divine commands?" Big Boy stuck a finger in her belly button.

"Are you a rebellious bitch?" Little Boy grinned. "Are you Eve in the Garden fiddling and flirting with the serpent?"

"I'm – ah – submissive," said V, thinking, what she was doing was entrapment; totally, but totally, unfair. She was being really *bad*, but she was really *hungry*. She felt the double shot of whiskey had given her strength, a surge of energy, a wave of feistiness, but it would quickly fade. She was salivating. She wanted the beefy guy with the tattoos and the silverware dangling in his ears. Big Boy was what she wanted.

"Submissive, huh?"

"Submissive is good," Little Boy gave Big Boy a wink.

"You can come out back and show us what you can do, kid, okay?"

"Sure! Yes, sir. You'll find it interesting, I'm sure."

Helen of Troy watched the two sadistic clowns play with the kid. She knew from experience that the playfulness was a prelude to the apocalypse and that the two clowns would warm themselves up into a paroxysm of pure violence – rape, then a beating, then maybe murder.

That kid is too young.

Letting them take her into the back room was not such a hot idea: the kid was doomed. Once they got her into the back room, and once they got excited, well, then the kid would be lucky if she got out of there with a broken nose and broken ribs, not to mention the rape which was like an *hors d'oeuvre* when Big Boy and Little Boy started to dance one of their homicidal duets.

Helen sighed and told the barman she could use another whiskey, and he said, "Yeah, sure thing, Helen; it's a quiet night, huh." He leered, setting down the tumbler, "Nothing much happening except maybe in the back room."

"Yeah, it's a quiet night," Helen said, feeling for the knife she always kept in her purse, but which she had never dared, until now, use.

Out back, V discovered, was a big empty room that gave onto the alleyway and it had a warped linoleum floor and a long zinc-topped bar at one end and a musty smell like an old dance hall or gym; and it also contained, V noticed as her nostrils twitched, the indelible perfumes of faded hopes, of dreams dashed in horror, of bodies dead and gone, of sweat and athletic socks and maybe washed-out eau de cologne and a spicy bouquet of wood rot, ancient urine, and creosote.

A big dirty plate-glass window that went right down to the floor looked out on nothing – or, rather, on the empty lot behind the club where, further down the alleyway, the mobile incinerator was working away – *puff, puff, puff* – turning garbage into smoke.

"Okay, kid, take off your clothes." Big Boy struck a judicious pose; he stroked his goatee; his eager little beady eyes were like black marbles.

"Do you want me to strip or just to undress?"

"Strip."

"Excite us."

"Show us what you're made of."

"Yeah! Show us the real you!"

"Well, I don't have the best – ah – props. But here goes!"

V was again feeling dizzy with hunger. But she managed to kick off Alex's hiking boots. She shuffled around in Alex's white athletic socks, again imitating a little boy reluctant to go to school.

Bending her knees, she slowly slipped out of the shorts, whipping them around herself like a skirt and bunching them up in front of her like a large flower, and then, using her cap, she mimed Charlie Chaplin's hobo figure, abashed and sly, and then she tossed the shorts away smoothly, very smoothly. The T-shirt was just long enough; it covered her nakedness like a short dress.

The two guys were standing now, and began to circle around her.

V lifted off the oversized T-shirt, but still kept the baseball cap.

She held the T-shirt in front of her as a teaser – she didn't have a bra or panties. The panties, already in agony from the trip across the desert, had finally, totally, perished in Alex's car in the morphing catastrophe. And then she let the T-shirt fly, so she was naked, except for the baseball cap, and the white athletic socks, and she shuffled around, doing some good soft shoe, and a few pathetic little burlesque ballet pirouettes; it was witty, full of seductive twirls, teasing hesitations, playful allusions, sensuous come-hither sideways slides …

But the boys were closing in. They were not interested in art.

"This is a club that's got entry fees," Big Boy said.

"You saw, there's no exit," Little Boy said.

"Once you're in, you're in." Big Boy grinned.

"Yessiree!" Little Boy's eyes twinkled.

"You saw Helen out there," Big Boy smirked.

"Yeah, you saw her!" Little Boy licked his lips.

"Helen of Troy," Big Boy said, grinning.

"Helen of Troy!" Little Boy giggled. "You always break me up with that, Helen of Troy!" He wheezed, doubling over, "Fuck!"

"Yeah, well, Helen of Troy …" Big Boy stroked his goatee.

Little Boy was smacking his thighs.

"Helen of Troy tried to declare independence. She disobeyed her masters. She defied the Word of God; she mocked the Scriptures."

"Yeah, the Word of God, she defied the Word of God." Little Boy was suddenly serious, his eyes narrowed. "You understand me, the Word of God!" He seized V's hand, squeezed as hard as he could, and breathed into her face: his breath was foul: "*Sin began with a woman and thanks to her we all must die!* Is it not so, Brother Big Boy?"

"Indeed it is so, Brother Little Boy, it is written: More bitter than death is woman – whose hearts are snares and nets and bonds …"

"Whosoever pleaseth God shall escape from womankind."

"*The sinner shall be taken by her* … Oh, yes, man, Hallelujah, and the Lord be Praised, I say, Let the Good Lord be Praised! The sinner shall be taken by her!"

V looked down at her toes and frowned. If she weren't so even-tempered, she would get mad right now, very mad, and perhaps spin totally out of control. This archaic patriarchal monotheistic misogynous nonsense was one of V's favorite *bêtes noires*; in fact, on this subject, V could go on a rant at the drop of a hat, and the rant would last for hours, she would go absolutely bananas, out-of-control hysterical, but right now ...

Big Boy loomed over her. He was breathing heavily, red in the face; he grabbed her other arm. "Pray to God!" he said, "Pray to the Almighty Lord!"

"No," said V.

"No?" Big Boy was aghast.

"No?" Little Boy was appalled. Blasphemy and disbelief were beyond the pale – unbelievable, unpatriotic, un-American!

"Why, you sinful bag of putrid woman flesh, you cunt," Big Boy glowed with fury. "Why in God's name will you not fall down on your naked knees and worship the Almighty, the God of Wrath and Thunder?"

"Because, Oh sirs, I cannot tell a lie, and because, oh, sirs, I do not believe in Him, The Almighty One, and I would not commit perjury in His Face, so I cannot pray to Him. No disrespect meant, good sirs, but – "

Both Big Boy and Little Boy roared: "Sinner! Sinner! Apostate! Unbeliever! Atheist! Darwinian! You must pay your dues! Now! Now!"

"To both of us!"

"To both of us!"

V thought, oh, oh, this is getting serious. I am not as strong as I usually am. I've got to play this very carefully, very carefully indeed.

"So I have to pay my dues," she said, breathlessly, mock humble, mock naive. "To whom, dear sirs, do I pay my dues?"

"Dear Sirs?" Big Boy laughed, but V sensed unease under his laughter: *Why was this woman playing it for jokes, why did she think it was funny?* Big Boy was not completely stupid, V realized. He was sadistic, evil, bigoted, and ignorant, but not completely stupid; this was not good news.

Big Boy swung her around and grabbed both arms, snatching her from Little Boy, and forcing her to face him. "You pay your dues to me, you stupid bitch!"

"Of course," V said, seriously, as if sobering up, as if realizing for the first time the seriousness of the situation. "Now?" she said.

"Now!"

"Does your pal watch?"

"My pal watches, and then he consumes."

"Consumes?"

"First me, then he – I consume, he consumes, we consume!"

Shit, thought V. She was fainting; her strength was fading; stars flashed in front of her eyes, blurry stars; she felt her limbs go limp.

Helen of Troy stood up and told the barman she was going to use the washroom, and she walked back to the johns and then stood, uncertain and undecided, in front of the door leading to the back room.

Should she go in, or shouldn't she?

She drew the knife from her purse.

She took a deep breath: Maybe I should go in – a suicide mission is just what I need right now.

As Little Boy waltzed away, dancing gleefully, Big Boy smashed V against the wall, pinning her against the rough plaster, and pressed his mouth against hers – his lips were fat and wet, his breath foul with onions, beer, stomach acid, and mustard, and the stubble of his beard was razor-sharp.

"I don't want to do this, not like this," V gasped. The light in her eyes was fading.

"You do it whether you like it or not, and you do it whatever way I want!" Big Boy breathed, his hot spittle splashing onto her face. "You do it, or Little Boy over there will turn you into a Helen of Troy, only worse, Right, Little Boy?"

V felt herself growing faint: I don't know if I can do this …

"It'll be my pleasure," Little Boy was grinning, ear-to-ear. "I love artwork; my ambition is a total work of art next time – no half measures, acid and razor from head-to-toe." Little Boy sat down on a bench against the wall and slapped his knees like he was a fan at a hockey game. "Rip her open, Big Boy! Show her the Wrath of God!"

V groaned. It was now or never.

She took a deep breath.

She gathered every last ounce of strength: she might be able to do *one*, but she wouldn't be able to do *two*, not now; usually, it would have been a piece of cake, but now …

But there is no choice, V, *there is no choice.*

It's now or never; it's do or die!

She said, "Okay Big Boy, Okay, Lover, I am all yours, and you are all mine!" She put her arms up over his shoulders, and she looked up at him as if she were worshipping him, as if she were going to kiss him, and then she slammed full tilt into him, giving him a shove, and coming on with another shove, she threw him off balance, making him spin across the room. He was spinning, twirling, trying desperately to get a grip, spinning, spinning, tottering, until he went smashing – in a huge explosive splash of glass – through the wall-sized plate-glass window, spinning down, into the empty lot behind the club, with V following, clinging, now on top of him, shielding her eyes from the glass and then down, still on top of him as he fell backward spread-eagled, belly up, arms wheeling wildly, ineffectually, in the air, smashing down with backbreaking violence, a huge thump, onto the cracked asphalt, between the trash cans and dumpsters, down in a shower of glass and cracked wood, onto the rough asphalt, and, V, howling like a banshee, with one sweep of her claws, now extended, slashed off Big Boy's nose, tore out both his eyes, and ripped out his tongue.

And then she swung around and faced the window where Little Boy had got up from the bench and was standing in the shattered window, his mouth gaping open, a pistol in his hand. Where had that come from? It was a Walther PPK, and Little Boy stood there, round-eyed, taking aim at her, just as V felt the momentary surge of energy falter and fail … and she thought, I'm not going to be able to do it, if he shoots I'm …

If he shoots, I'm dead …

At that moment, Little Boy's eyes went even rounder, his mouth puckered up in a comical "Oh!" He dropped the gun. He flailed once, arms wheeling out sideways, and he turned around, and tried to hit at something behind him. In his back there was, sticking out just below the right shoulder-blade, the handle of a knife, a pretty, ornate, knobbed, ivory-handled knife, and Little Boy, arms outspread as if he were doing a belly flop, fell straight down, face first, onto the floor of the back room, just inside the shattered plate glass of the window that looked out on the back yard.

The knife stuck up, neatly, from his back.

Standing over Little Boy was Helen of Troy.

She looked down at V and at the mass of red flesh that had been Big Boy's face. "Maybe, V, you'd better finish what you began."

"Yes," said V, through her fangs – she was merely in vampire, not scaly demonic mode, so the only alteration in her appearance was that, now, she had darker circles under her eyes, two neat vampire fangs, and very effective claws for hands, but she was without scales and other disturbing appurtenances of her superior she-devil form. "Thank you, Helen," she said, with a slight lisp, and …

… and she whirled around and leaped on Big Boy who was just getting up, staggering blindly to his feet, whimpering a bubbly glutinous tongueless something, and she said, "There, there, Big Boy, don't worry, it'll soon be all over," and plunged her fangs into his neck while he thrashed blindly, mute now, forever mute, and she fed, bloodily, with gore and blood spraying left and right, spurting, splashing, squirting, as Big Boy collapsed, like a puppet robbed of its strings, in monstrous slow motion, folding up in a fleshy heap.

When V, covered now in blood, with blood dripping from her fangs, looked up, Helen of Troy was still standing in the shattered window looking down at her, now holding the knife as if ready to defend herself.

"What the hell are you?"

"You do not need to be afraid."

"I'm not afraid." Helen of Troy stepped through the window, onto the ledge, and looked down at the crumpled mass. Big Boy's shaved skull was pale now, ghastly chalk-white. It made the writing, "The Will of God," even more prominent.

V returned to her feast, crouching, sucking the last blood out of Big Boy – *slurp, slurp, slurp.* She sucked Big Boy dry to the very last drop. Helen stood, arms folded, watching her. V stood up. "He's dead, he's truly dead," she pronounced, "He will not rise again."

"You mean he won't become –?"

"Like me?"

"Yes, like you."

"No. He won't become like me."

"Good. He's better dead, really dead; forever dead."

"Yes."

"Excellent! Big Boy would make a horrible, a dreadful vampire; that's what you are, right – a vampire?"

"Yes, in part," V blinked at Helen, "I'm a vampire."

Helen of Troy looked V up and down. V was naked except for athletic socks, and she was coated in a bright glossy sheen of blood, with thicker fresher gobs dripping from her lips. "You need clothes," said Helen of Troy, "and you need a shower; and what do we do with the bodies?"

"There's a mobile incinerator down at the corner. I'll take them," said V, looking up and down the alleyway. It was empty. "I'll chop up the bodies and dump them in the incinerator truck." She was now super-charged with energy. The two bodies needed heavy lifting, and they needed to be chopped up. This was easier to do as the reptilian she-devil. "I'm going to change into high gear. You don't have to watch."

"I'll watch."

In a twinkling blur, V changed into her demon form. In the twilight, her scales glittered and shone, with a rippling of rainbow colors on the turquoise and green, on the scarlet and gold, streaked with gobs and smears of blood. Still crouching next to the body, she looked up at Helen, and hissed, baring her fangs and flicking her forked tongue and blinking her reptile eyes.

"Well, well," said Helen. "My, my! I've seen miracles! Maybe I'll get religion!" She lit a cigarette – the match flared, and in the twilight, lit up Helen's twisted half-face. She blinked at V through the curling smoke. "Sure you don't need any help." And, "Can you talk when you're like that?"

"Yes, I can talk. And I can do it alone," V the she-demon said, "It will be a trifle bloody."

"I can stand it."

V carried Big Boy – now much lighter than he had been – to the incinerator, tore his body into digestible and burnable bits, and dropped them into the maw of the machine. His wallet, which contained money, a bank card, credit cards, and a tablet phone, she kept. His belt buckle would not burn, she decided, so she threw it into a garbage pail. The incinerator roared in pleasure and sparks, and a red glow emerged as the fat boiled and bubbled and burned.

Helen of Troy dragged Little Boy to the window's edge and threw him off the platform. "I'll mop up the blood," she said, looking V up and down through the ribbon of smoke, and squinting with her one good eye. "I like this new you," she said, "Almost as much as the old one, maybe even better."

V carried Little Boy over to the incinerator and used her claws to tear him into bits – two arms, two legs, two halves of a torso, one head – his eyes were staring and glassy, and his beard seemed even rattier than before. V felt maybe she should comb his beard and smooth down his hair but decided it was too late. Where he was going, nobody would appreciate grooming. She dropped the bits into the incinerator. She kept his wallet too: three credit cards, a bank card, a tablet phone, and some cash. The incinerator would reduce the two guys to ashes. When V got back, she saw that Helen of Troy, the cigarette dangling from the side of her mouth, was mopping up the blood from the dance floor.

"Thanks," V said, standing in the frame of the broken window.

"*De nada*," said Helen, squinting sideways, smoke rising from the side of her mouth; she pushed the mop and then wrung it out over the pail. "I'll do the pavement too. There's a side door to that shower you asked about, and the change room. You go. I'll be with you in a minute."

V went through the side door – the *Artists' Entrance* – peeking around the corner to make sure the room was empty; the girls might not appreciate a humanoid reptile covered in blood.

Nobody.

The strippers' change room was a thin narrow steamy corridor-like space with big speckled and smeared mirrors and cluttered makeup tables along one side and a wardrobe full of costumes and clothes and a shower and tiny toilet at the end.

The booming of hard metal rock vibrated through the walls.

V slipped into the shower and reverted to being human. She aimed her mouth, wide open, at the showerhead and let the warm bubbly water gush in. She gargled. The shower curtain was semi-transparent plastic, the space was tiny, and the plastic flapped against her skin and clung with clammy amorous affection to her wet backside.

There was a bottle of body wash-shampoo and hanging from a hook a bristly body brush. V took a handful of the goo and began to flagellate herself with the brush.

Scrub, scrub, scrub!

Helen leaned in and shouted, over the sound of the gushing water, "Here, you may want this," and handed V a large bottle of mouthwash. "We use a lot of mouthwash in a place like this!"

"Thanks!"

V poured the aquamarine mouthwash into her mouth and gargled and swished it around. One of the inconveniences of being a vampire was that she had to be intimate with all sorts of undesirable characters, the ones she ate in particular, and she did like to wash all traces of them away even while she was still delightedly digesting their blood and exulting in their life force.

Big Boy had led a sordid, tawdry, cruel life, and, in consuming his blood, V had also absorbed, in an unpleasant dizzying kaleidoscope of imagery, many of his memories. She was trying to wash these away as well. One of the cruelest of his memories, and one in which he had taken particular delight, was the maiming of Helen.

As V soaped herself down – using the foaming deliciously perfumed body wash – she shook her head vigorously, trying to chase away the images that her mind, with its ever active and extended electronic tentacles, had lifted from Big Boy's now defunct cerebellum.

"Ugh," she shouted, "Ugh! Phew, Phooey! Ugh!"

Go away, evil thoughts, go away dirty memories, go away!

Finally, she finished soaping and scrubbing. V always scrubbed very vigorously after a kill. There were times when she regretted she didn't eat slaughtered, over-bred, highly-strung, tormented pig, tortured, massacred cattle, strung up, butchered lamb, mass-manufactured eggs from filthy, unsanitary, battery-caged hell, and tortured, concentration camp, battery-raised, antibiotic-drenched, chlorine-soaked chickens, like everybody else.

She stepped out of the shower and took a towel from a rack.

"Okay, I've got clothes for you." Helen was holding out a skintight semi-transparent pink phosphorescent elastic dress, with matching purse and pink stiletto shoes.

"Boy," said V, "just my style." She held the dress out, arm's length.

The slender, golden-skinned, vixen-faced stripper came in, looked at V, looked at Helen, and said, "Well, that stuff belonged to Clara and she's certainly not coming back so you might as well take it – whoever you are – it'll certainly give you a different look from the urchin waif you were playing out there at the bar."

"Yes, Clara won't be coming back," Helen said, "This is V, by the way, and – "

"I'm Tracy, pleased to meet you." The stripper held out a slender, lightly tanned hand, which V shook, appreciating the fine, smooth, delicate bones, and Tracy said, "A guy told me the Mexicans are headed this way. Apparently, they're going to kill Big Boy and Little Boy and roast them alive. I think it might be a good idea if we skedaddle and make ourselves scarce. I think they're so mad they're going to burn the joint down. We've got maybe twenty minutes, half an hour."

"Right," said Helen.

"Good idea, let's vamoose," said V, who liked experimenting with the local lingo. Since entering the *Exotic Dancers' Oasis Club*, she'd tried to purge her speech of Britishisms and drop her British accent and syntax which she was delighted to use on snobbish trans-Atlantic occasions, and which had become second nature since she often hunted in London and environs, and liked to attend plays in the West End. She shimmied her way into the pink phosphorescent semitransparent dress – a *great* disguise, she was thinking – I'm supposed to be *dead,* and I'm strutting around in a *glowing* phosphorescent dress. She slipped her feet into the pink stilettos. They were utterly divine!

"Yeah, vamoose, let's vamoose," Tracy said, sliding into a T-shirt and jeans, and slipping out the door. "Bye, V, see you soon! And Helen … I still love you! You know that, I wish you wouldn't ignore me so!"

And she was gone. V let the image linger. Ships that pass in the night! V adored Vietnamese ladies with golden skin and fine bones and triangular vixen faces – but, she sighed, her tastes were so eclectic!

"Tracy was your girlfriend?"

"We had a moment."

The change room was still misty from the shower. V adjusted the stilettos and turned to Helen, "Do you want to get rid of that scar?"

"Are you kidding?"

"I'm not kidding."

"It's impossible."

"I don't think so. Let's see." V ran her fingers over the scar tissue, the blind eye, and the twisted scarred mouth. "I can do it if you want me to. I can make you the way you were before."

"This is what I have become, Helen of Troy, the two-faced woman." She turned the scarred side to V. "Tracy wants me in spite of it. It has its own beauty, like your reptilian scales, don't you think?"

V gazed fixedly at the scarred face. "Yes," she said, "But –"

"It's the mark I carry because I defied the Boys and their God."

"So …?"

"It's the mark they put upon me."

"So …?"

"It's the brand and mark of sin I carry."

"So …?"

"So – get rid of the fucking thing if you can!"

"Okay. Close your eyes."

"Just like that?"

"Yes, just like that."

V held Helen's face in her hands, and she closed her eyes and concentrated.

It took energy. She wasn't sure she was doing the right thing: deeds – all deeds – but particularly good deeds – had, in her experience, unforeseen and unintended consequences on this wayward planet, Earth. Perhaps Helen would be punished for having recovered her old face, perhaps …

All acts have infinite ramifications.

The meshes of the chain of being are infinitely fine.

Yeah, yeah, okay, so what, who cares! Every act is a risk! Go, V! Go!

The molecular structure had to be reorganized, the old molecular structure regenerated. The powers of regeneration V possessed and which she could apply to herself – she supposed it was a sort of dynamic biological nanotechnology – a sort of mobilization of some atomic or subatomic force field – she could also extend within a limited range to others.

V opened her eyes and looked. "Okay, you can look now," she said.

The mirrors were still foggy and streaked from V's shower. Helen used her elbow to wipe away the fog. And then she looked. For a moment, she was silent, and then she shrieked. "Oh, my God!"

"What?"

"It's me the way I was. God! What are you?"

She turned her face and, eyes wide, looked straight at V. Yes, V thought, Helen's face was perfect. It was the way it had been before, no sign of the scars, no sign of the knife cuts, and no sign of the twisted mouth. The right eye that had been blind and dead was bright, blue, and sublime. Helen of Troy was a very beautiful woman.

"Good. Let's get out of here," V said, "I'm a vampire; you saw that; I'll tell you the rest of what I am – so far as I understand it – some other time." A ripple of gunfire echoed from close by. V said, "What's that?"

"It must be the Mexicans. Let's go!"

V grabbed a large pink sombrero.

"What do you want that for?"

"You`ll see."

They exited into the alley. The incinerator was still wheezing and chugging out billows of black smoke. Big Boy and Little Boy were headed for heaven. The moon was high and veiled with dust. A sandstorm was coming, a big one.

A few minutes later, V, sheltered by the large pink sombrero from the overhead cameras, stood in front of a street ATM and emptied Big Boy and Little Boy`s bank accounts. Helen stood lookout.

As V withdrew the money, the machine asked her if she wanted to buy a new insurance policy, if she wanted to subscribe to a sadomasochistic bondage sex-flow holographic stream, if she was in the market for real-life anatomically accurate fully-functional sex dolls, if she wanted to buy a shipment of antique AK-47s. Then it said: "Your Profile has recently been Updated. Do you want to buy a sombrero, a top hat, a beanie, a fedora, a beret, a cloche, a fully-functioning Mauser MG-42, a German Waffen-SS World War II helmet?"

Clients and half-clad strippers were running into the streets, and shots were echoing in the sultry air. The Mexican gang had hit the *Exotic Dancers' Oasis Club.*

"They'll be down this street in a minute," said Helen, "and they'll be looking for Big Boy and Little Boy.

"Here," said V, "about $25,000. We can split it, if that's okay with you – I'd give you the whole thing, but I'm short of cash right now."

"How did you do that? Where'd you get the codes?"

"When I drink blood, I also absorb information – bank codes, social security numbers, other stuff …"

"Jesus Christ, Almighty! You are a real number!"

"Thanks," V grinned, "I'm like one of those gadgets with all sorts of accessories. I'm the Swiss Army knife of vampires."

"I owe you big time," said Helen.

While they split the cash, V said, "Here's a number. If you want to join me, you can find me through this number. Leave me a number to get back to you, and I will. I'd like it if we could get together."

"Me too, I'd like it very much!" Helen scribbled the number on the back of her hand. "I'll memorize it, and wash it off," she said. "I'm going to leave town tomorrow. I'll call you. I want to know more about you – and if I can help you, I'm your girl!"

"It's a deal! Till then!"

"Till then."

They shook hands, and then V kissed Helen of Troy on both cheeks – V was a girl from the Ancient pagan Mediterranean, after all.

Helen disappeared, and V headed toward the motel and a rendezvous with her friend, Alex.

V went clip-clopping along a back street in the stiletto heels. She was feeling extra frisky and oh-too-sexy in the glowing skintight pink dress. She could hear gunshots in the distance. She had about $12,500 from Big Boy's and Little Boy's accounts – and she'd used Big Boy's telephone-tablet to text a coded message to an address in Bern, Switzerland: *"Party was great, left early, have a headache."*

Buried in those words was a numeric code for a courier company delivery point not too far away from the desolate little desert town where she found herself. V needed new supplies – passports, identity papers, credit cards, access to money, and above all, new clothes and weapons. Andromeda Corp had stripped her naked except for the armored catsuit – and nothing was left of that. She was like Robinson Crusoe, tossed up nude on a desert island.

To confront just such an eventuality, over the years, over the centuries, V had developed backup facilities. Supplies were stored in various points of the globe. Containers were ready to be shipped at a moment's notice to dozens, to hundreds, of drop-off points. The people handling the containers didn't know what they contained. The various circuits were scrupulously isolated from one another. V tugged at the pink, tasseled hem. That damned Andromeda Corporation had better not have unlocked all her secrets. She hated the idea of having to build everything from scratch.

The only person who held the keys to V's life – and even she didn't have all the keys – was Maria Romano, the Italian criminologist, back in V's villa in Italy: Maria hacked computers, analyzed profiles, helped manage V's finances, and generally helped V choose her fodder – hardened criminals, murderers, sadistic killers, diabolical dictators, torturers …

V had decided she would not contact Maria until she was sure that she, V, was not compromised in some deeper way. V had set up many of the supply backup circuits independent of Maria so that Maria would not be exposed if those circuits were brought down and vice-versa.

V's new bio-identity would obtain most supplies. And she could change her bio-identity, or the appearance of her eyes, and her fingerprints, to about half a dozen variants.

And, if she survived and escaped the clutches of Andromeda Corporation – then she could return to Maria and to her old home base in Italy: the superb villa on the cliff, with its hidden beach and underground bunker.

Oh, to go swimming again! Oh, to watch the sunset over the Tyrrhenian Sea. Oh, to sit on the cliff, or go to the beach with Maria and reminisce about old times!

V came to the fire escape and took off the high heels – they were fun but inconvenient and not that comfortable – they were *killing* her arches – and climbed barefoot up the fire escape – to her new friend, Alex.

She climbed softly, panther-like, making virtually no noise.

She stood for a moment outside the window and looked back toward the strip club. Fires were burning. She heard more gunfire. She hoped her new friend Helen was safe. She was a stunning girl. V hankered after Helen, and also wanted her as a friend. Helen was gutsy, bright, and beautiful – and she might be very useful. V licked her lips. *I definitely see a future for Helen.*

Standing there, in the glow of burning buildings, V thought, for a second, of all the people who were gone, all the people who were dead. When you live so long, the dead keep you company; sometimes, the dead are your only company.

She was always talking to the dead! V stretched and yawned. The people she talked to in her head, her old friends, and her ancient lovers! There were so many of them, so many!

Yes, she thought, often people – human people – feel disconnected from their past lives, their past selves. They become strangers to themselves. But in her case, the detachment was even more extreme: she had lived so many lives, her rebirth had to be repeated, again and again, and it must begin now. *Each moment is a moment of renewal; each breath is a new self, a new performance.*

The red glow of burning buildings reminded her …

… reminded her of more than 150 years ago …

… London, England, in the Blitz …

An old song came back to her from one romance she had had – it was in London during the Blitz, when V worked for Winston Churchill, in one of his brilliant inventions, the Special Operations Executive, or SOE, an idea the British Prime Minister cooked up in the summer of 1940 when everything seemed lost, when Adolf Hitler was master of virtually all of Europe and Britain and its Empire stood alone against the Nazi Juggernaut. The Germans had just conquered all of Western Europe, including Britain's great ally and the anchor of the western alliance, France. Things looked hopeless. Democracy was doomed. Winston was in his element when things were darkest. "Well, V," the Prime Minister said, "Now things have become simpler, and more interesting. Now we are alone. And, V, alone, we in Britain know what we must do and what we shall do. We shall fight, and we shall fight, and we shall fight." And he explained: the SOE was to inspire and support Resistance

Movements, which were fighting the Nazis in occupied Europe. "We shall set Europe ablaze under the Nazis' feet," the Prime Minister muttered, looking slyly toward V to see if she appreciated the phrase. She did. Her bright, eager smile told him so.

"Cognac?" Winston held up the bottle; he was dressed in his special "siren suit," which looked to V like workers' overalls or buttoned-up long-johns with lots of pockets.

"Yes, Mr. Prime Minister," she said. Cognac was stretching her diet, which, in addition to blood, extended to whiskey, wine, and coffee, but in the eighteenth century when she had directed a convent in Normandy – full of luscious lusty young girls whose parents could not afford to endow them with dowries – she had developed a taste for the heady golden-colored stuff.

"V," the Prime Minister explained, "you will work for SOE, but in an unofficial capacity, of course. Having a vampire in the front line, you understand, V, is problematic. It's best that we keep it hush-hush. If it leaked, it would be a godsend for Doctor Goebbels." Winston waved a pudgy hand with its trademark cigar.

"I certainly understand, Mr. Prime Minister."

And they raised their glasses.

War is a hothouse of passion. Death and love go together. In the 1940s, fear and adrenaline and courage and desire made for an explosive mixture, a need to seize the instant. *Eat, drink, and be merry, for tomorrow we die.*

In the autumn of 1941, V fell in love with a young man who worked in SOE and who was later to be parachuted into France to set up and liaise with French resistance groups and teach them how to use explosives.

While the bombs were falling on London, and the night sky glowed red and gold, and the searchlights crisscrossed in the smoky air, and the drone of engines and the ack-ack of anti-aircraft guns were everywhere, and the sirens were wailing, people everywhere sang, *We'll meet again*, a song about lovers parted by war, but who were sure they would meet again, somewhere, sometime, someday when the sun was shining. But, from his mission to France, the beautiful explosives expert never did return.

Why did I think of that now? V wiped away a tear.

Oh, yes, it was the burning glow over the town, the flames over the club and the buildings around it; the scene reminded her of the night sky over London during the Blitz: German bombs raining down, explosions, the stuttering fire of anti-aircraft guns, the drone of aircraft engines, the big barrage balloons floating like dirigibles in the night sky, the smell of sawdust and beer – bitter hops – and broken masonry tumbling down, and dust, and blood spilt everywhere, innocent blood, it all came back in a flood, with the sweet-sharp apple taste of Cognac.

The lad's name was Mark Hill.

He was twenty-three.

The Gestapo caught him and, as V learned later, strangled him with razor wire, hanging him from a meat hook in the Flossenbürg concentration camp, after weeks spent torturing him, in vain, slowly breaking almost every bone in his body.

Winston said, "I'm sorry, V, I'm so terribly sorry."

"Thank you, Prime Minister," she looked away, toward all the maps pinned up on the wall, toward all the tasks yet to be accomplished. She hummed. *We'll meet again.*

V wiped away a tear and climbed through the motel window.

CHAPTER 5 – HUBRIS

Alex was lying on the bed on top of the sheets in his boxer shorts with the thick black and gold vertical stripes and with the lights off except for the bedside reading lamp with its little, frilly, red, bordello-style lampshade. He was reading a book, *Our Genetic Future*. "The air-conditioning doesn't work," he said. "I'm greasy with sweat. It's like glue."

"Greasy, hmm! I say, that's a very good-looking chap lying there," said V, passing the tip of her tongue over her lips. Alex looked very handsome indeed lying on top of the sheets in the reddish glow of the bedside reading lamp; his blond hair was sun-bleached and thick and tousled; he was tanned, had lots of nice neat dark hair with glints of gold and blond on his chest, good muscles, not an ounce of extra fat. Yes, he was a fine specimen of a man, thought V, and she considered herself an excellent connoisseur of human flesh.

"Did you eat?"

"Yes, I did," he said, "a pizza out of a machine at the corner." He put the book aside and sat up on the edge of the bed. "And you?"

She could see his eyes, widening in a comic way, taking in, and running up and down, the skintight, semitransparent pink dress. "I borrowed – I mean I appropriated – this dress. It was in the dressing room at the strip club down the road. What do you think? Do you think it expresses the essence of my personality? Do you like it?"

"You look good." He swallowed. "You look different."

She stood in front of him and put her hands on his shoulders – warm, solid, smooth, and furry manly shoulders – and looked down at him, coquettishly perhaps, but she couldn't help it; feeding always gave her an extra, almost uncontrollable, feeling of energy, and thinking of Mark Hill, so brave and so young, had made her, well, sentimental, vulnerable, in need of human contact, of human warmth; had made her, well, yes, horny, lustful, hungry for a form of satisfaction – orgasm – she could never fully, never adequately, or very rarely, fulfill.

"The bruises, the bruises are gone. That's what's different," he said.

"Feeding gave me more than enough energy to finish the healing, and get rid of the bruises; now I'm whole again."

"You fed?"

"Yes, indeed."

"Do you want to tell me?"

"Do you want to know?"

Alex put his hands on her waist, cupping them around her, holding her tight; he had big warm, strong hands; he said, "Yes, I want to know."

This was always a difficult moment for V. People she got to know, people she learned to love, wanted to know more about her. Sometimes the merest hint of what she was, of her true nature, would send people reeling away in revulsion, in disgust. "*You are an abomination,*" in the words of her old friend, Father Michael Patrick O'Bryan SJ, "*You are an abomination.*" Sometimes they accepted the abstract idea that she was a vampire, that she fed on human blood, that she was a predator living off humans, but then they would want to know more, they would want to see, to visualize and to feel what she was. And, once they had seen, very few could accept the truth – or her.

V frowned. She hesitated: I wear a mask all the time, a mask I can never take off, well, almost never. John and Maria, her assistants for many years, they had accepted her for what she was, though John, poor dear, was dead, killed in Sudan trying to save some girls from rape. Baron De Villiers, back in the seventeenth century, in his own wittily sadistic libertine way, had accepted her, knowing what she was; and he had fun trying to kill her, immuring her in a dungeon underneath his chateau, and then making up with her, most gallantly, once she had, with timely aid from one of his servants, foiled his dastardly plot, escaped from the dungeon, and fought him to submission in a duel which proved to be great fun for both of them. And Father O'Bryan, dear soul, he knew everything, and he loved her still; in his own way, he loved her.

She remembered how ashamed and frightened she had been when John watched her feed one night: she was crouched under the orange-colored moon, sucking blood from her victim; she was covered in gore; blood was dripping from her fangs and her lips, and John had said, "Don't worry, V. I've seen you feed before." She loved John and Maria for that; she worshiped them – they, like Father O'Bryan, truly accepted her.

And, tonight, Helen had stood coolly smoking a cigarette while she watched V, smeared in blood, dripping gore, drain the blood from Big Boy – causing V, more or less instantly, to fall in love with Helen.

"Okay," she said; she sat down on the bed next to him. "Alex, I did not choose to become what I am; but what I am is what I am."

"I understand that."

"So it is as if a panther were speaking to you, or a lion."

"Don't be afraid, V. Go ahead."

"Okay." V took a deep breath. "I'm not going to make it pretty."

"Okay," Alex said, and then he did a bold thing – given that he was dealing with a creature he knew to be a blood-drinking, reptilian, she-devil; he cupped her face in his hands, turned her face to his, and kissed her on the lips.

"Hmmm," V murmured, "Hmmm."

"Now, begin!"

"Okay!" V took a deep breath and told him how she had gone to the strip joint, how she met Helen of Troy, how she'd enticed Big Boy and Little Boy into the back room, how they'd tossed her back and forth while shouting Biblical verses and religious slogans, how she was feeling weak and uncertain and afraid, and how they intended to rape and then disfigure and maybe kill her; how she had danced Big Boy right through the plate-glass window, how he crashed down in the glass on the pavement; how Little Boy was about to shoot her; how Helen of Troy had come in with a knife, stabbing Little Boy in the back, probably saving V's life; how she, V, had ripped out Big Boy's eyes, how she fed on him (she was very graphic here); how she ripped the two bodies into shreds and dropped the pieces into the incinerator, how Helen of Troy helped her clean up the mess and helped her choose her costume – the cute little pink dress – nifty purse – and – stiletto heels!

"Well …"

"Yes, well …"

They sat side-by-side on the edge of the bed. V had shrunk into herself. She could see all the images as if she were living it all again; as vivid as when it was happening. She was afraid Alex would turn away in disgust.

Alex turned his face to hers and kissed her. "So," he said, "What do we do now?"

V took another shower. Using Alex's toothpaste and her fingers, she vigorously brushed her teeth, and she gargled. She stared at herself in the mirror, sweeping away the fog with the back of her hand: "So that is me, killer, vampire, and monster!" Her reflection stared back. "That is you, V, and there is nothing you can do about it. And what should you do with this wonderful man who has helped you?"

Leftover human blood is very unpleasant for another human when you kiss them – though she was pretty sure she'd gotten rid of all traces of Big Boy back under the shower at the strip club where she'd aimed her mouth wide open and the shower nozzle and used the mouth wash Helen had given her and gargled and gargled and gargled.

V came out of the bathroom, wrapped in a big white towel.

She glows, Alex thought, she looks like gold.

V said nothing but just draped the towel over a chair, carefully folding it, and lay down next to Alex and turned toward him and put her hand on his chest and moved it back and forth playing with the curls of his chest hair, exploring the muscles of his chest, gliding her fingers over the smooth and furry skin, and moving her hand gently down toward his belly – sculpting it with the palm of her hand, and tapping playfully – a little jig – a little martial drumbeat tattoo – with the points of her fingers on the muscles of his flat hard belly.

"You really are a darling, Alex," she sighed, "darling, darling Alex! You saved my life. When you stopped and picked me up, I was almost dead."

Alex turned on his side so he could look at her. "And what in the world were you doing out there, V?"

V moved closer, put her hand against his cheek, brought her lips close, and brushed them against his lips. "Well, my dear savior," she whispered, "It's a long story. It was my stupidity – and my arrogance – that got me there. I fell into a trap. I thought I was hunting, but I was the hunted, not the hunter. I was captured in California, on the coast. When I escaped, my captors were transporting me from California to Virginia – in a specially outfitted Boeing 777 no less."

"Was that the plane that, ah, crashed, what, three or four days ago?"

"Yes." V bit her lip, and her eyes burned into his. "I was the cause of the crash, Alex. I didn't want the plane to crash, but … I killed a lot of people, and a lot of people died."

Alex took a deep breath. "So that's why you were in the desert."

"Yes."

"It was a long way from anywhere."

"Yes. I'd been in the desert three days and nights. I almost died. And I'm virtually indestructible, for a biological entity that is."

"How did it happen? I mean, how do you live? You feed off people. Do you create vampires like yourself, like in the movies?"

V was stroking his hair, staring into his eyes; she had known human beings for thousands of years, yet she always found them fascinating. "No, dear Alex, I've never made a being such as I! I swore to my mentor never to make a being such as I am. It is my most sacred oath, and I have kept it."

"Mentor?"

"My father, a man – well an entity – he certainly seems human – you would like him, and he would like you, I am sure. So let's call him a man, a man named Marcus, though he is not from earth. I do not know, precisely, where he comes from. He is the alien side of my DNA. He is my father. And, as I said, he made me swear never to create other creatures such as I."

"Why?"

"Well, as he told it to me, Marcus wanted – he wants to protect the human race – even from itself."

"He wants …?"

"Yes, Alex. I use the present tense because Marcus is still alive, not here on Earth, I think, but somewhere, he's still alive."

"So, your oath is to protect humanity, in a sense."

"Yes. A herd of hungry vampires running around infecting other humans – it would be like a plague; it would only stop when there were no more humans! So my duty has been to make sure I remain alone – and I've done it for more than twenty-five centuries."

"Twenty-five centuries!"

"I hope you will not shrink back in horror, but you have in your arms, dearest Alex, a Phoenician girl from North Africa, born circa 608 BCE, brought up in a very fine family – my adopted family – in a Mediterranean port city not far from Carthage; that girl was transformed into what she now is – me and the simple vampire and the she-devil-reptile you saw – in her nineteenth year."

"Jesus!"

"Yes, Jesus! I spoke Phoenician and Aramaic, the language of Jesus, or a closely related dialect, similar in many ways to Hebrew; and I spoke Ancient Greek because my father – my adoptive father, not Marcus – was a merchant and, in his way, a philosopher."

"Jesus!"

V laughed. "I know, I know, you don't believe me!"

"I believe you, V, I do believe you."

"You are a very good boy, Alex, a true gentleman, and very understanding of such wondrous improbabilities, I must say, for a scientist of the twenty-first century." Her lips brushed his lips, and her eyes, so dark and deep and only a few inches from his, darted back and forth, gazing into each of his eyes in turn, drinking him in, or searching for his innermost, most hidden, soul.

"So," Alex said, as he breathed in her exquisite perfume, "The vampire and she-devil, the reptilian version, are two different things – two different versions of you."

"Yes, I have three states, Alex. I guess you could say I'm like some sort of extra confused sub-atomic particle." V climbed up onto Alex, and sat up, straddling him, perched on his thighs. She looked down, and smiled, and Alex felt it was the sort of smile of total trust that is so rare even between old-time lovers. "I can be as I am now, a seemingly normal human being. I can be a vampire, with the usual pallor, leaden circles under my eyes, claws, and fangs. And then, I can be my super-octane version, which is that adorable reptile you discovered sitting next to you out in the desert."

"Yes," Alex said, "V, the iridescent demon!"

"The iridescent demon: how very sweet of you to put it that way, Alex! It makes it – it makes me seem beautiful."

"You are beautiful. And your demon version is exquisite!"

V nuzzled down and pressed her nose against Alex's chin, and with her hand, she tousled his blond, sun-bleached hair.

"But who kidnapped you – and why?"

"Ah, that is the question! But I know the answer: Andromeda Corporation, the biotechnology firm. They set the trap, and they captured me."

"Andromeda Corp? I know them. The CEO is a brilliant woman scientist called Sabrina Jacobs. She's a Nobel Prize Laureate."

"Yes, Sabrina – that's the name the kidnappers kept mentioning. She is the big boss. They were all in awe of her."

"Well, she is one of the most brilliant bio-engineers in the world, if not the most brilliant; but why did she want you?"

"You have seen what I am, Alex." V crouched closer, leaning into him, brushing his lips with hers. "I'm a monster, a freak." She withdrew, just a touch, so she could look into his eyes. "And, Alex, I'm a weapon. I am good at killing, *very* good at killing!"

Alex pulled her closer, just for a second, and kissed her, lightly, on the lips. "Go on," he said.

"Yes, and, even more important, Alex, I'm a reservoir, a possible reservoir, of biological innovation. My genetic makeup is unique – well, almost unique, on this planet. I just discovered that they – that Sabrina Jacobs, that is – made a clone of me, so there is one other me, as it were, a copy of me: I don't know where or when they got my DNA – that's something I have to find out."

"Yes, if you are half-alien, why studying you could revolutionize … revolutionize everything. The possibilities are immense!"

"Exactly! It's rather disconcerting, but I am a treasure trove, an Eldorado!" V nuzzled down and gave Alex a quick kiss on the lips.

"But what was she going to do with you – you would have resisted … you would have fought."

"Well, your brilliant Sabrina Jacobs had a solution to that too. She wanted – she wants – to lobotomize me."

Alex's eyes widened. "That's horrible."

"That's what I thought." V laughed. "I didn't really fancy being turned into a bloody robot. I love my freedom!"

"But how was she going to …?"

"I got this information from my mental eavesdropping when I was a prisoner. Piecing it together, the bits and pieces, this is the story: Sabrina Jacobs planned to use chemicals to lobotomize me – there are classic techniques, as you know, for doing this. My system is pretty resilient, so who knows if her plan would have worked." V took a deep, dreamy breath, almost a sigh, and with the palm of one hand, she stroked the side of Alex's face. "But to be a robot, unable to feel desire, or love, or hate! Not to know, or recognize, or care for someone such as you! I shiver at the thought!" She leaned down and kissed him; her breasts brushed his chest.

He returned her kiss; his passion was rising. He had not felt desire since Judy had died; a fleeting sense of guilt cast a brief shadow, but it faded into an even stronger sense of yearning.

V broke off and drew back: "It's dangerous what we are doing, you and I, but I want to keep doing it for just a little while longer."

"Dangerous?"

"Yes." She leaned down and kissed him and swayed back and forth so that her breasts brushed lightly against his chest, offering herself to him. "I get excited, too excited, and then …" She bared her teeth, bright, and even, and very human. "And zoom, they grow, I bite, I can't help myself."

"Wow! Yes, that does make it very exciting."

"It does? For you? Yes, I guess it would. Men – some men – love danger."

"How did they capture you?"

V closed her eyes.

"Well, I was really stupid. As I said, I was arrogant. I took a risk I should not have taken. In short, stupid me, I fell into a trap!"

"A trap?"

V became thoughtful, as if she was living a horrible moment in her past. "Yes, Alex, I fell into a trap … It looked easy. You see, Alex, when I kill, I try to kill bad people – I know it's not a perfect solution, and it's not a just solution – I am judge, jury, and executioner, which is, of course, unfair. Father O'Bryan, a Jesuit friend of mine …"

"You have a friend who's a Jesuit?"

"Yes, strange, isn't it? The Jesuit and the Vampire – our friendship presented Father O'Bryan with some difficult moments and moral perplexities over the years."

"I'll bet!"

"Yes, in any case, Father O'Bryan, I adored him and I know he liked me, said only God can judge people, and I think that, in a way – even if I don't believe in God, not of the Judeo-Christian-Islamic monotheistic kind – that what Father O'Bryan said is true: Each person is a mystery and we never really know where evil and good lurk and, sometimes, we don't know which is which; we never know enough to pluck out the mystery of another person fully; so you would have to be omniscient, like God, to truly judge someone and to have the right to judge them."

"Yes," said Alex, and he ran his hand up, over her breasts, to her shoulders. She shuddered, took a deep breath, and continued. "But, aside from that caveat, I try to choose very bad people. Usually, I work with a brilliant criminologist, Maria Romano, and she helps me choose my 'targets.' But this time I flew solo, as it were, I didn't even tell Maria (which was lucky) what I was doing or who the target was. Sometimes, if I don't want to compromise Maria or expose her, I fly solo operations like this. My informant this time – and it wasn't the first time – was a Cambridge criminologist, Jed Barker. I trusted him. Now I'm not sure – either he was duped, or he duped me.

Somehow, through Jed, Sabrina Jacobs, or her people, prepared a trap and led me into it."

"You lead a complicated life, V."

"You are so right, dear Alex," V said, running her fingers through his hair, and staring down at him with something like adoration, "the life of a vampire demon is not always simple."

Alex kissed her. He wanted to console her for her difficult life as a vampire. He wanted her breasts to brush against his chest, which, as she leaned down and kissed him, they did.

"Oh, Alex, Alex, Alex," V sighed. "In any case, the 'target' was a drug dealer, a very rich Mexican, who had an ocean-side villa very close to the Mexican American border. He went running on the beach, my informant told me, and he had a little beach pavilion where he would meet girls – girls he would mistreat, usually."

"Ah," said Alex, "it would be easy."

"Yes, it seemed easy. I would come in from the sea. I would use a dinghy. I would anchor the dinghy off shore, and I would swim in, and I would catch him alone except for one or two guards and possibly a girl in the villa, and I would feed – and I would escape."

"Simple as apple pie," said Alex.

"When it looks easy," V added, running her fingers through Alex's hair, "that's when you want to watch out."

"Yes, you are certainly right," said Alex, thinking of how Judy died, just from running downstairs to help somebody.

"The water was warm and balmy. It was a go-it-alone operation: just me, nobody else. I parked my rented car five miles away on a deserted beach. I took the dinghy out of the trunk, took it down to the water, inflated it, and pushed it into the water, and I used its motor, which was electric and very quiet, to carry me to a position opposite the little villa – it was a bungalow really. My informant told me my target would be there; and, sure enough, the lights were all on."

V closed her eyes, and while she talked, she was transported from their hot little room in the Garden of Eden Oasis motel back to the Pacific Ocean almost a week before:

"It was going to be so easy. I could already taste the blood ..."

This will be so easy: I can already taste the blood.

I drop anchor, and I slip over the smooth rubber side of the dinghy into the cool water.

My face is painted in a camouflage pattern, matt black and khaki green. I'm wearing my standard, black armored wetsuit, slick and comfortable. I swim the distance slowly, carefully, watching for any danger signs – incongruous-looking lights, men on the beach, electronic surveillance, barbed wire, dogs, unusual shapes or shadows. There are none.

I should be more suspicious. But I'm not.

I swim to the edge of the beach. I lie absolutely still, in the shallow water, my belly flat against the sand, scanning the beach and the villa; I use night vision, and infrared. I don't sense any danger. Slowly I stand up out of the water. From where I am, the moon is hidden behind a bank of clouds, but it is shining full on the hills and on the villa, and they are coated in silver. The beach is dark, and so am I.

I'm invisible, I think, I'm invisible.

This will be easy, I think, this will be a coup, a public service, a cakewalk.

The man – Juan Rodriguez Alvarez is his name – is said to be untouchable. His uncle was the President of Mexico, and he had blackmail material – child pornography and child prostitution information – on the Governor of California. His gangs rampaged around northern Mexico and the southern states – nobody could touch him.

Alvarez had recently organized the killing of a school full of children. It was his revenge for the village calling in the Mexican Army to expel one of his drug laboratories. The kids had been shot or had their throats cut. The photos in the Mexican scandal sheets were full of the color red – my color: the color of blood.

His agents recruit girls to entertain the man.

He meets the girls in this isolated beach villa. And this is where he will die!

I leap across the beach and flatten myself against a wall of the villa: still no sign of surveillance, electronic, or other.

There is a window, and I see behind it the silhouette of a man and a woman. I wait a moment, and then I smash through the window, and the man and women freeze.

A wall of steel slams down behind me, and I turn to see that the window has shut, and I now know this is a trap.

The slamming down of the steel door is a distraction, and when I turn round …

The man has a gun, and he fires two bullets – silver nitrate bullets – I feel their poison enter my bloodstream and I hear a hiss and see that the room is filling with a gas, it must be a type of nerve gas – it is a neurological paralyzing gas, I think, it must be, for I feel I am losing control of my body: my arms and legs no longer respond to orders. The man and the woman topple down. I try to smash through the steel window, but, in my rapidly weakening state, I can't. My mind fades – I panic – fear floods through me – and I feel myself falling, and I see the floor rising to meet me, and I hear my pistol clatter onto the floor, and I feel my back suddenly flat against the smooth tile floor which seems somehow cool and restful, and I feel my body is utterly paralyzed and then I lose consciousness and my vision fades and it is all just blackness.

When I wake up, I am dazed and weak. I must have been pumped full of hallucinating drugs – and more neurological inhibitors. I am totally confused. I blink my eyes, looking around. Who am I? Where am I? What is happening to me?

Things gradually come into focus.

Bars, I see bars. I am in a metal cage, like a lion's cage at the zoo. I am looking out from behind metal bars. I try to move, but I can't. My muscles barely respond to orders. I realize I am manacled, neck, hands, and ankles, to what seems to be a thick wall of solid steel. It must be one side of the cage, and I am gagged, with a steel-and-rubber ball gag forcing my mouth wide open, and pressing my tongue down. I am still too dizzy to understand what is happening.

There are guards outside the cage, running around, shouting.

Then we are moving

The cage is being wheeled across the tarmac of what looks like a military airport. The airport lights shine on the greasy tarmac. There is a damp, warm breeze from the sea. I have a terrible headache, Oh, God, do I have a terrible headache, and …

I am seeing things double …

I am hallucinating. Hallucinations, they must be hallucinations: images of trees and jungles, full of serpents and I see trees turning into serpents and all of the vegetation of the thick jungle writhing and twisting like ravenous, starving monsters, gaping, teeth-filled jaws of tropical flowers, orchids like killers, vines like snakes, the flowers and leaves want to eat me, and I see myself, naked, bathing in blood, horns, and antlers springing up from my forehead, my fangs growing longer and longer, reaching down beyond my chin, my reptilian skin becoming thicker and thicker until I was encrusted with scales like an alligator or a monstrous gargoyle on some medieval cathedral tower …

… then I am me again but now I am covered in stripes, black and white stripes, like a zebra, running through a forest, then out onto a dry, dusty savannah, and I have hooves instead of feet, and a long tail, and mane, and a golden lioness is pursuing me, and I know there is something I should do, something which will set me free, but I can't remember what it is.

They are loading the cage onto a plane; up we go on a sort of forked lift, into the hold of a big cargo aircraft, a Boeing 777, and I think: Where am I going? Who are they?

There is a lot of noise of metal hitting metal, and of slamming doors, and shouting people, and closing hydraulic doors and then … it is quieter.

I am in a steel cage in an aircraft about to take off.

The pilot says, "Buckle up, ready for takeoff!" And I think, I don't need to buckle up, I'm already well and truly buckled up.

They take off.

There is a guard, a guy called Freddy. I'm beginning to focus: I can read his mind. He is sitting in a chair opposite the cage. He tries to be nice; he waves; he says hello: but of course, I can't talk, and anyway, I wasn't feeling very friendly. So, gaining more strength, I transmit a mental message. "*Sorry, Freddy, but I'm not in an especially friendly mood right now.*"

A woman came and stood outside the cage. She was holding a clipboard. "Well, honey, you don't look so dangerous," she said; she had a cute little black uniform with the Andromeda Corporation Logo, and she was very pretty. Toni Anderson was her name.

I want to say something to her, but I am still hallucinating – because I wanted to beg her – I see myself as the wild zebra girl or as a small child – I want to beg her: "Don't hurt me, please, don't hurt me!"

But I can only look at her. My mouth is jammed open by the gag. I can't speak. I can't utter a word, and for some reason, I can't transmit to her the way I did to Freddy; Freddy is more open; this Toni is an intellectual, her mind is too busy, too full of itself, to receive me.

Toni has a smile, part tender, part ironic, and part, I think, cruel, playing on her lips, very pretty lips, full and delicately sculpted, and very bright teeth. "What do I see in those eyes," she stares at me, "Fear, hatred, hunger?"

I think she sees all three – plus confusion: I am still caught in a phantas-magoria of images, and Toni Anderson and the interior of the aircraft and the guard sitting buckled in on a chair opposite me are still flickering presences seen through a veil of parading hallucinations.

I am still the hoofed zebra girl, my white tail floating behind me like silk, fleeing from the lioness through long golden yellow grass, hoping to reach a cluster of trees, where, I think, in spite of my hooves, I will be able to climb those trees and get up just out of the reach of the extended claws, that maw of teeth, that beautiful golden predator who wants to eat me.

So I kick up dust under my hooves in the dry African heat under the brilliant hot flattened sun, galloping flat out. Caught up in all of this, I can only stare mutely, my mouth jammed open, drool dripping from around the gag, at Toni Anderson.

Toni stands gazing at me with curiosity. Partly it is scientific curiosity – full of concepts and theories about my true nature: What part of this creature is human, what is alien, what is vampire, and how are these things coded into her DNA? Partly it is human curiosity – curiosity about what I am feeling, how I am seeing her, what I feel and what I fear, what a life like mine, an outcast living by murder and blood lust, must be like.

My eyes are dark and show no soul and Toni Anderson is puzzled, trying to get a grip on what I am. I realize, as these thoughts about Toni come to me, that my ability to read thoughts, foggy and limited in its range, is returning quickly, and intensifying, and with it, my sense of myself.

I catch another thought, vague at first, but then more and more precise: "It's too bad they are going to *lobotomize* her," Toni is thinking, "It would be much more productive to deal with her when she's still intelligent, when she's still a conscious being. Henry is right. Who knows what mysteries she might help us unveil. But Sabrina insists: this thing must be lobotomized, and totally; she is too dangerous to be left with intelligence. She must be turned into a robot."

I recoil. This wakes me up. To be turned into a robot, a slave, *a thing!* My pretty zebra self disappears; the lioness and the savannah fade; the vast flat hot afternoon African sun is no more.

I suddenly remember a precaution I had taken – a precaution I sometimes take when I go on a mission. And to think I almost didn't do it.

But I had.

Inserted beside one of my teeth is a capsule of pure amphetamine extract, vitamin concentrate, and silver nitrate antidote. It's a poisonous mixture, but it works in the short term, it gives me a huge spurt of energy.

Making a special effort, twisting my jaw slightly, I think I can crush the capsule.

The capsule, once broken, would give me a short-term spurt of super-energy, perhaps twenty minutes or an hour, maybe two hours if conditions were right, at the maximum level of energy.

I can become the reptilian demon if I need to, and I need to – only the demon will have the strength to smash out of this cage, and even then …

I think. Should I do it right away?

No, it will be better to wait until the plane lands, until they are transferring me, until we are safely on the ground. Then I can break out and spurt away and find a hiding place and figure out what to do next.

Toni Anderson is still musing, lost in her thoughts, and staring at me.

I realize that the steel-and-rubber ball gag will make it difficult to break the capsule; but, I think, I will be able to do it, I *must* be able to do it.

A man comes into the hold. "It's time to give this thing its injection of silver nitrate."

Silver nitrate, more silver nitrate, I shiver. Another injection will make escape impossible! It might even kill me!

"You could kill her if you give her another injection." Toni looks annoyed.

"I don't think so. The monster is stronger than it looks. Look at it – helpless. To think we went to all this trouble to get it. I think it's useless, just a freak of nature."

"Sabrina insisted – we keep her alive."

"I know. I know." The guy ran a metal cup along the bars, making a painful clattering sound. "How do you like it, you monster, you creepy-crawly obscenity, you *thing*? How do you like being a freak in a cage, huh?"

"Stop that!" Toni obviously hates the guy.

"Why? It's fun. Besides, I despise this creature. Have you dealt with its Clone?"

Clone, I think, clone? A clone of me! What clone?

"Yeah, I've studied the Clone."

Clone? What clone, where?

"Well, the Clone is just an animal, a slobbering incoherent idiot animal; it has no mental processes to speak of; it's just a freak and monster, like this one here – the original, the prototype. It looks human, but believe me, it ain't human!"

Clone – this is a violation of everything I stand for: I must never make a creature such as I! A Clone! How did they create a Clone?

"You are wrong about the Clone. She was fine until she was six. She was a genius. She spoke 5 or 6 or more languages; her I.Q. was off the charts. Then, at six, something happened. Her intelligence died."

"Well, I saw her after that – just a drooling idiot, see this one, she's drooling too, hey look at you, you *Thing*, I see those eyes, I see those eyes flashing hatred, I see that look – well, soon those eyes are going to be empty shells, soon, when Sabrina has finished with you, you will be an empty shell. There'll be nobody at home, nobody at all!" And he laughs.

I watch the man. I am thinking: Clone? When did they make a clone? And I thought of the first rule, the first oath: "You are not to make any more of your kind!" And I thought: I must destroy the Clone. And I must get away before he gives me the injection!

The guy makes some more clanking noises against the bars of the cage; it is irritating. He is staring at me with sadistic lust – he wants to kill me, he wants to torture me, he wants to fuck me. I can see the images parading, rushing, through his head. People, even mediocre people, can be so complicated! I have never understood why men get pleasure and perhaps some women too from making love to – from fucking – someone they hate, as if the act of love were an act of aggression, of hatred, of war. He is giving Toni Anderson the benefit of his wisdom, his experience.

"Yeah," he says, "I saw the fucking Clone when she was about ten. I mean, it screamed, it rolled its eyes; it threw its shit around; it fought like a demon when it didn't want to do something. To clean it, you had to chain it up, hood it, and spray it with a hose."

Listening to him talk (he is enjoying it, he even winks at me a couple of times), I think: *I must eliminate it, I must eliminate this Clone, this abomination and then, using the word abomination*, I remembered Father Michael O'Bryan, and I remembered that *abomination* was the word he used to describe me.

I am for a split second, stricken with a sense of guilt, of shame; then I think, No, I must eliminate the Clone – it is my duty, to Marcus, to myself, and to humanity.

"Maybe the Clone screamed because it didn't like you," Toni Anderson says.

The guy says, "Okay, I'll give our friend here the shot through the bars. It's neat. I don't even have to go into the cage to get at her. Her arms are close enough. See!" He takes out the needle and begins to prepare it.

I feel a rush of fear.

It's now or never!

I push my tongue around, pressing it up against the ball gag; the gag is held firmly in place by a sort of steel-and-rubber harness, with a broad band of rubber and steel that wraps around my mouth and the back of my head. Two lateral bands of rubber and steel hold it in place. My tongue is held down by the rubber ball. I move my jaw sideways, pressing the rubber ball against the capsule. The rubber ball is very hard, and there is just a chance that …

It might break.

The guy is squirting the needle.

I push and push and push with my tongue and then …

The capsule breaks.

The liquid touches my tongue and my gums; some of it makes it down my throat. It is like fire, like an explosion of electric energy. Within two seconds, it is in my bloodstream. A flare of strength rushes through me, like an explosion, arms, legs, hands, feet …

Out of my peripheral vision, I can see the guy squirting the needle, preparing to plunge it in. The drone of the aircraft is loud, deafening.

This is the moment!

Toni is standing back and watching, her arms folded, and she says, "I really don't think she needs more. It could be dangerous. I mean …" I reflect, in that instant, as the strength is washing through me like a tidal wave, that in the short time I have known her, I rather like this Toni Anderson even though she considers me a thing, a beast, and I would have loved, under different conditions or in a different situation, to have known her, talked with her, laughed with her, but … And I like the friendly guard, Freddy, but …

I morph into the she-devil, with all the she-devil's strength.

The guy was saying, "I don't give a fuck, if this *thing* – I repeat '*thing*' – dies …"

I gather all my strength and push. The steel manacles pop and snap like rubber bands, bits of metal flying here and there.

"Oh my God," says Toni Anderson.

"Fuck," says Tom Riley.

I smash against the bars – the bars pop, bend, and snap. Pieces go flying. Riley comes running at me with the needle. I break his arm, and then I break his neck.

Toni Anderson's body splits in two, the two halves careening apart in a wave of blood; she'd been cut in half by one of the flying bars.

"I'm so sorry, darling, I'm so sorry."

Another bar had cut a hole in the fuselage. The pressure is rushing out. The temperature is dropping. Red lights flash, an alarm is ringing, the wind howls. I can see my breath.

Poor Freddy leaps out of his seat. He tries to shoot me; I break his arm. First one, then the other.

Men rush into the hold. They are carrying submachine guns – not a good idea in an aircraft at high altitude (but I can feel we are losing altitude very fast), and some of their guns have, I realize, soft-nosed bullets, the kind that tear a baseball-sized or a football-sized hole in flesh – or in an aircraft.

I don't want to be hit by one of those.

I whirl around, leaping up to the roof, and then coming down behind the two gunmen. I break their arms, and I tear the head off one of them.

I am hit twice, but they are ordinary bullets, I can spit them out and fix up the wounds. I break another guy's neck, and since by now I am furious, I tear him in half.

When their guns went off, the bullets probably destroyed the control system of the aircraft and, going through the walls of the hold, they probably killed the pilot.

The plane is spinning downwards, and all the bodies and bits of metal bounce around, tumbling in total chaos.

I go forward.

Yes, the pilot had caught a stray bullet and was dead, slumped over the controls. The co-pilot stares up at me. He says, "Fuck! What next!" I push the pilot away from the controls, and I sit down, I try the controls. I am ultra-strong in my demonic state, as you know; so I think, maybe I can make a difference. Bug-eyed, the co-pilot watches me. I can't do anything. The controls don't respond. I shrug and indicate I can't help. The co-pilot goes back to trying to control the aircraft, but I know – and he knows – it's hopeless.

I get up, and I transmit the thought, "*They don't respond. I'm sorry!*"

He turns and looks at me, and he says, amazingly addressing me as if I were human, he says, "Yeah, I know. So am I. Sorry, I mean."

I climb back into the hold.

Freddy, the young guard, is still there, terrified, helpless. We were too low now, I know, for parachutes. I turn to him, and I project into his mind the thought: *I'd help you if I could – but there's no time.* He just gulps.

I don't think he even hears or understands me. After all, he is looking at a reptilian she-demon who has just massacred most of the crew and broken both his arms, and there is a storm of noise in the hold, the wind roaring and whistling, the engines screaming – and the whole structure on the verge of breakup.

Toni Anderson is crumpled in a corner, two blood-soaked rags. Her face is still unharmed, blond hair like bright gold, and her mouth is slightly open, bright lips and teeth, and her eyes too, very blue candid eyes, and I have time to think, *What a waste*, before I smash open a door and leap out.

I am leaping to my death, I think.

But there is no other way.

Caught in the air, I whip over the wing, flipping past and missing one of the engines by a few yards.

Then I float in the air, or so it seems, and I remember, once again, what Marcus had told me, that I wouldn't know what powers I had until I tried them, *well*, I think, *now is the time to fly or at least to glide*, and I stretch out my arms and legs and I concentrate and I feel my shape is changing … I am like a glider.

I can't fly, but I can *glide*. Vampires are supposed to be related to bats, after all.

It is night.

Below me, there were no lights, no lights at all. Far to the west, I could see a great orange and red glow, which must have been the reflection of the fires that were consuming what was left of California.

Above me are the stars.

The wind roars in my ears. I am truly gliding. I hear a dull explosion and see a distant flash. The plane had crashed. There will be no survivors.

I glide. I breathe the air that is warmer now, balmy even, and bone-dry, I am gliding lower. It is as if my arms and legs had sprouted wings, and, in fact, they had. Marcus was right. *But*, I wonder, *is this enough? Will the impact kill me?*

I concentrate. I focus my night vision. Below is desert, sandy dunes, pebbled plateaus, a few ancient ravines from when the water used to run free, small spots of scrub, nothing else – no human shelter. *How high am I now? How fast am I going?*

I have seen gliders land, I slow down, I turn upwards and gliding along the surface, slowing as much as I can, with the land rising and falling only fifteen feet below me, I use gravity, turning upwards, and then slowly going downwards, to slow me down, I bank up, now I am maybe ten feet above the ground, following the gently undulating contours of the desert land.

I crash down. It is a rough landing. I bounce and tumble, head over heels, and then smash into a dune, sprawling on a sandy slope, my claws stretched out in front of me, my fangs and snout buried in the sand, one of my arms almost ripped off, and I know I'm bleeding profusely from the impact, and I think, *am I alive, am I really alive?*

I'm shaken and dizzy and flat on the ground. Slowly I sit up. It is almost completely dark though I can see. I feel myself all over. I concentrate on stemming the flow of blood and on re-attaching the arm. I crawl on all fours. Then I stand up. Nothing is broken. The bruises, under the reptilian skin, are big – the soft tissue damage, I know, is extensive.

Then I remember – my jaw is still locked open by that damned ball gag.

Once I get my system stabilized a bit – and this takes a lot of energy – I unbuckle the gag, detach the metal-and-rubber straps, and pull out the rubber ball. I throw the thing down. Then I think better of it, and I bury it so it will be out of sight, though the sand is soft and may, of course, blow away. I stretch my jaw and try to make a few noises – and, yes, I can! I hiss in pleasure, and then I try words, almost human words, "Bow, wow! One, two, three, four, five …"

I haven't fed, not for almost two weeks. So here I am – weak, wounded, and in the middle of a desert. And the sun will soon be up. There is no shelter, no fodder. In my weakened state, without shelter or shade, a whole day's exposure to the sun will kill me.

When the helicopters came I dug myself under the surface and changed to vampire form, the vampire has cold blood and doesn't give off a thermal signature. I hoped this would make me invisible, and it apparently did.

The next three days were hard. I used the energy of the she-demon to dig my way under the sand just before dawn, keeping just my head close to the surface so I could breathe.

Once under a shallow roof of earth, I changed back into human form because that way, I used less energy.

During the night, I walked, in human form. If I heard a helicopter or drone coming, I lay down, curled up in some scrub, and changed into the vampire so I wouldn't register on the thermal imaging instruments.

Each night, toward dawn, I changed into my reptile form. I dug my grave and buried myself alive. Then I changed back into human form and lay there, a few inches under the surface. For hours, all day long, the sun beat down on the sand. The heat was like a furnace.

I dared not move since if the sand fell away, the sun would cook me alive, and in my weakened state, the sun would destroy me. I would die as my mother died, in a pyre of fire.

At dusk, I crawled out of my tomb, brushed myself off, stayed in human form, and, barefoot, and naked except for the ragtag ends of my wetsuit, I moved, walking all night, heading toward where I figured from the maps of the area I had once seen there must be a highway.

Once, a helicopter appeared, flying low, using floodlights to examine the terrain. I couched down, covered myself in dust, balled myself up into a shrub-like mass, and changed into the vampire.

The helicopter passed on – the sound of its rotors slowly fading until there was only me and the almost absolute silence of the desert and the stars overhead. And I kept walking.

So it was, day and night, and night and day, until I staggered up to the highway. I was so exhausted I lay down in the dust and waited. No one came. The hours passed. This is a desert road, I thought, it goes from nowhere to nowhere.

One truck went by, very fast, but it didn't stop.

I'd given up hope, and then …

"I'd given up hope, and then you came along, Alex," she said.

"And then I came along."

"And you saved my life," said V, feeling a catch in her throat, and realizing that her passion for this human, this Alex, was a rising tide, an inner tsunami, and was quickly reaching dangerous heights, fatal heights.

CHAPTER 6 – OBSESSION

In Moscow, on the other side of the globe, somebody else was thinking of V the vampire and of Sabrina Jacobs, CEO of Andromeda Corporation.

So the alien vampire had escaped from Sabrina!

In a Moscow skyscraper, Dmitry Pavlov, a Russian billionaire and scientist, CEO of Bio-Prom, one of the world's largest biotech companies, stared out of a plate-glass window at the distant walls of the Kremlin. The late afternoon sun reflected on the Kremlin towers, on rooftops, and on the Moskva River. Dmitry's hands were clasped behind his back; he twisted his fingers together, cracking the knuckles, something he did when he was obsessed, or thinking about a particularly vexing problem – or about a particularly vexing woman.

A tall, handsome, blond Russian with strong features, pale unblemished skin, and narrow gray eyes, Dmitry favored expensive clothes and prided himself on his physique. He was wearing a dark-blue pinstriped suit, a mauve shirt with a dark-blue tie striped with gold, and a red carnation in his button-hole. His eyes had a steely glimmer, a cruel light lurking behind the flinty irises and dark-gray pupils; there was an inch-long scar by his right eye, left over from a particularly wild night – involving a straight-razor and three prostitutes in Vladivostok.

Dmitry turned, walked to his desk, sat down, and stared at a photograph. The photograph was of a beautiful woman, and that woman, now his greatest and most deadly industrial and scientific rival, had once been his lover in a tempestuous, violent, passionate, and exquisitely perverse love affair, a story of sex-and-obsession, which had ended badly, very badly.

In the photograph Sabrina Jacobs was wearing a clinging diaphanous black evening gown and receiving a three million dollar prize for her scientific accomplishments – already at age 30 – in the Kremlin, a prize being handed to her by the President of the Russian Federation, an old friend of

Dmitry's, though Dmitry had had no role in the awarding of the prize. In fact, the whole affair had annoyed him tremendously – jealousy? Yes, perhaps he had been jealous even then of Sabrina's scientific accomplishments.

The bitch, he thought, the exquisitely perverse bitch!

But she did have a beautiful smile. Dmitry picked up the photograph and his mind – his senses – moved back in time; he could feel her skin under his hands, his fingers closing around her slender waist: she had the most beautiful skin and body, yes, he sighed, the most beautiful skin and body!

Looking at the photograph raised a whole host of violent memories and desires in Dmitry; but the greatest desire, now, was for revenge.

Revenge!

Exquisite, refined, prolonged revenge!

Dmitry would destroy Sabrina physically. He would redesign her. No one would ever desire her again. He would turn her into something he would own. She would be his property, his special pet. He would turn dear Sabrina into a freak, into a thing – a *Thing* – he could display to curious friends – his very own circus monster.

"You see, my friends, you see this grotesque creature before you, this thing crouching in the straw, this thing, this animal, was once the beautiful and talented … *It was once called Sabrina.*"

And he would also destroy Sabrina's legacy, the heart of her industrial and scientific empire – he would capture the Clone – Sabrina's greatest, most secret project – and he would sink Sabrina's pride and joy, the research ship *Andromeda*, her masterpiece, the most lavishly equipped scientific ship in the world. Total obliteration – that was the aim.

"You are obsessed," his brother Sergei had told him.

"Yes, I am obsessed."

"Obsession is unhealthy."

"No, Sergei, I don't think so: obsession is the spice of life. Obsession is an inspiration; obsession is creative; obsession is energy!"

"Well, you and Sabrina were well-matched, that's all I can say."

"And I will steal the Clone Sabrina so kindly created."

"Your plan is in place, then?"

"Yes. I have agents on Sabrina's flagship, *Andromeda*, and I have a submarine moving into position. Our agents will seize *Andromeda*, download all its computers and research information, capture the Clone and Sabrina. And then sink *Andromeda*."

"But, Dmitry, the security surrounding the *Andromeda* is extraordinary. It is usually accompanied by a British or Chinese or American or Philippine Navy frigate, sometimes several of them, and sometimes an extra torpedo gunboat."

"I have thought of all this, Sergei. Do you think your brother is so naive? The *Andromeda* is in the Pacific, in the southern Pacific."

"Yes, I know, it's headed toward the Philippines, toward the Sulu Sea. Sabrina has a project with the coral reefs and marine life there."

"Yes. And the British frigate *Darwin IV* is in dry dock. The Chinese escort has been tied up by some convenient sabotage. We have arranged for a last-minute "accident" to delay the other replacement escort ship, the Philippine frigate the *Ramon Alcaraz*. *Andromeda* will be alone. Thus I have created my window of opportunity."

"Yes, but –"

"A private security firm had been looking after security on board the *Andromeda* for the last six years. A convenient death occurred, and a new firm is protecting *Andromeda*. We have penetrated that firm. Virtually all the security personnel on *Andromeda* work for me."

"Yes, but what is the purpose of this act of war?"

"We get the hybrid, the Clone, the Alien-Human Clone; it will be invaluable. I will mine it for information and genetic material, then dispose of it. It is female – I will use it for breeding purposes, perhaps with animals, perhaps with humans."

Sergei said nothing; he just stared at his brother – the man was insane.

Dmitry despised Sergei's caution and his scruples. Sergei, alas, was an honest man. Soon he would eliminate Sergei. Yes, Sergei was his brother, but the man lacked imagination, he lacked 'vision' – As for Sabrina, she certainly had vision! Maybe she had too much vision, but, not for much longer – soon, she would have no vision at all!

"You do not understand, Sergei. This Clone may hold the future of the human race in its DNA. The DNA possesses features and powers that dwarf anything we humans currently possess. The present Clone is a drooling idiot, but that does not matter. It will be the source of an immense number of biological innovations – in medicine, in genetics, in genetic re-design, and in bio-weaponry. This creature may well render the human race obsolete."

"Are you sure you want us to be obsolete?"

"Ah, Sergei, my dear brother, Sergei, if only you had Sabrina's imagination!

The Clone is perhaps the greatest genetic treasure trove on the planet. Just think – alien DNA that can be integrated into a human subject and create a being that is viable."

"I can see that, but –"

"And I am going to turn Sabrina's creation against her. As you know, I have obtained a sample of the Clone's DNA. And I have developed a way of using the Clone's DNA that will genetically re-engineer any subject very quickly – in accelerated form, bringing out the most basic and alien qualities. I plan to try out this method on Sabrina."

"This is foolish – and horrendous."

"Sabrina will become the Clone of the Clone, and a drooling idiot, like the original." Dmitry favored his brother with a grin of childlike glee, but to Sergei, it looked more like the sneer of a diabolic and wild beast.

Sergei shrugged. "You are obsessed with Sabrina. It would be better just to kill her or to keep her somewhere in a drugged state and injected with truth serum so you could learn what she knows. If you turn her into an idiot or an animal, she will be useless. In any case," Sergei paused, treading on dangerous territory, "you are still in love with her."

Dmitry narrowed his eyes. Little brother Sergei had just pronounced his own death sentence. Too bad, Little Brother! Dmitry smiled. "I will give Sabrina a choice. If she wants to cooperate, I will give her a reprieve, a little extra time. If she is stubborn, I immediately use her for my little experiment. It will turn her into a drooling idiot, like the Clone – but much more interesting."

"Sabrina will be stubborn."

"Of course she will. I'm counting on it."

"So, that's the plan!"

"Yes. The submarine will transport the Clone and Sabrina, and all the computers and other material we've captured to my Pacific Research Institute. Everybody else on the *Andromeda* we will kill. And then we sink the ship."

"Does Sabrina know you already have the DNA of the Clone? That you have re-produced the DNA, and that you have prepared a morph serum …?"

"No, that will be the most exquisite part of what I have in mind for Sabrina."

"Your revenge certainly sounds baroque. It is a lot of effort."

"You can bet on it, my dear little brother. My revenge will be unique, and fitting. You see, as you so wisely said, I still do love and desire that bitch, so she is going to suffer in an absolutely unique way: no one before in history will suffer what she is going to suffer." The thought of Sabrina and of making her suffer and, above all, of humiliating her, excited Dmitry with an explosive, inebriating, transcendent, almost mystical mix of lust and sadism. "Sabrina will be superb material for this little experiment in transformation."

"The ways of love are certainly strange," said Sergei. He got up and took his briefcase and said, "Well, I'll see you tomorrow, Dmitry."

Out in the corridor, at the elevator, Sergei, who was CFO of Bio-Prom, frowned. He'd always liked Sabrina; he liked her still; he had hoped that she and Dmitry would marry, and they would spend family celebrations together; his wife Nadia adored Sabrina, and the two of them got on so well. Oh, well, it was not to be. Lately, there was something about Dmitry, something limitless in his ambition, something diabolic – and dangerous, very dangerous.

After Sergei left, Dmitry sat at his desk and flipped through photographs of Sabrina. He envisaged how the transformation would look – what the result would be.

It was an exciting exercise.

Then he put the photographs – old-fashioned black-and-white and color images – back in the drawer, locked the drawer, and left his office.

That night Dmitry hired a prostitute, a very high-class and beautiful call-girl, a blue-eyed blonde, a Sabrina look-alike. He wanted to recreate some of the thrill and violent heady emotions he had felt with Sabrina.

The girl was very good and very smart, and she tried very hard, but it was not enough. She'd probably need a month in the hospital – which Dmitry said he would pay for – to recover from what Dmitry did when he vented his fury and his frustration.

Dmitry walked along the Moskva, waiting for dawn.

A limousine and four security men followed at a discreet distance.

One could so easily be assassinated in Moscow!

Hate and love were so close, so similar. Dmitry glanced down at the river, the swirling water, lit up by reflected neon, giant floating advertisements. Lust and aggression overlapped, like intersecting waves. But why had love – or maybe it was merely desire – no, it was more than desire, it was, as his brother had said, obsession, absolute obsession – why had love or obsession so quickly changed to hate?

When he got back to his luxurious palatial penthouse, Dmitry sat down and gazed for a long time at a photograph of Sabrina Jacobs:

Ah, Sabrina, he sighed, I can hardly wait, I can hardly wait to see my creation, the new you – Sabrina Jacobs, you will no longer be human, you will be a pure animal, and you will be the Monster: *the Thing*. Ah, Sabrina, darling, I will turn you into everything you most hate and despise and fear in the entire world.

PART TWO – HUNTERS

CHAPTER 7 – TRUE FATAL LOVE

V straddled Alex and gazed longingly down at his – oh, so handsome – face. She frowned at something he had just said, leaned closer, kissed him, and then drew back. "So, Alex, you are saying this Sabrina Jacobs is a sort of genius, almost certainly the supreme genius in her field."

"Yes, she wants to push the frontier of research, always."

"She's a female Faust, then."

"Yes, or Prometheus. Her ambition is to give the divine spark to humanity – eternal life, among other things. When Judy and I had our biotech company, Sabrina saw we were doing some original, cutting-edge work; she wanted to buy our company. But we weren't for sale."

"She is beautiful too." V narrowed her eyes.

"People say so. I've never met her. I saw photographs."

"And she wants to use me for her experiments. She's the perfect human being, and I'm an alien, well, half-alien, and I am going to kill her."

"Kill her?"

"It's me, or it's her, Alex. And I'm going to eliminate the Clone Sabrina created."

"The Clone?"

"Yes. Sabrina created a clone, a girl; the creature is fourteen years old and based on my DNA. I'm going to kill it."

"Kill it?"

"Alex, there is only room for one being like me in the world. As I told you, I swore that I would never make another creature like me; and I never have. I didn't make the Clone, but she is based on my DNA, so it is as if I did make her."

"Well …"

"You made the calculations, Alex; you know how many people I have killed.

And I control myself. I only kill when I need to kill. And I have never created another creature like me. The epidemic ends with me. But, if the Clone is a vampire like me, then she will almost certainly not obey the same rules, and … Well, it would be the end of the human race. I have to kill her."

"So you're sure you must kill her?"

"Yes, I'm sure, Alex. I am a killer, remember, that's what I am, a deadly predator. If there were more creatures like me, there would be more deaths, more murders – murder and massacre without end. I swore to my mentor to avoid that."

"Well …" Alex frowned: he didn't like the idea of V killing a young girl, nor of her killing Sabrina Jacobs for that matter, but V's logic was … well, it was unassailable.

"Alex, can you forgive me for being what I am?"

"I have no right to blame or forgive anybody for anything, V. But I think I'm in love with you – so I will follow you and help you, whatever you decide to do – and, somehow, I'm sure you will decide to do what is right."

"Alex, you are a darling, probably a saint." V rose up, off Alex, slid out of bed, stepped over to the sideboard, and poured them both a shot of whiskey; and then as she came back to the bed, she said, "Let me give you a massage."

Alex turned over on his stomach, and V sat astride him and caressed his neck and then massaged his back. "You have a beautiful back," she leaned down and whispered into his ear. "It's big and broad and muscled and the proportions, between the shoulders, the shoulder blades, and the curve of the backbone down to those two dimples above your ass … it's … it's poetic …"

"Poetic?"

"Yes, poetic … and a beautiful ass too, the most poetic smooth muscular rising curve of the buttocks …"

"No one ever told me I had a poetic ass."

"People are blind," V said, sliding down next to him, turning toward him, and kissing him, very gently.

Andromeda – 350 kilometers southwest of Hawaii.

A conference call with Andromeda Corporation's experts had been arranged. Sabrina Jacobs swiveled in her high-backed synthetic leather chair, faced the tiny video camera, and made a little steeple of her long elegant, perfectly manicured fingers.

She gazed thoughtfully at the perfect – unvarnished – nails of her fingers, and she said, "So this creature, V, can break out of steel manacles. She can smash her way through steel bars. She can kill armed guards without blinking an eye, and she can bring down a Boeing 777."

"Yes, that's more or less it," said one of the experts, his image suddenly appearing on the screen above the camera.

"So, given her abilities," Sabrina lowered her voice and swung the chair around so she could look out the window at the brilliant, luminous Pacific, its glittering horizon, "how do we capture her? And how do we keep her, if we get her? Does anyone have any ideas?" She swiveled back to face the camera directly so that the other video conference participants would answer her.

A scientist from the Virginia Headquarters of Andromeda Corp spoke up. "What about those mini-drones, those little wee tiny insect-sized drones, could we send a fleet of them after her, like mosquitoes, in a swarm, and they could swarm her, covering her entire body, and inject her with the neuro-blocking drug so she would be paralyzed and suggestible and tame."

"There would have to be hundreds of them, maybe thousands," said one of the security experts, a thin-faced young woman based in Paris. Black bangs, cut short at the side, thin lips, and rimless spectacles that failed to hide large serious gray eyes and gave an air of schoolmarm severity to the young woman – an air which Sabrina found decidedly intriguing. *Hmm, perhaps drinks when I'm next in Paris?*

"Well, do we have thousands of them?"

"Yes," a product development expert in Shanghai spoke up. "We can mobilize thousands of them. We could adapt a whole fleet to a drug-injecting role, enough of them to cover every square inch of her body with dozens of the things. As you know, these mini-drones have a swarm mind, a hive mind, they act as a single entity, so the program would have to have a good three-dimensional visual profile of the target and be adapted to this purpose."

Sabrina envisaged a mass of buzzing black metallic insects covering every inch of V's body, like pushing the creature under a shower of living, squirming, pulsating, pullulating glittering black molasses. It would be sadistically picturesque, to say the least. "Good, let's prepare several swarms of thousands of mini-drones then."

"We also have the Medusa Gel," said the man from Virginia.

"What is the Medusa Gel?"

"The Medusa Gel is a new product that comes in aerosol form and can be injected through air-conditioning systems, heating ducts, or by spray-bomb in any given environment. The droplets cling to all living surfaces, biological non-plant surfaces, and, using a neurological blocking device, it freezes all the life forms in position, so that they are like statues, as if they had been turned to stone by the glance of the Medusa or by the gaze of the Basilisk."

"Does it kill or damage the subject?" Sabrina tapped a pencil on the desk in front of her, and quickly sketched a doodle of a severe, thin-faced woman wearing rimless glasses, a studious, French-speaking, Parisian dominatrix. "We don't want to damage the subject. I want this Thing, this V, intact."

"No, the subject can still breathe, and the pores of the skin still operate, so no damage is done to the target organisms."

"Is this 'Medusa Gel' weaponized?"

"It's in development. The compound can be put in an artillery shell or mini-missile warhead, for example, to explode in a given area, as big as a city block, as small as a bedroom. Once frozen, the targets still sense their environment – they feel and see and smell and hear – but they cannot move or talk or take any action whatsoever, the muscle structure is frozen in place."

"That's exceptionally perverse. I like it." Sabrina smiled. "How come I didn't know about it?"

"It had just been developed by one of our recently acquired subsidiaries, that unlisted Hong Kong firm *Universal Bio-Tricks*. It wasn't even included in the list of patents they presented us with; we only discovered it a few weeks ago when we took over their plants and talked in-depth with their people."

"Does it work?"

"It certainly does – we were able to freeze a whole herd of cattle, even out in the open, in Devonshire – or Devon as it is now known – even the bull was locked in place; unfortunately, the wind shifted, and the farmhands and the farmer and his family also got frozen."

"I'm not sure that is funny!" Sabrina glanced at Henry Rothschild, who was sitting beside her. "Were there any legal problems?"

"No, the farmer and his dependents were compensated; everybody has signed off on this unfortunate episode. It's all sealed up with airtight non-disclosure agreements. Inadvertently, the accident gave us good clinical results as far as humans went. There were no after-effects."

"Good. So the Medusa Gel didn't harm the subjects."

"No, as I said, they are frozen like statues, but fully conscious, and they can see and hear; but they can't move."

"I wonder if this would be strong enough to freeze V. She's pretty damn strong. How do you release the targets or victims?"

"The effect wears off after about two hours, depending on wind, temperature, etc. You can renew it by giving a repeat spray or by painting it on the subject."

"Okay, let's prepare the Medusa Gel too."

"You can also just simply wash the stuff off."

"With water? What if it rains or is humid?"

"No, it can only be removed using a special formula for which Andromeda Corp now holds the patent."

"Good. That sounds intriguing," Sabrina said. She smiled. She envisaged having the Thing – V – frozen in place like a statue. Hmm. Sabrina half closed her eyes: Let's see. I could walk around her, inspect her at leisure, poke at her, taunt her, experiment with her; that might be a quite thrilling experience.

The young woman in Paris cleared her throat, and adjusted her glasses putting the fingers of both hands flat against both sides of the frame. "What about the special slug, you know, the one that invades the brain and kidnaps the willpower of the subject?"

Sabrina gazed at the woman's face; she had an attractive little scar on her forehead and an adorable nervous twitch at the side of her mouth. Sabrina smiled. "That is a pretty disgusting thing, Nicole. It sounds like a horror film. Where did the slug idea come from?"

"That idea is from another company we bought," Nicole answered, "It's a Rumanian high-tech company. It's pretty hairy stuff. Some of the developers quit just before we purchased the company, and they have gone rogue, proposing to develop a variant on their own, a sort of group-mind slug, which could, I think, be very dangerous. One mind would control all the others."

"Does it work?"

"We suspect it does work," said Nicole. "We haven't tried it on humans because the effect, we suspect, is irreversible."

Out of the corner of her eye, Sabrina saw Henry go pale and raise an eyebrow; she shared his horror and disgust.

"I think we should develop an antidote or a cure," Sabrina nodded at Henry; this slug thing sounded like a scenario for the end of the world. "Does the slug reproduce?"

"Not yet," said Nicole, "But these slugs are very small; they can go anywhere."

"Nicole, you say 'not yet.' But you think it could."

"Yes, it could, probably, learn to reproduce. There are mutants in the manufacturing process that they set up. And mutants imply the possibility of evolution – if one or two reproduce …"

"So we don't know if it could reproduce. But if it got loose, and it could reproduce, my God, we would have a plague on our hands."

"Precisely," said Nicole in French, with a pedantically Parisian little twist of her lips.

"Okay," said Sabrina, thinking next time she was in Paris, she would definitely invite Nicole to dinner at, say, the Brasserie Lipp. *Let's see; I could wear that dark, tailored, clinging …* "We should try to develop an antidote and a cure. So we will have to continue to develop the slug to see how it works, to keep up with its evolving genetics, and fit the antidote to a possible future version of the – ugh – slug."

"Yes. I'll prepare the plan and set up the program," said Nicole.

"Good." Sabrina gazed at the woman's image.

Henry cleared his throat. "Now, the Thing – our friend V – seems to be able to eject or get rid of foreign matter – like bullets – that compromise her integrity."

Sabrina nodded. "That's a pretty way of putting it, Henry. You mean, she can spit out bullets."

"Yes, it seems, from some of the reports, that she can do this."

"A lot of our information is pretty shaky, isn't it," said Sabrina.

"Yes, admittedly, it is."

"The slug is different; it's organic," said Nicole, "not exactly a bullet."

"Good point," said Sabrina. "Well, Nicole, let's keep the slug in reserve, just in case, though I must admit, I don't like the idea. Let's prioritize study of the slug – so we will know how to neutralize it. I mean, if something like that could reproduce, it could infect people … and what would that mean …?"

"It would turn us all into zombies," said Nicole, again in French. "It would be the end of the world, or of the human race, at least."

"Exactly," said Sabrina in French, "and none of us, I think, wants to be a zombie. Not me at least – what about you, Nicole, what about you, Henry?"

V stared at the motel room ceiling and lay next to Alex. She was trying to resist temptation, but she found she couldn't resist temptation; so she turned toward him, kissed him on the shoulder, and ran her fingers through the hair of his chest. "I'm putting you at awful risk, Alex."

"I guess so," he said.

"I know so."

She pressed closer and kissed him, timidly, on the shoulder and then, more boldly, on the neck; and then, climbing onto him, she kissed him on the mouth, a soft, slow, tentative, exploring kiss. His muscular chest, tanned and with thick golden hair, shone with reflected light.

"You have beautiful eyes," he said.

"The better to see you with," she said, emitting a low growl from her throat.

With his fingers, he traced the outline of her ears,

"You have beautiful ears," he said, "like little seashells."

"The better to hear you with," she said, licking her lips.

"And you have beautiful teeth," he said.

"The better to eat you with," she said, brushing his lips with hers. She sighed, nibbling at the corner of his lips. "This is dangerous, Alex. I told you what happens when …"

"… when you get excited …"

"Yes." She whispered and then groaned. Alex ran his hands down her sides, down her flanks, over the smooth curve of her backside. She nuzzled her face close into his face, then down toward his neck, toward his broad, comforting shoulder.

He caressed her hair, softly, with his fingertips spread, each strand of hair a treasure, and the nape of her neck, delineating the delicate vertebrae; his fingers touched every nerve, every synapse of desire, every sleeping neural trigger, every eager nerve-end, and it was like a melody in which she could easily get caught, easily get lost, forgetting who and what she was, forgetting where they were – and it was an electric lullaby, too, soothing and tingling, and, when, after a long, slow, orchestrated crescendo, Alex entered her at last, it was the most natural – but most frightening – thing in the world. She sighed. A shudder went through her, "*Oh,*" she sighed, "*Oh, oh, oh,*" and then …

"Alex, darling, we shouldn't, we really shouldn't," and she drew back.

But he was still deep inside her; she looked at his face, her night vision sharpened by lust, by love, by excitement. His face shone, his eyes were wide open, though they could not see the way she could see (creature of the night that she was), he had the intense glow of absolute desire, the inner light …

Oh, foolish mortal, she thought, oh, foolish mortal, oh, foolish me!

"Alex," she said, "We must not …"

Alex answered by thrusting deeper, touching in an instant, touching some point, some feeling, some instinct, some image, taking her right to the edge, and, then, suspended on the edge, triggering a shudder that went all through her, and *Oh, oh, no,* she thought, *oh, no, oh no, oh, yes, yes, yes, yes, no …*

An orgasm once started is not something you can stop in midstream, as V knew quite well, at least with the part of her mind that was still capable of thinking anything, and she screamed, "Alex!!!!"

Oh, goddamn it, she thought, *what an idiot am I!* The tidal waves of pleasure, the ecstasy of abandonment, the surrender of self, the abolition of being, the obliteration of consciousness swept through her …

What the French call the "Little Death," *"la Petite Mort,"* overwhelmed them both.

At that very moment, uncontrollable, the *transformation*, the metamorphosis, the transmogrification, took place, in a split second, a nanosecond – *fangs and claws …*

The vampire …

She seized Alex by the hair, she bent his neck back, she leaned down, and, sighing the name *"Alex,"* she caressed his neck with her fangs, the skin was oh so tender oh so sweet, the blood was, oh so young, oh so rich, the scent of blood, his blood, the scent of life, the scent of love …

Tender skin, oh so thin …

The skin broke …

The skin broke …

Alex shuddered, and his body arched upwards, it all happening so quickly, so overwhelmingly, that his mind had no time to register what was happening.

There was no pain.

And, so, together, they came; they came – together.

CHAPTER 8 – ESCAPE

It was dawn. The sun rose, shining on little white clapboard cottages in Maine; it rose on the Carolinas; it rose on the towers of New York; it glimmered on the Atlantic beaches of Florida where joggers sprinted along boardwalks and on the cool damp sand, and it shone on terraces and balconies where people were drinking their morning coffee. It rose on the Appalachians: it rose on the vast sleepy Mississippi, and on the great wheat and cornfields and ranches of the west.

It had not yet risen in the desert.

It was just a ribbon of blood-red to the east, a ribbon of blood, lying along the eastern horizon.

In her one-room third-floor flat in a tawdry tenement building four blocks down from the smoking ruins of the *Exotic Dancers' Oasis Club*, Helen of Troy was up before dawn.

She was leaving town. She didn't want people to see the new her, the new Helen, the Helen without the scars. Her unblemished face was now her disguise. To escape from the town and to escape from her past, she needed to keep this new face a secret.

The only way to do that was to leave – right away!

It was weird – she thought – that her old self – the self before she had been disfigured by Little Boy's acid and Big Boy's razor – was now a disguise. She glanced into a mirror. *The new me is the old me. I feel like I'm wearing a mask.*

She laughed. She had become a stranger to herself. When she looked in the mirror and saw the unblemished skin, she thought: *Who the hell are you?"*

She tried out a smile, testing her new face. The one thing everybody remembered about "Helen of Troy" was how hideously disfigured she was. They remembered the half of her face that looked like a toothy, snarling clown, carved in barbecue-seared steak. She was a walking warning, a walking advertisement against trying to escape a life of prostitution and slavery; she was a cautionary tale, like one of those rotting corpses they used to leave hanging on a gibbet along the roadside in the Middle Ages and in England up until the early nineteenth century; or like one of those disobedient slaves the Romans would leave crucified in rows outside towns on the highways, for the edification of wandering merchants and preachers and slaves.

The new face, the new smile, didn't look bad, she decided. Excellent, in fact. She frowned, a clown's grimace. Who are you, really, Helen? In her years of servitude, she'd become a connoisseur of cruelty: she knew it inside out: she had studied it: the acid, the gibbet, the razor, the whip, the brand, the truncheon, the stocks, the rack, the cruel remark, the mocking glance, the cutting joke, the ugly caress, the slap, the punch, the rape, the beating, the bruises, the outer scars, and the inner scars.

And she had contemplated an infinite variety of forms of revenge, knowing all the time that it was a fantasy; knowing that she was too good-hearted, which was not a virtue in her books, to do what sometimes needed to be done – until V showed up – an unlikely savior.

If she found V and joined up with her, then perhaps she could learn from V. She could learn how to bring justice to an evil, fallen world.

Yes!

Maybe she could become like V!

She turned away from the mirror, stepped out of the bathroom, crouched down, and slid an old canvas backpack out from under her bed. She packed six black string-panties, three black T-shirts, two pairs of black jeans; she put her toiletries into a small bag and put it into the backpack.

She had a quick shower, dried herself, and pulled on a pair of black jeans and slipped into a black T-shirt and a black denim jacket. She put on a black baseball cap to hide her blond hair and slipped into black sandals. Dark glasses were a good idea too; she put on the dark wrap-around glasses she had used as a shield, so she didn't have to return horrified glances; she checked herself in the mirror. Okay, yes, okay. Not too showy, not too revealing. She took the backpack, hitched it over her shoulders, and walked out of the flat, locking the door carefully behind her. She went down the narrow wooden stairs. She didn't meet anybody: so far, so good.

Outside it was hot, even hotter than in the stuffy little flat. The weather was building up to another super-storm, and this one – she could feel it – would be a humdinger. The sweltering air pressed against her skin; it was an intimation, a foretaste, of the big wind – hurricane force and filled with waves and waves of sand. It could rip your skin from your flesh if it caught you far from shelter. Above her shone that livid, sticky, sickly, yellow-rose light that made you feel the end of the world was on its way. The whole damned planet was turning into a dust bowl.

Papers blew this way and that; the sun blazed down; the blue morning sky up above, above the dusty yellow-rose light, had that hazy pale blue that presaged a sandstorm, while closer to the ground the light was dense, misty and yellow, sick with some cosmic jaundice. The feeling of menace hung close, like treacle. She wiggled her shoulders, antsy, prickly, itchy all over.

She was heading to the bus stop when a car pulled up behind her. Two men jumped out and came running up to her – she sensed them coming, but it was too fast for her to do anything. They grabbed her, pinning her arms to her sides.

"Hey!" She stiffened in fear and turned around and faced them.

"Oh!" They let go. "Signora, sorry! We are looking for the Scar Face, the one known as Helen of Troy. Do you know her?"

"You mean the one with half her face like a seared steak?"

"Yes, that is the one we mean."

"Is she the friend of the Big One, the one with the bald head and the tattoos?"

"Yes. That is the one. We are looking for her, the friend of the Big One, the one they call Big Boy."

"She lives, I think, in that building – or the next one. I have seen her on the street or in the store over there – the convenience store."

"Thank you, Signora!"

"You are welcome."

They got back in the car and swung it around and in a cloud of dust headed toward the apartment building. Oh, well, apartment building was really too glamorous a description.

Helen quickly took a side street and walked to the next street over. She didn't want them to see her when they came out of the building.

One good thing: Three weeks ago, in an outbreak of hysterical self-hatred and physical loathing, she had destroyed all the photographs of herself that were in Big Boy's flat – photographs from before and after the acid-and-razor treatment.

They would not see, and they would not have seen, what she looked like.

Big Boy kept her photos off the net – too risky, he thought, though she was sure he would have loved the extra publicity and humiliation. But, still, these guys, whoever they were, must soon put two-and-two together.

Everybody knew her as Helen of Troy or as Big Boy's pet bitch, or sometimes as Big Boy's tragic-comic sex slave, "Scar Face." Boy, did they have fun with that!

Helen was her middle name. Nobody would match the name "Tamara" – her name before she became "Big Boy's Bitch" – and the image on her driver's license and identity papers, including the passport, which were all pre-acid, with the Scar Face Helen of Troy they all knew.

Maybe there's just a chance, just a chance I'll get away.

CHAPTER 9 – SHAGGY BEAST

Alex was dying!

Oh, how could she have been so stupid?

V lay flat on her back, staring at the dirty, cream-colored ceiling of the motel room. The curtains and blinds were drawn tight against the blaze of day, but her night vision showed a crack in the ceiling, and the old emplacement of a ceiling lamp that was no longer there, and a meandering yellowing, rust-colored stain, from when the roof had once leaked, from when there had been rain, long ago.

V blinked away the tears and stared at the ceiling. *How could I have been so stupid!*

Outside, the wind was rising, and the sun shone out of a hot empty blue sky. In the room, it was boiling, stinking hot, stifling hot and close. The darkness was wet with humidity; a thick layer of sweat clung like a coat of glue to every inch of V's naked body.

Lying beside her, Alex was in a high fever. He groaned from time to time. His skin was burning hot. V held his hand. She whispered to him. He didn't seem capable of speech.

When V had made love to him – or when he had made love to her – it happened. V cursed herself that she had allowed herself a luxury she rarely allowed herself; that she had done something she had vowed never to do: *she had lost control …*

…and, losing control, she *transformed*, as she knew she would, she *morphed*, into her vampire self, and with her fangs out and sharp and brushing amorously against his neck, she had *punctured Alex's skin.*

If only she could take back those few seconds, if only she could take back that very instant. But, no, she couldn't … that very instant …

Stiffening in horror at herself she closes her eyes:

That very instant …

That very instant …

It had been irrevocable, that instant.

That instant!

Oh, oh, oh, no, no!

And looking back in horror, she relived the catastrophe. She felt the wave of excitement mount and mount and mount …

She knows she must stop it, stop the excitement, the ecstasy mounting, radiating out from her belly, from her clitoris, from the wet pressed-back clinging lips, the tsunami rippling up from deep inside her, from her groin, down through her thighs, up her stomach, swelling like the tide, irresistible, the excitement rising in her breasts, the nipples straining, taut, erect, and the fever like liquid fire on her lips and tongue …

And with that rising liquid tide of excitement – with that tidal wave of straining ecstatic tension – she realizes the *transformation* is about to over-whelm her, possess her, take her; it is as if she is being taken, invaded, pene-trated, by two beings – by Alex and by her vampire self …

No, no, no, no! I refuse! I won't! I won't! I won't!

No, no, no, no …

And yet …

She couldn't stop it – it was a freight train rushing – Wham! – through the night.

She couldn't force him to withdraw.

She couldn't … stop the *transformation* …

She became, in an instant, in the instant just prior to, on the edge of, in the rising tide of, the final shuddering orgasm, she became *the Vampire* …

And her lips …

And her lips, tenderly caressing his skin, the tender skin under the jaw, at the side of his neck, her lips were pushed aside by the fangs, which cut into his skin.

She screamed in the delight and release of orgasm, and she screamed in horror, in absolute horror, at what she had done.

Alex's death sentence …

Breathing heavily, reverting instantly to human form, she kissed Alex on the lips; she whispered to him, "darling, darling, oh, darling."

He had come with her, at exactly the same moment – she felt his rich liquid flood deep within her.

She sucked on the pinpricks hoping to draw out the poison, but that too was dangerous.

He hadn't even noticed the pinprick of her teeth, her fangs, breaking his skin.

"Alex," she had said, "have you got alcohol, disinfectant, in your luggage?"

"What, darling, what?"

"Alex, alcohol, or disinfectant!" She was frantic. This was a very long shot, a desperate long shot. If only she could neutralize the effect of …

"What?" Alex's eyes looked like he was floating in outer space. "Oh, darling, that was fantastic!" Alex was still in the aftershock, the dazed afterglow …

"Alcohol, I'm serious!"

"What? No, no … I don't think … so …"

Then V remembered the whiskey – better than nothing. She disengaged, disentangled from Alex, from the dampness, from the glue, sticking to both of them, the liquids that wanted to keep her linked with him, entwined with him, and she ran to the dresser and took a washcloth from the bathroom, and she soaked the wounds – four tiny pinpricks – with Johnny Walker Black Label, pouring the whiskey onto his neck.

"Hold still!"

"What? What are you doing?"

"I bit you."

"What?"

"I bit you. I didn't mean to, but I bit you."

"What? You bit me?"

"Yes! I'm washing the wound. I'm hoping. I'm hoping."

"Oh, boy!" Alex's eyes went large: he stared into the darkness. He reached out and turned on the bedside light. "What does that mean, you bit me?"

"It means, dearest Alex, that I might have infected you."

"Infected me?"

"Yes."

"You mean …?"

"I mean that you might become a vampire."

"One like you?"

"Yes, that's what it means. It was just a scratch. I'm hoping the alcohol will stop it."

Like me: a vampire like me?

She didn't tell him that the change, the *transformation*, might not change him into something like her, something that could talk and even reason, but it would almost certainly change him into *an uncontrollable raging beast*, a beast she would have to destroy.

I cannot let him live!

Because she knew what that would mean.

Four decades before ...

Ghhhrrr, fangs bared, claws extended, the creature leaped on her.

His eyes were empty, utterly without intelligence or soul.

That was the last time such an accident had happened – the man, and she had adored him, had changed within the hour into an insatiable blood-drinker, a killer without conscience, a grotesque creature, a shaggy monster, a mindless beast of prey of immense strength, a merciless beast that could not be reasoned with or stopped.

They were in a boarding house in Mississippi, and she jumped out the window, barely escaping as he tried to tear her apart.

She ran across the lawn.

The moonlight shone through the magnolia trees. The air was damp, heavy and heady with perfumes – bougainvillea, oleander, orchids.

He was galloping behind her, his claws almost catching her heels.

Each time she slipped from his grasp, he roared – a sort of banshee yowl. *Yeeeeeehhhhaaa!*

She managed to reach the forest and the swampy ground. He followed. They were splashing through muck and water and mud, and there were alligators and snakes, but V figured alligators and snakes were less dangerous than what was loping behind her. *Yeeeeeehhhhaaa!*

She got enough of a lead to leap into a tree and wait on an overhanging branch, hiding behind the thick trunk of the tree, and when he was below her ...

She leaped.

She landed on his back, riding piggyback, her legs wrapped around his arms. Oh, but his arms were so powerful, and his fangs and claws were so long – she had one chance, if she didn't get it right, she was, well, she was doomed.

Plunging her claws into his face, she tore out his eyes.

The thing he had become threw her off and roaring in pain, his nostrils quivering, he came after her. She slipped behind a tree, and he stood, confused, sniffing the air, and howling in his blindness. *Yeeeeeehhhhaaa!* His skin was chalk-white, transparent in places, blue veins pulsing, white hair spurting out everywhere in tuffs; his fangs dripped saliva; his claws were long and curved. He had become shaggy and monstrous.

Do I look like that? V thought, peeking out from behind a tree. Surely not! She climbed up the tree, shivering in fear and shame. It was all her fault! The only way to win this fight was to become the demon – the full-octave, super-powered, demonic, reptilian she-devil killer. But it would consume lots of energy.

So be it!

Crouched on the branch, she morphed into her she-devil reptilian self – in the process exploding her black silk chemise into rags and fragments of fluff that floated down to the marshy ground. Then she tempted the shaggy shambling bestial vampire – to think that he had even been published in the *New Yorker!* – to come closer.

"Come on, darling, come to mummy!"

"Yeeeeeehhhhaaa!"

"Come, on, come on, over here!"

"Yeeeeeehhhhaaa!"

He approached, slobbering blindly, groping, sniffing and grunting – he sounded to V more like a wild boar than like a vampire. He was trying to sense her presence. He turned his bloody mask and blind empty bloody sockets to the moon and howled – a heart-rending, lonely, howl. "Yeeeeeehhhhaaa!"

V crouched on her haunches silently, utterly still, waiting patiently, on the low branch of the tree, the talons of her feet clamped into the bark, her fangs bared, her forked tongue flicking nervously back and forth, back and forth, her claws extended in anticipation, waiting for the right moment to pounce. She was feeling remorse and extreme guilt. After all, she had, in a moment of exuberant tenderness, and without intending it – but she should have known better – transformed a curly-haired, timid, charming *New York Times* correspondent, into a foaming-at-the-mouth, fanged, blood-thirsty, insatiable thing.

Then she saw that he was blundering into the path of a large snake, it was brown and black and patterned – a *Cottonmouth!* As V watched, the poisoned-fanged serpent undulated its way through the water, spinning out greasy iridescent ripples in the moonlight, alert, its head up, toward the shaggy blind vampire monster.

Then the snake stopped, poised to strike, but the vampire sensed its presence, and, with a lightning-fast movement grabbed the Cottonmouth in mid-strike, bit off its head, and began to eat it, with two ends of the snake wiggling desperately from the Vampire's mouth.

Ugh, thought V.

This is it, thought V.

She leaped, straight onto the Vampire's back, and with one sweep of her reptilian claws, lopped off its head.

His head flew off, with the snake still wiggling in its jaws, but even headless, the newly-minted shaggy vampire did not stop fighting; its claws reached up and closed on V's neck. But, without his head, without what was left of his brain, he moved jerkily, like a ramshackle makeshift creature created by Frankenstein; his claws dug into V's neck, pulling her off his shoulders. She kicked with all four claws; then, mustering every ounce of strength, she flipped over, and plunged her claws into his belly, ripping upwards, tearing out his heart; then, the two of them, Shaggy Monster and Vampire Demon, rolled into the mud, in a welter of blood and slime; finally his claws shuddered, relaxed, and opened, and let go, and she was free.

She took a deep breath, crouched on her haunches, and contemplated her work. Then she dragged the body through the slime toward drier ground. She waded back into the mud and retrieved the head. The snake was still writhing, but less so, just nervous spasms. V placed the head next to the body.

The dead shaggy beast was still wearing colorful fragments of his "I love New Orleans" T-shirt with the red heart that was torn in two. His wire-rimmed glasses hung from one elongated, hairy ear.

Crouching over the body, V was transported back to the moment she first caught sight of him, gangly, abashed, freckled, and tall, with those cute wire-rimmed glasses, dressed in faded jeans, a white T-shirt and a chamois leather vest. He picked her up in a small bar off Bourbon Street, they ran, laughing hysterically, up the narrow stairs, then they hopped in his car and drove to Mississippi and to the fatal guest house and its bedroom with the flowery wallpaper and the big bed and where V – lost control.

I am not made for love …

Crouching there, under the magnolias, she sighed, tore her very own *New Yorker* short story author apart, tendon by tendon, muscle by muscle, bone by bone. She put the tiny, bloody fragments on a funeral pyre of wood she had filched from the garage and piled up to make the pyre, very neatly, rather proud, in truth, of her handiwork; back in the lodging house, in her purse, was a lighter; she snuck back into their room, got the lighter, snuck back out, and lit the fire. She burned each and every bit of him, poor Eric, such a funny, unassuming witty fellow. She crawled close to the heat, reaching into the smoldering ashes; and she broke the bones apart, and she scattered the ashes on the waters of a nearby stream. She broke the rib cage into bits, and snapped the individual ribs. One hipbone gave her a lot of trouble, and she had to jump on it four times before it shattered into mortal dust.

For a moment, she held Eric's carbonized skull, shorn of its flesh, in her hands. She picked out the serpent bones, still trapped between his teeth, and tossed them into the fire. She caressed the parietal bone and the cheekbone and stared for a long time at the teeth, very fine teeth, now totally reverted to their pre-vampire harmony, where, so recently, such sweet, full lips so good for kissing had hung, where, until only a few hours before, such a witty tongue had wagged, where jokes and puns and amorous allusions had been spun – she could hear people laughing in many pubs and bars across the globe, and readers, too, delighted with his prose, with his elegance, with his humor.

Now – nothing!

I am what I am, she thought, I must always remember that; I must never forget it; I must never let myself go to … to what I most desire …

Love …

She kissed the skull and whispered: "You are truly dead, my love, truly dead, you will not rise again." She sighed. "Goodbye, my love." Then, gazing into the empty eye sockets, she crushed the skull in her claws, smashed the bits into pieces using a leftover femur as a hammer, and dropped the fragments and the dust into the fire.

Ashes to ashes, dust to dust.

If he had a soul, if there was such a thing as the soul, which V greatly doubted, then she sincerely hoped his soul was winging its way to Heaven or Valhalla, or Olam HaEmet, or that peculiar Paradise where all those dozens of beautiful eager waiting virgins rewarded virtuous pious warriors of old.

The moon was veiled in clouds.

V felt she should bay to the moon, but she didn't; she lay upon a branch; and, curled softly upon herself, V wept.

She remained there until dawn; the flesh had burnt away; the wood was aromatic; the night was full of perfumes, cedar, pine, magnolia, and oleander. She glanced up through the hanging vines and masses of foliage, at the moon, misty and white, and then watched it, approaching the horizon, as it became yellow and gold; then, in the cool milky light of dawn, she raked the coals and embers, doused them with water, and made her way, still reptilian, through the rising mist across the back lawn to the lodging house, the dew and grass were cool under her clawed feet, she managed to sneak in without anyone seeing her, went up the front stairs to what had been their room, closed the door, changed back into human form, had a shower, and after downing a quick cup of black coffee, she checked out, saying her husband had already gone into town to buy some groceries.

Two hours had passed. Alex was lying semi-conscious in a delirium of memory and terror. His skin had turned ash-gray, sweat bubbled from every pore; of his eyes, only the whites were visible. He trembled and cried out.

V stroked his forehead. "Oh, Alex, Alex – I'm sorry, I'm so sorry. It is my fault, my fault entirely."

Should she kill him now, or wait?

When the transformation came, he would be very strong – a mighty vampire – he was already exceptionally strong as a man – and he might easily overpower and destroy her.

She was in a pickle. If he killed her, then he would go on a rampage, and, inevitably, he would create others of his kind, others of her kind. It would spread like the plague – an army of unruly undisciplined zombie-like vampires, but fast, fleet-footed, and extraordinarily strong, with the cunning of agile wild beasts – and without the semblance of conscience that kept her in check.

Why was that? Why was she different? Why didn't she kill everyone in sight and sate herself in blood? Why?

If Alex got loose …

It would mean the end of human civilization.

To let this happen would be a violation of everything she believed in.

It would be a violation of her sacred oath to Marcus; which was dearer to her than anything in the world.

Now, while Alex was helpless, killing him would be easy.

And soon it would be night. Darkness was her friend. She had to move on – so she had to decide soon. The sun was low in the western sky; the clock was ticking.

Alex was delirious, and in the nightmare chaos of mumbling that came from his mouth, he seemed to become lucid for a moment, his eyes cleared, just for an instant, and they focused and he said, in a throaty, barely audible, whisper, one word: "V."

"V" – the search was on for V.

Out in the desert, under the pitiless afternoon sun, Edward Gunnarsson was feeling the heat, and he was feeling it bad. After all, he was originally from Iceland. His ancestors had evolved to face short summers, long winters, and long seasons with hardly any light or heat at all. His skin was fair, his hair was blond, and his eyes were crystal-clear blue – the worst possible combination for work under the giant southern sun and in the deadly heat. He wiped his forehead, and he squinted against the light – his eyes stinging from the salty sweat that poured down his forehead. The sweatband was soaked – it could absorb no more.

Edward was about ten miles from the crash site, and he was going over the area carefully, using a GPS to work his way through the grid he had established, and looking for anything that might have fallen from the aircraft.

The on-the-ground examination was supposed to find something the helicopters and drones with all their sensors might have missed.

He really couldn't see the point of it; they had recovered the black boxes, and they had the pilot's and co-pilot's voices as well, so how the accident happened would soon be pretty clear.

But Andromeda Corporation said there was very valuable cargo on board, genetic material, and a woman they were interested in, so that they wanted the whole area over and around the flight path preceding the crash, and even beyond it, covered.

It was hot, boy, was it hot!

The air-conditioning on his little desert buggy had given up the ghost, damn it. He was sweltering, and he was thinking of radioing in that he was going to quit for the day, that he was coming back to base, and that he'd pick it up tomorrow – when he saw it …

When he saw it, whatever it was …

There was something in the sand, something sticking there in a ribbed wave of sand, something that looked like it had been just uncovered by the wind and the shifting of a sandbank.

Edward stopped the buggy, wiped his forehead, took out his forensic kit, and, carefully watching where he was putting his feet, he walked over toward the object.

It was half-buried in sand.

It was a red rubber ball. Edward used forensic tweezers to pull it gently out of the sand He blinked. God, the sweat kept getting into his eyes! He saw that the red rubber ball was attached to a metal-and-rubber bar and harness. It was a gag, he realized, the type of gag used in sadomasochistic bondage sessions. He'd seen a girl gagged by one of these things back in Las Vegas, about ten years ago, on a 3-D video in the hotel room when he was lying there, dressed in a tuxedo, on top of the bed, sipping whiskey from a miniature bottle and waiting for the conference of forensic analysts to begin and waiting for his wife to get out of the shower. *"Ingrid …!"*

Edward dropped the gag into a sealed, transparent plastic forensic bag. He probed deeper: bits of tattered black synthetic elastic armored cloth, fragments of what might be flesh, and traces of what was probably blood.

Edward stood up and scanned the area. There were two other scraps of the black material on low scrubs about twenty feet away. Edward collected them, and placed them in forensic bags. Then he photographed and videoed the place and used various sensors – infrared, ultraviolet – yes, it looked like the sand around the red ball gag had been soaked in blood.

He collected more samples, and he fixed the GPS coordinates, and he radioed that he was coming back in.

They would have to do some DNA tests on the rubber ball and on the blood and the bits of textile – and then, maybe they'd have something, just maybe.

V sat on the edge of the bed and pondered. *How best to kill Alex?* She could break his neck. That would probably be simplest. It would be silent; it would not, initially, produce a lot of blood. But then she would have to separate the head from the body and dismember the body; and, ideally, burn it so that he would not rise again.

It would be complicated and difficult.

It was almost dark. She peeked out from behind the curtains. Most of the day, the air had been tinted orange. Now, the sun, sinking in the west, veiled by dust and by smoke from the fires in California, gave a sick, bleeding, livid tone to the fading light, streaked and mottled with ghastly shadows. A red sheen of gore was splashed on the storefronts, the neon signs, the gas stations, and the giant rotating hotdog, the flashing rooftop hamburger, which blinked on and off and, intermittently, sprayed out rose-colored sparks. When she opened the curtain a crack, a twilight gloom of blood and amber filled the room.

She had to move on; she couldn't stay here.

She could feed off Alex until he was absolutely empty – until she was sure he would not rise again – then she could just leave the body.

But, if there was a competent coroner in this god-forsaken, flea-bitten place, the blood-drained body would be a sign that something unusual, indeed unique, that is, a vampire, that is, V, was in town.

And if Sabrina Jacobs of Andromeda Corp leaned of this strange occurrence, she would put two-and-two together. Sabrina was obviously a very bright girl. She would realize that V was alive, and her minions would begin the hunt.

V paced back and forth. She didn't want Sabrina Jacobs hunting her. That would be a distraction. She wanted to concentrate on hunting Sabrina, finding her, and killing her; and she absolutely had to kill the Clone.

So if she drained Alex dry, she would have to put the body in the trunk of the car, and dump it somewhere – in the desert, in a grave she could dig in some isolated spot among the cactus and the rattlesnakes and the coyotes.

Yes, that was definitely the best solution – drink Alex's lifeblood, empty him down to the last drop, and tote him out into the desert and give him a dignified burial.

I shall be the only mourner, my darling. I'm sorry.

She leaned over Alex. The fever was still high. He groaned. His eyes were out of focus and blind like dead jelly, but they flickered into life. For an instant, they seemed to focus on her.

"V," he whispered. His lips were white as chalk, dry and chapped, and flecked with flakes of spittle.

"Yes, my darling," she said, leaning close and caressing his hair.

"V ..." His voice was a bit stronger, and his eyes seemed to be clearing,

"Yes, my love, I'm right here. What is it?"

"V, I'm hungry … I'm starving!"

Oh, oh, thought V. "What would you like to eat, my darling?" She tensed every muscle in her sinuous, lithe body, nerves tingling, on high alert, ready to spring into action. The thing he might most likely want to eat, the thing that was quite horribly and handily available, was … *her!*

"I'd like … I'd like … I think I'd like …"

"Yes, darling, yes …?" V surreptitiously extended her claws, energized her molecules, mobilized her neurons, marshaled her sinews, eager to morph, ready to transform: Alex may be strong, but she had more experience; she was quite adept, really, at killing. To disguise her anguish, she tenderly wiped his lips, hiding her extended claws, sharp as straight-razors, in the damp face-cloth. "What would you like darling, what would you like?"

"I'd like … I'd like … a … hamburger."

"A hamburger?"

"Yes." He was already stronger. He seized her shoulder. His grip was powerful, too powerful, his fingers dug into her flesh. "I'm hungry, totally hungry, famished!" He licked his lips.

"Good, my love, good."

He closed his eyes. "What I'm dreaming of, V, is a humongous hamburger, a triple-decker, super-size cheeseburger with tomatoes, onions, ketchup, hot peppers, gorgonzola, Swiss, bacon, pickles, and onions, lots of onions."

Edward Gunnarsson felt the chill in his bones.

Outside, even with the sun setting, it was sizzling hot. But inside the laboratory trailer was like being in a freezer.

Edward was leaning over the Andromeda Corp technician, Susan Little, who was doing the front-line DNA analysis. She glanced up. "There's no doubt about it. The DNA sample – and it really is a unique structure of DNA – comes from the prisoner."

"Bingo!"

"Yes, bingo," said Susan. "Great work, Edward!"

"But what does it mean?" Edward frowned. "Does it mean she's alive, or does it mean that she's dead? She might have just been blown apart, and the gag somehow ended up there."

Susan smiled. "Eddy, you are too critical; you are not giving yourself credit."

"Well, uh, thank you, Susan."

"Let's look at the elements," Susan took off her metal-frame glasses and swiveled around to face Edward. She was a slender blonde, tanned, with a thin but adorable schoolmarm's face, and a perky ponytail held in place by a knotted purple sweatband. She held up three fingers. One finger: "First, the gag-and-harness is not damaged. It was unbuckled – the buckle and lock are open – so I would guess she took it off."

"Yes, that was my conclusion. You're confirming it's a logical conclusion."

"Yes, you idiot, I'm confirming that. It is, indeed, a logical conclusion."

"Good."

Second finger: "Also, the sand was soaked with blood – right? And we have the photographs and analysis here: quite a lot of blood. So, she was wounded, badly wounded, but she obviously got away because there is no sign of a body at or near that spot – right?"

"Right."

"And – I'm not sure if you are aware of this, Eddy – but the prisoner is known to have incredible powers of healing and recuperation. So she probably regained her strength. That explains the lack of a body." Third finger. "And, here's a third point. there were fragments of her catsuit on bushes not too far away, plus flecks of blood. So she was moving, on her own steam, but losing blood, and maybe she was too confused or stunned or weak to avoid stumbling into the brambles. Does that sound reasonable?"

"Yes, it sounds reasonable."

"So, once she regained her strength, her only problem would have been to get out of the desert without being spotted – and then, of course, to find something to eat. She needs to feed every couple of days, I believe."

Feed – the choice of words was interesting. Edward rubbed his chin. "Yes, eat ... What does she eat anyway?"

"Oh, that," Susan grinned. "That is a *very* interesting story!"

"Onions, my love, onions?" V smiled her most trusting, reassuring smile. *Onions* and *cheese* sounded encouraging, But, almost certainly Alex did not yet realize what his real tastes had become. When he took a swallow of a real hamburger would he learn – with horror – who and what he was. He would gag, choke, vomit the burger up. In a flash, he would know, and, in an instant, the *transformation* would take place – *from man to vampire …*

And what kind of vampire would he be: a thinking, reflecting, cultured, literary vampire, or a wild, irrational bloodlust vampire, or a witty, amorous vampire?

She had no idea! Her only experience of vampires, other than herself, was of the wild, bestial, shaggy, uncontrollable, foaming-at-the-mouth, inarticulate kind. And, in the end, it didn't matter. Whatever kind of vampire he became, she was bound, by oath, to kill him.

"Okay, darling," she smiled, "Let's get you up and get you a hamburger, a big juicy, humongoous hamburger, with onions and gorgonzola! We have to get out of here anyway."

"Yummy!" He leapt out of bed.

He showered. He whistled in the shower. V frowned. Was whistling in the shower a good sign, or a bad sign, vampire-transformation-wise?

They packed, and got dressed.

V's spirits, she felt, needed lifting, so she insisted on wearing the skin-tight, phosphorescent, pink, semitransparent, nano-bio-plastic dress with ultra-thin spaghetti straps, and – she only noticed these features now – a classic 1920s Shanghai bordello-style side-slit going up to her hipbone, and an extra-short, slave-in-the-harem look hem, with tinkling tassels, which, she thought, gave the dress an adorably pertinent, extra naughty zing. She only now discovered how delighted she was she had borrowed this kitschy, trashy masterpiece from the *Exotic Dancers' Oasis Club* with Helen and Tracy's active connivance, of course, plus the perfect accessories, the fluffy pink purse, and the not very comfortable but quite amusing – adorable, really – pink stilettos. The whole ensemble made her feel so very much extra-alive! Weird, eh? Hmmm! She gave herself a quick once-over in the full-length mirror on the door of the weather-beaten old wooden stand-up wardrobe that graced one corner of their tawdry motel room.

Alex eyed her up and down. "You should always dress like this."

"The price goes up if I do," said V, giving him a look, and then, relenting, she turned to him, put her arms around his waist, pressed herself against him, and kissed him on the lips. "How do you feel, Alex?"

She wasn't sure if eager voyeuristic masculine lust – the high-octane, classic, objectifying, reifying, macho male gaze – that was concentrated on the skin-tight, translucent, phosphorescent pink plastic sprayed-on look that revealed an appropriately voluptuous, but also lithe and athletic female body – flat tummy, perfect abs from the blood diet – whether that particularly intense male gaze was a positive or a negative sign, vampire-transformation-wise.

"Hungry," he said, "totally hungry, ravenous!" And he gave her a disarmingly lustful human grin. "Famished, I am famished."

Sabrina Jacobs, seated, still damp from her morning shower, barefoot, and with a towel wrapped like a sarong around her torso, stared at the computer screen. They'd recovered the gag; they'd recovered traces of V's blood, and shreds of her clothes. So, the monstrous Thing was definitely alive. She must have jumped out of the plane before it crashed. Somehow, she had landed, and survived.

Sabrina glanced out the window – at the flat, sparkling horizon of the Pacific Ocean ... Somewhere out in the big wide world was V ... the ... the Thing ...

V – My friend, my enemy, V.

And, contained in the Thing's DNA, contained in its body – a body which had marvelous powers, a body which had lived for centuries, or even millennia, a body that was eternally young – contained in that body were, Sabrina was sure, genetic material that would enable humanity to take full command of its own evolution, to make a breathtaking leap in health, strength, intelligence, and longevity.

With that DNA, humanity could almost certainly escape from illness, disease, old age, and death. Humans would return to paradise, to the Garden of Eden!

It was Sabrina's dream – to remake humanity, to give to humans the means to transcend their finite, mortal destinies. *We will create the New Man, the New Woman.*

Eve and Adam ... freed from the fruits of sin ...

Sabrina closed her eyes. Savored the minuscule vibrations of *Andromeda*, its engines purring, its hull cutting sleekly through the water. It was her pride and joy, *Andromeda*, the most elegant, cutting-edge, state-of-the art research ship in the world and flagship of Andromeda Corporation.

Sabrina clicked a few keys and gave a verbal order, "Flight Path." Up came the computer map of the Boeing 777's normal flight path, and the path it had taken after the deadly struggle on board had apparently destroyed the controls.

There was one strange thing. Allan Carr had reported that on the cockpit voice recorder at one point, the co-pilot said, "Fuck, what next?" And about 30 seconds later he said, as if talking to somebody, "So am I," like he was agreeing with somebody – or something.

Who was he talking to? Sabrina wondered. Could it have been the Thing?

Had V been in the cockpit trying to save the plane, just as Alan Carr had suggested – *Claw prints on the controls?*

Sabrina superimposed on the flight path map the location of the red rubber ball gag that had been found, which was presumably where V had landed, since the sand was soaked in blood. Ah, ah! The point was about three miles off the path of the aircraft.

So the creature can fly ... or, perhaps, glide ...

And she's alive ...

Sabrina tapped her fingers on the desk. So, V's genetic treasures were even more valuable than she thought. Just think of it! A creature that can jump from a plane going 500 miles an hour, and land, and walk away, and disappear. Sabrina bit her lip: I need the original; I need to see, in detail, how she works.

She's alive. That's the *good news*, Sabrina thought, now we can capture her; but it's also the *bad news*. Now we know how strong and cunning and versatile she is. How in the world are we going to capture and keep such a creature?

"Would you like a massage, Sabrina?" It was Aimi's voice on their personal intercom. Aimi Hosokawa, a 23-year-old Japanese Ph.D. student, acted as Sabrina's personal trainer.

"Yes, Aimi, if you have time, I'd very much like a massage."

"I'll be right up."

V favored Alex with a motherly, compassionate smile. "Okay, Alex, if you are feeling weak, I can go in and order the hamburger. You can eat it on the way."

"No, I'm bursting with energy. Let's go in!"

They had stopped in front of a diner, a low oblong metallic structure pretending to be a 1940s railway dining car. The parking lot was full.

"Go in?" V sighed; she could see it now: the shock of his first bite of the dreadful humongous hamburger changes Alex changing into a vampire.. Onions and mustard and ketchup reveal to him what he has become. He rises up in the middle of the diner. He screeches "I'm hungry" and he eats all the customers. It was not an edifying vision. She pouted: "Can't you stay out here?"

"No." Alex pouted too. His lower lip stuck out, the corners of his mouth were curled adorably down. "I want to go in!"

V sighed. Was a childish pout a pre-symptom of *transformation?* She glanced out the car window across the pitted, dusty, wind-blown asphalt of the parking lot, past the assembled dust-splattered vehicles, and into the plate-glass windows of the faux-1946 transcontinental railway dining car – with its smooth, scalloped aluminum sidings and sleek Art Deco lines – somebody's dream of elegance in the desert – where the customers, all munching away, and virtually all colossally overweight, were brilliantly displayed, lit up like so many richly packaged bonbons, ready to be gobbled up. *Yum*, thought V, in spite of herself, *Yum, Yum.*

She had to admire, in particular – featured center stage right – a hugely fat fellow in a baseball cap, and wearing a loud, yellow, red, and blue, billowing, Hawaiian shirt, with two equally humungous, bulging children, one boy, one girl: they would total, altogether, she figured, about *ten* or *fifteen quarts* if you added them up, or *nine-point-five liters* or *fourteen-point-one-nine liters.*

Having lived most of her life in Europe, V was addicted to the metric system. She thought, mostly, in liters; since it made the arithmetic – particularly regarding fodder and calorie intake – so much easier. In the old days, pounds-shillings-and-pence had driven her nuts; and a pint of blood was still a concept she could barely wrap her fangs around. Liters, though, were as limpid as bubbly spring water. There was also a very fat lady in the second window, wearing a purple T-shirt and – when she stood up – revealing fine-grain fishnet tights, *230 pounds, maybe 9 liters: Yum!* The place was packed. *Lucky, I've just eaten*, V sighed. Big Boy had filled her up. She almost felt she should burp. But, now, what about Alex? She steeled herself. *What will be, will be.*

Alex, spoiled child, was still pouting, still mumbling, "I want to go in!"

"So be it," V growled, "Let us go in."

When they went in, everybody, or almost everybody, turned to look. Eyes widened, mouths gaped. Some people burped and tried to cover it up.

Glowing, skintight, elastic, pink, low-cleavage, waist-enhancing, fauxoriental side-slit, and mini-skirt hem, equipped with tinkling, titillating hem-tassels, jingling, and click-clacking in, on sequined pink stilettos, was maybe not the best way to pass unnoticed.

V frowned. It was too late to change.

In any case, maybe her cover – as the dead victim of an aircraft crash – had already been blown.

Exhibitionism was one of V's many weaknesses. Any occasion to show off, to strut her stuff, and she'd dive right in. And then … *What won't I do for love!* It was a pleasure, and a rare pleasure, she had to admit, having such a fine-looking human male specimen as her consort. Showing off, in such a situation, was extra fun, almost a duty, truly inebriating!

Alex had recovered his color, his hair was glossy, his tan glowed; she'd never seen him looking so good – but, then, she'd hardly ever seen him at all, and most of what she had seen had been in close-up working up a sweat in infra-red in bed, or in the half-dark in the car out in the desert when she was almost dead, almost beyond caring, certainly beyond fully appreciating, the splendors of masculine beauty. God, he really was a good-looking guy! She had been too tired the night before to really notice. *Looking good – positively glowing!* Hmmm! She wondered: Was this glow good or not good, vampire-transformation wise?

Their waitress was a very large woman wearing an oversized floppy red-and-orange polka dot cowbell bow at her neck and a big smiley badge saying her name was Big Bertha and a flared apron with a large screen-print representing a Krupp-made artillery piece – the classic WW I and II German howitzer – splayed across it, and her breasts were super-size. *Eight liters, at least eight liters*, V figured. The waitress smiled at them. "I'll leave you good folks with the menu," she said, and V noticed she had a marvelous smile, and, truly, boldly enormous breasts – with marvelous down-sloping curvature – like the ski slopes at Chamonix. Still, all in all, the waitress could produce *eight liters*, maybe *eight-and-a-half* of good blood, super-charged, excellent high cholesterol, of course.

The windows were fogging up. The eating humans were generating so much energy and heat eating: *munch, munch, munch, slop, slop, slop, slurp, slurp, slurp*. The room had a country-and-western sound-track about hopeless whiny love, a lonely guitar, and tumbling sage bushes, and coyotes wailing and horses and dogs being loyal, but that was overwhelmed in V's sensitive ears by the ruminant cacophony of little and big Homo sapiens, mandibles munching, tongues slurping, saliva gushing, gullets swallowing, and the peristalsis of at least seventy-five esophagi, and stomach gastric juices squirting like so many garden sprinklers.

V turned down the volume of her super-sensitive hearing. *God, I want to tune it out, Oh, I just want to tune it out!* All these people were *thinking* about food too – if you could call them thoughts – *Yum, Slurp, Grrrrhhhh, Slop!*

It was beyond horrible!

V usually avoided restaurants for just this reason. They were hell. She turned off, as best she could, her thought-reading stream. Silence, just silence. It was dangerous, like somebody turning off, or ignoring, or misinterperting, the radar readings at Pearl Harbor just when the Japanese squadrons of aircraft were closing in – but it was a price she was willing to pay.

"So, Alex," she said, organizing her mouth into a sweet smile, and gazing straight into his eyes, eyes which were glowing, sparkling, with energy. Hmm! "You want a hamburger?"

Big Bertha returned.

Alex looked up at her and licked his lips. V could almost hear his saliva gurgling.

"Are you folks ready, then? And what would you like, dear?"

"Black coffee. Thanks," V smiled her most ingratiating I-know-I'm-not-consuming-enough-and-hardly-have-earned-the-right-to-sit-here smile.

Big Bertha frowned and wrote down – black coffee.

Alex grinned. "I'd like the triple family-size cheeseburger with super French fries, dill, side bacon, breakfast bacon, peameal bacon, onions, mustard, hot pepper, green and red, ketchup, more French fries, coleslaw and a triple family-size chocolate milkshake, and three truly homemade hot Italian sausages on the side."

Big Bertha smiled, wrote it down; she turned to V. "Now there's a man who knows how to eat." And she turned to Alex. "You should tell her, dear sir, tell her to fatten up a bit – she's just a slip of a thing, look at that tummy, flat as a board, nobody has a tummy like that anymore! Sure you don't want something more, honey, maybe a milkshake, a special super family-size *frappatto grandissimo*, a hamburger, or a cheeseburger with the extra special trimmings; it's goodness itself!"

"No, no, thank you," said V, smiling tightly, boiling inwardly, and thinking, Oh, I *loathe* this woman!

With a radiant grin, Big Bertha headed off to fulfill their order.

A few moments of silence ensued while V tapped the tabletop with her immaculate, carefully filed and buffed fingernails, twisted a serviette into shreds, and contemplated emptying the salt and pepper shakers onto the floor, and, yes, perhaps pouring the contents of the supersized ketchup bottle over Alex's head.

Alex stared at V thinking how beautiful she was, and how perfect, and how strange it was! Such ecstasies as last night – and the utter ecstatic pleasure of sitting across from her here – they might be the last ecstasies for him of any kind whatsoever.

Am I a vampire?

Whatever!

Who cares!

Carpe diem, seize the day, gather ye rosebuds …

The monster burger arrived. Alex licked his lips and dug in. Food overflowed from his mouth. V took a careful sip of the black coffee and slipped her hand into the little spaghetti strap pink sequined fluffy shoulder purse – where she'd stowed Alex's glove compartment Beretta 9mm. It wouldn't kill him, but it would slow him down, and a Beretta 9mm would be more acceptable to the dining public in these gun-toting, gun-loving, Bible-thumping, patriotic Second Amendment parts of the Great Republic than *two vampires*, dueling with fangs and claws on top of the tables and upsetting the ketchup. That would not be family entertainment.

Alex gazed at her. "You look beautiful, V, you look radiant, you are flushed with – well, you just look beautiful!"

"Thank you, Alex," V said, carefully.

Alex picked up the monster burger again. He gazed for a moment at V, as if transfixed, and blinked, and then he again chomped into the burger.

How can he even grasp that thing, it's so big, and so full of juicy leaking horrible stuff! V shuddered.

Alex choked. His eyes grew round. They bulged out. His free hand drew desperate circles in the air. It looked like he was trying to fly!

Oh, no! V slipped the safety off the Beretta.

"Ohh, gghhhh, ghhhh," Alex groaned. His eyes spun in their orbits.

"Alex! Alex!" V cried out, thinking: Now, I have to do it now; now, I have to raise the pistol now, and, now I have to shoot, now, and now I really must shoot him now, now, now, I have to shoot him, I must, I have to do it, now, now, now! She gritted her teeth. And then I will have to kill him, really kill him, and chop the poor dear up, into itsy-bitsy little pieces … *Oh, God!*

Alex swallowed and grinned. "Just kidding!" he said. "It's delicious! Yum! Yum! Yum!"

V stared at him. Her mouth opened and closed, opened and closed. Finally, through clenched teeth, she whispered, "You bastard, you bugger, you absolute bloody bastard!" Deep in her throat, she growled, a true lioness. "You do realize I was going to shoot you dead."

"I guessed." Alex leaned across the table and gave her a kiss. It tasted of ketchup and mustard and onions and tomatoes and burnt beef.

"Ugh!" She wiped her mouth.

Alex took another supersized bite. She watched him eat. This is torture, she thought, but she smiled: *Whew, maybe he will be okay.* "You're sure you like it?"

"Absolutely! It's scrumptious!"

"Maybe – but when it hits your stomach."

"It already has."

"But when it gets to your intestine."

"I'm sure it's already dancing in my intestine. I can feel it."

"But when it poisons your bloodstream!"

"Ditto! Already there! Coursing through my blessed veins!" He patted his mouth with the serviette and took another deep, self-satisfied, grinning, overflowing, humongous bite of the hamburger.

V frowned.

As he munched, he said, "And what will you really do if I – what's the expression? – if I *change*?"

"You know what I'll do, Alex."

"Kill me."

"Yes."

He gazed at her and wiped his mouth. "V, I love you! You are a remarkable woman and vampire, and whatever else you are, she-demon and scaly voluptuous turquoise blue-and-green fanged reptile!" He speared some fries.

V leaned across the table and kissed him. "You are very forgiving, Alex."

"It's the first time," Alex said between bites, "It's the first time I've dated somebody older than me."

"Yes," said V. Her mouth was watering. "You know I haven't eaten *food*, real *food*, since the sixth century BC."

"Gosh!"

V gazed fixedly, as if they were a million light-years away, in another universe, at the crisp, salty, deep-fried fries; at the creamy, unctuous, overflowing strips of coleslaw, a singing diabolic chorus of scrumptious cabbage and carrot and onion; at the greasy bubbly beef, redolent of smoky blood sacrifice to Baal, of backyard barbecues in Minneapolis, and of the more tasty moments of the Spanish Inquisition. Little globules and sparkles of fat glimmered and shone and burst, like distant stars. *Ohhhhhhhhhhhhhh!* V wanted to scream.

"Honey, want a top-up of that black coffee?"

"Oh, what? Oh!" V blinked. She had been far away in an ancient Mediterranean universe of grilled lamb, of pomegranates, of flatbread, of lusciously ripe grapes she could press and let burst against her tongue, of sugared figs that melted in the mouth, of hot peppers that aroused even the most jaded appetite, of banquet tables sagging under excess. Being caught with such sinful thoughts, V blushed a comely, comic rose hue. "Oh, Yes, thank you."

"Your man has a real appetite!" said Big Bertha, pouring the coffee.

"He has indeed."

"Now, Honey, you don't mind my saying so, but what you do – you know, your profession – is nothing you should be ashamed of," said Big Bertha, noting V's blush, and then letting her glance slide, wide-eyed, down V's plunging cleavage and allowing her glance to drink in, with an tincture of wishful, wistful identification and charitable envy, the skintight, nipple sculpting, belly-button illuminating, iridescent, glowing, pink, elastic dress, and all it contained, a perfectly voluptuous, exquisitely toned human female body.

"What I do?" V was puzzled. She stared at Big Bertha's wide smile.

"The Good Lord forgives us all."

"He does, yes, He does," V repeated, "He sure does." She was still staring up at Big Bertha, still trying to figure out what the hell the woman was talking about and why Alex had such a silly grin on his face.

"Yes, even you," said Big Bertha, "Why, Mary Magdalene, who was the first to see the Lord rise again in all His glory, was pardoned, and the whores of Babylon and those of Sodom and Gomorrah walk among us still though their cities were reduced to ash and Lot's wife turned to salt for just taking a nostalgic gander back at the columns of smoke! Ah, *they gave themselves over to fornication, and they sought after strange flesh.* Just think! Picture it! *Fornication and Strange Flesh!* Hallelujah, All Praise to

Yahweh, and Amen! And, then, when you think of it, Salomé danced … daughter of a king but a whore like all the others, naked except for those veils that she quickly dropped (I have a reproduction over my bed) and asked for her John's head on a plate, but beautiful too, she was, beautiful, a true Child of God!"

"Whores," said V, "Yes, of course, whores!" She darted a look of fire at Alex and, again, blushed, smiled beatifically up at Big Bertha, trying to imitate one of Gentile Bellini's Madonnas she had so often admired in the *Accademia* Gallery in Venice and for one of which, sometime in the 1490s if she remembered correctly she had modeled readily, enthusiastically, admirer as she was of the Maestro's work, though it was rather chilly and damp in the Maestro's studio and she could hear even now the sloshing of the water in the canal outside the drafty and dimly clouded lead-and-glass windows, which gave her thoughts of escape – and of an escapade – in a gondola – and of romance by candlelight on a rooftop on the Grand Canal, and thus it was that she gazed up, blushing and beatific, saint-like, at Big Bertha.

"Yes, the Good Lord sees all, pardons all!" Big Bertha beamed. "The coffee's on the house, honey, you've hardly touched a drop!"

"Thank you. My profession …"

"A true vocation, honey, it's the oldest in the world, honey, the most respectable and honorable; Eve did it; the Serpent encouraged it; Adam fell into it; the prophets obsessed upon it, what with that begat and begat and begat and begat that never stopped; many even say that the Good Lord's son Our Savior did it, that He Himself did begat, though this may, of course, be an apocryphal tidbit designed to encourage the feminists or offend the righteous; the birds and the bees and the goats in the fields, it is said, do it, so why shouldn't you do it, that's what I always say! Why the first thing Abraham's servant did when he saw Rebecca was give her some trinkets for her ankles and wrists and put a ring in her nose – as the Good Book says – now, doesn't that just tell you something! I mean, we're all for sale, aren't we!"

V smiled up at the waitress. She drank some more coffee. "You are truly charitable, Big Bertha."

"Yours is not a badge of shame, honey, I reckon, but a sign of compassion. Why I imagine, honey, I can just see it, I can just see it before my very own eyes, how you lean down, and, with all your gifts, bring warmth to the lonely, comfort to the afflicted, succor to the perverse, joy to the maimed … A true good Samaritan, you are!"

"I sure do, give succor to the perverse. Take our friend here …"

"Now, now, now," Alex grinned.

"I can see that, honey. He's as fine a man as ever God laid eyes on."

"He is, he is, and since he's so fine, he has very special – very peculiar – needs. Supermen are very demanding, as you surely know, Big Bertha. May I whisper something to you, Big Bertha?"

"Of course, honey, we girls can't hold in our secrets forever."

V half stood up and whispered something long and complicated in Big Bertha's ear. As Alex watched, Big Bertha's eyes got wider and wider. "No, no, you don't say, but how did you? Oh, you did it like that, Oh, Oh, My God! Oh! Upside down? And the other way too? And backward? And hanging from *a what*?? And in the elevator of the Empire State!! And then you had to …?! Oh, oh, oh! And he wanted you to *wear a what*? Come again! And a *what*? Oh, the Lord be Praised!"

V finished whispering, and sat down – rather primly, Alex thought.

Big Bertha stood for a moment as if turned to a column of salt. "Why the Lord be praised. Now I understand the man's appetite! Such energy in a mere mortal! Honey," she said, looking at V and patting her on the shoulder. "You are a saint!"

When Big Bertha went off to serve other customers, Alex said: "I'm not even going to ask."

David Stanford Adams III was sitting, gloomily, in a far corner of the diner, alone. He wore a buttoned-down fine-weave paisley shirt, which he had buttoned up, at the collar, but without a tie; the shirt was complimented by a lightweight, synthetic, narrow-lapelled, pale, washed-out, cobalt jacket; and slightly baggy, deeply creased, ochre, corduroy trousers, with clunky, thick-soled, brown, tightly-laced shoes. David had a long, oval, pale, badly shaven face, reminiscent of a naked hard-boiled egg afflicted with late middle age teenage acne, and prominent dirty-looking black pores; his thin sandy brown hair was combed sparsely across the crown of his head, letting the ivory white scalp gleam fitfully through like a fresh snowbank partly hidden by flattened down reeds and giving the scattered flakes of dandruff a suggestive poetic air of wandering yuletide snowflakes.

David had ordered a no-calorie, no-fat, synthetic grapefruit salad with bio-engineered, zero-cholesterol goat's cheese, and colorless iceberg lettuce, and he was poking at a characterless hunk of feta and bemoaning his fate, stuck in this out-of-the-way, edge of the desert, ass-end of nowhere excuse for a town, looking for a woman outlaw who had probably died in a plane crash, when a couple entered the diner that looked like they were aliens from Los Angeles or stars from the set of some movie.

The girl – or woman – was dressed in some sort of pink elastic dress that glowed, and she had a very light tan and short raven-black hair, and she looked like ...

The guy was tanned and rugged and tough-handsome-looking. David Stanford Adams III already felt jealous on a number of counts – and – damn it! – it looked like the guy worked out a lot, his muscles positively bulged.

The woman, had extraordinarily dark sparkling eyes ...

In spite of the bright smile, she looked worried.

She looked ...

She looked ...

David Stanford Adams III pulled his personal assistant out of his jacket's inner pocket – this was not easy: The personal assistant got tangled up with six multi-colored ballpoint pens, a flat plastic package of breath-purifying anti-halitosis synthetic chlorophyll bubble gum, and two folded-up fliers for a local whore house, the lurid black-and-white cartoon illustrations of which – a girl disguised as Holstein cow eager to be milked and a girl in a scanty dominatrix latex bustier wielding a cat-of-nine-tails over an over-weight cowering Wall Street banker whose suspenders were undone and whose trousers were down – dispensed David Stanford Adams III of any need to avail himself of the services of said whore house, do-it-yourself being, if you have the right tools and the right inspiration, the true American Way, particularly if you're alone out on the road – but finally the personal assistant was in his hands.

The road warrior's friend.

He tapped in a code, and a miniature hologram, which only he could see, appeared. It showed the Andromeda Corp prisoner of a few days ago.

The hologram photos were not very good.

That was then: the prisoner was wearing a slatternly tattered black catsuit. She was drugged and dazed, so her eyes were out of focus and her muscles were slack, and the lighting was fitful and dull wherever and whenever those photos had been taken. She was manacled to something vertical, a wall of cold steel. She was gagged, and her hands and wrists, hanging from the manacles, were limp.

He looked back at the glossy couple; but they had now sat down in a booth, and the big bulk of the waitress – a yard wide at least – was between David and his two targets.

Gloomily, David speared a piece of watery iceberg lettuce. How are you supposed to search for somebody if you can't tell anybody that you are searching for that particular somebody or describe that somebody or circulate her specifications?

We want the woman, but we don't want anybody to know about her!

Andromeda Corporation sometimes asked for too much of its humble servants!

This was a hush-hush operation. Only those who *needed* to know were allowed to know. But David had a hunch. This was the lady, the lady who killed everybody on board the Boeing 777, and who somehow escaped the plane crash that left rubbish scattered all over the desert, a crash she had caused.

She is not to be harmed, so said the Directive.

She is extremely dangerous, so said the Directive.

She must be apprehended, so said the Directive.

Sabrina Jacobs was lying on her stomach, resting her chin on her wrist on a pillow in her private apartments on board *Andromeda* somewhere in the southwestern Pacific. She was watching the Clone on a monitor that showed the Clone sitting cross-legged, Buddha style, in its glass cage, staring into space, apparently looking at nothing.

Sabrina had just come from her shower, was naked, and was enjoying a very fine all-over massage. Her personal trainer and masseuse, Aimi, was working now on Sabrina's right foot and looking up, occasionally, at Sabrina, out of beautiful almond-shaped eyes, and occasionally, when Sabrina was distracted, Aimi would allow her hand to work up past the ankle and stroke the back of Sabrina's leg the calf of which had, in Aimi's well-educated opinion, a most graceful and elegantly muscled curve.

Sabrina had a cell phone planted in her ear, and she was listening to a man who had been put through to her and who could make the story of the

Apocalypse boring; it was something about the tone of his voice. She switched him to speakerphone so Aimi could enjoy the dialogue and be equally devastated by the man's charm.

"It was her, I'm sure."

"Good, great – so that confirms she's alive."

"She sure looked alive. And you know what she did then, when she noticed me, you know what she did then?"

"No, what?" Sabrina rolled her eyes. Aimi stroked Sabrina's ankle. Sabrina sighed, "What did she do then?"

"She looked straight at me."

"She did?"

"And that's not all she did."

"Oh?"

"She winked."

"She what?"

"She winked, and she gave me a great big smile, and she waved."

"She waved?"

"Yes, and that is not all she did."

"No?"

"No. At the precise moment she smiled, I heard a voice – it must have been her voice – in my head."

"In your head?"

"Yes. In my head."

"Well, well."

"And her voice, her voice in my head, said: 'Agent David Stanford Adams III, I know this is a boring shitty assignment, but it won't stay that way long, I promise.' That's what the voice, her voice, in my head, said."

"So, she knew your name."

"Yes, though there's no way I can figure out how she would know my name. And then she added something."

"I'm listening."

Aimi was now smoothing the oil up the inner side of Sabrina's right thigh.

"She added: 'See my friend here, he's healthy, and he's eating a bloody hamburger!' I don't know what she meant by that."

"Neither do I. You've sent me the photos?"

"Yes. Those from before she noticed me are okay. After she noticed me, they're all fogged up."

"I see."

"She and the guy seemed to be in love. It made me feel … well …"

"It made you feel sad and lonely. I understand. Thank you, Agent Adams."

Sabrina closed the communication, turned, and looked over her shoulder at Aimi. "I think, if you have time and if you can stand it, Aimi, I'd like a full massage tonight."

"It is always my pleasure, Sabrina. With oil?"

"With oil. You choose which oil." Sabrina sighed, and settled back down on her stomach on the white synthetic leather massage bench.

"Maybe we should have some music," said Aimi, flicking a switch and settling herself astride Sabrina's waist.

"Oh, yes, yes," Sabrina sighed.

Aimi began to smooth thick aromatic oil over the nape of Sabrina's neck over her shoulder blades and down to the small of her back.

"You know, I can hardly see it now," said Aimi.

"What – the scar?"

"Yes." Aimi traced the thin pale line. "You could have had it removed."

"The *Daddy Scar?*" Sabrina raised an eyebrow, "No, Aimi, I like to keep it, even if just a trace – it's a memento of Daddy, Sir Alfred Jacobs, Prix Nobel, and of the joys of childhood."

Aimi bent down and kissed Sabrina on the nape of her neck. "I would like to stay with you tonight, Sabrina, if you will allow me."

Outside the steamed-up diner, in the dusk, the wind was rising. Dust devils whirled in the parking lot. The garish parking lot lamps flickered, blinking on and off. An oversized garbage can flipped over and rolled across the lot, leaving a trail of rubbish behind. The can bounced over the broken, cracked asphalt, and suddenly veered, heading off toward the sands of the desert.

It was still hot.

Sand streamed through the air.

Standing outside was like breathing sandpaper.

"Are you okay to drive, Alex? You had a pretty bad fever."

"I'm okay, V."

"Good."

"You know, I don't think I'm going to turn into a vampire."

"Yes. If you were going to turn, Alex, you would have turned by now."

"So, boss, where are we headed?"

"Now we head to where I have a stash of clothes – and weapons; we head east."

"Yes, sir," said Alex, and they were on their way.

CHAPTER 10 – HELEN OF TROY

Helen of Troy was forty minutes out of town heading east. Her idea was she'd get lost in the Great Republic, retrieve her life, and maybe even resume her career as a lawyer.

Windshield wipers were not much good against sand.

The car was ten years old.

Out of the murk, the cops came, at least guys in cop uniforms, and they signaled her to pull over; Helen decided that, however dangerous it might be, she'd better pull over. Her car was ancient. It did have a souped-up engine, but it would be no match for the cops; and, down here, cops mostly shot first and asked questions later, if the cadaver was in any shape to answer questions.

She signaled and turned off onto the shoulder, creaking and rattling.

Yeah, the car was definitely a jalopy.

When she bought it a few hours before, the first thing the guy at the secondhand lot said was he didn't think a pretty girl like her would know much about cars; if she did want to take it for a spin, he'd come along and explain how it worked.

Helen gave him her special, disdainful glance. He had a fat face, dark stubble, large soft characterless eyes, big soft wet lips that were too red, teeth with gaps and dirty encrustations, and a heavy mop of greasy, slicked-back, black hair he kept smoothing down with the heel of his right hand.

She said, "Okay, you come along," thinking women's rights had regressed in recent decades at the speed of light. Now women were either Barbie-doll sex toys, or they were veiled from the crown of their heads to the tips of their toes, or they were dressed in calico and standing barefoot and pregnant in front of a wood stove and married, in some nutbar backwoods polygamous religious commune, to some asshole, bearded, unwashed, filthy, Bible-sprouting so-called prophet forty or fifty years their senior, and thinking: This guy, misogynous idiot asshole or not – at least he didn't have a beard – was … he was … *the first guy to hit on me since the acid attack*, thinking, *It's strange, it's really strange to be hit on. Christ! I'd forgotten what it was like!*

She had a carving knife in her backpack and a miniature stun-gun in the pocket of her denim jacket, next to the pepper-spray.

"Okay, hop in," the guy said, "I'll drive."

"No," Helen said, "Thank you, but I'll drive." And she gave him her brightest widest smile, thinking, *murder would be too good* …

"Right," he said. He was clearly disappointed, offended in his fragile masculine sense of patronizing, paternalistic gallantry.

She felt it. Anger and mortification were hot behind his eyes, which were suddenly flat as slate and not grinning at all, unlike his mouth with its drawn-back lips revealing all his unclean teeth in a mockery of a friendly smile.

She got into the car on the driver's side.

He's waiting for me to fuck up.

She put her hands on the steering wheel.

She started the car, and within twenty yards realized it had its rough edges, particularly the gearshift.

"Jesus! You know how to drive standard!"

"Yeah, I can manage it," said Helen, deadpan, thinking: Asshole, I know I can drive circles around you!

She skidded the car to a stop, gunned it. She made it do a couple of sharp turns. Acceleration was good, the center of gravity was nice, suspension held the road and didn't mind ruts, bumps, and quick hairpin turns … the engine was souped-up, and fantastic!

"Hey, lady, this is …" His eyes were round; he was holding tight, biting his lip.

Helen smiled. Scaredy-cat, I'm going to make you shit in your precious little undies, you pathetic drooling backwoods macho slob!

Going into a tight, fast turn, the car shuddered, moving sideways, quaking, trembling across the road, but it didn't fall apart. When she came out of the turn, the acceleration was fast and smooth; gearing up and down was a touch rough, but you had to be a connoisseur to notice.

She shifted down and gunned it, and shifted back up to high gear.

"Fuck, lady!"

"Just testing!" She gave him her best innocent grin – and she was only now realizing that she had regained *the power* – the power of the female smile – the power of female beauty. Since the acid, she'd stopped smiling, her smile was so grotesque – If she did smile, what she got in response was snide laughter. "Ha, ha, ah! This broad is really desperate, trying to smile, cowering to please!" What she got was mockery, or horror, or fear and repulsion, never a return smile – except from V, and, yes, from Tracy, adorable, clever Tracy who loved her. Tracy – beautiful Tracy!

"Yeah, but …" The sales creep was holding on tight as she swung out of a hairpin turn, gravel spurting every which way. "Lady, you are …"

"I'll take it."

She paid cash. She'd lifted all the cash out from under the floorboard of her kitchen. V had given her twelve thousand five hundred dollars from Big Boy's account. "It's all yours really," V had said, "I'll pay you back." "No need to pay me back," Helen said, "You've already paid me a thousand times."

"Cash?" the guy said.

"Yeah. Cash."

"Your cash?" He raised his black, unkempt, pimply eyebrows. In certain parts of the country, women alone weren't supposed to have cash; the Bible said …

"My cash."

He checked her papers – personal identity, passport, certificate of citizenship, Homeland Security permit, and driving license – making a great fuss and taking his time. He wanted to keep her around as long as he could. She was very good-looking, no, she was stunning, she was utterly unbelievable, and he wanted to bully her, intimidate her, make her feel *he* had the power, not her. If he could have made her grovel, get down on her hands and knees and drool, wag her tail and bark, he would have.

Desperate prick, she frowned, and then thought, *I'm uncharitable.*

Her documents, three years old, were still valid, and all in order; they hadn't been modified by her new-old post-acid, scarred look.

No infractions, no record, driving license in order, biometric identity card in order.

That was one good thing about Big Boy being outside the law and under the radar. Nothing she'd done as Helen of Troy had gone into the record anywhere or had been tied to her real name, Tamara H. Guerrera.

Tamara H. Guerrera was a virgin as far as the law was concerned.

Even her lawyerly life had been left untouched by her plunge into hell.

"What are you?" The guy said. He had dandruff on his coat lapels, and she noticed that his shirt collar was dirty. "What are you, huh, a ghost?"

The law had something on everybody, the better to screw with people's minds. Guilt and fear are great disciplinarians. She could see it in his eyes: *She must be guilty of something!*

"Maybe," Helen answered, "Maybe, just maybe, I am a ghost – and I've come back from the dead."

Now, she was forty minutes out of town and the dust storm – red-yellow dust streaming through the night – made it hard to see anything at all; and that was when she saw those cops – or at least guys dressed like cops – flagging her down. It was a roadblock with a six cars, blinking lights, blocking the road.

Traveling wasn't what it used to be.

Towns invented infractions so they could raise money, particularly from strangers; it was literally highway robbery.

Cops were underpaid and corrupt and often demanded at gunpoint bribes to let you go without a night in jail or worse – worse particularly if you were alone, particularly if you were a woman.

Gangs specializing in car theft, in kidnapping and in road heists leaving no witnesses, roamed the desert highways.

And drug transporters – mostly White Supremacists – killed people who just happened to be in the wrong place at the wrong time.

I've got no choice, she thought.

She pulled over.

She noticed, as the guys approached her, that they had their guns out – No, she thought, they are not cops.

They were all men – not a woman among them.

David Stanford Adams III patted his mouth with his napkin, put down sufficient change to make Big Bertha, the frightfully intimidating waitress, happy, and stood up.

The glowing glamorous couple had left the diner; they had turned right, so they were heading east. David Stanford Adams III took note of the make of the car and of the license plate – it was a California plate, he noted – and he had uploaded the information from his Personal Executive Assistant to the Andromeda Corp network, so they could give him a take on the car and its owner.

Alex Wolf – leading molecular biologist, geneticist, and genetic engineer.

David left the steamy, tropical warmth of the restaurant – where the air-conditioning was visibly struggling – and plunged into the torrid gusty heat of the night. Yes, it was night, but boy, was it sweaty! He popped two tablets of anti-bad-breath synthetic chewable parsley and chlorophyll into his mouth and began to chew. He put on his anti-dust helmet and Plexiglas shield, got on his motorbike, gunned it, and headed out, once again on the road, and, now, following the glamorous couple.

David crouched low and drove hard. His life, he felt, had essentially been useless and pointless up to this point. Now he had a chance to redeem himself and give meaning to his existence by apprehending the extremely dangerous fugitive – the woman who'd talked directly in his head, with a nice classy voice too, a touch of an upper-crust British accent. But she was the dangerous *Thing*; she was the enemy!

He wanted to apprehend her alive, and possibly without using violence, but if he had to use violence, then he might just use violence. There is no telling the lengths to which a totally desperate man might go to redeem himself.

He rode on, into the night, accelerating …

With luck, he'd catch up to the couple, and tail them, and when the opportunity presented itself, David Stanford Adams III would pounce.

The blowing sand made it difficult to see anything, but David floored the accelerator – he would sacrifice his life if need be to capture the Thing disguised as a woman …

In his mind's eye, he saw the Thing – flirting in that pink dress, flaunting her beauty and her smarts – and he saw the handsome devil she was with, tanned, glowing, happily in love. The world was definitely unjust!

I am jealous, I have to admit it, thought David Stanford Adams III, I am desperately jealous.

Alex consulted the GPS map. Yes, they were on course for the little town in which V expected to pick up supplies: how, he wondered, had she organized that?

Catching his mental question, V turned to him ... She *loved* turning to him; she loved *looking* at him; she loved feeling him *close*. "I have backup supplies and get them shipped to the most convenient point." She loved sharing information, information about her life with Alex. I'm in love. She bit her lip. And I'm absolutely not allowed to be in love.

She turned away from Alex, and concentrated on something else. Using the virgin Internet tablet she'd bought in a convenience store, she brought up files and news on Andromeda Corporation.

A deep voice intoned:

"Andromeda Corporation is an internationally recognized pioneer in advanced defense and security-related biotechnology as well as in medical research and fundamental research in molecular biology. It is a socially responsible, ecologically pro-active corporation. Under the visionary direction of CEO Sabrina Jacobs, Andromeda Corporation is determined to maintain its world leadership in research – that will help us create more secure, healthier, longer lives for all, and which will lead to a sustainable and prosperous future for humanity."

"What are you doing?"

"I'm trying to get more details on our friend Sabrina. The lady who wants to lobotomize me and who had the effrontery to create a Clone based on my DNA, which is, as I told you, totally unethical and absolutely against my basic tenant, the rule that governs my life!

"Under the dynamic leadership of Chief Executive Sabrina Jacobs, Andromeda Corporation has recently accelerated its R & D programs."

Sabrina Jacobs appeared as a hologram in V's lap, and she began to speak. This woman is beautiful, thought V. She's breathtakingly beautiful – and she has such a silken, soothing voice – I wonder if she's real.

"Hi, I'm Sabrina Jacobs. I work in molecular biology and genetics and in nanotechnology at Andromeda Corporation. It has been our aim at Andromeda Corporation to bring all of these fields together so that all of our knowledge – and all of our talents – can work to one aim: making life better for all of humanity. In the last few years, we at Andromeda Corporation have developed bio-nano air-borne drones, the size of small insects, used in many counter-insurgency and counter-terrorism situations, we have developed a new system of bio-metrics to increase the security of our great nation and our allies, and we have extended the boundaries of life-enhancing and life-extending drugs. Our cloning technology, the most advanced in the world, has led to a vast increase in agricultural productivity, and with our new 'Mindless Meat' line we have eliminated the need for suffering animals by eliminating the need for animals. Andromeda Corporation is a trans-world corporation, and our responsibility is to all the peoples of Earth. Our frontier-breaking research promises, in a not too distant future, to bring the human race close to some of its long-dreamed-of utopian goals: an end to poverty and hunger, the elimination of disease, and, also, an extension of the human life-span toward the ultimate limit, the dream of the gods, immortality. Thank you for taking the time from your busy schedule to listen to me, Sabrina Jacobs of Andromeda Corporation. We are only at the beginning. Let's strive for a better future – together!"

The Sabrina Jacobs' hologram froze and became a living statue of Andromeda Corp's CEO, and the announcer's voice returned – a deep resonant male voice.

"Thank you for listening to this message from Sabrina Jacobs of Andromeda Corporation."

"She's good-looking," said Alex, glancing over at the hologram of Sabrina Jacobs. V was now zooming in on the Sabrina image for a close-up examination of her enemy, her prey.

"Yes, she is," said V, "more than good-looking." V stared at the woman. She was a beautiful blonde with clear blues eyes, perfect skin, so far as one could judge from a nine-inch-high hologram, and her short blond hair perfectly but simply cut. "She's the perfect blond goddess type," V said, crisply, thinking, *When I lay my hands on that beautiful face and that perfect body, what will I do to them? Hmmm!* She let various delightfully sadistic scenarios unreel in her mind. *Now, now*, she frowned, *be surgical, V, not vindictive!*

"Yes, I can see that – the perfect blond goddess type …" Alex concentrated on driving. The dust storm was worse.

"By the way, Alex, we were spotted in the diner."

"Spotted?"

"Yeah, there was a guy in the far corner of the dinner."

"Was that the sad sack with the funny pale face, that pale cobalt blue jacket?"

"Very observant, Alex."

"I saw you transmitting some sort of message – telepathy of some kind, I guess – toward him, but I didn't catch quite what you said."

"Are you sure you haven't become a vampire?"

"I'll eat more hamburgers to prove my virginity, if it'll make you happy, my love!"

"Ugh! That was pure torture, Alex, and you knew it!"

"Well, I *am* psychic. You should have seen the faces you were making – pouting and grimacing like crazy – until the waitress started to compliment you on your dress – and your profession."

"Yes, well, I saw you left a very generous tip."

"She was trying to save your soul."

"Well, good luck to her; that's a hopeless task!" V looked out the window. "Problem is – now I probably need a soul, because I'm in love."

"Don't tell anybody, my love. But, back to the sad guy in the corner of the diner ..."

"The sad guy in the corner had a little electronic assistant, and he referenced photos of me – me a couple of days ago when I was prisoner of Andromeda Corporation. And he put two-and-two together and decided that I am the infamous freak V, the monstrous Thing that is supposed to be dead, and that he, lucky fellow, best of the hunters, had spotted me – or us – and I'm sure he was going to get this information to our beautiful friend, Sabrina Jacobs."

"So, now they know you are alive and that you are not alone but with this handsome hulk of a man-not-yet-vampire, me."

"Yes. What with you being so ultra-handsome and me in this dress, I might as well have gone in that place dressed as a Christmas tree."

"That's very poetic. I'd like to see it; can we try it some time?"

"Absolutely – next Christmas, I'll do it! I'll wear bells and balls and tinsel and wreaths and stars and maybe blinking lights." V leaned over – straining the seatbelt – and nuzzled against Alex; he put an arm around her. "I can see it now," he said – and he could.

"Hmm," V murmured.

"There's something else. I have, well, a connection, with this Sabrina Jacobs," Alex said.

"Oh?"

"Well, as I think I told you, she tried to buy our biotechnology company, Nano-Tech, a couple of years back; that is, her Andromeda Corporation tried to buy us, but we didn't want to sell. I never met the lady, but the negotiations went on for quite a while, and I met a member of the board, Henry Rothschild – a true gentleman, I thought – so Sabrina might know my name."

"That could be useful," V said. "Would you be valuable to her? I mean, the thing that kept me alive was the fact she wants to use me. Dead, I wouldn't be so useful, even if she could harvest the DNA. I think she wants to use me as a sort of lab animal – maybe to put next to the Clone. So, Alex, if you are valuable, she won't have you killed."

"That's nice to know. I had a bit of a name in biotechnology, and so did Judy. We did some pioneering work. Sabrina Jacobs might want to pickle my brain and put it in a bottle."

"I think the guy got photographs before I noticed him. After that I interfered, I fogged everything up."

"You fogged them up." Alex was thinking: this is beginning to be exciting: a battle of the giant females, V versus Sabrina, a detective story, who did what to whom, and, of course, a genetic mystery: how does V work, anyway?

"You are right, Alex, and, by the way, I would not mind if you deciphered my mystery – the mystery of my genetic makeup. It's time, and it already has been examined, but if you go deeper, it might get you a Nobel Prize. Humanity is ripe now, I think, to try to understand how I work. Since they discovered DNA and the Genome, humans are already re-designing themselves. So maybe it's time to examine what I am. And, after all, I was the result of an experiment."

"Sorry for the thought," said Alex, frowning. "I was looking at you like an experiment, like a guinea pig."

Sand battered in waves against the windshield. Alex squinted. What was out there in the sand blizzard? The wind had not reduced the heat, and the air-conditioning had broken down. Alex wiped the sweat from his forehead. He glanced at V. Her skin glowed, now lightly tanned a pale golden hue, her shoulders and breasts were beaded with sweat – salty water sequins – it was overwhelmingly sexy, Alex thought, and then thought: No, I must keep such thoughts in check, otherwise …

"Experiment with me all you like, darling. As I said, I am the result of an experiment, and it was a one-off experiment, more than 2,500 years ago. And the experiment, I might add, was not entirely a success. The alien scientists didn't intend to turn my mother into a vampire, but they did. And I inherited the trait. Otherwise, I'd just be a Phoenician girl born in 608 BCE. Not even that – I would never have existed, or I'd be dust and atoms by now." V leaned over and gave Alex an affectionate kiss on the cheek.

"Well, I'm grateful to the scientists – whoever they were – who conjured you up."

"The leader was my father. He was the one who carried out the experiments. And, yes, in the end, I am grateful. I find it difficult to imagine not existing."

V took a deep breath. "Death is such a … such a frustration! Living is such a privilege. Being here with you, now, is magic."

"Yes, the moment is magic," said Alex. How stunningly sensuous it was, mystically sensuous – whatever that meant – being in this car, driving in this desert, battered by this blizzard of sand, in imminent danger of being attacked by the minions of Andromeda Corp, with this extraordinary creature, and, while his mind flashed back to the previous night in bed, he tried to focus his attention on the road – a sign surged up through the streaming sand – and he turned right. It was like being in a snow blizzard, except this was the earth itself on the move.

"Hmmm." V licked her lips and glanced at Alex. God, he was good-looking! Her heart beat extra-fast. She took a deep breath. *No, V, No! Resist temptation, V!* She licked her lips again, cleared her throat, and spoke. "Okay, now, let's see about Sabrina." She tugged one of the spaghetti straps back into place – it had slipped off her shoulder – and called up Sabrina Jacobs' biography.

Up came a flutter of bio-pictures of Sabrina as a kid, as a teenager, as a young adult. Some of the images moved, some were three-dimensional stills, Sabrina in some deliciously seductive pose. A ribbon of text ran above the images while the captions ran below.

"She's got three Ph.D.s," said V.

"How old is she?"

"It says 34 years old."

"I don't think she's human," said Alex. "I've only got one Ph.D. and it was a sweat. You'd have to be superwoman … to …"

"She's been modified, I'm sure." V paused. "I wonder if you are immune, Alex." She glanced at him and passed her tongue over her lips and sighed.

"Immune?"

"I wonder if you are immune to becoming a vampire, like they used to make people immune to smallpox by giving them a little cut and putting in some cowpox."

"Could be. I'm not sure I want to risk …"

"No, you're right. I'll have to be good."

"It is a very interesting idea, though. If immunity can be created …"

"Yes …"

"Maybe we can …" Alex glanced at V and the memory of the night before came rushing back. In his mind, he felt her body against his, her lips against his, smelled her perfume, and ran his fingers through her hair …

"We'd better not ..." said V. Oh, what hunger! Not for blood, but for ... love. Maybe they could get away with a little tomfoolery, maybe a bit of nuzzling and playful foreplay ... And sex, oh, sex, oh, sex! No, better not ... *Grrrrhhhh!*

The hologram narrative babbled on, "Sabrina Jacobs completed three Ph.D.'s – one in molecular biology, where her thesis explored the future limits of DNA modifications and cloning; the second in nano-engineering, a pioneering study on integrating biological and non-biological engineering at the nano level in the development of bottom-up manufacturing and in the development of new entities, biological and non-biological, and in the creation of bio-metallic hybrids. The third Ph.D. dealt with the application of cutting-edge nano and biotechnology to security and the development of new 'intelligent' weapons and surveillance systems integrating human and non-human abilities."

"That's definitely my gal," said V.

"Your gal?"

"Sabrina wants to creat super-warriors; she must be the one who, personally, and I mean personally, wanted to lobotomize me and who created a clone from my DNA. I think I must have been one of her little pet projects for some time now, since she had me cloned maybe fifteen years ago."

"Where is this clone?"

"That's something we have to find out."

"If we find the Clone, we might find Sabrina Jacobs too."

"Yes. And I think you are right about something else, Alex." V made the tablet zoom in on the rotating image close-up of Sabrina Jacobs, bring it to ultra-slow motion. "She's not entirely human." V stared at the image, zooming in still further. "She's been biologically and genetically enhanced."

"When she was young?"

"Probably. Maybe later too."

"Who were her parents? Wasn't her father famous old what's his name, sir somebody something? I've got it on the tip of my tongue."

"Her dad, yeah, I think I know, but let's check." V scrolled downwards in the biographical section, and she scanned beyond the company website into journalistic and archival sources. "Sir Alfred Jacobs. I thought so. He was a pioneer of biotech and the founder of the Regal Cambrian Corporation, which became Andromeda Corporation. He held patents on 34 original life forms, and he got a Nobel Prize in Chemistry. Oh, and her mother was the German-Swedish film star, Alexandra Anders. Alexandra is still alive – and still working too."

"So, Sabrina comes by her beauty naturally."

"Shucks, Alex, I'm jealous."

"Shucks?"

"Well, you know what I mean." V sighed. "She's beautiful naturally and she's intelligent naturally and by household culture and by education – Sir Alfred was a stickler for childhood education, it says here, and he had all sorts of odd theories of how a child should be made tough to confront life and learn advanced math by the age of three or four and so on – the kid was probably tortured – I seem to remember there was talk that this Sir Alfred was a sadist – and I think Sir Alfred probably added some high-octane genetics to the little girl, for aesthetics and intelligence."

"So, if she was a human guinea pig …"

"She might not hesitate to use or to create other human guinea pigs."

"Only you are not human, not entirely."

"I have to keep reminding myself. Most of the time I feel human. My culture is human; the languages I speak are human. My mother was human, my father wasn't. My father used my mother as a guinea pig – he modified her DNA to try to make her immortal."

"That was an exciting project – 2,500 years ago!"

"Well, he succeeded, or so it seemed, in making her immortal. But, without wanting to, he turned her into a vampire – she was very thirsty, so my father told me, and so she was destroyed, by my father, I might add. He and she were lovers – that is where I come from, from their passion for each other. And my father killed my mother."

"This is like a Greek tragedy."

"When mother was pregnant with me, Daddy – Marcus – was away; and after I was born, mother hid me, sent me away; so Marcus didn't know he had a daughter."

'Which probably saved your life."

"Yes. My mother must have known what was coming; she sent me to safety, to another city, to a family which adopted me. Marcus had decided mother had to be 'terminated.' He tied her down and exposed her to the sun. She went up in flames, burned alive, on a bed where they had just made love. You see, I come from a complicated background: my father – and I love him very much – murdered my mother whom he worshiped."

"That is an extraordinarily cruel story."

"The world is full of cruel stories, Alex. When my father finally found me, he was going to kill me too. But he took a look – I was 19 – and decided that maybe I wasn't hopeless. So he trained me and helped me and laid down rules for me. That's how I've survived. I worship him, even now."

"He's the extraterrestrial, the alien."

"Yes. When he shows himself at least, he looks and acts human."

"Marcus – your father."

"Yes. He laid down the rule that I must never create any other beings such as I. I have obeyed that rule. So far, and so far as I know, I'm unique, aside from the Clone."

"So, there's nothing else like you on earth."

"No, I guess not."

"So, you are perfect for Sabrina. You are a mine of genetic and physiological information."

"Yes. You are a molecular biologist. You can understand the possibilities."

"So, what are we going to do?"

"Are you with me in this?"

"I'm with you."

The car shuddered, hit by a sand-filled gust that whammed into it from the side, almost pushing it off the road.

"Damn!" Alex squinted through the windshield. Visibility had zoomed down to zero. The desert storm engulfed them. "Impossible to see anything in this soup," Alex slowed down, driving blind.

"I don't like this!" V hunched forward, peering through the windshield.

"You want to stop?"

"No. Let's keep on, but real slow." V stared out at the withering streaking sand. "My program is simple: I am going to find Sabrina Jacobs, and I am going to find the Clone, and I'm going to kill both of them."

Gusts of sand swept against the car, battering it, almost driving it off the road.

Alex struggled with the steering wheel. He glanced at V. Her face was set in anger – or was it merely determination? *She wanted to kill; she needed to kill, and she was perfectly brilliant at killing. And she was going to murder two women, one of them a child.*

Her profile was exquisite, classical, beyond beautiful. She was on a quest – to save humanity from itself. Was she right? Or was she wrong? *Oh, love, oh, hopeless love …*

About 230 miles to the west ...

"Put your hands on the wheel!"

"Yes, okay." Helen sat very still.

"Would you step out of the car, please?"

"Certainly. Yes."

The men were all wearing bulletproof vests, Plexiglas masks, and they had their guns out and pointed at her. They looked tense, and nervous. Helen moved very carefully, very deliberately, keeping her hands visible. They must think she was extraordinarily dangerous.

She stepped out of the car and leaned forward and – following their orders – put her hands on the roof. The blowing sand swirled in behind her dark glasses, stinging her eyes.

"Documents!"

"They are in my vest pocket."

The man's gloved hand groped into her vest pocket and copped a feel of her breasts while he did it. He pulled out the documents. He spoke into the microphone.

"Tamara Guerrera!"

"Yeah!"

"Yeah!"

"No record. Okay. No police record. It says she's the daughter of Franklin L. Guerrera and of Marlene Hess, of Boston Mass. Yes, she's a long way from home. Okay, no connection?"

"Turn around, please."

Helen turned around.

"Take off your glasses and open your eyes."

Helen took off her glasses and opened her eyes, blinking against the blowing sand. There were floodlights set up on the side of the road. The guy did an eye scan with a retina and pupil scanner, a cross between a pistol and a flashlight. The bright light made Helen blink. "Don't blink," the guy said. She tried to keep her stare steady and deadpan. The machine flashed again, twice. "Okay, thank you!" He gave her a smile that was more of a grimace than a smile. The sand blew harder than before. Two other cars had been stopped. Helen kept her gaze steady. She wondered what they were looking for. Whatever it was, it was important. Then it occurred to her – it was probably V! Yes, V! Who else could be considered so dangerous? She put her glasses back on.

"Open your mouth." The guy was holding what Helen recognized as a DNA swab kit.

She opened her mouth.

He took a swab.

Helen thought of asking a question but decided it was best not to. It was best to be deadpan, to keep calm, and carry on. The new rules of civility – and survival: Tell no jokes, indulge in no banter, and display no personality or emotion. A number of what used to be considered the fundamental rights of American citizens were being violated right here, right now, but these guys did not care about rights – anyway, most of the old rights Americans used to care about had fallen into desuetude in the early the twenty-first century.

"You practiced as a lawyer?"

"Yes."

"You represented some of the Mexican gangs – the Rodriguez gang, the Navarre gang?"

"Yes."

"I see you haven't practiced lately."

"No."

"Three years. No sign of you on the lawyers and legal data bank."

"Yes, that's right."

"Why?" The guy smiled. He had very big teeth. "You don't mind my asking the question, do you?"

"Not at all. Why did I quit? I guess you could say nervous breakdown."

"Mexican gangs – high pressure, very tense work?"

"Very demanding clients, yes, you could say that."

"Yeah, very demanding. Well, Ms. Guerrera, this is a pleasant conversation we're having here. There's one more question I'd like to ask you and …"

The radio emitted a burst of static: DNA *negative, repeat, negative.*

"Well, we'll perhaps continue this conversation some other time, Ms. Guerrera. Here are your papers. Have a pleasant evening."

"You, too, officers, have a very pleasant evening."

Helen got back into her car and slowly drove past the roadblock. The "cops" – only they weren't cops – waving her forward through the floodlit sand-blasted gloom. Helen concentrated on driving very, very carefully. Being alone in this world was not going to be easy. She could contact V. Yes, as soon as she could, she would contact V. One of the parked trucks, she noticed, had a logo: Andromeda Corp. A laboratory trailer, perhaps. A group of men and one woman were conferring together, sheltering from the sand. Helen saw a tall, very pale blond man – he looked Scandinavian, maybe Norwegian or Icelandic.

David Stanford Adams III caught up with the fugitives in less than an hour. There weren't many roads, and he'd followed his instincts. His bike was fast, so he'd even been able to take it easy. He'd considered asking for helicopter backup, but the sandstorm was blowing too hard, and then he thought maybe he should ask for ground backup, and then he thought, no, if I do that, then all the glory will go to other guys, and I'm the one who found the trail, and I'm the one who picked it up.

As his Internet tablet and Andromeda Corp had informed him, the car belonged to one Alex Wolf, a scientist, former CEO of Bio-Tech, a company that had gone bust nine months ago because of a fire and possibly because of sabotage. Alex Wolf, the Andromeda Corp voice told him, was a valuable commodity, just like the woman, and Alex Wolf should not be killed, damaged, or harmed in any way.

David thought it unjust that not only did the guy look like a movie star, not only was he with that incredible babe – whatever she was, killer or psychic or psycho, she looked beyond luscious – but he was also a "valuable commodity." The world was not just.

I'll capture them myself, David thought, just me, just old David Stanford Adams III, I'll do it all on my lonesome, like the heroes of old, like the gunslingers of the West, like Yojimbo, the samurai. Just me and them, that's the way it's got to be, and that's the way it will be.

David had a Smith &Wesson .357 Magnum pistol; it was loaded with hollow-point bullets; one shot of that and you blow the leg off a buffalo; and you could kill a person, through shock, even if you just winged them; and that's the way it was; tough titty and tough bananas! David had never before fired the pistol, and he had never used hollow-point or soft-nosed bullets against anybody, much less against a broad in a clingy pink phosphorescent semitransparent spaghetti-strap dress. David was getting close now, real close.

The rear lights of Alex Wolf's car blinked.

The storm was bad.

David slowed down. They were entering one of those desolate sorry excuses for a town that you see strung out like carbuncles along every highway in North America.

V gave Alex directions. The town was one of those towns that used to live off oil. It was now a dust bowl, neo-rust-belt relic, a rectangle of streets with the names of old battles and dead Indian chiefs and dead owners of empty oil wells; the sand blew through the town like it would through an empty playground, all the old toys, oil derricks, truck depots, power-lines, empty assembly plants funneled the streams of sand that swirled and danced and rattled. V said, "We need to make space in the back seat."

V's phone tablet rang.

"Hey!" It was Helen.

V smiled at Alex and spoke into the phone. "Come and join us, Helen. I'll give you some GPS coordinates and a time." V already had a half-formed thought of the destiny she had in store for Helen. Of course, that destiny might not *take*. Human beings were fickle and unpredictable, and the best-laid plans of mice and men – and of one lonely vampire – could easily go awry.

On *Andromeda* …

"So, now we know she's alive, how do we capture this … this *Thing*?" Sabrina paused. "We've had the chemical ideas – first, a swarm of drones armed with neuro-paralyzing drugs that simply paralyze the victim; second, the Medusa Mist that turns people into living statues; and third, the – ugh – the Mind Slug. I propose we definitely pass on the Mind Slug." Sabrina was in *Andromeda's* conference room, in a teleconference with various experts from Andromeda Corp's Security Branch. Henry Rothschild was on her right, and sitting on her left was Aimi, who had come to take notes.

Sabrina had showered and was dressed in a perfect, lightweight, charcoal-toned, pleated-skirt business suit, with a crisp white shirt, a coil of pearls, sheer black stockings, and high-heeled black patent leather shoes. Aimi was in a T-shirt, tight jeans, and sandals.

"First, we have to find her – we can assume she is heading east. She must have an objective. What is that objective, I wonder."

"No idea, Sabrina."

"She probably needs money and equipment," said Henry.

"Yes, I see."

An assistant had just handed Sabrina a set of photographs and biographical notes. Sabrina nodded. "I knew it was him. The man with the creature in the diner, it was Alex Wolf."

"*The* Alex Wolf – the molecular biologist?" Henry took the photographs and glanced at them.

"Yes," said Sabrina, "that's him – one of the most ingenious, most independent-minded bio-engineers and nano-engineers on the planet. I'd die to have him on our team."

"I like that young man," said Henry. "Remember, Sabrina, we tried to buy his company, but he and his wife didn't want to sell. I did the preliminary negotiations – they were a brilliant couple, and served very good coffee."

"I remember." Sabrina flipped through the file. "What we wanted was them, not the company. His wife is dead, and he wound the company up."

"It was a tragic story," said Henry, "Judy was a charming woman, idealistic – and hugely talented."

"It was disgusting. The rabble killed her when she was trying to save some poor guy, a vagabond who camped outside their offices. I read about it. She burned to death." Sabrina shivered, and then frowned, scanning the report. "It says here Alex has been adrift since Judy died, and has stopped working. So what is our creature, the *Thing*, doing with a brilliant burnt-out scientist-engineer?"

"Maybe she needs help of some kind. Who knows?"

"In any case, if we find her, we have to be very careful. She is more than dangerous."

"Maybe we could kidnap somebody she cares about – if she cares about anybody – and then blackmail her into surrendering to us," said one of the security men in Shanghai.

Sabrina shook her head. "I don't like that, it's logical, but we've already had too much innocent blood spilled. Besides, the only person we know who is close to her is Alex Wolf: and that may just be a business relationship."

"It doesn't look like it, not the body language, not the way she is dressed," said Henry.

"They look like they're in love," said Aimi.

"I wonder." Sabrina gazed at the photographs, "if Alex Wolf knows what she is; maybe she just picked him up and is going to feed off him, if that's what she does; picks up guys and feeds off them."

"That is sexy!" Aimi grinned and nudged Sabrina, "Like a horror film: pick up guys and drain them of their blood! She is certainly dressed like bait … I *love* the dress!"

Sabrina smiled at Aimi. "I know you're joking, but I don't think she's going to kill him. He's valuable in his own right. If I can get my hands on Alex, I'll offer him gold, pure gold, to come and work with us."

Henry coughed. "There's another reason for not harming anybody close to her. Her revenge would be terrible."

"Yes, absolutely, she would take revenge." Sabrina waved her hand over the table, gently brushing away, dismissing the kidnapping idea.

"No kidnapping or blackmail, then." Aimi put a negative sign beside the two possibilities in her notebook.

"Maybe Alex Wolf could persuade her to work with us." Henry glanced slyly at Sabrina, "After all, we don't want to kill her. We just want to analyze and work with her DNA. And I imagine she could teach us a great deal if we asked her."

"Yes, it would be easier if she could be brought on side, as they say," said Aimi gently, glancing at Henry: *See, I'm backing you up, but you and I know it absolutely won't fly.*

Sabrina smiled: *the Gang of Two.* "Are you guys kidding? This creature is pure evil, a pure killer, look at what she did to the crew of the plane. She must have killed thousands of people in her career."

"Yes, okay, so we rule out a diplomatic approach." Aimi made another negative tick in her notebook.

"If we find her, we could try to use our quick-freeze weapon," the security guy from Shanghai was saying.

"You mean instantly take her down to absolute zero. Yes, that would involve little or no damage to her cells." Sabrina sighed. "It's cumbersome to set up, though."

"But what happens when you melt her? She might go berserk. She'd be mad as hell." Henry was doodling with a pencil. He drew a cartoon of the *Thing*, V, pinned to the wall of steel.

"True. Melting's not a process that can be controlled."

Aimi raised an eyebrow, and wrote: "Deep freeze – no go."

"That leaves us with the swarm of drones – injecting her with a neuro-logical blocking agent that will paralyze her willpower, she'll just collapse and fold up, and with the Medusa Mist that will freeze her like a statue, fully conscious but unable to move."

Aimi wrote: "Yes, drone paralyzers! Yes, Medusa!"

"What happens when she regains control?"

"She could be released very gradually, once we've got her in a secure location."

Sabrina nodded. "That's a good solution."

"But how do we design a secure location?"

"I'm not sure any location can be secure. She's got superhuman powers, and she's not stupid."

"I suggest we starve her for a week, maybe two, or three, and then she'll be weak, too weak to break out." It was that severe-looking, sexy schoolmarm, Nicole, from Paris.

Sabrina gazed at the screen. "Not bad, that's good – that just might work."

"And how do we feed her once we've got her? We have to keep her alive."

"Fresh blood from somebody living, passed through a filter, so she can drink; we give it to her in very small doses, just keep her alive, but very weak."

"I'll feed her myself," Sabrina said, "I mean with my own blood – if that will keep her alive."

"Me too, I volunteer. I'll feed her," said Aimi. Wow! It would be pretty cool to talk to the *Thing*, and to nurture *it*, or *her*.

"Then maybe you can talk some sense into her." Henry said, "Maybe she'd cooperate."

"*Sense? Cooperate?* I doubt it," said Sabrina. "Have you ever tried to talk sense into a lion or a tiger or a leopard?"

"So, shall I sum up the plans?" Aimi glanced at Sabrina and Henry; they both nodded. "Okay, when she is located, she is not to be harmed; she is to be immobilized either by a drone swarm attack, injecting neuro-blocking agents into her bloodstream, or by a Medusa Mist spray attack, freezing her in place like a statue. While immobilized, she is to be starved, so she is very weak, and then she is to be fed very little, just enough to keep her alive and conscious, so she will be unable to harm anyone or escape. The dosages of neuro-blocking agents will be reduced gradually, cautiously; then we feed her blood through filters – blood from living subjects such as Sabrina or me – just enough blood to keep her alive. At that point, experiments and perhaps, if she proves amenable, interrogation can begin."

"Good. That sounds right," said Sabrina. "So now, ladies and gentlemen, let's intensify the search, let's find V, and let's look at other weapons in our armory, and once we've found her, let's not let her go."

CHAPTER 11 – GENIUS CHILD

The sun had set. *Andromeda* was entering the Sula Sea, a sea in the Philippine Archipelago surrounded by strings of islands and by some of the most beautiful and rich coral reefs in the world.

Sabrina's stateroom was lit by low, discreet lighting. Porthole windows looked out on the vast Pacific. Sabrina was in a black silk bathrobe that perfectly complimented her sharp blond beauty, blue eyes, and golden tan. Aimi, whose raven hair was tied back in a ponytail, wore a white silk bathrobe that threw her delicate features, dark eyes, and arched black eyebrows into splendid stark relief. She looked like she had stepped out of a black-and-white glamour studio photograph from the Hollywood of the 1940s.

"You and this creature have a long history." Aimi poured tea. She gazed at Sabrina, bowed, and held Sabrina's cup out, like an offering. She was eager to console Sabrina, to make her happier, but she couldn't resist asking a question: "Why do you hate this – this Thing – this V so much?"

"Hate her?" Sabrina frowned. "Do I hate her? I'm not sure … Yes, you may be right. I hate her. She is a blood-thirsty killer, she revels in human sacrifice, like an ancient pagan goddess covered in human gore. She is the enemy of the human race."

"Is she the enemy of the human race?" Aimi brought her cup to her lips, tilting her head to one side and raising a skeptical eyebrow.

"She is a predator; we are her prey. But, Aimi, it's not only that. We humans must make scientific progress. There are almost ten billion people on the planet. The climate has gone haywire. Disease is rampant. Poverty is everywhere. Food is running out. Governments are collapsing. Humans are not up to it – to surviving. We must pass to a new stage of human existence, a new stage in human history."

"And how will we do that, Sabrina?"

"Oh, you girl of little faith!" Sabrina sighed. "How long have we existed as a species? Six million years? Three hundred thousand years? Now, after less than six thousand years of what we fondly or foolishly call civilization, we have come to a moment of truth – we either change, or we die. And V may hold the key to change. Science is the only way we will survive. V, like an ancient goddess, stands for all that is archaic, ancient, and violent. She is our enemy."

"That may be," said Aimi, "But I think, in a way, you – let's say you dislike her – because, in some ways, you are like her, and she is like you: you are both, how shall I put it, rather like, well, rather like superwomen."

"Superwomen! I do love you, Aimi! You are so good for my ego! And what about you, my darling, you are no slouch – daughter of warriors and samurai, a brilliant researcher, precocious scientist, crack shot, and martial arts champion …"

"You are too kind, Sabrina." Aimi bowed her head.

"I never have told you much about my life have I." Sabrina put the cup of tea down and gazed at Aimi, such an exquisite, beautiful, talented young woman.

"No, you are always discreet. You know much more about me, Sabrina, than I know about you. You know how my mother and father were killed, how I was brought up by my grandmother and grandfather in a town near Kyoto, what sports I played, what boys I fell in love with, all the exams I have ever taken, and the marks I got …" She stopped. "So now it's your turn – tell me about yourself, Sabrina, tell me your story."

"I'm feeling expansive tonight. Here is my confession. I guess I can start with our friend V." Sabrina closed her eyes, "In a way, you are right, V and I are old friends – I first learned of her many years ago. I dreamed of her often."

For a long time, Sabrina said nothing. Aimi drank her tea and read a book, glancing up from time to time to look at Sabrina. Tears were running down Sabrina's cheeks. Aimi decided to say nothing. She would wait.

Sabrina was thinking, it was an old story, a story with deep painful roots. More than fifteen years ago. She gazed at Aimi.

"Okay, Aimi, here goes: here is my story and how it is linked to V. I was twenty-one years old when Daddy, Sir Alfred, died unexpectedly on a business trip to Germany. Well, actually, he was in the arms of a twenty-three-year-old Russian girl in Bremen and had a heart attack. Mother was annoyed but, as always, *very* discreet! When Daddy died, I inherited the Andromeda Corporation Empire."

"That was a challenge, I imagine, at 21," said Aimi.

"Yes. It was. Where to begin?" Sabrina frowned. "Maybe I need something stronger than tea."

Aimi stood up, went to the bar, and took down a bottle of strong red wine, *Amarone Valpolicella.* She poured them both a large brimfull glass. She sat down, and waited. There was a long pause, then ...

"Okay," Sabrina began. She closed her eyes and told the story in the third person, as if it were the story of someone else; this was a mental trick Sabrina often used – looking at herself from the outside, talking about herself, even when alone, even to herself, as if she were someone else.

And so ...

When Sabrina inherited Andromeda Corporation Empire, she was twenty-one years old and already had a reputation as one of the world's leading biological engineers, a child prodigy, a woman of incredible talents, a freak of nature. But her gifts – and this was a secret – did not come from nature alone.

She was eager to prove herself the equal of her father – in fact, she was determined to prove she was *better* than her father, more brilliant, more creative. It would be her *revenge.* Now that he was dead, she could never gain his love and respect; but she could, at least, prove that she was better than the Master – the Master with his novel techniques of radical genetic modification, which he had used on Sabrina, as he had used his black leather whip, his antique rattan cane, his handcuffs, his electric shocks, his subtle and scientifically refined forms of psychological torture, all of which he used – frequently – on Sabrina.

And so, plotting her revenge upon her father, she had allowed herself to dream of an incredible breakthrough project in genetics. She had to do something that would utterly transform the human race.

And one day, she found what she thought might be the key to her Faustian or Promethean project. The kernel was contained in the myth, or the story, of a creature that had incredible powers. At first, it seemed merely a fable, too good to be true, with all the trappings of an urban legend, or a fairy-tale, or a piece of maverick religious folklore.

There existed, somewhere on this planet Earth, it was said, a fantastical creature, a vampire-like creature that drank human blood. It was a woman, this creature, and it reputedly had several forms or manifestations, human, vampire, and reptilian demon.

The key for Sabrina, though, was the suggestion that this vampire was half-alien, that its DNA was, in part, literally not of this world.

When Sabrina first heard the rumors – and they were rumors moving in British government and intelligence circles, she didn't believe them; she dismissed them as urban legends, old wives' tales.

Then, through a friend of her fathers', she came into possession of some top-secret documents on the "events" of 2027, as they were known – a wave of earthquakes and volcanic eruptions which had done huge damage.

There, in these top-secret official documents, were reports of a woman who had lived for centuries and who had played a crucial role in stopping the catastrophe.

In some of the documents, she was referred to by what Sabrina decided must be a code name, *V*.

The people who wrote the reports about the creature (and some of the reports preceded 2027 and dated back many decades, into the mid-twentieth century) seemed positively to be in awe of the creature. It was as if they were in love with her. But this creature – this *Thing* – was also, apparently, and by her own admission, an outlaw, a mass murderer; she lived by killing people, by drinking their blood.

She was a vampire.

She was a predator, and people were her prey.

Sabrina was fascinated. First, the creature was reputed to be immortal, and had, it seemed, extraordinary powers of recuperation – it could be shot, it could be hit by explosives, and it had the power to regenerate itself; there were even reports that it could heal the wounds of others – by a sort of magical laying on of hands.

The information was spotty. Great effort had been made to keep the existence of this half-alien vampire from the general public. Many of the documents, even though their distribution was "highly restricted," had large swaths blacked out.

The second point was included in a DNA report. Reading between the lines, Sabrina could see that the report *suggested* that the creature's DNA was unique, that it contained elements never seen in any living creature; that it was almost certain that the creature was indeed a half-breed, a hybrid of human and alien!

If any of this were true, then the creature could be the Holy Grail of genetic research – the creature would, in short, be a gold mine.

Then the impossible happened. Fifteen years ago, Sabrina had managed to obtain some of the *Thing's* DNA.

The *Thing* had gone to England, near Cambridge, to hunt down and kill a serial killer, a kidnapper and killer of little girls. The man was a solicitor named Tillotson.

This was serendipitous. Cambridge was the old base of the Jacobs family. It was in Cambridge that Sir Alfred Jacobs had established his first research center and then his first biotechnology-nanotechnology hybrid commercial company. It was in Cambridge that Sabrina had gone to school.

It was in Cambridge, too, that her father had carried out some of his more daring experiments – and he carried many of them out on his own child, on Sabrina.

He turned her into a *genius* – and a *freak*.

Sabrina was already an extremely gifted student, and she was already showing signs of being an extremely beautiful woman. Her mother, a film star, was one of the fabled beauties of the age.

Sir Alfred decided that he would accentuate his daughter's perfection, her intelligence, and her physical prowess. At first, when she was a child, it was fun, playing games in her father's laboratory, and being with him in his office. He was her god. She worshiped him. She sat on his lap or next to him while he worked.

But with time, Sir Alfred became more and more demanding, less and less patient, and angrier and angrier. Nothing was ever enough. Whatever Sabrina did, however brilliant she was, she did not do enough to please him.

He began to experiment on her. She became his guinea pig. He tried out newfangled types of genetic engineering and new teaching and studying methods. The experiments worked, but were never repeated: Sabrina nearly died – several times – and her mother, who was often away on film shoots and who usually allowed Sir Alfred his way, threw a spectacularly hysteric fit and declared she would kill Sir Alfred if he continued using their daughter as a guinea pig.

"But," said Sir Alfred, "She is going to be a new model for humanity – she is going to be the perfect woman, the salvation of the human race; she is the future."

"Balderdash," said her mother. "Rubbish! Poppycock! You do speak the most horrible rubbish, Alfred, and whatever theories you have about the future of the human race, that is no excuse for being sadistic to your daughter!"

Sabrina recovered, with enhanced physical resistance and a mental brilliance that turned her into a freak, so she learned when at school or when dealing with any of her classmates.

She no longer had any friends – her moodiness and outspoken opinions didn't help. The fact that she was ultra-beautiful – and rich – made it worse. She received many painful lessons involving bloody noses – usually, if not totally outnumbered, she gave back more than she got. One winter, she suffered a near-fatal dunking in the icy River Cam.

It was twilight on Christmas Eve. Sabrina was suddenly mobbed by some very jealous girls who pretended they wanted to be her friends – "Let's go for a walk along the river," they said, "I'm not sure I have time," she said, "Oh, loosen up, Sabrina, it's Christmas Eve, you have to be human once in your life!"

"Okay," she said. She was suspicious, and even afraid, but she was damned if she was going to show her fears, and one of the girls was a lithe and charming, rather intellectual, beautiful, and very funny black girl from Jamaica whom she found ever so poetic and desirable; she did so desperately want to make friends with her and –

Mistake …

Once they were far from any houses and people, the girls suddenly turned on her and seemed intent on killing her.

The four girls wrestled her to the ground, and pushed her, face down, head and shoulders underwater. The bank was slimy and icy and muddy and slippery.

Sabrina fought, thrashed, squirmed, and kicked.

But they were stronger; they held her down, her face underwater, two of them pressing her shoulders down, and one, she felt, sitting on her back.

At first, she struggled, but then she mimicked being dead, jerking a few last desperate spasms, and then going totally limp, holding her breath and turning blue.

Her head was underwater for almost four minutes.

She hoped to survive by stealth. She hoped they would have the bloody bejesus scared out of them and run away. If they kept her under for a second longer, she was going to push and kick herself deeper into the water – it was freezing cold there was even a film of ice here and there – and try to swim to the other side and get away from the bloody bastards.

But, just at the last second, they pulled her out, thinking they had committed murder. She remained limp and pretended to be dead; she locked herself into a non-breathing mode, though she felt her chest was caving in for lack of oxygen, and she was so cold she felt she was an icicle.

"She's dead! Oh, fuck! She's dead!"

"Yeah, she's not breathing! Oh, fuck!"

"What do we do?"

"Shall we hide the body?"

"No, you idiot! Where would we hide it?"

"The story will have to be: she fell in, she drowned, she crawled to shore, but she died."

"That's right! That's the story!"

"There is no story. We were never here. We don't need a story."

"Right! We were together all the time!"

They ran away, leaving Sabrina lying on the frozen grass, limp, not breathing, her eyes open, staring blindly toward the dark night sky.

When they were gone, she choked and gasped for air – her lungs and throat burning liquid fire. She lay there without moving for several minutes before getting up, shivering with cold, soaking wet, and furious, absolutely furious – against herself: I am a bloody freak! I'm a monster. Against the girls: Those idiot murders, I will crush them! And against her father – he turned me into a freak! And against her mother – she abandoned me to that sadist.

Sabrina walked home through the Christmas Eve dusk. Her shoes and socks made a spooky squishy sound that was extra humiliating. She took them off, tucked them under her arm, and walked barefoot. It was already turning to night; the street lamps were on; the streets were empty; the high old brick walls along the pathways looked like prison walls; she was soaking wet and icy cold.

Snowflakes began to fall, heavy, crisp flakes, ice-cold and bright in the lamplight, beautifully drifting sideways through the air. Some stuck on her lashes.

She walked out of the park and onto the narrow road leaving Cambridge, and then down the side road that led to the family "chateau" – a mammoth red brick Victorian mansion, surrounded by high brick walls, and with a pebbled and flagstone courtyard, and a separate gatehouse and garage. Strands of her hair, she noticed, had grown stiff with ice. Her shirt was rigid like a piece of glass.

She went in the chateau gateway, being careful not to be seen by anybody and headed straight to the kitchen, Old Bess's room. Once inside she stood at the entrance, making a puddle, and then took off all her clothes and hung them on a rack, and Bess, who had come to help her, said, "You poor child! You can be brilliant in this house, you *have to be brilliant* in this house, but it's better to hide it when you are out there among ordinary mortals. The dim ones don't like bright lights. Here, take this towel! Make sure your hair is dry!"

"Thank you, Bess." Sabrina took the towel and looked at it, eyes wide, uncomprehending – *What is this thing and what am I do to with it?*

Bess suddenly realized the depth of the girl's shock. Her eyes were staring; her mouth hung open; her lips were blue; her skin was covered in mottled goosebumps, and she was violently trembling. Her teeth were chattering, literally going clack, clack, clack. Sabrina, staring at Bess, wondered if she'd break her jaw from the chattering, and wondered if she was shaking from cold, or from fear, or from humiliation and rejection. She'd really *liked* the Jamaican girl, more than liked her, even dreamed about her! She could have been my friend! I should have so liked her to be my friend! But, like everybody else, she hates me!

"No, I'll do it for you, child!" And Bess took the towel and toweled Sabrina down so vigorously that Sabrina shook herself, coming alive again, and turned to Bess with a timid, shivering grin. "You're toweling me down like I was one of the horses."

"Well, you are not a horse, Sabrina, but you are a little rascal, so I'll towel you down just the way I want to towel you down!"

Bess had a large, almost walk-in fireplace in the kitchen – three logs were burning, sending up high flames and glowing with embers – the heat was intense – and the naked teenager stood in front of the crackling fire and was toweled down and dried off. Slowly, the trembling stopped; slowly, her lips took on their usual healthy gloss; slowly, her skin was again smooth, and slowly …

"And, now, don't tell anybody, but I think, if you would like it, I'll give you a little glass of brandy with some sugar in it, you've had such a shock," said Bess, "and then you need a hot bath."

Sabrina had been trained by her father and her mother to be indifferent to nakedness – Sir Alfred had a theory that going naked was good for the mind.

In their villa in France, they never wore any clothes at all, unless there were visitors and even then … So Sabrina let the towel drop and sat down cross-legged, naked, on the rug in front of the fire, and she drank the hot brandy and felt all warm inside.

Old Bess gazed at her and said, "You really are the little pagan, aren't you, my love."

Cupping the glass of brandy in her lap, Sabrina looked up and said, "Yes, Daddy is at least right about that, I think. I like the old gods, Bess, I like the things they do, always running around killing each other and loving each other and turning into willow trees and lampposts and swans and things, and the men being women, and the women being men, and the gods and the mortals making love and making children. The gods are like us; we should be like them."

"I doubt any of them ever turned into lampposts," said Bess, who was poking at something that was steaming on the stove. "I think you had better eat with me and stay with me tonight. We don't want you catching a fever all alone in the middle of the night."

"No, we wouldn't want that, would we," said Sabrina, rather primly, and laughed. "And I suppose I should sleep with you, Bess."

Bess gave her a sideways glance while stirring the broth, "Well, that might be quite a sweet idea, if you have no objections, Sabrina."

"No objections." Sabrina stood up and turned around, pirouetting, warming herself like something roasting on a spit. "But I would like another glass of that brandy."

"Well, you can have that when we eat, which will be in about three minutes," said Bess.

And so Sabrina ate, a rich broth and fresh bread with big slobbery slabs of creamy butter, and drank the brandy and then even a glass of wine with the roast beef and mashed potatoes.

Then, she had a hot, steamy, perfumed bath, and then she and Bess watched videos in bed, and then they turned out the lights, and Sabrina really liked it in that big, slightly sagging bed that smelled warm, warm from Bess's body, but also from cooking.

"You know what your bed smells like, Bess? It smells like freshly baked bread."

"Well, that is sweet," Bess said, and Sabrina sighed, and she thought how much she adored it, sleeping with Bess, whose body was smooth and athletic and firmly soft like a very comfortable pillow.

Sabrina liked to lay her head on Bess's stomach and feel the gentle rise and fall of Bess's breathing as Bess stroked her hair and told her stories.

Both her mother and Sir Alfred were away in the Bahamas, so, yes, it was logical that Sabrina spend Christmas Eve and Christmas morning with Old Bess.

And Old Bess wasn't really old at all – she was a handsome slender woman of maybe forty or forty-two and very loving. Not having had children of her own, she showered affection on Sabrina, and she made Sabrina feel that she was a person, a serious real person, not a monster, not a freak. Bess had been a school teacher before she decided pots and pans and soufflés were more agreeable than rowdy children and when she was young she had hitchhiked her way around the world, Europe, and Asia and the Australian outback, and the Americas, so she had plenty of stories to tell.

Beth's praise and her common-sense approach to things were good antidotes to Sabrina's father, who continually told his daughter that she was a monster; that she was ungrateful; that she was incompetent; that she was stupid; that she didn't appreciate the advantages she had been given.

He made her climb mountains with him, clinging to ropes, dangling over the void, terrified and trembling; he made her swim naked in icy waters pouring from glaciers, and stay in the water until she turned blue; he made her pass tests on advanced – university-level – mathematics and Ancient Greek and Latin when she was ten.

Daddy taught me so much, Sabrina later thought, but he would have destroyed me – killed me or driven me mad, literally hopelessly irredeemably mad – if it had not been for Bess – and for mother. Without them, I'd be dead now, or totally insane – and I'm pretty much insane as it is. She wondered what perverse form of love – because he did love her, there was no doubt about that – had turned Sir Alfred's affection for her into an unhealthy, sadistic, almost homicidal obsession.

She could remember, vaguely remember, when he was an affectionate, doting father. But then, suddenly, that all changed: she had to be *perfect*.

"I think he loved me, Aimi, but he loved me, probably, in the wrong way. He was attracted to me, I sometimes think, the way a man is attracted to a woman – or even, perversely – to a child – at least I think that was it, part of it, but maybe I'm just projecting my love for him, my yearning, and its perverse side – I'm sure there *is* a perverse side – onto him. But if he was attracted to me like that – maybe, then, he had to destroy me."

Once, coming back from school, Sabrina announced that she had not been first in her class in a competition in mathematics – she was second. *What a bloody disaster!*

Sir Alfred was furious.

It was a cold stormy November day. Sir Alfred decreed that Sabrina must kneel in the courtyard until she promised to do better.

Sabrina was furious too. She felt – and it turned out she was right – that the examiner had misunderstood one of the bloody examination questions and had not understood Sabrina's bloody brilliant answer, which was, in fact, the damned correct bloody answer – so Sabrina bloody well refused to promise to do better. "If the teachers are bloody idiots, and can't get their bloody sums right, it's not *my* bloody fault," she said.

"Young lady, you go out and kneel in the courtyard, kneel, on your bare knees, until you are ready to apologize and to say you are sorry and to promise to do better!"

Sabrina went out into the back courtyard in her school uniform, a short plaid skirt, and a thin white shirt, and she knelt, shoeless and without socks, on the hard cobblestones in the middle of the courtyard.

It was raining, an icy November rain laced with wet sleet and hard pieces of hail that came in sudden cutting bursts. It was a dismal gray afternoon. Soon, by about 4:00 o'clock, it was dark. The lights went on in the house. The large windows looked bright and comfy and warm.

Sabrina could see Bess in the kitchen preparing tea and muffins. She wanted to be inside the kitchen with Bess and be dry and warm, and she wanted to drink strong tea; she could even taste, in her mind, the strong tea laced with sugar or honey; this was an abomination her father said, sugar or honey in extra strong tea, what a horrible heresy, only an imbecile like you, Sabrina, could even envisage such a thing! And she wanted to smell the perfume of baking bread, and she wanted to press her cold, wet body against the slender, hard, dry body of Bess and feel Bess's hands, reddened from cooking and washing, but which could be so tender, stroke her hair, stroke her neck, and she wanted to hear Bess whisper endearments and warm common-sense comfort.

And she wanted, too, to be forgiven by her father. One of her ongoing fantasies was that her father would suddenly see he had been unjust; that he would suddenly pardon her; that he would take her in his arms; that he would caress and kiss her; and that he would be warm and compassionate, and not the tall, cold, abstract, and inhuman – icily handsome – man he had become.

He was God, her father was. She would do anything, but anything, to win his approval, except, of course, admit she was wrong when she bloody well knew she was bloody well not wrong!

Sir Alfred never did play his role in this fantasy reconciliation – the fantasy had many variants, it was a long-running inner soap opera with dramatic gestures, characters falling on their knees, swelling music, tears, embraces, kisses, caresses. Sabrina played it over and over in her head; it obsessed her. And, of course – it never came to pass.

"Your father is certainly a genius, and he means well, I really think he does," her mother once said, "but I think the gods somehow left out parts of his heart."

The rain continued, icy. By now, it was totally dark. Sabrina saw Bess look out the window several times, raising her hand against the reflections from the bright inside to see if the "poor child" was still out there in the darkness and even blindly waving encouragement. Bess had tried to persuade Sabrina to come inside – to no avail, and Bess knew better than to try to force the girl. Sabrina, like Sir Alfred, was stubbornness itself.

Sabrina's clothes were soaked through; a tiny crust of ice had formed on strands of her hair. Her nose was running; she let it run, the snot coursing down, gelid and thick, glutinous and freezing, over her lips, down her chin. Her eyelashes were icy. She blinked. It was hard to see. Things were blurry.

At some point, her mother – the famous Alexandra Anders – came home, was told of the drama by Bess, and came running out and said, "Get up, Sabrina, come in; he won't even notice; hide in the kitchen with Bess."

"No, I hate him. I'm going to stay here, right here, I don't care if I die! I want to die: I want him to see me dead! I want him to know he killed me!"

Her mother, Sabrina could see, was exasperated. Alexandra Anders was standing, hands on hips, legs slightly apart, water pouring down and ruining her perfect little Chanel dress, the very picture of theatrical impatience.

"Look, my child, my brilliant wayward genius beautiful child," Alexandra got down on her knees. "I will kneel here and beg you until you relent. Come in and get warm, or else we'll both die of pneumonia!"

"No, mother, get up, you'll ruin the dress."

"I do not, my dear child, give a flying fuck about this dress. I know I'm an egotistical actress bitch, and I know I'm not with you as much as I should be, but in spite of appearances, I do care about you! I do love you! And I don't want you to die – if you were to die, dear child, I would feel very guilty, and it would absolutely ruin my season!" And she poked Sabrina in the tummy. Sabrina had to smile, but she bit her lip and hid the smile. Her teeth were chattering too much to really smile.

Her mother continued to kneel there, as it if were a scene in one of her movies, water coursing down over her, her makeup running, giving her eyes a tragic cast, circles of mascara forming streaks and waves, charcoal tears running down her cheeks, the icy water turning the dress transparent in the lamplight, and her mother was obviously not going to give up, not going to move, so Sabrina finally said, "Get up, mother, let's go in, I'll hide with Bess, and don't you tell father."

"Your father," her mother said, "Sometimes I would like to tan his hide!"

"Tan his hide," Sabrina said, suddenly laughing, "That I would love to see!"

"Well, perhaps you will, someday!" Her mother stood in the rain, opened her arms, and said, "I love you, my dear, crazy, wayward, stubborn, genius child." She hugged Sabrina and held her as close to her as she could.

Sabrina spent a delicious evening with Bess, and she also caught pneumonia and almost died and was in bed for three weeks.

Occasionally, particularly if her mother was away, and Bess was out for the evening, Sabrina was rewarded with electric shocks if she didn't live up to Sir Alfred's expectations and once with an old-fashioned whipping with a sharp, oily rod which left a series of scars across her back that only slowly faded – and one switch mark never faded entirely but left a faint scar that Sabrina refused to have removed.

The genetic experiments were carried out in secret, and they had the effect of making Sabrina hyper-nervous: her mind was running too fast; she couldn't slow it down; she couldn't sleep; she read, and studied, and absorbed information at a hugely accelerated rate, but the nervous tension risked destroying her.

Only Bess could calm her down.

The genetic and chemical experiments also had the side effect – though no one knew it at the time – of making Sabrina sterile.

Her mother, when she was at home, which was rare given the demands of her international film and theatrical careers, occasionally rebelled, making operatic scenes, running her fingers through her hair and turning in circles like a ballerina: "Alfred, you are making of our daughter a monster; you are transforming her into a freak!"

Sir Alfred stood there, lofty, handsome; he did not reply.

"Alfred, you are torturing the poor child. She is perfect, as perfect as any young person I have ever met, and yet that is not enough for you! I am taking Sabrina to Italy for six weeks, just to get her away from you. I want her to be able to live for a few days without doing differential equations and quantum theory or whatever it is called or two hundred and forty-five push-ups: girls are not meant to do push-ups! I, for one, have never done a push-up in my life!"

Alfred Jacobs could not resist his wife when her ire was up – which was rare, she was a very easy going, even negligent mother. But that one time she and Sabrina did leave for Italy.

The Italian interlude was glorious and left Sabrina with a love for that country which never faded. It was in Italy that she discovered who she was, and she later learned that there was a long tradition of travelers discovering in Italy their own selves, their true, or truer, identities. Sabrina wondered why this was – why Italy was a place where you could discover yourself.

"It's beautiful," she said, "But why is it so wonderful?"

"Italians have no shame," her mother laughed, "That's their charm – and that's why they are so useful to the rest of us. They are very wise. They know that life is opera and theater and that you can always create your own role. Of course, all of that is a myth; but, for we privileged foreigners, it's a useful myth. Italy frees us from guilt, from shame, from ourselves. All the world's a stage, Italians know this, and Italy is a wonderful place in which to practice being the actor – and dramatist – of your own life."

Sabrina and her mother hiked along mountain trails, wearing backpacks. They were greeted at little inns with their luggage, and wonderful meals of pasta and meat and salads and fresh fruit, and Sabrina was allowed to drink wine.

There seemed to be laughter everywhere.

Strangers talked to strangers; people they'd never met greeted them like old friends or long-lost relatives!

Sabrina felt alive, and she felt like her mother was a sister, not a mother.

They sat in cafes and gossiped. They wandered slowly through museums and galleries – often getting in after hours. Sabrina's mother was so famous that museum directors and curators would arrive to give them a private tour, avoiding the crowds, avoiding the rush, and getting very special treatment.

It was the first time, really, that Sabrina realized her mother was a truly separate entity, as famous as, perhaps even more famous than, her father.

Sometimes in cafes – though her mother wore very big dark glasses – waiters and waitresses and customers asked for her mother's autograph. Her mother was very gracious, and carefully asked for everyone's name before signing a napkin or a photograph or a book. It was the first time too that Sabrina began to realize that she – Sabrina – was also beautiful.

"Signora Anders, is this your daughter? Why she is stunning! She is *bellissima!*"

"May we take photographs of both of you?"

So Sabrina found herself on the cover of several magazines with her mother, sitting in cafes, "Famous Actress Alexandra Anders and her Beautiful Daughter visit Urbino!" Boys and men turned in the streets to stare, and shout, "*Ciaò, Bellissima!*"

"Why are they doing that?"

"Because you *are* beautiful, dear. It's a compliment." Her mother put her hands on Sabrina's shoulders and looked into her eyes. "You really don't know, darling, do you, you really don't know how beautiful, how exceptional, you are!" Alexandra took Sabrina's hand. "You know, Sabrina, sometimes the people who most need love, are also the people who don't know how to accept it, even when it is offered to them. It's too risky. To love and to accept love requires courage, and it is a skill, like differential calculus or playing the piano."

They stayed with a friend of her mother's in a large villa up on a cliff side on the Amalfi Coast, and they visited Capri. Sabrina loved the water and the sun, and she learned to scuba dive.

She fell in love with the sea, and with life under the water. "I shall be a sailor," she declared to her mother one evening as the light settled over the Mediterranean, and they ate *spaghetti vongole* by candlelight on a terrace amid the bougainvillea. "Admirable ambition," her mother said, "And I shall be the captain."

Sabrina returned from Italy with a tan, more self-confidence, and a determination to be her own person.

"That trip really did you good," Bess said.

"Yes, Bess, I'm grown up now, or almost."

"I'm not going to lose you, am I?"

"No, Bess, you will never lose me."

Even as she grew older, even when she went to university, Sabrina did make a point of coming to the kitchen to do her homework; she set up her laptop on a corner of the big kitchen table, and she did revel in Bess's company and she continued, even into her late teens, sometimes, to sleep with Bess and enjoy watching DVDs or video streams in bed with her and gossiping and criticizing the films, and cradling her head against Bess's shoulder.

And then Bess fell ill, suddenly, of cancer; Sabrina was with her, holding her hand when she died, listening to Bess, talking to her:

"Let people love you, Sabrina," Bess whispered; her voice was almost gone, "Let people get close, Sabrina, don't push them away."

"Yes, Bess, I will."

"Don't refuse, love, Sabrina … Don't push people away … You know, there was a boy once, a long time ago. He loved me, and I loved him, but we were both poor and … Well, you know what life is like, Sabrina."

"Yes, Bess, I know," Sabrina kissed Bess on the forehead.

Bess didn't say anything else; Sabrina sat there, watching, talking, and Bess smiled and squeezed Sabrina's hand, and then the light faded from her eyes – it took only an instant – and her hand went limp and cold in Sabrina's hand. Sabrina held the cold hand for a long time, and, finally, she closed Bess's eyes, just the way she had seen people do in the movies, and only then did she call out, "Nurse!"

It was strange, Sabrina thought, I was the closest person to her, the closest person on earth, and it seemed too great a privilege, too great a tragedy; Bess should have had other people to love her, better people, more people, she should have had …

Love …

Bess was cremated, and following the instructions in her will Sabrina scattered her ashes on the River Cam from a little bridge just at the edge of Cambridge. Sir Alfred was in China. Sabrina's mother flew in from Germany for the funeral. She stood beside Sabrina while Sabrina opened her hand and let the ashes fall and drift away. It was a bright warm spring day. The sun shone in ripples on the river.

Aimi poured another glass of Amarone and said, "That is a very sad story, Sabrina."

Sabrina gazed at Aimi as if surprised to see her there, she had been so lost in the past. "I'm not sure it was sad, Aimi. I think Bess did, in some ways, have a good life. I loved her, and she knew I loved her. But I was just a child and, of course, there was that whole other life, the life she might have had, with her childhood boyfriend, with marriage, with children, maybe with grandchildren, the life that never happened – but I think that everybody has a life, or lives, that never happened ..."

"And Cambridge led to V?"

"Yes." Sabrina emptied half a glass, and glanced at the bottle: *more, please, more.*

CHAPTER 12 – A STRAND OF HAIR

Yes, it was Cambridge that put Sabrina on the trail of V.

Having spent her childhood in Cambridge, and then going to university there, Sabrina had many contacts in the town and in the university.

One old friend of hers – a friend who dated from her university days when Sabrina had ceased to be a freak and had become a star – was a criminologist, Jed Barker. Jed had thick red unruly curly hair that stood up straight, an upturned pug-nose that gave him a goofy look, widely-spaced teeth, an infectious impish grin, and pale creamy skin with large freckles.

Jed was in love with Sabrina – and had been since the first time he caught a glimpse of her – but he believed that his love could never be reciprocated by such a beautiful, brilliant, and rich young woman, so he played the clown and entertained Sabrina and hid his passion. And so, with Jed playing the jester to his queen, they had become friends.

Jed liked the Mitre pub in Cambridge and the Tickell Arms out in Whittlesford, not too far from town.

Sabrina, when she was at Cambridge University, would sneak off with Jed – he was so amusing – and drink beer and gossip and just do nothing for an evening or sometimes even a whole afternoon.

Jed had fantasies that he would become rich and famous – and handsome – and that Sabrina would fall in love with him and be his wife.

He also had less admissible fantasies that he would learn hypnosis or concoct some sort of diabolic aphrodisiac, and cast a spell over Sabrina, making her fall in love with him Thus she would become enslaved to his sexual charms – which he knew, or thought he knew, were truly mediocre, or maybe non-existent. She'd have to be under a spell, he thought, with a wry mixture of sadism and masochism, to fall for somebody like him.

These fantasies made him blush and feel guilty. He believed such thoughts were very unusual and very wicked, so he began to study other wicked people, perverse minds like his own, serial killers, bloody tyrants, and other obsessive criminals. And so, out of his secret love for, and obsession with, Sabrina, Jed Barker became one of the world's leading criminologists.

Jed easily got inside the mind of the worst criminals and inside the "psychological logic" of the most sadistic crimes and often, when he was doing this, he used Sabrina, the image of Sabrina, the idea of Sabrina – Sabrina as the victim, Sabrina as the imaginary object, Sabrina as his mental puppet in these inner homicidal dramas, and, yet, though soaked in cruelty, mutilation, and murder, these were perhaps the highest, most intense moments of his adoration for her, his worship of her.

Sabrina sensed the inner currents of desire and violence that swirled inside Jed – after all, her first experience of men had been her father – but she enjoyed the erotic edge, the cruel ambivalence, underneath Jed's clowning. And she instinctively realized that the man or woman who plays the clown outside, is often melancholy and tragic and all alone inside – and, knowing this, she trusted Jed and wanted him to be happy. And she knew that, whatever fantasies he might harbor about her, he would never do her any real harm, and she trusted her own strength to make things right if ever anything did go wrong. Sabrina had been taught in a hard school; she was physically very tough, and, psychologically, she was perceptive and sly, devious when necessary, and not at all judgmental. She had needed subtlety and subterfuge, an open mind, and patience, to survive.

So fifteen years ago, long after Sabrina had left Cambridge, Jed phoned. "This is about something hush-hush," he'd said, mysteriously, to Sabrina's secretary who protected Sabrina from too many calls – and to Sabrina he said, "I have something interesting for you."

"What?" she asked.

"You know the mythical alien-human hybrid, the mysterious V."

"Yes?" Sabrina said, cautiously, thinking that maybe this was going to be a practical joke on the part of Jed, who did, alas, like silly pranks.

"Well, I've got some of her DNA."

"What? You have got some of her DNA? How did you get it?"

"Come to Cambridge, and I'll explain everything. And I'll give you the DNA."

"Jed, if this is a joke, if this is one of your pranks, I shall execute you, I mean it; I shall take that old sword that hangs over the fireplace in the pub in

Whittlesford, and I shall bloody well cut off your blinking head! I shall scissor off your balls and dangle them from a lamppost. I shall draw and quarter you and display your bloody remains on King's Parade! I shall use that old mace in the Tickell Arms to bop you over the head twenty times!"

"No joke, Sabrina; come to Cambridge."

Sabrina caught the first flight she could, and just before noon the next day, she was in Cambridge, in the forensics lab of Cambridge University.

The official explanation they put out was that Sabrina Jacobs, the illustrious CEO of Andromeda Corp, was in Cambridge to consult on some new surveillance devices that Andromeda Corp was developing which might be of interest to the Home Office, the British equivalent of Homeland Security.

"This is a hot potato for us, and we don't even want to recognize, officially or unofficially, that we have found what we have found," said the senior Home Office official, who was waiting for her in Jed's office, and who stood up and shook hands.

The Home Office official said his name was Geoffrey. He didn't give his last name or tell her what his position was. Sabrina examined him carefully. He had a thin pale ascetic face, gray eyes, thin, neatly delineated lips, and a very expensive, well-cut, dark pinstripe suit. He had a self-conscious way of gesturing, rather excessively, with his long thin pale hands, which, Sabrina noticed, were almost entirely hairless and very beautiful. From time to time, leaning forward in his chair, he caressed his ankle, touching his very fine dark-blue stockings, and highly polished Oxford shoes; he was extremely intelligent, Sabrina concluded, highly aware of the fact, and narcissistic, but very scrupulous in weighing the pros and cons of any course of action, a true civil servant, and the exact opposite of Jed's mischievous, exuberant, wildcard love of risk and improvisation.

"And what have you found?" said Sabrina carefully. They were sitting in Jed's office amid piles of papers, files, documents, books, and about a dozen state-of-the-art computers all busy doing something. And, out beyond the tinted one-way plate glass, researchers and technicians were hectically helping detectives and officers solve terrorist attacks, murders, kidnappings, robberies, and cases from all over the United Kingdom – and far beyond – as well as researching basic problems of criminology.

The Home Office official glanced at Jed and then back at Sabrina: "What Doctor Barker has discovered is this: a murder committed by a person, well, by a creature, by something, whose DNA is only partly human."

"Partly human," said Sabrina, "What's the other part?"

"The other part is …" The official glanced at Jed and said, "Well, Doctor Baker can explain …"

"Well, Sabrina," Jed said, grinning enthusiastically, "what we had was a cadaver floating underwater out on the fens, the cadaver had been drained of all its blood, and I mean *all* its blood, and the cadaver had those classic vampire fang punctures on its neck. And this cadaver was an alleged serial killer."

"Alleged?"

"There's no doubt he was guilty," Jed said, "but you know we legal types, we Home Office officials, we forensic psychologists, we ivory tower professorial wankers, we have to keep to the forms; we are sticklers for legal niceties and linguistic exactitude."

"Hmm." Sabrina smiled. *Good old Jed!* She nodded. "Go on."

"In any case, the creature had killed this chap, draining him of all his blood, and here's the interesting thing, the creature rescued two little girls who were prisoners – they would have died had they been held by the … by the victim … much longer."

"That's undoubtedly true," said the Home Office official, "so in a sense … So in a sense, the vampire – let's call her that – is a hero, a heroine. We should have offered her champagne."

"In any case," Jed stood up and started pacing back and forth, "she drove into Cambridge – we presume she didn't fly on a broomstick – and she delivered the two children to the police, to a policeman standing guard outside one of the children's homes. Just walked up to him and said, 'Here, I think you were looking for these two little chaps.'"

"Cheeky," said Sabrina.

"Indeed, Sabrina, it was exceptionally cheeky." Jed paused, drinking in Sabrina's presence. She was sitting very still, in a classic charcoal gray business suit, with a straight but short skirt, and dark stockings, and flat heel black patent shoes. Her golden hair shone, and her tan set off her large, strikingly blue eyes; she was smiling, patiently, one finger tapping lightly on her skirt. Jed swallowed. "Well, it turns out, Sabrina, that our heroine had leaned down and kissed the little girls and perhaps carried one of them on her shoulder and so some of her hair, just a few strands, got caught in the sweater of one of the girls – so that's how we got our clue."

"Otherwise, she left absolutely no trace," said the Home Office official, "no trace at all."

"Impressive," said Sabrina.

"Yes, very impressive," said the Home Office official. "We could certainly put someone like her to good use, I mean legitimate good use."

"Now," Jed sat down, then stood up again and put his hands in the pockets of his baggy corduroy trousers. "We did a routine analysis on the hair, because, though we were very grateful to the lady for getting rid of a very sick and dangerous individual, we can't very well have a girl vigilante running around the peaceful English countryside, killing people and drinking all their blood, can we?"

"Do you know who she is? Did you find her?"

"No, no idea. She probably came from abroad, but ... millions of people come in and out of Britain all the time. And, from a purely crime-solving point of view, this was not a hugely high priority, you can understand."

"How did she pick her victim," said Sabrina. "She must have known ..."

"Well ..." Jed looked down at the floor; he looked embarrassed, "I suspect that she does extensive research, I suspect this is not the first time she's been here, I'm quasi-certain of that, and I suspect too that she has ... friends ... in the law-enforcement and security forces. She may have friends here in Cambridge even ..." Jed nodded at all the detectives and criminologists busily working out beyond the one-way glass window of his office.

"So they should know ... somebody should know ... who she is ..."

"Her files – there are files on her it seems though their very existence is denied of course – her files are not available. I certainly have not been able to see them. I believe I have been, as the Americans say, stonewalled." Jed shrugged and gave her one of his hopeless grins.

Sabrina glanced at Geoffrey, the Home Office official.

"I have not been privy to these files," he said, "and not even the Prime Minister has access."

"Wow," said Sabrina, "So, we have a vampire with friends in high places."

"Yes, very high places, you might say," said the Home Office official. "This is even a rumor that she did work for Winston Churchill, during the Second World War, for the SOE."

"Special Operations Executive," said Sabrina, "the outfit that backed resistance to the Nazis in occupied Europe?"

"Precisely, and, it's also rumored that two hundred and fifty years earlier, she worked for Churchill's ancestor, the Duke of Marlborough, in his wars with Louis XIV." He coughed.

"Winston Churchill, the Duke of Marlborough, but …?" Sabrina stared at the two men. "How could that be …?"

The Home Office official nodded, "Yes, yes, impossible, I know …"

"But …" Jed began, but stopped when he saw the Home Office official was about to speak.

"Now, there is a little problem, you see," the Home Office official said, leaning forward and stroking his ankle, "to try to do *public* research, research financed by His Majesty's Government would present difficult and delicate problems of accountability and budgeting and reporting."

"I can see that." Sabrina began to get the drift.

The Home Office official nodded. "Jed told me of his friendship with you, and we put our heads together, and we thought … we thought that …"

"You would like Andromeda Corp to do research on the DNA of this hybrid creature, this half-non-terrestrial vampire."

"Yes, no strings attached, but we would like, discreetly, of course, to be kept informed of your results. Jed could be the liaison."

"Why do you think this is so important?" said Sabrina, "I know this is a stupid question, but I want to ask it anyway."

"Let's see. Well," the Home Office official shifted in his seat, looked down at the perfect crease in his trousers, "I think that, from your point of view, Doctor Jacobs, such research could, let us say, offer immense advantages in terms of pure and applied research – products of various kinds – and since your Andromeda Corporation is registered in the UK – even if largely based in the US and China – and as you personally are a joint UK-EU-German-American citizen it is in our interest to help promote your company's well-being, let us say." He paused.

"Yes, of course." Sabrina waited.

"But from a national interest and national security – indeed, world security – point of view, we are right, I think, to want to know as much as we can about this creature."

"Yes." Sabrina crossed her legs. She smiled and nodded patiently. Even the most intelligent bureaucrats tended to be long-winded. Or perhaps methodical was the right word. Like lawyers, they didn't want to leave any contingency unexamined or unformulated.

"First, purely as a weapon, she offers immense possibilities – intelligent, invisible (largely), near invincible, and – immortal. What if the Russians or the Chinese or the Japanese or the French, even if they are presently our friends and allies, were able to 'produce' such a creature?"

Sabrina nodded, her forefinger tapping impatiently on her thigh.

"Also, perhaps even more important, if she is truly a half-human, half extraterrestrial alien, then either she has come from outer space, and was bred on another planet or space ship or something like that (You can see why we can't let this fantastical story go public!). Or, equally disturbing, it means that aliens, or at least an alien, visited earth and bred with a human female." The Home Office official raised his fine pale hands, palms up, as if weighing imponderables, or as if he were offering up an invisible gift to an invisible deity.

"I see the problem." Sabrina held his gaze.

"So, Sabrina, what do you think?" Jed's overbite was showing; he looked like an eager rabbit.

Sabrina furrowed her brow, pursed her lips, and stared at the floor, pretending to think, even though she knew that both men knew she didn't need to do any thinking at all. "Yes, I'll do it," she looked up, "I'll start a top-secret research program at Andromeda Corporation."

"Good," said the two men in unison.

"Let's go out and have a drink!" Jed was already standing.

"Just one question," said Sabrina, "I'm curious: what does she look like?"

"Well, we don't have any photographs, but the policeman said: she's beautiful. Here's a sketch done by a forensic artist from what the policeman and the two little girls said."

"Yes, I see," said Sabrina, "very beautiful."

"The two little girls called her the funny angel – apparently she told them funny stories."

"And there is one more thing," said the Home Office official. "You were surprised by my mention of Winston Churchill and the Duke of Marlborough."

"Yes," Sabrina said, "I was surprised, shocked even."

"Well, our preliminary tests indicate that our friend is, well, rather old."

"Old?"

"Yes, she was apparently born roughly 2,600 years ago, and the human side of her DNA, the female line, is Phoenician."

"You mean Phoenician as in Sidon and Tyre, or Carthage?"

"Yes, rather Carthage it seems, North Africa in any case, one of the Phoenician cities of North Africa; and, here is the analysis." He handed Sabrina a sheet of paper. "She was born at least 600 years before the birth of Christ."

"So, you see, Aimi, it was true – the few documents that I had seen earlier – and some of which I had never mentioned to Jed – told a patchy story, a story that seemed like mythology. The creature from the fairy-tale existed – and I had her DNA!"

The bottle of *Amarone* was almost empty. Aimi stared at Sabrina. "I think I'm drunk," Aimi said, and drank some more. "And so the Clone, Claire, is a result of the DNA, the DNA picked up on the little girl's sweater fifteen years ago, the DNA of this part-alien vampire."

"Yes. And I think we need another bottle of that Amarone," Sabrina didn't slur a single syllable.

Aimi went to the wine-rack and pulled out another bottle of Amarone. "You're sure?"

"Quite bloody sure, yes," Sabrina smiled. "I like you, Aimi; in fact, I love you; in fact, I desire you; in fact, I'm crazy about you, and that is not just the Amarone talking!"

"Sabrina, your crazy feelings are more than reciprocated," Aimi carried the bottle over to the table and sat down to uncork it. "And you know it."

"Yes, I do know it."

"Good." Aimi concentrated on the bottle.

"So, yes, and the other thing that is crazy is this: Claire is the daughter of a microscopic speck, a wee little droplet, a tiny fragment of jet-black hair caught in a wool sweater one rainy night about sixteen years ago and that's where the whole adventure started."

Aimi looked up from uncorking the bottle and blinked. The wonders of life and of human life never ceased to amaze her. "And, of course, we all come from such tiny cellular fragments."

"Yes." Sabrina's eyes took on a dreamy cast. "As you know, it took many attempts to create the Clone – Claire. We tried, we failed; we tried, we failed; we created monsters that died within hours or minutes; I tinkered, I changed the recipe; I inserted new elements, I fiddled around. I almost gave up, and then I threw everything – almost at random – at the problem. Hundreds of attempts – then, almost by accident, when I had given up hope, a bit of material we were going to reject worked. Bingo, abracadabra, eureka! We had our Clone! We had stolen the soul of that mysterious creature, V."

"Yes." Aimi said, "It was a miracle!"

"Only, it didn't work." Sabrina looked down. Her eyes were wet. "For six years Claire was like, well, she was my child – the child I could never have. She was a genius, beautiful, and loving … and then … it all turned wrong, she ceased to develop, oh, of course, she has grown, she is growing, and she is beautiful, exquisite, remarkable, but, but … there is … nothing … in here …" And Sabrina knocked on the side of her head. "Nothing, nothing, nada, rien, nichts, nichivo … niente … Oh, God, I'm so miserable!"

Aimi knew the story. Clone-1, a new kind of human, the future of humanity, suddenly changed, age six, from a shining hope, to an utter catastrophe – a seething cauldron of violence, idiocy, and madness.

Sabrina glanced up, her eyes shining. "But you know, Aimi, I think I've discovered something about the Clone. It may change this whole story. I'm not sure yet, but I think she is not exactly what we think she is. I think she is different, a different creature altogether."

"Oh?" said Aimi. She put her hand on Sabrina's shoulder, and kissed Sabrina on the cheek, lightly, tentatively, daringly.

CHAPTER 13 – FACE TO FACE

The dust storm abated. Alex kept driving.

"We're going to be meeting a friend soon, maybe in Virginia," V said.

"What? Who is it? That person you were speaking to on the phone?"

"Yes."

"Hmm," said Alex, "not another vampire."

"No," V said, snuggling close to him, examining him closely. She laid her hand on his forehead. "Not another vampire. I think you will be pleased."

V was cooking up a plot. If she couldn't be Alex's lover, if she couldn't have Alex, not in *that* way at least, then she wanted Alex to be with someone who would be her friend; she wanted to keep two people she liked, perhaps even loved, close to her – for how long she didn't know – and so she had developed a little plot, an equation in her mind; the equation added Alex to Helen and gave, as a result, happiness for all, V included: though, of course, she knew she would be jealous and bereft, in spite of her best instincts.

She would have to wait to see if the recipe worked, if the attraction was there, and then, if it was, she would ease herself out to the edge of the newly minted couple and let them live their life; and, then, if they wanted to be close to her, sometimes, so be it; if not, well, so be it too. They would be free, and she would be free.

I'm a stupid romantic, she thought, I'm a bloody old romantic, a spinster match-maker. Always a bridesmaid, never a bride!

She unbuckled the seat belt and swiveled around to look behind – sure enough, there it was: the motorcycle.

"Yes," said Alex, gazing into the rearview mirror, "He's still there. Who do you think it is?"

"I bet it's the guy from the diner."

"The sad sack?"

"Yes, the sad sack. His name, by the way, is David Stanford Adams III."

"David Stanford Adams III. Well, well." Alex glanced into the mirror. "And he rides a vintage, Harley-Davidson, looks like a 2026 model. Is he alone, I wonder, or are we about to be attacked from all sides?"

"He looks alone," said V, "I think he's a loner."

"Well, we should find out if he's really alone."

"How?"

"We entice him, somehow," said Alex.

"Well, we have to stop anyway, to pick up the equipment."

"Yes, how do we arrange that?"

"We just go into the lot and pick up the stuff and see if David tries to ambush us there."

"Or if there is an army waiting for us," said Alex.

"Let's be reckless," V grinned. "Let's just go pick up the equipment, and then we'll see."

"Reckless?" said Alex. "That's new! When have we ever been reckless? You jump out of planes, you bite me on the neck, you dress up like a Christmas tree, we jump into a diner full of horrible food – well it was scrumptious really – I bite into that hamburger that might have turned me into a bloodlust vampire … You attack and eat gang member Big Boy – When have we been reckless?"

"Oh, stop, stop," V was laughing. "I say we just go and pick the stuff up, and we shall see what we shall see."

So, they drove to the warehouse. V's nostrils quivered, her mental radar tuned up to high alert, she scanned the parking lot, the warehouse, and the surrounding few blocks. She found nothing alarming. "Well, it looks like we are here, and my senses don't indicate a major ambush, though, of course, I could be wrong."

"I have infinite faith, almost infinite faith in you," said Alex. He glanced at his scantily clad, pink, phosphorescent vampire. She looked more like a perky super-buff raven-haired cheerleader than like an ordinary garden-variety, pale, languorous, perverse, nocturnal, melancholy, sleepy-eyed vampire.

"Okay, let's go."

"Yes, now!" V took a deep breath. "You drop me off at the office and then you drive the car around to the back, to loading dock number three, while I go to the office. If they are going to attack inside, then they'll come after me. But they'd have to know we were coming here, and I don't think they do. And if they do attack outside, well, you will be the first target – bait, as it were. Don't resist, Alex, don't resist. We'll see what they want, and then we'll decide what we have to do."

"Fantastic. I always saw myself as bait – luscious, handsome bait!" He leaned over and gave V a big, bold kiss, a prolonged smackeroo, rounded off with a tender, nibbling, passionate, deep probe …

"Hmmm," V murmured, "Hmmm! You are going to make me forget," she took a deep breath. "You are going to make me forget my good resolutions."

"And you are going to make me forget mine!" Alex ran his hand down the back of her head, caressing the fine jet-black perfumed hair, the fine down and curls, and then down the nape of her neck and over the lightly tanned satin smoothness of her shoulder. He toyed with the spaghetti strap.

"Oh, Alex, oh, foolish mortal! Oh, V, oh foolish me!"

"Oh, foolish us," Alex kissed her again.

"Well, here we are," said V. "I'm going in. Wish me luck! The box will fill most of the back seat."

V went inside. The door closed behind her. Alex watched her enter the office. There was a plate-glass window, and she was leaning over the counter, talking to some guy in a baseball cap who was either very short or was seated, and the brutal fluorescent light lit up V's raven-black hair, her startlingly dark eyes, her light golden tan, and the marvelous curve of her shoulder, her collarbone and her breasts, and that beautiful crazy damned pink dress, as if V were a display in a show window. V was obviously putting on the charm. Everything seemed okay.

Alex backed up and drove around to the side of the building; he backed in next to loading dock number three.

There were no other cars, and there was only a big tractor-trailer parked at the far end of the lot. Alex thought that would be an ideal place to hide a SWAT team or an electronic stake-out. He glanced toward the truck. A driver seemed to be snoozing in the cab. Maybe it was just what it seemed: an exhausted driver taking a snooze.

Alex glanced toward the entrance to the parking lot. There it was – the Harley-Davidson. It had stopped in the entrance to the parking lot, under the sagging arched gateway. Either the guy was trying to make up his mind what to do, or he was waiting for backup. Either way …

Yes, it was David Stanford Adams III.

David Stanford Adams III skidded his bike to a stop at the entrance to the Holy Beatitude Storage Facility. Why had the lady come here? Then it occurred to him that she needed supplies, that she probably had supplies in storage, and that she had come to pick them up. What if the supplies included arms, weapons? If she got the weapons, then she would be doubly dangerous. So, maybe it would be a good idea to stop her before she got the weapons. But she was known to be totally deadly, even without weapons. Well, her guy, even if he was a buff, tanned, blond, handsome muscle-bound guy, looked normal – he was a human being, reputedly, at least.

David gunned the bike and headed straight for Alex Wolf's car. He skidded to a stop and jumped off the bike, knowing he was taking a risk. He drew his S&W .357 Magnum, and approached the car.

He wondered what he'd say when he got to the car. It was stinking hot. The car had its motor on to keep the air-conditioning running.

Alex Wolf saw David coming. He opened the door and got out and, seeing the pistol, he put his hands up, and grinned, and said, "Hi, David, how are you?"

David Stanford Adams III was not used to polite felons or fugitives or terrorists, so he didn't know what to say, so he just said, "Hi, how are you?" keeping the pistol level, pointed at the guy's midriff.

"I'm fine," said Alex, "I'm doing great, though it is a stinker, isn't it. My name, by the way, is Alex Wolf."

"Ha ... Pleased to meet you, Alex; I mean, I knew your name already. It's Doctor Alex Wolf, isn't it? My name is David Stanford Adams III, my father insisted on the Third." David frowned and wagged the pistol at Alex. "I'd like to get rid of it, frankly, the Third in the name, I mean, if you know what I mean. I mean, it's awkward and it sounds pretentious, I try not to seem pretentious, and I'm not pretentious. I think I'm not pretentious."

"I don't think you look pretentious at all, David, though you do have an S&W .357 Magnum, and you are pointing it at me; but I must say I understand your position, so I don't mind."

"That's kind of you," said David, "where's your friend."

"Oh, V, my friend – she's quite a card, isn't she?"

"Yes, she makes jokes, I guess you could call that being a card, I mean she seems to be able to talk inside your head, you know what I mean?"

"Yes, I do." Alex nodded. "It can be endearing, but it can be annoying too, the way she can get into your head and chatter away nonstop and all."

"Well, where is she now?"

"She's inside getting some supplies. She'll be out in a minute, I'm sure, David. She'll be delighted to meet you."

"In a minute, you think?"

"Yes, I'd say any minute now, though women can be a little unpredictable, you know."

"I know," said David, "I know, I mean, I've heard tell, but out on the road all the time I don't meet many women, not real women, I mean, I'm sort of shy, I mean, I know I don't look shy, but I am shy, it's something people don't seem to understand about me, and it creates a lot of problems if you know what I mean, because they think I'm being bold and sassy or disrespectful and standoffish, but I'm just being shy. I hated dances at high school." With his free hand, David tugged at his buttoned-down, buttoned-up paisley collar.

"I hated those dances too," said Alex, "Standing with sweaty palms against the cement blocks of the gym wall watching the girls and pretending not to watch them. I do know what you mean. I'm shy myself."

When V came into the office of the Holy Beatitude Storage Warehouse, she could see, out the plateglass window of the office, Alex sitting in the car watching her and his gaze made her feel all excited and desired and desirable. The office was lit up like a stage set with naked tube fluorescent lighting, and the walls were white with calendars and schedules pinned up and one image of the Holy Virgin holding a Baby Jesus while two or three Holstein cows – bits of hay hanging out of their mouths – and some guys wearing crowns looked on.

The guy on duty was sitting at a low-slung ancient wooden swivel chair. He was wearing a baseball cap and a knotted red-and-black bandana under the baseball cap. The baseball cap said, "*Anarchy Über Alles.*" His big glossy name card said, "Ralph." He looked up and grinned and said, "How you doin'?"

"I'm doin' fine; and you?" V leaned over the counter, giving her suavely tanned cleavage some extra clout.

"Hunky-dory, honey," Ralph said, focusing his watery eyes on the display. "I'm hunky-dory."

"Here's the number," she said.

"Right, right!" He stroked his graying stubble as if he had to think long and hard. "The shipment came in yesterday. And there's a word you gotta say," he said.

"Yeah," V said, "the word is puffball."

"Puffball, eh?"

"Yeah, it's puffball." V leaned further over the counter, chewing her gum – tutti-frutti flavor. It came in a brightly-colored plastic-wrapped package, something she particularly adored.

"Well, bingo, sister, you got it right!"

"Well, that's good, then."

"Yep, it sure is, it's good. It sure is good." Ralph sighed and levered himself out of his low-slung leather-backed wooden swivel chair, which creaked as he got up and, when freed of his weight, spun backward in slow motion over the black-and-white streaked faux marble linoleum. "I got a new hip. It makes moving slow, you know what I mean. I never thought the old body would fold up on me; but you're young. They'll probably have an answer to everything when you get to my age."

Ralph led V down the stairs under the glare of the fluorescent lights. With each switch, Ralph magically flipped the long corridor and locked storage doors out of sleeping darkness into garish brilliant light.

They came to a wooden freight elevator and stood waiting while the elevator creaked its way down to them. The place smelled of pinewood and lemon-scented wood wax and metal grease and cable and wire.

V's nostril's quivered. She was on high alert: if Sabrina Jacobs and Andromeda Corp had penetrated V's backup system – and had discovered V's system of resupply – then this would indeed be an ideal ambush site.

So far, she did not sense any danger: just the motorcyclist. The big tractor-trailer parked out in the parking lot was, her radar told, her just that – a big tractor-trailer, with a truck driver from Omaha Nebraska snoozing fitfully and dreaming of – his dreams were not quite clear – two kids, the girl eight, the boy eleven, a wife with a yellow-and-black polka dot kerchief over her hair, a clapboard bungalow somewhere near a muddy narrow little stream and, in the unkempt backyard, a rusty squeaky swing for the kids, Marie and Atticus Junior, that they'd set up one sunny, windy afternoon, and … And Ralph, her mind-radar told her, was exactly who he appeared to be.

They stepped onto the freight elevator. Ralph pushed a big button and held it down, and the elevator lurched upwards with a sudden jerk and whining complaint. Ralph, still holding the button down, inspected V carefully and with evident pleasure. She was, of course, still wearing the semitransparent pink phosphorescent dress – she'd washed it in the shower the night before – lucky it was quick drying and didn't shrink. Boy! That would have been a sight! And so she thought she looked her very best, according to some lights, that is.

"I like the outfit, Sister. It's bold. You don't see bold these days."

"Thank you, Ralph."

"I got the locker key," said Ralph. "You gotta do the bio-identification, and then it's all yours, pre-paid, and all. You got a truck?"

"A car, out back; it's by loading gate number three."

"That's the right one. Good, that makes it easy."

V passed the bio-identification test with flying colors, putting her eye to a little hole, which immediately recognized the iris and pupil pattern she had slightly re-arranged for the occasion: Eye Version 34X-B.

Ralph handed her the key and V opened the storage locker, and there it was – the package, a two-meter by one-meter by one-meter rubber and steel box, with new clothes, new documents, new communications gadgets, hacker equipment and programs, and new weapons.

Ralph limped off to get a wooden cart to wheel the box out to the loading dock. V could have hoisted the box onto her shoulder and waltzed away with it, but she didn't want to reveal her strength and she thought that Ralph was so pleased to be of help that it would be a shame to refuse his old-fashioned courtly gallantry. She watched Ralph come back and she kissed him on the cheek and he seemed even more pleased.

"You are a true gentleman, Ralph," she said, still keeping all her senses on alert – having present in her mind a three-dimensional real-time X-ray model of the building and its surroundings, dynamic schematics which were speculative to a certain extent, but which helped her locate each sound, each source of biological energy – a mouse scurrying one floor below them – a cat prowling not far behind it – the tractor-trailer parked in the parking lot with the driver, Atticus Payne, sleeping off twenty hours of illegal overtime to help pay for the mortgage on the clapboard bungalow, slumped over the steering wheel, snoring ...

They loaded the case onto the wooden trolley and began to trundle it toward the elevator. And they went down in the elevator and Ralph said, "Those shoes are pretty classy."

V said, "Yes, pretty cool, huh!" She swiveled her ankle and inspected the stiletto heel, displaying a luscious silhouette of human female calf, shin, and thigh for Ralph's delectation. "They are party shoes and they're not very comfortable, but I left all my other stuff at home, and I was invited to this party, well, it was sort of a surprise party, and so since I left there, the surprise party I mean, I haven't been able to go home, I didn't have anything else to wear, but my man outside there who's waiting for me, he's very understanding – so he doesn't mind my having, let's say, this flashy showbiz look."

"He'd better be very understanding, Sister! Otherwise, I'll have a stern word with him," said Ralph, as the elevator jerked to a halt.

Ralph had to maneuver the elevator up and down two or three times to get it exactly level so that the trolley could roll off smoothly. Then, finally, all systems were go!

When the corrugated metal door rolled up with a bang and V appeared on the loading dock with a bent-over limping codger in a baseball cap, David Stanford Adams III was still talking to Alex. David had meant to put the gun to Alex's head and to threaten to blow Alex's brain's out if V didn't do what he wanted – and when he saw it was too late for that scenario – he was standing about two yards from Alex – he also realized that he didn't know what in hell he wanted V to do.

"Hi, David," said V, grinning, "Hi Alex. Ralph, this is David, and Ralph, this is Alex; and Alex, this is Ralph, and David, this is Ralph."

Ralph looked at the gun and at Alex and at David and the men all looked at V and then at each other and everybody said, "Hello, glad to meet you, pleasure … is mine."

"Gee, I'm glad you caught up with us, David!" said V. "I wanted to have a chat; in fact, I've been longing to have a chat."

"Okay …" David Stanford Adams III didn't know which way to point the gun. So he kept it pointed at Alex.

"Just let us get this box down – we're not going to open it! – David, and then we can have that little chat."

"Maybe you need some help," said Alex, noting Ralph's limp. "Do you mind, David?"

"No, no, go ahead," David waved the gun toward the box.

V and Alex got the box down and slid it – it was pretty bulky and pretty heavy – into the car. With the back seat flipped up, it fit, just barely.

"Well, Ralph," V said, "Thank you very much for your help, and I'm really delighted you like my dress. As you said, bold is rare these days. I think it's important we make these little statements for the liberty of female attire, don't you, Ralph?" And she handed Ralph a substantial tip.

"You got it, Sister. You're a mighty lucky man, Alex! I'm jealous. Now, if I were eighty years younger, I'd, well, I'd set myself up as a rival, that's what I'd do, I'd come a-courting. Nice meeting you, David, but you might want to put that gun down. These are mighty nice folks, and I'm sure they mean no harm."

V kissed Ralph on both cheeks, and he stood there for a moment, a touch flustered, and said, "Well, God Bless, I guess. There's times when it's awkward saying goodbye … so I'll just say goodbye." And he disappeared, pulling down and closing the corrugated iron door of loading dock number three with a bang.

V jumped down from the platform, so she was within a foot of David Stanford Adams III. "Well, David, I guess you work for Sabrina Jacobs and the Andromeda Corporation. Am I right? I'm V, by the way."

"Well, yes," David didn't know which way to point the gun, at V or at Alex, and so he gave up and put the safety on, and he stuck the gun in his belt holster. "I work for Andromeda Corp and for Doctor Jacobs."

"I'm dying for a coffee," said V, "Let's find a place to get some coffee!"

"That sounds about right," David said. His collar felt extra tight; he tugged at it.

"Now you know," V took David's arm and shot Alex a glance, "Sabrina – I mean Doctor Jacobs – wants to capture me, and I don't want to be captured."

"That sounds about right."

"And poor Alex doesn't want to be captured either, do you, poor darling, though I don't want to speak for you."

"No, I'd very much prefer not to be captured," said Alex.

"Maybe we could talk to Sabrina," V said, "What do you think, David?"

"Well …"

With David following close behind on his Harley-Davidson, they found an all-night coffee joint – it was full of obsolete, redundant, off-the-books truck drivers doing off-the-books runs – and took a booth and ordered coffee and David used his tablet phone to try to get hold of Sabrina Jacobs.

"Hello, may I speak to Doctor Jacobs?"

…

"Yes, I know it's late … well, this is important, it concerns something very important to her … Yes, I'll wait. Thank you."

…

David held the phone – it had a little TV screen so this would be a video call, which V thought, in the circumstances, was really cool.

"Hello, Doctor Jacobs. No, no, I'm not as lonely as I was. Thank you, thank you, for thinking of that. It's amazing you remembered; you have so much on your mind." … "Ah, yes, I guess that's good, no, in fact, I`m not alone right now, well, there's somebody here who'd like to speak to you." He handed the phone to V who positioned it so she could look at Sabrina and so Sabrina could get a good look at her.

"Hello, Sabrina, I'm V."

There was a pause; then, Sabrina said, "Hello, V."

"You are really beautiful, Sabrina, as beautiful as your photographs. I like that. I like your beauty. It makes me hungry, famished hungry: yum, yum, yum. But, Sabrina, here's the thing, as I believe they used to say, here's the thing: Your brilliant agent, David Stanford Adams III here, has tracked me down, and he has also tracked down Alex, Alex Wolf – say hello, Alex!"

"Hello, Doctor Jacobs."

"Hello, Doctor Wolf." Sabrina Jacobs was smiling, but it was not a particularly happy smile.

"Well, Sabrina," V piped up, "the problem is this: you want to capture me – and I suspect you want to capture Doctor Wolf too – but neither of us particularly wants to be captured. So, I just thought I'd tell you that, so we are clear."

"We are clear."

"Thanks. I like things to be clear."

"So do I; I like things to be clear," Sabrina paused: "There's one thing: David …? Will he be okay?"

"Yes, of course, we are going to have coffee and then we will go our separate ways. David will not be harmed. I give you my word."

"Good. Thank you."

"Don't mention it. But, Sabrina, you and I will meet someday. In fact, I have set my heart on it – and my appetite, you might say, my fangs are itching to meet you. Goodbye, my dear Sabrina."

A little less than eight thousand miles away, on board *Andromeda,* Sabrina sat in the swivel high-backed synthetic leather executive chair in her bedroom in a short, black, silk, T-shirt-like, nightgown, staring at the screen: so there she was, V, the redoubtable killer, charming, mischievous, beautiful – and deadly.

Sabrina stood up and stretched. *My fangs are itching to meet you!*

Oh, boy! Sabrina glanced over at the empty bed, at the bedside lamp, at the open book. Could she go back to sleep?

No.

My fangs are itching to meet you!

Sabrina slipped on sandals and went up on deck and stood leaning on the rail looking out over the vast calm ocean. The Pacific was really behaving very well. The moon sent silver ripples over the slight swell, a slow, lazy, silky undulation; a few wisps of cloud, high-level cirrus, curling up, and drifting slowly west, were a silver gossamer tracery high up in the sky.

Sabrina took a deep breath. God, I love living, I really don't want to die.

The breeze was warm. The short black nightgown fluttered gently, a silken caress against her skin. But Sabrina felt a hollowness, a chill inside. The deck was empty. The floor plates and railings gleamed silver under the moonlight.

There was no one on deck or anywhere about, except the watch on the bridge and a watch at the stern. She could just see the uniformed silhouette at the stern pacing back and forth. The radar antennae turned and the various communications and satellite dishes traced a dark calligraphy against the sky. The breeze and the movement of the ship created delicate rattling sounds as cables moved and metal strained.

Sabrina let the stillness, the little sounds, and the sense of movement invade the silence in her mind. *Andromeda* was a living thing, a friend. Sometimes, inanimate things seemed more alive than people. An officer on the bridge was silhouetted and lit up slightly by the lights and instruments and control panels, his peaked cap making a sharp curved line.

About 500 yards astern was the Royal Navy frigate, *Darwin III,* which usually accompanied *Andromeda.* Red and green lights twinkled. All was calm as the two ships cut smoothly through the water.

Darwin III was like an old friend – it would soon be leaving *Andromeda* for two weeks of repairs, maintenance, and upgrades. I'll miss you, Sabrina thought, I'll miss you, but you'll be back.

My fangs are itching to meet you! Sabrina shivered. She'd better get some sleep. She turned away from the railing.

Oh!

Standing there …

Standing there like a moonlit ghost, was Aimi, barefoot, in a gleaming oversized white T-shirt and white spandex shorts. "You can't sleep?"

"No."

"Would you like me to come to you?"

"Yes, Aimi, I would, I'd love it."

"Let's go, then." Aimi stepped forward and took Sabrina by the hand.

"Aimi, I just spoke to *It*, to the *Thing*."

"What?" Aimi said in her soft, calm voice. "How did that happen?"

"On the phone. She was with that strange fellow, David Stanford Adams III; and, yes, she does call herself V."

"V?"

"I thought it was a code name, but that's what she calls herself. I liked her, in spite of everything I know about her." Sabrina laughed. "And she likes me, I think. She finds me appetizing. She's going to kill me, or so she implied. And I think she means it. And if she wants to kill me, and drink my blood, she will."

"Let's go, Sabrina. I'm here. No one is going to kill you. You need to sleep."

"Yes. You're right. And so do you, Aimi, you need to sleep – let's sleep."

Aimi led Sabrina, as if she were leading a child, hand in hand, down to Sabrina's stateroom.

CHAPTER 14 – INSTRUMENT OF DEATH

"So this is it," Sergei Pavlov turned to his brother, "Your instrument of revenge; your instrument of death?"

Dmitry and Sergei Pavlov were standing at the railing of the research ship *Gogol*, in the Western Pacific at a Russian naval base near Vladivostok. The *Gogol* was in no way as glamorous as Sabrina Jacobs' *Andromeda*, but it did the job. It was a converted Russian navy ship, a powerful ship, with lavish laboratories and storage facilities.

Below Sergei and Dmitry, in the same harbor, its dark round hull rising only slightly above the water was the sleek black form of the old attack submarine the *M.I. Kutuzov VI*.

"Yes, that is it." Dmitry leaned against the railing and stared at the dark shape of the submarine. "Our agents on *Andromeda* will take control of *Andromeda*. They will capture Sabrina and the Clone and transfer them to the *Kutuzov*. Once Sabrina and the Clone have been secured on board the *Kutuzov*, and all the computer files on *Andromeda* have been secured and transferred, the *Kutuzov* will sink *Andromeda* and then it will rendezvous with the *Gogol* which will deliver everything, including Sabrina and the Clone to my research facility on New Shangri-La."

"Ah, yes, New Shangri-La." Sergei nodded. It was an island Dmitry had bought, lock, stock, and barrel, from a tiny bankrupt island state in the Pacific. It was Dmitry's own little kingdom, from which he had driven out the entire native population, using any means, including murder.

"Yes, my own little paradise," said Dmitry. He turned to his brother and gazed at him with a sinister smile, a dark twinkle in his eyes. He clapped Sergei on the shoulder. "There, in New Shangri-La, I will exact my revenge on Sabrina. And, using Sabrina as a guinea pig, and the Clone as an experimental subject, I will push my genetic and biological warfare research to new heights. And, Sergei, let me tell you this – Sabrina will be my masterpiece – transformed into a freak of pure grotesque horror!"

Sergei nodded and held his brother's gaze. He was tempted to ask Dmitry what Sabrina had done to merit such a fate. But he knew better; he would be rewarded with a furious rant about the woman …

Sergei also began to wonder if he should change his routines, and hire new – independent – bodyguards. Maybe he and his family should seek refuge somewhere. But where? Dmitry's reach extended everywhere.

Sergei hated the thought – but he was convinced that his brother, whom he loved, intended, at some point, to kill him, and probably his whole family.

M. I. Kutuzov VI began to move, its low dark hull cleaving the sleepy water of the harbor. It was leaving for its rendezvous with *Andromeda*. The rendezvous would take place in the Sulu Sea of the Philippines.

"So it begins," said Sergei, suppressing a sigh.

"It will be an appropriate setting," said Dmitry. "Sabrina loves the Sulu Sea, particularly the coral reefs. She always dreams of the sea. For her, it is paradise. So it will be fitting when her dreams end there."

Sergei shook his head. He felt that this whole exercise spelled doom, and not only for Sabrina Jacobs. "I don't know," he murmured. "I really don't know."

"All will be well; all will be well," Dmitry smiled and clapped his arm around Sergei's shoulders. Sergei was so transparent. You could see what he was thinking – and you could see too that he had once loved Sabrina – a platonic brotherly love, perhaps, but it was still love, and therefore, dangerous. Sergei's emotions and his lack of imagination were a problem, and an obstacle to Dmitry's plans, since Sergei owned enough of Bio-Prom to block Dmitry's wilder and most brilliant projects. But the obstacle would soon be eliminated. Soon, alas, Sergei would die – victim of an assassination attempt that would also kill his wife and children – so that all shares in Bio-Prom would devolve on Dmitry.

"All will be well, little brother, all will be well," Dmitry repeated, his smile getting larger and larger.

Helen of Troy suspected that the so-called-cops had put a tracking device on her car. They were not really cops, she figured, they were agents for somebody else, somebody who was looking for V, and that meant, probably Andromeda

Corporation, since she'd noticed its logo on one of the trucks. She'd also noticed, out of the corner of her eye, when she was standing, legs apart, hands on top of the car, one of the officers leaning down pretending to examine the trunk of the car, the taillights, and the license plate.

She pulled into a roadside garage-restaurant.

She had a quick coffee, and went into the washroom; she came out of the washrooms immediately by another exit and, pretending to look at boxes of chocolates near the cashier's booth, she glanced toward the parking lot. It seemed that nobody was near her car or watching it.

She left the restaurant, went to her car, leaned down, and checked, and, yes, there it was, right behind the license plate; she looked to see if there was a second, backup device. She didn't see one. She took the device and placed it behind the license plate of the car next to hers.

She drove out of the pit stop and onto the highway and then took a side road, cross-country.

CHAPTER 15 – AVATAR

As soon as they disposed of David Stanford Adams III – and that had been lots of fun – Alex and V had chosen, for themselves, an extravagantly upscale motel. They signed in under elaborate false identities, which was equally fun since V's equipment case was a treasure trove of highly adaptable – and sometimes positively goofy – false documents.

So, after a long day on the road, they found themselves in a luxuriously spacious suite, one with soft lighting, a well-stocked bar, and a marvelously equipped bathroom in white marble.

They showered together, making lots of use of creamy liquid body wash and a smooth perfumed shampoo, and then, wrapped only in towels, and soon abandoning those, they lay down on the bed, naked, and vowed total mutual self-control. "Just a bit of tenderness, that's all we need," was V's way of putting it, "Just a little tenderness, a little amorous teasing, just a little …"

And then lying on her side, facing Alex, and playing with the thick curly hair on his chest, she returned to the serious business of the day, the game of cat-and-mouse with Sabrina Jacobs and her Andromeda Corp.

"So, Alex, you are an expert on biotechnology, nanotechnology, and weaponry, right?"

"Yes, I guess you could say that."

"So, put yourself in Sabrina's place. What sort of weapons will she use to capture me?" V punctuated this question by kissing Alex three times on the lips, then withdrawing, slightly, dreamy-eyed.

"Ah," Alex cleared his throat. "Well, let's see: she knows that you are very powerful, that you can break out of anything, that you can repair damage to yourself, but that you are vulnerable to a few things; so she'll probably, let's see, she'll probably shoot you with sliver nitrate, or try a swarm drone attack – yes a swarm drone attack might be a good idea."

"What's a swarm drone attack?"

"A swarm of tiny bioweapons, little things like bugs – like tiny mosquitoes – all following one program, working as one brain – would fly into a room, say, perhaps through the ventilation system, and swarm all over you, and, maybe, drug you, say, inject you with some paralyzing drug or poison. All the little pinpricks would add up. It might knock you out. And there would be too many of them for you to swat away. That would be one possibility."

"Ugh! Yuk!"

"Yes, it's not very pleasant. The swarm would probably deliver something to paralyze you – not a poison and not the nitrate thing. She doesn't want to kill you. I imagine she wants you physically intact."

"Yes, I guess she would."

"Then there's the Medusa Drug. She just acquired a company that was fooling around with that and then there's the Mind Slug –"

"Mind Slug?"

"Yes, it's a nano-biological weapon, something like a tiny worm that gets into the blood supply. It can climb through any orifice or wound or maybe in some cases burrow right through the skin."

"Ugh!"

"Yes," Alex caressed V's hair, "The Mind Slug can invade the cerebellum, and it sets up residence in the cerebral cortex and takes over thought, planning, and action. And I think some people are trying to develop a group-mind version. People would be reduced to robots – zombies, sort of – programmed to work for some sort of central puppet master."

"Slug, ugh! Mind control! Ugh!"

"Yes, in any case, as I said, there's also the Medusa weapon – I think it's a sort of aerosol spray – it turns people into statues. You're conscious, but you can't move. It blocks part of the neurological system. You stand where it caught you, in whatever pose it caught you."

"Ugh. So I'd become a statue in Sabrina's little garden of horrors, a trophy. It reminds me of my dear friend Baron de Villiers in the eighteenth century – or was it the seventeenth? He built a thick, solid, brick wall down in the dungeon of his castle, leaving me, sealed in, behind the wall, manacled and naked, walled up in a little alcove, deep underground, so I'd starve and suffocate and die; and once I was ripe, I guess, and the flesh had rotted away – or of course they could boil it off – he was planning, as he told me, to have my skeleton polished, burnished, and mounted on a stand in his bedroom so I would be the witness, the skeletal, silent witness, of his amorous pursuits and conquests and cavortings by candlelight in his finely furnished boudoir."

"Very kinky," said Alex, who was running his fingers, amorously, through V's hair and staring at her lips, and hanging on every word, every breath. "Very perverse."

"Yes, perverse, kinky, and refined. He was a splendid chap, I was extremely fond of him."

"You would be," said Alex, kissing her, gently, on the shoulder.

"Alex, this is fun," said V. She ran her hand, fingers extended, down Alex's chest. "Oh," she shuddered, "I absolutely adore, adore, your chest! Like this little curl of hair here, and this gentle muscular slope here, perfect pectorals, perfect abdominals; the rectus abdominis and the transverse abdominis are to die for."

"Hmm," said Alex, kissing V, gently, carefully, on the lips, and then, with the tip of his tongue, he gently forced her lips open, which was, he knew, a very bold move, aware, as he was, of the sharp and virtuoso nature of her canines and incisors.

"Hmm," murmured V.

"Hmm," murmured Alex.

This amorous waltz in extreme mutual close-up continued for some time. Then, with a sigh, V pulled back. "I must introduce you to someone."

"Right here, right now?"

"Yes, right here, right now – why not?"

"Well, we don't have any clothes on, for one thing, and for another …"

"Don't worry, she won't mind, Alex. Naked is good. You know, as an alien vampire, I am not supposed to have a soul. My Jesuit friend, Father Michael Patrick O'Bryan, used to go on about how I didn't have a soul. He really did break my balls on that particular subject."

"He broke your balls, the good father?"

"Metaphorically speaking, Alex. I'm a poet; I'm not always literal."

"Of course. You are not always literal."

"In any case, Alex, I do have a soul, and I did show her to Father O'Bryan. He was totally charmed, I think, because she flirted with him. I try not to evoke her too often because she is – well, she is exhausting, and she can be annoying."

"Your soul is annoying?"

"Absolutely – she is beyond irritating! It's time you two met." V squished her eyes closed. "I am evoking her. Oh, this is painful! Ouch! Ouch! Ohhhh!"

Alex who was lying dreamily by V's side thinking that he was ready to take the plunge and once again risk becoming a vampire, once again risk death at the hands of his beloved, and while he was having these feverish amorous imaginings, he saw a sort of mist, a sort of swirling distortion of space, just in front of the giant paper-thin flat-screen television that was on the wall opposite the bed. The mist crystallized into a cloud. The cloud took the form of a ghost. The ghost sketched out the form of a woman wearing, well, wearing V's phosphorescent pink dress. Then, the colors filled in. A woman was standing there, in flesh and blood, or so it seemed, no, not a woman – it was V! V herself was standing there.

"My God," said Alex.

"Is she there yet," asked V, concentrating, keeping her eyes squished as tight shut as she could.

"Yes, I'm here," the double said, "and about time too!"

"Alex, meet my soul and my Avatar. And Avatar, meet Alex," said V, opening her eyes.

"We already met, in a manner of speaking," said the Avatar, "and I must say, Alex, I enjoyed that last orgasm almost as much as V did. Thank you very much! We rarely get orgasms these days in my part of the universe."

"What?" Alex sat straight up.

"Now, Avatar, don't upset Alex!"

"As for using me as a decoy, V, doing that will require me to be glamorous."

"Yes," V said, cautiously.

"And you, you should be in disguise. You should be a frump."

"A frump? Me? A frump? Me?"

The Avatar struck a sexy pose, one leg cocked out as if she were loitering on the edge of a road somewhere outside some steamy glamorous Latin city soliciting burly truck drivers or randy five-o'clock-shadow evening commuters. "Yes, you should be absolutely frumpy!" She licked her lips. "Oh, this will be fun! I can see you now, V, in a baggy frumpy dress, thick stockings and slouch-heels, or maybe Birkenstocks or something hideous like that, and maybe a really tacky, heavy, greasy, gray wig, askew on your head, and thick glasses, you know, like the bottom of an antique Coca Cola bottle and maybe with silly spinsterish frames."

"Silly spinsterish frames! Silly spinsterish frames! This is outrageous!" V swung her legs off the side of the bed, and sat up, naked, feet on the floor; she looked, Alex thought, furious, outraged, and the absolute opposite of frumpy.

Alex was also puzzled, speculating about the sudden appearance of the Avatar. How had this creature suddenly appeared out of nothing and nowhere? This could not be mere biology, nor mere genetics, it must have something to do with physics too – if it wasn't just pure magic. But Alex was a scientist and he didn't believe in magic or – except in a metaphorical sense – in miracles. That meant that somehow V evoked other dimensions, that might explain her ability to transform herself so rapidly too; maybe forms and transformations were being plucked out of another dimension, from the interface between alternative or parallel universes. And if you could concoct genetics that gave such powers to a human organism, well, then … Sabrina Jacobs was definitely on to something – V was a gold mine, a key to the secrets of the universe, a possible recipe for …

The Avatar was saying, "Absolute frumpiness, that would be your disguise, darling V, while I put myself on the line for you, and for Alex too, I might add, you both must remain invisible – therefore you both must be unimpeachable frumps."

"Hmm," V frowned.

Alex glanced at V. She was fuming, but that, at the same time, it was clear that V, with infinite regret, could see the Avatar's point.

The Avatar had placed herself right in front of V, looking down at her as if V were the audience in a concert hall – or at a political rally – and the Avatar was about to make an important speech. Whatever she was going to say, she'd obviously, Alex thought, been storing this up for some time. She was like a Roman candle, about to explode.

Hands on hips, the Avatar began. "You don't realize, V, how much I sacrifice for you; you don't appreciate how special I am! I'm your very own soul, and I *am* special. You really don't realize how special, and that's because you don't really realize how special *you* are!"

Sitting very erect, knees pressed together, like a naughty school girl receiving a tongue-lashing, V blinked up at the Avatar and nodded. "Yes. Okay."

The Avatar was just warming up. "Most souls are watery, insipid undistinguished, indistinguishable, empty-headed, characterless little things, tiny damp squibs, flickering wet little gutted candles, empty little vessels that really don't do much of anything except at the end of life dissolve into the great Sea of Being or the Great Sea of Unbeing and I must say it's difficult to tell them apart, Being and Unbeing, I mean."

V blinked and glanced at Alex.

The Avatar waved her arms as if she were haranguing a vast mob. "Really, I ask myself: is the *Great Fullness* equal to the *Great Emptiness*, is *All* equal to *Nothing*, and vice-versa or not? Bonafide mystics kill each other over this stuff! Go figure! Anyway, here I am, wandering around in *Limbo* or *Purgatory* – I can never get *Limbo* and *Purgatory* straight! – which one is which? I've been around for centuries, working on the problem, and I still don't understand it! If they don't end up in Buddhist semi-annihilation, it seems that, by Divine Ordinance, those anodyne useless pathetic little souls end up, once dismissed from their day jobs, they end up, I say, drifting around on pink little clouds, perhaps strumming lutes and fluttering miniature impotent little wings, singing the Praises of the great *What's-His-Name*, the Infinite, Omniscient, Omnipotent, Omnipresent, the Jester-in-Chief, who is, it seems from all reports, All-Hungry for Praise and Very Jealous, and Who gobbles up praise and sacrifice and flattery! But otherwise, down here on earth, such souls as these aqueous little things are singularly, my dear V, and my dear Alex – you really are a beautiful specimen – such souls are singularly absent from the daily humdrum quotidian struggle and travails of life, from the great battles and crusades and jihads of our time!" She took a breath, and, then:

"But I, V, your most annoying and petulant and personal Avatar, I am a different breed of soul, I'm that sort of soul that rattles the cage, that screams and hollers, that protests, and ululates, that whistle blows, that hurls herself into the front line of strife, that gives advice and that complains, that occasionally threatens to go on strike, but never does.

"In truth, V, dearest V, however difficult I am, I am truly yours, I will sacrifice anything for you darling V. I am truly here for you. I will ride in my shining armor to the ends of the earth and beyond, into the Valley of Death, yea, into the Very Valley of the Shadow of Death, sword aloft, breastplate gleaming, chainmail rattling, to defend you, V, to defend you from all and every danger, V, my darling, my love!"

And with this tearful, angry, amorous, feverish declaration of love, the Avatar tossed herself down on her knees, and lay her arms straight beside V's thighs, and laid her beautiful head straight down snugly in V's naked lap

V looked at Alex and rolled her eyes. She ran her hands through the

Avatar's short raven-black hair. "There, there," V murmured, "there, there – I do love you, I do appreciate you, and I do realize how unique you are."

Alex who had gotten up out of the bed, and who was looking around for something to drape over his prelapsarian nakedness, glanced at the tableau – two beautiful, absolutely identical women, one dressed in phosphorescent pink and wearing pink stilettos, and one dressed in nothing, the clothed one kneeling in seeming obeisance before the other, who was sitting, naked, poised rigidly like an Egyptian Sphinx carved in stone, on the edge of the bed, and he thought it was a splendid tableau, of course, worthy of Helmut Newton or somebody like that, but the whole thing – this stormy Avatar materializing out of thin air and the immortal vampire who was comforting her – was certainly more than unnerving for a twenty-first century molecular biologist who had been brought up in the cult of the scientific method and whose metaphysics, simplified to their essence, were rather materialistic at heart, allowing of course for quantum mechanics, and the indeterminacy principle, and the unanswered and unanswerable questions of *Why there is Anything rather than Nothing at All*, and *How come, eh, this Whole Universe seems designed by Divine Fiat to make life for Us Possible*, eh, *Explain that Please, eh*, and he was thinking, I have to get to the bottom of this. He said, "I think I need a drink."

"Me too," said V.

"Me too," said the Avatar, tearfully, her tearful voice muffled and her head still buried intimately in V's lap.

Alex appropriated three tumblers from the suite's kitchenette, and, with a newly-acquired blue-and-white-striped hotel towel slouched enticingly low around his hips, he poured three whiskeys from the bottle of Glen Grant that sat on the dresser.

"So, boss, what's the plan?" The Avatar looked up from V's lap and stared straight into the eyes of her most demanding mistress.

The glasses frames were what Alex described as wire-coat-hanger-frames for sixteenth-century spectacles, and the lenses were about as thick as could be managed. V's dark eyes stared out, google-eyed, from behind two inches of rippling glass. She felt she was swimming in an aquarium.

"I'm sure I stand out like this," said V, "I mean nobody wears glasses like this anymore; they all have their eyes redesigned."

"Your eyes look cute," said Alex, who had picked up some of the Avatar's sadism. "What I can see of them. Anyway, they are about the only thing I can see of you."

V was dressed in a baggy sort of neo-puritan American Gothic Mennonite gingham burka over which she wore faded blue denim farmer's overalls, and she had a faded kerchief knotted over and imprisoning her hair but hidden by the burka, and big flat Birkenstock sandals with white socks underneath the leather straps and poised on thick wooden soles.

"She always does this to me." V's voice was muffled, "or something worse."

"Well, she *is* making a sacrifice," Alex said.

"Indeed she is," said V.

They shuffled anonymously along the pitted sidewalk of the small mid-America town where they had hooked up with the Avatar. Their shoulders were slumped, and their steps constrained, as they inched forward, in a good imitation of bearing with dignity the many weights and constraints, the slings and arrows, and indignities of old age.

Alex was buried under a wig of long wild gray hair, an unkempt biblically-approved, angry-prophet-style mustache-and-beard, farmer's overalls, duly flavored with authentic manure and wheat dust, and big muddy rubber boots.

"We are to lie low," said Alex.

"Yes," said V. "So why don't we go back to the hotel room and lie low in the bedroom in the bed."

"That's not a bad idea," said Alex. He was continually in danger of being transformed into a vampire. The night before, with the Avatar sleeping beside them, or pretending to (she had refused to evaporate for the night and occasionally she slapped an idle arm over Alex's backside; perhaps she was having a nightmare), V insisted on nibbling his ear; but, she assured him, she had not broken the skin, and she was doing it with her ordinary teeth, not her dangerously serrated vampire dentition.

"It's not a bad idea," Alex said again, "but we've already checked out. And we are supposed to skip town while we're in disguise, frumpy disguise, and we're headed toward Virginia, aren't we, dear?" He lifted V's American Taliban Veil and kissed her on the lips.

"Indeed we are," she said, breathlessly, "We're headed to Virginia – the Headquarters of Andromeda Corporation, the lair of that beautiful evil witch, Sabrina Jacobs Ph.D., Ph.D., Ph.D."

They climbed into the car – all the supplies had already been stowed in the trunk and in the back seat and, with a lurch and a burp, they started off, for Virginia – the home of Sabrina Jacobs and the Clone.

The Avatar meanwhile was making a display of herself in a local Wal-Mart, hoping to attract attention so that Andromeda Corporation would reveal its hand.

And, when she saw they had cottoned on to her presence, she left the Wal-Mart and moved on to a Blow-Out Super-Bargain Superstore, and began to make a fuss in the girdle section. She insisted on trying on oversized girdles. The sales lady said that she didn't need a girdle. The Avatar stamped her feet and shouted, "I do so need a girdle," and she screamed, "I know, only I know how desperately I need a girdle." The sales lady said that given her figure, "a girdle was inappropriate." "*Inappropriate!*" shrieked the Avatar, "*Inappropriate!* What the hell are you talking about, woman?" The sales lady pushed a button for the manager. The manager wondered whether bouncers would be in order. Girdles were a tricky item.

So, Andromeda Corporation would now have to decide whether to reveal its hand.

And, soon, it did.

"She's not that stupid," said Sabrina Jacobs. She didn't enjoy conference calls. She was dressed in her bikini bottom and eager to go for a swim, preferably with Aimi, if Aimi could spare a half an hour from her studies; Aimi really was an adorable swot – study, study, study! Sabrina tugged at the bikini string – if they went to the right beach, they wouldn't have to wear anything at all.

"Well, maybe she's just challenging us, but she's been reported in some superstores making ridiculous purchases, three cases of pink bubblegum for example, and wearing that pink phosphorescent outfit she wore in the diner, you remember, the one that David Stanford Adams III, pointed out and where he took the photographs of her and Doctor Wolf. Right now she's in the girdles section –"

"Girdles?"

"Yeah, girdles – the girdles section of a suburban Super Blow-Out Super-Bargain Superstore."

"I didn't know girdles still existed." Sabrina raised an eyebrow. "Do they still exist?"

"Yes, apparently they do. There's a whole section for them."

"Okay." Sabrina frowned. *Girdles*! Maybe she was still just a naive kid, maybe there were more things in heaven and earth than her philosophy encompassed, maybe she should start life all over from the beginning, learn her A, B, Cs, learn about girdles, and see if she could build on that and maybe figure out the origins of the universe and the planet Earth from there, from … *girdles!*

"Well, we can take her out – I mean to say, capture her – anytime."

"Hmm …" Sabrina used a sharp-pointed B12 pencil to doodle a sexy cartoon of V in a tight-waisted bodice and garter-belt, hog-tied with Scotch tape, and begging for mercy. "What happened to David Stanford Adams III?" Sabrina swiveled around to look out at the ocean rippling off in the distance beyond the plate-glass windows. "The last time I spoke to him, he was a prisoner of V and her friend Alex."

"Oh, David Stanford Adams III is back on the job," said the voice. "He was the one who signaled the presence of V in the Wal-Mart and who followed her to the Super Blow-Out Super-Bargain Superstore. He did say there is something fishy about the situation; and he said, from his experience, we should proceed with caution or, better yet, not proceed at all. 'She's a trickster,' he said, 'and this might be a joke.' Those were his very words. He also said that the lady, when in the girdle section, gave one of the salespeople the finger, which he said, and I quote, 'is totally out of character.' So we are going to mobilize our special bio-weapon-equipped SWAT team to corner the creature in the girdle section and take her down, no questions asked, no quarter given, no joking accepted. Of course she will be unharmed, as per instructions."

"Well …" said Sabrina. She was doubtful about this whole heavy-handed SWAT team, gun-slinging approach. "I guess you are the experts. But, I'm curious, how did David Stanford Adams III escape from the creature, from V?"

"Well, that's the funny thing. David Stanford Adams III apparently fell asleep after they had that coffee V had promised – they undoubtedly drugged him – and he woke up in a luxury hotel on a beach in Florida in a hotel room with a big cellophane-wrapped vase filled with fruit and a card which said 'From V and Alex with love' and …"

"From V and Alex with love …"

"Yes, that's right. And, sitting in a chair reading that day's *London Finan-cial Times* was a young woman wearing a short pleated skirt, charcoal gray Armani business suit, with charcoal gray jacket, white Cashmere sweater and a four-layered choker of smoky white pearls – with an ivory-white-and-robi n's-egg-blue cameo featuring Britain's Queen Victoria in embossed profile – and dark sheer stockings, and flat heel black patent leather shoes and she said, 'Oh, you are awake. Well, David Stanford Adams III, I have been pre-paid to fulfill and satisfy any and every unsatisfied and unslaked desire you may have.'"

"Uh-uh," Sabrina added a few lines to her doodle of V.

"There was also a bottle of champagne in the fridge and a bowl of peanuts – and a coupon covering dinner for two all-inclusive in the luxury restaurant of the hotel – or the equivalent in room service."

"I see."

"The trouble was, David Stanford Adams III had too many unslaked desires and he was too shy to express them, or so he tells us anyway, and the girl con-firmed his story; she's a partner in a merchant bank, by the way, and told us she occasionally does charity work; and so David merely asked her to dinner and told her all about his complexes which made it impossible for him to tell her about his desires and he had already alerted us, so we debriefed them both, but as far as the setup went – and the source of the money – we could not get beyond an anonymous booking agency in Chicago which had set up the whole deal. The credit cards led to Switzerland then to Outer Mongolia and then to Kyrgyzstan and then to some new form of encrypted bio-currency and then to nothing."

Sabrina sighed. She knew this would end badly. "Okay, do it, try to capture her, but be careful not to hurt her and let me know what happens and be very careful when she is in your possession. Don't let anybody get killed trying to stop her from escaping. If she regains her powers and insists on escaping, well, just let her go, okay?"

The SWAT team decided that they could not alert the customers or staff of the store, because, given the extraordinary intelligence and quick reflexes of the target, that would give the game away, so the swarm of nano-bugs, much smaller than mosquitoes and all directed by one computer program and all carrying tiny needles to make a million tiny simultaneous pinprick injections of a nerve-paralyzing drug, zoomed into the Super Blow-Out Super-Bargain Superstore; they were programmed to seek out V, having a visual Gestalt implanted in their tiny brains – and in the hive brain – which would invariably lead them to the right object in the midst of all the confusion of a Super Big Blow-Out Super-Bargain Super Store.

The moment the swarm was released, the store was flooded with the Medusa Vapor, as it had now been renamed, or the Medusa Mist, because the SWAT team decided a Double Whammy was called for.

The Mist entered through the high-powered ventilation system – people buy more in a torrid climate when they are cooled down, so the theory goes, and thus the big cool is worth the expense – and the result was that the people in the store were hit by a paralyzing mist just as the nano-bugs stormed through the aisles of the Girdles Department.

When the nano-bugs swarmed the Avatar, she immediately evaporated and then re-materialized on the far side of the store, and when the nano-bugs, now getting confused and even angry, headed for the newly constituted Gestalt or Avatar, over on the other side of the store in the Perfume section, she did it again, evaporating instantaneously just as the nano-bugs stormed in, attacking her, but there was nothing there, so they all bumped into each other, and while they were recovering and buzzing around fighting, she popped up, like a mirage, in the Garden Tools section, so the nano-bugs, furious and some of them badly bruised, had to swing around and buzz their way through fertilizers and garden overalls, holly and honeysuckle trellises and … and then she was gone again, and some of the nano-bugs had already emptied their stingers and dropped dead, and some of them were so confused and fed up they began to disobey the hive mind, which, in any case, was suffering a nervous breakdown, and the remaining nano-bugs, about 15,835,000 of them, began attacking each other and the customers and staff of the Big Blow-Out Super-Bargain Super Store and the plate-glass windows and some even attacked the hapless store mannequins which toppled over in the assault, shedding most of their clothes, which had been punctured to ribbons in the process, while the living people, the customers and staff, including the manager, a voluptuous and ripe and extremely competent Lebanese woman who spoke five languages, couldn't even topple over, since they were frozen in place, having been whacked by the Medusa Mist, which instantaneously transformed everybody living into a statue, but they were bitten and injected all over by the outraged nano-bugs who also tore all their clothes to shreds, leaving all the customers and staff and the manager, stark naked and immobile, frozen in the weirdest poses, and it would take the fire department five hours to finally enter the place and clear up the mess and release those under the spell, though they were all, the customers, the staff, and the manager, clearly visible, garishly lit by the fluorescent overhead lighting, through the plate-glass windows, to passers-by, and the show soon gathered a large public and lots of TV and Internet coverage and the images were splashed around the world. There were enticing headlines, all over the Net, featuring the phrase, "Shocking Wardrobe Malfunction …" You had to click through all the ads to see what the fuss was about – and tens of millions did.

While this was going on, about five hundred miles away, in Houston Texas, a young woman, wearing a pink phosphorescent elastic dress, and outfitted with pink impossibly high heels, materialized out of thin air in front of an ice cream parlor on South Main street, and ordered a triple scoop of vanilla, with chocolate syrup on top, and sat down, in full view of the busy sidewalk and of a TV studio, on the terrace, and proceeded to hitch up her skirt, and cross her legs, and began to spoon up the ice cream, while reading an antique facsimile of *The New Yorker* magazine.

A small boy was the only person who noticed that the lady had appeared out of nothing and nowhere. He sat there, clinging to his chair, his mouth and eyes wide open, staring at her. His mother, who was thumbing into her Miniature Personal Assistant an urgent vitriolic text about her recent visit to the nail parlor and how dreadfully impolite the indentured teenage Bangladeshi manicurist had been – had noticed nothing.

The Avatar winked at the little boy and said, "Eat your ice cream, kiddo!"

The mother glanced up. "Do not talk to strangers, Hubert!"

The boy said, "Huh?"

The mother glanced at the Avatar's pink fluorescent elastic dress and pink stilettos. "I'd ask you, Madam, not to talk to my son."

"Why not? Is this not a free country?" The Avatar put down the *New Yorker*. "Is not Hubert free to speak to whomever he wishes? Am I not free to address anyone whom I please to address in this the Land of the Free and Home of the Brave, in this the Great Republic for which our forefathers fought so valiantly and our forbearers bred so boldly?"

"No, you are not – you slut!"

"Slut, me?"

"And don't talk dirty around Hubert!"

"Talk dirty? Me?"

"Yes, you, you hussy, you slut, you ..."

"Me? Hussy, Slut, Me?" The Avatar jumped up and came over to the woman's table. "Why look at you, you mammary monster, you tummy-tucked, rubber-enhanced lips, blown-up boobs, spray-on-synthetic-tan freak, and that's not your real hair color either!"

"What? What? How dare you? Who do you think you are?" The woman stood up. The Avatar slapped her. The woman grabbed at the Avatar's dress and ripped it away, stripping the Avatar to the waist ...

A waitress screamed.

The manager came running.

When the police arrived – and the photographers and TV crews – the Avatar waited long enough to be handcuffed. The woman, by now utterly hysterical and half-naked, was also handcuffed, in front of her son, Hubert, who was taken in as a material witness. The Avatar, clutching her ruined phosphorescent pink dress modestly to her breasts, lingered long enough to be photographed and to give an interview to Reuters and do a standup with an eager, breathless 18-year-old girl reporter from the local Volpe TV News. Then, a few minutes later, the Avatar evaporated, leaving a woman cop with an empty handcuff dangling from her wrist.

Just before she evaporated, the prisoner said to the cop – the cop was a 23-year-old black woman of considerable charm, "Sorry, darling, I'd love to stay, I really would, but it's off to limbo for me, alas!"

And she kissed the cop on the cheek and was gone.

Nothing but empty air ...

The cop, Armanda Sinclair, stared at the dangling handcuff, and wondered if she was hallucinating and should apply for post-traumatic stress disorder leave, or claim she had had a nervous breakdown, but the kiss had been so sweet, so utterly luscious and memorable, and the disappearing lady so polite, that she decided she would merely whistle her way back to the station, explain the "daring escape" as best she could, and take her husband out to a five-course meal in some fine restaurant.

Alex and V, meanwhile, skipped town and headed east.

"Okay, Mother, now we get this buggy on the road," said Alex from deep behind his beard, and V answered, her voice muffled by her American Taliban tent-like attire, "Yes, Grandpa, we're are heading out of town, finally hittin' the road, in search of liberty, grandpa, in pursuit of life, liberty … and … the pursuit of … happiness … whatever the dang hell *that* might be."

They had previously changed cars, abandoning Alex's vehicle and using one of V's multiple credit cards, this one ostensibly based in Montreal, Canada, to rent a new car, and now, dressed like somebody's idea of two dustbowl hillbilly Bible-bashers, they were headed east, toward Virginia.

The car radio was full of reports of an infestation of itsy-bitsy wild bugs that had invaded a Super Big Blow-Out Super-Bargain Super Store and spread a strange plague that left everybody petrified in place.

"The authorities are still trying to clarify …

"At the center of it all was a mysterious woman, captured by security cameras, but who slipped away in the midst of the mayhem and who is still at large though police say she is wanted as a witness and is, at present, not suspected of having committed a crime."

About fifty miles out of town, Alex and V drove off the main highway and down a side road, and when they found an isolated spot far from any prying eyes, they stripped off their disguises and dressed in jeans and T-shirts, V now, once again, in her trademark black T-shirt, black jeans outfit, and Alex in the same, to be in harmony with his vampire lover. Alex buried the beard and wig and their odious clothes in a deep dry hole and stamped down the earth over the burial site and pulled a few dead bushes over the grave.

The stop-over provided an opportunity for about five minutes of languorous smooching, and then they were, once again, back on the road.

CHAPTER 16 – STRIPTEASE

The Virginia Headquarters of Andromeda Corp was based in a newly-created artificial city, *Walden VI*, which was designed, with high walls and electronic defense devices, to keep out all undesirables and to create a perfect utopian world conducive to high scientific and industrial productivity and to a healthy family life. Outside the walls of Walden VI, the world was going to pot – sewers didn't work, supermarkets were empty, once prosperous suburbs had become slums. But inside the walls, everything was prosperous and impeccably clean, sprinkled and scrubbed daily. No signs of poverty were allowed within the gates.

Stigmata of any kind were *Absolut Verboten.*

Andromeda Corp itself had its own on-site "campus." The Corp's HQ and Sabrina Jacob's residence were housed in a skyscraper, the Sir Alfred Jacobs Memorial Tower.

Alex had friends in the biotech and intelligence community who gave him the low-down on Andromeda Corp's Corporate Headquarters, and they also finagled an invitation for Edward van Duyn (Alex) and Ingrid Siegel (V) – well documented aliases with impeccably false scientific biographies and bibliographies from V's data bank – plus their assistant – Melody Brûlé (Helen Guerrera) – to a Bio-Fair which was just about to take place inside Walden VI, and which invitations provided the key to getting inside the kingdom.

Helen had phoned V, and V told Helen to phone back from a freshly purchased tablet phone, which Helen did. V said, "Dump your car on some side street, buy all new clothes, including underwear, take a full and careful shower, dump all your old clothes, dump your suitcase, purse, dump your toiletries (everything!), and all possessions except vital documents, scan those, and then hop a flight – pay with cash or bio-crypto currency – to Virginia, and we'll see you there."

"Yes, sir," said Helen. She scrupulously followed the instructions and stepped off a flight into sultry, wet, pre-hurricane Virginia.

V and Alex picked her up. "Alex, this is Helen. I told you about her." And V watched Helen and Alex shake hands, warily at first, but with an underlying current of electricity and excitement that V immediately picked up on, and which fitted in, tragically, unhappily, with the perfectly diabolical plan she had put together in her very own very devious little mind. V was preparing to make a great sacrifice – Tears welled up; she held them back; there was a catch in her throat; she suppressed it.

She had already hacked into the Andromeda Corporation website and into parts of the internal Andromeda Corp-Net, and she had obtained schematics of the building and of the "campus," and she obtained, with Alex's help, an interesting tidbit.

Jeremy Keenan, 35, the Chief of Security for the Alfred Jacobs Memorial Tower, had just gone through a nasty and expensive divorce, and he had fallen into the habit of seeking solace by drinking, alone, at the Shadow Club, a classy strip joint which was one of Walden VI's few concessions to the darker more lively side of human nature. Only sanitized filth should, it was argued, be allowed into Paradise.

"Perfect," said V. She had concocted a plan, and, looking up from her computer in their hotel suite – where they were all booked, sinfully, into the same suite – she told Alex and Helen her plan.

"You've got to be kidding." Helen was folding some underwear.

"No, I'm not kidding."

"You say we're going to get into Andromeda Corps HQ by staging a striptease?"

"Yes," said V. "It will be a classy striptease."

"Sure! I'll bet!"

V took a deep breath. "It will be a feminine and feminist striptease, a striptease expressing and enacting feminine empowerment and the symbolic castration of the male."

"What?" said Alex, "I'm not sure I like the castration of the male even if it is symbolic."

"We shall tear away the hollow phallus!"

"What phallus?" Helen looked at Alex.

V was undeterred. Once, decades ago, eons ago, she had gone out with an excessively cute paleo-feminist, and she had proudly acquired a vocabulary she rarely had occasion to use. "We shall reveal that the patriarchy is a hollow shell, a travesty, a charade, an impersonation – men being men by pretending to be men – but when you strip it all away, all their phallic decoration, all the flimflam macho facade, there's nothing left. Masculinity is a masquerade."

"What?" Alex was alarmed.

"Do you understand her?" Helen was sitting on the edge of the bed, legs crossed.

"No, I'm trying, though."

"Well," V crossed her legs demurely, imitating Helen. "I read all about it a long time ago, and I also saw, about one hundred and fifty years ago, a great performance in London and always I've wanted to try it out myself – a truly liberating striptease, a definitive and courageous feminist statement."

"Who does exactly what in this thing," Helen said.

"I strip, and you make me strip," said V.

"How do I make you strip?"

"You cast a wicked female witch spell on me."

"Oh, that sounds nice. I'd love to cast a wicked female witch spell on you."

"What do I do?" asked Alex.

"Alex, dear, we are the bait and the decoy, and you are the hunter; you sit in the audience and drink some malt whiskey, and then you spring the trap."

"The trap," said Alex, "What trap – Oh, you mean, Oh, I get it, the chief security guy, the guy who was recently divorced, the guy who –"

"The guy who goes to mourn," Helen rolled her eyes, "every night, at the Shadow Club and …"

"… and gets hammered," said Alex.

"Precisely. Drowning his sorrows," said V, "our duty will be to give him a good time, a really good time, high-powered, high-octane solace. For that, we've got to get ourselves hired."

The manager stroked his beard. "Now, feathers are important …"

The Shadow Club manager's office had a one-way plate-glass window that looked out over the floor of the Shadow Club. The other walls of his office were plastered with posters, and the shelves were cluttered with memorabilia. There was a poster of Josephine Baker wearing bananas; there were stills from the Moulin Rouge, les Folies Bergère, and the Crazy Horse, in Paris; there were signed photos of Gypsy Rose Lee, of Carol Doda, and of Dita Von Teese, and there were stills from ancient films like … *Striptease, The Blue Angel, It Happened One Night, Blade Runner, Vixens, Sweet Movie, Freaks,* and *Ninotchka.*

"Now, feathers – feathers are important," said the manager, "particularly for the historical acts." The manager was an overweight portly man with a neat goatee, deep circles under his eyes, and a fatigued avuncular manner, amiable, but giving the washed-out impression that everything he said he had said a thousand times before. "And we use skin-like materials, lots of body paint, lots of spray-on, lots of drip technique, like Jackson Pollock, and poses adopted from Allen Jones, girls as statuesque furniture, girls as ponies, girls as idols, and synthetic girls, and special lighting, and props, lots of props, all of which creates our special ambiance – a sort of dreamy paradise where all bodies are perfect, and all desires can, of course, be realized and all dreams consumed – where women feel they are goddesses and men feel Eden was never tossed away by Eve and the Serpent."

"Synthetic girls," said Helen.

"Systematically enhanced girls," said the manager.

"We are not enhanced. Are we enhanced?" Helen glanced at V.

"I'm not enhanced," said V, looking down at herself. "This is the way the gods made me."

"You don't need to be enhanced," said the manager, perking up, the light glinting off his monocle. "You two are naturally enhanced."

"Thank you," said V.

"Your eye is exquisite." Helen crossed her legs and hitched up her skirt, ever so slightly.

"Thanks. So tell me about this act of yours," said the manager. He yearned for a cigar. But smoking was forbidden.

"Well, this is an act with social content," said V.

"Social content," said the manager; he glanced at the calendar on the wall. "I find social content threatening; maybe even inappropriate. You know I only agreed to see you, girls, because I've got a sudden gap in my programming."

"Yeah, gosh, it's too bad Trixie and Tinsel got sick," said V.

"Food poisoning," said Helen, "very unfortunate."

"Well, those girls, you know, they'll eat anything. Those hotdogs spiked with LSD were particularly unfortunate." The manager twiddled with an eraser, doing invisible doodles on a notepad, breasts, thighs, haunches, ankles, "So you were saying, V, 'social content'?"

"Yeah," said V, "This act pitches a girl clown disguised as a femme fatale dressed in a multicolored revealing skintight catsuit motley, an icon of femininity as imposture, the subtext being that being a girl is really just clowning around, being female as farce, womanliness as disguise, the feminine principle, being derivative and parodic, is naturally deconstructive – a parody – of that false front patriarchal phallic facade called reality, if you wish. The sexy clown will be played by Helen here. Her antagonist will be an evil rakish playboy in a tuxedo, a caricature of archetypical masculinity, a hollow resonant tin can phallic pompous narcissist villain, which is me."

"Okay …" The manager sighed and made a thoughtful steeple of his fingers, or perhaps it was a tee-pee; his eyes, while seemingly glazed over, were spinning picturesque visual conjectures based on the two female bodies seated in front of him – breasts and thighs and haunches danced like sugar plum fairies in his cerebrum; lips and eyes and ankles and collarbones did impossible things, on a well-lit interior stage in a theater which would forever be for him alone: these two were knockouts; it was too bad the brunette – a stunner if he'd ever seen one – was wacko.

"You see," said V eagerly leaning forward, "I play the role of the masculine chauvinist imperialist patriarchal stuck-up pig, albeit slender and glamorously languorous in a campy vampy sort of way, a mélange, as it were, of Marcel Proust and Charlie Chaplin, Rudolf Valentino and Marlene Dietrich, decked out in tight-fitting trousers, wasp-waisted jacket, white carnation boutonniere, black tie, waving my ivory-topped cane, my top hat set at a rakish angle, black overcoat fluttering, and flourishing a white silk foulard, my black mustache which I can twirl –"

"Transvestite, that's good, that's good," said the manager. "I can identify with that! Guys get off on that. I mean, look at Dietrich, Greta Garbo, Katherine Hepburn, even Audrey Hepburn, and … I'm beginning to see possibilities here. So what happens next?"

"Yeah, what happens next?" Helen grinned at V.

"I am a cruel cad. I beat and subdue the clown. I tie the clown down."

"A little s&m, huh, a little bondage, maybe," said the manager.

"Precisely," said V, "But, but …"

"Yeah?"

"The clown liberates herself. She rises from patriarchal macho-imposed bondage. She casts off her femme fatale mask; she throws away her leather chains. She reveals herself as the evil clown, the abyss of androgynous ambiguity, the evil jester let loose, the surrogate Big Bad Mum, the dark void of amniotic abjection, the womb where all individuality dissolves, all frontiers are moot. And she turns the tables – she hypnotizes and seduces the cad. His desires are his chains. Her curves reduce him to slobbering servitude. She leads him around by his ... phallus. She turns him into a puppet, makes him strip, and turns him into a naked cringing gal – sans phallus, sans trousers, sans cane. Guys, underneath, are really girls."

"Old-fashioned role-reversal," said the manager, "the master-slave dialectic so praised by ... ah ... that great German philosopher what's-his-name?"

"Hegel, Georg Wilhelm Friedrich Hegel," said V, "And, yes, that's exactly it, an inebriating tincture of the master-slave dialectic, stirred in with an enforced, antic, clownish, sex change – from boy to girl – and a feminist message, as dark mustachioed top hat and voluptuous particolored clown struggle for ascendancy, who will be hegemon in our post-patriarchal ruin-strewn multicultural hodgepodge morally relativistic brutally secularized postmodern landscape."

"Two broads duking it out on stage, eh?" The manager closed his eyes: it was not quite mud or liquid sequin wrestling, but ...

"Exactly," said V.

"And one of them gets naked," said Helen.

"Which one?" The manager raised an eyebrow.

"Her." Helen pointed at V.

"Yeah, me!" V grinned. Her exhibitionism, she knew, knew no bounds; even after 2,500 years!

"And you?" The manager wagged a thick finger at Helen.

"I'm virtually naked from the beginning."

"Virtually?"

"Latex catsuit equivalent of body paint – the fetishist's delight – hell to put on, I might add."

"Talcum powder," V said, "Talcum powder helps, and, darling, I'll apply it, and I'll help you wiggle and squirm and snap into your outfit."

"Thanks, darling," said Helen, half closing her eyes and giving V a particularly sleepy look that combined the tender, the salacious, the mystical, the amorous, the grateful, the transcendent, the ...

"You girls have vision."

"Thank you."

"And you can whip this dish up for tonight? The nine o'clock special?"

That night, in the dressing room, V was bubbly. She sketched out a two-step; Helen gazed at her and said, "You can dance."

V did a soft shoe swivel, and kissed Helen on the cheek, "I've done the gavotte, the minuet, the waltz, the Charleston! You name it, over the centuries, I've done it. Now, let's get you ready."

V did Helen's makeup. First smoothing down Helen's hair, then tucking it under a tight-fitting rubber cap, then applying the gooey thick makeup smoothly all over so it even hid Helen's eyebrows, and then she painted Helen's lips bright red, and curved them upward into a permanent smile, and she painted Helen's nose red and gave it a slightly bulbous end and drew big startled triangular charcoal eyebrows high up on her forehead.

Then she plopped on and fitted down the wig, curly red hair, and added the neck ruff. V stood back and considered her work. "There, great!"

"Is that me?" Helen stared into the mirror. A startled pixy clown face stared back.

V powdered Helen down with talcum powder, and then helped her – snap, squeeze, snap, snap, ouch, gosh, stretch, snap, squeak, snap – into the skintight, more than skintight, latex, vivid, particolored clown catsuit.

"Thou art a motley fool, a wise fool, a sublimely beautiful fool, my very own fool!" said V.

"Same to you!" Helen gazed into the mirror and then back at V who had just put on her false mustache and eyebrows, but nothing else. "Thou hast made me, V, in thine own image," Helen proclaimed, "Oh, my lord and master, my majestic fool, my lovely vampire, whom I adore and worship and who is, verily, crazier than a coot."

"I'd kiss you, but you're icky." V was pulling on her trousers. "And I'd smear your beautiful lips."

"Now, where's my glamour girl femme fatale mask?"

"Here," V handed Helen a mask, like a Venice carnival mask – to be held on a stick in front of her face. It was a mask of hypnotic beauty. "Once you whip it off, you reveal the clown, the jester, the shaman, the ambiguous, androgynous abyss beneath … The macho monster will be terrorized, I mean, I'll be terrified, and I'll be your slave."

"Excellent," said Helen.

The lights went up for the 9 o'clock special floor show presented by the Shadow Club, and the guys and girls were all sitting at little tables drinking cocktails and eagerly waiting for the spectacle.

Waitresses dressed as mid-twentieth century bunnies moved among the tables taking orders and delivering drinks. One girl was hitched, pony style, to a little trolley, and she jingled back and forth among the tables, conveying sweets and appetizers.

One girl, rotating on a circular platform, emerged from a bath of sticky blue bubbles so, as the lights played over her, she was covered in drooling bubbles which fell gradually away leaving her crouching, vulnerable and naked, painted blue-silver, and going, *Oooo, Oooo, Oooo,* her bright scarlet lips rounded in a heart-shape Marilyn-Monroe-style pucker-up kiss, brilliantly illuminated in the spotlight; then she fell back into the bubbles only to emerge again, slowly, pucker up, *Oooo, Oooo, Oooo,* and splash back down – in a never-ending cycle, like Sisyphus pushing that rock up that hill, over and over and over …

Then, with a roll of drums and thunder, with flashing lights mimicking lightning, in a *son-et-lumière* worthy of Jehovah or of Baal, V appeared at the top of a ramp, surrounded by clouds of smoke, imitating real celestial clouds, and enrobed in ribbons of light.

She was attired in a natty tux, an overcoat, a false mustache, false heavy dark eyebrows, and wearing a monocle, tightly screwed into one eye. She came down the steep ramp slowly, waving her cane in jaunty, arrogant, phallic macho fashion

As she approached earth, the thunder gave way to a syncopated 1920s beat, a bit of the Charleston in the mix.

Twisting her mustache and twirling her cane, V began to dance, and the spotlight shone straight down, focusing all attention directly on her.

Alex was sitting alone, halfway to the back, and he thought that V looked pretty hot. This transvestite thing had something going for it.

V was playing the snob, with her nose in the air, and with her hat at a jaunty angle, she added a bit of the rake and decadent dandy to her attitude, and even, twirling the mustache and rolling her eyes, a bit of the villainous nineteenth-century cad to her subtle patriarchal portrayal.

Then, below the ramp, under a cartoon Tree of Knowledge, appeared Helen, aka Eve, the clown, in her tight clown catsuit, she was dancing with a synthetic, six-foot-long, glossy, black bio-designed python, writhing with it, enrobing herself in it, curling herself around it, lying on the floor, in intimate congress with it. The snake, a well-trained old ham who knew many of the routines, was taking an active part in all of this, and visibly enjoying itself.

"Eve!" thundered V, in a hugely amplified voice.

Helen squirmed, cowered, the snake – feigning guilty terror – skittered away and disappeared. Helen – Eve – rose up, shielding her clown face with her femme fatale mask

The divine cad descended from heaven to earth, sidled over in a slithery menacing way, and began to inspect Eve closely, haughtily, through his arrogant macho monocle. Eve made eyes at the cad. After at first trying to resist, he responded, as if hypnotized, adopting a slavish, syncopated dance, reacting, like a sinuous, entranced cobra, to every gesture Eve made.

Then undulating in one place, like the serpent in the Garden of Eden, Helen wiggled her hands at V, as if she were about to cast the presumptuous macho cad under a spell – and V, waking from her initial fascination and enslavement, responded by wielding a whip, subduing the clown, imprisoning the masked femme fatale in a cage of light, bars of smoky light projecting straight down from the heavenly ceiling above.

The masked femme fatale pretended to swoon, and when V came closer, too close, Helen's femme fatale dropped her beautiful Venetian carnival mask, revealing evil satanist androgyneous clown.

Oh, Horror! V shrank back, stunned, raising an arm to defend herself from the evil clownish objectifying, petrifying gaze.

Undeterred, the sexy clown weaved her serpent-like spell. V, the suddenly unmanned man, slowly succumbed, becoming puppet-like, her movements jerky and uncoordinated, a marionette whose strings were being pulled by the diabolic clown.

Alex thought Helen looked pretty hot. He frowned. Hmm. Did he have a clown complex? Was a woman clown particularly enticing? If so, why? Hmm. Perhaps he should see someone about this.

The spotlights blinked and flashed. V went rigid, jerked several times, and then bowed low as if enslaved and took off her black tie, and then staggered back, blinded by Helen's clownish beauty, one arm up trying, in vain, to protect her eyes, while she struggled out of her jacket.

Now V was reduced to a shirt, trousers, and bow tie – but still she wielded the phallic cane, still she attempted to twirl the mustache.

The femme fatale clown broke free of her cage, its shimmering bars of light shattered into smoky filaments. She closed in – weaving around V, fluttering her arms and hands. V struggled, tormented, caught in the whirlwind of an invisible, luminous, mote-filled spider's web, arms wheeling. Her trousers fell down around her ankles.

Abashed and startled, V stepped out of the heaped up, shriveled trousers. The long white shirt was now the only thing, or so it seemed, that sheltered her from the lascivious gaze of the audience.

Alex leaned over to the next table – one of the tables for Andromeda Corporation employees, where one guy was sitting all alone, and said, "I really like this one!"

The guy said, "Yeah, the two dames are hot. I like the one in the catsuit, but the other one is hot too, except you can't see for the shirt."

"I'll offer you a drink," said Alex, "the atmosphere makes me feel, ah generous."

"Buddy, I never refuse a drink!"

Helen struck a very bold pose and closed in on V who cringed and shivered and backed up, using her gentleman's cane to try to fend off the she-demon-clown.

It was all in vain!

Now, surrendering, V threw off her shirt.

V was now naked except for a G-string and the top hat and her cane, and she went down on her knees before the clown demon and took off her hat, letting her long hair – a wig – tumble down over her shoulders. She handed her cane to Helen who then mimed spanking her with it – *Whap! Whap! Whap!* The sound, monstrously amplified, resonated throughout the whole club.

Both girls stood up then, faced the audience, and took a bow. The applause was loud and long. People shouted, "Bravissime! Bravissime!"

"I know those girls," said Alex, "I must say I'm proud of them."

"You know those kids! Wow, I'd love to meet them!"

"You'd like to meet them?"

"Absolutely!"

"Well, let's see, maybe we could go backstage, while they're getting out of their costumes, and then maybe we could have a drink."

"Wow, I'd love that!"

"Sure, no problem. Let's wait for a bit, and we can go backstage."

Backstage they went and then to the hotel room booked by V and Helen and Alex where V offered Jeremy a glass of whiskey, and then another, and then a truth serum which made him cough up, in friendly fashion – he was having a really, really good time – all the codes, and all the plans of Andromeda Corporation HQ.

"There's a part you can never get into, though," Jeremy said. "Nobody ever goes there, and that's the center where they keep some secret experiment."

"What secret experiment?"

"I've heard say it's a clone, some sort of human clone, a girl; she's about 14 or something, cooped up in there all the time, a prisoner."

"Doesn't seem fair," said Alex.

"No, it doesn't seem fair. And in there too, right next door to the Clone, are the living quarters of the big shot, Sabrina Jacobs, she's the brains behind Andromeda Corp since her father died, she's the real brains, and she lives in there, they say, like a monk, or a nun, plotting how to take over the world. You need special passes to get anywhere near that part of the building."

They took Jeremy's fingerprints and created a synthetic mold print of his fingers, and they photographed his eyes, and from the photograph created eye-replica contact lenses.

And they got the formula for the identity passes used for different levels of clearance in Andromeda Corporation HQ.

"I had a good time, I really did!" When he left, Jeremy was convinced he had made love to the two women and that they had been just as delighted with the cavortings as he was.

"He was sort of nice," said V.

Helen, standing in the middle of the room, arms akimbo, gazed at V and said, "V, you are the sweetest, most generous, most undiscerning vampire I have ever met!"

"Thanks, I think," said V, but she did find the guy's eagerness to please rather endearing, his boxer shorts were cute, and his frankness in spilling the beans was very encouraging.

It was one o'clock in the morning when V and Alex presented themselves cheerily at Andromeda Corp Headquarters at the entry to the Alfred Jacobs Tower.

Both were dressed in night maintenance uniforms, a sort of overall with a logo, and both had the proper papers, and V had hacked the security system so that they were indicated as arriving at precisely one o'clock to fix a pipe that was leaking on the 35th floor. The computer monitoring system had been tampered with, too, to indicate a leaking pipe on the 35th floor. Of course, the pipe was not leaking at all.

The security guard at the main desk took a cursory look at their documents and at V's tool kit. He was watching, Alex noted, a football game. Alex made knowledgeable comments on the teams and their tactics. The security guard got interested and started a conversation that could have kept them there all night.

V shot Alex a glance.

Alex said, "Well, the boss says we've got to attend to that pipe."

"Right, work before pleasure," said the guard.

V's tool kit looked like a plumber's tool kit, but it contained concealed weapons and break-in equipment, miniature cameras, and a few bugs and nano-drones, which might, V thought, be usefully left behind. Even after she killed Sabrina and the Clone, other, future, mischief might be brewing inside Andromeda Corp.

V and Alex rode up in the elevator.

The numbers and floors zoomed past.

"Well, here we are," said Alex.

They got off on the 35th floor and cased the joint. They went to the place where the pipe was supposed to be leaking. They put biomarkers in the room so, if anyone checked, it would seem that they were there.

In a small storage room, where it seemed there were no cameras, V took the Beretta 9mm out of its case and slipped it into the pocket of her overalls.

"This is a spooky place to live," V said.

"Well, corporate chiefs are often spooky paranoid people," said Alex.

"Okay, I'm ready," V said, "Let's go."

Using the building's key code, they went up a service stairs to the 38th Floor. This floor was home, according to the intelligence gleaned from the security guy Jeremy and from their perusal of the building's secret schematics which had been pilfered through hacking by Alex, of both the Clone and its owner and creator, Sabrina Jacobs.

The Clone, well, V thought she would shoot the Clone. It was young, so it would be vulnerable. She could just shoot it and then make sure it was "dead, truly dead, forever dead, and would not rise again." This might require dismemberment – tearing the body apart – and a full draining of its blood and perhaps an office bonfire or maybe just a few toilets and the building's plumbing and waste disposal systems. She'd send Alex out of the room for that part.

As for Sabrina Jacobs, V had a more elaborate plan. She wanted, if time permitted, to talk to Sabrina, to discover what made Sabrina tick; she wanted to kiss Sabrina and make her feel desire; and then, when they understood each other, V planned to feed on Sabrina, slowly, a sip at a time. Sabrina, she felt, would be exquisite fodder – V would do it leisurely, thoughtfully, she would drain Sabrina by degrees, drip-by-drip; it would, V thought, be a gorgeous experience – *to incorporate into my own being the genius and sensibility of such a woman!* It would be an act of love; well, almost.

Alex didn't really think V would kill the two women, and V was aware of these foolish thoughts – and hopes – drifting through Alex's very fine, very human mind.

Oh, foolish, wonderfully just and splendid mortal, oh admirable man, oh superb and sensitive lover, oh, all that is best in humanity's brief flame, oh wicked and deadly me. She smiled at Alex. You will judge me, Alex, you will judge me harshly, and perhaps you will be right, and perhaps you will hate me and leave me! But, Alex, the survival of the human race, of your race, Alex, is at stake, and if I squeeze some extra little pleasure out of destroying the Clone and its creator, is that so great a sin?

The service stairs did give access to the 38th floor – but you needed three codes to get in: a numeric code, an optical (pupil and iris) bio-check, and a palm-and-fingerprint check.

Under the impression that he was wooing her while singing a Neapolitan love song, Jeremy had given V the numeric code. Using the false eye and the false palm-and-fingerprints, V and Alex managed to get to the 38th floor, the holy of holies. Inside the service stairs, they were standing on the threshold of the laboratory, which contained the Clone. Strangely, so far, there had been no guards, no humans. Already, V had a suspicion that all of this was a wild goose chase. *But, nothing ventured, nothing gained, as Maria often says, and out of errors come new truths; detective work, like science, is a matter of trial and error, progressive approximation, conjecture and refutation …*

V took out her dart gun.

Alex raised an eyebrow. V motioned toward the door and raised two fingers – two life forms were on the other side of the stairway door and not far away.

Alex edged the door open. This was the sacred 38th floor.

V stepped through the door.

A guard was sitting at a desk – a guy – and another guard, a woman – was standing, looking out a plate-glass window. The guy began to turn toward V. The woman began to turn away from the window, and she began to draw her pistol out of its holster …

V fired the dart gun twice – *whish, whish* – the guy crumpled over his desk. The woman, turned in slow motion, her face in profile, her Beretta 9mm half-way out of its holster, she put her palm flat against the plate glass, and slid slowly down, making a scratching, squeaking sound – *my, my, what long nails you have, my dear,* thought V.

"They'll be out for an hour at least," said V.

"That should be enough for what you want to do."

"Yes, it should, dear Alex, be enough time for what I want to do."

First, they went to the top security lab holding the Clone. Again it meant numeric controls and eye controls and hands-on controls.

"There will probably be technicians and guards inside, V whispered, but I don't sense any life forms inside, which is strange. I'm beginning to think …"

The door whooshed open.

An antiseptic smell, a specially scrubbed smell, an electric smell, of computers and high-powered electronic instruments, leaked out. V's nostrils quivered.

The lab was empty.

Cautiously, guns drawn, Alex and V edged their way into the space. It was a huge, vaulted, bio-secure room, at least three stories high. It looked, in some respects, like a movie sound stage, or a very large and airy television studio.

A huge armored glass cage stood in the center of the room, which was full of control panels and monitors.

Inside the cage was a bed, a huge computer screen, built into the walls, a bookshelf with rows and rows of books, some exercise equipment, a bathroom, and a shower. There was a tray to put things into the cage and take them out – food.

"I suppose that's how they feed the Clone," V said. She felt, for a single second, sorry for the creature, locked inside its whole life because it was a clone, half-human, half-alien, a monster, a freak, a dangerous freak made from dangerous DNA – *A freak just like me*, thought V, *well, I'll put her out of her misery.*

"So," said Alex He was relieved. He did not like the idea of killing a child, even if it was an extraterrestrial alien or half-alien. The whole thing was perverse. This child was, in a way, V's child, or her sister, depending on how you looked at it. When she killed the child, V would be killing part of herself.

"I've seen enough," said V, standing hands on hips, looking around. "It's impressive, isn't it?"

"It's horrible."

"Sweet Alex, you really are a most kind and considerate person! I think that's where they wanted to put me, perhaps, or something like it, maybe much worse, since I'm not a child."

"Well, as I said, it's horrible, and nobody is going to put you anywhere you don't want to be, not while I'm alive, at least."

V blinked at him and puckered up a kiss, offered, just for him. "Well, let's go check on Sabrina."

Again, they had to go through a complex rigmarole of security; finally, the door slid open, and they were in the holy of holies, the lair of Sabrina Jacobs.

Empty!

"This gal sure lives well!" V examined the magnificent bed, the tailor-made reading lights, the choice of books on the bedside table, the rows of clothes, all of impeccable taste, hanging in the built-in invisible wardrobe cupboards, the large flat-screen television, the state-of-the-art computer connections and music equipment and the absolutely splendid bathroom, with a cornucopia of soaps and cosmetics, of mirrors and beauty instruments. No wonder Sabrina looked so glamorous! V was tempted to take a shower or a bubble bath, but she decided that would be unwise.

"I'd like to take a bubble bath, Alex. Do you want to stand guard?"

"Really, V!" Alex did a good imitation of an exasperated husband from some early Leave it to Beaver TV decade.

"What?"

"I'd love to see you in a bubble bath, but not here, not now."

V examined herself in one of the full-length mirrors. She slipped the plumber's overalls off one shoulder, and stuck out her tongue at the polished glass. "I could take off all my clothes and lay them out on this big flat Art Deco bed, and I could ..."

"V!"

"Okay, okay, Alex." V gave him a big grin. She made faces at the mirror, suspecting, rightly, that there were cameras behind the mirror.

Alex frowned. How could a vampire be so frisky? Aren't they supposed to be mournful and morbid? "Let's get out of here," he said.

"Right! Right! You are right, Alex." V took a running jump and bounced up and down on the bed. "Whoopee!"

Alex, hands planted firmly on his hips, in the classic pose of masculine exasperation, growled, "V!"

"Yes, Alex! Yes, sir! Yes, sir!" V jumped off the bed and took his arm, and – then she stopped. A small personal organizer was sitting on the bedside table. She snatched it up, and they left Sabrina's suite, carefully closing the door behind them, and began to walk down toward the bank of elevators.

"We'd better look working-team-like, or the monitors will not be very happy."

They walked seriously down the corridor, V swinging her plumber's kit jauntily.

"You seem happy, V."

"Yes, the chase is still on. Climax is anticlimactic somehow, don't you think? The excitement of the hunt's the thing! My blood runs wild! You know I'm a predator!"

"I have never doubted it, not for an instant," Alex gave her a smile, "I was almost a full meal myself."

"Don't remind me," V rolled her eyes. "I have never been so terrified in my life. The thought of eating you made me sick!"

"Thanks," said Alex, as they arrived at the bank of elevators. He leaned over and pushed the elevator button.

"And, by the way, Alex, though I love you dearly, it is frustrating to see you so near to me and yet so far because we both agree we should not make love, and so this is unfair to you because you are young and feisty and have your life before you; so my idea is, my dear …" They stepped into the elevator. "My idea, my dear, is that you should have an affair with Helen."

"What?"

"Now, don't play innocent – admit it, you find her very attractive."

"Well, yes, I do, but you and I …"

"You and I are everything and nothing, Alex. We are friends, we always will be, I hope, but we cannot be lovers," V paused, blushed, and ran the tip of her tongue along her lips, "though I do like to smooch with you and flirt with you and even tease you!"

"You certainly do, unprincipled wench," said Alex. He took her in his arms and kissed her, in spite of or perhaps partially for the benefit of the camera that looked down from the corner of the elevator ceiling.

Her lips, as always, were sweet and warm and soft as satin; her eyes fluttered, her heart beat, and she looked at him with those deep dark eyes, pupils and irises like depths into which you could throw yourself and out of which, once gone onto those depths, you could never return.

"Oh, boy!" Alex sighed.

"Helen is the girl for you, and she really does know how to kiss."

"How would you … know?" said Alex.

V gave him a big bright smile, and they arrived, *ping, ping, ping.* "*You are now at the rez-de-chaussée,*" said a smooth female voice.

And as they came out of the elevator, Alex, pretending to be shocked, asked, "Did you two really … ah …?"

"Yes, of course, Alex, we girls are curious, vampires especially so! You know that!"

The guard looked up from the television screen. "Hey, six-zero," he said.

"Told you so," said Alex, "See you next time."

"Anytime," said the guard, "Have a great night. And thanks for coming in so late!"

"Don't mention it. It was our pleasure!"

With a soft proprietary hiss, the big glass corporate doors slid shut behind them, and the soaring marble columns – pure Carrara – channeled the balmy, perfumed night breeze into a river of airy sensuous delight. The fronds of the palm trees rustled in a sharp feathery way like chiffon paper being crumpled. Arms outstretched, V spun around in a pirouette. "I'm so happy!" She took Alex's arm, and twirled him around in a short, improvised waltz.

Alex realized – yet again and not for the first time – that he didn't understand anything at all of female or vampire psychology.

Helen was waiting in the "getaway car" as she called it. "Thank God you guys are back. There have been three security patrols around and I had to say that I was waiting for you and that we didn't have our regular plumber's van because the call was so late and the van was locked in the company garage, and we thought we'd hurry right over instead of taking the extra time to get the van out of the garage and etc. and etc. and etc. and I had to refuse three offers of dates, and one offer of marriage, and it was really hard to get rid of them. Boy, I'm glad you are back! Let's get going! And what happened in there? I don't see any blood. I would have thought, V, that you would be covered from head to toe in bright gooey scarlet gore, your two victims coming out of your ears."

"No such luck," said V, sliding in next to Helen and kissing her on the cheek, "but I love the way you describe it."

"Well, you know, your eating manners, V, are …"

"I know, I know, I'm a messy eater."

"Yes," Helen said, "like remember Big Boy, I mean, he was splashed all over you in big bloody dripping gobs and a shower of blood all over the …"

"Girls, please, please," said Alex, who was in the back seat.

Back at the motel, for security reasons, they shared the same room, the three of them. V took a shower, and then Helen took a shower, and then Alex was allowed into the bathroom.

There was no hot water left, so Alex, swearing under his breath, took a cold shower, and then shivering and coated in glittering icy droplets tried to dry himself on two towels which were soaking wet.

He and Helen ate Chinese from a take-out while V contented herself with a cool glass of Chivas Regal from a bottle she'd left lying sideways in the room's refrigerator.

For this picnic, the three of them sat cross-legged on the rug on the floor. Alex was wearing orange and black striped boxer shorts, and Helen and V were wearing matching, black silk, teddy-style nightgowns.

"Look at those abs," said V, "Alex is a gorgeous specimen."

"He sure is," said Helen, "good enough to eat."

V punched Helen in the side, and Helen punched back, and they both began to giggle. Alex was terrified. They might start to wrestle and roll around on the floor in their nightgowns or begin a pillow fight. And yet there was a part of Alex that was delighted to witness such simmering female hijinks – every pubescent boy's dream after all – but another part of him – also a little boy – wanted to be watching television somewhere alone in a quiet room with no female antics and a good cool beer clenched in his fist.

Men!

Women!

Alex thought perhaps he should read some books on the subject. There must be some key to unlocking the infinite mysteries of …

They slept on top of the covers on the same big hard bed, V in the middle, Alex and Helen on either side.

It was a steamy night The air-conditioning was not working, so Helen and V of one accord and with one motion threw off their flimsy little nightgowns.

Alex kept his boxers shorts on and rolled over on his side and stared at the alarm clock radio that told the time minute by minute and second by second. He watched a lot of time go by.

Females are the true Dionysians, he mumbled, they are the Furies, the Banshees, the free spirits. Yes, he fumed, girls are the true polymorphous and the perverse; we males are poor pitiful, single-limbed, up-tight, inhibited, phallocentric, single-minded, pathetic …

At one point, V put an arm over Alex, she began to play, gently, with the hair of his chest. Then her hand ceased to move and just dangled, warm and soft and smooth, and Alex sensed that Helen had put her arm over V, and …

03:02, click, 03:03, click, 03:04, click …

Finally, he fell asleep.

V was wearing glasses and a towel and sitting at the breakfast table sipping black coffee and reading the screen of the miniature personal organizer she had filched from Sabrina's bedroom.

"I didn't know you wore glasses," said Helen.

"I don't. It's just that wearing them makes me look like I'm thinking, and I find it helps me to think. Like – if you smile, it makes you feel happy. If you frown, it makes you sad. If you wear a nifty tight uniform, you become a soldier and kill people. The get-up makes the girl. The mask is the man. The habit makes the monk. Outer dictates inner. Science says so." V slid the glasses up onto her forehead. "I've discovered some interesting stuff in here. I figure this HQ, and its 38th floor is largely a decoy as far as Sabrina, and the Clone are concerned. They are rarely there."

"Oh?" Alex came out of the bathroom, wearing a fluffy towel around his waist. His skin glowed with humidity. V and Helen gave him the once-over, exchanged glances, and grinned.

"Now, ladies ..." said Alex.

V blinked at him, licked her lips, slipped her glasses down onto her nose, and put on her serious, professional expression. "Sabrina has a research ship, *Andromeda*, and it's now in the Sulu Sea in the Philippines. It was built fifteen years ago and outfitted and designed for advanced genetic and biological research. It has very high security – there's even a British frigate, the *Darwin IV*, and sometimes a Chinese warship, the *Deng Xiaoping III*, or a Philippine stealth frigate, the *Ramon Alcaraz,* to accompany it. Sabrina is passionate about oceanic biological research – you know, it's the sort of thing she would be interested in, the untold riches of genetic diversity to be found in sea creatures, in sea plants."

"The ship would be an ideal high-security environment," said Alex.

"An ideal place to keep the kid, you mean," said Helen.

V glanced at Helen. "Yes, it would be an ideal prison for the Clone, and it has big, specially designed, biosecure, high-security environment, to isolate, as far as possible, the Clone and her DNA."

"A prison for a baby – or a kid."

"Exactly – but they anticipated her growing up. It says here the studio-prison is equipped with a library, with computer connections, with gym materials, a big wardrobe space ... It's just like the space we saw at the HQ."

"Where did you say the ship is now?"

"Well, there's a diary or calendar here. And, as I said, it indicates that *Andromeda* should be in the Philippines in the Sulu Sea."

"So, is that where the Clone is, and is that where Sabrina is?" Helen, wrapped in a big white towel, was fluffing out her hair under a remarkably sleek and silent blow-dryer.

"I'm monitoring their communications."

"I'm impressed." Helen turned the blow-dryer off.

"Much of this is encrypted, but I've broken the code." V glanced up at Alex, and continued. "The texts refer to C-1. I think that's the Clone, Clone One. And Sabrina is on the ship regularly. I think it's her headquarters. She loves scuba-diving."

"She loves scuba-diving?" Alex raised an eyebrow.

"Huh, huh."

"That's interesting."

"She's big on saving the oceans. She thinks biotechnology can help us repair what we've destroyed; I mean, what humans have destroyed."

"So this Sabrina of yours is, in some ways, an idealist," said Helen, as she put her towel down on a chair, went to the wardrobe, made a selection, and pulled on panties, black jeans, and then a black T-shirt.

"Yes, in a way," said V, twisting and biting her lip, staring through the glasses, and concentrating on the organizer.

"She's an interesting creature, our Sabrina. Is she sincere about this?" Alex, who'd pulled on his boxer shorts, was fiddling with the coffee machine.

"Oh, yes, I think so." V flipped through more pages and files of the personal organizer. It contained budgets, learned articles, press reviews. "She has poured huge amounts of money into trying to regenerate coral reefs and save marine creatures – without any immediate profit. She's written a little summary here: 'With more carbon dioxide in the atmosphere, the oceans absorb the carbon dioxide, and in the oceans, the carbon dioxide dissolves, reacting with seawater, creating carbonic acid, and increasing the acidity of the water, and the increased acidity corrodes the calcium in bones, coral reefs and shells and so destroys the basis of much marine life, causing whole parts of the food chain to collapse. That and nitrogen fertilizers which, draining from the land and from rivers, leak into the sea, super-charging the water with super-food and creating huge islands of toxin-releasing, oxygen-consuming algae that suck the oxygen out of the water, and you add in plastics and waste, and over-fishing, and we get dead oceans, acidic and full of poison and plastic rubbish, and empty of oxygen and empty of life.' Sabrina is trying to reverse the process," said V, frowning

"So she's not all bad," said Helen, as she pulled on her sandals.

"Hmm." V clasped her hands in front of her. "Well, I'm in a bad position to judge people. After all, I do what I do so I can feed."

"You've done the best conceivable with the hand you've been dealt, my darling," said Alex, turning away from the coffee machine. He came over, pulled her up from the chair, and kissed her, and held her tight.

"Don't get me excited, Alex!"

"Oh, do get her excited, Alex," said Helen, "and let's see what happens."

PART THREE – ANDROMEDA

CHAPTER 17 – IS EVERYBODY ASLEEP?

"Is everybody asleep or what?"

On *Andromeda*, in the Sulu Sea, Sabrina opened the teleconference call by asking:

"Is everybody asleep or what?"

Sabrina was seated next to Henry Rothschild; but the video conferencing camera stayed focused, 90 percent of the time, on Sabrina. She was dressed in an impeccable charcoal black power suit, crisp jacket, and white shirt open at the throat. Her blond hair glittered like gold. Her tan, too, was golden. She looked, to the cowed executives, mesmerized and trembling in front of screens around the world, like the goddess she was.

"Look at this." She held up a photograph of V and Alex kissing in an elevator at Andromeda Corporation HQ.

"And look at this!" It was a photograph of Alex and V inspecting the Clone's cage.

"And look at this one!" It was a photograph of V making faces in the mirrors in Sabrina's very own bedroom at HQ up on the 38th floor of the Sir Alfred Jacobs Memorial Tower.

"This is my favorite. Here are the Alien and her boyfriend Alex Wolf, *Doctor* Alex Wolf, prancing around in my bedroom – *my bedroom!*"

V was jumping up and down on the bed, and Alex looked exasperated. Sabrina sighed. "What sort of security do we have, anyway?"

"Well ..." somebody somewhere began.

"This is extremely frustrating," Sabrina looked stern as the various executives stumbled over themselves in apologies and explanations and excuses. "Indeed, after the incident at the Super Big Blow-Out Super-Bargain Super Store – it's lucky we weren't sued, and the only reason for that is nobody knows who let those damned bugs loose – after that, we have this ..."

While looking stern Sabrina was gazing at the pictures of V in her bathroom: one showed V smirking, another showed V wiggling her hands behind her ears and crossing her eyes, another showed V doing a sultry film star imitation, sideways to the mirror, eyes wide open, lips puckered in the smooching pose, and in that photograph, Alex Wolf was at the edge of the photograph, leaning in at the bathroom door, looking perfectly exasperated. Sabrina sighed. *I rather like this impertinent V!* But then she remembered: V was ultra-dangerous, a one-woman invasion from outer space, to be hunted down and neutralized and neutered and tamed and domesticated and enslaved and lobotomized and robotized and put in chains, and exploited for every wiggle and kink in her very unique alien-human DNA. However charming V might be, she must be neutered and enslaved! *I shall put her in an escape-proof cage, that's what I'll do,* Sabrina thought, dreaming of how titillatingly erotic it would be, *I'll turn her into my personal slave!* She snapped to attention and perked up: "*What* did you say?"

The Vice President Security Virginia HQ was explaining, apologizing, that he had gone to the Shadow Club; he said, "You know the Shadow Club?"

"Of course, I know the Shadow Club!"

"Well, I was there having a few drinks, you know ..."

Sabrina rolled her eyes, "Yes, you were having a few drinks, you know, and then ..."

"... and then these two girls did a striptease, well only one of them really stripped, I mean 100%, or almost, I mean down to a tiny G-string, you know, and that was that lady, V."

"What?" Sabrina sat up straight in her chair. "A strip act, V did a strip act?"

"Yes, she was dressed, like, like a gentleman, you know, bowler hat, cane, tuxedo, and then this clown comes along –"

"Clown? Clown?"

"Yeah, this clown, a girl clown, a blonde, but in tights and in a wig and ..."

"How do you know she was a blonde if she was in a wig?"

"Well, that's the thing, I spent time with them, hum, and I got to know them ..."

"You got to know them!"

"Yeah, this guy was sitting next to me at the Shadow Club, you know, down in the audience, table right next to mine, you know, nice guy, real friendly, you know, good expensive suit, nice cufflinks, super-polished shoes, and he offered me a drink, and he said that's quite an act isn't it, and I said, Yeah, and he said, Well, I know those two girls ..."

"He knew those two girls." Sabrina's thin-lipped smile was deadly, "and of course, he looked like this guy, right, like the guy in the photograph, like Alex Wolf, in short."

"Ah, yeah ... yeah, he did, matter of fact."

"Okay, so what happened next?" Sabrina tilted her head to one side. "Wait – Let me guess: He invites you to meet them, and you go to some room in some hotel or motel, and you have some drinks, and it's a bit fuzzy after that, you probably think you had sex with V, and that other one, the clown, the blonde, and you remember you were very witty and wonderful, and they loved you mightily, but when you go happily home, it's all more than fuzzy. And they have extracted from you the schematics of the security system, finger molds, eye prints, and the whole shebang, right?"

"Yeah, well, yeah, I guess you could say ..."

"Yes, I certainly guess I could say ..."

"Henry, I'm going for a swim," Sabrina said. The conference was over. She stood up and revealed that though she was wearing the jacket and shirt, from the waist down, she was wearing only the bottom of her skimpy black string bikini.

"You know what we've learned, Henry?" Sabrina slipped out of her jacket and shirt and put on the top half of her bathing suit. "We've learned that V is definitely coming after us. We are the bait – me and the Clone." As she said these words, a chill rippled up her spine, goosebumps blossomed on her arms. What were V's exact words? *My fangs are itching to meet you, Sabrina, itching to meet you.*

"Yes, it would seem so," said Henry, "unless it was some sort of practical joke on the part of this ... ah ... creature."

"Well, she is a prankster," Sabrina rubbed her arms. "Perhaps she gets bored being a vampire, so she has to fool around. And she's got a female buddy, this blonde, this clown, this ... Which is quite strange, and a new development. And what she is doing with Alex Wolf, is something I still haven't figured out at all."

"Maybe they're in love, Sabrina."

"Love!" Sabrina rolled her eyes. "What is love? Have I ever heard that word? Have I ever heard of love?"

"Now, Sabrina, you know very well what love is," said Henry. He had known Sabrina since she was in diapers, he had held her in his arms and fed her from a bottle, he felt that, as a colleague and friend of her father, Sir Alfred Jacobs, he had a duty to try to save Sabrina from herself – and from the damage Sir Alfred had inflicted upon her.

"I'm not so sure, Henry, I'm not so sure I do know what love is, though I do of course love you." She gave him a kiss on the cheek, a warm kiss with her hand and lips against his skin and a kiss which was, in a chaste way, passionate and lingered ever so slightly.

Henry gazed at her – Sabrina was a marvel, of course, a wonder; but she was so deeply damaged ...

"Okay, I'm going swimming," she said. And she walked out of the conference room and onto the deck and into the sunlight.

Ah, the warm sunlight, the tropical heat! Sabrina shivered. *My fangs are itching to meet you, Sabrina, really itching to meet you!*

Aimi was waiting, and Tania, the captain of *Andromeda's* launch number one, the *Zeus*.

"Let's just have fun, girls." Sabrina stepped into the launch.

The Launch was swung out, lowered down into the water, and slowly began to move away from *Andromeda*.

The "girls" – Aimi, Sabrina, and Tania – were accompanied by six armed guards from a newly contracted security company; Sabrina received a great many threats – from pirates, from kidnappers, from ecological terrorists, and, most seriously and above all, from Dmitry Pavlov's giant Russian biotech company, Bio-Prom. Protection was needed. And when their old chief of security, Amos Herzog, died of a sudden heart attack, leaving everybody feeling bereft, a new company had been contracted to fill the gap.

The 14-year-old Clone was safely locked as always in its transparent, armored cage, two decks below, in the top-secret ultra-secure central lab of *Andromeda*.

As the launch moved away from the Andromeda, for the afternoon of swimming off Paradise Island, a tiny uninhabited island where Sabrina had established one of her automatic robot research bunkers, she looked back at the ship. She felt a pang of guilt. She had not paid her quick ritual daily visit to the Clone. Oh, well, that could wait! She would see the Clone when she got back to *Andromeda* at dusk.

In any case, the visits were never very productive. The Clone never recognized her, and seemed entirely unaware of her presence.

But, in the last two weeks, something had changed. Sabrina's ideas about the Clone had been turned upside down. Terrifying new possibilities had opened up – possibilities that might force Sabrina to revise all her ideas, about the Clone, and about V's DNA.

But Sabrina didn't know how to confront these possibilities – they opened up a frightening void. She hadn't yet decided what to do.

They anchored off the coral reef that surrounded Paradise Island. Tania stayed on the launch with three guards, while Aimi and Sabrina and three guards put on their wet suits and masks and plunged off the launch into the water – into a world of blue bubbles and dark depths.

Sabrina and Aimi, followed by the guards, swam along the reef, following schools of fish, and Sabrina stopped to check on some of the underwater installations that were meant to measure temperature, acidity, and salinity, oxygen levels, the presence of toxins, and, generally, the chemical contents of the water, while Aimi took photographs of the evolving flora and fauna of the reef – and of the conditions of the coral – and also, using a hand-held gage, made some independent measurements of acidity.

"I love it down here," said Sabrina over her aqua-phone.

"Me too," said Aimi, "it's like being able to fly."

"Yes," said Sabrina, "perhaps someday we humans will return to the sea."

"Whence we came," said Aimi.

"Yes," said Sabrina, "Whence we came."

CHAPTER 18 – IT SPEAKS

While Sabrina scuba-dived with Aimi and enjoyed a snack on the launch with the warm sun blazing down and the gentle breeze caressing them, the Clone was being watched by Sally Blake.

And Sally Blake, an eager and ambitious child developmental psychologist, was thinking back to two weeks ago – to the day her world changed.

Two weeks ago ...

Two weeks ago to the day. The Clone, the female hybrid – half-alien, half-modified human – had just taken a running jump and smashed herself against the rubberized foot-thick glass wall. The wall bent and rebounded, bouncing her back into the middle of the glass cage.

The girl howled. Her eyes turned toward the ceiling so that just the whites showed.

"They should put her out of her misery," said Jack Yong, one of the technicians.

"*She*? We are not supposed to use the word *she*," said Sally, "You are supposed to call her *It*. In any case, she's the only one we've got – so we can't eliminate her. It took hundreds of tries just to get *It*." Sally was exasperated by the hopelessness of it all.

"Yeah, but what use is a howling idiot?"

"I don't know. I don't know what purpose *It* serves or will serve; only Sabrina knows that – and maybe not even Sabrina knows." Sally shrugged; the whole thing was terribly discouraging. This research program probably led nowhere; besides, it was cruel.

The girl smashed herself against the barrier again and then retreated to a corner of the cage and sat down and sucked her thumb. Drool and saliva dribbled from the corner of her mouth.

On the far side of the cage a 140-inch flat computer screen, built into the flexible wall and immune to the creature's temper tantrums, showed a news channel, then flicked to a multiple screen with, on one screen, a mathematics seminar on advanced differential equations, on another screen, a lesson on stochastic or random processes in mathematical modeling, on a third screen, a nature program on mating rituals among baboons, on a fourth screen a TV drama series, and on the fifth screen, a news broadcast in Russian.

In the girl's ice-blue eyes, the multiple screens reflected blindly.

"How does it do that?" Jack Yong was staring at the monitor that tracked what the girl watched on her giant screen, "I mean, how does *she* do it? – I mean, how does '*it*'" – how does *it* change channels like that?"

"She exercises mind control of some kind, apparently," Sally stared at the girl, "She controls the computer streaming and the computer programs by thinking – just by thinking."

"Yeah, but the psychologists say she has virtually no mental abilities at all – what do they say, 'no higher cognitive functions'? So how does she do it? And what is she getting out of all that streaming?"

"Patterns, colors, patterns, I guess." Sally sighed, "At least that's what Doctor Starr and his committee of experts said."

The girl was crouched in the corner of the cage, her eyes wide open, staring, or seeming to stare, as if rapt, at the screens.

It was too bad, Sally thought, that a unique experiment in cloning, absolutely unique, had gone so wrong. They had created a monster, well, less than a monster, a freak. It was infuriating! *If only I could communicate with her, talk to her.*

The cage was still furnished with a large bookshelf – full of books in a variety of languages (it was strange, but the girl had not destroyed the books) and with a large wardrobe. Sabrina had insisted. "In case she becomes human, part human, again, then she will have lots of choices. I know she likes to look good."

"Well, good luck," said Jack Yong, and he left the laboratory.

The problem is, thought Sally, the kid has no mind, not a human mind at any rate. Sally sipped her coffee and stared at the girl.

The girl had closed her eyes now and was sitting back, leaning against a cushioned section of the wall.

Sally gazed at her. The Clone was beautiful, really, and perfect skin, perfect features, an athlete's body, the body of a sublimely beautiful 14-year-old girl. Up until the age six, she had been perfect – an ultra-fast learner. Her name, then, was Claire. She spoke and read and wrote five languages when she was four-and-a-half, and she could do college math. Sabrina had been so proud. *I feel like her mother,* she had said, *I really feel like her mother.*

Then, close to her sixth birthday, everything changed. The girl threw a super-tantrum, the tantrum of tantrums – she refused to talk, she threw her food at the walls, she threw her excrement at the walls. The bright, happy, trusting child they had known had disappeared.

She never came back.

Gone forever ...

Claire became *It*.

She was the only successful clone from the DNA material Andromeda Corporation had managed to obtain – to steal – from the mysterious V. It was DNA that was unique in the world, probably unique in the universe.

"Claire, it's time for breakfast," Sally spoke into the speaker.

The girl opened her eyes, sprang to her feet and walked – her walk was lithe and smooth and rhymed like that of a dancer – or perhaps a panther – across the cage to the tray that dispensed her breakfast – two eggs turned over light, bacon, fried potatoes, fried tomatoes, and one sausage. The utensils were plastic – plastic fork, plastic knife, and plastic spoon – so she wouldn't be able to use them as a weapon or to hurt herself – in case she ever tried.

Strangely, the girl had never attacked anybody. She would fight only if they were forcing her to do something she didn't want to do – and she had never attempted to harm herself. When the girl fought, Sally suspected she was holding back, not using her real strength.

And the girl dressed very carefully; usually in jeans and a T-shirt.

Today she was dressed in white ballerina tights.

The girl took the breakfast tray and sat at a small table. She had become a careful eater, strangely for a creature without a mind – or, more accurately, with the mind of an animal.

The giant TV screen shifted to a two-screen split. One side was a National Geographic show on the nature of volcanoes on Mars. On the other was a text display, a book: what was the book? Sally checked: *Great Expectations* by Charles Dickens.

Where the heck does she dig that stuff up? I mean, why volcanoes on Mars? Why Charles Dickens?

Random stimulus, random results, thought Sally, repeating the conclusions reached by the clinical psychologist Rudolf Starr. But, Sally frowned, suddenly, silently, objecting: I don't think so. I really don't think so.

And no mental activity, there were no organized patterns in her head, just pure random chaos – was that the result of various scans they had done – when the kid let them perform scans, which was rarely.

Sally frowned and looked down at her notes: Well, it's not exactly true that there is no mental activity, there is, in fact, too much activity, it's a scrambled mess, every time they checked it was a super-charged chaos of activity with no pattern.

The girl was cutting the eggs carefully, her eyes flicking every half second up to the screen. The pages of Dickens were flashing past, probably a page a second, maybe a bit slower.

Up to age five, the girl's mental patterns had been perfect for a tiny humanoid female genius. Then came chaos, pure chaos

Sabrina had wanted twenty-four-hour continual surveillance by cerebral implants. Installed in the child's brain, the implants would monitor Claire's mental progress 24/7, but the child's body rejected the implants, literally spitting them out – the wounds closing up within seconds as if there had been nothing there.

So they had given up continuous monitoring.

The girl – *It* – would grow, and then they would see what she would become. She was to have been the model, the prototype, for a whole generation of new humans, possibly of warriors, possibly of drinkers of blood, though Sabrina had tried to engineer the blood-drinking out of the girl's system; the girl would have been the mother of a race of superwomen, and if they could engineer it, of supermen – the grandchildren of the vampire, V.

Through Claire, Sabrina had hoped, the human race would transcend itself, escape from its limits.

Claire would be a new Eve – and from her would be born a new race. Claire would be the Gateway to Perfection.

"If we create them, Claire and clones of Claire, they'll make us obsolete," Henry Rothschild had argued, and Sally remembered sitting in on the discussion in the boardroom on *Andromeda*, "They will be smarter than we are, they will be stronger, they will be immune to almost every disease, they will live longer than we do – in fact, potentially, they will be immortal. Sabrina, you are setting humanity up for extinction. At least until we merge with them."

"We lobotomize them," Sabrina had answered (to Sally's horror), "We lobotomize them; we turn them into obedient robots."

"So it's a return to slavery, is it?" Henry had answered.

"No, Henry, it's not a return to slavery," Sabrina answered, "These creatures will not be human. They will have no rights. Legally, they don't exist. They are tools, bio-machines, not people."

"But this particular experiment is a failure," Sally had said. "The girl – I mean 'It' – I mean *Claire*," she added defiantly, "cannot be used for any coherent purpose."

"So we start again!" Sabrina tapped on the table. "We start from the beginning. We start from V. We find V, this mysterious V. And we use V to build up the DNA bank from scratch – to see where we – to see where I – to see where I went wrong."

That had been six months ago.

Then, recently, they had sprung a trap and captured V; but – or so the rumor in Andromeda Corporation went – V had escaped and had killed several Andromeda Corporation employees. Nobody was talking, no details were available.

This was all hush-hush. Sally did know that her friend and colleague Toni Anderson had disappeared, killed in a plane crash they said, and that both Henry and Sabrina had seemed gloomy the last two weeks. Henry, in particular, had aged ten years.

Sally watched the girl. Few people dared use her name: "Claire." Sally, who was one of Sabrina's favorites, was one of the few who did occasionally dare use the name.

Claire ate delicately, but her eyes were now focused on the screen. *Great Expectations* was over – or finished. It had been replaced by what looked like a geology textbook; Sally checked: Yes, it was all about mineral structures, quartz, feldspar, silicates.

The pages flashed back.

Sometimes, but rarely, the pages whipped back, then went forward again.

Sally frowned. Does that mean she missed something, and she's going back to check?

The girl finished breakfast. She tapped her mouth with the paper napkin. She stood up and carried the tray to the slot, put the tray on the platform, and then went back and sat down, facing the screen. Sally kept one eye on Claire and one eye on the monitors: and then she noticed it: When Claire moved toward the tray slot and back, the screens slowed down, the pages of the geology textbook turned more slowly.

Pages turning more slowly …

Then speeding up again …

My God, thought Sally, it's so obvious: she's actually reading those books; it's not just visual patterns and the distraction of movement. *She's disguising her intelligence.* She's playing games with us. She's deliberately scrambling her mental signals. She understands everything! Shit!

Is it possible?

At that moment, the girl did something she never did. She looked outside the cage, through the glass – and directly at a person. She looked directly at Sally, in fact, she stared at Sally as if surprised by something, and she then flashed a glorious smile. Sally had never seen the girl smile. The girl winked, and then, even more extraordinary, she put her index finger up to her lips: the signal was clear: "*Don't tell anybody!*"

Then she turned her attention back to the screen.

It was like a lightning bolt!

Sally sat absolutely still, in shock. She glanced at the monitors. The cameras were set at angles, and moved back and forth, and it was clear they had not captured the smile and the wink. Sally glanced at Tony Brant, one of her research assistants. He was reading a scientific magazine. He had not seen anything.

"So," thought Sally, "I'll keep your secret."

The girl turned briefly, looked straight through the glass at Sally, smiled, gave a thumbs-up, and went back to watching the screen.

Sally sat numb for about five minutes, trying to keep her mind blank. Then she said to Tony. "I'm going up on deck for a bit of fresh air. You okay down here alone for ten minutes?"

"Sure," Tony smiled and yawned. "I'm okay down here. Nothing ever happens down here in any case."

Sally went up onto the deck of *Andromeda*. A warm breeze was blowing. The ocean was calm as the ship headed on a steady course toward the Philippines. *Darwin-IV*, the British frigate that almost always accompanied *Andromeda*, was slightly behind, maybe half a mile away.

Sally took a deep breath, tilted her face up to the sun, closed her eyes, and breathed in the wonderful ocean air. So – Claire reads thoughts; she is intelligent, almost certainly a genius, probably far beyond any human genius; and she can hide her abilities for … for years at a time … And, unless she's just playing games and bluffing, it seems she can read and absorb information much faster than any human being who has ever lived.

She's a goddess with god-like powers!

My God! What will happen when she grows up, when her vampire nature awakes – when she undergoes the "change"? My God!

Thumbs-up …

Sabrina Jacobs had had a similar insight, just after Sally made her discovery – the evening of that very same day, two weeks ago.

Sabrina had gone to a meeting with some officials in Hawaii, and her helicopter had returned to *Andromeda* just before dusk. She made a quick visit to the laboratory and glanced at the glass cage. The Clone was sitting cross-legged in a corner, eating supper and watching the multi-screen television. She totally ignored Sabrina's presence even when Sabrina went to the monitor and pushed the button, and said, "Hello Claire. How are you?"

No response.

So, everything seemed normal.

"I see you call her Claire," said Sally, who looked up from her files and who, it seemed, was working late on something.

"Yes, I do, sometimes, Sally. Goodnight."

Sabrina returned to her stateroom. She went over the reports for the day; then, she undressed and took a long shower. She closed her eyes and let the hot water pour over her as she scrubbed and then sponged herself down, and she thought, as she so often did, of the Clone, of Claire, of the failed experiment.

The girl was now fourteen years old, tall for her age, and, like her prototype, extremely beautiful, but, due to a genetic modification Sabrina had introduced, Claire had blue eyes and blond hair – the opposite of her DNA prototype, the vampire, V. In her Plexiglas ultra-secure cage – Claire was probably watching video streams or sleeping or exercising – things she seemed to do automatically, without any sign of intelligence or consciousness.

Eight years ago, something had gone terribly wrong. The child – the only successful clone of its genetic material out of more than 500 attempts – had been bright and ultra-precocious up to that moment. She was six years old.

And, up to that moment, Sabrina had been like a mother, a distant mother, but they did play together, and the child would leap into her arms and kiss her.

Then it all changed. The girl became a wild beast. Her violence was uncontrollable. She refused to talk – or she lost the ability to talk – it was unclear which – she threw her food around and sometimes smeared the walls with her excrement.

Then she calmed down. But she remained mute, and distant, never looking anyone in the eye, never speaking.

She exercised.

She ate her meals.

She kept her glass cage home scrupulously clean.

She watched videos – streaming on a giant computer constantly, capturing material from all over the world, and it was clear she could control the programming by her mind. She speeded up the screening, so it went at speeds much too fast for human comprehension, images flashing past, and the sounds reduced to a high-pitched whining stream of garble.

"She's just watching patterns," the psychologists said, "She doesn't understand what she's watching; besides, the brain scans, when she lets us do them – often she violently resists – show a chaos of brain waves, no higher organization, and no higher conceptual activity at all."

"But she cleans her room. She eats and uses a knife and fork! She exercises."

"Yes," said the psychologists, "but those are things she learned to do before she regressed. They are instinctual patterns, residues of earlier learning."

"I don't know," Sabrina had said. She was bitterly disappointed – the only successful clone of a half-alien, half-human creature, the opening of a whole new world, and it had ended in failure, in a dead-end.

The Board of Directors of Andromeda Corporation had wanted to "terminate" the experiment – to kill the child – but Sabrina, who held a majority of voting shares and who was supported by Henry, vetoed the idea, though to avoid an open split she had had to allude to "weaponizing" the Clone, of the possibility of creating a race of lobotomized warriors and slaves – some investors liked such talk.

Sabrina finished her shower and sat down at her desk. Out of idle curiosity and perhaps out of a feeling of frustrated love – if you could call it love – she ran a fast-forward replay of the day's events in Claire's cage. Then something suddenly caught her eye. *A thumbs-up? Claire giving a thumbs-up?*

Sabrina stopped the stream and ordered a replay.

She ordered the stream to freeze.

She couldn't see Claire's face, but it was definitely a thumbs-up.

Claire never communicated with anybody. A thumbs-up meant a measure of mutual understanding, of previous communication; it meant playfulness, intelligence, even mastery.

Who was she communicating with? Who was Claire looking at when she gave the thumbs-up?

Sabrina went down to the lab. Claire was asleep, or seemed to be asleep. Sabrina signaled to the night-watch not to make a sound and, without revealing what she was doing – she pretended she was looking for a document – she worked out the line of sight of the thumbs-up.

It was Sally Blake's work station: that was the aim of the thumbs-up. So, unless somebody else had been sitting in Sally's place or standing behind the chair, Claire had been communicating, in a very human way, with Sally Blake.

Sally was a developmental psychologist. She had been with Andromeda Corporation for three years. She had started to monitor Claire's video streaming three weeks ago.

If Claire used a thumbs-up, she was agreeing with Sally or congratulating Sally on something.

What did that mean about Claire's intelligence – and about the video-audio-streaming?

The theory held by the guy who preceded Sally, and by all the other experts, was that the video streaming was nonsense: it was just an animal's delight in fast-moving colors and sounds, very fast-moving, beyond human comprehension, and therefore, so the psychologists thought, nonsense.

Sabrina decided to investigate starting afresh. She would talk to Sally, but first, she wanted to do a little sleuthing of her own.

An idea had come to her. She had a new theory, or a hypothesis as they say in science, and she wanted to test it. She called one of her assistants and asked him to compile a registry of all the video streaming watched by Claire in the last five years. She asked the assistant to catalog the streaming items by categories – nature shows, mathematics, physics, chemistry, history. Sabrina suspected there was a pattern, and she wanted to know what it was.

"Put them in chronological order and by level of difficulty for each subject if you can, from basic studies, through intermediate, to advanced. And, this is essential, absolutely essential: I don't want you to talk to anybody about this, and I mean not to anybody – not even Sally. And don't ever go near the laboratory. Stay away from the laboratory. Work in the Archives. Pain of death! Understand?"

"Right," the assistant said; he was a very serious young man; Sabrina could almost hear him clicking his heels.

Sabrina went back to bed, but she couldn't sleep. There was another mystery: if Claire was intelligent, if she really was communicating and studying, then why had she gone "crazy" at age six – and *why, now, was she hiding her true nature?*

Sabrina pondered. She tossed and turned; she lay on her side, and stared at the reflected light of the moon entering through the large porthole window.

What had happened to Clair at age six that had made her regress suddenly, absolutely? They had always looked for the solution *inside* Claire – They'd always looked for a neurological or psychological or genetic problem.

But what if the answer was *outside* Claire? What if it was something that happened? Sabrina opened her eyes wide: *What if it was something I did?*

Sabrina felt a cold sweat of horror – and overwhelming guilt.

What if it was something I did?

She got out of bed, slipped on shorts and a T-shirt, and sat down at her computer. She accessed her diary and the ship's diary. She went back to the year, to the month, to the day the change had come upon Claire – turning her into an "idiot."

The date was engraved in Sabrina's memory.

What had happened that day? Nothing, in particular, had happened – except that Claire, from the morning on, acted like a wild thing. So whatever had happened, the triggering event, had either happened during the night or the day before.

So, what about the day before?

Sabrina frowned and concentrated, consulting the diary: Let's see: I was giving a top-secret tour to some leading investors in one of Andromeda Corporation's subsidiaries. I showed them Claire in her transparent little house. Claire was reading a book, but she smiled and looked up and waved at me, and I waved back.

Sabrina closed her eyes and went back in her mind to that day.

Yes, yes! I remember: then, a few moments later, one investor asked me what use the child was – in industrial and military terms. "I mean, it's a unique genetic entity, isn't it?" He was a venture capitalist from Brazil, a deep tan and a cynical and slick manner and lots of money. "What money is this creature going to generate? What's the revenue stream?"

I was annoyed – yes, I was annoyed by the question – but I also wanted to show off, to show the guy I was as cynical and hard-headed as he was, even more than he was (my macho side showing through – the part of me that wanted – that wants – to be a boxer), so I said something like, "We foresee contracts with national defense, Homeland Security, and with some of the leading private security firms and private military companies. We can harvest it for genetic material, and we can experiment on it to see its strengths and weaknesses, and, of course, it is the prototype for a whole generation of future genetically modified warriors – of course, the personality and decision-making power, or free-will, will have to be eliminated."

"Such a creature would have to be lobotomized, in effect," said the Brazilian.

"Yes, that's right."

We were not within hearing range of Claire. We were not in her visual field. She couldn't see us. But could it be that Claire somehow captured what I said? Could it be that she had *understood* what I said?

Sabrina brought up the video recordings of the tour – the insurance companies insisted that all visits and all events be scrupulously recorded and that all the records kept, virtually forever. *Andromeda* even uploaded every day's material – all material – to a satellite and to several separate highly secure storage facilities twice every day, in case something, God forbid, should happen to the ship.

Sabrina followed the visit from beginning to end. She could see exactly where she was – when she made those atrocious statements. She brought up the audio, and she listened to herself saying those atrocious words. "*We lobotomize it.*"

Sabrina sat very still, in shock. *What an idiot I am!*

But – Claire could not see me when I said those things. And, no, not even with ultra-sensitive hearing could Claire have heard me – no sound waves whatsoever made it into the Plexiglas housing; it was triple sound-proofed.

Was it possible? Could Clair read thoughts?

Was it possible that she could read the thoughts of people out of visual and audio range? How far did her thought-reading power reach?

Sabrina sat back in the chair. If her hunch was right, this was horrible! Claire, who was extraordinarily precocious, had understood that she was going to be treated like an animal, like a thing, that she was going to be tortured perhaps, reduced to robot status, used and abused like a thing – a lobotomized robot.

That had not been Sabrina's intention, and it never had been: her idea was that the bio-warriors would be designed from the beginning without a "soul" without independent free-will or decision-making capacity. She wasn't even sure she wanted to make the damned bio-warriors! The defense angle was essentially a way to ensure that she got funding for basic research – the basic research that was designed to create a new type of human being, to allow humanity to transcend itself.

Claire, depending on how violent and thirsty her "vampire" side was, and what would be needed to satisfy it, would be allowed – indeed encouraged – to live her life.

Claire is the child I never had.

Claire *is* my child!

Sabrina didn't sleep that night. She lay in bed, with the bedside light on, staring at the ceiling. She thought of calling Aimi, but she knew Aimi was working on an article, and she didn't want to disturb her. Aimi tended to go on coffee jags and not sleep for two or three nights when she was finishing an article or a part of her Ph.D. Finally, Sabrina watched a movie, and then toward six in the morning, sprawled stomach down on top of the covers, she fell asleep.

A week later, Sabrina had the results. Mixed in with a great deal of video entertainment, were educational video-audio streams, courses from MIT, Oxford, the University of Shanghai, the University of Heidelberg, the Sorbonne, Moscow University, Barcelona, and so on, plus independent educational material from a host of private sources and private schools, think tanks and institutes of every description.

The material was *not* random.

There was a definite logic.

The video streams would treat, say, the basics of a subject, and then would be interrupted by an entertainment or travel program or a video stream on a totally unrelated subject. But the next video stream on the subject would be consequent, in the logic of learning at least, building upon the previous videos in the same subject, or would explore an aspect of that subject, or a byway, sometimes an arcane side alley, picking up a reference, or exploring some concept or idea that was perhaps not clear.

My God!

The little rascal!

She was educating herself, and she was disguising the fact by throwing up "static."

And she can absorb and understand information at least 100 times faster than any human being, probably thousands of times faster.

Sabrina sat at her desk thunderstruck: Claire wants us to think that she is an idiot, an animal; she wants us to think that the experiment is a failure; that she is useless, so that … so that she won't be exploited … because she's not worth exploiting …

Let's see: in the last few days, this "animal," this "thing," this "alien," this 14-year-old girl, had been studying, in an ultra-high-speed manner, let's see …

Florentine Art in the 15th Century …

String theory and cosmology …

Advanced economic equilibrium theory …

The history of sport in Ancient Greece …

The Zoroastrian religion of Ancient Persia … and the roots of Monotheism …

Sabrina went back further – years before; she flipped through the archives: mathematics, lots of mathematics, okay, mathematics are fundamental if you are going to understand the sciences. So, had Claire educated herself in mathematics?

And, of course, the answer was – *Yes!* Claire had studied mathematics from the ground up; she'd done arithmetic, set theory, symbolic logic, number theory. Algebra, trigonometry, geometry, pre-calculus, calculus. She'd zoomed through everything and then gone back, occasionally, for refreshers. Sabrina did a quick check – if, say, there was a problem in physics, that needed a special type or branch of mathematics, then, sure enough, soon after the problem popped up, at least half the time Claire went back for a refresher.

How did she even know *what* to study?

My God! And we thought she was an idiot!

No, she's not an idiot – she's an *alien*. And, in human terms, she's a *genius!* *No, more than a genius, beyond genius …*

Sabrina stared at her desk. She shifted a few pencils around. And she had another thought: What about the "entertainment" video streams, the "static" or "noise" that blinded the experts and blinded me too to the continuities and logic in the "educational" streams? *How stupid I have been!* Sabrina banged her fist on the table.

She checked the catalog of entertainment video streams, and the order in which they had been viewed.

Bingo!

Claire had done her studying – the "entertainment" videos – in checker-board fashion; but it was clear: she was building up a systematic knowledge of culture, of human culture – of the history of cinema, for example, or opera, or music, or warfare, or weapons technology, of Sumo wrestling, of Japanese flower arrangements, of shipbuilding, of bridge-building, of Chinese literature, of the histories of the wars and politics of the nineteenth, twentieth, and twenty-first centuries, she explored epics, romances, best sellers in half a dozen languages ... TV serials ...

Sabrina took a deep breath. And Sally knows this. Sally must know this. I have to talk to Sally. And I have to regain Claire's trust – but how?

And Claire can control computers by thinking ... and she can read minds, or so it seems. Jesus Christ! She's probably hacked into our computer systems – she's probably read my bloody emails! She's probably just as familiar with the research we are doing on *Andromeda* as I am! And she is half-human, half-alien.

Half alien ...

It occurred to Sabrina that Claire might not only be absorbing knowledge – she might be transmitting knowledge too ... but where and to whom ...?

Was such a thing possible?

A living encyclopedia of what the human race had created and done ...

Being transmitted elsewhere?

To whom?

And – why?

Two days after this discovery, Sabrina screwed up her courage and decided to talk to Sally Blake about Claire.

Sabrina went out on deck. By now, they were in the Sulu Sea, and the nearby islands lay low on the flat, glass-like water. It was absolutely calm, and the sky was a sleepy faded blue. It was exquisitely beautiful, all of it.

Sabrina was suddenly flooded with happiness. The research vessel *Andromeda* was a thing of beauty. All who saw her agreed with that – elegant lines, powerful engines, a model of the best in human design and ingenuity. And, now, *Andromeda* was where it belonged, anchored in deep water just off a reef in a southern part of the Philippine Archipelago – close to Paradise Island.

Paradise …

Sabrina put her hands on the railing and leaned forward, breathing in the glories of pure sensation, the smell of the air, the gradation of colors, the calm, the flat distant hazy horizon, and the gentle, rhythmic sounds. A flock of birds flew low over the water – pelicans. She adored their elegant clumsiness – what a marvel of evolutionary design!

She wished she could have Claire up here, beside her.

She wished she could grant Claire her freedom.

She wished …

"You wished to see me, Sabrina?"

"Oh, yes! Hi, Sally. Yes. Isn't it beautiful … so beautiful."

"Yes, it is. The quiet that precedes the storm, I guess."

Sabrina turned to look at the young woman. Sally was a pretty, 32-year-old, open-faced blonde, wearing a white shirt, jeans, and sneakers. She was athletic, a great ping-pong player, and had an open sunny disposition, unlike so many psychologists, and unlike the gloomy arrogant Doctor Starr, who had preceded her, and who treated Claire as if she were a particularly stupid rat caught in a rather simple maze. Sometimes, Sabrina sighed, we don't want to see what is in front of us, and I have been the stupidest and most criminal of all.

"Yes, you are right," said Sabrina, turning to look up at the rotating radar above the ship's bridge. "The typhoon! But it's not supposed to get here, I think, for two days."

"Nature sometimes springs surprises," said Sally with that open disarming and slightly wry grin that had caused half the crew of the ship – and not only the guys – to fall in love with her.

Sabrina leaned back against the railing and gave Sally a big smile in return. "Sally, I think you and I have made a similar discovery about Claire – I may be wrong."

Sally's smile faltered only slightly: keeping a secret from the boss – particularly this boss – was not good politics. "Go on …"

"I understand you don't want to betray Claire. I think she has confidence in you. Alas, she's lost all confidence – rightly, from her point of view – in me."

Sally nodded and then added. "I like Claire. I like her very much."

Sabrina didn't say anything for a moment. She turned away and leaned on the rail and looked away at the horizon. She wiped her eyes and took a deep breath, still staring at the horizon. "Okay, what I think I've discovered is this: Claire is extraordinarily intelligent and totally sane."

"Yes, I think that's right."

"And she's been hiding this from us. In the beginning, her 'madness' may have been a result of anger, of fear, of shock, of disappointment – it was because of something I said, something I did – but then it became an act, camouflage. She is hiding her intelligence, her delicacy, even."

"Yes, I think that's right too. She's afraid."

Sabrina turned to face Sally. "Yes, she's afraid of me, mostly. I think she's afraid of me."

"Yes," Sally said quietly, "She's afraid of you."

"I was just thinking that it would be wonderful to have her up here, with us, as one of us. She's never seen the outside world. She's always lived in a lab. She's never, not once, been outside. She's never breathed air like this."

"She's been educating herself."

"Yes, I know."

Sally took a deep breath. "She's been brilliant at hiding. She's been all alone. No one to confide in, no one to talk to, no one to share with. To think of the courage, the tenacity!"

"Yes, superhuman."

"Superhuman," said Sally, "and, let's admit it: *non-human.*"

Sabrina ran her fingers through her hair. The admission that she had failed in one of her great "experiments" wounded her to the quick. She was furious at herself for inflicting so much pain on a creature who was – whatever else she was – a mere child. "Sally, I think I want you, if you are willing, to try to talk to her more, communicate with her. I would frighten her; she hates me and fears me. Maybe soon, we can have her up on deck with us. Maybe we can, in a sense, set her free."

"Yes, I'm willing. I'll try." Sally hesitated; she was, after all, talking to one of the richest and most powerful, and most brilliant, persons on the planet. "You know the risks – she is, after all, half-alien – and we don't know what race of alien that is. If she gets out, into the world? And if her DNA gets out – into the world?"

"Yes, you are right. We have no idea, really, of what she can do – of what potential powers and abilities she possesses – she probably doesn't know herself – and we don't know what potential dangers she poses for us, mere humans, and she probably isn't totally aware of those dangers either."

"And one thing," Sally touched Sabrina on the arm, "I'll have to be absolutely up-front with Claire about what we've discussed, I'll have to be absolutely honest with her because –"

"… because she can read thoughts. Yes, I know." Sabrina laid her hand on Sally's hand. "Be completely honest – then Claire will do with us what she will."

CHAPTER 19 – I HATE HUMANS

Be patient, be patient!

I don't want to be patient! To hell with being patient!

In her glass house, suspended on its platform in the middle of the midship lab, Claire paced back and forth. She knew very well she was on a ship, *Andromeda*. She knew the ship was near an island in the Sulu Sea, in the Philippine Archipelago, a scattering of islands. She could reel off in her head thousands of facts about the Philippines and the Pacific and the Sulu Sea and *Andromeda* itself.

She knew all these things, but she longed to taste and to feel them and to smell and to touch them.

She had never been outside; when she was transferred from the ship to the shore or from one facility to another, it was always done with her inside an armored container. The containers were comfortable, like little rooms, with games and books and monitors, but once or twice, she had caught a whiff of smells and heady bouquet of ozone and frying onions and grilled meats. Then the doors slid shut, and the air was once again purified, odorless.

Her nostrils quivered as she pressed her hands against the foot-thick armored glass. Not too hard, she warned herself, not too hard – *You might break it.*

I have never been outside.

Her strength and appetites were growing day by day. I am fourteen, she thought, I'm tall for my age, tall for my human age, and I've just entered puberty.

What happens now?

Using her mind and not a keyboard, she had hacked into the computer systems of *Andromeda*. She had accessed her own files, the files on the experiment of which she was the result, the files on the mysterious "V" from which her DNA came, and so she knew a great deal about herself, about her history; but it was all abstract, all theory, and she had absolutely no idea *what* would happen to her or *when* it would happen to her. It was terrifying.

I still eat human food, she thought. What if I change, what if, suddenly I need to feed on blood, on human blood?

What if I truly go mad?

She had learned many things. She discovered her powers by trial and error, by trying things out. And her powers, she discovered, were increasing day by day. She stopped pacing and pressed her hands against the foot-thick armored glass. "I'm a time bomb. I'm a time bomb, ticking, ticking, ticking, and I'm going to go off."

And I don't know what to do!

She was learning new things every day – seizing and absorbing information through video streaming and audio streaming, doing research through the Net, accessing libraries, and texts from all over the world. Her desire to learn and to know was ferocious; and she didn't know *why* – but it was, with exercise, her one remaining source of joy. This morning she had studied the structure of two Beethoven sonatas and compared them to the works of Haydn and Mozart, as well as working on some problems of cosmology that she still found rather puzzling.

She had learned to work and control the computers merely by thinking. Then, following the electrical connections, she had penetrated the control and communications systems of *Andromeda*. It was as if *Andromeda* had become an extension of her own nervous system, of her brain.

She knew its navigational codes, she knew, if she cared to follow that particular stream, when the captain was giving orders to the engine room, when he touched the controls, port, starboard, faster, slower, revolutions per minute, etc.

She knew – from the way they communicated – the personalities of many of the people on board; of Duncan, the captain, of Ian, the chief engineer, of Henry Rothschild, of Sabrina (of course, of Sabrina!), of Sally, of Aimi, the beautiful Japanese friend of Sabrina's.

But she'd never talked to any of these people

She'd never been on deck. She'd never been in the bridge. She'd never been in the marine laboratories or the radio and chartrooms. She had never been in the crew's quarters or the scientists' quarters.

She'd never been in Sabrina's stateroom though she'd overheard thoughts about it, and she had pictures in her mind of what it looked like: a large flat ultra-modern bed with very white sheets, cupboards flush with the white walls, and containing a vast selection of clothes.

She imagined herself combing Sabrina's hair, she imagined herself playing chess with Sabrina, she imagined herself giving Sabrina a massage, she imagined herself helping Sabrina choose her clothes for the day or for the night. *Here, Sabrina, try this. I think these shoes are divine, don't you? Yes, Claire, you have such wonderful taste, Claire, you are ...* Claire had many secrets, and one was that she adored *clothes*: if she had been human, one career she would have loved, for a month or two, would have been as a model, and then as a designer of *clothes* and *shoes*. She knew she would look great on a runway. She would design very extravagant and very sober dresses, pantsuits, jackets, nightgowns, catsuits, evening robes; she would explore the depths of psychology by decking out her models in revealing yet deeply symbolic dresses, she would explore and express people's most secret inner desires, she would exploit the newest technologies in textiles, and she would ... She could see the flashbulbs flashing, she could see herself giving an interview in a dressing room in Paris, she could see ...

It's all a dream: I am not human, not fully human; I am something different – I am *alien*.

She had watched the ancient Alien movies with woeful fascination. That is me, she thought, *that is me*, when the drooling monster appeared, when the baby monster burst out of the man's stomach, when the jaws opened and closed and ... *That is me!*

I hate humans – hate, hate, hate, hate ...

No, that's not true; I don't hate humans.

She was now pressing so tight against the glass that a red light went on in the control room, and a buzzer sounded in the monitoring center.

Claire stopped pressing on the glass and stepped away. There was a full-length stainless steel mirror in her room. She looked at herself in the mirror.

She did a quick pirouette.

She *loved* to move with *grace*. She again glanced at herself. One day, I shall be the prima ballerina in the Bolshoi Ballet or perhaps Covent Garden! She cast a carefully critical and appraising eye on the image in the mirror, on the leg held up, the toes pointing down, the heel levered up. I look human. I still look human. I am fourteen years old, damn it!

There was one human she wanted to talk to and confide in, one human who would, perhaps, just perhaps, understand, and that human was a cold, distant, beautiful creature, that human was her greatest enemy and the object of her most desperate love and most intense hate; that human was her jailer – *Sabrina*.

I want her love. But she fears me and hates me and wants to use me and destroy me. For her, I am a *"thing,"* an *"it."* I am a dangerous virus, a plague that, if released, could destroy everything ... And, yet, before, she was like my mother, and then ...

Claire sat on the floor and looked down. *I want to kill myself.* Maybe I should just stop eating. But then they would try to force-feed me, and I'd have to accept the force-feeding or reveal the truth, the dangerous truth – my strength: I could kill them all.

... kill them all ...

... Sabrina suspects something ...

... She will ask Sally ...

... Sally will feel duty-bound to ... talk ...

... then Sabrina will know ... and ...

... will kill me or turn me into a robot.

... kill them all, kill them all, and escape ...

... but where do I escape to?

... I've never been outside ...

... I don't know anybody outside.

... Kill them all, all the humans, even the ones I love, especially the ones I love.

She frowned and stood up, did a ballerina's pirouette, on tiptoes, closed her eyes, thinking: I might as well let them see my "human side." Sally already knows, Sabrina suspects and is investigating what I've been studying, and she'll soon figure it out, if she hasn't already. And, in any case, the others are about to discover it.

She closed her eyes, and danced slowly around her glass prison cell and called up in her mind Franz Schubert's *"Death and the Maiden"* and played it through, in her mind, using as her model a 2022 performance by the Shanghai Schubert Quartet she had listened to three weeks ago. The other thing I'd love to do, she thought, as she twirled on tiptoes, arms outstretched, and played the quartet in her mind, is this: I'd love to chew gum, bubble gum, wear a baseball cap, and play baseball, just one sunny afternoon, someplace, and hear all the people up in the bleachers, rise up and cheer and scream and yell my name when I hit a home run!

One of Sally's assistants, Karl Ambrose, a 25-year-old Ph.D. candidate from Chicago, who was on duty in the monitoring room, looked up from the genetics research paper he was reading and saw, through the glass of Claire's cage and on the control monitor screens, the girl dancing, in her white ballerina's costume, as she turned once, twice, a third time, flawlessly, and he had an involuntary thought: *God, she's beautiful, she's really fucking beautiful.* He made a quick note – "*Sally, this kid has talent and grace; she can't be all crazy. Check out the videos at today's time code 13:12:02 – New Series.*"

And yet ...

Kill all the humans.

Kill, kill, kill ...

Two images flashed in her mind, and they flashed with a mixture of anguish and hate and love. One was Sabrina, dressed in a crisp white shirt, with a small dark tie, a dark pleated skirt, black stockings, high heels, Sabrina running her hands through her hair – it was a typical gesture when she was self-conscious or nervous – and examining herself in a full-length mirror, and then turning to see Claire standing behind her, and realizing that Claire had escaped, that she was out, that she was free, and that she was going to kill Sabrina, and Sabrina gets down on her knees and begs for forgiveness, and begs for her life.

And there was the image, the shadowy image, of the mythical and mysterious V whom she had never met, V, who she sensed, she somehow sensed, was coming to kill her. *To kill me? Why? Why are you coming to kill me? Because I am you, and you are me.* That was the phrase that echoed in her mind. Because I am cloned from her, she wants to kill me. Why?

And there was another voice that came to her mind, occasionally, only very occasionally and as if from very far away. It was a man's voice, a sweet and understanding, and very masculine voice, and this man seemed to understand everything and be very friendly, and he never said much, just "How are you, Claire?" And "What are you studying today?" "Set theory? Oh, that's good, that's very good. What do you think of the inclusion principle? Yes, hmm, very interesting. And, Claire, do you think Sergio Leone's spaghetti westerns changed America's view of itself? What about nuclear fusion, Claire? That, I think, is a very interesting subject. You might want to look into it. Now the difference between Jesus Christ and Socrates has always intrigued me, Claire, what do you think about those two gentlemen?" And Claire answered him, and sometimes he told her jokes, or she joked with him – rather impertinent of her, she thought, since she was a child and he was undoubtedly an adult – but she had no idea who he was, or what he was, or where he was.

CHAPTER 20 – LOST AND LONELY LOVE

"Well, this certainly is an island paradise!" V peered out from behind some palm fronds at the beach where the ocean rolled in gently, just making a thin line of sparkling white foam at the edge of the sand.

Alex and Helen and V were lying on their stomachs, gazing out over the flat calm of the Sulu Sea of the southern Philippines, a sea containing some of the most beautiful coral reefs and islands in the world.

Out on the horizon, about four miles away, a graceful white ship floated on the waters – it was Andromeda Corporation's research vessel, *Andromeda*.

The computer files that V lifted from Sabrina Jacobs' apartment in Virginia indicated that Sabrina and the Clone were going to spend the next six months on *Andromeda*.

Andromeda was, for many purposes, the real corporate Headquarters of Sabrina and it was her residence for most of the year. It was clear too that she always kept the Clone close to her.

And V had learned that *Andromeda* would be dropping anchor off Paradise Island and remaining there for almost a month while Sabrina did underwater research.

"I'll bet they're just here to have a holiday," said Alex.

"Well, we can make it a holiday, too," said Helen.

Paradise Island was uninhabited and deserted except for an Andromeda Corp research installation full of instruments but which was locked tight, a sort of nondescript squat cement bunker, with some instruments on the roof.

Two days earlier, they had arrived on the far side of the island, brought by a helicopter that V had rented, claiming – and they had all the papers to prove it – that they were journalists doing a tourist "adventure travel" reportage and that they would camp on the island and would radio when they wanted to be picked up. If they didn't radio, they were to be picked up in four days.

They planned to stay even though the hurricane was predicted to arrive in less than two days.

"You are very foolhardy people," the helicopter pilot had said, as he prepared to take off.

"We'll do anything for a story," said Alex, shaking the guy's hand and jumping down from the helicopter, "See you in a day or two."

"Right," shouted the pilot, and the helicopter had taken off, keeping low to the water; since it was on the far side of the island, it was invisible to the radars of *Andromeda*.

"Look," said Helen, the frigate *Darwin IV* is leaving." She handed the binoculars to V.

"Yes," said Alex, "that's right on schedule. They were supposed to have a Philippines frigate, the *Ramon Alcaraz*, as a replacement to cover for the *Darwin*, but it's had engine trouble and has returned to base for repairs; at least that's what the material we've picked up says."

Alex was staring at the screen of his solar-powered computer: they had hacked into *Andromeda*'s communications systems and were following, real-time, developments on the ship and its communications with Andromeda Corp HQ.

"I don't like it." V peered through the binoculars. "It's fishy. They lose the *Darwin IV* for the first time, in what, two or three years, and, now, they've lost the Philippine replacement. And for some reason, the usual Chinese frigate is not available."

"Do you think it's a trap?"

"It might be. After the Avatar stirred up hell in Texas, and after we pulled our caper in Virginia, Sabrina knows I'm coming for her."

"So Sabrina's setting herself up as bait? She's making *Andromeda* look vulnerable on purpose?"

"I don't know, but something is going on. In any case, I'm going to go in and find out."

V, Helen, and Alex had set up camp just inside the tree line on the side of the island facing the Sulu Sea and facing *Andromeda*.

Their camp – a tent made of ultra-modern camouflage material – blended in totally with the forest greenery and was designed, chameleon-style, to adapt to the shifting light and to the changing color and texture conditions that surrounded it.

It was invisible unless you actually bumped into it, and it was powered by solar energy and by batteries and designed to give out almost no biological or heat signature.

Helen and V and Alex were also wearing light-absorbing chameleon camouflage suits and chameleon makeup that made them virtually undetectable. They blended perfectly with sand, with water, with reeds and bamboo and jungle foliage.

"Let's go for a swim," said V.

They cut through the jungle to a cove where they were invisible to *Andromeda*, took off their camouflage outfits, and they swam. After an hour swimming, they stepped out of the water, and Helen and Alex cooked and ate ready-made food – on the small solar-powered stove, and they all had coffee.

"Tonight, I'll go to *Andromeda*, and I'll case the joint, and then I'll do what I have to do."

"So, you really are going to kill Sabrina and the Clone?" Alex gazed at V, so elegant in her bikini, so seemingly human.

"Yes. I'll stay on board *Andromeda*, hidden, all day tomorrow to get a sense of the place, and of what they are doing, what experiments they are carrying out. Then, tomorrow night, just after sunset, that's when I'll kill Sabrina and the Clone. Right after that, I'll leave *Andromeda*. I may need you, Alex, to come and meet me, and if I do, I'll make the agreed signal."

"We'll be watching for it," said Helen. She put her hand on V's arm.

It was strange, now, to V, being with the two humans, Alex and Helen, and seeing them grow more and more fond of each other, and realizing that, however much she loved them, she was drifting farther away from them, becoming, with each passing day, more *alien*, more distant from their intimacy, which was clearly growing, day by day.

Well, she thought, that is what I have chosen, that is what I planned. I want them to be happy, and they are going to be happy with each other, I can see that already.

"I'm going for a walk," she said, picking up a cup of coffee.

"Do you want us to come?"

"No. I just have to think about things."

V walked down the beach. She stopped and looked at some fish swimming in clear shallow water; she waded in and looked down at the fish, slivers of silver running hither and thither. "Hi, little guys." She crouched down to watch them, to be close to them. Then she waded back to the shore, walked on a bit, looked down and kicked at the sand. *Damn it, damn it, damn it!*

She glanced back. Helen and Alex were laughing. Alex was laughing with his mouth full, and gesturing to Helen, who was making fun of him.

V's mind went back to the hours and days she and Alex had spent together, on the road, to the time they made love, to the laughter and teasing, and to the terrors and ecstasy, to the caresses and intimacy. It seemed long ago.

Well, this is the way I wanted it to be, this is the way it has to be. I am alien; I am dangerous; I must protect Alex and Helen from … from … yes, from me.

She sat down in the shallows, cross-legged, and let the warm water lap over her, up to her waist, and let the sand ebb and flow under her thighs, under her backside.

She drank the coffee, now grown cold, holding the cup close, like a friend, clasped in her hands.

The sea was a deep blue, then, farther out, a smoky blue, striated with cobalt and turquoise, and then, off toward the horizon, it grew pale and hazy, milky and calm, and the water merged, vaporous and white, with the sky.

What I would like to do, right now, is I would like to change into the demon, right here on the beach, change into the demon, all scaly and turquoise and blue and green and gold, with touches of scarlet, and I would like to make love to another demon, and just howl and scream and yodel and purr and meow and bark and hiss and laugh and cry and extend my claws and dig up the sand.

And maybe build a sandcastle.

She cupped some water in her hand, let it run though her fingers. V, you are an imbecile, a romantic fool, full of unslaked cravings and yearnings that are utterly ridiculous.

She sniffed the rich ocean air, lifted the cup of coffee, and took a deep swallow. I am an idiot. That delicious kill in Manila, where I fed oh so deeply, that kill has left me with a superabundance of energy, a superabundance of yearnings and desires. In short, I'm as horny as hell, I'm yearning for unity with another person, transcendence, escape from myself, total abandonment, like the very worst of the mystics. Oh, foolish me!

The fodder in Manila had been gratifying. She frowned. A school of minnows played around her toes, slivers of silver and gold, all flashing around in unison. Do minnows ever feel lonely?

Her meal in Manila was a very fat Chinese gentleman from Yunnan who specialized in child prostitution and had a chain of offices across South East Asia, in Europe, and South America, catering to sex tourists. V sighed in pleasure. Lao Zhang had been absolutely scrumptious. He wore red-and-black suspenders or braces, as the British would say, and a white, patterned shirt, open on his chest, with his white, neatly pressed linen trousers hitched up high, hanging on his ribcage, like somebody from a 1940s gangster movie, and he had a genial, paternal, and joking manner that was quite attractive. V felt a surge of affection for Lao Zhang as she sat in his office offering to deliver up to him a shipment of one hundred and forty-five Russian orphans, aged five to ten, girls and boys, to be used sexually, in bordellos in South America and Eastern Europe.

But then when he was about to drive her to his villa by the sea so that they could celebrate the deal over drinks she caught his thoughts – to wit, that she was a real babe, that though it was against his better judgment, which generally dictated that he avoid mixing business with pleasure, he was going to drug her and rape her and then if he needed to – if she objected strongly to the rape – he would kill her. While he was chatting pleasantly, he was envisaging, with a great deal of inner pleasure, just how he would rape her, and just how he would eliminate her. She caught the full vision: her body mutilated and then stuffed into a barrel of cement, and the barrel, once the cement had dried, being taken out in a fishing boat and dumped in 3,000 meters of water.

She decided he was not so avuncular.

Which made her task so much easier, so much more pleasant.

They were in his Mercedes with a driver and a guard in the front seat and the great man and V in the back seat. This was a delicate situation. If she killed Lao Zhang now, she would have to kill the driver and the guard. V usually tried to limit collateral damage.

So, she would wait until they got to the villa. It was isolated. It was on a beach. There was a dock with boats, a promising escape route. There was a separate villa, in the garden, for the man's trysts. It was a very luxurious compound, with lots of exotic plants; the perfumes, to V's super-sensitive sense of smell, were exquisite; her nostrils were twitching.

Lao Zhang led the way along a flagstone path through the bougainvillea, with little mushroom-shaped ground lights on either side, giving a flickering suffused light to the path and the undergrowth.

Here, wondered, V, here?

But then they were already at the private hideaway, an elegant bungalow. As they entered, V got a clearer vision, from the man's mind, of his plans, which, of course, were not terribly nice.

They entered. He put on music. He served the drinks. V said she would be more comfortable in the room next to the terrace – it gave onto the ocean, and there was a dock with a few boats tied up. She said, "We are alone, aren't we, I'm rather shy. I think I'm falling for you – I have a weakness for older, distinguished men – so I'm going to take off my clothes now."

"No hurry," he said.

"No, I insist. It's so warm: I'm feeling really hot."

"Hot? You are feeling hot?" Lao Zhang could not resist a smile.

When she could, V stripped before a kill. Being naked spared her wardrobe, made the clean-up afterward simpler, and the getaway faster.

"We are all alone," he said, "There is no one here but us."

V slipped out of her clothes, still not having taken a sip of the drink. She folded the clothes neatly on a deck chair while Lao Zhang, stout and paternal-looking, watched her – and she slipped out of her sandals and she said, "Well, here I am," and, holding the glass, she moved toward him as if to touch glasses and propose a toast, and then, within a foot of him she said, "I'll come from behind, turn around and I'll give you a surprise."

Lao Zhang was suspicious by nature, and ultra-cautious. But he was now under the spell of V's beauty and her nakedness – which seemed to make her vulnerable – and he knew now that to possess her, he would not have to rape her. So, thinking he was perhaps being foolish, he turned around.

V gave him her surprise.

Her claws ripped across his face, blinding him. Her fangs sank into his jugular and severed the commands of his nervous system – he couldn't speak, he couldn't scream, he was just barely able to breathe – just enough to know that something horrible was happening – and that it was happening to him.

Lao Zhang fell forward. She rode him down onto the Persian rug. Toppling down, the man almost knocked over a priceless green-and-gold Ming vase with a goldfish motif, but V, who had a great respect for art, steadied it with a quick scoop of her claw-like hand.

Lao Zhang was a big man. He contained a lot of blood; it was high-quality, healthy blood from a good life and many years of expensive eating and carousing.

While she was drinking, slurping away, with the stout sex merchant sprawled under her, his white shirt unbuttoned, and open on a hairless chest, a black cat entered the room and started to rub itself against her leg. It purred.

V looked up from her feast, her eyes aflame with excitement and soaring energy, her tingling fangs and mouth and tongue dripping blood, her shoulders and breasts glistening in a bright lacquer of thick delicious gore.

The cat blinked and again purred.

V replied, a deep-in-her-throat gurgling purr. She stared deep into the cat's amber-and-yellow eyes, and transmitted the thought, *Do you want some?* The cat meowed, arched its back, and began to lick at the pool of spilled blood.

Then, as V plunged back into the feast, the cat sidled up began to lick the back of V's leg, which was a ticklish and comfortingly intimate gesture. V growled: *We can share the feast.* The cat purred in delight and rubbed itself against V's thigh, slithering sensuously along, and stopped and licked up more blood.

V drank Lao Zhang dry – not a drop was left. She stood up and looked fondly down at the splendid red-and-black suspenders, now stained with blood. She was tempted to keep them as a souvenir. But that would be unwise, an indulgence.

Standing astride the emptied bloated body, she proclaimed, "You are dead, truly dead, and you will not rise again."

The cat was still licking up the small pools and extra splashes of blood.

V used Lao Zhang's shower to wash the blood away. And she rinsed her mouth and teeth with his toothpaste and mouthwash. When she came out of the bathroom, wrapped in a brightly-colored towel, the cat was still licking up the blood. It looked up at her, blinked, and meowed.

Wrapped in the bright festive towel, V sat down at Lao Zhang's silver-colored laptop that was perched, open and turned on, on a corner desk. Using the codes and account numbers she had absorbed while drinking his blood – she unlocked his business files – shipments and transfers of children and the accounts of various child bordellos – and a long list of sex tourist clients – and transferred them to various police authorities.

She also emptied one of his accounts of 4,453,000 American dollars, 3,587,000 euros, and 153 million yen, and transferred the funds, through a cascade of intermediaries and "empty boxes" to an account in Switzerland, from which she made a donation for 1,000,000 dollars to a charity that worked on freeing child prostitutes. She eliminated all trace of these transactions from the laptop, but then decided to take the laptop – a razor-thin Apple – with her. It was cute.

She dressed carefully, putting on her light jacket, short skirt, sandals; she said goodbye to the cat, holding it in her lap and stroking its back, and she picked up the man's computer, slipped it into her briefcase, and went down to the dock.

The cat insisted on walking with her, its tail held high.

"So it's not goodbye, then, not just yet," said V, and the cat meowed.

When she got to the dock V chose a sleek-looking motor launch; she untied the mooring ropes, and jumped aboard. The cat, sat down, stared at V, and stayed on the dock.

V hotwired the ignition. The motor started, and V eased the boat out of its slip and sped away. She looked back. The cat was standing on the dock watching. V waved. She was saying goodbye to an old friend. Seeing V's wave, the cat stood up, arched its back, turned, its tail held high, and walked back up toward the villa.

So that was that; now, three days later, V was brim-full of energy – and desire – and it made being alone so much more … ah … lonely.

Oh, I am so, so, so …

She picked up a handful of sand and threw it into the water. She rubbed the sandy, gritty palm of her hand against her face. *Grrhhhh!*

Grrhhhh!

Grrhhhh!

"Are you okay, V?" Helen had come up behind her. She sat down in the water next to V, and put her hand out, resting it on V's thigh.

"I'm okay," V said, "I'm pissed off, I'm an idiot, I'm sad, but I'm okay."

"Do you want to talk about it?"

"Do I want to talk about it?"

"Yes."

"No, I don't want to talk about it. But I will. You know I love you, and I love Alex, and you know Alex and I had a fling, and you and I have fooled around, and now you two are going to be happy – and that's what I want – but, well, I feel useless, irrelevant, *de trop*, as the French say, the extra wheel on the chariot."

"You are not useless. We both love you."

"Oh, Helen, you are crazy," said V. She turned and grabbed Helen by the hair and gave her a long passionate savage kiss. It lasted for maybe three minutes.

"Wow," said Helen, when she was released, and catching her breath.

"You and Alex are already lovers even if you don't fully realize it and you are going to be a couple – I'm pretty sure of my judgment when it comes to these things – and you are a wonderful couple, and so I am not going to invade your life together."

Helen gave V a long gentle, thoughtful kiss, and she transmitted an extremely clear thought: Alex and I love you. We always will. And I am sure Alex agrees with me that you can invade our lives whenever and however you want.

CHAPTER 21 – V THE KILLER

V left just after dusk. She paddled out with the smaller of the two dinghies. Alex and Helen walked with her out into the water.

V was all business – hijinks and sentimentality were a thing of the past. She was in a skintight armored black wetsuit; her face, once again, was painted in camouflage. She had her usual kit – dart gun, stun gun, and Beretta 9mm, plus magnetic clamps and plastic cables for climbing up the side of *Andromeda*.

"See you later, guys," V whispered. She turned on the silent electric motor and disappeared into the darkness.

Alex and Helen stood there, waist-deep in the water, watching until V disappeared. Then, hand in hand, they headed back toward the beach. They climbed up onto the beach and then turned to look at the sea.

There was no sign of V.

The moon had disappeared. The sea was dark. The air pressed against their skin. It was a heavy, damp night. The surface of the water was flat, dead calm, presaging a storm – Typhoon Akiko was, so the forecasts said, heading directly toward them.

Helen leaned against Alex. "V is sad," she said, "She feels she's losing us."

"I know," Alex took Helen in his arms and kissed her. "V knows she is different, and she is alone, but she also knows she can count on us; V is hungry for love, and love is difficult for her, even impossible. And so she's alone – she's been alone for centuries."

"Yet she wants us to be happy, and she wants us to be together."

"Yes, she does."

They walked up the beach and disappeared into the foliage and then into the camouflaged tent. The tent flap closed, and they were invisible.

Her face a few inches from the surface of the water, V lay flat on her belly in the small dinghy – it contained just enough space for her and her backpack and possibly, just possibly, for booty she might take from *Andromeda*, computer files – and maybe a souvenir or two, and a body, too, if she decided to keep one of the cadavers, or, maybe Sabrina, kept alive, just barely, so V could feed on her slowly – and make the pleasure last.

The small motor purred quietly.

V kept her eyes fixed on *Andromeda*, as it loomed out of the darkness, all its lights blazing. It was a very beautiful ship, yes, that was clear. Sabrina had exquisite taste.

V imagined Helen and Alex would be talking about her, for a bit, and then they would make love, as they had before, because the attraction between them had been growing, and she could see in the way they touched each other, glanced at each other, helped each other, and laughed at each other's jokes or smiled at each other's little ironies and allusions, that they were truly in love and that they wanted to touch each other, to kiss, to embrace, and to consume their love, their mutual desire, their mutual hunger.

V sighed. It was exactly what she had wanted, and exactly what she had expected.

For a moment, she was back in Alex's arms. They were making love. Her fangs spouted, and she bent down and kissed his neck and … broke the skin.

She shook herself. Oh, V, don't even think about that. They will be happy, and they are your friends, and your allies, and that is all you should think about.

She was now within sixty yards of *Andromeda*. No one seemed to be on deck. Some people were on the bridge, just vague silhouettes lit up by the control instruments. Somebody, somewhere on the ship, was playing a guitar; and somewhere someone – a woman – was laughing; it was a frank, happy laugh, a delightful and delighted laugh.

V slowly and cautiously came close to the side of *Andromeda*. The fact that the British frigate was being refitted and its replacement – a fast Philippine navy frigate – had had engine problems at the last moment and had not come to escort *Andromeda* was an opportunity, and it had forced V to seize the moment. V was capable of many things, but she was not enthusiastic about doing battle with a fast, heavily armed warship; the coincidence also made V nervous and suspicious – part of her mind told her it was a trap. Something was not right.

She frowned. She'd been a fool. By invading Andromeda Corporation's HQ and by showing off to Sabrina, she had revealed her hand. Sabrina would be expecting her to attack *Andromeda*, so a trap would be a natural counter-move. V cut the engine. The dinghy slowed, and then it bumped, gently, silently, against the side of *Andromeda*.

V buckled on the waterproof backpack, attached the magnetic metal clamps to her hands, and to her knees, and she slipped into the dark water. The water was warm and comforting, almost amniotic, womb-like, as it soaked through the wetsuit.

V deflated the dinghy and let it sink and attached it and the motor, underwater, to the hull of *Andromeda*. The magnets, when activated, were strong and even if *Andromeda* were to shift position, or indulge in a boat race, the dingy would cling loyally to the hull. When V left *Andromeda*, she could automatically inflate it. The dinghy would release itself, except for a light magnetic – and easily detachable – anchor line attaching it to the ship's hull, and in less than 15 seconds, it would pop to the surface, ready to go.

V climbed out of the water. She attached herself to the hull and, clinging by means of the magnets, she shimmied her way silently up the side of *Androm-eda*. Then she stopped, and hung in space, a few inches below the floor of the deck.

A man was leaning over the railing.

He was only three yards away.

In the invisible chameleon tent on Paradise Island, Alex kissed Helen and moved behind her and unzipped her camouflage suit. He bent down, and, kneeling, he peeled it off her, inch by inch.

Helen turned and gazed at him as he knelt in front of her; she gazed at the lamplight gleaming on his sun-stained, copper-blond hair. She smiled and licked her lips. He stood up. She pressed herself against him.

Alex cupped her face between his hands and kissed her. And they slid down onto a sleeping bag and made love as humans make love.

V hung by the magnetic clamps to the side of *Andromeda* just underneath the railing. Holding her breath, she peeked sideways to get a better view of the man who was leaning against the railing not far from her, maybe three yards away, smoking a cigarette.

Damn it!

She waited, dangling on the side of the ship, twenty feet above the water. The moon came out and shone on the railings, on the buttons of the man's open vest, and on the visor of his cap and on his high clear forehead. The man was thickset and had a white mustache. He took a slow puff on the cigarette, held the smoke, and exhaled, making a small white moonlit cloud.

He was staring off toward the horizon.

V felt that her matte black skintight wetsuit, the tight-fitting cap, and her face painted in matte night camouflage, should make her almost invisible. Her backpack was beside her, held by a rubber-coated magnetic clamp to the ship's side. But if the man turned her way, the moon would outline her silhouette; he would certainly see her.

Slowly, silently, she took a knife, with a matte blade and handle, out of its sheath and clenched it between her teeth. She slid the pistol with the silencer out of the backpack, unsheathed it. If she killed the man, it would have to be quick and silent, but killing someone now would force the pace and ruin her whole plan. She needed time to learn all she could about *Andromeda*, all she could about Sabrina and her projects – what Sabrina knew, and what she didn't know; whom she had shared her secrets with – and from whom and how had she obtained V's DNA.

Hanging on a steel wall was not a reposeful position. She forced herself to remain absolutely still. The dripping wetsuit was not that comfortable. Oh, if only I could wiggle and scratch and peel the whole thing off!

Another, younger, man had just joined the thickset man with the white mustache. The newcomer also leaned on the railing.

Damn! V squirmed. She was going to be stuck here all night, and she really had to find a place to hide and get dry. Still, it was a balmy night; the moon was almost full; the warm air was soft, perfumed, inebriating; it was a truly poetic, romantic setting. She calmed herself and listened. The man with the white mustache spoke.

"Don't worry. Nobody can hear us here."

"You're sure?"

"I've been on this ship for three months. I know *Andromeda* like I know the back of my own hand."

"So when do we do it?"

"Tomorrow, toward evening. The submarine will be in position."

"Good."

"Everybody here is expendable; orders are to shoot them all, except the Clone and Sabrina Jacobs. We have to deliver those two alive – that's essential. The rest we kill – no witnesses."

"And the ship?"

"Once we've unloaded or uploaded the information, and taken the documents and key personal computers, we sink *Andromeda*."

"I'll be glad when this is over."

"Don't worry. It will be smooth. They suspect nothing. The surprise will be total."

Clinging to the warm metal flank of the ship, suspended over the water that quietly lapped against the ship's side, V held her breath.

The two men stood for a moment, and then the thickset older fellow threw his cigarette over the side. V watched the bright ember fall, and she heard the hiss of the cigarette when it hit the water.

The ocean was so calm, and the air was so still that V scarcely dared breathe. How had they not seen her? How had they not sensed her presence? She held her breath.

The two men stood at the railing for a few more seconds. The silence was immense.

"Beautiful night," said the thickset man. The moonlight glittered, briefly, on his white mustache.

"Yes."

"The calm before the storm. There is a typhoon headed this way, and it's a really big one, a doozy. Our work will all be over by then, and we'll be far away on the open sea or in the submarine."

"Get a good sleep."

"Right, mate; you too."

And they were gone.

V waited. Her eyes were exactly level with the deck. The storm – a humdinger? Yes, that could be a complication. Still, right now, it was beautiful. The moon shone on the capstans, on the sealed canvas edge of a cargo hatch, on the steel framework of the winch that was used to haul up equipment and to lower and raise the deep-diving vehicle that was sitting, outlined in the moonlight, on the open deck aft.

V grabbed her backpack and climbed over the railing. She took off the magnetic hand and knee clamps and stowed them in the backpack. She crouched down behind the nearest cargo hatch, and then she carefully threaded her way aft to the storage room indicated on the schematics and that she planned to use as her hideout until she went into action. She would wait until the next evening, just after dusk, carry out the murders – she thought of them as "murders" to intentionally steel her heart against pity or doubt – and then she would leave *Andromeda* the way she had come.

She went down a staircase soundlessly. She heard a voice, a woman's voice. It was a very pleasant voice.

"I feel really guilty."

"Don't," said another woman's voice, "Don't feel guilty."

"She reads thoughts. If I had told you, I would have felt I had betrayed her, and ..."

"I know, I know. You have to be honest with her. What's happened is my fault. I don't know if I can, but I'll try to make it better."

"Goodnight, Sabrina."

"Goodnight, Sally. We'll talk to Claire tomorrow night – when I get back."

V slipped out of sight and made her way aft to the storage room. She had a universal key set. On her second try, the door opened.

She went in, and, without turning on the lights, she found a place to lie down on the floor where she wouldn't be seen from the entrance. She took the dart gun out of her backpack, and she took off her wetsuit and underwear and draped them from a shelf so they would dry and yet be invisible from the door.

Using a padded flap of the backpack as a pillow, she lay down, hidden from the door by a work table, and waited.

V needed to sleep. But first, she had to think. The men who were leaning on the rail were plotting a takeover of the ship, and they planned to kidnap her two targets. They also intended to murder everybody on board and sink *Andromeda*.

She had to do her work first, or she had to forestall and destroy the plotters, and then do the deeds she had come to do. How many plotters were there? And who were they working for?

Almost certainly, it was Bio-Prom Corporation – a Russian company specializing in advanced biotechnologies; it was the biggest rival and enemy of

Sabrina Jacob's Andromeda Corp. And it was absolutely unscrupulous. So if they got the Clone … They would do God-knows-what with it. And if they got Sabrina and drugged her, they would be able to access her genius, and so then, too, they could do God-knows-what with her ideas, her intuitions, and her plots. And, as for killing the whole crew …

Hmm! V frowned. And hadn't Dmitry Pavlov of Bio-Prom and Sabrina Jacobs been lovers?

Hmm!

And there was another thing; hearing Sabrina's voice gave her, once again, a different picture of the woman. So that is the evil monster I intend to kill, so that is the person who drugged me, kidnapped me, and wanted to lobotomize me.

Me …

Her …

V shivered. To be reduced to a near-vegetable state, to a zombie-like slavish existence, just the idea filled her with horror. It was more horrible than death.

She tried to imagine it: to be a zombie … and to be in the hands of unscrupulous killers, terrorists, revolutionaries, or dictators, a tool, a puppet, a weapon of mass destruction.

All the old anger boiled up, fresh and furious. She growled. Then she took a deep breath, clenched her fist, and bit her knuckles: Calm down, V, don't be an idiot! You are much too impulsive, young lady! Okay. Okay! What to do? Wait, wait and see what happens, wait and see when these pirates go into action, how they do it, who they are, and how many they are.

And then there was that other thing – Sabrina said she was going to be away for the day and would be coming back at night. So V would have to either act now, right away, or wait for tomorrow night, until Sabrina had returned, which was the original plan.

V closed her eyes. She lay for a long time listening to the small sounds of the ship, the anchor chain groaning, the generators humming, the air-conditioning in the cabins, a winch creaking from the slight rocking movement of the ship, the gentle lapping of the water against the hull, faint country-and-western music coming from somewhere.

She thought of the lives on board the ship: Sabrina, the Clone, the captain, the crew, the scientists, the interns, the students, and the people who worked for Andromeda Corp, the security people … The security people … hmmm!

She had a dream, or was it a waking dream?

She was back with Marcus, the moment she first became and first discovered what she truly was – a vampire.

It was as vivid as if it was yesterday. But it was more than 2,500 years ago. She was crouched, half-naked, covered in the fresh blood of Gaius, the soldier friend of Marcus. She had just fed on Gaius. His blood dripped from her fangs and from her claws. Suddenly Marcus was standing over her. His sword was drawn. His eyes were cold. "Your first kill, I believe." She looked up and knew that this warrior standing so close, his broad sword already in his hand, was going to kill her. And yet, in his eyes, she saw … interest … and compassion.

And then, standing next to Marcus was Sabrina as V had seen her in the holograms and photographs and in their telephone conversation. She was dressed in a crisp jacket, white shirt, short, pleated black skirt, the epitome of sexy corporate elegance, and Sabrina was saying, "It's my fault, it's all my fault; now I'll make it better; I'll try to make it better."

Sabrina reached out her hand and clasped Marcus's free hand. And Marcus turned, looked at Sabrina, and smiled. "Yes, we will make it better," he said. "Together, we will make it better."

V blinked. She shivered. She was awake. For a second or two, she didn't know where she was. Then she remembered. She was on a ship, and she was there to do a necessary thing, the thing she was best at, she was there to kill.

Kill, kill, kill!

Kill, kill, kill!

V fell asleep.

It was past midnight. It was the 10th of August, 2059

CHAPTER 22 – STORM WARNING

At precisely 5:00 AM, August 10, untracked by any radar or sonar, the submarine *M.I. Kutuzov VI* slipped into the Sulu Sea and came up to the surface, briefly, invisible, and sheltered by a low string of island reefs from *Andromeda*.

Radio communications confirmed that *Andromeda* was right where she should be, in shallow water, just off a deep part of the Sea, almost 4,000 meters deep. *Andromeda* would be seized, gutted of all her electronics, then sunk in the deep water, making recovery next to impossible.

Unseen, except by a pair of pelicans, the *M.I. Kutuzov VI* slipped beneath the waves to wait for dusk – the moment planned for the takeover of *Andromeda*. And, shortly after the takeover, and massacre of all the crew, and the final destruction and sinking of *Andromeda*.

It was 5:30 AM and still dark when Sabrina Jacobs slipped out of bed. The coffee machine had automatically prepared an Americano with a dab of raw sugar added.

Sabrina picked up the cup, took a sip, and tapped out a code on the computer that sat on her desk; she took another sip of coffee and unbuttoned the white silk pajama suit and slid out of it. "I do pamper myself!" she sighed, as she stared at the computer screen.

The screen showed weather patterns over the southwestern Pacific. Typhoon Akiko was advancing directly toward the Sulu Sea and toward *Andromeda*. Sabrina gazed at the screen for a moment, absorbing the information: wind velocities, barometric pressures, relative humidity, all along different zones of the storm front, the inclination of the warm front, and the Estimated Time of Arrival of Akiko.

Sabrina took another sip of coffee, and then she whispered, "BBC World," and the computer shifted to the BBC World Service Radio: "News Hour."

She walked over to the built-in cupboards. Carefully, she placed the pajama suit on a hanger and smoothed down a few wrinkles and straightened the hanger. Then she slid the door shut. She went back to the bed and spent a minute making it up – with perfect military precision – the sheets taut and flat and without a wrinkle.

The news was read by a suave female voice: An unexplained outbreak of the new HTX-T virus, a strain of last year's HT-Z, has caused a rising wave of panic in San Francisco. Schools have been closed and …

Sabrina stood for a moment, eyes closed. Then she walked into the bathroom, inserted a tiny waterproof earphone in her right ear, and turned on the shower.

Closing her eyes as the hot soapy water flowed over her, she listened to the radio news as it continued – drought here, flood there, rising sea levels everywhere, failing crops, new diseases, low-lying coastal lands to be evacuated, soil exhaustion, wars over water supplies, terrorist attacks throughout Africa and the Middle East, and the failure of governments everywhere.

She clenched her fists and swore to herself. Damn it! Everything going wrong everywhere! Andromeda Corporation had been founded by her father, in part, to anticipate the problems of a crowded world and to invent solutions. She continued the tradition. But the problems were overwhelming – and getting worse. No one had the courage to confront the facts, to tell people the truth, to adopt bold solutions – climate change was accelerating into a spiral, the environment was collapsing, more than half of the forms of life on the planet had disappeared in the last one hundred years; people were starving, people were panicking, and political leaders – well, political leaders were not sure what they should do, and, for the most part, having evaded the truth, and kept the public in ignorance, they lacked the courage, the simple guts, to fess up to decades of evasion, lies, and double-talk, to finally tell the bare unvarnished truth, and to do the things that they, at least the wisest among them, knew had to be done. In any case, it might be too late.

Her own problems were, for the moment, more modest: What to do with the Clone-Child, Claire?

Claire fears me and hates me. I imagine she'd like to kill me if she could.

Tonight, with Sally's help, I'll try to talk to Claire.

It is time.

And what to do about the search for V, the prototype, wherever she was, who had been tracked down here and there, the joker and trickster and shape-changer and vampire? V always escaped the net.

V is a wild card. If I could only talk to her, really talk, but I imagine it would be, however charming, like talking to a lion or a tiger: she is a predator, and we humans are her prey.

And V enjoys the hunt.

My fangs are itching to get to know you!

Sabrina shivered. And what to do about the criminal companies, such as Dmitry's Bio-Prom, who defied their governments – even the Russian Government! – and who were stealing patents, sabotaging research stations? *Dmitry wants to destroy me – and he may well succeed.* And then she thought, *No, Sabrina, that is the masochist in you speaking. He will not destroy you; he will not destroy Andromeda Corporation; he will not destroy the future!*

Oh, well … each day is a new fight – and we shall win, in the end, we shall win!

Dmitry – I still miss him.

Dmitry – he tapped into parts of me I didn't know existed.

Dmitry – even his hatred was … stimulating!

Stop thinking such thoughts, Sabrina!

Today she would inspect a set of monitoring devices on a coral reef; she would be scuba-diving, a delight. She was never happier than when she was swimming alone, underwater or on the surface, far from anybody, and far from everything.

The shower stopped, and she stepped under the dryer – hot air whooshed down over her body; it fluttered around her, from the sides, from above, from below.

When she stepped out from under the dryer, Aimi, who every year spent four months with Sabrina on *Andromeda*, was standing there, holding out a towel.

"Oh, Aimi, you are up early."

"Thesis work," Aimi sighed. "They told me I had to email a whole extra chapter today. Didn't sleep!"

"So, you won't be able to come out to the island?"

"Oh, boy, I wish I could; but I have to hang in here. Otherwise, Professor Wasserman will shoot me. We can spend some time together when you get back – if I finish the damned chapter and send it."

"Don't worry, Aimi, I'll bring you a snack if you are still slaving away. Otherwise, we can eat here – by candlelight or something romantic that will make us feel like human beings."

"Great!"

"Off you go!" Sabrina gave Aimi a kiss.

Sabrina stood for a moment thinking how much fun she and Aimi had and how it was great having her around – in fact, she had to admit she was obsessed with Aimi, in love with her – *and* she was stealing Aimi from her delightful boyfriend in Osaka.

I'm starved for affection; I'm bloody pathetic!

But Aimi seems really like our times together, so …

Sabrina pulled on jeans and a T-shirt and sandals. Fieldwork was a holiday – somehow, swimming, underwater, she felt purified.

Aimi – she's so generous and discreet. Her affection makes me feel like I'm real.

Even these thoughts are so bloody egoistical!

What is this called – negative narcissism?

She glanced at her watch. She wondered if she should go and visit the Clone – visit Claire, her child – Claire was usually up at this hour.

No. The crew was already waiting in the launch and Claire didn't particularly like to see her; an early morning visit would probably just upset the girl; Sabrina would have to earn her way back into Claire's heart – and she didn't know if she would ever be able to manage that particular feat.

Tonight, I'll see her. With Sally, I'll sit down and see if she will let me talk to her. I'll sit down and see if she'll let me listen to her – really listen.

Sabrina went up on deck to meet Tania, the skipper of *Andromeda's* number one launch, the *Zeus*, and the two scientists – Bill Griffiths and Hans Hoffman – and the security men – the security people were all men, Sabrina noticed, with a tinge of disquiet – who would go with them on this little excursion.

It was 8:10 AM. The sun was already high in the sky. Claire paced up and down. She did thirty push-ups. She turned on music; Mozart's String Quintet Number 3 in G major. Then she tried some Philip Glass. It didn't help. Nothing helped. She turned the music off. Something was wrong. There was something wrong in the ship. Something was going to happen. She lay face down on the exercise mat, took a deep breath, and began some more push-ups.

Forty push-ups; no, fifty ...

During the night, she had had dreams of blood. She had seen herself dismembered, broken into little bits. She was lying on a laboratory table, and they were cutting her up. She saw her legs, torso, arms, lying, bloody and separated, on a white Carrara marble floor in a large room where white muslin curtains were blowing in, and sunlight was shining outside. Her head was sitting, blind and bloodied, on a platter. In the nightmare, she had also seen Sally, lying dead in a pool of blood.

She finished the push-ups and got up.

Maybe it is the change coming upon me, she thought, a surge of uncontrollable power, and the beginning of sexuality, explicit sexuality, new yearnings and fears that were difficult to control.

Her periods had begun. She had prepared for it. She was prepared for it, she knew all about it, or she thought she did, she had learned as much as she could, but then, she knew, too, that, with her genetic makeup being unique, there was no real precedent for what might happen to her with puberty, and with growing up, no real knowledge about what she might become. There was no entry for *her* in all the encyclopedias.

She stood still in the middle of the cage, thinking. Maybe a shower would calm her down.

So she took a shower and carefully dried herself. She went to the wardrobe and changed into the white ballerina costume. She felt the power surge through her body; it was super-charged, like electricity.

She sat down on a mat in the lotus position. This might help calm her down. It usually did.

But something was still wrong.

The *vibes*, as she remembered they used to say, the *feelings* in the ship were not right. There were stray thoughts, bits of dialogue, inner or outer dialogue she wasn't sure, chattering and whispering in her head like static from a distant storm, just on the edge of consciousness: *We kill them all, except Jacobs and the Clone.*

The ship, we destroy the ship.

Whispers, murmurs ...

Shoot them all, sink the ship.

The submarine ...

The Clone, yeah, and the Jacobs bitch …

The night shift was coming to an end. Outside, the sun had risen; outside, it was day. Inside, things didn't change much. The night technician, Karl Ambrose, a nice young guy who was doing his Ph.D. in developmental psychology, was preparing to pack it in, and go back to his cabin to sleep. He didn't watch the monitors or the cage very carefully, and he didn't bother her, but he always said, when he arrived, "Hi, Claire, how are you doing?" and when he left he always said, "Goodbye, Claire, see you tomorrow night."

She had never answered him though, lately, she had begun to smile at him when he came and when he left. And two mornings ago, she had even waved, shyly, and he had waved back and given her a very big smile.

This morning when she saw him get up and gather up his books and notes and his laptop, she somehow felt sad, and anguished and eager to say something, what precisely she would say she didn't know.

"Goodbye, Claire, see you tomorrow."

"Goodbye, Karl. And, Karl – take care," she said, though the speaker; she hesitated. Should I say more? Can I say more? But what should I say, I should warn him, but about what? Should I say I've had dreams? Still sitting in the lotus position, she looked up and waved and, again, said, "Take care!"

Karl paused, shocked. She had never spoken before, not in his memory, or not in any of the documents and transcripts he had read; she had been silent for more than six years. He sat down. "Right, Claire, I'll take care. Thank you."

"I don't know what it is," Claire said, "but I think something terrible is going to happen."

The door to the lab opened, and Sally, summery, cheery, beautiful Sally, came in, with her usual radiant morning smile.

"May I share what you told me with Sally, Claire?"

"Yes. Of course, I have no secrets – well, not many, from Sally."

Sally's eyes opened wide; she looked astounded; she sat down at her console. Claire had never spoken before, not in years. "Good morning, Claire – My goodness, what are you two chatterboxes up to?"

"Claire says –"

"I have a feeling," Claire rose from her lotus position and came to the glass wall, pressing her hands flat against it. "I have a terrible feeling. I don't know exactly why – that you are all in mortal danger. And that I am in danger. There is a threat. There is a plot, but I don't know exactly what type of plot."

"Whew!" Sally and Karl stared at each other.

It was 8:15 AM. Sabrina sat on the gunwale of the *Zeus*, her back to the water; she checked her mask, her audio phone, the oxygen supply, gave Tania a thumbs-up, and pushed off backward, letting herself fall into the sea, splashing down, twirling down, and then, suddenly, swimming and plunging, straight down, into that wonderful weightless world of bubbles and aquamarine blue.

The coral reef was like the wall of some vast undersea castle. It soared up, or down, depending on your perspective, for more or less two hundred meters, and it perched on a 400-meter cliff, so that the water descended straight down into deep dark blue and then to blackness, more than 600 meters below.

Sabrina swam down and then along the wall of coral. She was going to take it easy and just enjoy looking at things. Hank Hoffman, *Andromeda's* geologist, and Bill Griffith, one of the marine biologists, and the two of the guards were swimming above her. Sabrina decided she would go off on her own – she wanted to be alone, and she wanted to feel that she was at one with nature, with the creatures swimming and swirling around her.

In fact, something was bugging her. Five security guards were too many. She felt a prisoner with so many guards around. And she didn't like the guards from the new security company – there was something about them. They had been suggested by the insurers in London. Henry had mentioned his unease with the new men and had said they should change companies. He was right, there was *something*. She'd speak to him about it when she got back tonight.

Sabrina was not only one of the world's richest persons; she was, with her scientific knowledge and entrepreneurial flair, one of the world's most valuable commodities, and in recent years kidnap threats and assassination attempts had increased in frequency for the daughter of Sir Alfred Jacobs, the Nobel Prize winner and founder of Andromeda Corporation.

She swam down further, thinking about the conversations that had just taken place on the launch as they had approached the island. As the launch accelerated away from *Andromeda* and sped across the glassy, smooth water, four pelicans had lifted off and glided along parallel to the *Zeus* – and a gaggle of seagulls swirled around above the launch's wake.

The weather was perfect. "Let's hope it's a quiet day," she had said to the guards' leader, Milo, when she stepped onto the launch, "and you guys don't have anything to do."

Milo had looked her in the eye and, lifting his coffee cup, he smiled with his very bright even teeth, and he had said, "I'll drink to that, Doctor Jacobs."

It gave her a funny feeling somehow, that bright, even smile; it didn't seem quite right. It was, somehow, as if there was a secret message in his smile, a hidden meaning – a hidden threat.

The rest of the trip had been quiet. Sabrina sat next to Tania and read through her work notes. The coral reef had been damaged by carbon dioxide and by increases in the temperature and acidity of the water; but a bio-agent, genetically-engineered and invented and supplied by Sabrina and Andromeda Corporation, had, it seemed, restored the health of the reef. It was growing again and populated by a host of fish and marine creatures.

And, when she plunged underwater she discovered – success! The coral looked in splendid shape. Sabrina followed a school of brightly-colored damsel fish downwards and along the edge of the coral. Life teemed, in all its bright colors and wondrous forms.

Sabrina, for the first time in weeks, felt truly happy.

Just after 8:00 AM, on Paradise Island, Alex was in camouflage gear and camouflage makeup and lying on his stomach just above the beach and just inside the tree line. He had been watching *Andromeda* since before dawn. There it was, at anchor, the very image of elegance, luminous, in the flat milky-blue morning light.

V was, hopefully, safely hidden, on the ship, waiting to accomplish what she saw as her sacred duty. Alex was worried about V, her safety, her sadness and her determination to kill Sabrina Jacobs and the Clone.

The air was still cool and utterly delicious, and, in spite of his worries, Alex felt almost drunk with happiness. This was what paradise must be like!

He glanced back at Helen and gave a low whistle and waved. She looked up and gave him a neat little wave and a big smile, and went back to making adjustments to the camouflage tent.

Yes, this was paradise, being on a deserted, lush, uninhabited, tropical island, with food and drink, and with two of the most beautiful women in the world, both of whom loved him – that was pretty clear – and, even if one of the women was a vampire, she was a most charming vampire.

And his interest in genetics and its possibilities had, under the influence of

V, come alive again. She was utterly unique – what if her talents, her capabilities – the good ones, not the homicidal ones – could be adapted, harnessed for the good of the human race? The possibilities were endless!

Andromeda looked ethereal, dream-like, ghostly, smoky blue-and-white, floating on its own reflection in the cool blue of the ocean, suave and calm as it was, in the early morning.

Alex sighed. God, it was a beautiful ship!

Soon the breezes would rise. The sun would begin to ripple in its reflections on the water. Waves would come. And somewhere out there to the east, an enormous storm, Typhoon Akiko, was moving toward them.

The typhoon would bring with it a different world, a world of violence, pain, and death, of chaos, confusion, and danger. And soon that world would be here, but, for the moment, here all was calm. Here, it was indeed paradise.

Then at 8:03 – he'd glanced at his watch, *Oh, oh, what's this?* A launch was moving out from *Andromeda*. It was a dark speck on the water, a smudge, and then it began to move quickly toward the island.

Oh, oh, Alex used his elbows to crawl back further back into the shelter of the brush and trees.

"What's up?" Helen crawled up beside him, keeping low, sheltered by the leaves of a large fern. Her hair was held back in a ponytail, and she had already acquired a tan. Her shirt was open at the neck, and she was wearing khaki shorts, and boots with white socks.

"A launch – from *Andromeda*; it's headed our way."

"Do you think they caught V?"

"No, and in any case, if they did, V would not talk."

"Besides, how would they keep her if they did catch her?"

"Exactly."

"Okay, let's take cover and test the camouflage."

"It looks good to me. You disappeared a few minutes ago."

"State of the art, so V says; it reflects the surroundings and picks up the exact coloration and patterns that are needed to blend in perfectly; it also absorbs the sounds from inside and radiation, so that it's virtually invisible on infra-red and other wavelengths."

"You sound like a brochure."

"I do. I love gadgets." Helen smiled. "And I've been having fun setting up the tent and testing out the equipment. V has an amazing collection of technical toys. I love it!"

Alex thought Helen looked deliriously happy and just too beautiful! He sighed. What perfection! And they slipped behind the camouflage net and immediately became invisible.

V opened her eyes and wondered, for a split second, where she was. Then she remembered: she was on Andromeda Corporation's research ship and floating headquarters *Andromeda,* and she was here to hunt down Sabrina Jacobs and the Clone.

V lay flat on her back on the floor of the storage room and looked at the ceiling. Everything was sparkling clean, everything was ultra-neat. Everything she had seen on this ship was impeccable.

She could feel – and it was a strange thing to feel – but she could feel that *Andromeda* was a ship that was *loved.*

Andromeda – the nest and headquarters of her enemy; *Andromeda,* Sabrina Jacobs' own creation.

V listened to people walking past in the corridor; she heard the motors and generators; she heard the little sounds of the water against the hull.

Once a man opened the door and came in to get some office supplies – but he didn't see V or sense her presence.

Sabrina had left the ship at dawn. Through a porthole, V had watched the launch leave the ship, slowly move away and then accelerate. Sabrina was standing next to a tall blond woman who was the pilot or captain of the launch. There were nine people on the launch.

V took a deep breath. She must wait until Sabrina returned to *Andromeda* before taking action. And then there was the question of these plotters – kidnappers – when were they going into action?

It was 8:30 AM. Sally had settled in and was sitting at her console, puzzling what to do with Claire's "intuition" of danger.

Claire was talking. For months, for years, Sally had been waiting for this moment.

"You talk," she said, "I mean, you're talking."

Claire smiled. "I talk."

"Well, I'm amazed."

"Silence is no longer useful."

"Good. I mean, that's good – I think."

"Sally, I want to thank you for not telling Sabrina, not telling her earlier, I mean."

Sally blushed. "I'm sorry ... I ..."

"No, that is quite all right. I know she figured it out herself. She accessed the video and audio archives. She had someone analyze the logic and sequencing of what I studied. So now she knows about me, but I don't think that will be a problem."

"Thank you, Claire."

"I am going to be silent for a while now, Sally. You are staying with me all day, are you not?"

"Yes. I am."

"Please don't leave me, Sally. Please stay here. Ask them to send your lunch in here."

"I'll do that."

Sally was perplexed. What was going on? The girl spoke for the first time in six years, and now she sounded so adult, so serious, but, something more, she also sounded – so afraid.

"Do you have a weapon, Sally?"

"A weapon? What do you mean?"

"A pistol? A sidearm? Anything?"

"In my cabin, I have a pistol ... for going on expeditions, you know, snakes, things like that. Sabrina insists we know how to use firearms."

"Please, Sally, go and get it and come back to this room and stay with me."

"I don't know if ..."

"Please!"

"Okay. I'll be right back."

It only took Sally two minutes. She hurried to her cabin. She got the pistol out of its packing case; she checked that it was loaded. She took a small box of ammunition. And she hurried back to the lab.

Claire was still sitting in the lotus position.

"Thank you, Sally."

"You're welcome, but –"

"Please don't let anybody into the lab – unless you trust them, trust them absolutely."

"Why? What?"

"I don't know. But … I'm worried."

"Okay."

"Now I shall be silent."

Sally watched Claire for a couple of minutes, but the girl didn't stir or look up. She was still as stone. She looked like an exquisitely slender female version of the Buddha. So Sally went back to the report she was writing; but then she stopped and typed out a few notes on this morning's events.

The creature, the *alien* they thought was an idiot, a chaotic, burnt-out relic of a brain, a brain-dead failed experiment, was, in fact, a genius, maybe more than a genius, and an extremely articulate and feeling person, yes, a person – Claire was a person! She was articulate beyond her years, far beyond her years. How in the world did her tongue, if not her brain, know how to articulate such complete precise sentences and thoughts after six years of silence? Sally paused and thought about it: If I've been working alone, silently, for a couple of hours, or a couple of days, I have to clear my throat and pitch my voice, and find my tone, before I'm a real social human being again; but Claire has done it without effort, perfectly, on her first try.

And the girl, this alien creature … Sally had to remind herself that Claire looked human, but half of her DNA was alien, half of her DNA was not even of this planet, and what precisely she was, they didn't know – not even Sabrina knew – and what powers she had – they were evidently far beyond those of any human – no one knew either – probably not even the girl herself.

Claire looked up. "Yes, Sally, you are quite right: even I don't know what my powers are. I really don't know." And she smiled – and even winked, goddamn it! – And then closed her eyes and returned to her contemplative pose.

Sally blushed. *What do you do when you are around somebody who reads minds?* So, yes, now she talks. Now, she confides in me. But she is worried – frightened, terrified even. She wants me to carry a pistol to protect her, and maybe to protect myself.

Sally didn't know whether to rejoice or to be terrified – or both.

But, in the event, the day was peaceful, and Sally was scheduled to leave shortly after 5:30 PM. She glanced at her watch: It was 5:29 PM.

She was just thinking that, when the moment came, just before she left, she'd say to Claire, "Well, Claire, was that a false alarm, or do you still think something is going to …?"

She was just about to say it, when …

CHAPTER 23 – DEATH OF ANDROMEDA

Henry Rothschild sighed with pleasure: the bridge of *Andromeda* was an extremely pleasant place, much better than a corner office in Virginia or in the City of London.

Henry had been CFO of the Andromeda Corporation for many years; he had founded the company with Sabrina's father, Sir Alfred Jacobs, and he felt an affection and a passion for everything to do with the company and its vast ambitions. He had come up to the bridge to talk to the captain, Duncan Robertson, who had been with *Andromeda* since she was launched in 2047. Duncan had also helped Sabrina and her architects design the ship.

They had also worked closely, all three of them, Henry, Duncan, and Sabrina, on *Andromeda's* sister ship, *Andromeda II*, which was in the final stages of construction in Germany – it would be ready for launch at the end of the year.

Henry loved it when they were based on *Andromeda* and, while he could have stayed in company headquarters on dry land, he loved the rhythm and feel of shipboard life, he loved the idea of being in the front line of scientific research, of being able to feel and touch things, he loved the sonar, the radar, the hum of the motors, the minuscule vibrations you sometimes felt – and these were hardly perceptible since *Andromeda* had been designed to be exceptionally agile and exceptionally stable; he loved the sea air, the vast flat horizon, the huge towering clouds they sometimes encountered, and the brisk salty breezes.

Above all, Henry loved the fact that Sabrina was happiest when they were at sea. He had watched his great friend – that genius of science and invention, Sir Alfred Jacobs – inflict tremendous damage on Sabrina when she was a child. He had remonstrated, he had argued, he had protested, but Sir Alfred descended into a dark fury, and Henry was told, many times, that it was none of his damned business!

And now there was one other thing that haunted Henry. And that was this other child – the Clone, Claire. He sometimes went down to the lab and sat with her, well, sat just outside the glass, and he would watch her – even when she was absolutely still, she was extraordinarily graceful. She had never looked at him directly, not that is, until recently.

One day, a week ago, he had gone down to sit there, peacefully, and watch her. She was dressed in ballerina tights and slippers – this was already unusual; usually out of the vast collection of clothes available to her, she just wore jeans and a T-shirt and went barefoot or in sandals. Whether she was a genius or an idiot, some of the experts had said, was hard to tell. Perhaps she was an *idiot savant*, with a couple of highly developed mental talents and no coherent human or social personality; Henry had not decided, but he was somehow convinced there was something more, some mystery …

Henry was thinking about a chess problem when he sat down in the deck chair and began to watch her. She was reading a book – and that, too, was unusual, very unusual – usually, she merely stared at a whir of high-speed videos or listened to music, and sometimes, rarely, she speeded the music up too. And she was reading slowly, at a normal human pace, not flipping the pages over. It was a big thick book she must have taken from the massive bookshelf that occupied one side of her glass house.

Henry squinted to try and read the title. It was *War and Peace* – Henry could read Cyrillic script – and she was reading it in Russian! Was she really reading, or was she just mimicking what she had seen people do?

Claire glanced up and looked directly at him and held his gaze and there was just a hint of a smile on her lips – and a thought came into Henry's head as clearly as if she had spoken it, only she hadn't uttered a word for the last six years: "*I like you, Henry, and the answer to your chess problem is …*"

Henry didn't know what to do – so he just smiled at her and waved. She waved back, timidly, he thought, and winked, and went back to reading Tolstoy.

Henry sat for a while. She gave no further sign she was aware of him. But when he got up to leave, he waved at her, and, without looking up from her book, she waved back.

Henry checked the chess problem when he got back to his private apartment: The answer Claire proposed *was* the solution!

Whew! Henry didn't know what to do or think. Either it was a fluke, or Claire was changing, or she had always been this bright, this aware, and had decided to come out of the closet and reveal what she really was – he didn't know. Maybe she was growing up. Maybe she was tired of hiding. *She reads minds; she can transmit thoughts: she knows chess, she is a genius, undoubtedly a genius, and … What else is she?*

He waited for a week, and then he decided: he would talk to Sabrina; he would talk to her tonight, when she got back to the ship.

Captain Robertson was saying, "I think we`ll swing her around and take her out into deeper water. That typhoon is coming in faster than we thought."

Henry said, "That sounds like a good idea, captain."

The captain ordered the anchor raised, and the clinking sound of the anchor chain coming up could be heard dimly from the bridge. The engines hummed into action, and *Andromeda* swung slowly around.

"When are Sabrina and her team scheduled to get back?" Henry asked. He looked out the windows at the flat horizon and at the low, shadowy, blue profile of Paradise Island. On the other side of that island, Sabrina was probably working underwater, or maybe – and she deserved it – just having fun.

"She's supposed to be back in three hours, just before dusk," the Captain said, "She should be back well before the first storm. Its ETA is now about midnight, and close behind it is the main storm, Typhoon Akiko."

"Sabrina will be able to find us?"

"Yes. I told Tania I might take *Andromeda* four miles further out. They won't have a problem. In any case, they will still be able to see us when they come out from behind the island.

Just as the ship swung around, the chief of security, a heavy-set beefy red-faced man with a white walrus mustache entered the bridge. He was carrying a pistol, and he leveled it at the captain.

"What is this?" Captain Robertson barely blinked.

Henry stared at the security chief. Damn! We've got traitors in our midst! He'd been worried about security, and he had been doubly worried since the *Darwin IV*, which usually accompanied *Andromeda* was being refitted. The Chinese frigate was unexpectedly not available, and the Philippines frigate, *Ramon Alcaraz*, which was to have taken *Darwin's* place, developed engine trouble at the last minute and wouldn't arrive until the end of the week. Too many coincidences – he should have thought about this more clearly, and sooner.

"What is this about, Jim?" Henry stared at the Security Chief.

"Shut up, Henry!"

Jim Delgado, head of security for the *Andromeda*, was an ex-Marine, highly recommended, and he'd been on the job for only ten months, replacing Philip MacArthur, the old-time head of security who had suffered a sudden – and totally unexpected – stroke.

Jim brought a new company and new men – and no women – with him, re-assigning virtually all of MacArthur's old hands to duties on other stations, on shore, not on *Andromeda*. Henry had been uneasy about this. He'd ordered extra background checks on Jim and his key people – they all came up smelling roses.

Two other security officers had come onto the bridge. They both carried submachine guns.

Well, thought Henry, now we know this is a real plot, not just one nut case. And what about Sabrina? What will happen when she gets back? My God! She's got security people with her, and she and Tania are isolated out there – No, there's one of the old guard security company with them ... and two scientists.

"Captain," said Jim Delgado, motioning with his pistol, "all you have to do is take the ship out into deeper water – here are the coordinates."

Captain Robertson looked at the coordinates and the chart.

Henry didn't say anything. He wondered why they wanted to take the ship out into deeper water. Then he understood. They are going to sink us! They are going to steal all the equipment, kidnap Claire – and Sabrina. And they are going to sink the ship. And, if they sink the ship and kidnap Claire and Sabrina, they won't want witnesses – so they will almost certainly kill everybody on board. Who was doing this? Dmitry Pavlov! He was the only person who could organize something like this. Henry wondered if there was any way to stop the madness.

The Captain was saying, "But –"

"No buts, Captain. We have people here who can replace you if you want to be a martyr and shark bait!"

The captain glanced at Henry. Henry shrugged and nodded. *Do what he says.*

"That's very reasonable, Mr. Rothschild."

The engines began to accelerate. As always, *Andromeda* responded immediately and to the lightest touch. They were on their way – out into deep water.

Dmitry Pavlov glanced at his watch, 5:30 PM. He was pacing on the deck of his research ship *Gogol*. Radio silence and Internet silence were frustrating. He didn't like suspense, he didn't like not knowing. The plan was going into action now, or shortly.

Soon he would see Sabrina again. Had she changed? No, probably not, not if you judged by the press photographs – the TV interviews. She was still the arrogant beautiful bitch she had always been, still the elusive beauty, the …

He smashed his fist on the railing. When I get you in my power, Sabrina, when I get you in my power …!

It depended on surprise, on acting quickly, before the crew of *Andromeda* realized what was happening.

It should be all over in an hour – the prisoners, Sabrina and the Clone, taken; *Andromeda* stripped of its computer records and useful equipment; the crew and staff executed; and the ship sunk. Then *Kutuzov* would rendez-vous with *Gogol* and deliver the prisoners, and Dmitry would turn Sabrina into his slave! No, she would be less than a slave; she would be an experiment, an animal, and his pet, his zoological oddity, into his pet *Thing* – his cowering, monstrous, slobbering *freak*.

What a feeling of elation! Dmitry was tempted to pirouette around the deck. Hate and love, lust and obsession, all in one heady mixture – and all embodied in one woman! How beautiful! How sublime!

It was 5:30 PM.

"*Okay! Go!*" the launch radio spluttered.

"What?" Tania was puzzled. "What was that?" She turned to the radio.

"*Okay, go, guys, go!*" The radio sputtered again. Tania glanced at the security guys. They had their pistols out except for one.

Ted Lacroix – he was the only old-timer, the only veteran from the previous regime.

"Ted, what are those guys doing ..?"

Ted drew his pistol slowly. "Guys, what is going –?"

The tall Ukrainian, Milo, shot Ted in the forehead and in the chest.

Double-tap, thought Tania, shocked into lucidity – seeing the impact, the shots, Ted – dead in a split second! Ted, who had been a friend for years, *double-tap. These guys were not fooling around.*

She put up her hands, her heart beating extra-fast. What the fuck was going on? Sabrina was underwater with the Hans and Bill and the other security guys. All the security guys underwater and up here were from the new security firm. *Cripes, this must be a plot to kidnap – or kill – Sabrina.* An intake of breath. Had they taken over *Andromeda?* She had to warn *Andromeda!* How? But they must have already taken over *Andromeda*, because the radio signal came from … No, not necessarily, the signal could have come from anywhere in the ship or from somewhere else. We're on an open frequency.

"So guys," Tania still had her hands in the air, "What do you want me to do?"

"You do nothing," said the Ukrainian with the very even, very white teeth. He'd already confessed to her that he hated Russians, Russians like her; and she had said, "Yeah, I understand, Milo, you Ukrainians have got lots of reasons to hate Russians." And now she thought: He'd love to kill me, I bet, well, let's hope he doesn't, not yet anyway; maybe, if I have time, I can …

She'd installed, all by herself, a pistol, just under the controls, on a spring-operated, slide-out drawer. Nobody else knew about this, not even Sabrina. Tania hadn't trusted the new security guys; there was something weird, something fishy about them.

"Okay, that's easy." She smiled a tight smile at Milo and the other guys, their guns were all aimed at her, and thinking: What the fuck am I going to do, alone on a boat with four guys who have guns? And – if I do what I'm going to do, will I have time to do it?

5:35 PM. On the bridge of *Andromeda*, Henry Rothschild faced a dilemma. What, precisely, should he do?

Andromeda was still swinging around. Next to Henry, but out of sight of the machine-gun-toting guards, was a large red button; the emergency button. If Henry slammed his hand into the red button, sirens would wail. What effect would that have? People would be alerted to an emergency, but they wouldn't know what emergency. They might even turn to the security guards for help. There were probably about forty-five people on *Andromeda* right now, including eleven security people with arms. And the rest were scientists, crew members, technical support staff, and Claire … Claire counted in Henry's mind as a person, perhaps as more, as much more. Sabrina was probably underwater at this moment, on the other side of Paradise Island. She'd gone with the usual contingent of guards – seven of them – including Ted Lacroix, who was an old-timer, and, Henry felt, could be absolutely trusted; but all the others were part of the new team. Ted Lacroix, Henry would trust his life to Ted anytime, and he actually had in a couple of tricky situations. But the other guys, no, the other guys he wouldn't trust – not one of them, not now, not with their boss Jim Delgado pointing a pistol at Henry's heart. No, he didn't trust them. Then, out there with Sabrina, there was Tania, the Russian tiger. She was ferociously loyal, and she was ferociously competent. Henry was just a bit in love with Tania – *if I were fifty years younger!* But what could one woman do, even if she was a Russian tiger?

So I have to do something, yes, and I'll do it!

Better than doing nothing …

Henry slammed his fist into the red button.

When the siren went off, Aimi was just starting her sixth cup of coffee – *after seven of these I'll get the jitters and then go totally nuts* – and was inserting the next-to-last footnote into her chapter on the genetic analysis of deep-sea thermal-vent life forms that are independent of oxygen and light and the way in which those life forms may give clues to the colonization of hostile environments, eventually extraterrestrial environments, by genetically designed bio-servo-mechanisms that can survive, produce oxygen and … And, then, when the siren went off, she thought, *Oh, boy, what now?*

She got up from her desk and went to the door of her cabin, quietly opened the door, and peeked out. She saw a guard down the corridor pushing one of the researchers in the stomach with a pistol. The researcher was Karl Ambrose. He was a nice guy, actually, a great guy – and Aimi had often kibitzed with him at lunch about his work with Sally and with the Clone, Claire, and just two days ago she'd said to Karl, "You're in love with the two of them!" "Well, they are both damned cute," he had said, adding, "and the Clone, well, my secret theory, Aimi, is that the Clone's a genius." Aimi hadn't told him that Sabrina had reached the same conclusion – that would be a breach of confidence. Sabrina shared her every thought, well, almost her every thought with

Aimi – Aimi had long had her own suspicions about the Clone: *Claire* ... She was a girl, a person, not a thing ...

Aimi softly closed and locked the door. Was Karl Ambrose guilty of something? It was hardly possible. No, something else was going on. Spending a lot of time with Sabrina had made Aimi acutely aware of the threats to Sabrina – there was V, the vampire alien-human hybrid, and there was Bio-Prom's Dmitry Pavlov, Sabrina's former boyfriend. Boy, had they had a lively, steamy relationship! Wow! Now, Dmitry was Sabrina's greatest enemy. So, if the guard was the bad guy in this scenario, then he would *not* be acting alone. It didn't look like he was crazy, a maverick; it looked like he was doing a job; so it was probably a plot, and it was almost certainly Dmitry and Bio-Prom.

Aimi took her pistol out of the drawer, and unwrapped the soft cloth wrapping. Since her sideline – the way she was paying for her Ph.D. research – was as a personal trainer, Aimi knew about martial arts – and she was an excellent shot, more than excellent, actually.

Let's see, she thought. I need to know what is going on. Who can I trust?

"Damn it!" When the siren went off, V had just pulled on her gloves. She frowned. This was too early; Sabrina was not back; it was not yet dark: *Damn it, damn it, damn it!*

But, except for the bad timing, V was ready for action. She had spent the day studying schematics and tuning into life on board *Andromeda*. She now had a perfect sense of the layout of the ship, a masterpiece of design, she had to admit. The black armored catsuit, which doubled as a wetsuit, had dried completely, and she had put it on just two minutes ago. The Beretta 9mm was in her hand; she was equipped with soft gloves, quiet-soled elastic traction shoes, a stun gun, a knife, and a submachine gun on a strap over her shoulder. The backpack, already strapped onto her back, contained everything she would need for her getaway, and then some.

When she left *Andromeda*, she would be alone.

She stepped out of the storage room, closing the door carefully behind her. Just at that moment, the engineer – a thick-set man with close-cropped gray hair and a broad, honest, deeply tanned face – V was particularly struck by his candid blue eyes – came out of the engine room wiping his hands on a white cloth.

"Who are you?" He said, his eyes opening wide, looking her up and down. "What's the siren about? What's going on?"

"Someone is trying to take over your ship."

"The hell they are!"

"If you've got a weapon, you'd better get it."

"Christ!" He blinked again, taking in the black catsuit, the Beretta 9mm, the goggles: "Who are you? How can I trust you?"

"You can't trust me. But you'd better hurry."

"The Devil!" He wiped his broad, tanned forehead with the white cloth. He stood for a moment, staring at V, and then he went back to the engine room, cut the power, so *Andromeda* would be adrift, and came back out carrying an antique Walther P-38.

"You have traitors aboard," V said, "but I don't know who they are."

The engineer stared at her. "The security people; it must be them. Everybody else's been with us for years – except some of the youngsters on scholarships and some of the visiting scholars – but it can't be them. We're family, except for the new security people. I had a bad feeling about them, from the beginning. Are you with me – or against me?"

"I'm with you."

"Then, come! Let's go forward and see what's going on."

They went forward.

The siren was still ringing in his ears when Jeff Turnbell – radio operator and radar-sonar specialist – took a punch at the guy who was holding a gun to his head and sent the guy flying.

Jeff thought: If only I can get the gun.

The guy was down on the floor, stunned, but he still had the pistol. Jeff jumped on him and tried to wrestle the gun away, clamping down with all his might on the guy's wrist. The guy gave Jeff such a punch in the gut that Jeff reeled back – seeing stars as he went – and let go of the guy's wrist, and that was fatal …

… fatal …

… almost fatal because the guy, dazed and bleeding as he was, raised the pistol, aiming it right at Jeff's chest, but Jeff kicked out and dropped sideways and the shot brushed by him, punching a hole in the cabin door, and Jeff grabbed again for the guy, meaning to get a hammerlock on him ... but ...

... to think ...

... to think that just five minutes ago Jeff had been pouring over the latest hydrological soundings and instrument readings and preparing a report for Sabrina on the changing salinity and acidity levels and how they were influencing the viability of coral regeneration, and he glanced up at the Doppler radar and saw that Typhoon Akiko was progressing mighty fast and might arrive sooner than expected and ...

... and at that moment the door burst open and one of the guards, a guy named Brent Fairchild, was standing there with a pistol in his fist, saying, "Back off from your toys fuckface and don't touch anything or I'll blow your fucking head off." And the guy stepped into the cabin and closed the door behind him and said, "Now, then ..."

And the siren went off distracting ...

... distracting Fairchild and Jeff went at him, but Fairchild was slippery with sweat and he was much bigger and stronger than Jeff and though Jeff now had him down – Christ, this was hard – Fairchild tossed Jeff away, and again they fought.

Fairchild threw Jeff down, got the gun, and twirled around and ...

... and, while Jeff was just getting up and thinking he was going to butt headfirst into Fairchild to take the wind out of him, Fairchild pulled the trigger and blew Jeff Turnbell's sorry fucking highbrow wanker fucking snobbish Ph.D. noggin away. No more cerebellum, buddy! Bright red blood all over the radio sets and the charts, fucking good thing too!

The last thought Jeff had when he saw it coming was: *Fuck ... I tried ...!*

"Are you a friend of Sabrina's then, lass? You look like her type."

"No, I came to kill her."

"Kill her? God in Heaven! Over my dead body! I'll kill you first."

"She's not here and I won't kill her; not now anyway." V raised her hand. *Someone coming.*

Around the corner came a guard; seeing the engineer and V, he narrowed his eyes, whispered fuck, and raised his pistol, but the engineer, whose pistol was already raised, shot him between the eyes.

"You are a stout man, and true," said V.

"A stout man and true," the engineer laughed, "Lass, you speak like an Elizabethan."

"Maybe I am, in part," V said softly, partly to herself, as they stepped carefully over the dead man.

"Now, lass, about Sabrina …?" The engineer glanced sideways at V. His twinkly blue eyes darkened. He was dead serious.

"People love her, I see."

"Well, lass, she's a grand lady, beautiful, and young, difficult, yes, pig-headed sometimes, yes, but in her way very kind, compassionate; she's rich, amazingly rich, and a genius to boot. But she's not stuck-up, she's not a snob. And she's loyal, fiercely loyal. Yes, people who know her love her."

"I see."

"And yet you do not …"

"I don't know her."

"Well, lass, perhaps when you do …"

"Perhaps …" V hesitated, whispering, "I have come to see … the child, the Clone."

"Claire? Ah, lass, that's a tragic story. She was a wonderful child! Then, age six or thereabouts, she suddenly went mad, from one day to the next, stark raving mad! She became – how can I put it, lass? – She became an animal, worse than an animal, crying, howling, and screaming. Her mind, so bright before, it lit up a room, became just a storm of darkness and confusion. It made me weep to see it, lass, it was tragic and cruel – for, you know, lass, it is like we are all family, all family on this ship."

"Tragic," said V, thinking: So that is my heritage – a storm of darkness and confusion and utter madness. How close have I come? How dangerous am I? Marcus was right to make me promise – *never create one of my own kind!* The fundamental law, the basic rule!

They were out in the open, on deck. The sun was shining, but low on the horizon; within half an hour, it would touch the ocean's edge. Night would come in an instant. The siren was still wailing.

A guard came running toward them. V whispered, "Enemy?"

"Enemy!"

V felled him with a single shot. The body fell forward and skidded along the deck and ended up face down one arm reaching out under the railing, dangling toward the ocean.

A ripple of shots came from the center of the ship.

Thank God for the siren, Aimi thought. If it hadn't been for the siren, I would have had no idea something was going on; but now, I'm ready.

She stepped out of her room, and closed the door.

She had just uploaded her thesis to a satellite-based server, and she had sent out a message to a friend at Andromeda Corp HQ, with a copy to his home address, saying she was not sure, but *Andromeda* might be under attack: Alert whoever has to be alerted. "Our position is just southwest of Paradise Island, coordinates, 8° 25' 6" N, 120° 19' 10" E," she added, giving her cell and text number. "And, hey, I've got my cell phone!"

Then all computer and internet connections were broken off.

So, she thought. What do I do? Wait for trouble or go out and look for it? Aimi had samurai and warrior ancestors, and tales of heroism ran in her family. *If there's trouble, go out and look for it!*

She put the cell phone on silent nerve-tingle alert, slipped it into her jeans pocket, held her pistol ready, and went down the corridor, heading toward the research offices. Turning a corner, on the way, she came across the bodies of three crew members – she knew them all. They were dead, their bodies sprawled on the deck. She heard a series of shots and she hurried. She heard more shots, a ripple of shots from an automatic.

The door to the main open-plan office space was open. Aimi peeked around the edge of the door into the research offices. Two guards stood over a line of bodies – all researchers and research students. The guards were both holding automatic weapons.

Aimi took a deep breath – no time now for thinking – she stepped into the door and said, "Hey," and shot the two guards, one in the back of the neck and the other, as he turned around, in the side of the head.

She turned to check the corridor. Nobody. She stepped into the research office, closed the door behind her, crouched down, and checked the bodies, all covered in blood. They were all dead – or so it seemed.

Karl Ambrose

Ted Ramsay

Hiro Hamsaki

Jenny Bridges

Sarah Wells

Isabelle Moreau

God! How horrible! For a moment, she could hardly breathe. She stood up. What should she do? Sabrina was out at Paradise Island with – what? – Maybe six or seven guards. That left how many guards on *Andromeda*?

What was happening to Sabrina, she wondered, and to Tania and the two scientists? They were great guys, mentors to all the students, Hans Hoffman and Bill Griffiths.

Then she heard banging from the office storerooms. She went to the door and whispered, "Who's in there? Who are you?"

A chorus of voices answered her. It was the other researchers.

Aimi said, "It's me, Aimi. It's okay, for the moment it's okay. Unlock the door."

On the bridge, Captain Duncan Robinson was looking down at his friend – and his boss – Henry Rothschild, lying wounded on the floor, bleeding to death.

Henry had been shot within half a second of punching the alarm. Henry was lying half under the desk. Delgado apparently didn't realize that Henry was still alive. The siren was wailing.

Whaaaa! Whaaaa! Whaaaa!

The moment the siren sounded, and in the confusion, just as the shot echoed on the bridge, the captain turned and with his back to the wheel, pushed a hidden small button and shifted a lever that would immediately send out the GPS coordinates of *Andromeda* and which would signal, "Distress, distress, distress," to the Philippine, US, British, Australian, Chinese, and allied navies. He knew a French destroyer was maybe sixty miles away, heading for Manila.

The captain had not bothered – had somehow neglected – to tell the security personnel about this particular device; it was absent from the ship's schematics; and the only people privy to its existence were the captain, Henry, and Sabrina.

"Don't do anything foolish, Captain."

"No, of course not."

"So let's proceed. Your course is –"

"There's a problem: we have no power; the engines are not responding. We've lost power. We're adrift."

"I will shoot you now."

"That won't solve your problem. The problem is in the engine room."

"That damned engineer ... And can you turn that goddamn siren off!"

"Of course." The captain pushed a button; the siren ceased; suddenly, *Andromeda* was uncannily quiet.

"Talk to the engineer. Get us under power. We need to be in deep water."

"Of course." Captain Robertson took the microphone, "Engine room, Engine room – Ian, can you hear me? Ian, please pick this up. Why have we no power?"

There was no answer.

"No answer. I don't know what to do. We'll have to send somebody." Captain Robinson stared straight at Jim Delgado, and in his eyes, it was clear that he would kill Delgado if he could.

"Okay. I'll send somebody." Delgado hesitated. "Okay, Knox, you go. Go to the engine room and make that bastard give us power."

Shots rang out in different parts of the ship. A fight was obviously going on. Captain Roberson was tempted to smile. By pushing the alarm, Henry had given people time to grab their weapons and get organized. There was hope, maybe there was hope.

Surreptitiously, the captain gave Henry a thumbs-up. Henry, lying on the floor, was clearly bleeding to death; Henry blinked and nodded, blood dribbled from the corner of his mouth.

The captain knew Henry only had minutes to live, that he needed urgent medical attention, but he also knew that if he drew attention to the fact that Henry was still alive, Delgado would shoot Henry again, but this time in the forehead.

V and Ian moved forward, carefully, corridor by corridor, room by room. So far, they had eliminated four of the traitors and they had liberated about fifteen members of the crew; but only a few of the crew members had sidearms, so the engineer told unarmed personnel to wait aft until the ship was back in friendly hands.

"We part ways here," said V. This, she knew from the ship's schematics, was the entrance to the central experimental laboratory, Lab Number One, the home of the Clone.

"Getting into mischief then, lass?" Ian squinted at the mysterious lady warrior. God, but her eyes were beautiful – and dark! What, he wondered, went on in there, behind those eyes? What had made this young woman the way she was?

"Yes. No. Maybe." V extended her hand.

The engineer took her hand. "Well, good luck to you, lass."

"And to you, Ian."

The engineer – and the armed crew members he had gathered with him – three sailors and two women crew members – carefully made their way forward, toward the bridge. Strange woman, that lass, Ian thought, maybe he should have disarmed her, or tried to disarm her; it probably wouldn't have been easy, maybe it wouldn't have been possible. For some reason, whatever she said about killing Sabrina, he trusted her. She didn't look at all like Sabrina, but there was something, some spiritual quality, something that was similar. In some mysterious, intangible way, they could be sisters.

They came upon one of the research assistants, Jane Wu. She was soaked in blood. A whole group of researchers, she said, were being held hostage – the gunmen were threatening to shoot them.

"They shot me, just grazed me really. I was in a hallway, and I managed to run and hide in my room."

"Okay, Jane, go to your room. Lock yourself in. We'll look after this. We'll get the doctor to look at you shortly."

So, this would be their first priority, clean up amidships, and then move in on the bridge where, Ian hoped, the captain was playing for time – for time against whatever these criminals had in mind.

The engineer and his small team made their way to the research quarters.

They found the door open to the main research hall, and when Ian peeked around the corner, he saw a vision from hell, a heap of bodies – mostly young people, mostly Ph.D. students on scholarships, laid out and covered in blood.

And two of the security guards – the killers, the traitors, undoubtedly – were lying dead too, shot neatly, each killed, Ian could see as he stepped cautiously into the room, by a single surgical shot.

One body was moving. It was a girl – Isabelle Moreau, she was pushing her way out from under the other bodies; she was covered in blood.

Ian scanned the room.

He knelt down next to Isabelle and whispered. "Isabelle, Isabelle, are you hurt, lass, are you hurt?" She looked up at him with wide, terrified eyes that made her look as if she were blind. "Isabelle, come on now, lass, look at me, talk to me." Ian glanced around. There might be more of those bastards about. He did not want to give them a chance to shoot him and then finish off Isabelle.

He saw a flash of dark to his right, just at his peripheral vision, and he swung around, his finger on the trigger, ready to press, and he saw that it was Aimi in her trademark black jeans and black T-shirt; she was holding a pistol leveled at him.

"Ian?" she had blood streaked on her face.

"Yes, lass, it's me."

"Thank God, Ian. There are more researchers back here. Some of them are wounded. I shot these two, but I think these – these murderers – have still got control of the bridge, and they must be trying to kidnap Sabrina. She's out at the island –"

"I know." Ian looked down at Isabelle. "I don't think Isabelle here is hurt, but she is in shock. I'll take her up into the air. And we'll take the bridge away from the bastards. I cut off the engine power, so they aren't going anywhere unless they know the codes on the bridge. And I don't imagine Captain Robertson is going to tell them."

"Okay, I'll get the doctor – if he's still alive – and bring him here to help the researchers. Do you need help taking the bridge?"

"I might. By the way, if you see a stranger, a beautiful woman in a sort of military getup-type black catsuit, she is on our side – so far, at least."

"Okay … good … that's good to know," said Aimi, frowning, and she turned away, thinking, a beautiful woman in a military-type catsuit …? Could it be the vampire, could it be V?

In the last seconds of her life, Sally Blake wondered: *How did Claire know?* How did Claire know that something horrible was going to happen, well before it happened?

Such power to see the future would be the Holy Grail of psychology – a kind of almost supernatural intuition and knowledge, an ability to see into the future.

How did she know?

It happened just as Sally was about to end her shift and leave. Clair was sitting in her lotus position. Suddenly, she stood up and came to the glass wall and put her hands – palms flat – against it, and said, through the speakers, "Sally, it's happening. Can you lock the door, please! Get your pistol out!"

"What's happening?"

"They're going to kill us."

"Who? Who's going to kill us?"

"Hurry, Sally, hurry!"

Sally pulled the pistol out of the drawer. Yes, Sabrina had insisted Sally learn to shoot, but she really didn't know much about it. She went to the doors. They could, in theory, be locked – super locked – only from the outside; that was in lockdown mode, designed in case the "virus" – Claire – escaped or ran amok; but there was a secondary lock system, designed for just such an eventuality, an attack from outside, or an effort to destroy the "virus" or the "alien."

Sally bolted the door and pushed a series of buttons; bars slid across the door – the only entry to the lab. Still holding the pistol, she went back to her console. "Happy now? Did I do the right thing?"

"Yes."

"Good."

"Now let me out."

"Let you out?"

"Yes."

"Claire, you know I can't do that. It's against the protocol."

"Fuck the protocol!"

"What did you say, Claire?"

"Fuck! I said, fuck, okay? I watch movies. I said, 'Fuck the protocol.' This is a matter of life and death, your life, my life, maybe even Sabrina's life."

"But I can't. I mean, Claire, I don't have the authority."

"Authority, authority, authority! Look, I'm sure Sabrina would approve."

Sally couldn't believe her ears; this was a 14-year-old girl talking; she was talking as if she were thirty years old and in command of the bloody ship!

The emergency siren began to wail: State of Emergency! Lock Down! Emergency procedures …

"See, Sally, it is happening. I am getting very annoyed, Sally!"

"Let me think, let me think …"

"There are times for thinking, Sally, and there are times …" Claire was almost crying; her hands were white from pressing against the glass wall; the wall was buckling – a fact Claire took note of.

A huge flash engulfed the lab – the door to the lab flew open – the security bars spinning through the air –

"Christ! Get down, Claire!" Sally spun around, leveling the pistol toward the entrance, just as she'd been taught: the shooter's stance.

A guy appeared in the smoking doorframe – one of the security guards – and he shot at her.

"God," thought Sally, "it's an inside job." She pulled the trigger, firing back and ducked behind the console.

"Sally!" Claire screamed, "Watch out! Leap away!"

A small object, a small round object came flying toward Sally. It was like a baseball, and for an absurd instant, Sally felt the impulse to catch it.

It landed at her feet. She was paralyzed – she felt she was paralyzed, though in a second thought, she realized she didn't have time, no way, no way …

"Sally!" Claire screamed.

The grenade exploded.

The pain was instantaneous, then it was gone – far away – and Sally was lying on the floor, staring through the smoke and fog at the ceiling of the lab.

Aimi knelt over Jamie Smith. "It's going to be okay. I'm going to get the doctor and I'll be right back."

"Okay, okay, I'll be okay," Jamie could hardly speak; she'd been shot at least three times; blood oozed from her shoulder, and her crotch was stained a deep red and purple, and one leg had been shattered.

Aimi turned to Jerry Edwards. He was the oldest of the group. "Keep that tourniquet as tight as you can, okay? You guys stay right here, I think that's safest. Can anybody shoot a gun? You can? Here, take this." She handed them a pistol she had lifted off one of the assassins. "The safety is off. All you have to do is aim and pull the trigger. Each little bit of pressure will shoot a bullet. You probably won't need to use it, but if you see one of the security guards, don't hesitate, shoot."

"Right!"

Aimi paused. "You may see a woman you don't know – in a black military sort of catsuit … don't shoot at her, okay? She's with us."

Aimi knew she was taking a risk here, but she was following Ian – he had a good eye, solid nerves, and good Scottish common sense, so if he said the mysterious woman was on the side of right, well, Aimi would accept that – until proof to the contrary. She stood up. "Okay, I'll see you guys later."

Keeping her pistol drawn, Aimi took an inside corridor back to the medical office. Two sailors – Ben Akoui and Sam Laskin – lay dead in the corridor. Aimi knelt down. They'd been shot in the chest. The door to the infirmary was ajar. Aimi went in. Doctor Cohen was tied up in his chair and gagged, and the nurse, Anita Chong, was lying on the floor hooded and hog-tied.

"I will definitely kill more of those bastards if I meet them." Aimi closed the door, propped a chair against the handle just in case, and she ripped off Doctor Cohen's gag.

"Thank God, Aimi," Doctor Cohen breathed.

"I'm going to cut you two loose," Aimi said. "I think we're regaining control of the ship – I'm not sure. Quite a few of the crew are dead. There are some wounded people up front … research staff mostly."

She cut Doctor Cohen and Anita loose. Anita was flushed and angry, "It's the security guys, I never liked this new group, you can't trust them; they were going to kill us, but one of them said we might be useful, so we got a last-minute reprieve."

Doctor Cohen and Anita followed Aimi forward along the corridor to where the researchers were waiting.

The instant the grenade exploded, the two killers, Max Broad and Tim Baikov, rushed into the lab. The woman at the console had been hit by the grenade, so she was dead or dying. She was not going to be a problem. The only thing they had to do was to get the Clone. They looked around.

"There's nobody else, just the Clone or Alien Hybrid, whatever you want to call it."

"Okay, we get the little bitch. She's right there."

"What? That's her, that's the package?!" Max pointed at the slender girl in the glass gage. She was wearing a white ballerina's costume and white ballerina slippers. Her fists were curled into tight balls of anger; her eyes blazed. Max said, "It's just a kid!"

"Yeah, that's the package."

"She's just a fucking kid!"

"Nope, she's dangerous, an alien."

"An alien – you mean, like from outer space – fuck! I don't believe this!"

"Get the gas canisters, Max. We have five minutes, not more. We have to paralyze the kid, otherwise she could be dangerous. We knock her out, and then we take her –"

"Right! Okay!" Max grinned. "She's cute, almost a woman, eh, hah! Maybe we can have some fun with her! Good-looking, God, is she good-looking!" He headed for the smoldering exit, twisted and blackened metal, a gaping smoking hole.

Claire took a deep breath; she thought: *I don't know if I can ...*

"Hey, don't worry, honey! We're not going to hurt you!" The one called Tim – she caught their names and some of their thoughts – was grinning. "Hey, don't run away!"

Claire ran to the furthest side of the cage; she took another deep breath; she closed her eyes ... and she projected herself, full speed, against the wall of glass.

Some scientist in later times – if she or he had all the elements and information – might have been able to calculate or discover that Claire hit the glass at a speed of 300 miles – 480 kilometers – per hour, and that her flesh had for several nanoseconds hardened to the consistency of solid stainless steel, and that the shock wave, which really may have been the element that hit the wall, consisted of a pressure level of ...

When she hit it – or when the shock wave that preceded her hit it – the glass buckled out, fractured into a million pieces, and Claire landed, delicately, and unscathed, still in her white ballerina costume, she landed gently, time having slowed down, or so it seemed to her, she landed gently, with a spray of shattered glass still flying around and past her, but not touching her, she landed, on her toes, and turned, gracefully, miming a ballet move she had seen, a sort of delicate and coy pirouette, and she turned to face the kidnapper who was called Timothy Baikov.

Timothy Baikov was being shredded by a thousand shards of shattered glass, blinded, pierced, slashed, spurting blood everywhere, with one large shard cutting, at that very instant, through his jugular, almost decapitating the man, and Claire watched, blinking, as he fell, in slow motion, ultra-slow motion, his body falling sideways, slowly, slowly, slowly, but without even time for him to say "fuck," he fell to the floor, collapsing, arms outstretched, fingers curved inwards, eyes bloodied but wide open, the pistol he had been holding bouncing away, across the glass-strewn floor, with glass still raining down, with a crashing and slashing sound, and now, as time sped up again, slightly, but still going very slow, each instant stretching out, the glass rained down, making a playful tinkling sound, along with a sort of sonic boom that seemed to be reverberating, a much louder, deadlier sound.

The other kidnapper, the stupid, arrogant one, the one called Max, came running through the shattered door. His mouth was open in shock and surprise, but, even with his mouth open, he was speechless, Claire noted, as she watched him, again in slow motion, as she watched him put down the gas canisters, dropping them really. And slowly, slowly, they fell from his hands, they fell, slowly, tumbling slowly sideways; she watched him as he raised his submachine gun – now a submachine gun, Claire knew, was not a thing to be trifled with – and before the man could pull the trigger or even aim or even, really, clearly understand what was happening – glass still raining down like hail and some of it bouncing and making a god-awful racket and there was, too, the echo of something, yes, something like a sonic boom in the air, echoing and echoing and hurting his eardrums and his eyes – creating black splotches and stars in his vision – and before he understood what was happening, Claire was upon him …

… she is upon him …

Claire realizes as all these events unfold that she doesn't know how she is doing what she is doing – no idea, really. And, I'm so careful, so calculating, she thinks, frowning inwardly, thinking, I must think this through, I must analyze all of this once it is over – if I'm alive when it's all over. It is very annoying, to be so mysterious, even to one's self. The unexamined life, she thinks, is not worth living, though, truth be told, she was – she isn't – really sure Socrates was right about that. I mean, she thinks, if you consider, say, a fox, or a rabbit, does it know what it is doing, does it reflect upon the methods it uses when it is chasing chickens or nibbling grass, does it care, should it care? Perhaps Friedrich Nietzsche was right – that action without thinking, without the pale cast of Hamlet-like thought and excessive, reflective, dithering ratiocination – a veritable hall of mirrors potentially – was the better, the more aristocratic and warrior-like way of existing, a loftier, simpler style of life – just do, don't think, a more …

… she is upon him …

She is upon him and she has – and, *So this is what it is like, she thinks, this is what it is like* – she has grown fangs, two teeth suddenly extending, she feels them, pressing against her lips, pressing down and outward, and she knows what they can do, and claws ... claws ...

... claws ...? Gosh! Who knew!?

Her claws wrap around the man's face and tear out his eyes, scraping off his nose and one cheek, a flapping fatty envelop of strawberry colored flesh, and scraping the bone. Her fangs sink into his jugular, quickly, easily, into the soft, warm, smooth, luscious, bloody weakness of his neck – *food.*

Blood!

So this is what I am!

Blood and power!

Energy explodes, rushes through her! Her flesh is incandescent. I am a bright flame burning, she thinks, wondering, in the rush of sensation, where such thoughts come from. I have been alone too long, she thinks, I think too much. *Ooops, I'm doing it again!*

Don't think, Claire, drink!

She drinks, she drinks her full. Some instinct tells her to empty the man completely, to drain every last and possible drop of blood from him, She lets him fall away, a dried-up empty husk, a bag of loose flesh and bones, no longer a man.

A broken puppet.

She stands up; she is soaked in blood; blood splashed on her hair and face, blood dripping from her mouth, the perfect sleek ballerina costume drenched in blood, the white has become scarlet. She looks down at the fallen mercenary. "*You are dead, truly dead, my friend, and you will not rise again,*" she pronounces, and then frowns, wondering where that phrase comes from, and why she felt impelled to say it.

She steps delicately away from the emptied body, steps lightly, with a ballerina's grace, over the broken glass, and looks down. Timothy Baikov, the other mercenary, is dead – dead before he hit the ground, probably; his bloodied shattered eyes stare from a twisted mask of gore.

She pushes Sally's desk aside. She steps over Sally and kneels down beside her. She takes Sally's hand. Sally's fingers close around her fingers. Sally's hand squeezes her hand. Sally's eyes turn toward her; Sally's lips whisper, "*Claire, Claire, I'm sorry, so sorry ...*" and then the light fades from Sally's eyes – they become bits of empty glass, blue and colored, striated and glutinous, all surface and no depth; there is no longer anyone there.

Claire breathes out, "No!"

An instant too late!

Too late!

Crouching over Sally's body, and covered in blood, Claire raises her eyes toward heaven – toward the high, stainless steel, arched ceiling of the lab, toward the sky and heaven that had limited her world, toward the steel sky and heaven designed by Sabrina Jacobs, and Claire howls, she howls like a beast, a soul in torment, she howls, a demon in hell, she howls …

Doctor Cohen leaned over Jamie. "Jamie, you are going to be okay. You are going to be just fine."

Anita was bandaging the others, distributing aspirins, making those who were in shock drink water.

Aimi held her pistol ready, covering the entrance to the researchers' quarters, and then she heard it. "What is that? Somebody is howling! Somebody is screaming!"

V heard the howl – a savage beast, a thing, was howling, and now the howl became a wild keening sound. So that was it! That was the Clone! That was the monstrous, mindless *Thing*.

Cautiously, V approached the door to Lab Number One. A red light was blinking: *Security Breach! Security Breach! Security Breach!*

Huge letters were written in red over the entrance: "NO ENTRY! AUTHORIZED PERSONNEL ONLY! LEVEL RED!"

The security doors had been blown away. It was an open wound of raw steel and twisted metal, and it was still smoking. V's nostrils quivered. It smelt of burnt metal and of explosives and of blood. There was an overwhelming smell of blood. V swallowed her saliva. A tingling excitement rose, and an unnamable fear, acute anguish.

I am going to meet myself in there; I am going to meet part of myself.

She put one hand on the door frame, and she swung through the door, pistol ready, in the shooter's stance, ready to fire in an instant, ready to spring, ready to kill.

Carnage: that was what it was – sparkling glass, bits of a body, and walls of blood.

Yes, utter carnage, it was a scene of massacre, a gore-soaked scene from a horrendous battlefield. Blood was splattered everywhere, on the walls, on the lighting, on the computer installations, on the screens, on the scientific instruments. A body lay near the entrance; it was one of the security guards, V could tell by the uniform, his flesh was deathly pale, his face torn away, his limbs covered in blood.

Another body lay just a bit farther on; it was dead by a thousand cuts, more a bloody shambles than the shape of a human being; that body too was one of the guards – tatters of a uniform were still visible woven into the ribbons of skin, blood, and raw, peeled flesh. One eyeball, glassy and naked, protruded from the skull; the flesh from half the jaw had been sheared away.

All around lay shattered glass; and there was a great wall of glass, or what remained of it, it must have been the Clone's cage, part of it still standing; and the stink of blood, the delicious stench of blood, and the acrid reek of explosive hung like a mist in the room. V sniffed the air. Her nerves were taut; she was about to meet her nemesis: *herself!*

And there it was – V's DNA, the *Thing*: the Clone.

V leveled her pistol and took a deep breath.

The Clone was crouching covered in blood, and her long straight blond hair was matted and clotted with blood and fragments of flesh, and she was looking toward the ceiling howling like a banshee, only the whites of her eyes showing.

She certainly doesn't look like me. V took her shooter's stance and leveled the Beretta at the howling creature: Just how crazy is this creature? And just how dangerous is it?

V's finger was on the trigger, nervously tense, ready to fire, but she hesitated. The Clone was still a child. She might not have reached puberty. And she might not yet have fully undergone the transformation.

V moved forward carefully. She stepped over the body that lay just inside the doorframe. She stepped over the other body that lay, sparkling with shattered glass, in front of the creature.

Then there was yet another body. This was the body of a woman, bits and pieces scattered here and there, and it lay just where the Clone was crouching. The body had been torn apart – by what? By the girl?

The Clone's mouth dripped with blood – Oh, so she has drunk. She is a vampire; she is one of my kind; she has undergone the change, the transformation; I must destroy her. V's finger tightened: Shoot her to stun her, then tear off her head and tear her apart and burn the pieces.

And yet – she is my flesh and blood; more than my flesh and blood.

In a sense, she is me.

Cautiously, V moved closer. The smell of cordite and explosive was stronger – a grenade, almost certainly a grenade.

V took another step.

Maybe the dead woman had been disemboweled by the grenade, then that would mean that the Clone had drunk from the body at the entry. If that were so, the Clone was crouching over the woman not because the woman was her victim, not because she had just been feeding, but because she was mourning. *She is mourning, mourning a friend.*

V stopped and stood absolutely still. The Clone is aware, she is finally aware of my presence.

Slowly, carefully, the Clone raised its eyes, and looked directly at V. The Clone blinked but showed no emotion whatsoever.

Slowly, carefully, the Clone stood up and faced V. The Clone licked its lips. She was, V saw immediately, exceptionally handsome – a blonde, pale-skinned, and not like dark, raven-haired V at all – a perfectly symmetrical face, a body that was strong, beautifully balanced, and large eyes, blue eyes strangely: If she's a clone from my DNA, then my friend Sabrina has certainly tinkered with the genetics! The girl's gaze seemed, now that she had stopped howling, to indicate calm, depths, intelligence, and focused awareness.

Not like my eyes either, thought V, my eyes are so dark that nobody sees anything in them. Sabrina Jacobs must have modified the genes – engineered a different appearance, more like herself, more like Sabrina. The girl's eyes looked like Olympian eyes – eyes of calm contemplation, but what was going on behind them?

Is she the "blond beast" – the perfect Aryan killer?

Is that what Sabrina has created?

Has Sabrina created a mindless but beautiful killing machine?

The girl put her hand to her mouth and coughed. Her lips were trembling. The blood on her body and on her face was drying. "It was a grenade," she whispered, and then cleared her throat and repeated, louder, clearer this time, "It was a grenade."

"A grenade?"

"Sally was trying to protect me."

"Sally – she's the dead woman?"

"Yes."

V hesitated. "You talk. You can talk."

"Yes. Sally was the only one that knew about my secret."

"Secret?"

"That I wasn't – that I'm not – crazy. Sabrina guessed it, and almost certainly Henry too."

"What happened to these two?" V motioned with the pistol toward the dead men.

"They killed Sally. I killed them. One died when I broke the glass. I killed the other one – I drank … I killed him by drinking his blood. It was my first time. The first time I drank. I can move very fast – like you."

"Like me?"

"Yes. You are V."

"Yes, I am V."

"They are afraid of you."

"Who is afraid of me?"

"Them. Sabrina, Henry, all of them."

"And you?"

"I am afraid and I am not afraid. I don't know. You have come to kill me. You swore that you would make no more of your kind, and all your life, all your existence, you have kept that oath."

"Yes, I have kept it. But you? How do you know this?"

"I'm connected to you. I don't know how. In the last few days, I have begun to hear – to feel – your thoughts, sometimes, rarely, but sometimes you whisper in my mind. I have become a vampire just now. I still have to grow up. I don't know what I will become, not exactly."

V hesitated. She took a deep breath; she stared at the girl, so beautiful, so calm, so needy, so confused, so like V had been when she first began to discover who and what she was; V took another deep breath; she hesitated; the girl has just woken to her vampire nature – Now she will need blood, and more blood, or will she? V sensed something different about the girl – some new form of discipline and extreme self-control. "Well, well," V murmured, and she put her pistol away, buckling it into its holster. I may regret this, Marcus may never forgive me, I may never forgive myself. Marcus may decide I must die. If it will be so, let it be so. If Marcus decrees I must die, I shall die, I shall accept his judgment gladly – whatever it is.

But I am not going to kill this girl.

She came up to the Clone and put her hands on the girl's shoulders. She looked directly into the girl's eyes, blue eyes that seemed curious, focused, but not afraid, not really afraid.

The girl was shivering, shivering uncontrollably.

V put her arms around the girl and kissed her on the forehead. The girl leaned into V, embraced her, and hugged back, and began to cry. "Now, now, now," V said, feeling suddenly helpless before such pain, such need; it was an echo of her own pain, her own need.

"I'm sorry," the girl said, "I'm an idiot – but no one has ever held me like this."

"I will hold you," V said, suddenly falling into an acute, abyssal, spinning, vertigo of love and desire, of abandonment and yearning, "I will hold you whenever you want to be held."

"What shall I call you?" the girl said, blinking through her tears, "Mother or sister?"

V leaned back, tried to blink away the tears, and smiled: "Well, that is a conundrum! I guess I'm both. Call me both, or just call me V, call me whatever you wish to call me. And what shall we call you? I heard the engineer say –"

"They call me, officially, C-1."

"C-1."

"Clone-1."

"That's not a very romantic name!"

"No. But my name, and many call me by my name, is Claire. Sabrina and Doctor Starr thought it would be dangerous if I had a name, a real name; people, the lab workers, would identify with me, Sabrina thought, that's why she always used the word '*It*' when she talked about me in the lab though I know in her mind she used '*she*' to refer to me and she calls me '*Claire*' when she thinks about me – I can read thoughts, just a bit, when people are up close. Sometimes I caught Sabrina smiling at me, but sadly. I think, particularly before I pretended to be crazy, that she liked me – but she didn't want to like me. She even loved me, for a time, but she hated herself for loving me. It was a problem for her."

"Well, Ian, the engineer, called you Claire, and for me, you are Claire – let's go … Let's go, Claire, up into the fresh air …"

Just as they left the Lab, they ran into a young Japanese woman in black jeans and a black T-shirt, her face smeared with blood, a pistol in her hand.

Aimi stopped and blinked. "Claire?" she said, "Claire, are you okay?"

"You are Aimi, the friend of Sabrina."

Aimi blinked. "Yes, I am Aimi, the friend of Sabrina."

"Yes, Aimi, I am okay. Sally is dead, and I killed the men who killed her."

"Sally!" Aimi eyes filled with tears.

"And this is V," said Claire, "She has come to help us."

"V, yes, V," said Aimi stared. So this was it, so this was the monster, this was the creature that brought down aircraft, and slaughtered crews, and was on the hunt for Sabrina. "I have heard about you, V. I am Aimi. I work with Sabrina. We must save Sabrina." Tears streamed down Aimi's face.

"Sabrina is not on the ship, Aimi," V said.

"No." Aimi wiped her eyes. "Sorry. I apologize. Sabrina is at the coral reef with Tania and two scientists, on the other side of Paradise Island. They have six security people with them. I'm afraid Sabrina may be dead by now."

"No, she isn't dead," said Claire, "I feel it. She isn't dead, not yet. But she's very frightened."

"Then we must rescue her," said Aimi. "I have to join the doctor. He's trying to save some of the wounded. V, can you help Ian? He needs help to take the bridge from these … these … these murderers …"

Ian had taken Isabelle Moreau up onto the deck to be with the rest of the crew. And now they were joined by V and Claire. Both Isabelle and Claire were soaked in blood – they looked like twin survivors of a horrendous accident.

Staring at the two girls soaked in blood, and then glancing at V, the engineer said: "The bastards have still got the bridge, lass. Can you help me?"

V considered Claire and the other girl. Claire will be okay. She can look after herself – and she can look after the other girl. But, just in case, she asked: "Will you be okay, Claire? Ian and I have to liberate the bridge. I won't be long. But I won't go if you want me to stay."

"Yes, we'll be okay," Claire said, looking into V's eyes.

V kissed her on the forehead.

"Let's go, lass."

Ian had told most of the crew to move to the stern where they would be safer. He and V moved forward.

Claire and Isabelle Moreau sheltered in a doorway. The sun was low in the sky, and the sea was sparking with evening light that flooded in on both of them.

"You're covered in blood," said Isabelle, looking Claire up and down.

"You too," Claire said, gazing at the girl, examining her closely. It was the first time, in a very long time, that she had been able to look at a human being up close, without a wall of glass between her and the human being – now nothing separated her from this girl.

The girl's teeth were chattering. "They shot five of my friends," she said, "I fell down and pretended to be dead. Then Aimi, she works with Sabrina, came along, and she shot the murderers dead. Then Ian found me."

"They killed Sally too." Claire put her hand on the girl's arm. "But the ones that did it are dead."

Isabelle's mouth formed an "O" and her eyes went wide. "Sally, Oh God, I loved Sally!" she said, and then she stared at Claire with a light slowly, then suddenly, dawning. "You … you're … you're … you're the …"

"I'm the Clone."

"But they said you were crazy, they said you were absolutely raving nuts."

Claire frowned and said something she had not even thought about saying and which was, of course, as she knew when she said it, a lie, a pathetic, childish lie. "Sabrina wanted people to think that. She wanted people to think I was crazy, an animal. So I wouldn't be bothered. So people wouldn't get at me. You know, pester me. I mean, they'd want my autograph for Christ's sake!" As she said it, she hated herself and realized she was saying it because she wanted it to be true. It was so damned silly! I want love, how pathetic I am, I want love, and she realized that she loved Sabrina, desperately, hopelessly, and that she needed love, but what the fuck – movies again – does the word "love" mean? It's a human word, and I'm not human, so what do I mean, *I love*? So – what do we have but words, she thinks, sneaky unreliable, lying, slippery, fucked-up human words – *I love* – and I need the love of – which is different, needing love, and loving, are two totally different things, she thinks – I need the love of, and perhaps the respect of … V … from whom I spring, I need the love of Sabrina, who created me, and … of Henry (who, she somehow knows, is lying on the floor of the bridge mortally wounded) and of Sally, who is dead.

Love …

The girl is saying, "That was a brilliant idea. Of course, people would be all over you." She extends her hand. "My name is Isabelle. Everybody calls me Izzy. I work on marine biology; you know, rescuing dying species."

"I'm Claire," she says, shaking the offered hand, thinking, this is the first time

I've introduced myself to somebody, and saying, "Didn't you write that paper about genetic drift in the Paradise Island coral reef?" She'd read somewhere that it's a good idea to talk to people about themselves and their work and their kids, if they have any, and the house they bought, if they bought a house – but she doubts Izzy has kids and she doesn't see any houses around here – just ocean and a little island low in the sea – so it's best, probably, to talk about Izzy's work.

Izzy's eyes light up. "Yes, I did!"

"I learned a lot from it. I know Sabrina liked it." And, in fact, she did know that. She'd read the paper, and, hacking into Sabrina's files, she'd read Sabrina's notes – she thinks: They have a name for what I do when I do this, "hacker" and "hacking," but I do it with my mind, which, from what I've seen, is unusual.

She likes the girl. Izzy has pale creamy skin, a bridge of freckles across her nose – obscured, slightly, by a sheen of blood, gray eyes with shards of emerald green in the irises, a perky, slightly upturned nose, red hair, and a bright smile. She must be about 22. And I am 14. And yet I am so much older, so much older already. I will grow until I'm about 19 or 20, then I will stop; Claire knows this, but she does not know how she knows it.

Perhaps V, unknowingly, has shaped me in her own image: I must love her to become what I must become. *I am you, and you are me.*

Love ...

Destiny ...

Izzy is talking about genetic drift; her eyes are bright, and she has laid a hand on Claire's shoulder; they are both so bloody they seem like twins. Claire likes the warm feel of the girl's hand on her shoulder.

Contact ...

Izzy talks on. Claire knows the girl is suffering shock – so am I, she thinks – and is talking so she won't fall apart, talking, talking, talking, and Claire smiles warmly, and looking straight into Izzy's eyes, and she nods and says, "Yes, yes, that's right."

Words like a wall, Claire thinks, keeping away the images, words like a barrier, a dike, keeping away the ocean of fear, of terror, the images of blood, the tsunami of ...

The sun is setting, and Claire thinks for a moment that, being a freshly minted vampire, she should be burning up, like in the movies, covered with fire, falling apart into embers and ash and bones and then nothing but dust and then nothing ... and *I've never been out in the sun before!*

But the distant flush of the sun only radiates a sultry heat that makes Claire feel she is glowing and extra alive. *This is the very first time I've been outside!*

As Izzy talks and smiles at her, Clair smiles back and seeing the beautiful curve of the girl's cheek, the delicate comic freckles, the moist young lips, the bright teeth, and, beyond the girl, the vast flat smoky line of the ocean, the sun breaking softy, breaking apart, like a huge fire, falling into embers, into pieces with dark traces of charcoal, black as night, framing them, all of it changing slowly, and Claire smiles at Izzy and breathes it all in. *This is life; this is the world.*

The world!

I will hunt night and day, she thinks, V will teach me how.

Ian and V were on the forward deck, watching the bridge.

"There are three of them left, I think, lass, and they are all on the bridge."

Ian was wondering about the black-clad warrior woman. She certainly did seem like Sabrina's twin – not physically, but in her – what was it? – Yes, in the way she was so focused. She was like a laser beam when she looked at you – that glance, oh, yes, like a laser beam, a dark laser beam; she's the dark version of Sabrina's blue eyes and blond hair. It's as if the spirit of the two of them were one thing!

They went along a narrow gangway to get close to the bridge. The gangway was sheltered from the bridge, and so they couldn't be seen from the bridge which was a very good thing, thought V.

"The captain's still alive, I think," the engineer whispered, "he's been buying time. They intend to sail us to Russia or someplace or sink us."

"One of the pirates is just beside the door frame." V signaled: "I'll take him."

"Yes, lass, if you wish." He didn't know why but for some reason the engineer now had great faith in the lady's ability to do things – maybe it was just the spiritual resemblance to Sabrina, and maybe it was the special ops getup; he had an eye for technical details, and he knew this stuff was top-of-the-line, cutting-edge, and beyond.

V readied herself. She had a small mirror-like device, Ian noted, which allowed her to look around corners. She unsheathed the Beretta 9mm, gave Ian a finger count-down signal, three, two, one …

It all happened in a flash.

How she leaped so far so fast Ian could not for the life of him figure out.

I'm fast for a man of my age, but … He heard shots, six shots, he thought. When he came storming through the door, the young woman was crouched, in a shooter's stance, next to the captain, who was standing there, his back against the control panel, with his eyes staring and his mouth open.

The three traitors lay dead on the floor of the cabin. The engineer leaned over them; each had been shot twice: once in the forehead, between the eyes, and once in the chest, right over the heart, neat little holes. Not much bleeding.

She'd used the double-tap, two shots to make sure, and, to judge from her pose, she'd used the classic pistol tactic.

"Well done, lass!"

"Thank you, Ian."

"That was done so quickly I didn't even see it happen," said the captain who seemed to be waking up from a dream or bad shock. "I still don't believe it."

V was on her knees, leaning over Henry. "You are Henry Rothschild," she said; he whispered, "Yes," a trickle of blood came from the corner of his mouth.

"Hold still, Henry." V put her hand on the bullet wound, and she closed her eyes and concentrated.

Henry felt a flood of warmth spread through his chest. V took her hand away and handed something to Ian.

"The bullet," she said; and turning to Henry, "You should feel better, now, Henry."

Henry stared at her. "You are … the vampire … the …You're the one who …"

"Yes," V said, "I am V. I'm the vampire, I'm the prototype for Claire, the source of her DNA. I'm the creature, the *Thing* that Sabrina wanted to … what was she going to do to me?"

Henry was beginning to sit up. He grimaced.

"… She … Sabrina … I don't think Sabrina understood – understands – exactly what you … what you are … what you seem to be …"

"Well, thank you, I think," said V.

Henry felt his wound. He gradually sat up, and then, with V's help, he stood up.

"I seem to be healed," He was astounded. "What did you do? How did you do it?"

"I have never understood how I do it, but I can do it, sometimes, if I get there in time. But be careful, Henry. You've lost a lot of blood."

"You seem to be a miracle worker," said Ian, who had been conferring with Captain Robertson. "What's your name, lass?"

"My friends call me V," she said; and Ian noticed, for the first time, there were streaks of blood on her 'uniform' and on her hands – probably, he thought, from when she had embraced and probably saved Claire.

Claire …

"Well, I'm pleased to meet you, V," said Ian, and Captain Robertson echoed his sentiment.

"The pleasure's mine, Ian, Captain, but you – and we – have another problem now."

"What?"

"A submarine; if the mutineers lost control of *Andromeda,* they intended to sink you. I overheard some of their chatter. Look at the sonar."

At that instant, the sonar began to beep a warning, and on the screen, just behind the captain, there was an oblong dark shape.

"It's coming up to the surface," said V. She looked around, and knelt next to one of the dead mercenaries, the leader, the older man with the walrus mustache. She extracted a small phone device and held it up. "This is probably an open connection."

"So, they've been listening."

The captain made a cutting motion and V turned the device off.

"Ian, can you give us full power?"

"I can do it from here." The engineer flipped a few switches. *Andromeda* trembled as power surged to its engines; a light whirring sound ran through the ship.

"You are right, V, if I may call you that, they are coming up … and …"

"… and …?"

"They are opening their torpedo hatches."

"They are too close."

"They are too close for their own good – and for ours."

The captain swung the wheel and switched the engines to full speed ahead. He flipped a switch and turned to a microphone. "This is the captain speaking. Everyone – hold on to something. And hold on tight. The mutineers have been overcome, but we are now under attack from a submarine. Those who are below decks should get to the upper deck, close to boat launch numbers two and three. Prepare to hold on tight – I repeat, hold on tight – wherever you are since we may be hit by a torpedo shortly and get ready, when I give the order, to abandon ship."

Andromeda was an agile, high-powered ship, equipped with ice-cutting blades, the latest in super-strong nano-construct plastic-metallurgical technology. As *Andromeda* swung toward the sub, the sub launched a torpedo. The captain flipped on the electronic defenses, which were designed to make an incoming torpedo explode well before impact with *Andromeda*, but as he flipped the switch, he was thinking that the submarine was too close, and the torpedo already was too close, for the defensive shield to work. The submarine launched a second torpedo.

"This is a good ship," whispered V.

"She's a darling," said the engineer, "everybody aboard adores her."

"She's Sabrina's great love," said Henry.

"We have an electronic screen," said the captain, "we have an electronic screen to deviate or detonate torpedoes. It's not perfect, of course, and these torpedoes are starting from too close in. I don't know if –"

The first torpedo exploded just ahead of *Andromeda* – a great shuddering column of water rose up and *Andromeda* plowed straight through it.

The second torpedo exploded under *Andromeda*; the ship shuddered, rose slightly out of the water, but plowed on.

The submarine had been slow to react, slow to understand what was happening. It was still coming to the surface when *Andromeda* smashed into the submarine's hull, rising up over the submarine, crashing into the conning tower and snapping it in half. A third torpedo exploded just as it was leaving the torpedo tube, blowing the bow of the submarine into fragments.

The captain flipped a switch and the giant bulkhead doors inside *Andromeda* slid shut, isolating different compartments of the ship. It was a desperate act, an effort to seal off the damage, and probably in vain, since … The captain glanced at the monitors. Little red lights flashed in a row – *there was one red light too many*.

Captain Robertson glanced at Henry, at Ian, and at V. "This is it," he said, "*Andromeda* has been too deeply wounded. Four of the bulkheads have been compromised. We will not have enough buoyancy to keep her afloat, even with all our pumps in action. *Andromeda* is going down. I'm giving the order to abandon ship."

He turned to the microphone. "This is the captain. Prepare to abandon ship. Gather on rear deck B. Prepare to lower number two and three launches and the six annex lifeboats. Prepare all inflatable dinghies."

"I'm going to get Claire," said V.

"I'm coming with you," said Ian. He turned to the captain. "No false heroics, now, Duncan."

"I'll be the last off her, Ian. But I fully intend to command *Andromeda II*."

"Good!"

"Goodbye, Captain."

"Goodbye, V, and thank you."

"Goodbye, V," said Henry. "Thank you. You saved my life. Perhaps you can do the same for Sabrina."

"Goodbye, Mr. Rothschild," V shook his hand.

The engineer and V hurried aft.

The sun had set. It was night.

CHAPTER 24 – MOTHER, SISTER, DAUGHTER

Claire glanced at V for permission, and then, seeing V's eyes wet with tears, she threw herself into V's arms. V held her and then, still holding the girl, she drew back and, looking Claire in the eye, said, "Together?"

"Together!"

"Goodbye, Izzy," Claire turned to the girl. "We'll meet again."

"Goodbye, Claire. I loved talking with you! You are great!" Izzy grabbed Claire and hugged her and held her close, and then drew back and kissed Claire on both cheeks. There were tears in Izzy's eyes, Claire noted. She reached out and brushed away one of the tears and kissed Izzy again.

Being human, Claire thought, was, in some ways, not so hard: You just did what you felt like doing, you just did what felt *right*.

Aimi had come up from below. She went straight to Claire, held her in her arms, kissed her on both cheeks. "Claire, we never talked."

"We will, Aimi, someday we will."

Aimi – her eyes wet with tears – turned to V. "V, I just want you to know. I love Sabrina. I love her very much."

"I understand."

Ian offered his hand to V. "Well, V, you and Claire, you are not coming with us?"

"No, Ian. I have a dinghy attached to the ship. We are going to find Sabrina."

"You'll bring her back to us?"

V, glanced at Aimi, looked Ian in the eye for a long time, and, still holding his hand, she said, "Yes, Ian, if we can, we will."

V pushed a small button on her belt, and the dinghy magnet released its hold on *Andromeda's* hull. The dinghy instantly began to inflate, and sprang to the surface.

Aimi looked over the side, looked at V, and went to the railing and pushed a button. "This will help, I think." A synthetic rope ladder suddenly appeared, dropping down the side of the ship.

"Thanks, Aimi." V glanced at the young woman, thinking, Yes, I understand. You are in love with Sabrina, and she is in love with you.

Claire stared down at the surface of the ocean and at the rope ladder that was swinging against the side of *Andromeda* and that led to the dinghy. It seemed a long way down.

She took a deep breath. The lights from the ship – and flecks of the pale moon – reflected in the dark water like wiggling serpents. The sea, with its reflections of the sky, was like another sky, but upside down. Which way was up? She felt she could fall upwards, or fall downwards. Up was infinity, and down, she knew, was a long way down! The Sulu Sea, Claire well knew, having researched it thoroughly, was about thirteen thousand feet deep – two-and-a-half miles. She felt a sudden surge of vertigo, as if she were standing over nothing. "I've never been outside before," she said, looking up at V.

"I know." V put her hand on the girl's shoulder. "You'll handle it. The water is deep, but it's warm and, if you fall in, you'll float. This is going to be a spectacular introduction to the outside world, Claire, but you'll like it. I'll climb down. You follow – just do what I do, and I'll lift you into the dinghy. If you fall out, you'll float, just keep calm."

Claire felt that everything around her was moving and shifting and jiggling. She'd played video games, and mind-stimulation games, lots of them, ultra-fast and accelerated so that nobody – at first at least – would know what she was doing – but this was different. The side of the ship, the cord ladder, the surface of the ocean, the dinghy, the sky itself with the moon and cloud streaks and lights and tones, the vast expanse of water, the air itself, all of it was moving, and her body was part of it, swaying and moving with the ship, touched by the air, touched by the smells and sounds which were coming from every direction. Oh, the smells, they made her drunk with possibility, the blood drying on her clothes and on V, the lemony perfume of Aimi, the soapy smell – under the blood – of Izzy, the oil and manly sweat of Ian, the salty fertile smell of the sea, the oil and paint and wood polish of the ship. And the blood, of course, the blood! It was endless!

Her fingers tightened around the rungs of the ladder, and she backed away from the side of *Andromeda* and then, hanging free and close to the side of the ship, she felt a rush of vertigo, like when she wanted to throw up – a sense of panic rising like a wall of water.

She closed her eyes and said to herself, *Don't be an idiot, a little self-control, Claire, a little self-control.* She opened her eyes and was suddenly filled with euphoria, a rush of exhilaration and freedom. She quickly climbed down the ladder, and turned, still hanging on the ladder, to lower herself gently into V's waiting arms. V helped her into the dinghy. "Hold on tight, darling, and lie low. This is a small dinghy for two people."

In fact, water was already sloshing over the sides of the tipsy but brave little dinghy.

V cast off, the electric motor purred, and the dinghy began slowly to move away from *Andromeda.*

Now, for the first time, Claire saw that *Andromeda* was tilted at an angle in the water; that all its lights were blazing; she stared at it, her eyes wide open. And then they heard the captain's voice through a megaphone, "Everybody on B Deck!"

"Will they be okay?" Claire glanced, her eyes wide, at V, and thinking, that's my whole world dying – everybody I know, my home, my books, my clothes …

"They know what they're doing, Claire. They'll be okay." V put her hand against Claire's cheek. "You'll see them again."

The Bio-Prom submarine was nowhere to be seen; it had sunk immediately after the torpedo exploded in its bow, going down, with all hands, to the bottom, thirteen thousand feet below.

Night comes quickly in the tropics.

Alex had left the island when he saw the green flashes of light from just below *Andromeda.*

Something was wrong – sirens had wailed on *Andromeda* half an hour earlier, and then there were explosions, and Alex had seen what looked like a submarine approach *Andromeda* – and there was a collision – more explosions.

Now *Andromeda* was tilted on an angle. God! She was sinking! Christ! He hoped V was okay. He wondered about their expedition – was it V? Had she done this?

It was unlike V to be vengeful. But she had sworn that no creature like her should be allowed to exist – her sacred oath. Yet to kill a 14-year-old child, however monstrous the child might be, however dangerous!

Then he saw the three green blinks – *blink, blink, blink.* That was the signal that V was returning – and with a *long flash, repeated twice*, it meant that he was supposed to go and meet her.

Helen waded out with him, and held the dinghy while he climbed aboard. Then Alex shoved off. "Be careful," Helen whispered.

"I will. I'll be right back. I love you."

"And I love you!" Helen's voice came, whispered, across the water.

Alex accelerated. He was worried. Maybe V was hurt and needed help. Otherwise, she would have come back the whole way in her own little dinghy.

Things had gotten very complicated very quickly.

All day, Alex and Helen had been eavesdropping on the radio of the pirates who apparently intended to attack *Andromeda*. And they knew that Sabrina Jacobs was somewhere on the island and that she might be dead. The kidnappers, who had attacked her, some of them, were dead, that was pretty clear. The kidnappers had been talking a lot, and then they fell silent. The ones who had come to the island may have died. Then the kidnapper giving the orders from the launch stopped talking too.

"I wonder what happened on Sabrina's launch," Helen had said.

"I don't know."

"Silence; that's all we've heard – and the connection is still open."

"Maybe they're all dead," Alex sighed, "the good guys and the bad guys."

After Alex headed off to pick up V, Helen went back to the camouflage shelter to see that everything was in order. She glanced at the radar and satellite images on her laptop.

Typhoon Akiko was fast approaching. It would probably arrive sooner than expected, sometime around midnight. Would their shelter survive? Would the island survive?

And was V wounded, or hurt, or captive?

What if Alex was heading into a trap?

Helen went back outside and walked down to the beach. What she saw was spectacular, and tragic. She put her hand to her mouth. *Oh, God, oh, God, oh, God!*

Fireworks shot up from *Andromeda*, now tilted dangerously, the prow down, the stern up, the propellers rising out of the water. It was a dark night, but *Andromeda* was lit up, all lights ablaze, sparkling like a Christmas tree. Above the dying ship, Roman candles burst in a huge display of fireworks.

Then music began to play. *Andromeda*'s loudspeaker system was playing music, what was it? It was *Auld Lang Syne*.

Should auld acquaintance be forgot,
and never brought to mind ?
Should auld acquaintance be forgot,
and auld lang syne ?
For auld lang syne, my dear,
for auld lang syne,
we'll take a cup o' kindness yet,
for auld lang syne.

Helen's heart skipped a beat; she put her hand to her throat.

Somewhere out there, Alex was speeding toward the sinking ship.

After the signal, V had left the green light on so Alex could find the dinghy in the vast open flat ocean. The immense expanse of water seemed to hang in tension, in immobile stillness, with the music rippling across the silk-smooth water, the lights of *Andromeda* reflecting, and fireworks exploding –

Boom, boom, boom – big echoing festive booms, showering sparkles of stars, the Roman candles bursting overhead, reflecting on the silent sea, a taut and tense mirror, waiting for the incoming typhoon.

Alex thought he was getting close; he must be getting close.

He stared at the brilliant, sinking ship. Bloody defiant! They're saying they are going down all flags flying, spirit unbroken. They're saying, We'll be back, that's what they're saying!

Alex squinted through the darkness. There she was! The shape was strange though – were there two people in the dinghy – it wasn't made for two people. Had V brought a hostage? Was V prisoner and was this a trap? Alex slowed down and picked up the submachine gun. "V?" he shouted.

"Yes, Alex. It's okay. Come ahead."

Alex pulled up to the dinghy, slowly, so the wash from his larger dinghy wouldn't swamp the smaller boat, and so his bigger dinghy wouldn't bump into the smaller and overturn it. Then he saw that the passenger was female, a girl, in tights, a sort of ballerina costume, long blond hair ... at first, he could only see the silhouette, in the moonlight – the moon had just come out. It looked like a stage set. The girl was covered in blood.

"This is Claire, Alex," V said, "Claire, this is Alex."

"Delighted to meet you, Claire," Alex said, reaching out for the girl and thinking, so this is the Clone! Whew, so V didn't kill her after all! I somehow didn't think she would – or could.

"Is he one of …?"

"No, I'm human, Claire," Alex gave her his best smile, and helped her into the dinghy. "Though V did bite me once, so I sometimes wonder."

"Alex is a man, Claire. Men are dangerous. I couldn't resist."

"You made love?" Claire smiled, and Alex saw that she had a radiant smile, rather like V. Of course, you idiot, he thought, she's a clone or partial clone of V.

"Yes," said V, and Alex, who was busy stowing away material from the smaller dinghy, could have sworn that V, impeccably perfect V, blushed.

"I would like to make love someday."

"Well, I think that will happen," said V, stroking the girl's hair. "We'll just have to see how it can be arranged. Now, my child, my friend, my sister, you sit down and hold on tight. Alex is going to take us to our campsite."

Alex made sure Claire and V were snugly aboard, and then, towing the small dinghy, he put the motor in gear and slowly accelerated toward Paradise Island.

Behind them, about half a mile away, the lights of *Andromeda* shone , ever more brilliant, across the water and the speakers were still playing *Auld Lang Syne*, then the ship shuddered – vast hollow explosions echoed across the sea – hollow, echoing, ghostly underwater explosions – the lights flickered, and then went on again, with seeming new brilliance, and kept shining and the music began again and still brightly lit, still broadcasting the old Scottish song, beautiful *Andromeda* slid beneath the sea and disappeared.

For auld lang syne, my dear,
for auld lang syne,
we'll take a cup o' kindness yet,
for auld lang syne.

PART FOUR – SABRINA

CHAPTER 25 – MONSTER

They are going to kill me.

They are fucking well going to kill me.

Damned bloody idiots!

When Sabrina first realized something was wrong, she was in a black wetsuit with two oxygen tanks, ten meters below the surface, swimming alone along the edge of a coral reef that was about ten miles distant from *Andromeda*.

It had been a long day. Diving, and working on the *Zeus*, and then a quick lunch, just a light sandwich and black coffee, and then three more dives. She was on her last dive of the day – oh, how luscious – and she'd slipped away from the group, just to enjoy the solitude of the sea. She'd been following a large manta ray along the bank of coral: it was lazily undulating along, feeding; it had stopped and turned to swim alongside Sabrina for a few minutes, before turning away and resuming its feeding cruise. Sabrina was pleased to see the large creature feed; food was abundant – one more sign that the reef was regenerating.

Sabrina knew there was a large and fairly aggressive moray eel with its nest – its favorite hole – close by. So she'd left the manta ray, who was progressing slowly along scooping up food, and moved out from the reef, and down several yards below the moray's nest, when her ultrasonic underwater phone spluttered into life, and she heard Hank Hoffman, her top geologist, yelling something like, "*What the hell ...?*"

And the phone spluttered into silence.

Just as Sabrina was about to ask what the hell Hank was shouting about and what the hell was going on, somebody else's phone burst into life – it must have been Bill Griffith's – and all he said was, "*Hey, Sabrina ...*" And then it was just a scream: "*Hell, no! No ... What!*" And then nothing: The earpiece was filled with static.

Sabrina swirled around. Was anybody nearby? No, there was nobody. She was alone. She was floating, just her, in a vast blue space, rays of smoky sunlight going down and down, into a deeper and deeper blue that shaded into utter darkness – more than three hundred yards straight down, and then, a little further out, more than a thousand yards, over half a mile.

Usually, for Sabrina, this was a place of joy. Suddenly, now, it seemed dark and threatening.

A chill shiver rippled down her spine. Goosebumps!

The outer edge of the coral reef was perched on the precipice of a cliff, an ancient geological fracture. The reef itself went down and down, like the roughhewn and beautiful wall of some ancient underwater castle, about four hundred feet, right on the edge of the cliff, then there was the cliff, the thousand-yard depth, and, a little farther out it was deeper still – an abyss.

Sabrina swirled around again to check if anyone was close by, and she wondered if she should try the phone, speak into the little mike inside her mask: *No, silence was best.*

It must be an attack. And the attackers knew – or probably knew – where she was. Was it just an attack on their little boat – or was it also an attack on the mother ship, on *Andromeda*?

She thought of trying to warn the ship, but her phone was only short-range: it wouldn't reach *Andromeda*.

She looked up toward the surface, the light of day. The sun shone on the water. And there, near the surface, she saw the body of Bill Griffiths, the marine biologist, a big, gruff man, brilliance itself, and fond of sly jokes and silly puns. He was dead – she could see from the way he was floating, motionless, arms and legs spread out, and surrounded by what looked like a spreading stain – of blood.

Jesus Christ!

Sabrina swore. She'd better try to raise the launch; she clicked on the phone. "Hi, Tania, what's going on up there?"

Nobody answered – there was just silence and static.

"Tania, come on, Tania, what is going on up there?"

"Tania, are you okay?"

"Speak to me, Tania, talk to me, please!"

"Tania?"

Nothing – just static.

So the launch was taken.

Who were they? Pirates? There was a fair amount of pirate activity in the zone. But would they attack a small boat with not much in the way of booty? And would they kill people? No, they'd want to hold people for ransom. And if the boat had been attacked by another boat – there would have been a warning. There were four armed guards on the *Zeus* and two guards underwater. So Tania, the skipper, would have had time to warm the divers. Sabrina could just hear Tania shouting: "Get your asses up here, lickety-split!"

Tania was very proud of her English.

No warning! That meant one thing: *betrayal!* One or more of the guards must have overpowered or killed everybody up top – and the two diver guards came for those underwater.

The guards! Yes, that must be it, the guards! Yes, yes – Henry had been suspicious of them, and then there was that smile Milo had given her, and she had even thought, in that moment, that she should talk to Henry, tonight, right away, about changing security companies.

I woke up to this too late!

It was planned, and had been planned for quite some time. It was not an improvised pirate attack; it was calculated. Could it be V, the Vampire? No, she was a loner, maybe with one or two accomplices, Alex Wolf and the mysterious blonde, no more than that. This had to be a bigger operation – and she had one thought: it was Dmitry, Dmitry Pavlov and his company, Bio-Prom.

She circled around again, looking above and below.

No, nobody.

So, they hadn't found her yet.

She swam in closer to the reef, being careful to stay under the moray eel's lair. Sabrina had nicknamed the moray Hector; she didn't know why. He was very large – maybe eight feet long, had razor-sharp teeth, was black with red stripes, and most evil-looking eyes you could imagine.

But he was beautiful with his red-and-black patterned scales.

Sabrina rather liked Hector – predator and indomitable fighter.

If it was a planned attack, she thought, it must be Dmitry and the Bio-Prom Corporation. Maybe the idea is to kidnap me, and use me as a hostage, as leverage, to seize our research ship; after all, *Andromeda* is the best in the world, and it is chock full of industrial and scientific secrets.

And – it contains the greatest secret of them all: Claire.

Sabrina cautiously edged in under an overhang of the coral reef; then, she saw the two divers, the guards, the traitors, swimming downwards, toward her.

Okay, so now they are coming after me.

She moved quickly along the reef, dove in closer, swimming just under Hector's nest, hopefully out of Hector's line of sight, hoping that Hector would come out, but *not just yet.*

The two divers spotted her and began swimming down and along the reef. Sabrina went in closer, just behind an outcropping, and unsheathed her speargun. It could do five shots in quick succession – and she was a good shot. She was just below Hector's lair, and about five yards beyond it, partly sheltered by the outcropping.

The divers came quickly, swimming close to the reef.

Sabrina thought: Come on, Hector, come on, come on, baby, show your stuff, do this for me!

Just as the divers passed in front of his nest, Hector swooped out at one of them – a distraction. Both divers turned, their attention distracted by the charging eel.

Sabrina pulled the trigger; the spear flashed through the water, and slammed into the chest of the first diver. Blood billowed out in the clear water, the man's arms went out, limp, floating.

As the second diver turned toward her, swirling around, he lifted his speargun, Sabrina let go a second shot. It hit him in the middle of his face mask, shattering it, and probably going through his skull.

Both divers were either dead or badly wounded. Hector didn't attack humans; Sabrina had fed him, three or four times, being very careful and using a pronged stick; but now – sensing the blood and violence – he attacked one of the men, sinking his fangs into an arm of one of the dead – or dying – divers.

Sabrina swirled around – there were no more divers in sight. She began to swim along the reef as quickly as she could, going deeper, down to twenty meters. Her options were limited. She couldn't surface, and she couldn't go back to the boat. If she surfaced near the boat, they could shoot her or take her prisoner. The speargun was clumsy and ineffective if you tried to fire it from the surface at something like a boat. If they shoot to wound me, then I'll be helpless. And, if Tania was still alive they would use the Russian as a hostage: *Drop the fucking speargun and come on up, Bitch,* they would say, *or we cut your cute Russian girlfriend's throat!*

Sabrina thought, Okay, what's the balance sheet here?

Tania – maybe she was still alive, unarmed but canny and tough and gutsy.

Bill Griffith – most certainly dead (taken by surprise)

Hank Hoffman – probably dead (taken by surprise)

Ted Lacroix, the old-timer security guard – dead or prisoner; probably dead; they knew he had a weapon, and he'd use it to defend us, so Ted is almost certainly dead.

Damn it, damn it, damn it!

She had about twenty minutes of oxygen. What to do and where to go? Trying to cross the top of the reef – it was partially above water – would be risky, maybe impossible; and she'd cut herself to ribbons. There was an opening in the reef about three hundred yards further on. If she went through it, she could get to the lagoon and to Paradise Island. She had to get to land. That was the only way!

The break in the reef was a narrow opening with heavy crisscrossing currents and it was not big enough for the launch, hardly big enough for a dinghy or a canoe, but it was deep.

She could get through the opening; and, if she was lucky, she could get to the island at the center of the reef. Paradise Island was fairly big, maybe a mile long and half a mile wide and uninhabited; she could hide there. She had used the island as a temporary research base, and she had left supplies on the island, in a concrete research bunker, so she knew where she could find water, food, and even a can-opener, though she'd have to break into the bunker. That would take time, *if* she could do it at all. It had combinations and heavy locks. The doors were of steel, and it was watertight.

Did she remember the combination? Hmm – yes, she thought she did.

So, if she survived, she could get into the bunker.

Then what? Well, dear Sabrina, we'll just cross that bridge when we come to it, won't we?

Okay, I've got to try: I've got twenty minutes. She swam up to a depth of about fifteen feet, and then swam as quickly as she could along the reef. Every few seconds she swirled around to see if anyone was following her, if anyone was approaching from behind, or from above, or below. Nobody was – or so it seemed.

She came to the break in the reef – the current swirled this way and that. Still, she was lucky – the sea was calm; but it wouldn't be for long.

Swirling through the narrow opening, where the currents ran back and forth, violent foam bursting – exploding – high above, cliffs of coral towering on either side, She plunged down deep, glanced up at the yellowing light from above, and then, being careful not to scrape against the razor-sharp coral, she swam, as fast as she could, zigzagging, through the narrow breach in the reef – until, finally, after two or three close calls, she came out on the other side.

She was in the lagoon; the water was limpid, and the bottom sandy, and it was, mostly, shallow. In this space, there was no place to hide. She had to get to land, and quickly.

She came up to the surface. The lagoon was utterly still, dead calm. Night was fast approaching. Steel-dark clouds were piling up on the eastern horizon; a storm was brewing already – the leading edge of Typhoon Akiko. Right now, it was the deadly quiet before the storm – an eerie, ghostly stillness, so tangible she could touch it. The white sand-line of the beach and the spinach-green tree line made neat, horizontal, almost painterly, strokes above the deep cobalt blue of the water that in the shallows shaded into turquoise.

Sabrina scanned the shoreline; there was no sign of a boat, no sign of anybody. Maybe she had a chance.

She swam slowly toward the beach, ready to dive at the slightest sign of anything – even though in this shallow water, she wouldn't stand a chance. There was absolutely no place to hide.

She got to the beach and stood up, holding the speargun ready. It might be ineffective, but it was better than nothing; and, at short range, it could still be deadly; she hitched it over her shoulder and pulled her pistol – a Beretta 9mm – from its watertight case.

Holding the gun in one hand, she slipped out of her flippers, picked them up, and walked straight up to the tree line. She took off the tanks and the wetsuit and hid them under the brushes, mentally marking the spot relative to a particularly high palm tree and to the froth she could see at the narrow entry to the lagoon.

She was barefoot, and dressed in a string-bikini bottom and a skintight T-shirt. She took stock: She had a pistol, a knife, and the speargun.

She pulled more branches over the hidden wetsuit. Then she saw it: a tracking device had been placed between the two oxygen tanks: a small black box. *Damn it! So they know I'm here.*

She glanced around, found a large enough piece of bamboo, split it with the knife so it made a sort of vice, like a tuning fork; she jammed the tracker inside the bamboo; she knelt by the water's edge; the bamboo held the tracker solid and the bamboo still floated. Good!

She looked up and down the beach and out toward the break in the reef.

Nobody. Nothing. Holding the knife between her teeth and with the speargun slung over her shoulder, she swam out to the reef, swam through the opening. This was tricky, the surface water swirling and bubbling and surging around her, the current racing, sloshing, reversing, reversing again, swirling this way, and that, and the razor-sharp coral only a few feet away. Out beyond the reef, she released the bamboo. The current and the breeze, which had now picked up, carried it quickly away. It was not much, but it was something.

She swam back through the reef, again fighting all the way, and, miraculously avoiding the sharp, beautiful coral. She made it to the beach. She finished camouflaging the wetsuit and oxygen tanks. Then she began to trek toward the interior of the island to see if she could find the store of supplies she had left inside the research bunker when she set it up.

Did her enemies know about that too?

She swore to herself. Bloody, bloody Dmitry! Even if Dmitry managed to destroy everything, she would claw her way back – the work was too important to be stopped by bloody pirates or traitors or competitors. *I'll be back, you bastard!*

She turned for a moment, looking out to sea, where she couldn't see the *Zeus* – or any trace of human presence, just the vast flat ocean and a gathering, towering mountain of charcoal-black clouds.

She came upon a hollowed-out tree. She remembered seeing it when she'd last been on the island; it was not far from her landing point. The tree might be useful for setting up an ambush. If she hid inside the hollow of the tree, they wouldn't see her at all, and she could pick them off, hopefully one at a time. She poked at the hollow, and prodded it with the point of the speargun. Good! No snakes, no scorpions. So, now, I have to lead them into the ambush. She went back to the beach and got the two flippers and she put one about fifteen yards inland and then the other just beyond the hollow tree.

If they came to check out the flippers, she could shoot them. If only one came, she'd have to be silent: she would stab him, or shoot him with the speargun, and wait for the next man.

They would probably fan out to look for her; if they did, she could pick them off one at a time. She passed her hand over her brow. Sweat was getting in her eyes. Her body was sticky; the heat was building up, the humidity heavier and heavier, like being coated in glue.

Typhoon Akiko was not far away and coming fast.

She went back to the edge of the beach, opposite the opening in the reef, and peeked out from behind a thick tangle of fronds and vines. Sure enough, a dinghy was coming, the backup dinghy from the *Zeus*. There were three guys aboard her.

That would leave one hostile guard back on the *Zeus*.

Sabrina retreated into the jungle. She stood beside the hollowed-out tree and waited and listened. She could see the men in silhouette against the bright water – yes, they split up, they fanned out …

At least one of them was coming toward her. Sabrina slipped into the hollow of the tree – if he approached from the right direction, she would be invisible until the last second, and maybe even beyond the last second. He would, if things went right, have his back to her.

She heard the footsteps, they were very gentle; she heard a few braking branches; she heard him push aside reeds and vines. She held her breath.

He came up past the hollow of the tree. He was about three feet from her. He spoke into his earphone mike, whispering, "One of her flippers, it must be hers, is here. Why would she take her flippers into the..?"

She stepped out, he heard something, her foot on the ground perhaps, he started to turn, but she already had the knife at his throat, slashing it just above his Adam's apple, cutting in one swipe the man's windpipe and jugular. He had no time to say anything. He gurgled. She spun him around, pushed him against a tree trunk, plunged the knife into his guts, ripped it upwards, twisting it deep, and feeling it scrape against his ribcage. *That is for Bill Griffiths*, she whispered in her mind, careful not to make any noise his phone might pick up.

He was a young man. *Frank*, yes, that was his name, *Frank Something*. His eyes, looking skywards, up toward the canopy of palm fronds, up toward the brightness of the dying day, were mostly whites. Blood sprayed all over her. He fell back against the tree, with one arm reaching up, as if he were trying to grab at a branch of the tree. She twisted the knife savagely, feeling it dislodge his heart and rip open his lungs. The blood spurted and squirted and splashed. The last trace of light left his eyes.

She pulled the knife out. Frank Something slid down the tree trunk and toppled sideways. Sabrina stepped back, holding the dripping serrated knife, panting, wild-eyed, her hair matted and soaked with blood and spittle and gore. Only now did she realize how hard her heart was beating, how her adrenaline was rushing, "God, this is exciting," she thought, "God, I like this – I actually like this!"

She took the Frank Something's earphone and stuck it into her ear. The voice spoke. It was Milo, Milo with the beautiful teeth, the steely eyes, the even tan, and the cruel smile. *What's up, Frank, What's up? Come on, Frank, where the fuck are you?*

She dragged the body, so it was about four yards from the hollow tree and left it, face up, the head toward the hollow tree, as if Frank had been attacked from the far side of the small clearing and fallen backward. She moved back into the hollow tree. It didn't take long. *Charlie, can you go check out Frank … He was at high noon, 12:00 o'clock, straight in from the landing site …*

Perfect! Saliva flooded her mouth, she swallowed it back, she licked her lips. Her pulse was racing. Perfect!

And soon Charlie was there. He said, *Oh fuck*. He knelt over Frank Something's body. She stepped out and shot him with the speargun: one shot in the nape of the neck, severing the spinal cord. *Wham*!

Charlie fell face down onto his friend Frank Somebody, without so much as a whimper. She stepped forward, leaned down him, rolled the man over, knelt down, and cut his throat, just to be sure.

Charlie had a nice honest face. It had a startled expression, sun-tanned, fair-skinned, blue eyes open and staring, and …

Were those tears …?

Yes, he had already been mourning, shedding tears for his buddy, Frank Somebody. She remembered. The two of them, Frank and Charlie, out on the back deck or in the mess, a chessboard set up between them, always together, the two of them, always laughing.

She crouched and stuck her fingers into the blood, quickly coagulating. She gazed at her bloodied fingers, the bright, darkening gobs of blood, and she was tempted, for some reason, to lick the blood. *Yummy!* What would V say? *Yummy?* She sighed. Well, I'm sorry, guys, but for you this is the end of the game. No more moves. She took a deep breath. There was one more to go. The earpiece spoke again. *Charlie, what's happened? Frank, where the hell are you?*

She laid Charlie face down next to Frank. She jerked the spear out of Charlie's neck – it brought a flap of skin and flesh with it, leaving the spinal cord visible, a giant zipper. She took his pistol and she slipped into the hollow tree, and waited, and sure enough, after about ten minutes, good old Mike turned up.

She used the Beretta this time. She shot Mike in the back of the neck and then, as he lay on the ground dead, or already paralyzed, she pulled out the knife and cut right through his neck, hacking the head half off; then she ripped open his belly, plunged in, and carved out his heart and lungs. She was angry, and for some reason which she didn't understand, and which appalled her, she was rejoicing in the death of these young men she only vaguely knew and against whom she had, personally, nothing, against whom she felt no animosity at all, except that they wanted to kill or kidnap her, and that they had killed her friends, but that, she knew, was, on their part, not personal; for them, it was just a job.

Well, for me, it's not just a job.

Heart of Darkness, she thought, Heart of Darkness.

Lord of the Flies.

She looked at the other two bodies: one lay face down, his arms spread out like he was about to catch a basketball. She had slit his throat and rejoiced in the gurgle of blood and air escaping and when she turned him around, she had exulted in the helpless stare in his eyes: "*That is for Bill Griffiths,*" she had whispered, "*For Bill,*" and she had slashed him again, and again, and again – it was redundant: he was already dead. But feeling the spray of blood was good, oh, so good!

Mike was sitting propped against a tree trunk, chest and belly an open wound; his head, half hacked off, dangled on his shoulder, his half-closed eyes staring, askance, a sly look on his handsome ruined face.

Sabrina crouched for a long moment, contemplating her handiwork.

She shook herself, as if waking from a dream. She relieved the three bodies of their weaponry – three pistols, three knives, one submachine gun.

She gathered the ammunition and a banderol to hold it. She took the submachine gun, a 38 Special pistol, and a dart gun with its tranquilizer darts. So they did want her alive. But not now, not any more, not after this. Now they would want her dead.

She took off the smallest guy's boots and socks and pulled them on and buckled up the boots.

The radio crackled. Again, it was Milo's voice. "Come in! Hey, Come in! Charlie! Mike, Frank, Frankie boy! Come in! Come in!"

She was exhausted. She picked up the submachine gun, but then leaned against a tree trunk. Everything was spinning around. She slid to the ground, letting the gun fall beside her. She shook her head, and settled herself, next to Mike's cadaver, propped up where she had left him, sitting lopsided, her dead companion, her buddy. It was nice to have company.

The sun was by now at the edge of the horizon, shining in golden glints through the palm forest. It was sinking below the towering bank of cloud, the thunderheads edged with gold. Yes, Typhoon Akiko was on its way. Soon it would be here.

She half closed her eyes. I like killing! I actually like it! What is happening to me?

She ran her fingers through her blood-matted hair. How bloody weird all this was! I mean, these guys, these guys, they were alive a few minutes ago; these are guys I have had a beer with, guys who worked for me, guys who have wives, girlfriends, kids, mothers, fathers ... And they were just pawns, just hired hands, they didn't deserve ...

She should get their dinghy and move it and hide it, or maybe use it, use it to make a run for it. She glanced at the sky. The sun was gone. The world went dull, the color drained away.

In a moment, it would be dark, pitch black.

Yes, night in the tropics comes fast.

She dipped her fingers into Mike's chest, into the coagulating mass of blood, thick and sticky and still warm; she looked at the clotted mass on her fingers, and ran it through her hair.

War paint ...

No, don't get their boat. If she took their dinghy to sea, she would be taking a huge risk. Milo was out there on the high-powered launch, *Zeus*. Milo was the most dangerous one. He would see her, he would hear her, and out on the ocean, there would be no place to hide, not yet, not until the typhoon came, or night, and even then, with radar, and *Zeus* did have its own radar set ... And, then, in a dinghy, in a typhoon ...

The radio spluttered into life. Again, it was Milo. "Hey, Charlie, what the fuck you guys doing! Remember! We want her alive! Whatever happens, get her alive!"

The sky turned black.

The radio spluttered: "Hey, Charlie, what the fuck! It's getting dark, guys, fuck, what the fuck is happening?" Poor sod, she thought, he has no idea.

She roused herself and stood up. She looked down at the dead bodies. Part of her wanted to bathe in their blood, to revel in it. She yawned and stretched, thinking that the obverse of masochism was clearly sadism; somebody's theory – was it Freud? – must be right. I must be both, she wiggled her shoulders, I must be prey and predator, victim and oppressor. How weird was that?

What the hell is happening to me?

She walked out to the beach to check the boys' dinghy. She pulled it farther up on the sand, to the tree line; she secured its anchor rope around four different trees. She took a second rope, and tied it to other trees. The typhoon would almost certainly carry it all away. But if *Andromeda* was in the hands of Dmitry and his men, the dinghy might well be her only way to get off the island. It was a long way to the next island, and that one was uninhabited too. She walked back to where the bodies had set up their little camp, dead and bloody, attracting flies. Yes, the boys were camping out.

Andromeda …

What will they have done with Claire?

Claire was too valuable to kill – if this was Dmitry's work, he would want Claire alive; so I must somehow find a way to rescue her, to get her back.

But the others – the crew, the researchers, Henry, Ian, Duncan, my oldest friends, Sally, beautiful Sally, and Isabelle Moreau, so naive and yet so bright, and Jeff, the radio operator, and Aimi …

Aimi …

Oh, God!

Claire …

Her eyes filled with tears. She bit her lip, vowing to save them or avenge them or do both.

The sky was pitch black. Was there a moon tonight? Yes, there was, almost full too, if she remembered correctly. Well, where was it? Oh, moon, come on moon, come out moon!

She would hunker down and wait it out. Then what? If *Andromeda* had been taken, then she was alone. She would have to make her way from island to island – fight her way back and find out what happened and save those who could be saved. Even if the dinghy survived the storm, it wouldn't have enough gas for an island to island hop, but it would get her somewhere at least.

She squatted on her haunches, thinking. The submachine gun and other weapons were ready-to-hand, protected by a small plastic sheet she'd lifted from the dinghy.

She left the dead behind and walked farther inland. She was suddenly exhausted. She settled herself against a tree. Now, she just had to wait.

I reek of blood, she thought, I reek of blood and murder, and part of me likes it, rejoices in it, celebrates it. More clearly than ever before – I am a murderer, a killer.

Suddenly, it was night, dark, heavy, and with the electricity-filled calm that precedes a storm.

Then she heard it – the *boom, boom, boom* of fireworks, and she saw, dimly, through the canopy of trees, the flashes of fireworks, Roman candles, the explosions, the great brilliant cartwheel sprays of light. *Andromeda* …

Then the music, faint and distant …

Should auld acquaintance be forgot,
and never brought to mind ?
Should auld acquaintance be forgot,
and auld lang syne ?

For auld lang syne, my dear,
for auld lang syne,
we'll take a cup o' kindness yet,
for auld lang syne.

So her great love, *Andromeda*, was dying. If ever anything happens and we go down, Captain Duncan had once told her, then we shall go down singing, and we will sing that song: *So we will come back. Yes, we will come back, my dear, we will come back!*

The fireworks stopped; the song ended in mid-phrase.

There was an explosion, a distant muffled explosion.

Andromeda must be gone.

Andromeda was gone.

The jungle was silent.

Time passed, how much time, she had no idea; time just passed, and she stayed there, immobile, crouched in front of the tree, waiting – but she didn't know what she was waiting for, and she was thinking: *Claire, Aimi, Claire, Aimi* …

It was night, deepest night.

Lightning flashed, and the rain began.

Lightning flashed again. There was something in the trees, something close by, something dangerous, something deadly. Sabrina went totally still. She scarcely breathed. Now I am about to die, she thought. Her hand reached for the Beretta.

CHAPTER 26 – TIGER, TIGER, BURNING BRIGHT

V morphed into her demonic version. It was, she found, easier and easier, and more and more pleasurable, to parade around as her reptilian demonic self; and, on the hunt, the reptile was so much more fun, so much more efficient – a top-notch, cutting-edge, absolutely merciless killing machine.

And now, fully aroused, she was hunting. The pleasure of the hunt made her drunk with excitement. She followed the scent, the scent of blood, the scent of murder. It led her along the edge of the beach, away from Alex and Helen and Claire and their camouflaged shelter.

And it led her into the forest.

She moved silently, cautiously; she glided between the trees, she parted the reeds and vines, making barely a whisper; her claws stepped softly, delicately, their talons gripping the soil deftly, firmly.

Blood, much human blood, had been spilled here or nearby.

She stopped. Her nostrils quivered with pleasure and anticipation – saliva dripped from her forked tongue, from her fangs. Her prey was close.

She crouched on all fours; she slithered forward, now even lower, zigzagging on her belly. Her reptilian eyes gleamed between the foliage, her claws parted the vines, her body clung sinuously to the soil, her scales merged with the jungle.

Then she saw her, it was her enemy, her worst enemy, the woman she now felt she knew so well, the CEO of Andromeda Corporation, the star of international conferences, the most brilliant of minds, the TV personality, the Nobel Prize – Sabrina Jacobs.

The woman she'd vowed to kill, the woman she'd promised to save.

"Oh, Sabrina," V purred, "beautiful, beautiful Sabrina."

V's night vision, when she turned it on, was near perfect. Her serpent eyes blinked, greedily drinking it in, an exquisite vision. Sabrina was crouched in the shelter of a tree, she was covered in blood, her hair was matted, her eyes were wild, she was armed, she had a banderol of shells over her shoulder, and her hand, palm flat on the ground was next to what was probably, yes, a submachine gun. A hunting knife was in a holster, and a handgun too, and propped beside her was a speargun, maybe some stun darts too.

The girl doesn't travel light – T-shirt, string bikini bottom, military boots, and a whole arsenal. V's eyes gleamed, her tongue flicked back and forth in anticipation of pleasure.

She would love, she would absolutely love, to drink Sabrina's blood, to drink it slowly, to drain, amorously, every drop, to gain knowledge of all the science, all the emotions, all the passions contained in that beautiful, head-strong, brilliant, mortal female.

V climbed onto a thick tree trunk that had collapsed sideways. It gave her a perfect balcony seat, about six feet off the ground. Now, she could look down on Sabrina, facing her, examining her every move, her every expression. V crouched, on her haunches, her pose echoing that of Sabrina.

The rain poured down.

V in her demonic form was naturally camouflaged. Her green and turquoise scales matched the dark tropical night in the forest in typhoon weather, though she did have a tendency, when excited, to glitter and glow, and flash little ripples of gold and scarlet.

The rain glistened, pouring down her body, streaming down her sides, slipping easily off the scales. Natural waterproofing, V thought, like water off a duck's back, it's like the ease with which I kill. Doctor Sabrina Jacobs would probably want to patent me as a new form of raincoat, the latest in iridescent turquoise and green, colors to suit your every mood.

She focused, examined Sabrina. The lady had been in a fight, a couple of fights, and she had come out on top. She's tough, and, so they say, a genius, which is certainly true. But she's hungry, and she's confused, and she's alone; she's almost naked, but she's certainly well-armed – heavily armed.

V concentrated on Sabrina's thoughts. Through the interference of the rain, and of the electricity in the air, she got snippets. Sabrina was worried about the ship; she knew it had sunk; she was anguished, about her friends, about Aimi and Henry, and, above all, about the Clone, she was calling the Clone "Claire," thinking of it like it was a human child, *her* child. That *is* interesting! I should have guessed! And Sabrina was worried – appalled even, and scared – that she had taken so much pleasure in killing.

Welcome to the club! V grinned.

Sabrina looked up. She was looking straight at V. V was utterly motionless. Sabrina's gaze did not waver.

She's aware of something, V thought, but she doesn't know what it is.

She saw Sabrina's hand edge, imperceptibly, toward the Beretta. Then she saw Sabrina's eyes focus, and widen, in fear and probably – in horror.

She sees me, thought V, *and she sees me seeing her.* Staring straight at Sabrina, V wagged one finger-claw in front of her fangs. The message, she hoped, was clear. *Don't reach for that gun!*

Sabrina's hand stopped. She clenched her fist and slowly brought her hand up in front of her, and opened it, the palm toward V, the fingers spread *See, there's nothing, I've got nothing in my hand.*

The girl is *good*, thought V.

Lightning flashed and in the blue-white flickering flash of the lightning – it seemed to go on for a long time.

V stepped off the branch, and, in one leap, she was across the clearing, swooped close, and crouched in front of Sabrina. The two women, the reptilian demon and the scientist-billionaire, faced each other, their lips inches apart.

Sabrina didn't move. She took a deep breath. Now this creature will kill me, and there is nothing I can do about it, and nothing I *want* to do about it.

The reptilian creature stared at Sabrina; its eyes glowed; it reached out a claw and it ran its claws through Sabrina's hair. Sabrina stayed rock still. And the two of them crouched for a long minute, staring at each other, neither moving, the predator and the prey, the hunter and the hunted.

The reptile's forked tongue flickered between its lips, and it seemed to have a smile on its face, and Sabrina allowed her lips to reflect that smile, ever so slightly. How do you communicate with such a thing? Henry said you could look into its eyes and reason – but how, how?

The reptile hissed, a long, voluptuous hiss, its forked tongue flickering in pleasure in the moonlight.

My God, thought Sabrina, my God, it is so pleased to have me at its mercy! What do I do now? She cleared her throat; should I try to talk to it? Can you talk to such a thing?

The reptile smiled. "Hello, Sabrina," it said, "Or should I say 'Doctor Jacobs'?"

Sabrina was utterly shocked. The thing – V – in this demonic shape could still speak. It had a mind. "You know my name," she said, swallowing.

"You are famous, Sabrina; and besides, we have met before, I have a special interest in you. My name, by the way, is V."

"Yes, I know. We've spoken. Pleased to meet you once again, I suppose."

"The pleasure, once again, is all mine," said V, her claw caressing Sabrina's hair, which was dripping wet, matted with blood and gore.

"Your fangs are quite prominent," Sabrina said, her curiosity aroused, "I didn't realize."

Lightning flashed again, and thunder echoed through the jungle. V smiled, tilting her head slightly to one side. "Yes. They're awkward. They give me a lisp. Or perhaps it's the forked tongue. I don't think they're my most attractive features."

"No," Sabrina said, "You're wrong. They are very attractive. You are quite beautiful, you know, unique, just the way you are. It's startling, actually."

"Well, thank you, Sabrina." V placed her other claw on Sabrina's shoulder and registered that Sabrina didn't flinch, not in the least, not a tremor, not a shiver.

"There is one thing," Sabrina said, clearing her throat, "Well, there are many things I don't understand – but there's one thing I didn't realize, that I didn't know, and I apologize that I didn't know it."

"What was that?"

"I didn't realize that when you take on your … your … demonic form …"

"She-devil, demon, reptile, serpent … People call it different things." V shrugged. Coin-like glimmers of moonlight danced, reflecting off the scales of her shoulders and breasts.

"I didn't realize that you keep all of your … ah … human intelligence … that you …"

"It might be my *alien* intelligence."

"Yes, you are right. I didn't think of that – how stupid of me, how anthropocentric – my father would definitely not have approved of such stupidity – I would have been whipped or received a session of electroshocks – you keep all your intelligence … your personality, you don't just turn into … a monster."

"I'm monster enough in all my forms."

"May I touch you?"

"Of course," The tongue flickered; the golden eyes flashed. "Help yourself."

Sabrina reached out and touched V's cheek and her lips and her chin and her forehead.

"Amazing," she said, "Utterly amazing! How does it work? How can it be done? The human epidermis transformed into overlapping scales, keratin scales, and so quickly. How can it work?"

"I don't know, Sabrina." Even in the gloom of the tropical storm, in the light of the faint periodic moon, in the flashes of lightning, V's eyes glowed with an inner light. "But, Sabrina, I am rather annoyed with you. In fact, I tracked you down to kill you."

"I understand. That's what you came here for. You are right, of course. But ..." Sabrina, for the first time, seemed frightened. "You didn't hurt Claire?"

"I came to kill her too."

"Oh, no, you must not. Claire is innocent. She is not what she seems."

"And what does she seem?"

"She seems crazy, mad, an animal, wild, dangerous."

"But she's not?"

"No."

"What *is* she, then, Sabrina? I believe you call her '*the Thing*' and '*It*,' terms you use when referring to me, too, if I'm not mistaken."

"Yes, but I was wrong. I am wrong. I have done wrong. I wronged Claire terribly – and you, V, I apologize. I beg not for pity – you will be right to execute me – but for forgiveness. Claire is a person, that's what she is; she's intelligent and sensitive, she's a genius in fact, but she's hiding it."

"From whom?"

"From me."

"It is too late for all of this. It is too late for Claire – what I've done to Claire, I've already done."

"Oh, God, no, please, no, V, no!"

"Ah, I see." V frowned. "*Now,* you care! That is too bad. A mere animal, a demon, you can kill, or perhaps lobotomize ..."

"Yes, I am sorry. Nothing I can say or do will make that right." Sabrina stared into V's eyes. "Do what you will, V. Do what you must. You hate me; you are right; I tried to destroy you."

V reached out with her claw, its razor-sharp points extended. "I like you like this, Sabrina, half-naked, covered in blood, crouching in the jungle, a killer, a wild animal which has just fought to survive and now – all messed up, under the rain, alone, hating herself. It's a beautiful image."

With a quick swipe of her talon, V slashed Sabrina's face, from the forehead, across the left eye, across the cheek, to the chin; it was a neat, clean cut. The blood began to ooze. "You arc beautiful, Sabrina. I saw that when I saw the hologram on your website. But you are more beautiful than I thought. Now I have put my mark upon you, a very visible mark, like a brand."

Sabrina didn't flinch, barely dared breathe.

V took Sabrina's bleeding face between her claws and cradled it in a vice-like grip, rocking Sabrina's head gently back and forth. "You have a long delicate neck, Sabrina. It's a very appealing feature."

As the two crouched, facing each other, V holding Sabrina's head between her claws, weighing possibilities, enjoying the moment. Sabrina didn't move, didn't say anything, she just stared into V's eyes where she could read nothing; then she bit her lower lip. "Is it now?" she whispered.

She stared steadily at V, waiting for the death blow – a quick twist of V's claws and her neck would be broken, and she would be dead.

V said nothing. Her claws held Sabrina's head tighter, in a death-like vice. One pointed claw-finger lightly, teasingly, caressed the lobe and rim of Sabrina's ear.

V's tongue flickered beyond her lips. She leaned forward, so her face was within an inch of Sabrina's face. V's tongue flickered out, it touched Sabrina's lips, flickered along Sabrina's lips, flirting with them, and then V kissed Sabrina, a full kiss, on the mouth, and Sabrina, holding her breath, hesitating, fearful, slowly returned the kiss, her lips caressing V's lips, her tongue answering V's tongue, and thinking, *This is kiss of death, she will kiss me, and then break my neck!* The blood, welling up from the slash, was getting into Sabrina's left eye; she tried to blink the blood away; it stung, blinding her. The kiss continued, V's reptile lips nibbling at Sabrina's human lips, V's reptile tongue exploring Sabrina's human tongue, V's fangs pressing on Sabrina's lips, and Sabrina thought: *This is a very strange way to die.*

V slowly, almost reluctantly, drew back, gazing with reptile eyes at Sabrina. Sabrina's heart stood still. Now, she thought, now she will kill me. "Is it now?" she whispered.

"No, it is not now," V said. She released her grip on Sabrina and stood up. "Come with me," she said.

Sabrina stood up, wiping the blood from her eye with the back of her hand, half her face now covered in a zigzag of fresh blood, her blood. "Where?"

"You'll see." V turned away and added, over her shoulder, "Bring some weapons. We might need them. Don't forget the submachine gun."

Sabrina stared for just a second and then bent down, hoisted up the machine gun, slung it under her arm, and followed.

V looked back. "I'll show you what I've done to your Clone. I want you to see for yourself the body of the Clone."

Sabrina gazed at the elegant reptilian back, that the glittering scales, the narrow waist, the powerful shoulders, thinking: V has turned her back on me, and I could shoot her, pump her full of lead, but it wouldn't kill her, and besides if she wants to kill me, she can kill me. I'm not going to try to stop her. "You can see in the dark?" she said.

"Yes. My night vision is excellent."

"Can you control the sensitivity?"

"Yes. I can control the sensitivity. Always the scientist, Sabrina?"

"Always curious."

"That's good. I guess. No, it is good. I'm sure it's good."

"But Claire?"

"You'll see the Clone's body; you'll see what I've done. Sacrifices must be made. Don't worry. My mentor made me swear that I would never create any of my own kind. And Claire is a clone of me – she is 'of my own kind.' So …" V stopped and turned. "By the way, Sabrina, I read minds too."

"Oh, oh!" Sabrina suddenly felt ashamed.

"Don't worry. You didn't think anything to be ashamed of. And, in any case, things work out. Some things work out."

V pushed away some heavy vines, and turned, eyes, gleaming, to gaze at Sabrina.

"And, Sabrina, *Andromeda* sank. Many of your staff were killed – murdered by the security staff – but Ian, the engineer, and the captain, and your friend Aimi, and Henry, organized the resistance – so most people were saved."

"And you helped," said Sabrina, catching a surprising and unspoken thought. Can I read thoughts now?

"I'm sorry," said V, "that thought sort of just leaked out. And, yes, Aimi, Henry, Ian, and the captain are all alive, and, yes, I did help."

V led Sabrina out onto the beach.

"I`m finding it difficult," Sabrina said, "to control my thoughts."

"Don`t control them; think of me as your confessor – you can tell me anything. I am part of you, and you are part of me. We belong to each other." V took Sabrina's hand in one of her claws.

"Just let it all flow?" Sabrina took a deep breath, thinking, Claire cannot be dead, I cannot believe she would have killed Claire.

"Yes, just let it all flow."

The rain whipped down; the clouds were low and wild; the sea was high and raging. The moon appeared and disappeared. Tangles of cloud were being dragged down to the level of the sea, skimming along the horizon, closing in, lowering, racing on the surface. Silver and black, it was all silver and black. "It's beautiful, isn't it?" said V.

Sabrina was startled; but then she said, "Yes. Yes, it is."

"It's strange perhaps for a creature such as I, Sabrina, but I do love the world," said V, "I love the night: the power of it, the majesty!" Now they were walking side by side, hand in hand, as V led Sabrina along the beach, up toward the tree line; then they entered the forest and stopped about ten yards behind the tree line.

The moon appeared and disappeared behind clouds racing high in the sky. V said: "Let's stop here for just a second. I'm going to morph back to being human – well, *my* version of human. You may watch. You will find it interesting."

Sabrina stood very still. The moon came out, the clearing was bathed in silver light. V became a blur, and where the demon had stood there was now a naked human female. "My God, that is amazing," said Sabrina.

"The first time was traumatic, let me tell you, I didn't know what was happening to me," said V, "and clothes are always a problem. I could wear big baggy things in my demonic form, but I think it would not really be very aesthetic or impressive. Scales beg to be worn naked, if you see what I mean," and she smiled at Sabrina. "And, now, let's meet our friends."

"Friends?"

V pulled aside an invisible curtain. The camouflage was so perfect Sabrina had no idea they were standing next to a shelter. She blinked, shocked. There were candles inside, just a few. The whole place was invisible unless you knew it was there. Three faces, lit by the candles, looked up at them. A handsome man – Alex Wolf – cocking an automatic weapon, a beautiful movie-star type blonde, with her hair cut short, and Claire!

Claire!

Sabrina's heart almost stopped: Claire was still alive, and she was looking up, in a focused, intelligent, very human way, startled, but fully aware.

"Hello, Claire," Sabrina said, swallowing hard. The girl who probably hated her, the girl whom she had kept prisoner all her life, the girl whom she should have loved but had not dared love, the girl who was a genius – and who was undoubtedly eager for revenge, rightly eager for revenge, she was alive!

"You didn't kill her?" said Claire, looking at V.

"No, Claire, I didn't kill her. She wants to tell you how sorry she is, don't you, Sabrina?"

Sabrina looked at V and then gazed at Claire. "I know you can't forgive me, Claire," Sabrina looked down at the ground and then at the girl. "I did terrible things to you."

Claire stared at her for a long time, then she said, "You're all wet and covered in blood, Sabrina. Come here, and I'll help clean you and dry you off. And what is that cut on your face? First, you'd better take off those clothes."

Sabrina stared at Claire: she was fourteen years old, and giving orders like an adult, like she was somehow in charge. Suddenly, Sabrina felt doubly ashamed, morally and physically exposed, a prisoner.

"Go ahead, Sabrina, join V – strip," said Alex, "I won't look!" And he grinned, "By the way, as you know, my name is Alex, Alex Wolf, and I imagine you could use some coffee." He poured a cup and held it out.

"Thank you, Doctor Wolf … I know you, I mean about you, I know your work."

"Just plain Alex will do. We're all family here."

"I'm Helen, Helen Guerrera," said the blonde. She came over and helped Sabrina lift off the bloodied T-shirt. Sabrina pulled off the boots and socks and the bikini bottom. She was naked.

Doctor Sabrina Jacobs … the New Eve … bloodied, and a killer, and now branded and scarred – a prisoner …

Claire said, "Sabrina, we'd better go outside, for a minute, in the rain. It'll act as a shower."

Outside, in the dark, Claire shampooed Sabrina's hair, and pummeled her scalp cruelly, working her fingers into the foam, and working up the suds.

"Lean over, Sabrina, bend down, that's right, that's good, thank you, Sabrina! I've always dreamed of doing this for you. And I wanted to tell you what to wear, too."

"What to wear?"

"I wanted to look after you," Claire said, "You see, I hate you and I love you. Do you mind my speaking so frankly? I have not yet learned how to be human."

"If I have time, Claire, I'll try to earn the love, at least. I suppose I've already earned the hate."

"I love you more than I hate you," Claire said, "if you want to know. But the hate – maybe it's not exactly hate, it's probably something else, something more subtle. Human words are so inadequate, don't you think, human words are such gross, clumsy, galumphing, leaky things; but whatever this emotion or feeling is, it adds, how do they say, it adds spice, it adds an edge to my love, to my yearning." And she gave Sabrina's scalp a particularly vigorous rub.

"Ouch!"

"Hmm, I *love* doing this!"

"Ouch!"

Sabrina began to soap herself, but Claire insisted on soaping and scrubbing Sabrina's back – she was very thorough.

And then they came back into the tent, and Claire toweled Sabrina down – again, she seemed to take pleasure in making it as vigorous and rough and humiliating as possible. "This is fun," Claire said, smiling and glancing at V.

V was finally putting some clothes on, and as she pulled on her T-shirt and jeans and buckled her holster onto her belt, she watched the girl towel Sabrina's neck and back and, though Claire was staring at V – with an expression of love and gratitude – and smiling and nodding – *This what you want me to do, right?* – V felt almost jealous, but she lifted another set, panties, black jeans and black T-shirt, out of the equipment box. "I think we are about the same size, Sabrina. These will fit you."

"I've been an idiot," said Sabrina, shaking her head, "a criminal idiot."

"No, you're a genius," said Claire, roughly toweling Sabrina's hair, "and that is worse."

CHAPTER 27 – TSUNAMI

Helen handed Sabrina a sandwich and another cup of coffee. "The typhoon is coming in quickly. We need to find shelter, a real shelter. Do you want a sandwich, Claire?"

"Yes, thank you." Claire took the sandwich and took a deep bite and swallowed, and then drank some coffee. V watched with interest. If Claire doesn't get sick, that means … That means she can still eat food; she is a vampire – she can drink blood – but she can also eat food, that means … that means … that may possibly mean that part of the curse is lifting, that may mean that Sabrina really has created a new race out of my DNA!

Marcus had suggested, once, that this merging – this new entity, this new being born out of a marriage of human and alien, might, some day, just possibly happen – a new *hybrid* …

Could it be that Claire …?

"So, what is this scar, this cut?" Claire glanced at Sabrina and then knelt next to her; she traced the scar that V had made with her claw – a single straight razor cut that cut from Sabrina's hairline, down across her forehead and eye and mouth to her chin.

"I did it," said V, "I put my mark on her, but it can be removed, and I'm thinking that right now I will –"

"… remove it?" Claire looked up at V.

"Yes. It was a stupid, cruel thing to do. But I was excited and still angry."

"May I do it?"

"Yes, you may," V raised an eyebrow. So Claire knew about her healing powers! "Of course you may, darling. Do it!"

"What?" Sabrina looked from the one to the other. "Do what?"

"You'll see, Sabrina," said Helen; she was kneeling in front of the computer following the path of Typhoon Akiko. "We don't have much time, folks, the typhoon will be hitting us in about an hour and a half or two hours at most, and it's apparently got some really big waves with it, mini tsunamis – or worse."

Claire cupped Sabrina's face between the palms of her hands and she concentrated and she frowned slightly, and Sabrina watched the girl's face, and felt a sort of radiant warmth penetrate her own face and skin, and she wondered at how vastly things had changed, at how vastly their relationship had changed, in just a few hours. When the day began, Claire had been a prisoner, an experiment, and now she was ... well, what was she? My boss, my mistress, my jailer? And what am I?

"There," said Claire, and she lifted her hands from Sabrina's face, and smiled. It was perhaps the most radiant smile Sabrina had ever seen.

"Well done, Claire," said Alex. "Well, Doctor Jacobs, we shall be forced to rewrite the laws of molecular biology, and physics, and this is just one reason – what Claire did to you right there."

"What, what did you do, Claire?" Sabrina asked, gingerly feeling her face with her fingers and wondering what had happened.

"The cut is gone, repaired, gone as if it had never been," said Helen, "V did the same for me. Half my face had been scarred by acid, and cut by a straight razor. V cupped my face in her hands, and all the damage was gone."

"Well," said V, "all those who eat should eat something, a sandwich or an energy bar, and then we'd better prepare for the storm – and that's going to be a problem."

"There's a bunker on the island," said Sabrina. "It's made of reinforced concrete, it's very strong, it's supposed to be waterproof, and it should resist anything the storm can do. There's room for everybody inside, if we can get into it."

"How far?"

"I think about a quarter of a mile."

"Can you find it?"

"Yes, I think so."

"Okay, eat, drink, and let's pack up and go," said V.

They were already deep in the forest when Claire held up her hand, and they all stopped. They waited a moment.

"What is it, Claire?" V put her hand on the girl's shoulder.

"The typhoon – or something – has caused a giant tsunami," said Claire. "I can sense it, it is coming. We must hurry."

"Okay, everybody, run," said V, running beside Sabrina, and leading the way.

They found the bunker easily, and Sabrina remembered the combination to the armored door, and they got inside.

But then a horrible thing happened. V thought she would never forgive herself for allowing it to happen.

Sabrina said she had to shut the vent on top of the bunker and get the recorder.

"If the ventilation system is open and the water sweeps over the island, the bunker will fill with water, and we'll all drown!" She rushed out of the bunker and climbed onto the roof.

"Come back, Sabrina! There's no time!" V followed right behind, leaping onto the roof.

"The recorder has absolutely essential information, vital for the survival of this archipelago." Sabrina was fiddling with the ventilation system hatch.

V, right behind her, shouted, "No, Sabrina, there is no time, come back here!"

Claire peeked out the door. "It's coming; the tsunami is coming! I can hear it, it's coming!"

"Throw me that rope, Claire," said V, "and tie the other end to the bottom rung of the steel ladder next to the door. If you have to, close the door – and leave us outside."

Claire grabbed the rope, tossed it to V, and tied the end of the rope with a triple knot to the steel ladder. Claire was continually surprised and shocked at what she knew how to do.

V caught the rope, tied it around her waist, and leaned over Sabrina,

Sabrina was unscrewing the clamps of the recording device, "It will just take a second."

"We don't have a second." V heard a roaring: a huge wall of water was sweeping over the island. Claire was right. Alex shouted, "It's coming, and I'm going to close the door, but I'll open it for you!"

"Yes, close the door, close the damn door!" shouted V. The roar of the oncoming wave drowned out her voice.

"Just give me a second!" Sabrina had the instrument free; she shut the vent and locked it in place.

V looked up. "Damn it!" A twenty-foot wall of water, gray and green, was plunging, foaming, through the forest, sweeping everything in its path, trees tumbling over, everything, absolutely everything, was lifted up and torn away,

"Shut the door," V shouted, "Come on, Sabrina!"

Sabrina stood up, holding the instrument, and smiling, and then she saw the wave. "I was so distracted," she said, "I'm sorry." In that instant, Sabrina looked like a child who knew she had done something naughty.

V grabbed her. The wave slammed into them, swept them up in a wall of water. V clamped her arms around Sabrina's waist, clinging desperately. The water swirled them, round and round, upside down, right-side up, upside down, a thundering, whirling maelstrom of water, tree trunks, planks, vines, sand, pebbles. V was hit on the head. Dizzy. Stunned. Sabrina slipped from her grasp. Suddenly, they were on the surface. Sabrina, her eyes wide, breathed out, "V!" With a roar, they were swept under, then back to the surface. Sabrina was far away, then she was slammed back. V reached out. The tips of their fingers touched, slipped away. V was plunged down, in a torment of whirling water. She bounced up, suddenly on the surface, a boiling churning vortex of foam, waves, water, flotsam and jetsam. Gasping, she looked around. No Sabrina. V was still, to her surprise, attached to the rope, tied around her waist. Suddenly, she was in a freight elevator, going down, and down, and down … She spun like a top. Wham! She was in the open, sitting on soaked ground amid piles of dripping debris, heaps of rubble. The wave had passed by. No sign of Sabrina. A roar raced toward her, the thunder of an oncoming freight train. Another wave! V staggered to her feet. The bunker was still there. Pulling on the rope, she stumbled drunkenly back to the bunker. The door opened. Claire and Alex standing there.

"Get in," Alex shouted, "Where is Sabrina?"

"Sabrina! Sabrina was swept away! I held onto her, but then she … she was swept away."

The look in Claire's face was of total devastation. She threw herself into V's arms and began to cry.

"Another wave is coming," Alex said, "get inside."

They got inside. Helen and Alex locked and barred the steel door. "We may drown in here," said Alex. "If the roof doesn't have any holes, and we are lucky, it may trap air, and, maybe, just maybe, we'll survive."

The wave hit, the blockhouse trembled, water flooded in under the door, but the door was low, and there were no windows, so maybe … just maybe, they would not drown. They were waist-deep, then neck-deep, in water. Light came in below the door, lighting them up, in a ghostly green light, from below, loops and circles of light, and then, as the water went deeper, dark green and blue and ghostly gray, and then hardly any light at all. Darkness. The voices echoed in the bunker.

For the next twenty minutes, the bunker was underwater; inside, they were now up to their necks in water. And they could hear the ocean swirling around, thundering down on the roof of the bunker, a chaos of crashing sea and objects smashing against the concrete.

"By closing that vent, Sabrina saved us," said V. "If she hadn't, this whole bunker would be full of water by now."

"Worst comes to worst, we can open the door and swim up to the surface," said Alex.

"You don't want to be on that surface," said V.

Claire looked into V's eyes. "V, you told me the outside world would be interesting, well it … is." Claire closed her eyes and put her arms around V. She held on tight, and leaned her head against V's shoulder. Boy, thought V, the girl is strong; her embrace is sweet and loving, but like a steel trap.

It was totally dark. Claire opened her eyes. "Sabrina is still alive, I know she's still alive. I can feel her."

V held Claire and kissed her, stroking the girl's hair.

"I'm connected to her, I know I am," Claire was trembling. "She's not dead. She can't die. She won't die."

"We'll find her," said V. "When we get out of here, we'll find her."

The hours passed – after the tsunami, the typhoon itself hit with all its thunderous force, sweeping across the island, ripping up forests, lifting waves of sand, carrying whole beaches and sections of the island away.

Then, after hours of thunder, after hours of enormous waves, there was a dead calm – silence, like the silence of death, and just the dripping of rivulets of water.

They had to push the door open. It was buried in a bank of sand, and a tree trunk blocked the way. V changed briefly into her demon version, and she clawed her way out through the sand, with Alex shoveling debris away behind her. When they got out of the bunker, what met them was a scene of utter devastation.

Claire was awestruck by V's transformation, and curious about it. She ran her hands over V's scales. "This is one version of you?"

"Yes, darling, this is one version of me. I'll tell you all about it later."

"It's beautiful."

"Thank you, darling." The reptilian V kissed Claire on the forehead with a sweet, lingering flicker of its forked tongue.

They were outside. They looked around.

It smelt like they were underwater.

"Let's go," said V. "Let's look for our dinghy." Helen and Claire carried the equipment and supplies. V and Alex led the way. They climbed over mountains of debris, broken, shattered tree trunks, dead animals, dead fish, and immense tangles of vines. It was as if the world had been destroyed and then only half reborn, out of chaos. "It smells," said V, "like the bottom of the sea."

"Sabrina is hugging something," said Claire.

"Hugging something?"

"Yes, it's ... it's ... it's an iguana."

"An iguana ..." V looked deep into Claire's eyes and cupped her hand on Claire's head. "Yes, darling – You are right, you two are connected, and she's ... she's on a raft ... a sort of raft."

"Our dinghy is still there, but it's out in the water." Alex waded into the water, now calm, but still boiling and seething in that quiet insidious oily way water does after a violent storm. He lifted a rope from the dinghy and towed the dinghy back to the beach.

"So now we begin again," said Helen.

"And we look for Sabrina," said V.

It would be a long search.

They would, perhaps, with luck, find Sabrina, many days or weeks later, but when and if they did, she would no longer be Sabrina.

CHAPTER 28 – REPTILE

"This installation will be destroyed …"

An alarm was blaring: *beep, beep, beep …*

A suave mechanical female voice was saying, in Russian, "This installation will be destroyed in 15 minutes. This installation will be destroyed in 15 minutes. Please follow the agreed evacuation procedures. This installation will be destroyed in 15 minutes …"

The heavy-lidded eyes blinked open. The eyes stared at a set of large bright rectangular lights, and at a ceiling. *Where am I? Who am I?*

Whoever she was, whatever she was, she tried to turn her head. She couldn't. Her neck was paralyzed. Various complicated surgical and scientific devices hung over her, close-focus lamps, video cameras, knives, drills … She tried to sit up. She couldn't. Slowly, dazedly, she realized she was manacled, ankles, neck, wrists, and waist, to an operating table.

An operating table!

Where am I?

Who am I?

"This installation will be destroyed in 14 minutes and thirty seconds; this installation will be destroyed in …"

The heavy-lidded eyes blinked, and blinked again. There was, she thought vaguely, trying to organize her thoughts, there was something wrong with the eyes, with the lids – something definitely wrong with *her* eyes, with *her* lids. Something *very* wrong with her eyes – *my* eyes – with the way she was seeing. The spectrum of light was wider; she was seeing some infrared and ultraviolet, and the 3-dimensionality of space seemed accentuated; it was like scary 3-D special effects in a video simulation, or like an extremely vivid drug trip; and the field of vision was wider, quite a bit wider – how could that be? She could see to both sides, as well as in front. They must have drugged her, whoever they were and whoever she was. What sort of drug? Was it a drug that was making everything seem so strange? Why had they – whoever they were – put her on an operating table? Why was she tied down?

Who am I?

She experienced a sudden intake of breath – an inner light dawned.

Sabrina? Is that my name?

They – who are *they*, what had happened? Where am I?

Sabrina Jacobs. That is who I am, that is what I am.

Where am I? Who brought me here?

Images began to form.

Dmitry Pavlov!

Dmitry Pavlov – suddenly some things became clear: her life, who she was, and one vivid, frightening, image – a man: Dmitry Pavlov. It must be him. But what had happened? What had happened before? Where was she?

The body – which seemed a stranger's body – tugged and strained against the manacles. Ah, the right hand! It was not tied down so tightly! She realized there was something strange, something weird, about that right hand that was, it seemed, her hand; she couldn't see it but she flexed it; it strained against the manacle, as she tried to remember …

This installation will be destroyed in 14 minutes. This installation …

She tried to remember.

What had happened?

What had happened to her?

Memories? Were these memories? They were like a dream, a nightmare, a phantasmagoria of elongated tortured images, stretched out on a rack, monstrous, like paintings by Goya or Ensor or … The memories were disconnected, flash images, *flash, flash, flash* …

She remembered …

The killers who followed her onto the island; V, the beautiful demon, her turquoise scales running with water, her breasts dripping silver streams of water, her claws outstretched, her claw slashing my face. I was taken prisoner by V in the jungle. V and I walked on the beach, hand in hand, we saw how beautiful it was. Suddenly, she sees Claire, the Clone, her grandest experiment, suddenly become a person, an adult, a friend, like a daughter, suddenly, like a daughter, an angry, beautiful, loving adolescent daughter, transformed in one day also into a masterful adult; Claire washing and shampooing her as if she were Claire's pet dog; Claire, adopted by V, in the tent, by lamplight; and she remembers kneeling in front of Claire and receiving some sort of forgiveness, some sort of benediction; and she remembers the handsome man Alex – a famous molecular biologist – and his friend, the stunningly beautiful blonde, Helen, both of them crouching over a computer. Then they were all in the storm, and they ran to the research bunker – and it took some time to open it; but she did remember the combination, and so they got inside just in time – just before the tidal wave hit and she'd insisted on going on the roof to close the ventilator opening, and to get the atmosphere recorder. And then a wave hit, perhaps a tsunami, and then she was underwater swimming for her life: *And V tried to save me, but she couldn't, and we were both swept away. Oh, God, I hope V is okay! I hope I didn't cause her to drown!*

And Claire, and Alex, and Helen. They are alive. I pray they are alive!

We are one family, all one family here, Alex had said.

And then she was underwater swimming for her life, and then relaxing, letting the current take her, thinking, now I am dying, how foolish, but in the end, I don't care, I've lived my time … But, no, damn it, I'm curious, I want to know what will happen next, I want to live, I want to help Claire find herself, I want to make up for the damage I have done! And the dark water swirled around her, bubbles of air, trees, vines, earth, animals, all swept up in the thundering maelstrom of water, and then, suddenly, she was on the surface, sputtering, coughing, vomiting, in the moonlight, in the crux of a wave, the valley between two waves, and she could see a wave towering over her, its foamy edge, white-silver, and sharp in the moonlight, so she just let herself float, she was turned upside down, swept down, underwater again, swept into the bubbling gurgling frenzy, then, splash, she was up again, once again, in a strangely calm and flat valley between two waves, and she didn't know how long it continued, underwater, above water, underwater, then again above water, and finally, she bumped into a log, which was part of some sort of floating ruin of a structure, a few boards attached to it, and she held onto the log, and finally, in a moment of calm, the water oily and swirling slowly, and vomiting up all sorts of things in miniature whirlpools, vines, tree trunks, leaves, weeds, plastic bags, she climbed onto the log, and found that it was part of a wall or something, planks and logs tied together, and she jammed her arms down between two logs that were bound together, and she lay face down, thinking that maybe she would drown that way, spread-eagled, face down on a raft, or maybe the thunderous sea – the roar was deafening – would break the raft apart and tear her arms out of their sockets. She felt the logs creak and groan and scrape against her face and her arms and her belly, her legs were flopping and flipping, as if broken, but not really, carried this way and that by the thundering water, but she was wedged there, stuck between the logs, and didn't lose her grip.

Then she doesn't remember anything until she wakes up. She is lying face down on the logs, bound round with ropes and with vines and seaweed, and sharing the raft with an iguana. It is staring her in the eye. It comes closer to her when she disentangles herself, and sits up. It raises one paw-like foot, as if wanting to shake hands.

The sea is flat and glassy and oily, and the sun is high in the sky, and it is hot – stinking, salty, sticky hot – and the smell of seaweed and wood rot is overpowering. The iguana looks at her with his funny little pivoting eyes that resemble a side gun turret on one of those early First World War tanks. It's an interesting design feature, Sabrina thinks, perhaps she could adapt for a bio-creature, a reptilian robot. The iguana moves close to her, when she turns onto her side, so it can shelter in the narrow band of shade cast by her body and she likes the feel of its leathery skin against her skin, at least it's alive, pressing against her hot burning skin. She whispers.

"Right, Come to Mama, Mama will keep you in the shade, don't worry, Mama's here, that's right, Mama's here."

She passes out again lying face down sprawled across the logs and when she wakes, the iguana is still there, but farther way now, blinking at her, perhaps wondering whether she's dead or alive.

She thinks of Tania and wonders if Tania survived – alone on the launch *Zeus* with the guards. They had guns, Tania didn't, so Tania too is probably dead, and then she thinks of V. I owe V, that creature, now my friend, I owe her my life, and I owe her Claire, too, I owe her Claire's rebirth, and Claire's forgiveness – of me.

I am an idiot, she thinks, *Sabrina Jacobs, you are an idiot, and that is* not *the fever talking.* She knows she is dehydrating. Here in the middle of the ocean, she will die, probably, from thirst, from lack of water. The sun will burn her brain away. She will go mad.

The Vampire is my friend.

Claire is my daughter, and she is the Vampire's daughter, too – or sister.

It's a tangled family tree.

It's a tangled web we weave …

She sinks into delirium. Her mind is feverish, disconnected, hallucinating; it drifts back to her love affair – no, "love affair" is not the right phrase – her sex liaison – her obsession, her beautiful, sublime, sick, violent, sadomasochistic obsession – with Dmitry Pavlov, the man undoubtedly behind the murders of her friends, and the sinking of *Andromeda* – the man she had known perhaps better than she knew any other man, except her father; the man who wanted to kidnap her, or kill her, or worse – *Dmitry, my master, my slave, my love; once upon a time …*

Most fairy-tales end badly.

Dmitry Pavlov, tall, handsome, strong-featured, blond – one of the richest men in Russia. She sighs. I thought he wanted *me* – well, he certainly liked to *play* with me – but really what he wanted was Andromeda Corporation.

Sabrina Jacobs – Dmitry's plaything.

Sabrina Jacobs – Dmitry's sex toy.

They first met in Paris at an International Biotechnology Conference. Dmitry immediately charmed her with his intelligence, his brilliance. He was a molecular biologist, so they shared a great many interests, the talk flowed easily, dazzlingly. And then there was his sense of romance – candlelight dinners, cheek-to-cheek dancing, long intimate conversations – and then, having hooked her, he revealed, playfully, and tidbit by tidbit, his darker side, his penchant for cruelty, for erotic cruelty, for calculated psychological cruelty, and, of course, in revealing his darker side, he was revealing hers too. She'd been well trained by Daddy: Sabrina Jacobs, the pre-formatted slave girl. You just had to have the key, and you could open her up, and – eureka! – You would discover, behind the cool facade, behind the stylish arrogance and apparent mastery, an anxious, adoring, slave-in-waiting. Dmitry knew what she was; he knew the key was there; and he knew how to find it. He started with literary allusions, with little hints, with talk of the Marquis de Sade and of the *Story of O*, and then he began to buy her clothes, provocative, slightly humiliating clothes, *Sabrina Jacobs, sex object*, and then more and more provocative clothes, and shoes with punitive stiletto heels, tight skirts that got shorter and shorter, slowly challenging her, slowly pushing the frontier, slowly changing her – *Sabrina Jacobs, classy exhibitionist slut.*

Oh, but it was exhilarating, inebriating, and it was, for a time, fun!

One evening in Moscow he took her to a club where people were tied up and led around like slaves and one man in black leather was hanging in a cage from the ceiling; he was a famous violinist, apparently, and others, men and women, were crouching in things that looked like the stocks, hands and necks sticking out through big round harnesses of wood, and some girls were dressed as ponies, with tails and harness and shoes which were designed to be like hooves. One of the pony-girls came to the table and sat with them for a while, but girl couldn't say much or take a drink because of the bit in her mouth, and she had to turn all the way around to look at you, if you said something to her, because of the blinders sticking out beside her eyes that restricted her field of vision, but not much of interest was said anyway because the music was high-volume ultra-decibel, hard metal rock, or whatever they call it, and Sabrina was in a tight black leather dress Dmitry had insisted she wear and stiletto heels which made her arches and toes ache and Dmitry told her to lead the girl around by the little chain attached to the girl's pony halter which Sabrina did, and then brought the girl back to the table, and Dmitry took the girl away, and Sabrina sat alone thinking that this night-club master-slave stuff was maybe a good concept in theory, but in reality it was a very boring way to pass an evening in Moscow, maybe a good conversation by firelight, time in bed with her guy, or an evening at the Bolshoi, or even better, a good book, would have been more entertaining – but she did like the submissive glances the girl sent her, looking up from between the blinders and the halter, her mouth held open by the bit, and flapping her eyelids. When Dmitry came back from doing whatever he did with the girl, Sabrina said, "I'm bored, I'm going," and he said, "But the night is young," and she said, "Maybe for you it is," and she left and he stayed, but, still, when she went back to their hotel room, and she was in bed reading a book, she found herself waiting for him, anticipating with guilty, half-repressed excitement his return. When he got 'home', well, it really wasn't home, just the Imperial Suite at the what's-it's-name hotel not far from the Bolshoi Theater, he made love to her in a way that was so violent, it appalled and yet thrilled her, and she said, *What are you doing to me?* And he said, *I'm doing to you what you want me to do to you, I'm doing to you what you really desire. You are like the slave girl, like the pony, just like her, only worse.*

One stormy night in Hamburg, Germany, in a small specialized hotel near the port, with lightning flashing and rain hammering the window, Dmitry stripped her, blindfolded her, and tied her down to the bed; the bed was made for tying a girl down – or a guy. It was that kind of place, the lobby wallpaper was black leather, the waitresses in the hotel restaurant dressed as dominatrixes; whips and chains and handcuffs hung from the walls of the bar. Dmitry said that he wanted to try it out that way, with her blindfolded and tied down, and she said, *Okay, why not!*

She had trusted him that far, and she felt, though she *sometimes* blushed to admit it, a strange tingling thrill in being completely, as they say in the sexual jargon, "submissive," in being completely in somebody else's power, a thrill that became, briefly, in waves, overwhelming, a sort of absolute abandonment of self, and she wondered if it was related, this implosion of the self, to the rapturous abandonment, total submission to God, the mystics talked about. Meister Eckhart spoke of emptying the soul. The Sufi mystics rhapsodized about the abandonment of self, and about dancing, whirling, into ecstasy, into unity with the other, into oneness with the divine. She wondered: *Is mysticism sex? Is sex mysticism?* She thought that, maybe for her at least, they were, mysticism and sex, one and the same thing. Dmitry was a true priest and poet of this private little cult. He was systematic and merciless in reducing her to nothing, a pure object, a quivering slave.

She sensed, she feared, she worshiped, his violent Will to Power, to dominance. His urge to dominate, above all other things, *her!* He touched her everywhere, every inch of her body, every millimeter, with his lips, his hands. He took his time about it, often tenderly, as if he were exploring an unknown continent; she closed her eyes, and her body seemed, as she submitted to his body and his will, to become both very intense, concentrated in one small place, in one small fiery locus of sensation and feeling, and also, spread out, disintegrated, vast, sprawling this way and that, dispersed and ramified over continents, and hardly belonging to her at all, bits and pieces, distant light-years from the lost center that once was her, like the stars of another galaxy.

And then, finally, he made love to her, he penetrated her, and, here too, he took his time, infinite time, and during all of it, tied down on the bed, blindfolded, in the dark room, she was both in total abandon, as if non-existent, and ultra-alert, her hearing and her sense of touch seemingly magnified. The storm had moved on. The thunder was distant. The rain had ceased. She heard a woman talking in the street; she heard the woman's heels on the sidewalk, she heard a man, walking by, whistling, *Lili Marlene*, and she heard a ship's horn, as if through the drifting white fog, throaty and resonant, in Hamburg's port, and a distant siren, *whooo, whooo, whooo,* and music, intermittently,

Hey Jude, and then *Pink Floyd* she thought it was, something from a radio, far away, *oldies,* she thought, *oldies,* and she thought, *that is life, out there, but what do they know of me who am here, me who am nothing, I am nothing, but I am this emptiness into which the sounds and music of life flow, that is all I am, that is all that is left of me, an empty space, an empty dance floor, where the music plays.*

Oh, Dmitry – we could have been happy, in our own perverse way.

Okay, Sabrina, sober up; maybe you could have been happy, maybe not, most likely not.

It was all a lie, a lie from the very beginning.

It was all a calculated performance – push the right buttons, and the little girl is yours, and all she has will be yours too.

Which was, alas, the real point of the exercise.

Damn him!

In fact, Dmitry certainly wanted control of *her* – he wanted control of her body and her mind. But, much more important, he wanted control of her *company* and her *patents,* her intellectual property. And he evidently wanted V's DNA and, above all, perhaps, he wanted the Clone, he wanted Claire.

He had inserted spies, a few young researchers, into Sabrina's office. She discovered them and fired them. He stole key documents. She discovered that too – and, as bait and decoy, she set out forged and inaccurate, documents, so he would waste time with misleading hints. She set Cyber Traps, and they quickly revealed who the hackers and thieves were – Who was working, secretly, against her and for Dmitry.

The magic, perverse affair had begun in Paris, and it ended in Paris. Dmitry spiked her drinks one night and tried to get her to talk about some of her most important discoveries, to reveal some of Andromeda Corporation's deepest, best-kept secrets.

"What about that Clone, you are rumored to have made from some alien DNA?" She realized her drink had been spiked – how she knew it she never figured out – and she mumbled incoherent evasive things about confidentiality and projects that are not interesting and really not worth talking about. And then, sobering up, she flatly refused to tell him anything, and she told him she knew about the spies and the stolen documents, and that she would never tell him anything.

By slow degrees, he became furious. Calculated escalation – and then ... He lost it. He slapped and punched her. She would come out of that little argument with two black eyes and for two weeks wore extra-large wrap-around sunglasses; she hid the strangulation marks around her neck by wearing a high turtleneck sweater, though it was summer and extra hot.

He screamed at her. She was a whore and a slut and a sexual freak; he had only made love to her because he wanted control over her company, and, "If the price to pay to get control of Andromeda Corp was fucking you, you stupid freakish cunt, then I was willing to pay that price."

"Fuck you!" She pulled on her dress. "I'm leaving, and I am not coming back, ever! Forget about me and forget about Andromeda Corp!"

He grabbed her at the doorway – they were in his penthouse in Paris – and he punched her, dragging her back into the apartment, slapping her so hard she fell across the bed.

"You bastard," she shouted, "You bloody bastard!"

He picked her up, ripping her dress, and slammed her against the wall. Pushing his face into hers, he snarled, "You are not leaving! You are not leaving, not ever; you belong to me!"

"I am leaving," she snarled back, "and right now!"

He held her by the neck, pushing her up the wall, her feet dangling, only her toes touching the rug; he was choking her; she clawed at his face, she raked his cheeks, going for his eyes. He dropped her. She crumbled on the floor and tried to crawl away.

He straddled her. He ripped the clothes from her back – everything – as she kicked and squirmed and tried to wiggle free.

"God, I hate you," she shouted.

"Go, naked, if you want to go."

"I will, I will go naked! But she grabbed other clothes – shorts, a T-shirt.

He watched her pull the shorts and T-shirt on; then, he tore them off, punching her, pushing her away, pulling her to him, ripping, tearing, and slashing – until nothing was left.

She started to head out the door, naked, *who cares, naked, I don't care*, and he grabbed her by the waist, lifted her up, and pulled her back and forced her down onto the floor, clamped her waist between his thighs, and held her down, naked, and poured whiskey into her mouth, it gurgled down, her jaw forced open by his fist – she bit his hand, over and over, but he kept pouring, and then, finally, he stopped. Sucking his wounded hand, he said, "Here, dress in this, you whore," and, as she tried to crawl away, he slapped her down, and while she sat on the floor, her back flat against the wall, rubbing her jaw, he threw her one of their play costumes – a collar, a skimpy leather halter, an ultra-short leather mini skirt, boots with stiletto heels.

"Fuck you," she said, "I will."

She pulled on the skimpy dominatrix outfit, buckled the collar around her neck, slipped into the high boots, laced them up, and then she grabbed for her purse. He held it away, up, out of her reach.

"No, no, no," he said, "beg, get down on your knees and beg."

"Fuck you," she said, and, as she made a grab for the purse, he punched her, and she fell back against the bed, dizzily getting up. As she charged back at him, he retreated out onto the balcony and tipped the contents of the purse and her wallet over the edge of the balustrade and threw the purse after.

Documents, money, wallet, personal organizer, all tumbling down, falling down eight floors. And purse flying after …

She stood in the balcony doorway fuming, thinking, You Bastard, If I ran straight at you now, and pushed with all my might, you might just lose your balance, topple over, and go all the way down, all eight floors. *But he's not worth murder*, a voice inside her head told her; it was probably Henry, she thought, her CFO, wise old Henry, Uncle Henry, his voice whispering of a guilty conscience, a murder charge, a trial, a scandal, and jail – and so she turned on her heels and walked out of the apartment leaving Dmitry Pavlov standing there, stunned, arms akimbo.

He shouted after her: "You belong to me! In the end, I will have you, you will be mine! You *are* mine!"

In the hallway, the elevator arrived, making a discreet little noise – *Bing!*

She stepped in and pushed the button – lobby. The door closed behind her: Thank God! She closed her eyes and took a deep breath. Music was playing – Mozart, *the Piano Sonata Number 8.*

She opened her eyes: the polished walnut wood-paneled elevator had a full-length mirror. She turned and looked in the mirror. God, my hair is cut so short! The bruises, there undoubtedly would be bruises, hadn't started to show. The high stiff black leather slave collar, with its iron ring, hid the strangle marks, if there were strangle marks. It felt like there probably were.

A dark-haired young woman got on the elevator two floors below. Her skin was the color of milk-chocolate; she was very handsome and dressed in a sleek skintight one-piece silver jogging suit.

She gave Sabrina a cool inspection and then said, "Business or pleasure?"

"Pain," said Sabrina.

"Indeed," said the woman, "You see all kinds."

"Indeed you do."

In the lobby, Sabrina said, "Goodnight, Henri," to the night duty door-man. Henri gave her a startled look, did a second take, and said, "Goodnight, Madam Jacobs" and hurried to open the door.

On the sidewalk, the woman turned to her, startled, "You're Jacobs, Sabrina Jacobs, *the* Sabrina Jacobs?"

Sabrina nodded, "Yes. Carnival," she said, "Carnival." She felt like crying, "Masquerade."

"Great costume," said the woman.

"Thanks," said Sabrina, "have a good run!" and she stood on the glossy sidewalk suddenly alone – it had just stopped raining, and the air glowed with silken lamplight and silver reflections.

She watched the woman's lithe figure, a sexy silver figurine, as she ran off toward the Champs Elysees. Somehow she wanted to run after the woman and beg forgiveness – but for what?

Standing on the wet sidewalk, Sabrina sniffled. Now I really want to cry, but there is no fucking way I am going to cry. She looked around. The store windows glowed with fashionable clothes and jewelry in elaborate presenta-tions, and one of them was of a supposed bordello with a dominatrix in black leather – fashions by somebody in the tradition of Jean-Paul Gaultier – tow-ering over a cowering wax stockbroker or banker. How perfectly appropriate, thought Sabrina. If I stepped into that show window I'd be right at home. Just give me a whip!

She walked around the corner into the side street where Dmitry had thrown her purse and all its contents – her whole life in a little Hermès bag! The street was narrow and dark, with no shop windows, but a bar on the far corner, *Le Chat Bariolé*.

There was an improvised mattress of rags – lots of faded black & white tar-tan in the white-marble-and-brass doorway of an Import-Export company, *Oriental Delights*, where a vagabond – she figured he was probably a classic old-style Parisian *clochard* – had been sleeping.

Yes, that was probably him; he was bearded, with wild gray hair, spilling over an old black-and-white square pattern tweed jacket. He was gathering up her stuff.

"*Bonsoir,*" she said.

He looked up, he was on his hands and knees in the midst of the street, he had very sharp features, a pointed chin, a pointed nose, dark stubble, and a red point to his nose.

"*Bonsoir,*" he said.

"Can I help you," she said, "I think that is my purse."

"I wondered," he said, "Here. The purse almost hit me on the head, it bounced off the Mercedes there and landed in my bed, my bed is over there, and this is my bedroom, and here are some credit cards, but, Madam, since we have just met, may I ask your name, before I hand over these cards – and I see a driver's license too and a passport, you travel often, Madam?"

"I do, I travel fairly often, recently to Israel, China, and Japan," said Sabrina, "and my name is Sabrina, Sabrina Jacobs."

The *clochard* perused the passport, looked down at the handful of credit cards, and said, "Indeed, Madam, that is the name on the cards, and you do match the photographs. Here you are, Madam, and I believe there are more over here, and over there: lipstick, a compact, and some coins. Let us recover everything that is to be recovered."

"And what is your name, Monsieur, if I may ask?"

"Indeed, Madam, it will be my pleasure to introduce myself. My name is Jean-Pierre Emmanuel François Saint-Poix Junior." He got down on his hands and knees to gather up some change, and a scattering of euros and dollars, and she crouched next to him.

A flash lit up the scene, and Sabrina looked up, furious, just in time to be shot, flash, again, by a photographer, and then again, she was about to get up and give chase, but the photographer high-tailed it out of the street and Sabrina thought: Oh, what the fuck! Who cares!

"Here is your PEA," Jean-Pierre said, "It looks like it might still work."

Lucky, she thought, there's not much traffic on this street, and Jean-Pierre Emanuel François Saint-Poix Junior is an honest man.

He handed her the bills.

"I owe you. I am greatly in your debt, Monsieur," she said, "What can I do for you?" Everything seemed to be there. She folded the wallet and put it back in the purse – all black leather, so both purse and wallet quite harmonized with her dominatrix outfit.

"I would very much like it if you would have a drink with me," he said, "over there, in the Bar at the corner." He indicated the *Le Chat Bariolé*, an all-night neighborhood bar, which was quite fashionable during daytime when offices were open, but which offered refuge for denizens of the night after 11:00 PM.

"Of course, Monsieur," she said, "I would be delighted."

The barman, Charles – the classic Parisian barman who does not allow his persona as barman to be unhinged or shocked or flustered by anything – knew Sabrina. "Madam Jacobs, what would you and your gentleman friend, Monsieur Saint-Poix, desire this evening?" he said, smiling knowingly, amiably, and with the glance of a connoisseur's appreciation, at her costume.

"Good evening, Charles, a double shot of Black Label," said Sabrina, "no rocks, water on the side."

"Perfect, Madam." "And you, Monsieur Saint-Poix?"

"I shall follow madam most faithfully," said Jean-Pierre Emanuel François Saint-Poix Junior.

The two high-class XVI arrondissement prostitutes who were standing at the bar, eyed Sabrina, nudged each other, and the taller of the two, a fluidly slinky voluptuous brunette in furs, came over and said, "Sorry, honey, but this is restricted territory; you are muscling in where you shouldn't; it could be dangerous."

"She's with me," said Jean-Pierre Emanuel François Saint-Poix Junior, "And she's a friend; this is not business."

"Oh, she's with you, Jean-Pierre," said the prostitute, "then there's no problem."

"Indeed!" "Jean-Pierre is an old friend," said Sabrina, "May I offer drinks?" The whiskey had taken effect, she realized. Fuck Dmitry! "Charles, drinks for our friends here."

"Of course, Madam Jacobs," Charles said, "And, if I may say so, your costume is very fetching."

"Thank you, Charles."

"Yeah, honey, that's top-of-the-line stuff – where did you get it?"

"There's a little shop on rue de Buci," Sabrina said, "It supplies theaters and film companies, and they have the most marvelous ..." And she began to give them details of the various items she had purchased, the items she had had specially designed, the halters, the bustiers, the three catsuits, the collars, the G-strings, the whips, the ...

Sabrina didn't remember entirely clearly what followed – she just had little vignettes: sitting in the corner of the bar talking with the two prostitutes, Dijana and Miranda, and with Jean-Pierre, who knew lots of French troubadour songs by heart, and began singing some of them, and there was a bottle of whiskey and then a bottle of wine on the table and at some point she ate a steak tartar – the others had steak-and-fries – and the Dijana and Miranda told her about the problems they had with the various "johns" – the violent ones, the baroque ones, the unwashed, the diseased, the obsessive ritualists, the –

And then she was dancing with Miranda and then Charles and Jean-Pierre were helping her into a taxi and then she was standing in front of her apartment building on the other side of the Seine, in the Latin Quarter, near the Église Saint Germain-des-Prés, thinking, with that double vision that sometimes comes to the very drunk – being both *inside* herself and *outside* herself, lucid and detached, in some distant galaxy, inside, and discombobulated and wavering or stumbling, outside – thinking, *Somehow, I have to manage a dignified entrance,* and the doorman, Ahmed, she realized, was already standing there, and smiling and holding the door open, and he said, "I wondered when you were going to notice me, Madam Jacobs," and, "I'll accompany you upstairs," and she said, "Yes, thank you, thank you, Ahmed," feeling the blood rush in shame, but thinking, too, it had been quite a night, and Ahmed said, "Quite a night, I imagine," and she said, "Yes, Ahmed, quite a night."

When she was inside the apartment – luckily, she had the keys (Jean-Pierre Emanuel François Saint-Poix Junior had been very thorough in vacuuming up the sidewalk, crawling in between and under parked cars) – she checked her voice mail: there were twenty-five messages, all from Dmitry.

She listened to them all. He threatened, he begged, he declared eternal love, he begged, he threatened, and he said he worshiped her, he hated her, and he would get his revenge – and he detailed some of the ways he would obliterate her: her identity would be gone, he shouted – physical, psychological, industrial …

You will cease to be you!

You will cease to exist!

She was going to erase all the messages; then she thought better of it and had them archived on an Andromeda Corporation server, as well as sending a copy of the file to her personal lawyer in New York, to her Paris legal firm, and to Uncle Henry, CFO of Andromeda Corporation with the note, "*Don't bother opening now, but do keep on file: if anything happens to me …*"

What a hangover!

Still clad in the dominatrix outfit, she swallowed two aspirin, made herself coffee – Oh, boy! I need a gallon of coffee!

She put two chocolate croissants into the microwave and sat down to drink the coffee, spiced with two more aspirins, her elbows on the table, and to try to figure out how to disentangle her emotions – hate, desire, love, fear, thrilling abasement, mystic exaltation, fetishist self – the outfit she was wearing: she glanced in the mirror, *not bad, still not bad* – disgust, self-disgust, pride, masochism, overweening pride, ambition, obsession – his eyes, his touch, his smell, his sadism, his mastery. And, how would she put her life back together?

Work was the answer.

The next day several Paris newspapers and Internet Sites and tabloids and then the weekly magazines – in France, Italy, the UK, the US, Spain, Russia, Japan, and China – featured Sabrina Jacobs, billionaire and scientist, CEO of Andromeda Corporation, on her hands and knees in revealing S&M regalia in the middle of a glossy rainy nocturnal side street in front of a wild-looking bearded man who was wielding what looked like a purse but could have been a whip.

Asked to comment, Sabrina said, "It was an interesting night."

She never spoke to Dmitry again.

From that moment, it was war between Sabrina's Andromeda Corporation and Dmitry's Bio-Prom.

Bio-Prom sabotaged Andromeda Corporation's shipments. Dmitry triggered a hugely ambitious campaign of Cyber spying and Cyber sabotage. Bio-Prom tried to steal Andromeda Corporation's patents. Bio-Prom kidnapped Andromeda Corporation researchers – and, sometimes, murdered them, poison being a favorite weapon. At every stage, Sabrina fought back – and, mostly, she won. Except when people died, that was irredeemable.

And, now, in the most recent battle, as she vaguely began to remember, Bio-Prom had tried to kidnap her, had murdered her friends and employees and research partners, and tried to capture Claire – and had sunk *Andromeda*.

Claire had been saved by her own strength and brilliance and by the alien-human hybrid V and by the efforts of the crew of *Andromeda*.

Then what happened?

Then?

Waves were lapping over her arms.

She was lying on her back, staring up at the sky, now a cloudless pale blue.

Oh, God, where am I?

Oh, yes, now I remember – raft, Pacific Ocean, iguana …

She blacked out.

Later, still later, she woke up, vaguely woke up, and her body – she thought it was her body – felt like a vast disconnected continent, an archipelago, of aches and pains.

She was face down, lying on her stomach on the raft, and the iguana was sprawled over her outstretched arms when she heard a helicopter overhead, or thought she did, she wasn't sure of anything, she had a horrible headache and a fever.

Slowly, carefully, she dislodged the iguana – it hardly moved at all and just blinked at her – and she turned over and, shielding her eyes from the glare, looked up: there was a helicopter. And written on its side: "Bio-Prom" and the Bio-Prom logo.

"Oh, shit, my friend," she whispered to the iguana, "this is worse than dying. These people will kill us, and it won't be pretty."

She didn't wave or make any sign. She just sat up, adopted the lotus position, picked up the iguana, and cradled it in her lap and said, "Don't worry, my child. We'll get out of this. Mommy will look after you."

The helicopter dipped down, circled, dropped a small buoy, and then flew away. Sabrina watched it disappear, and she thought, they'll be back, that buoy must be a position marker, and it will float with current just like us. "Just like us," she said to the iguana, "And so they'll come and get us and then let the gods have mercy on our souls."

The sea was oily and calm now, weirdly silent and still. The sun was lower in the sky. Great coils of seaweed floated near the raft. A school of dolphins jumped out of the water, and then were gone. Other fish jumped, and then were gone, and then there was silence. The sun was getting lower, and soon it would be night.

It was night – dark and still and humid clinging air – when a Bio-Prom launch came up, bright floodlights glaring, and sent out a dinghy to pick up Sabrina. She refused to be separated from the iguana. They humored her and let her bring it on board.

She really didn't remember much of what happened next. She knew she was taken to the infirmary. Everybody was speaking Russian.

It was like a dream. A nurse took off what remained of her clothes and gave her a shower, propping her up and scrubbing her down. She was given intravenous and strapped down – manacled – to a cot in the infirmary. She was blindfolded with a sort of tight-fitting elastic hood, and the iguana was put in the cot with her.

"Here's your friend," the nurse said. Her name tag, Sabrina had noticed before she was blindfolded, read *Sonia*.

Sabrina, tied down and cloaked in darkness, could feel the weight of the iguana as it walked over her, and then curled up on her belly, and maybe it went to sleep because it didn't move for a long time.

They must have injected her with sedatives because after that, she remembered nothing, but had the impression at one point that she was being wheeled on a gurney, and then she looked up and saw Dmitry.

The memories came back in fragments. Dmitry was looking down at her, and he said, "You are my guinea pig now, darling."

What?

"You are my guinea pig now, darling," he said.

What?

He was dressed in surgical greens. His face was shielded by a tip-up plastic visor. Above Dmitry's head were the big bright panel lights of an operating theater; there were instruments on automatic arms – surgical knives, suture machines, drills, lasers, saws …

Operating theater? What the hell was he going to do? She tried to say something, but she couldn't – no words came – and she realized again, vaguely, as if from afar, as if it was all happening in a dream, that she'd been drugged; she realized too, that her mouth was gagged, and she was manacled down – *gagged and manacled down on an operating table.*

What the hell?

"Did I tell you, darling Sabrina? We obtained some DNA from your precious *Clone*, that useless insane animal, but its DNA certainly does offer some seductive possibilities. We've re-engineered it a bit – touched it up here and there, made it into a powerful brew – and I'm eager to try it out."

What the hell is he talking about?

Dmitry lifted a syringe. There were two nurses behind him, wearing protective masks. She can only see their eyes – pale skin, dark almond-shaped eyes, and neat black eyebrows.

"We are ready now," Dmitry said, "Get the intravenous ready – and the radiation gun."

Radiation gun?

One of the nurses applied what Sabrina guessed must be alcohol to her arm.

"When I finish with you, Sabrina," Dmitry said, "you won't recognize yourself, nor will anybody else."

The wife of Frankenstein ...

She wanted to act like the tough guys in the movies; she wanted to say "Fuck you, Dmitry!" but she couldn't say anything, and she had to admit the truth: In her confusion and fear, wherever she was, and whatever was going to happen, she was *terrified*; so, she just stared and tried not to show any emotion, but she could feel tears welling up – *Damn him, damn him, damn him!*

Dmitry smiled and leaned over her. Tenderly, using a white serviette, he wiped away the tears that were running down her cheeks. "Tears," he said, "How moving, Sabrina, how moving."

That was then ...

This was now ...

In twelve minutes and thirty seconds, this installation will be destroyed. Beep, beep, beep ...

What did he do to me? Where is he? The gag is gone. Her jaw is sore and feels weird. Sabrina swallows and runs her tongue around her mouth – it feels unfamiliar; something is not quite right.

In fact, nothing is quite right. *Everything feels terribly wrong!*

Where is everybody?

Everything is terribly wrong!

Sabrina tries to speak, but out of her mouth comes not words, but a sibilant hiss. The hiss of a snake. Her throat is dry.

She runs her tongue along her lips and then along her teeth. She is drowsy and confused and only half-awake, but something definitely does not feel right. Something about her mouth is wrong.

Very wrong ...

What feels strange? She concentrates; she tries it again, she runs her tongue along her teeth, touching incisors, the incisors, the lateral incisors, the canines, with the tip of her tongue.

This is impossible.

I'm hallucinating; I've been drugged. It must be the drugs.

She tries again. She feels her tongue flicker *outside* her lips; it runs along the upper and lower lips. *Her tongue* – it feels longer, thinner, and, it is *split* in two at the end – *split in two* – the two sections operating independently, the curling tips touching, separately, her lips.

In eleven minutes and thirty seconds, this installation will be destroyed.

She shivers. Christ, my tongue is forked!

She closes her eyes in horror.

This is definitely a bad dream, a nightmare, a hallucination.

And *my teeth* – my teeth are sharp, pointed, and two are longer than the others, much longer – the incisors. So I have *fangs,* she thinks, *fangs,* and she shivers, then thinking, yes, this must be a bad dream … a nightmare …

But then she remembers – Dmitry's sadism. "You are an animal! I'll turn you into an animal!"

Oh, boy, oh boy, oh, boy!

She closes her eyes in horror – *What has Dmitry done to me?*

Oh, boy, oh boy, oh, boy!

She has a pretty good idea what he has done to her, but she doesn't want to think about it; she shuts her eyes, squeezes them shut; even that action feels *strange …*

The lids …

The form of the eyes …

She feels her nostrils quiver – *quiver:* this place smells; what is that smell? It's the sweet sickening smell of rotting flesh – *necrosis.* Is that me? Am I dying, is my flesh rotting? What has happened?

She tries to move. She can't.

Okay, analyze this, she thinks: *Sabrina, analyze calmly, analyze the situation,* Yes, okay: so I know that I'm manacled down, ankles, wrists, and neck.

The radio – she only now notices it – is playing Russian songs and giving the local news in Russian from Vladivostok: *the temperature is 23 degrees Celsius, and traffic delays of up to 20 minutes are foreseen on the M-60 …*

A siren is sounding somewhere: *beep, beep, beep …*

In ten minutes, this installation will be destroyed.

When she'd been brought, dehydrated and half-crazed, with her new iguana friend, on board the Bio-Prom ship, Dmitry had said – what had he said? – Yes, now I remember, he had said: *Now you will tell me everything!*

"Now you will tell me everything."

"I will tell you nothing." Her voice was so dry she could hardly speak.

"You will be mine."

"I will never be yours."

And then he said, with his diabolic smile – he had a wonderfully diabolic smile – she still adored it, that smile, even now, even terrified, even transformed – *transformed* – into what? – "If you are not mine, Sabrina, you will belong to nobody. And if you won't tell me your secrets, I'll make sure you never talk to anybody about anything ever again."

Then she was strapped down, being wheeled somewhere on a gurney, and Dmitry was walking along side, looking down at her, almost fondly.

And now he takes on a professorial tone: "I'm using DNA material we obtained from your lab, material taken from that Clone you are so proud of, hair clippings, spittle, and so on. It was easy to do. I had spies in your Headquarters and on the *Andromeda*.

He pauses to give some instructions to a nurse, and then he continues.

"So, Sabrina, we will turn you into an animal, into a *Thing*."

She wants to speak; but her tongue, her lips refuse to move.

"I'm sure you'll like it, Sabrina; it's what you've always wanted. You are going back to the Garden of Eden, Sabrina, to a world before consciousness, before intelligence. Your mind will cease to be a mind. You will experience the blind ecstatic innocence of the wild unconscious unshriven Beast."

Damn you, damn you, damn you, she arches up against the straps.

Dmitry smiles, from on high, he smiles. "It's your own personal voyage, Sabrina, back to the Garden of Eden – or perhaps to Hell, your own private Hell, from which there will be no exit, no redemption, and no salvation."

She was being wheeled into the operating theater. Yes, now she remembered, and Dmitry said, "We'll try a bacterium on you too, just as an extra gift, and see what happens – it's a weaponized version of the bubonic plague, updated to be very quick-acting, almost instant death. Two birds with one stone, you might say."

Damn him! So he used me as a guinea pig – as an experiment, damn him!

Beep, beep, beep …

The President of the Russian Federation said today that his talks in Berlin with the German Chancellor and the French President had been very productive on the economic front and that the problem of climate change had been added to the agenda for the next meeting of the …

In eight minutes and thirty seconds, this installation will be destroyed

Destroyed, this installation will be destroyed. Wake up, Sabrina, wake up!

She again realizes – *I'm going around in circles* – *I'm still under the influence of the drugs* – And she remembers, too, that one of the wrist manacles is loose, looser than the others.

Maybe I can get out of here. She bends her hand around and picks at the buckle: these are old-fashioned buckled manacles, she thinks, not steel or synthetic, thank the gods.

The small bars slip out of the holes. The leather loop pops open. She pulls her hand out. *This is too easy! This is too easy! My nails are too long! And my fingers are* ... She tries to undo the other wrist manacle; they all consist of buckles, and it will not be too hard. As she brings her right arm across her chest to pluck at the buckled manacle holding down her left hand, she catches a glimpse of her arm and she sees while doing this ...

And she sees while doing this that ...

Her hand is a claw.

Both hand and arm are a bright glitter of black scales – with touches of scarlet – snake-like, the limb of a reptile.

Fuck this!

She frees her left hand.

She liberates her neck – this is hard, takes a long time – and she realizes she has an additional collar attached to her – what is it? A GPS tracker, a control mechanism. Damn! It could control her mind if it had electro-connections. It was not too tight, not too snug, but that didn't matter. It could still trans-mit messages to her neurological system, and she'd be the man's puppet. The bastard!

A collar ...

She levers herself up.

The long hard claws are useful.

Jesus! She catches a glimpse of herself for the first time, just a glance: her body, in any case, is reptilian, covered with fine black scales with a few bright red stripes. Her feet are human in shape but elongated with more articula-tions, and they end in long, viciously pointed nails.

In seven minutes and thirty seconds, this installation will be destroyed.

Only her ankles are tied down now. She uses her claws to tear open and unbuckle the ankle straps.

Her mind is turning over in a carnival of horrors.

Sabrina, do not panic!

She swings up and sits on the side of the operating table, grasping the table with what she now sees clearly are claws with sharp, pointed, bright yellow nails. She takes a deep breath. *Take stock, you idiot, you are a scientist after all.*

Her body is much more voluptuous and muscular than before, she already senses this; it has a tense, sinuous, serpentine muscularity: she looks down: yes, smooth, glittering, black scales with decorative stripes of bright scarlet.

How did Dmitry do this? How did he transform my epidermis into this thick armor of keratin, of black scales? And my whole body into ...?

She growls, deep in her throat. It must have been done by genetic modification. But for such a morphological transformation to happen so fast, and so totally, he must have deciphered the mechanism that allows V to transform herself from human to demon within a second or two.

Or they've simply used Claire's DNA to re-program me, somehow accelerating the transformations into Claire's most extreme form: *I'm a new species, a hybrid, a thing, an It! Just like he said!*

A freak!

A monster!

I'm a *Thing*!

She growls and slurps back saliva with the long, thin, flashing, forked tongue. Of course, Dmitry didn't know that Claire is not an idiot, because Sally and I didn't know it; it was not recorded in any of our files – so Dmitry probably assumes I am an idiot, or that my intelligence is an animal intelligence, no longer human, or just barely human – Hmm, this might be useful!

Well, maybe I am an idiot! Maybe I am just an animal! Who knows?

Dmitry had said: "You're our guinea pig, Sabrina. I think we'll rejig your genetics – Sir Alfred did it once, but we will go further."

She hadn't said a word; she just stared at him. So he knew that her father had used her for his experiments. He had the details. How did he know them?

Dmitry had squeezed her jaw between his fingers. "As I said, we are also going to try out a new version of the bubonic plague on you – it is designed to work very fast, to kill people within minutes, even within seconds."

She lay there, paralyzed, incapable of saying a word – a test animal, man-acled down, in a laboratory.

"You see," Dmitry said, "I am turning the tables on you, Sabrina. You made monsters. Now you will become a monster."

Did he actually say that or did I dream it?

She stood up. The claws of her feet echoed, clicking on the floor; claws are not meant for smooth floors, she thinks, remembering her cat *Bojo* who used to skid on the marble when chasing a ball or galloping after her specially-designed and very clever robot mouse. Sabrina is tempted to say, *Miaow!* In some ways, this is really *funny*!

Funny!

Ha, ha, ha!

Who's laughing now?

A body is lying on the floor of the operating theater; another body is lying in the doorway, which is half-open. Sabrina kneels by the first body, a man; she touches it with her claws, turns it over so she can see the face. Her nostrils twitch. *So that was the smell!*

The man is Russian, or he certainly looks Russian, with that translucent waxy skin, the washed-out, coarse, straw-blond hair, combed straight side-ways, a few wart-like beauty spots, and his rimless glasses, askew on his face and cracked, undoubtedly from the fall. His skin has burst in various places, the mouth is surrounded by sores, the eyes, staring wide open, have already started to rot. Advanced necrosis, she thinks, and yet the body is still warm, or so it seems. So this is accelerated necrosis. The body is rotting in fast-forward, super-fast putrefaction. And the way the man fell, right here, means the bacterium kills within seconds.

That's unheard of, that is something entirely new.

If it kills so fast it will burn itself out, the dead can't travel, so, unless it can live in hosts that are not suffering from it, the bacterium won't be able to travel either.

But you could certainly weaponize it – in a big city or crowded army base, it would spread like wildfire!

Damn it! So Dmitry had done it, he had used the bacterium – *maybe just on me* – but he lost control of it. This was too horrible. Was she awake or was she dreaming? Wake up, Sabrina, wake up! She pressed down with her fangs on her lips: *Ouch!*

I *am* awake!

The dead man is holding a clipboard. The notes are in Russian. Well, I can still read, thinks Sabrina: "Irreversible cellular transformation successful. Keratin transformation complete in 13.5 seconds. Muscular and mammary modification was simultaneous: less than 12 seconds. Subject showed Genetic redesign triggered by our N-23 blocking intervention has been successful. Subject seems to be viable."

Irreversible, thinks Sabrina, I don't like the sound of that. Does that mean I can't return to being human? *Viable*, well, that's good: I exist! *Muscular and mammary transformation* – so I have more muscles and bigger tits, yes, bigger tits: she looks down at herself and thinks: I noticed that with V too, she's more statuesque – really stacked – when she's a demon – a demon like me. We are cartoons!

Fuck and bloody damnation!

She taps on the clipboard with the yellow tapered points of her claws, thinking: "Yes, well, okay, so I've been morphed, fairly completely; that means a few genetic switches were able to reorganize the whole map of my body and its surfaces in less than 15 seconds; that is interesting; I wish I knew how Dmitry, the bastard, did it. It can't be just biology and genetics; it must involve physics, quantum mechanics, some sort of spatial-temporal interface maybe. 'Neurological blocking devices are working successfully.' *Neurological blocking devices* – I *really* don't like the sound of that! It must mean that parts of my mind have been switched off, or blocked, or neutralized. Okay, what? And *why* would Dmitry do that, if he thought I was an idiot? And how could he do it? Hmm! What parts of my mind have been switched off or destroyed?"

In five minutes and thirty seconds, this installation will be destroyed. Beep, beep, beep …

What had he said? Dmitry had said: "Sabrina, if you won't talk to me, you are never going to talk to anybody again." I thought he meant he was going to kill me, but maybe that wasn't it. *Well, let's try; let's see what we have here!*

She tries to say her name; the result is a hiss, but no words. She tries to count to ten. The result is the same: a serpentine hiss. Damnation! I sound like a rattlesnake, she thinks, *I can't talk.*

I can't talk!

V, in reptile form, can talk. But I can't talk.

I can't talk!

An icy chill ripples down her spine. Panic mounts. She shivers. *I'll turn you into an animal, a monster,* that's what Dmitry said, and, yes, that's what he had done.

There is a pen attached to the clipboard. Sabrina takes it in her claws, and tries to write ... Her mind becomes a blur, and the writing is a scribble ... She tries again; she concentrates; her mind blocks, blurs, and the result is the same, a meaningless scribble. *I can't write!*

Damn that bastard!

Damn Dmitry! Panic is rising fast. I can think, but I can't communicate. *I'm locked inside my own mind.*

Dmitry, that sadistic bastard, has put me in a mind-prison. Even as an animal, I can't express myself! If I get my hands, okay, my claws, on him, I will tear him apart – *I will eat him alive.*

She takes a deep breath. Her nostrils flare. Her fangs tingle. Saliva drips from her tongue. Okay, okay, Sabrina, calm down, it could be worse. You are alive, healthy even, full of beans, sparkling with energy. Where there's life, there's hope.

She looks down at the clipboard – Injection of Subject with *Modified N-A23 Versinia pestis bacterium* at 9:45 am. She glances up at the clock on the lab wall. It is now 13:50. So, if 9:45 am was today and that would be logical, they injected me with an updated version of the bubonic plague a couple of hours ago, and I am still okay, bubonic plague-wise at least, while this guy is dead; and the woman lying in the doorway is dead. Probably everybody in this laboratory is dead. Maybe Dmitry is dead. And outside; what's happened in the outside world? There should be chaos, police, ambulances, emergency crews in masks.

Instead, there is nobody.

Is everybody in the city dead? Is everybody in the world dead?

Her tongue flickers along her lips. She feels the hungry luscious thick saliva. It bubbles. A thrill ripples up and down her thighs and belly, tingles at the tips of her breasts. She runs her claws over her breasts. Yum! An electric fan is creating a small breeze, rattling a few papers. The overhead lights burn brightly. The instrument graphs blink, and the registration lines – which are all flat because not connected to anybody or anything – unroll, bright green, red, orange. She studies the dials, the graphs, the controls: Machines and things can live without people. When all the people are gone, the world will continue – the breeze will move through the corridors, the vines will twist around the trees, the sun will rise and set, the ...

The electricity is still on, but that doesn't mean anything: power generators often operate themselves, automatically, for hours, days, months, even years, if everything is computerized, and automatic, and run by Artificial Intelligence.

The radio! The radio is still broadcasting: it's giving weather reports and traffic conditions in Vladivostok. So, unless it's a recording or delayed broadcast, the world is not dead after all. It doesn't sound like a recorded broadcast: they are giving weather, traffic reports, the news … Everything sounds normal. No, the world probably still exists.

In five minutes, this installation will be destroyed …

She puts the clipboard down on the operating table. She goes to the half-open door and kneels by the woman. She turns the woman over – the woman has the same symptoms as the man; blood has erupted from her mouth, nose, and eyes, the sores have burst like bubbles, little pus-filled greenish-blue volcanic craters in the skin, necrosis is advanced. The flesh is already rotting, putrid, dissolving.

Sabrina goes into the corridor. Bodies are lying here and there. They must have dropped where they were standing. Dmitry's little toy, his modified version of the Black Death, certainly did escape. *Maybe I sneezed. Maybe a needle leaked. Maybe an airtight chamber wasn't quite airtight.* The corridor is brightly lit; three bodies are lying in the middle of it. There is a sort of nurses' station, with computers.

Sabrina walks up and pushes a cadaver off a stool. It flops heavily down sideways, the skirt riding up, white sheer stockings, shapely legs. *Too bad darling, and I'm sorry to push you off your perch like this, but I will make Dmitry pay!* Sabrina bends over, and glances at the keyboard – Cyrillic characters, she sees – but she knows Cyrillic, and she speaks – *she used to speak* – Russian, so she should try.

She takes a deep breath, poses her claws, ten bright yellow pointed claws – at least the shape of the hands is not *entirely* non-human, the fingers are still articulated – *maybe too articulated!* She poses her claws above the keyboard, concentrates, and tries to type.

Her claws clack on the keys, but her mind freezes up, the keyboard becomes a blur, and the result is gibberish, just random letters on the screen – letters which she can read. *Damn!* She hisses in frustration, curls her claws.

She is tempted to hammer down on the desk, and rip the computer from its moorings, and toss it across the corridor, but she resists the temptation. She doesn't want to break anything. She curls her lip, her tongue flickers in anger, emitting a long serpentine hiss. *So that is the neurological blocking device in action. It's a neurological inhibitor. I wonder if there is a way of working around this or an antidote for it.*

She tries random letters – x, z, b, m, s …

Surprise!

Yes, that I can do … random individual letters …

But articulating a sentence, or writing a word, that I can't do.

How sophisticated, what sophisticated targeting!

They somehow neutralized a very select set of sub-programs of sub-programs.

It's like having a mini-stroke, a very selective mini-stroke.

Okay, Sabrina, now you are mapping the problem – Good! That is progress!

She sees a full-length mirror and takes a deep breath, and thinks: Okay, now I'd better get the full-frontal bad news – the mirrors, the mirrors, the mirrors.

And I am so bloody vain! I've always been so proud of my very impeccable person, my very human good-looks. I've been a self-regarding idiot! And now it's payback time!

She sees in a flash the way she used to look into mirrors – the flawless, well, almost flawless, beauty, looking back, her public image, which she carefully nurtured, even when alone. Sabrina Jacobs, voted by *Time Magazine, Le Figaro, Die Zeit, The South China Morning Post, The Times of India, el País,* and Russia's *Pravda,* the most beautiful …

Mirror, mirror on the wall
Who in the land is fairest of all?

The lights are bright, and the mirror is full-length. This is a very luxurious hospital or research station if it is in Russia! *Well, that is Bio-Prom, only the best will do for Dmitry!*

She takes a deep breath, closes her eyes, turns *away* from the mirror, and opens her eyes: she's staring at a blank wall and a clock.

Okay, Sabrina: do it, do it – look at yourself!

She takes another deep breath, and spins around, in front of the mirror, facing it straight on. She shrinks back in horror – the demon in the mirror shrinks back in horror. The appalled reptile expression is almost comic. *I am a cartoon!*

Mirror, mirror on the wall
Who in the land is fairest of all?

In four minutes and forty-five seconds, this installation will be destroyed.

How horrible, how awful …! Can that be me …?
Yes, it is.
She takes a deep breath: Okay, what do I see? I see a *she-demon*, like V. But with a different color scheme. I have black scales with a few bright red – maybe scarlet is the right word – stripes. I have fangs like V's fangs, though smaller, I think, than V's. My tongue is forked, thin, and quite long. She sticks it out and examines it. The forked tongue is black. Interesting! *Hmm.* I have the eyes of a snake, almond-shaped eyes with vertical lozenge-like slits; the eyes tilt upwards, gold and amber-colored, and marked or framed by pointed upward tear-shaped or triangular-shaped stripes which are scarlet in color. She blinks at herself. *How bloody elaborate! How bloody interesting!* She uses her claws to examine her scale-like epidermis. The scales are triangular, are organized in an imbricated or overlapping structure; they look like snake scales, but they are quite smooth, silky smooth, pure satin, almost as if they were coated in oil, perhaps adapted to the water, so maybe she is amphibious. *Maybe I'm amphibious! Jesus!* In the snout or muzzle, the nostrils are finely etched, two vertical slits. She can see a suggestion of the features of the old her, the human Sabrina, inside the reptile design, inside this *Thing* she has become. *I am no longer human. I am a Thing.*
What if I can never get out of this?
A delicious thrill of horror ripples up her belly.
And, there it is, around the *Thing's* neck – a rubber and steel collar. It has, in red glowing, blinking letters, a neon sign, a text, the letters are backward in the mirror.
She feels the collar, exploring it, cautiously, with the points of her claws. It is thick, not attached to her physically, it's just a collar. Still, it could have electronic implants, GPS, and electronic neurological stimulators and inhibitors. But, somehow, she doesn't sense any such devices.

The words and letters are backward in the mirror, but she can still read them, and quite easily. She growls, she snarls, she hisses. She clenches a claw. It's her name, her human name: "*Doctor Sabrina Jacobs*." She hisses. It's the old me!

The name blinks, red and neon-bright. It's a circus sign! There is a steel ring on the collar, too, just under the bright, flashing name. Ah, ah, Dmitry plans to lead me around like a pet, a circus animal!

Nice touch, Dmitry! I really have to admire the refined thinking – even down to the bloody title "*Doctor*." You've bloody well branded me, Dmitry, and you're going to make sure people know *who* I was and *what* I now am, and delight in the comparison!

Let's make the masochistic humiliation as thrilling and complete as we can, shall we? She sighed, a long, hissing, sibilant sigh. Yes, indeed! Dmitry had learned the art of cruelty from the more notorious s&m clubs – where branding was popular among some of the clients, and some cool cruel tricks from *Liaisons dangereuses*, from the *Histoire d'O*, from the Marquis de Sade, and other classics, mostly French. And he has applied the lessons to me. Probably that's how he intends to use me – some act in a Moscow s&m zoo or circus! Or strobe light mudwrestling in the Urals! *The absolute bloody bastard!*

She considers her image again. The snout is red and black, the body is, well, certainly statuesque, a pin-up parody. With my face markings, and this scaly stark naked body, and it is stacked – as they used to say – with this stacked and spectacularly patterned body, I look like a superheroine dragon lady from some old horror comic book. Well, maybe that's a selling point!

I'm a second V!

My God, what if I am a vampire?

Somehow she thinks she isn't. Hmm. Her tongue slips out of her mouth and licks at her snout and chin. I'm not even hungry, she thinks, but then, at the thought of blood, the two longer fangs tingle … a warm, intense, titillating, tingling … electric … as if they had thoughts of their own. Oh, oh! The thought, the imagined taste and smell, of blood makes her own blood rise in sexual excitement; her body tenses, turgid and hard, in a rising liquid tide of anticipation, breasts, sex, claws, tongue, all eager, aroused, as if ready to copulate, ready to attack … ready to feed.

Yes, I am ready to feed.

Oh, my God! I hate this feeling! It is so exciting, so overwhelming, so wonderful, so sexy, so blood-curdling, so ecstatic, so blood-thirsty …

Yummy!

Calm down, Sabrina, I order you to calm down …

Blood, the image of blood, floods her consciousness.

Sabrina, stop this, right now!

In four minutes and thirty seconds, this installation will be destroyed.

She hears banging. Someone is hammering on one of the doors – somewhere. Following the sound, the *Thing* that was once Sabrina Jacobs – this is how she now thinks of herself – the *Thing*, anticipating how others will see her, the *Thing* – knowing how she, her *old* self, would have seen her *new* self – how she would have seen the *Thing*, the *Freak*. Following the sound, she rushes along the corridor.

Somebody is trapped behind a high-security door. Red lights are flashing everywhere.

Beep, beep, beep …

I have to get out of here! I've been fooling around gazing in mirrors, babbling about the subtleties of sadomasochism, while this place is ticking down to zero, and it's going to blow me and everything else to kingdom come.

She comes to the door, source of the hammering. Inside, behind the thick porthole window, is a woman in a laboratory uniform with the Bio-Prom logo. She's been crying – her face is streaked with tears – and when she sees Sabrina, she starts back in horror – her mouth opening in a silent scream, her hands flying to her mouth.

Sabrina frowns: *I don't blame her!*

Then Sabrina realizes: it's Sonia, the nurse who gave her back her pet iguana.

That was in another life, when I was a human being.

You are still a human being, you idiot, stop this operatic wallowing in morbid self-pity.

The door has a thick high-security glass window; the door itself is armored steel closed from the outside – the keypad is next to the door – and there is a large extra security bar across the door.

Behind the nurse are dead bodies – so Sonia must be immune, like me, thinks Sabrina – But she'll be valuable, she'll be worth her weight in gold, because even if I'm immune that doesn't mean anything for humans; my genetic makeup is now not human, and so, in a way, irrelevant. But if this woman, if Sonia is immune, that really means something!

Sabrina tries to smile through the glass. Sonia recovers a bit – she's crying, tears streaming down her cheeks – "Help me, get me out of here!" she screams in Russian.

Sabrina twists her snout into a quizzical expression, shrugs, and points with one bright claw at the keypad. Sonia understands." A-27-ZQ-549," she shouts, in Russian, spelling it out slowly, as if for an idiot or a child.

Sabrina thinks: Okay, this has no syntax and no semantics; it's just letters. I should be able to do it: one peck of one claw at a time. And it's a standard security Cyrillic keypad.

She closes her eyes and pushes the buttons quickly, automatically, by feel. *Do it fast, without thinking, like an ATM code.* Bang, bang, bang: the buttons are all pushed.

Spatial memory!

And for a Russian keypad!

A suave electronic female voice says, in Russian: "Welcome! Security Door X-55 is now unlocked. Proceed with caution. Make sure to observe all Security Regulations! Thank you!"

The light goes green. Sabrina lifts the lock bar, shifts it over, and pulls open the door. The woman called Sonia comes out. She's a slender blonde, and she's very young, probably a nurse in training or a research fellow. She looks at Sabrina in terror.

Sabrina points to her collar, to the blinking neon red sign: "*Doctor Sabrina Jacobs.*"

"Oh, my God! You … you are the experiment? You're Sabrina!"

Sabrina nods: yes, *I'm the experiment.* And: *this is what has become of me.* And she points at a sign "EXIT" and takes Sonia by the arm, her claws closing gently, thinking – I must not puncture her skin!

In four minutes, this installation will be destroyed.

Sonia allows herself to be led. As they run past the nurses' station, Sabrina notices the iguana, her iguana, in a cage, sitting on a metal trolley. The cage has a handle. She lets go of Sonia, skids to a stop, her clawed feet making a squeaking scratchy noise on the marble floor; she grabs the cage; the iguana, startled, looks up; Sabrina reassures it with a friendly hiss.

"Let's get out of here," says Sonia.

"*Hisssssss*," says Sabrina, which is meant to mean, "Yes!"

"Your pet," says Sonia, running to keep up.

"Hisssssss," Sabrina nods, meaning, 'yes,' and thinking, I hope my hiss didn't sound hostile.

"You were really clinging to that iguana when you came in!"

"Hisssssss!"

The massive steel exit doors are shut and locked. Sabrina looks at Sonia. Does Sonia have the keys? These are high-security doors.

"No, I don't have the keys. I don't know the code – not for these doors."

The count-down gives them three minutes and thirty seconds.

Sabrina knows that V has exceptional powers. *Maybe I have been given some of that too*, she thinks. *Okay, let's see.*

She hands the iguana to Sonia, and she steps back, and she takes a short run and rams into the steel security door, shoulder first.

WHAM!

The door pops open, and Sabrina is so surprised – it's as if she hardly touched it – she shoots right through the door into the outside, and, as she staggers to regain her balance, she sees that about 100 yards away there is a dock – and a large cabin cruiser tied up in the slip beside the dock.

Sabrina looks back at the building. It dominates the whole space.

It looks like we are on an island.

If the building blows up, the whole island will blow up.

She beckons to Sonia and starts running down to the wharf.

Sonia, carrying the iguana in its cage, runs behind her.

Sabrina unties the ropes from the cleats. These long articulated claws are *very* useful, she thinks, I've never been this fast with ropes before!

I could get used to this!

This installation will be destroyed in exactly one minute.

She jumps aboard. Sonia climbs aboard and crouches down on the deck, holding the iguana's cage in her arms.

Sabrina knows engines, and she knows boats. There is a key in the starter lock and a cadaver, a young blond man wearing a blue jacket with brass buttons and a yachting cap, sitting in the pilot's seat; his handsome face is a drooling mass of bubbles and sores. Sabrina grabs the body under the armpits and heaves it overboard. The man must be six feet tall, but he seems as light as a feather. *Okay, so I'm super strong,* Sabrina thinks, *I'd better keep that secret.*

She turns the key. The motor roars into life. She puts it in gear and steers the boat out and away from the dock.

There is a large rocky outcropping, a separate little island, soaring up, maybe four or five stories high, about fifty yards beyond the entrance to the small harbor.

This installation will be destroyed in 45 seconds. The suave voice echoes over the water: they have speakers outside, but my hearing is extra good too – I'd better disguise that as well.

Sabrina takes the boat up to full speed and swerves around the big rocky outcropping, into its shadow. She slows the boat quickly, hoping that the rock is not mined with explosives as well. The outcropping is large, an ideal shield, in theory – *in theory.*

Thirty seconds!

She brings the boat to a full stop; it rises and falls in its own backwash. There is a moment of calm, the motor idling. The instant overflows with sensation: the smell of gasoline, of brackish water, the fragrance of rocks and lichen, the oily iridescent reflections on the surface of the water, the distant caw-caw-caw of a seagull. Sabrina's nostrils quiver. She tenses and flexes her muscles. She glances at Sonia, and she goes to crouch next to the girl and the iguana. She puts her arms around them and locks her claws onto the boat, and curves her reptilian armored body over Sonia and the iguana, like a shield.

Fifteen seconds!

The iguana blinks its armored swivel-eye up at Sabrina and raises a foot as if in greeting. *Hi cousin,* Sabrina thinks, *Hi Little One.*

Ten!

"I'm afraid," says Sonia.

"*Ssssssss!*" Sabrina hisses in reply, nodding and thinking, *Me too, I'm afraid, this may be the last few seconds of our lives.* As she covers both of them with her scaly body, her scales are gleaming, and she notices that there is an extra glow, something like an inner light: *Yes, my black and red arms and claws are positively glowing, all my scales are glowing, my whole body is glowing; is this some sort of excitement? Do I glow when my adrenaline is racing?*

Five!

She closes her eyes and waits.

It seems an eternity – then a huge explosion WHAM echoes, and a shock wave ripples across the water. Rocks and stones tumble down from the rock. Debris, timber, rocks, and metal fly overhead, splashing down just beyond them, and a huge wave comes roaring out of the harbor. The cabin cruiser bounces up and down in the backwash, and above the towering rocky out-cropping a huge cloud rises up, ash drifts over them.

But, yes, they are still alive, sheltered in the shadow of the towering rock.

"You saved us," Sonia says, still cradling the iguana.

Sabrina smiles, baring her fangs in what she hopes is a friendly manner, nods, and runs her claw through Sonia's hair. Sonia seems to understand that this is a friendly, not a hostile gesture.

Sabrina stands up and goes to the pilot's seat and looks at the gasoline gage. The tank, according to the gage, is full.

There is a map case. Sabrina pulls it out. She is surprised to see her claws, the glittering black scales, and the long yellow pointed nails. *I keep forgetting what I am!* She unfolds the map and turns to look at Sonia, who is sitting staring up at her and holding the iguana's cage in her lap.

Sabrina crouches next to Sonia and shows her the map and shrugs and stares quizzically at Sonia. The question is: *Where are we?*

Sonia points at a group of islands lying between the Philippines and Viet-nam. "This island has been rented, I think, on a long-term lease by Bio-Prom to carry out experiments and because Dmitry Pavlov loves the tropics. Dmitry left the island before the epidemic, so he's probably alive."

Sabrina now has some complicated ideas to discuss, but she doesn't know how to express them; this is going to be very frustrating: *I'd better explain the problem.*

She points to her mouth, and then shakes her head and her finger: *I can't talk.* Then she mimics writing, and makes the same gesture, shaking her head and her finger: *I can't write.*

Sonia repeats, "You can't talk, and you can't write."

Sabrina nods.

"I know," Sonia says, "Dmitry said that, even if you were reduced to being just an animal, with no human thoughts, he still wanted you to be totally incommunicado – no words, no writing – 'locked in the prison of her mind,' was what he said, 'locked in the prison of her beautiful mind,' that's what he told me, 'locked in her own private hell.' He also joked, 'In any case, she will have nothing in her mind – she will be an animal, a pure, unthinking animal, an idiot.' That's what he said."

Sabrina shrugs. What's done, is done!

Sonia gazes at her.

Miming and mimicry are fun, maybe, Sabrina thinks – *if I keep this up I'll be a champion at charades* – but it is a very clumsy and slow way to communicate; and I don't know sign language and I reckon Sonia doesn't either.

And we don't have much time!

Then she remembers. There was something that she – and Sally, poor dear Sally – something they thought they had discovered about Claire, right at the last, and which was *not* in any of their reports or correspondence – so Dmitry, no matter how many spies he had, wouldn't have known about it!

And what they had discovered was this: Claire and V can transmit thoughts directly to other people without speaking, and they can read other people's thoughts too! And she had seen V do it, with her, that night in the forest.

Okay, what about me? Can I do it?

And she tries:

She concentrates. Sonia, can you hear me transmitting this thought to you – This is Doctor Sabrina Jacobs transmitting a thought to you, Sonia!

Sonia looks up, startled: "Yes! Yes! I hear the thought. It's as if you were speaking in my head, and your accent in Russian is excellent!"

"Thank you, Sonia, you are very kind," Sabrina transmits, and then she thinks but does not transmit, Oh, Dmitry, I've got you now! I'm going to get you, you bastard!" Then she says, mentally, to Sonia: "Now, I think we have a problem. Let's try to get away from here. Do you understand?"

"Yes! You said, 'Let's get away from here!'"

"Good. Now, if Dmitry finds us … Let's see, let me think this out …" Sabrina pauses, trying to organize her thoughts.

"Well, he won't want any witnesses to what happened here, on the island," says Sonia, anticipating Sabrina's thought, "but he will want to keep you because he wants to torture you – he's obsessed by you, I saw how obsessed he is by you – his brother Sergei was on the phone from Vladivostok and furious because of what Dmitry planned to do to you. Sergei was also furious about the plague experiment. He was coming out to try to stop it."

"That's interesting," says Sabrina, projecting the thought, "I always liked Sergei."

"Yes," says Sonia, "Everybody likes Sergei, and the people in the experimental station were against the experiment too – but they were all terrified of Dmitry and too frightened to stop him."

"Yes, I know," says Sabrina. "Dmitry was my boyfriend. He is terrifying."

"Yes, I knew he was your boyfriend. He has photos of you in his office."

"Oh, even now?" Sabrina raises a reptilian eyebrow – really an arched triangular red stripe, emphatic, comical.

"Yes, even now. In any case, I think I know what you want to say. Dmitry thinks you can't communicate – he also thinks you will probably be reduced to idiocy and so you will not be dangerous – and he will want samples from me, blood, and so on, to try to find out why I am immune, apparently, to the bacterium. So he will keep me alive for a while. But he will want to eliminate me shortly afterward. So he will kill me. He won't want any witnesses, witness who can talk, to what happened – the plague that escaped."

Sabrina stared at the young woman and nodded, hissed her agreement, and said, "Yes," in her mind, "Yes, exactly!" What a bright young woman! "If we survive this, do you want to come and work with me?"

"Absolutely!" Sonia's face lit up in a smile.

Sabrina – or, rather, she had to remember what she was: the *Thing* that had once been Sabrina! The *Thing* stood up and started the motor. "Yes, you are right. Dmitry must *not* know that I have a mind – he must think that I am a reptile without human intelligence, with – perhaps – just enough of a sense of myself, and of my past, to suffer, be humiliated, and feel shame, just enough to know that I am his slave, his pet. I have to be entertaining, but not dangerous, a toy. He must be led to believe that I can't communicate, that I'm terrified, essentially harmless."

"Yes." Sonia was now standing next to Sabrina.

"Sonia, if Dmitry finds us, you must put me on a leash."

"On a leash?"

"Yes, I will be like our friend, the iguana. I'm just a thing, a frightened, helpless, passive thing. When the moment comes, I will take vengeance on Dmitry, and I will liberate you, me, and, hopefully, our friend, the iguana."

"Yes," said Sonia, glancing at the iguana, "He – or she – is cute."

"He … He's in love with me," Sabrina said, "I feel it, he knows I'm female and that I'm fit for breeding. I must be in heat."

Sonia laughed. "Let's get out of here, and let's hope we don't meet Dmitry before we are ready …"

Sabrina revved the engine then she said. "Can you drive this thing? You'd better drive. I'll get something that can serve as a leash."

Sabrina went below and after a few minutes came up with a length of chain, some hooks, and some locks. She put herself on a leash, attaching the chain to the hook on her collar. She hissed, a long, languorous hiss. Now I am a thing, a thing on a leash, a thing in a cage. Weirdly, she did feel an illicit erotic tingle. Truly perverse! Her masochism – spiced up with a bit of fetishism – was revving up, truly she was excited – and amused at her excitement. It was thrilling, really, exquisitely humiliating, titillating, just like her old master-and-slave games with Dmitry.

Sonia overheard the thought. "You played those sorts of games?"

"Yes, we did – those were the days."

"It's an interesting life," Sonia said.

"You could say that," Sabrina transmitted, "and getting more interesting all the time."

"You *are* funny!" Sonia laughed, accelerating now that they were away from the island, and Sonia was thinking that maybe if they hopped from island to island, they could get to a port somewhere, and maybe they could survive, and thinking: *Do we, who are immune, carry the bacillus? If we do, are we carrying with us the recipe for the end of human civilization? Will we infect all we meet?*

"That's a good question, Sonia," Sabrina transmitted, as she crouched down next to the iguana. Hello little friend, little Brother, now I am a pet animal on a leash, just like you, well you don't have a leash, do you? But you do have a very nice little cage.

The iguana came close and stuck a foot through the mesh of the cage. *I love you too*, Sabrina said, projecting the message in her mind and touching the iguana's little foot.

Then she began to practice looking scared and cowed and confused, a drooling, submissive, frightened animal. There is not much need to practice, she thought, I've been trained, since I was a child, to be on a leash – and part of me certainly likes it, part of me thrills to it, damn it!

Strangely, Sabrina realized she was no longer angry. More than anything, she was curious. This new her, whatever else it is, is an adventure! And the new body tingled and rippled with excitement and new sensations, new sights, new smells, a new sense of touch, new feelings – and new powers! True anger and despair, if they came at all, could come later.

She settled down, her chain dangling from her neck, lazing, sitting with her back against the sun-warmed hull, basking in the bright hot equatorial light, next to her friend, the iguana.

And so she waits, Sabrina Jacobs three times Ph.D., Nobel Laureate, sleepy-eyed, a gleaming, slick, scarlet-and-black humanoid reptile, dozing in the sun. She yawns, a wide-mouthed, fanged yawn, her black forked tongue flickering in the light.

Smooth and slippery and sly, that's what I am, a serpent I am, crouching, waiting, gazing out from under my heavy, half-closed, scaly lids, from my scarlet-and-black serpent's mask, contemplating with my golden serpent's eyes – revenge, calm and resolute revenge, revenge for Sally, for the crew of *Andromeda*, for *Andromeda* herself, for Ted Lacroix, for Bill Griffiths, for Hans Hoffman, and for Tania Klimova.

CHAPTER 29 – RUSSIAN GIRL

Long ago and far away …

In the past, days ago, August 10, at 6:10 PM, when the future had not yet turned into the past.

The sun was about to set.

Andromeda, in all her splendor, was still afloat. V had just met the Clone, and Dmitry's conspirators were in the midst of their takeover of the ship, the submarine was moving into attack position.

On *Andromeda's* number one launch, *Zeus*, Tania Klimova watched Milo sweat. The man was afraid, terrified even. He wiped his forehead with a clean, white handkerchief. The other guards, those he had sent to capture Sabrina, more than half an hour ago, had gone silent. Something had gone wrong. Well, Tania thought, they had underestimated Sabrina; I'll bet that's what went wrong.

She said, "Milo, it's not too late to reconsider."

Milo looked at her and narrowed his eyes, still holding the sweat-drenched handkerchief in his hand, and said, "Shut up, Russian bitch."

"Okay, okay, relax," said Tania, "cool down, Milo."

Milo was sweating heavily and on edge. He clearly didn't know what to do. The radio – wherever it was coming from – asked again: "Have you got the Jacobs woman?" Milo didn't know what to answer. Tania sensed that he was terrified. Failure was not an option. Failure meant death. The three guards – the traitors – that Milo had sent to the island to capture Sabrina had stopped broadcasting. The connection to them was open, but there was only static coming through the phone.

Somebody was alive – but it wasn't the guys. It was probably Sabrina. Somehow, all alone, Sabrina had killed or neutralized the kidnappers.

Milo leveled the pistol at her: "Okay, bitch, we are going to the island. We'll get Sabrina ourselves."

"How, Milo, how are we going to get to the island? We have no dinghy, and the launch can't get over the coral reef."

"You go through the opening in the reef, where the dinghy went."

"No way, this launch can't do that. It's too big. We'll wreck her and sink if we try to go through the opening."

"Bitch, I'll do it without you, in fact, I think I'll kill you now and rape you when you're dead, or I'll rape you and then kill you. What do you prefer?"

"Milo ..." Tania's hand slipped behind her as she pretended to lean against the control panel while her hand groped for the pistol and she smiled and she said, "If you want to make love, Milo, I've always found you attractive, why don't we just make love and forget the past, forget about Russia and Ukraine," and her fingers closed over the pistol and she pulled it out of its slot and slipped her finger onto the trigger.

"It's not love, Tania, it's hate, it's hate, I'm talking about," and Tania was just about to pull the pistol out and shoot him when Milo shot her in the stomach.

The shot echoed, yet the sound seemed tiny in the vastness.

Tania jerked back, still holding the pistol, invisible, still hidden behind her back, and she felt the pain flood her stomach and the blood spilling, warm, and a sort of loosening of her bowels and bladder and she slid slowly down to the floor of the boat, breathing out, "Oh, Milo, Oh, Milo, Oh, I'm sorry, so sorry!" She somehow managed to keep the pistol in her hand, behind her back, under her, pinned under her, as she slid down to the floor and feeling her lips go numb and how it was suddenly difficult to speak and her tongue felt heavy, and she just stared, glassily, at Milo, and he was smiling at her with that bright even smile in his healthy tanned face, with his blue eyes and blond hair, and he said, "This way, Tania, you die slow, real slow," and she thought, *Am I dying, what can I do now, how can I help Sabrina?* And she saw that Milo was unzipping his fly, and she thought, *Oh, boy, he's going to try to rape me, and, shit, I've shit and pissed myself, and I'm dying, and this bastard is going to try to fuck me while I'm dying, fuck him!* She levered herself up slightly, and pulled out the pistol, aimed it, saw sudden fear and realization in Milo's bright blue eyes, and she shot him five times, in the groin, in the belly, in the chest, and twice in the neck. He flailed, waving his arms, grabbed his pistol, shot wildly, smashing the control panel, smashing the radio, and then he dropped the pistol, his eyes still round and staring in surprise, his cock, now decapitated and bloody, half a cock, just a smear of mangled meat, hanging in a splash of blood and long stringy dribble out of his fly, and he stumbled back, hit the transom, tried to grab it, toppled, his arms still flailing, and fell over-board, his boots being the last thing to disappear, banging on the gunwale, kicking upwards – upwards toward the empty sky.

He was gone.

It was silent. Tania lay in the pool of her own blood and shit and piss. She could smell it. *What a mixture,* she thought, *this is not a pretty way to die; this is a totally useless way to die.* She tried to move, but she couldn't, her legs were paralyzed. *Maybe the bastard shot me through the spine; maybe I'm never going to get up, never walk again.* She tried to use her arms to pull herself up. Nope, can't do it – too weak.

It was getting dark. Is it just me, or is night coming on? Maybe I'm going blind, that happens when you're losing a lot of blood, or in a lot of pain, you go blind, you think it's night, but the sun is shining. No, it really is night, the beginning of night; and the typhoon is coming.

Then she heard it.

Explosions – fireworks.

And, far in the distance, music, echoing over the water, faint, but still, Tania could distinguish the melody, and the lyrics. She thought, for a moment, she was hallucinating.

Should auld acquaintance be forgot,
and never brought to mind?
Should auld acquaintance be forgot,
and auld lang syne?
For auld lang syne, my dear,
for auld lang syne,
we'll take a cup o' kindness yet,
for auld lang syne.

She understood. She knew what it meant. Once, when she and Ian were out on deck, leaning on the railing, watching the sun go down, Ian had explained it to her. "Lass, if ever *Andromeda* is attacked – and we know it could happen, if ever *Andromeda* goes down, she'll go down singing, Lass, she'll go down singing *Auld Lang Syne*. And with fireworks!"

Yes, she understood. *Andromeda* – *Andromeda* was sinking! Then, there they were, fireworks, in the distant sky, beyond Paradise Island, flashes, and one distant, giant Roman candle, high in the sky. Fireworks!

Andromeda was saying goodbye!

Finally, there was a dull, distant roar – an explosion. The music ceased. *Andromeda* was gone. Tania realized she was crying. Crying! God damn it! Crying! She wiped away the tears. *God damn it! God damn it!*

Time, now, was a blur. The pain seemed far away, not part of her. She presumed, in a moment of lucidity, that the nerves must have been cut, so, of course, she would feel nothing. She was probably bleeding to death. How long, she wondered, would it take to die?

She blinked and looked up. High above, in the endless heavens, there were towering clouds, dark and silver and gold. The wind rose. The launch began to rock. The launch was moving. It must be adrift. The anchor she had attached to an outcropping of the reef must have slipped, and so now the launch was in deep water, and the typhoon was coming. *If one thing doesn't get me, another will … and …*

She lost consciousness – she must have lost consciousness, blacked out, disappeared, dreaming, into another world, lying in the bottom of the launch *Zeus* in a pool of piss and blood and shit.

She woke up feeling nausea and as if she were riding on a roller coaster – being swooped up, then plunged down, then up, then down. The launch was rising and falling, scooped up, and dropped down, scooped up, and dropped down. She was unconscious again, and then the launch was being lifted way up, and let fall, way down. Much higher than before, or so it seemed.

She managed to crawl along the bottom of the launch. She pulled herself under a bench; she tried to wedge her body under the struts. She was only half-conscious, half-aware of what she was doing.

She was unconscious again, and then the launch was being lifted up, a long way up, and it almost turned over, she almost fell out, water rushed in, then it rushed out. The launch righted itself, and then it seemed to be sailing through the air, and then it crashed against something, and stopped. A wall of water poured over it, and Tania spluttered, and spluttered and tried to move but couldn't, and then the water receded, and the launch remained where it was in a warm twittering dripping sticky darkness. Tania slept.

When she woke, she was lying twisted in the bottom of the launch that was filled with vines and rubbish and then, *Oh, God,* she saw it – a large mottled brown thing, the color of the foam on a cafe latte, a long thick rope-like thing, its hooded head raised, and it was looking at her, and it was only a few feet away, and, she recognized it: it was a Philippine cobra, and Tania thought, this cannot be true, this is just too fucking much, this is not really possible! What a day, what a night!

She lay absolutely still, hardly daring to blink, remembering the courses she had taken – Sabrina had insisted on it – covering the dangers of fieldwork, and one of the lessons covered the most venomous snakes in the world. This guy, staring at her right now, was exactly that – one of the most venomous snakes in the world. He could spit his venom and blind you. He could bite and kill you; and with his hood extended like that, he was clearly in a foul mood, annoyed, or mad about something, or scared, none of which was good.

She remembered, or she realized, that in her right hand was the pistol, but she didn't know if she could move her hand and she wasn't going to try to right now, and she didn't know if the pistol would work after the drubbing they both had taken, water pouring over everything, a night in the inferno of Dante.

The snake slithered closer, sliding up, oozing up and over a shattered tangle of bamboo. It opened its hood a bit more; it looked like it was ready to strike. Tania froze, literally froze.

If the cobra bit her, then she would die. She knew the symptoms. It would not be a pretty death. Sabrina had explained it all in graphic detail. The poison was a neurotoxin. It would paralyze the nerves that control breathing. She would not be able to bring oxygen into her lungs. She would suffocate, and she would know she was suffocating, drowning in the open air. It would take, maybe, thirty minutes.

This way, Tania, you die slow, real slow.

Maybe Milo was going to get his revenge.

It was fitting that a snake would deliver the death blow for Milo.

The moment seemed to last forever. It must be morning. She really did not want to die. Up above a thin strand of cloud caught the morning sun, it was a delicate rose and white, and the sky itself was a deepening morning blue, robin's egg, delicate at the edge, a deeper darker blue overhead, and the air, after the violence of the storm, was saline and fresh, and there would be so many days that she still could live, and even if she couldn't walk – she was not sure whether she was paralyzed or not – and she wanted to live those days, and she wanted to know that Sabrina was alive and safe, and if possible she wanted to help save Sabrina and all their friends from *Andromeda*. If their mission had been destroyed, Tania was determined to help build it all up again. After all, the folks on *Andromeda*, they were her family – her real family.

The fingers of her left hand groped for some weapon, making a tiny movement, and she discovered, squinting out of the corner of her eye, that there was a stick just next to her hand and it was maybe a yard long, and she thought that, perhaps, if she gave it a shove, or a poke, would distract the cobra, for just enough time ...

She pushed with her finger, quite violently; the stick, a broken length of bamboo, jerked; and the Cobra struck, whipping around and attacking the bamboo; and in that instant, as the snake plunged down, Tania grabbed the pistol and shot the snake through the neck, and as if flipped over and tried to come at her, she shot it again – through the head. The snake jerked backward, flailing against the side of the launch, and was still.

It was dead; it looked like it was dead.

She poked it with the end of the bamboo: it lay still; *yes, it was dead.*

Tania tried to lever herself up. She managed to get into a sitting position; she had no feeling in her legs. *Damn it, damn it, damn it!*

Gripping the transom, she pulled herself higher and peeked over the side of the boat. *Oh, boy, now we have one more challenge!* The launch was halfway up a tree, smashed and hanging from the branches.

She looked around for other snakes, holding the pistol at the ready. She must get down to the ground. She could not move her legs, and there were shooting pains coming down from her back, and she felt horribly weak. Must have lost a lot of blood. Maybe she'd better risk it, and so she tried to shout, but her throat was so raw that hardly any sound came out. She swallowed, and again she tried to shout.

"Hey, is there somebody, is there anybody?"

Nobody answered. She waited maybe for ten minutes and then she tried again

"Hey, is there somebody, is there anybody?"

And she heard a man shout.

"Yes, who are you? Where are you? We'll come and get you!"

Tania had gotten into a sitting position, leaning against the tree trunk.

"I'm here, I'm here," she shouted.

A very good-looking man appeared. Boy, he was a dish, and behind him were two, no three, women, and Tania realized from the prisoner's photographs – Oh, My God! – that one of the women looked like the infamous V, the vampire Sabrina had tried to capture, and that the next one was a blonde, a very good-looking blonde, and then there was a younger person – and Tania was astounded. It was the Clone; it was Claire.

What had happened? Were these the people who had tried to kidnap or kill Sabrina? Was the vampire behind everything? She pulled the pistol from her belt. "Who are you? What do you want?"

They were now at the bottom of the tree, looking up at her. Claire, the Clone, looked fully intelligent, like a normal human being.

"Tania, are you hurt?"

Tania looked down. "Who are these people, Claire, what did you do with Sabrina?"

The vampire spoke up. "Tania, Sabrina was with us, she was swept away when the first big wave hit. But we think she is still alive …"

"We *know* she is still alive," said Claire, "I know she is still alive! So we have to find her. We are her friends, not her enemies."

"We'll come up and help you down," said Alex.

Alex and V climbed up the tree and brought Tania down.

When they got her to the ground, V said, "We have to find out where Sabrina is – and what has happened to her."

"The radio might help," Tania said, as they lowered her to the ground.

"The radio?"

"The radio in the launch."

"Right."

"It was tuned to a Bio-Prom frequency." Tania coughed up some blood. She paused. Then she managed to speak. It was hard. Her throat was raw. She was so damned weak! "The Bio-Prom station was giving instructions to the kidnappers. Maybe they found her after all, they had a ship nearby and a submarine from what I could understand. The radio was hit by a bullet, it's damaged, but it might be just the casing and the batteries."

Claire said, "Tania, you are hurt, you are hurt bad, and you need to be cleaned up."

"I know," said Tania, "Milo shot me."

"Well, let's have a look at it," said V. She and Claire bent over Tania, like two consulting surgeons or beautiful witches from some ancient time. V turned to Claire. "Do you want to do it, or shall I?"

While V and Claire concentrated on Tania, Alex climbed up the tree, and got the radio from the launch and brought it down.

As Tania had guessed, it was the battery and the connections that had been damaged, not the radio itself.

In their kit was a sun-charged battery that might make the radio work;

Alex crouched over the radio, hooking up wires here and there, and testing the dials.

Tania was studying V and Claire, as they conferred and examined her. "What are you guys talking about? Are you going to kill me, or drink my blood, that's what you guys do, don't you?"

"No, I'm not going to drink your blood, at least not before you've had a bath," said Claire. "Right now, you are not at all appetizing."

"Claire!" V grinned. Having a genius teenage vampire – her daughter, her little sister, a new version of herself? – All those things – was even more fun – and challenging – than she could have imagined.

"They are kidding, Tania. They are not going to drink your blood," said Helen, who was helping Alex with the radio, "They are going to try to heal you."

"How?"

"We don't know how or why it works," said V, "but it works – it's sort of like a laying on of hands."

"Okay, try it," Tania, who was beginning to feel the pain, shooting up her back, and her legs – *damn it!* – She couldn't move them at all, and no feeling from her waist down. *Damn it!* She tried to smile. "I like witchcraft."

"I'll do it," said Claire.

"Good!" V nodded her approval.

Claire concentrated. She closed her eyes and laid her hands on Tania's belly and moved her hands up and down over Tania's stomach. Tania felt a warm glowing sensation that spread through her belly and to her back and down her legs, and then she felt the pain dissolve as if it had never been. "I feel better. This is weird, but I think I'm okay."

Claire lifted away her hands, and looked Tania in the eyes. "Try to stand up."

Tania hesitated, but then, slowly, doubtfully, she bent her legs, flexed them and then she stood up and said, "Gosh, this is a miracle, I feel like it never happened."

She lifted her T-shirt, and underneath, there was no sign of the entry wound.

"Now, Tania, you need a bath," said Claire, "and fresh clothes."

While Alex and Helen worked on the radio, V and Claire went to the beach with Tania and swam in the water while Tania washed. Tania stood waist-deep in the surging swirling calm water, took off her soiled clothes, and scrubbed herself with a bar of soap, then she shampooed.

She plunged up and down in the water, delighted to be alive, delighted to be able to walk and swim and talk. When she came out of the water, V handed her a new set of clothes, the standard V issue: a black T-shirt and jeans and tough walking boots.

As she pulled on the jeans, Tania said, "Okay, I'm reborn, thank you, and now, Claire, V, I have questions – and I want to know – what happened to Sabrina and how can we help her?"

Using one of the batteries in their kit, Alex and Helen were able to fix the radio and they listened in on Bio-Prom communications and learned that the research ship *Gogol* was somewhere between the Philippines and Vietnam.

"Sabrina might be on that ship. We need a plane out of here."

"Well, our pilot is supposed to return this evening," said Helen

"He may not, what with the typhoon and all."

"We have to hurry," said Claire, "We have to save Sabrina."

The pilot did return – but several days late. The interlude was spent, living off the land. V was glad she could live a fair bit of time without a fresh meal – of blood.

The helicopter settled down on the beach.

"Sorry for the delay, folks! Terrible damage. Had to get a replacement copter."

"We are just glad to see you," said Alex.

"You can say that again," said V, who was feeling a trifle peckish; black coffee was fine, but …

"You folks were crazy to stay here, but it looks like your gamble worked – you've even multiplied, I see, two more than when you went in. Well, we're lucky this copter is made for crowds."

The flight back was over the sea that now seemed so calm and so beautiful, but when they reached the islands they saw the scenes of devastation – villages plowed to the ground by huge waves, nothing left but a few walls and miles of rubble; forests and farms swept away; ships carried far inland; and roadways that had ceased to exist. Then began an overland trip – not easy, and it took several days – to get to Andromeda's local headquarters, in the City of Jolo.

V managed, one dark and stormy night, to catch a snack – a serial rapist who preyed on young children in the refugee camps and who murdered anyone who suspected him of his misdeeds – and, of course, he murdered the children too. Claire accompanied V, and watched. She was eager to learn how to hunt.

Wearing a heavy, fully-packed rucksack, Aimi Hosokawa fought her way through a ragged and sweaty and desperate crowd in the city of Jolo, the capital of the Philippines Province of Sulu; she elbowed people aside, as politely as she could, repeating, over and over, in the local language Tausug and in Filipino, "Sorry, pardon me, sorry!" Finally, she got to the Andromeda Corporation office, situated in a busy downtown street, saluted the guards, who all knew her, crossed the lobby, climbed up to the third floor, and entered the executive offices. "It's pure chaos out there, so many people have lost their relatives and their friends from the Typhoon. I'm not sure we'll be able to rent or buy a boat, but I did get a bag of food – mostly chocolate bars and rice and peanuts and cans of tuna."

The survivors from the sinking of the *Andromeda* were camping inside the local Andromeda Corporation offices, since all the hotels and guest houses were overflowing with refugees and the hospitals were full.

"Welcome back, lass, you've been working overtime."

"Well, we all are," said Aimi. "How are we doing?"

"We've got the kitchen up and running, and we've got food – though the chocolate and peanuts and tuna and more rice are a welcome addition – and we've got bunks and cots for almost everybody, which is a miracle, considering."

"Great." Aimi began to store the chocolate and peanuts and cans of tuna away in improvised shelving and cupboards.

"So, now, lass, would you like to join Henry and the Captain and me in a little meeting with some of the rest of the staff? We are trying to see if we can find Sabrina and if she's alive, and if we can figure out how to save her. As you know, there are some indications that Sabrina has been captured by Dmitry Pavlov's Bio-Prom."

"Absolutely," said Aimi, and she followed Ian into the conference room where Henry Rothschild and Duncan were standing in front of a large map of the western Pacific.

"Greetings, Aimi," Henry said, "We've received information that Bio-Prom has a very long lease on an island, and the island is here," and he pointed to the map, "and that would be the logical place for them to take Sabrina if they have captured her. So if we could –"

The door opened, and an assistant came in. "Mr. Rothschild, there is someone to see you."

"Who is it?"

"She is not alone. She gave her name as V."

"V? Show her in, with her companions."

So V penetrated, for the third time, into the heart of the enemy empire, Andromeda Corporation, though now it no longer seemed like the enemy – it was beginning to seem more like family, the first family she had had for centuries – except for her long-time assistants, John and Maria.

Henry saw amazement on many of the faces of the Andromeda Corporation regulars – Who were these people? He introduced the newcomers. "Hello, Claire," he said.

"Hello, Henry," Claire said; she came up and kissed him on both cheeks.

Henry blushed. "Claire … Thank you!"

She winked and gave him a radiant smile.

"Oh, dear," Henry sighed. "Well, hello, V, welcome, and Doctor Wolf, it is a pleasure to see you again! Tania! Welcome, we were very worried about you! And you are …?"

"I'm Helen Guerrera," said Helen, "I'm with V and Alex."

"Welcome, Helen." Henry glanced at Claire and at V, "Perhaps I'd better explain to some of our colleagues – what has happened. And, V, who you are, perhaps – can that be revealed?"

Claire and V nodded. "To this limited company, yes, you can reveal who I am," V said. "Besides, Ian and Aimi and some of our other friends, like Izzy here, already know – who and what I am."

Henry turned to the others. "Yes, well, then, Claire, as some of you will have possibly have guessed, has been with us for a long time."

"Since I was created, actually," Claire said, brightly.

"Yes, that's right, lass," said Ian.

Claire favored him with her very special smile – it was dazzling.

Several people opened their mouths in shock. This beautiful, accomplished, poised young woman was the mad Clone they had heard so much about? It couldn't be! And how had she come here? And who were these people with her?

"And V, here," Henry put his hand on V's arm, "V is the prototype – the origin of the DNA – almost all of the DNA – from which Claire was created. You have probably heard quite a bit about her."

"But ..." Jack Park, one of the researchers, was about to say "She's the monster, the absolute enemy, she's the one who brought down our plane, who killed our friends ..." But before he could say any of this, Ian cut him off.

"V helped save all of us." Ian glanced at Jack. "She was on *Andromeda*, and without her, we wouldn't have been able to take the bridge, foil the damned plot, and save all of you, all of us."

"She saved my life," said Henry.

V stared for the briefest of moments at Jack Park and transmitted the thought. "You're right – I caused the plane to crash. But I didn't mean to. I tried to save the ones I could – but I couldn't. I'll explain later if you wish. But the important thing now is to save Sabrina." She smiled.

Jack stared at her for just a second. "Okay," he transmitted back, knowing somehow she would understand. "Okay, later – if you have time, if we have time."

V nodded.

Nobody else had noticed their silent exchange, except Claire, who edged closer to V and put her hand on V's shoulder.

"We have had some tragic misunderstandings with V, which have cost much, both for V and for us and our friends," said Henry, "But I can assure you that V is a friend – and that whatever has happened in the past, she meant – and she means – us no harm."

So, the meeting went into a working mode, Henry acting as Chair, and Aimi as Committee Secretary and note-keeper. The program? They would try to locate and to save Sabrina.

V and Claire explained how Sabrina had escaped her kidnappers – and how V had sought out – well, hunted down – Sabrina on Paradise Island, and how Sabrina had then been swept away, trying to save all of them by closing the bunker's vent. "She also wanted," Claire said, "And this is so typical of Sabrina – she also wanted to save some vital research material." And, yes, V added, it was almost certain that Sabrina had somehow been captured by Dmitry Pavlov.

The meeting decided that, yes, Sabrina had probably been on Dmitry's research island; but the island, it seemed from Alex's monitoring of Bio-Prom's broadcasts, had suffered some sort of unspecified catastrophe; so if Sabrina was still alive it probably meant she was somewhere else.

Claire assured them that Sabrina was still alive. "I'm connected to her somehow, and I sense it, I am sure of it, she is alive."

Using the radio that Alex had fixed, they listened in on *Gogol*'s broadcasts, and though the transmissions were veiled in something that resembled a very primitive code, V and Claire deciphered it in an instant, completing each other's sentences.

They pieced together the following picture: Sabrina and someone else who was with her, Sonia, who was apparently a Russian nurse and researcher, had been taken on board the *Gogol*; and they were being submitted to some sort of torture or experiment there. It seemed to have something to do with the plague. The bubonic plague! Other broadcasts they intercepted indicated that Sergei Pavlov, Dmitry's brother, was not happy with what Dmitry was doing – a violent confrontation loomed.

V proposed that they locate the *Gogol* and that they liberate Sabrina.

Everyone agreed.

But how best to do it? The discussion was a long one.

Finally, a strategy was decided upon. A commando raid would try to capture the *Gogol*, or at least board the *Gogol* and liberate Sabrina.

The members of the raid would be Ian, Alex, V, Tania, Aimi, and Claire, plus a few crew members. Helen would remain with Henry and help coordinate logistics.

"Claire … but Claire is a child!" Henry exclaimed.

"Claire is virtually indestructible," said V. "She is like me."

"Yes," said Claire, "I must go. I *have* to go."

So it was agreed. Andromeda Corporation had a high-powered, fast, long-distance launch, used mostly for exploration and supply; it had just come into the port, and so was available; it would be used, by V and her crew, to track down and attack the *Gogol*.

CHAPTER 30 – VENGEANCE

When the *Gogol* appeared, Sonia waved, and turned the cabin cruiser toward it, as if eager to be saved. She jumped up and down and yelled. The *Gogol* sent out a launch, and when the launch came up next to the cabin cruiser, Sonia shouted, "The laboratories have all blown up, I got away. I brought the reptile woman – and her pet iguana – with me. Don't worry about the reptile woman; she's tame, and terrified of me. She's like a pet, a rather stupid pet, in fact."

The people on board the *Gogol*'s launch were in protective suits.

They sprayed the cabin cruiser and Sabrina and Sonia and the iguana with disinfectant – and kept them at a distance for a full hour – before allowing them on board. Sonia kept Sabrina on a leash, and led her around like a pet dog or monkey. Once they were settled in, Sabrina crouched in a corner of the launch. She whimpered, and occasionally snarled like a cowed, frightened dog, and her collar blinked, in scarlet, off and on, *Doctor Sabrina Jacobs*.

Even from inside their protective suits, the men from Bio-Prom had a good laugh at that. "Look at her!" "Look at the Thing!" "She'll sure as hell make a good pet!" They were delighted that their leader, Dmitry, had finally vanquished his rival, the famous Sabrina Jacobs of Andromeda Corporation. The iguana perched on Sabrina's shoulder and clung to her as if its life depended on it.

As soon as they had Sabrina, Sonia, and the iguana safely on board their launch, the men in the protective suits sprayed the cabin cruiser with gasoline, set it on fire, and using a short-range armor-penetrating missile, sank it. Then they headed off to rendezvous with the *Gogol*.

On board the *Gogol*.

Sabrina was wide awake, but she pretended to be dazed, a confused and cowering animal, but tame, absolutely tame.

They gave her an injection. She sniffed at it, decided it was not dangerous, and that she had better let them to it.

She had to give the impression that she was helpless – mindless and harmless. She wanted to wait for the right moment. She was afraid that if she attacked now, they would gun her down before she could get to Dmitry – wherever he was. So she curled up and whimpered and drooled and pretended to be afraid. It turned out the injection was an anesthetic, and so she really was, for a time, unconscious.

When she woke up, she didn't know how much time had passed. It took her a few seconds to realize where she was and what had happened to her – and what she had become – the *Thing*. But it all came into focus. She knew what she was, where she was, and what she was going to do.

Without moving, she peeked around, carefully, staring out from her heavy-lidded, half-open, reptilian eyes. She was lying on the floor of a large cabin in the Bio-Prom Research Ship – well, to be more accurate, she was lying on a mat of straw – *How thoughtful!*

The chain leash rattled; she turned her reptilian head to look: the chain went from the ring in her collar to a bolt-and-plate on the wall of the cabin; the chain was a thick, strong chain of steel, and it was about six feet long allowing her to shift around just a little bit. She wondered where her iguana was. She hoped they hadn't harmed it. She would kill anybody who harmed it.

She lay still, blinking, like a sleepy lizard in the sun. It was warm, tropically warm, in the cabin. Two guards were in the room. They were sitting on chairs; they had protective suits and submachine guns in their laps, and, behind their protective masks, both looked bored and sleepy.

Sabrina shifted slowly onto her side, thinking the chain would make a neat – possibly deadly – weapon, and thinking that if she cowered and begged and groaned and drooled, and if she were a convincing enough actress – true Oscar material – then maybe Dmitry would be fully persuaded that she had become a helpless animal, a pet, and he would let his guard down. After all, he believed Claire was an idiot – and he had used Claire's DNA, with a few tweaks and additions, to design her, to design the new Sabrina, the scarlet-and-black reptilian *Thing*.

She could hear the motor of the *Gogol* and the swish and splash of water against the hull. *So they were still at sea, and they were on the move.*

Dmitry entered the cabin. He was not wearing a protective suit – arrogant bastard – he thinks he's invulnerable – and he was looking very natty, decked out in splendid cream trousers and a fine mauve shirt. He grinned. "Is the *Thing* awake?"

The two guards stood up and pulled the submachine guns down on their slings so they would look like they are at the ready, fully alert, doing their duty.

With her nostrils quivering, her mind on the alert, Sabrina sensed that the two guards were terrified of Dmitry and didn't like him one bit. "She moved a bit, sir," said one of the guards, "She may be waking up."

"Good, good!"

When Dmitry crouched down next to her, she started back, as if terrified. And then, lying on her side, curled in on herself, she whimpered and hissed, baring her fangs, cowering against the wall, as if terrified.

Dmitry grinned. "Well, Sabrina, I don't know if you understand me. It's natural for you to be confused and frightened in your new ... ah ... condition. But you have turned out better than I could have dreamed. And you even survived that stupid accident with the plague. Do you understand me?"

She whimpered, cowered, and hissed, pressing her back against the cabin wall, her belly and claws exposed, as if she wanted to be scratched or patted.

Dmitry reached out his hand – his shirt cuff was impeccable, she noticed, and his hands, as always, were perfectly manicured, and he had that Royal Gold cufflink she had given him, and there was that slight perfume of eau de cologne, the German brand he liked so much, and as he reached out his hand, she whimpered, cowered back farther, and, baring her fangs, she hissed a warning, and tried to curl still further into herself, the defensive fetal position.

Dmitry grinned. "You shouldn't be afraid of me, Sabrina, we have been lovers. Now I am your master. I own you. I shall look after you."

He put his hand on her reptilian head and stroked the smooth, silken scarlet-and-black scales. "There, there, there!"

Sabrina curled and stretched in a parody of submissive pleasure; she trembled and, suddenly, made a purring noise deep in her throat. And she blinked at him, in slavish voluptuous ecstasy. *God, I can purr, I can purr!* She purred some more, a soft throaty ripple. *I will kill him, I will kill him, I will bloody well rip him into a bloody thousand pieces, I will drink him dry.*

He was still grinning, rather fatuous really. "I really did love you, Sabrina, and perhaps we can become lovers again."

She purred and blinked, with adoration in her golden reptilian eyes; a tear ran down her cheek; she listened, with her ears and with her mind, hearing his words, and hearing his thoughts, hearing – with her mind radar – all that he left unspoken, all the thoughts lurking behind his cool gray eyes and his smug, patronizing smile. He was thinking: "She will be a wonderful experimental subject. I will keep her in a high-security cage in my laboratory just outside Moscow. I will modify her further, slowly draining any remaining humanity from her, if I find any remaining humanity, which is doubtful. I will transform her step-by-step, until she is merely a beast, a monster; after all, this is what she has done to others, and the material I used to transform her came from her own laboratories. *She is her own creation,* which adds to the irony. And, yes, she will be good entertainment, perhaps for some private parties. He could see it now: She would be put on display for his friends, led around on a leash, kept in a cage. Perhaps she could be taught a few simple tricks – sit up and beg for a cookie, roll over on her belly and beg to be scratched, run after a ball and retrieve it, wrestle in mud with a python."

And, with these delicious thoughts as background, he stroked her reptilian scales, and gazed into her eyes, smiling amiably. "We had some good times, didn't we, Sabrina? Maybe we can have good times again; maybe we can go to some of those great clubs you liked so much." And he was thinking, Yes, I can take her on a leash, how splendidly appropriate, perhaps festooned with a gag and blinkers, her collar blinking her name in scarlet, so everyone will know who this *Thing,* who this *Animal* is."

She purred gratefully, and shivered with pleasure. *Bloody Hell! I will drink his blood, every last drop of his blood …*

… and he was thinking: I could not dream of a more exquisite revenge, the great, the beautiful, the powerful, the brilliant Sabrina Jacobs, reduced to a slobbering, purring helpless grateful reptile under my hands … a show reptile, spectacularly, voluptuously human in her forms, but a slavish mindless beast … my very own pet …

She purred and simpered and trembled – *from fear or from pleasure, let him guess!* – seeing clearly in her mind, the pictures were very vivid, the plans he had for her. *The myriad ways he will put me on display, the bastard,* and at the same time, with the anger, she did remember the good times, the sensuality, the funny naughtiness, the outrageous parties, the long nights, and his quirky delicious sadistic sense of humor. *As evil goes he is bloody refined, if only he hadn't been really evil, but of course I too have done what I ought not to have done, and left undone that which I ought to have done,* and she thought of

Claire and V and Alex and Helen, running for the shelter of the bunker, and she prayed to her gods that they had survived the storm.

"Do you need anything, Sabrina?" Dmitry asked, his face close to hers, his eyes looking straight into her eyes.

With one stroke of my claws, I could rip off his face.

With one plunge, I could sink my fangs deep into his jugular.

She blinked her heavy, reptilian lids, worshipfully, amorously, and remained curled, defensively, in on herself, and purred and hissed, a low friendly, loving pacified hiss – clearly, she was, by now, a tamed and grateful *thing*, an *animal, a pet.*

Dmitry stood up. "Maybe we should give her some water, perhaps something to eat. She is not infectious. You can discard those suits."

"Yes, sir!"

"Goodbye, Sabrina. I'll come back later to see how you are doing. You will find your new life interesting, almost as exciting as our old life together."

He left, and one of the guards got ready to follow him out, saying, "I'll get some water, and I'll see what the cook can rustle up – what do you feed a creature like this?"

"I don't know, maybe spaghetti – maybe meatballs?"

"Does it use a knife and fork?"

"I doubt it, but bring some just in case – the little plastic ones."

"Right!" The guard disappeared out the door.

Now, she was left alone with one guard.

Sabrina slowly moved into a sitting position, being careful not to frighten the remaining guard. She didn't look up, she purred softly, thinking, *I hope the purring sounds reassuring,* and thinking, *I'm not sure I can do this,* and thinking, *I'll try, just a little tug,* and she tugged at the chain, feeling strength surge up, muscular strength, mental strength, such as she had never known before.

She braced herself, thinking, now or never. She jerked at the chain. It broke away from the wall, carrying the bolt-and-plate with it. In a single bound, she sprang to her feet and swung the chain – it slammed into the guard, wrapping itself around his neck, and she gave the chain a light tug; and, not realizing her strength, she broke the man's neck, seeing his eyes bulge, his tongue protrude, and hearing his spine crack.

"*Sorry,*" she thought, transmitting the message to his mind, which was, in any case, unfortunately, already dead. She leaped across the room and caught the submachine gun and the dead guard before they hit the floor. *I don't know my strength, I've become like V; maybe I can smash my way through walls! But, no, Sabrina, you are a neophyte, don't get ideas above your station.*

Feeling remarkably little remorse – none, really – she propped the dead guard in his chair, turned the chair away from the door, and then she hid behind the door – her straw mat was invisible from the door, luckily, so the guard who had gone for food would not see that she was missing from her mat of straw – not until the last minute.

She broke the chain off from her collar. For a brief second, she thought of ripping off the "*Doctor Sabrina Jacobs*" collar. Then, she hissed. *No, I'll keep it. As Sonia said, it shows I'm not a wild animal – I'm a domestic animal; it might keep me from getting shot. Also, and this is really perverse, I rather like it!*

When the other guard opened the door – he was without his protective suit and he was carrying a tray with a glass of water and a plate of spaghetti – yes, spaghetti and meatballs, *how thoughtful* – Sabrina stuck the submachine gun under his chin and put her finger vertical in front of her fangs to indicate – *Silence!*

The guard looked at her with bug eyes. She motioned for him to put the tray down on the table and to lie face down on the floor. He was trembling and almost spilled the spaghetti and glass of water.

And she thought: *What do I do with prisoners?* She took the guard's submachine gun. And she realized she was hungry – perhaps for spaghetti and meatballs – but, above all, hungry for blood.

Oh, no, Oh, God!

And whose blood should it be? She found a rope and electric tape in the cupboard in the cabin, and indicated to the guard – transmitting the thought in very vivid terms – that he should undress. When he was naked, she bound him with the tape and rope and wrapped tape around his eyes and mouth, so that he couldn't see, and he couldn't shout. She sniffed his fear; her saliva rose; she was tempted to bite into his jugular, but she resisted the temptation. *Blood, blood, blood …*

Dmitry … Dmitry's blood!

Sabrina found Sonia in the next cabin. She was half-sedated and lying strapped down on a table. They were taking a sample of her blood, presumably to examine what made her immune to the bubonic plague bacillus. In a corner of the room, the iguana was in a cage, munching on some sort of vegetable. He turned toward Sabrina and waved one of his feet – she transmitted a message of *love* – and her friend stared at her for a long moment and went back to munching.

Sabrina removed the drip and looked down at the girl. Sonia opened her eyes, blinked, her eyes widened, and Sabrina raised a finger – she still thought of them as fingers – of one claw to make the *Quiet Don't Talk* sign. She unbuckled the straps that were holding Sonia down.

"Thank you," Sonia whispered in a dazed, dreamy sort of way. She sat up, and rubbed her forehead. "What do we do now?"

Sabrina transmitted the thought: "Now we find Dmitry, and we take over the ship."

Sonia and Sabrina headed toward Dmitry's office. The corridor was empty. Everybody seemed to be outside, perhaps distracted. There seemed to be some sort of commotion on deck. Dmitry's office was not far away. Sonia – now totally awake – stood outside, holding one of the submachine guns Sabrina had lifted from the guards, while Sabrina opened the door to Dmitry's inner sanctum.

Dmitry turned, surprised, "Sabrina, my pet!"

She transmitted no thought. She stood in the doorway, a submachine gun hanging by its strap from her shoulder and a semi-automatic pistol in her right claw. Her collar blinked, delivering its message of humiliation, branded in neon: "*Doctor Sabrina Jacobs.*" Her scales, she noticed, glowed and glittered. *I must be excited. I'm almost iridescent.*

She saw in Dmitry's eyes the dawning realization that she was carrying a submachine gun and a pistol; that no chain was attached to her collar; and that she was probably not the helpless animal he thought she was.

"What do you want, Sabrina?" he said, and then he smiled, "Oh, I forgot, you can't talk, can you. I shall have to help you express yourself."

Oh, he looked so smug! Still, she said nothing; but she could read his thoughts, and what he was thinking was this: there is a pistol in the drawer by my right hand, and I can get it and shoot the bitch before she has the smarts to shoot me.

He still thinks I'm a dunce, oh, such overweening pride, Dmitry!

"So," he smiled broadly. Sabrina remembered how that smile had, so many times in the past, had been her reward for "good" behavior, her cherished reward, and how, even now, the smile gave her a warm thrill of satisfaction, it was somehow, she imagined, though she was totally irreligious, like the pardon dispensed by a priest after confession. It was somehow the incarnation of redemption and salvation. It was what she had mistaken for love – it had been the benediction she had longed to receive. But, no longer.

"So," he said, smiling broadly, "What do you want?" And his hand was sliding, imperceptibly toward the drawer.

"What do I want, Dmitry?" she projected the words directly into his mind, "I want you, my love, I want you!" She shot him twice, once in the right arm, once in the left arm, just below the shoulder in both cases, splintering the bones. She did not want him dead, not yet; she wanted him helpless, but alive; she wanted a little lovers' conversation before she drank – and she knew it was essential to drink the blood while the food was still alive – and so she wanted to give him time – time to know what he had lost, time to realize he was going to die – and she was going to kill him.

Dmitry's chair shot back from his desk and bumped against the wall, blood blossomed on his arms, and both arms hung, smashed, shattered, limp, and useless. "Sabrina," he said. His mouth and eyes were round in shock; his face was chalk-white. "Sabrina. Let's talk. I love you, Sabrina, I love you."

Nervously holding a submachine gun, Sonia, was standing just behind Sabrina, standing guard.

"I'm going to lock the door now," Sabrina transmitted.

"Okay. I'll stay here, on guard, outside."

"Thanks, Sonia." Sabrina shut the door and carefully locked it. She sauntered over to Dmitry's desk, came around to his side, sat on the edge of the desk, and looked down at him. She favored her old lover with a hiss. He was sitting, helpless, both arms dangling and bloodied, against the wall.

She closed one claw around his tie. *He loves expensive ties.* She pulled the tie, almost strangling Dmitry and pulling him toward her as if he were on a leash.

The chair rolled forward and Dmitry choked, his face turned red. Sabrina relaxed her hold on the tie. He gasped for breath. Looking down on him, she caressed his face with her razor-sharp claws, leaving only the thinnest traces of blood, being careful not to touch his eyes, not to blind him; she wanted him to see and to experience fully what she was and what she was doing.

"Beautiful tie," she transmitted, staring into his terrorized eyes, "Where did you buy it? Did we buy it together? Perhaps we bought it together. Maybe, now that I think of it, I bought you that tie, perhaps in Paris, Place Vendôme, or was it during that stop-over, that very romantic stop-over, you remember, in Zurich?"

"Sabrina, my love," he stammered.

"Ah, love, my love … What is love?" she said, delivering the thought – *What is love?* – like a flaming sword directly into his mind. She gazed steadily at him with her reptilian eyes. Her tongue flicked; she hissed and bared her fangs. They felt longer now, and more eager.

She reached out with one claw – the other held the pistol ready (though she knew she really wouldn't need a pistol), she reached out with one claw, and tousled his hair tenderly, and speaking in French in her mind, she breathed out the thought with a prolonged and melancholy hiss, "Ah, my love, my Dmitry, my very own, you were – you are – so beautiful!"

"Sabrina …" And, as he said it, he was wondering if he could kick out with his legs, if somehow he could kick her off the desk, maybe run for it, call for help. But how? He needed his hands; he needed his arms! Nothing worked! He tried twitching his fingers; there was no response, no response at all. Just pain, awful, fiery pain.

"Naughty, naughty, Dmitry, such thoughts of escape will get you nowhere. Kicking out with your legs would be useless. You won't be able to push the buttons. And you couldn't open the door even if you made it to the door, which I sincerely doubt you would be able to do – given that I seem to have acquired, from your little experiment, superhuman strength, among other talents I am only now beginning to explore."

He looked at her, startled. *She can read thoughts!*

She stood up and lowered herself down on him, sitting astride his waist, moving her thighs, as if eager to couple with him, to make love. *Now I am a true lap dancer, Dmitry. You always had a fondness for those performances.*

He shrank back. She hissed and lowered her scarlet-and-black snout, nostrils wet and quivering, toward his face, baring her fangs and hissing, her eyes sparkling. And she spoke softly, alluringly, again in French, into his mind, "We really did have some good times, Dmitry, and I did love you, in my own way, and I think you loved me, in your own way, and I think we still do, in our own ways, love each other. Even your 'revenge' on me was a form of love, is a form of love, a form of possession. You wanted me all for yourself. And I am so happy you feel like that! Such desire is sublime, I suppose, in its perversity."

She nuzzled his forehead with her snout and licked the sweat from his brow with the long black forked tongue. He was so terrified, and she felt it, that he didn't dare breathe, that he didn't dare say a word. "Maybe I would have liked it, being led by a leash – as a reptile, an animal, your trained pet

– into Moscow's Wild Cat Club. Part of me, shivering in shame, would have adored it, I'm sure, the part you knew how to explore and exploit so well. It might even have been fun – fodder for my exhibitionist and masochistic side – if we had decided this little reptilian caper together. You don't know – and now you never will – what I would have done for you, what I would have sacrificed for you."

She paused, leaned down, and with her forked tongue extended, she licked the blood which was flowing down his right arm, and licked, and licked again, and then straightened up, using her long forked tongue to lick the blood from her muzzle. "Do you find me beautiful, the way I am? I am your creation, Dmitry! I am your work of art."

She ran her claws down over her breasts and belly, showing off, voluptuous and deadly, a parody of a night club stripper caressing herself. "No, you do not like me? Ah, Dmitry, that is too bad. We could have such good times together!"

She stood up and with her claws extended, she loosened his tie, and pulled it from his neck, and folded it neatly, and walked over to hang it in his wardrobe. "I am what you have made me. And you know what I am? I don't like it, it horrifies me, but I am … among other things, I am … I am a vampire. I drink blood. Human blood. Isn't that interesting? Isn't that charming and picturesque – I drink blood."

"Sabrina …"

"Yes, Dmitry?"

"Sabrina, let us talk. There is still time."

"No, Dmitry, I don't think there is time. I am hungry, you know, I am very hungry. I am starving, in fact. The last few hours have been so stressful!"

She turned from the wardrobe. "You have such wonderful clothes. I always admired your impeccable taste in clothes." She turned back and opened a drawer: "I like the collection of Cashmere sweaters particularly. And these heavier sweaters in merino wool, I love them too. And the mauve shirt you are wearing, Dmitry, well it is just so … so *you*! Now, as for me, Dmitry," she opened the two swivel doors so that she could see herself, back and front, in their full-length mirrors. "As for me, I don't think I need clothes at all. I am perfect just as I am. I am back in the Garden of Eden, as you suggested, sex and death and nakedness no longer trouble me." She gazed at herself in the mirror, turning this way and that, like a model considering a new dress from various angles.

"You are beautiful," he said, and coughed, "you are extraordinarily beautiful, now, just as you are."

"Why, that is so sweet, Dmitry! If we had world enough and time, Dmitry, we might recreate our own little paradise, right here, or somewhere else. I was willing, you know, I was willing to play all your games, I'd be willing even now, even as I am, I would parade for you, I would strut for you, I would get down on all fours and crawl for you, I would let you lead me on a leash, but …"

"But …?" he gasped.

"I don't think there is time, Dmitry, because …" She turned toward him and hissed angrily, baring her fangs, "because you murdered my friends. Your thugs, killed Jeff and Ted and Karl and Sally and probably Tania, and a whole slew of innocent young people on *Andromeda,* and you wanted and intended to kill them all, and you sank *Andromeda,* and you know how much I loved *Andromeda.*"

"Sabrina …"

"I really did love *Andromeda!*"

"Sabrina …"

"I am hungry, Dmitry. I am hungry for you." And she leapt across the room and over the desk, landing astride him. "Ah, Dmitry," she loosened his collar, affectionately caressing his neck, and she gazed into his eyes. He tried to kick and struggle. But she was too strong, far too strong. He was pinned down, locked between her thighs. She gazed at him. "You made me this way, you know, Dmitry! Now you and I will truly be one! In a true consummation, as it can only be dreamed of, you will be absorbed into me. I shall drink you to the last drop."

"Sabrina," he whispered, hopeless now.

He screamed – and he screamed again – as she bent down, amorously, fondling his hair, hissing, in a friendly fashion, her tongue licking at his skin and she said, "Now, Dmitry, now, you will become me, and I will become you, and all the barriers that separated us will dissolve, it is a mystical marriage, a marriage made in heaven!" She sank her fangs, slowly, deliciously, as if they were sliding into soft butter, into his throat, and she drank and drank and drank until the great oligarch Dmitry Pavlov was an empty shell and she was ready to stand up and to say, and she knew she had to say it, she had not been taught, but she knew it was in the code, and perhaps in the DNA, she knew she had to say it, and so she said, "You are dead, you are truly dead, and you will not rise again."

The rush of energy and power was immense, but at the same time, she was overwhelmed by sadness and horror.

As she was draining the blood from Dmitry, as she was sucking it all up, slurp, slurp, slurp, and as it gurgled like a thick milkshake coming through a straw, a wave of images flooded over her – all of their life together, all of their love for each other, all of their hatred, all of the elaborate and silly and passionate games they had played. She had killed not only Dmitry – and part of herself hated herself for killing him – but, in killing him, she had killed her own past, her own love, her own desires – she had killed so much that was truly her and that only he had understood: he was her brother; he was her lover; he was her mirror.

Oh, the horror! The horror!

And then, too, I am a vampire, I truly am, a horror, an abomination!

She was covered in blood. Blood dripped from her fangs. The hollowed-out cadaver that had been Dmitry Pavlov sat rigid, like a statue of chalk-white papier-mâché, in his executive chair, chalk-white splashed with gobs of crimson and scarlet. The eyes were hollow, the mouth frozen in a silent scream. He was a grotesque work of art, an installation.

So this is the death of love.

Sabrina raised her head, opened her jaws, and howled in anguish. She howled and howled.

The door sprang open, and Sabrina turned toward it, ready to kill whoever or whatever came in the door.

It was V, the human V. She was holding a pistol, and she held it level straight in front of her. She was crouching in the shooter's posture, and she was wearing her warrior's gear, the black catsuit, stun gun, knife, and machine gun over her shoulder, and the matte black-and-green camouflage makeup. She looked exactly the same as she had when Sabrina's team had captured her a month before. Still holding the pistol in front of her, she stepped into the room.

From behind Dmitry's desk, Sabrina hissed, ready to spring.

V said, "Sabrina?"

Sabrina hissed and bared her fangs. Slowly she stood up. She pointed at the collar, blinking: *Doctor Sabrina Jacobs, Doctor Sabrina Jacobs, Doctor Sabrina Jacobs.*

"Jesus Christ!" breathed V, the pistol wavering.

Covered in blood, with blood dripping from her fangs, Sabrina was whimpering, mourning, keening; silver tears ran down her black and red reptilian cheeks. In front of her, slouched back in his high-backed leather chair, was the bloodless, chalk-white cadaver of Dmitry Pavlov, its pale open vacant eyes staring straight ahead.

He looks like a mummy, V thought, he looks like he has been dead for centuries.

"Oh, Sabrina," V put the pistol back in the holster, and buckled the holster. She came to Sabrina, and she put her arms around Sabrina and held her tight; she ran her hand over the crown of Sabrina's head; and she looked into Sabrina's eyes; she pressed her human lips to Sabrina's bloodied reptile lips, and she kissed Sabrina – it was a long, firm, loving kiss – and she said, "I'm so sorry, Sabrina, I'm so sorry."

Then she pulled away slightly, and, smiling slyly, V said, "But welcome, sister, welcome! Now we truly are one!"

EPILOGUE

Years had passed.

Claire was terrified. Swimming underwater and afraid to rise to the surface, she glided along, within an inch of the sandy bottom, aware of the gentle waves, just above her, lapping against the beach.

Just above her, on that beach, her destiny was waiting. The death sentence, she knew, would be absolute. There would be no appeal. Execution would be instantaneous.

Her very existence was a violation of the fundamental law.

I have no right to be alive.

I don't really exist.

And why did judgment have to fall now, when I am so happy!

V had told her to go ahead alone, to be brave – and to face her destiny whatever it might be!

"My destiny – my destiny?" In an instant, Claire was plunged into an abyss of anxiety. Until that moment, it had seemed such a beautiful evening for a swim.

Claire, who was almost nineteen years old and could now take on demon form – and who had exactly the same scarlet-and-black patterns as her mother-sister-daughter Sabrina, had been visiting her older sister-mother, V.

The day before, V had taken Claire hunting. Near Monte Carlo in a luxurious cliff-side villa overlooking the Mediterranean was one very fat African dictator and his tall, broad-shouldered, muscular Chief of Security – who was also his principal interrogator and torturer.

A high-class and very exclusive escort service based in Zurich had offered the dictator and his henchman "two extremely beautiful young women, one with jet-black hair and extraordinarily pale skin, and the other blonde, with blue eyes, with a golden tan," as companions and playthings for a long weekend of pure pleasure – refined pleasure – "Such as nothing you have ever experienced before."

The dictator was delighted when V and Claire arrived, in a chauffeured antique Rolls Royce, and entered, dressed in extremely elegant evening gowns, and carrying only their slender overnight cases.

"You are even more beautiful than your photographs," the dictator said. He was a vastly overweight, jovial, charming man, witty and quick, with a face which, not too many decades ago, before it was buried in fat, had been extremely handsome.

He offered drinks. He and his henchman took the two elegant and slender creatures, who both spoke impeccable French, out onto the terrace of the villa.

The dictator was so fat he waddled, his shirt ballooning over his trousers; and, when he bent over to serve the drinks, he huffed and puffed, running out of breath. The henchman – or Chief of Security – was muscular, obviously a bodybuilder, with heavy powerful shoulders and a strangely gentle and sensitive face for a man who had organized the massacre of more than 200,000 people and who, personally, had murdered several hundred, often in the most gruesome and prolonged ways, since, in his well-publicized opinion, murder and torture are more entertaining if you can take your time, do it slowly, and savor the moment.

Below lay the Mediterranean, glowing softly, gray-silver, in the evening light. The lights of a few fishing boats sparkled, here and there, far out on the dimming vastness.

The two women were charming and funny and sophisticated – in fact, thought the dictator, they were extraordinarily sophisticated and accomplished for creatures so young. If they hadn't been prostitutes, he would have considered adding them to his considerable harem, or even marrying both of them.

He had arranged for the foursome to be very intimate. The servants had been sent away, and the bodyguards were discreetly placed out of sight at the entrance to the villa and, below, in the garden.

The women suggested they might change into something "more comfortable."

"Of course," said the dictator, bowing graciously.

"Close your eyes! This will be a surprise!"

And change they did – into reptilian demon form.

And it was a surprise.

By now, Claire did not need lessons in feeding or killing.

The dictator and his Chief of Security lay dead and drained of blood on the terrace. It was dark and the candles were burning in the candlesticks, and the cicadas were still trilling in the trees, and the gentle sound of the waves on the beach below made the atmosphere particularly romantic. It had been a soundless event – both men having their windpipes and their nervous systems paralyzed in a single instant. None of the guards were aware of anything unusual.

Claire and V had changed back into human form, taken a shower, and then, once V had used a dart gun to immobilize the guards, they had gotten back into the Rolls. Joseph, V's trusted butler, would drive them back across the border into Italy and down the coast to V's seaside Tuscan villa.

"I trust it was a profitable meeting," Joseph said, with the perfect aplomb of a long-time partner and servant.

"Yes, Joseph, it was quite profitable."

V and Claire had mastered the dictator's computerized accounts and after a bit of computer mind-control and wizardry on Claire's part, and a few keystrokes on V's part, 800,000,000 euros had been transferred to a charity account for the people the dictator had bilked and murdered and 200,000,000 euros went into a fund administered by V through a bank in Paris.

"It covers expenses, research, travel," said V to Claire, "and you can use some of it, if you wish, to expand your fashion business."

"No. Maybe next time I'll take a share, V," said Claire, "I'm still learning. And, you know, I really don't need the money."

In fact, Claire, who now had a large interest in Sabrina's Andromeda Corporation, didn't really need the cash at all; she had plenty of sources of income of her own. But she did *adore* going hunting with V.

They both slept through the next day until late in the afternoon. Then Claire got up, and leaned over V and whispered, "Okay, time to get up sleepyhead!" And so they had begun their day.

By six o'clock, the sun was low in the west, brilliant and warm over the Mediterranean.

Claire suggested a late afternoon swim – and V agreed and asked Joseph if he would bring down drinks – coffee, whiskey, wine – and perhaps a sandwich or two for Claire – to the beach in about half an hour.

Joseph said, "Of course, V and Claire, I'll see you down there! Have a good swim!"

Claire and V went down the white wooden stairs, to the secluded cove, surrounded by soaring cliffs, and which possessed a splendidly private sandy and pebbled beach.

"You know," said Claire, "when I am in reptilian form, I have gills – I can breathe underwater."

"You have what?" V raised an eyebrow.

"Gills, I have gills – you know, gills, for breathing, like a fish." Claire took off her clothes, hung them on a deck chair, and morphed into her scarlet-and-black she-demon form. "I'm amphibious," she said, rather proudly, V thought.

V sniffed. She was vexed. "Hmm. I've never tried that." She slipped out of her dress and underwear and stood doubtful for a moment and then morphed into the green and turquoise she-demon – with sparkles of gold and scarlet – and stepped into the water. "Where are your gills?"

"Here," Claire said, "just on the side of my neck. Look!"

"Hmm," said V, "I see." The water sloshed gently around her thighs; her foot claws gripped the shifting small smooth round pebbles; she curled her lip in a slight reptilian frown, emitting a perplexed and quizzical hiss. *I like to think I am the most advanced design; this is very annoying.* And, seeing Claire give her a mischievous, golden, sparkling reptilian glance, she shot Claire the thought: *You are a proud annoying little wench, my adorable little sister!*

Claire winked, an adorable, mischievous reptilian wink.

V concentrated – "*gills, gills, think gills!*" She felt the side of her neck – *lo-and-behold* – fluttering gills emerged from her smooth scales, ready to filter and extract oxygen from the water. *I wonder if they work,* V frowned. *Well, the only way to find out was to try.*

"Claire," V said, "now I understand why humans live such short lives and turn things over to the younger generation so quickly."

"Why?" Claire was grinning, her fangs bared, her forked tongue flicking up and down in a very self-satisfied manner, and it was clear what she was thinking: *Well, well – I have taught the marvelous V, my mistress and mother, and teacher and older sister, something she didn't know about herself. Bravissima, Claire!*

"Well, Claire, you new biological entities – to speak like Sabrina or Alex for a moment – you new, young biological entities try out things that just don't occur to us older life forms." V paused, "I mean, Marcus told me I would discover powers I didn't know I had. I just never thought of gills and of breathing underwater!"

Mentioning Marcus gave V a tinge of fear and guilt and an ominous premonition of a coming encounter – discovery, criticism, guilt, judgment, and – death. Claire was the proof she had failed to enforce the oath that there never be any other creatures such as V. Marcus might insist she enforce the oath, or principle, or he might enforce it himself. She suddenly felt sure that Marcus was somewhere watching over her, somewhere close. It was an intuition – like a body blow –stronger than knowledge, stronger than seeing, stronger than touching. *Ouch!*

She glanced at the lithe scarlet-and-black demon wading into the milky, pink, twilight water, so beautiful, so feisty, such a wonderful hunter, and so talented: *I cannot believe I did the wrong thing.*

Claire, as if sensing a thought that concerned her, glanced back over her shoulder, and then put her arms out in front of her, ready to dive. "So, are you coming in?" she said, still with that mischievous smile.

"Yes. Okay, here goes," V said, and she dove into the water, skimming smoothly along the bottom and expecting to choke when she began to breathe. But, no, it was smooth and automatic, her nostrils had closed automatically, and the gills took over.

Now, why didn't I think of this before! She frowned, skimming along the bottom and following Claire, who was about twenty feet in front of her, and glittering black against the white rippled sandy bottom.

For about half an hour, they swam close together, exploring the bottom of the little cove and the sea life on the cliff walls along the edge of the cove, and going out to the very mouth of the cove where a few flat rocks rose just above the water.

They crawled out of the water and slipped onto the rocks like two mermaids and lay on the flat wet stone allowing their scales to dry in the gentle evening breeze. The sun was by now just above the horizon, a huge milky-rose globe, melting, dissolving, and spreading out its white-rose light over the sea.

"We are sirens," said Claire, lolling back, "like the mermaids in the old stories."

"Yes," said V, thinking what a joy it was to have someone who was not exactly like her, but so much like her that she could share everything: and the fact that they could breathe underwater – that was, V, thought, positively awesome.

V was sometimes jealous – though jealousy was not really in V's makeup – of Sabrina. "I'm so happy when you are here, Claire, and I must admit I am a wee bit jealous of Sabrina, who sees so much of you. Perhaps Sabrina should come here too sometime."

"She'd like that," said Claire, "though she does love life on the ship, and she loves to work all the time. But, here, we could all go swimming together. And she could bring her work with her. I'll ask her."

They slid off the rocks into the sea, dove down, deep, undulating down, along the underwater cliff that fell away right at the entrance to the cove, there where the water descended into dark depths, the rays of the sun fading into pitch-black far below and where V felt a little chill of fear – as she always did – it was so deep.

They swam back slowly, keeping close to each other and close to the bottom of the cove.

Then V received a mental message, a very strong one, a message aimed at her alone, an imperious message, an order: "Hang back, V, stay underwater! Tell the Clone to go ahead. Tell the Clone there is someone, on shore, who wants to meet her."

V felt a shudder of fear, but then she felt, somehow, reassured. She knew that nothing could go wrong; she did not know how she knew, but she knew; she had faith, "Claire," she said, transmitting the thought, "You go ahead, I'll swim for a bit longer; there is somebody on the beach who wants to meet you."

"Somebody wants to meet me? Now, like I am, I mean, in my present form?"

"Yes, Claire, he wants to see you in your present form."

"He wants to see the demon?"

"Yes, he wants to see the demon."

Claire was doubtful and suddenly afraid.

In my present form, she thought, in my present demonic reptilian form, who would want to see me? She was perfectly aware of the basic law, the interdiction: *Thou shalt create no other Beings such as Thyself.* This was her death sentence.

Claire V. Jacobs became a reptilian she-demon shortly after her sixteenth birthday. Her stateroom was next to that of the Sabrina she-demon on *Andromeda II*.

For Claire, there was no warning.

Claire had come back from working with Aimi in the ship's library. She left the lights off in her room and was undressing by the light of the moon. It was streaming through a large porthole – and she was listening to the sound of the water against the hull as *Andromeda II* cut through the waves.

Being in the moonlight was very romantic, and it was one of the things Claire really liked to do, just bathe in the silvery light of Earth's ever-loyal satellite.

Just then, the moon went behind a cloud; the room was plunged into muffled, silken darkness.

Suddenly, she felt a trembling, a fluttering, all over her body. It was as if army of ants had been let loose and were crawling all over her, their little feet going patter-patter-patter and tickling and nibbling and generally making a fuss; and there was a burning itch everywhere, on every inch of her skin, an itch that she wanted to scratch, and which made her feel she was going crazy, and then it all suddenly ceased, and her body was calm again, but *changed*, definitely *changed*.

Even in the dark, even without a mirror, she knew she had *changed*. The itchy rippling creepy-crawly feeling was gone. But her body was not the same body it had been a minute ago. She had become another being, another type of being – it was thrilling, absolutely thrilling, but scary too, really scary.

What do I do now?

She stood absolutely still. She didn't want to do anything; she didn't want to touch anything. She felt the claws of her feet grip the carpet; she opened and closed her hand-claws, the long pointed nails felt powerful and sinister, as if they could rip her – or anything else – apart: she would have to be really, really careful if she touched any of her clothes, the Cashmere, the silk, the new synthetic tissues she and Andromeda Corporation had developed, since Claire, it turned out, was a genius at textile and clothing and fashion design. Slowly, cautiously, standing naked in the dark, she hugged herself, wrapping her reptilian arms around her chest.

Yes, scales, definitely scales, her skin had become the skin of a reptile, and muscles, more muscles, and her breasts … Yes, bigger breasts! They felt truly comic-book voluptuous! With her claws, she caressed her arms, trying to get used to the idea – scales, smooth warm scales!

She was afraid to turn on the light; afraid to move in front of the mirror; afraid to look at herself: *What if I'm monstrous? What if I'm too horrible to look at?*

She felt fear – cold terror. What if I can't speak? What if I can't change back? What if I'm locked inside this body?

Finally, taking a deep breath, she walked over to the light switches, and, closing her eyes, she turned on the lights.

With her eyes still closed, she thoughtfully, carefully, bit her lower lip, making sure that her newly sprouted fangs were not breaking the skin – or, rather, she corrected herself, the *scales*.

She opened the door of her wardrobe and, eyes still closed, positioned herself in front of the full-length mirror.

She opened her eyes.

Standing in the mirror was a scarlet-and-black she-devil, and – Claire moved closer just to be sure – the pattern was exactly, but *exactly*, the same as Sabrina. With the index nail of her right claw, she traced the red markings of her face, above her eyes, around her lips, on her snout. Yes, the markings were exactly the same. She turned around, and she swung the side mirror out so she could examine her back – yes, yes, and yes! *I'm an exact echo of Sabrina!*

Maybe not quite so tall, maybe not quite so voluptuous – a more slender, younger version, but the design was exactly the same, with precisely the same scarlet-and-black patterns.

I still have to grow. In a year, maybe two, I will be exactly like Sabrina, a carbon copy, only, of course, she's a carbon copy of me!

How confusing!

Am I the mother, or is she?

Are we V's sisters, or her children?

Are Sabrina and I sisters, or are we the same person, or are we twins, but only when we are reptilian? Of course, Sabrina is *only* reptilian now – that is what she is, she's locked in, and she can't speak, and she can't write.

Can I speak?

She took a deep breath, closed her eyes, and tried to say, "One, two, three!" She took a big breath, jumped up and down and shouted "Yes!!!"

"Yes, yes, yes! I can talk!"

Then she thought: Let's try something more challenging! And she acted it out, the dagger-speech from Macbeth, one of her favorites, and so, adopting a gruff, archaic, king-like tone, she uttered …

Is this a dagger which I see before me,
The handle toward my hand? Come, let me clutch thee.
I have thee not, and yet I see thee still.

Art thou not, fatal vision, sensible
To feeling as to sight? Or art thou but
A dagger of the mind, a false creation,
Proceeding from the heat-oppressèd brain?
I see thee yet, in form as palpable
As this which now I draw.

Well, she thought, contemplating the effect in the mirror, my Shakespear-ean acting has not suffered at all. Indeed, in this guise, I might be quite a hit at the Royal Shakespeare Company, or in Berlin playing in the Deutsches Theater.

Claire's knowledge of literature was immense – and still growing – and she loved to act, both for herself and others; and she felt, seething within her, the call of a multitude of lives, a multitude of professions, a multitude of passion-ate love affairs. *I will never grow up,* she sighed.

Again …

Is this a dagger which I see before me …?

Okay, that's enough, Claire! Now: Can I change back?

V had told her how she had learned to do it. In fact, V had given her instructions, preparing her for this moment: "You close your eyes. You con-centrate on the image of yourself as a human being, you concentrate on how you look as a human being, and you keep concentrating."

She did it.

Nothing happened

Oh, oh, there goes my modeling career!

A cold wave of fear rippled down her spine.

I guess I could join a circus.

Or hide in my cell as a Top Secret Freak on *Andromeda II*, like Sabrina.

Concentrate, Claire, concentrate!

She closed her eyes and she envisaged herself in her ballerina costume, dan-cing, she envisaged herself in jeans and a T-shirt, she saw herself in the dinghy with V when they were leaving *Andromeda* as the ship was sinking, and she felt the same fear she felt then, with the water lapping around – and even into – the tiny dinghy, on the huge deep ocean, in the darkness, leaving virtually the only home she had ever known, out in the vast world for the first time …

Should old acquaintance be forgot …

A rippling, shivery, warm feeling engulfed her body.

Wow! How utterly voluptuous!

Wow!

She opened her eyes. She was Claire again, the human Claire.

She changed back and forth three or four times, just to make sure, just to practice, then she showered, and then, smiling slyly – this will be a surprise – she changed into her girl-demon form and knocked on the door to Sabrina's apartment.

Usually Aimi was with Sabrina in the evenings; but Claire knew Aimi wouldn't be this evening since Aimi had explained – lamenting and making a whole comedy routine of it – that she was on a deadline, an article for a Japanese scientific magazine, that had to be finished by three o'clock in the morning, so she would be down in her own rooms.

So Sabrina was alone.

She was sprawled on her stomach on the bed, under a bright lamp, reading Marcel Proust's *À la recherche du temps perdu*, and making a clicking and hissing sound – *God, his prose is so rich and insightful, but some of it is bloody complicated* – when Claire knocked and then entered.

Sabrina looked up and saw a reflection. It was a mirror image of herself – a slender scarlet-and-black she-demon version of Sabrina. She hissed, swiveled around on the bed, and sat up straight.

"Hisssss!" she said again, and "Claire?" She asked in her mind.

Claire hissed back, and then said, out loud, "Yes, it's me."

"You can speak," Sabrina said in her mind. She got up and went over and took Claire in her arms. "Now you are me and I am you."

"Yes," said Claire, "Now we are truly one!"

The next morning, when she was under the shower – and in demonic form which she adored testing out like a pilot maneuvering a new type of aircraft – Claire discovered that in she-demon form she had little fluttery appendages, normally invisible, on the side of her neck; these became visible and active only when she stepped under the water.

She had gills!

She was a bit hesitant to try them out, but try them out she did, watched over by Sabrina, in shallow water on an island near *Andromeda II's* anchorage.

Yes, she could breathe underwater!

And so, it turned out, could Sabrina, though her collar made the gills less efficient than they normally would have been, so Sabrina compromised with her principles and had the collar modified so that it could be removed.

But she always clicked and locked it back on, immediately after each underwater swimming expedition. With its blinking "*Doctor Sabrina Jacobs*," it was a reminder of her punishment – and a reminder and incarnation of her masochistic exaltation in her punishment. *Oh, how complicated I am, even now!* She sighed a reptilian sigh, and letting the perverse thrill ripple through her, she licked her reptilian lips.

"We are amphibious," Claire shouted, exulting. "I love it underwater!"

Three days later, it was almost midnight, and Sabrina was lying on her stomach on her bed under a warm reading lamp flipping through a book of fashion photographs: clothes that she – now locked forever into her reptile form – would never wear.

Claire, in human form, was lying on her back beside Sabrina, dreamily looking at the ceiling and lightly caressing the scales of Sabrina's arm – the scales were so smooth and warm.

Claire turned on her side and put one finger through the steel ring at the front of Sabrina's collar and flipped it, up and down, one, two, three, four times, and she said, "For years, when I was crazy, or pretending to be crazy, I contemplated revenge."

Sabrina's attention pricked up. She hissed gently, quizzically.

Claire gave the ring a final little flip, and then ran her hand, possessively, down the smooth curve of Sabrina's neck and shoulder.

"You kept me in a cage, and now *you* are in a cage," Claire said and kissed Sabrina on the snout. "And the cage is *you*." And she pulled away a bit and ran her fingers over the feathery scales at the top of Sabrina's head, and the small delicate reptilian ear, "And I, who love you, am the key to the cage."

Sabrina extended her long forked tongue, coiled it, hissed, and ran the tongue over Claire's extended hand, licking the palm.

"So now my revenge is to have you like this, my pet, and to love you, to love you without limit," Claire said, gazing with her human eyes into Sabrina's gleaming, narrowed reptilian eyes.

With her fingers spread delicately, Claire again slowly stroked Sabrina's side and shoulder. Sabrina's tongue flicked and her eyes glowed, and the reptile she had become groaned – and purred – with pleasure, infinite pleasure, at having inspired such cruelty – and such love.

A few nights later:

Claire came into Sabrina's bedroom. Seeing Sabrina, Claire felt almost breathless with power and pleasure; Sabrina was, as usual late at night, lying on her stomach reading a book. The reading lamp gleamed on Sabrina's shoulders, on the deliciously delicate small of her back, on the sublime rising curve of her ass. Claire came to the bed and knelt next to Sabrina and ran her fingers down Sabrina's back. "For you, I was a thing, an experiment, a clone, a caged animal, and now I'm a woman: but what am I, what am I, really?"

Sabrina put the book on the bedside table, and turned, looking at Claire with a quizzical, reptilian smile, and hissed, gently, curiously.

Claire kissed Sabrina on the cheek and stood up. "I don't want to sleep alone tonight," she said. She took off her nightgown and hung it neatly in the built-in wardrobe and slides the door closed; Claire knew she would be in deep trouble if she were not ultra-organized when in Sabrina's space; Sabrina may have become a reptilian demon, but she was still obsessively neat and organized; her bedroom on *Andromeda II* was an Art Deco masterpiece of creamy white with a decorative motif of black and scarlet, and everything had its place and everything was always in its place. Aimi, who often slept with Sabrina, and gave her massages, had warned Claire and instructed her on the rules. "If you are going to stay the night with her, Claire, you must be absolutely neat; everything has its place, and everything in its place."

Claire turned to face Sabrina who, coiled on the bed, blinked her reptile eyes, and watched Claire intently.

Claire stood very still for perhaps fifteen seconds and then, in an instantaneous blur, she morphed – and her demon self stood there – its forms and patterns – the black and scarlet scales – exactly echoing those of Sabrina; they were identical twins.

"Alex had this made for me, I insisted on it," Claire said, picking up a thick steel-and-rubber collar that she had put on the dresser. "When I wear it, my vocal cords are paralyzed and I can't speak: I become like you: I *am* you."

She put the collar on, clicked it in place, and locked it. It had her name on the front, blinking in neon-like scarlet, *Claire V. Jacobs*, blink, blink, blink, and, just under the chin, it had a large steel ring just like Sabrina's.

Claire walked across the soft thick rug to the bed and lay down next to Sabrina and, hissing softly, her forked tongue flickering between her half-opened reptilian lips, Claire asked with her mind. "Do you like it?"

Sabrina put one clawed finger through the ring, flipped it up and down playfully, then gave it a gentle but forceful tug, right, then left and then down, so that Claire had to nod her head and then lower it in obedience, and Sabrina said, with her mind, her tongue flickering, "Yes, I love it." And she ran her claw gently along Claire's cheek.

Sabrina reached up and turned off the light. With her mind, Claire said, "I love you, I love you so much, and I always wanted you to love me, and now, I think you do," and she rolled onto her side, put her arms around Sabrina and held on tight.

And Claire was thinking as she clung to Sabrina that she herself, Claire, did not really know who or what she herself was and that the world was a vast abyss where you can go on falling into the darkness forever, but now, clinging to Sabrina, it was into an ecstasy of abandonment and happiness and comfort that she was falling, not caring who or what she was, just drunk with joy that she was alive and with Sabrina.

Claire was an optional vampire – like Sabrina – she could eat ordinary human food, or she could live off human blood, and sometimes she would leave Sabrina and *Andromeda II* to join her other "sister" – V.

V and Claire would hunt together as Claire accompanied V on her nocturnal travels, to find those among the human tribe who deserved to be sacrificed.

Claire had become very successful in the "human world." She designed clothes for both men and women and her brand, CVJ Fashion, had within the space of two seasons, become famous, and she had even modeled her own clothes, twice, in Paris and Milan, and she was regularly on lists of "the most beautiful women in the world."

Now, all of this, all of this perfect life, was, Claire feared, about to come to an end. Her life would be extinguished; she would discover that she was mortal, after all.

V had said, "You go ahead. Someone on the beach wants to meet you."

Claire swirled around in the water, to face V. "Somebody wants to meet me? Like I am now?"

"Yes, go ahead, exactly like you are now," V transmitted the thought, "Don't worry. I love you, Claire. I always will."

Claire gave V a timid wave and a doubtful look and – reluctantly – she swam toward the beach. She skimmed along the bottom, gliding with the ease of the aquatic creature she had become – it was like flying, she thought, the almost weightless sense of freedom.

The waves had left ripples in the sand, and then, at the edge of the water, just where the beach began, there were pebbles, little pebbles, polished and rounded by the waves, slippery, and clattering softly, like gentle castanets, as the water moved them back and forth, rubbing against each other.

A school of tiny fish, golden and silver in the waning light, were swimming frantically, darting here and there, in the shallows along the waterline, and Claire thought how varied life was, how beautiful and unique each instant was, and how the world was vast and full of adventure, and how she wanted to live, and to keep on living, and yet she knew, too, that her very life was an anomaly, that Sabrina had violated the basic law laid down by Marcus in creating her, and that V had violated her basic oath to Marcus in not killing Sabrina, and in not killing her, the Clone, *the Abomination*.

Perhaps her whole existence had been a mistake, a short reprieve, and now she was going to die – it would be as if she had never been.

The basic law would be enforced – she must die.

Am I to die now, she wondered. Am I to die now, just when I am so happy, just when people love me and when I love them? She thought of all the people she knew whom she loved and who loved her – V, Sabrina, and Aimi, Sabrina's special friend – and lover – who had become like another sister to Claire, Alex, Helen, Ian the engineer, Duncan, the captain, Henry the CFO who was like an uncle, and Izzy, goofy beautiful brilliant Izzy who worked with Claire on special biology projects and who liked to put her feet up on pillows at the end of Claire's bed, and eat popcorn as they watched old movies together.

Okay, Claire, be brave – dying is nothing; it is merely non-being.

It was hard to imagine, though, not existing; it was hard to imagine the whole universe, disappearing, *poof*, and no longer there; all the people gone, and me gone too … All the other people continuing to exist, but me gone, gone, gone …

Nothing there at all …

No there at all.

Death.

She took a deep breath through her gills and burst through to …

… and burst through to the surface, taking a deep breath of air – her gills automatically closing and disappearing, and the webs that had extended the claws of her feet – making them into superb flippers – automatically folding into the skin, giving her back her prehensile claws, and she stood, slightly awkwardly, the claws of her feet gripping the slippery sliding and rolling pebbles.

Her vision had shifted, instantaneously, from underwater vision to earth atmosphere vision, and she saw the fold-up wooden beach table had been brought down from the villa and that the table was set with a bottle of whiskey, a bottle of wine, a battery-powered espresso machine, and dishes and cups and wine glasses and whiskey tumblers – and a plate of food. Several large white fluffy towels had been laid across one of the sleek white wooden deck chairs.

Standing beside the chair was a man – the sinking western sun accentuated his sun-bleached blond hair – with tiny streaks of gray – his tan, his white, even teeth, which were grinning at her, his blue eyes, and thick eyebrows, and the scar, a tiny scar in truth, on his brow.

"Well," said Claire defiantly, as she came out of the water, but she hung back a little, intimidated and afraid, "Well, well."

The man tilted his head to one side and was staring at her as if drinking in an astounding freakish sight. "Well, well," he echoed, as if amazed.

Claire, who was stepping free of the water, and of the rolling pebbles and getting a foothold on the sand, shook herself like a dog, sending off a luminous spray of silver drops, an instant rainbow in the rosy milky twilight.

She noticed that the man was wearing a very fine open-necked sweater and soft-fabric very fine trousers, and a wide false-leather belt and sandals.

The clothes carried her logo, her design: CVJ.

She swallowed. Good sign or bad sign?

She walked up onto the sand and hesitated to hold out her claw to shake hands. He had not offered his. He was still grinning though, and though she could not read his thoughts – he must have a thought barrier up, she thought – she felt that a grin was probably a good sign. So she didn't hold out her claw. "Hello," she said.

"Hello," he said, very gently. He was now only about a yard away.

"Turn around," he said, "Let me have a look at you! Do one of your dance pirouettes, but slowly, arms in the air."

Claire gave him a sideways glance, almost a smirk, and then turned around, tip-toe, on her claws, her arms raised straight up, wrists slightly bent; she was thinking, this is amazing: He looks totally human and yet he's totally, so far as

I know, alien, and I'm half-human, and I look totally alien. Is he going to tell me that I, the hybrid, the clone, have no right to exist and that I must be put down like a rabid fox? Is he going to strike me dead, here and now, with a bolt of lightning like the gods of ancient – human – times?

He was stroking his chin. He said, "Amazing, utterly amazing! Yes, this is quite exceptional. Utterly amazing! Turn again, Claire, please."

She turned twice, then three times, then four. "Am I a horse being auctioned off?" she said.

"No, not quite," he said, smiling with his bright, even teeth. "Could you be so good as to open your mouth wide? I'd like to look at your tongue and your fangs." His voice was familiar – she knew his voice.

She gave him another look and stuck out her tongue and hissed, but she did as she was told, and opened her muzzle wide and let him peer at her snake-like fangs, her forked tongue, and the roof of her mouth.

"Hiss," he said.

She hissed.

"Purr," he said.

She purred, managing to purr, in a short medley of tunes, the *Star-Spangled Banner,* the *Marseillaise*, and the *International*.

"Brava," he said, "You are a virtuoso!"

"Really," she said, pouting, and purring again to show off, "This is just too much. I'm not a show animal, you know."

He laughed. "I'm sorry, Claire. No, of course not! You are not for sale! And you are not a show animal."

"Well, thank you, I think."

"But you do like to perform on runways, I believe, and you did model your own clothes in Paris and Milan last year. And you are an accomplished dancer, among your many other accomplishments."

"Thank you again," she said, and she could not resist a quick pirouette, hissing in pleasure. "And you, I know your voice. You have been following my reading, my studies, from the beginning – why?"

He picked up one of the big white towels, and put it over her shoulders and helped her wrap it around herself. If she could have blushed in her reptilian form, Claire would have blushed.

"Why? Ah, I wonder."

"Your voice was in my head, and you asked interesting questions. So – thank you."

"You are welcome."

"And I see you have good taste in clothes." She moved close to him and used her claws, delicately, to adjust his collar, and the front of the sweater.

"Indeed, I have."

"You like the designs?"

"Yes, I do. I'm very proud."

"Proud?"

"Well, it seems my daughter designed these clothes."

"Your daughter?"

"Yes, I am Marcus, and I am, if we look into things closely, your father."

"My father …?"

"And a very proud father, too!"

Claire stared at him. A feeling she couldn't define rushed in and tears welled up in her eyes. Marcus opened his arms, and Claire fell into them. He kissed her on the forehead, and she clung to him and let her tongue, her long forked tongue, flicker along his cheek, hissing and purring her happiness. "You are extraordinarily beautiful, Claire. You are perfection! You are a marvelous design! I've never seen anything like it before."

"Perfection is too … too kind." Claire whispered, grinning self-consciously, drawing back a bit and shifting uneasily on her foot claws. She drank Marcus in – his perfect teeth, his rich tan, and his thick golden hair. "May I dare to love you, father?"

"If you agree, daughter, we shall love each other; as for me, I have already fallen head over heels."

"Head over heels!" Claire laughed, "You are so idiomatic," and she fell into his arms again. "Now, I have a father!"

Splashing awkwardly, V came out of the water, using her foot claws to get a grip on the slippery pebbles, and then she was on dry land. Marcus grinned, "And here is your sister, the other prodigal daughter!"

"Hello, Marcus."

"You haven't changed, V, perhaps more beautiful than ever."

"And you are just the same Marcus, the little scar on your forehead, the tan, just as handsome as ever."

V kissed Marcus, let him hold her, and ruffled his hair with her claws. "So," said Marcus, "This is our brave new world." He poured wine for V and for Claire and a whiskey for himself. "Joseph said I could bring the drinks down. He didn't mind at all."

"So you accept Claire," said V.

"Absolutely! You have brought me – us – a great gift, V."

"And Sabrina, it was her doing."

"Yes, Sabrina," said Marcus, "I shall thank her someday."

Claire picked up a chunk of gorgonzola, smeared it on a biscuit, and popped it into her mouth. Marcus followed this small act with interest. V's tongue flashed, guiltily and hungrily, across her lips.

"Yes, V, you are jealous," Claire smirked, taking a big bite, and turning to Marcus, "You should see the way V stares at me when I eat food – there! She's doing it right now!"

V laughed. "Yes, I can't help myself."

Claire let her towel drop away and lowered herself into a deck chair; she had the lithe, rapid smoothness of a dancer, or a panther, and the intelligence and extreme physical self-consciousness of a young human.

V changed into human form and wrapped herself in a towel. "Claire, I think, prefers her alien or reptilian form, don't you, Claire?"

"It's simpler," said Claire, stretching back in the deck chair. "One doesn't need clothes"

"And yet you adore clothes."

"That's true too. I'm a bundle of contradictions." Claire sighed. So it was not to be death, after all. "Oh, I'm so happy," she said, and she opened her arms as if to embrace the whole world, and the whole universe and the star – or planet, really – called Venus, which began, just then, to sparkle in the evening sky.

Sonia, the Russian researcher and nurse who had accompanied Sabrina in her adventures on the *Gogol*, joined the research team on *Andromeda II*, and her own DNA was used to create cures and antidotes for a number of diseases, including Dmitry Pavlov's weaponized bubonic plague.

Adjacent to Sonia's laboratory, was a rather large cage, a miniature jungle inside it, and with its own sun deck, and in this cage lived a very spoiled iguana who was extremely popular with the crew and who, soon, when encouraged, and given a mate, produced a family of little iguanas.

Alex Wolf became the chief bio-engineer at Andromeda Corp. He worked with Sabrina and her team; he developed a series of breakthroughs in biological engineering.

Four years after Claire's *change*, Alex and his team managed to engineer a reversal for Sabrina. She could now shift from her reptilian to her human form at will, just like V, just like Claire.

For months, Sabrina refused even to contemplate changing back into human form; she had gotten used to her monkish existence.

Sabrina's reptilian transformation was top secret, and any hint of it had been kept from the world. With the help of a double, and lots of computer effects, the human Sabrina continued to exist. Now, the reptilian Sabrina had to be reassured that she could go back to being her reptile self whenever she wished. She was doubtful. Everybody – Aimi, Claire, Alex, Helen, Tania, and Henry – had to work hard at convincing her.

Finally, she agreed, and the old Sabrina Jacobs, brilliant, beautiful, human, and articulate – she could even speak and write – returned, in all her glory.

Sabrina's mother, the actress Alexandra Anders, who had visited her demonic reptilian daughter on *Andromeda II* many times, said, "Well, I'm delighted to have this human version back, Sabrina, but I rather like your excitingly wicked demon version too – don't drop it altogether."

Sabrina, in her human guise, once again became, with Claire V. Jacobs and Alex Wolf, the public face of Andromeda Corporation.

Helen Guerrera became chief counsel for Andromeda Corporation and spent much of her time with her partner, Alex, on *Andromeda II*, "the best, most luxurious corporate headquarters in the world," as she put it.

One evening, about six months after Sabrina had once again become a part-time human being, Helen and Alex were in their apartment on *Andromeda II*.

Helen was about to start dressing, and she shouted, "You'd better hurry with your shower, Alex, they are expecting us at the dinner in an hour and remember – it *is* black tie."

Alex, she noticed, had laid out on the bed his tuxedo, and the little medals which indicated the various distinguished scientific awards he had been awarded by various nations and scientific academies.

On the program, this evening was an official dinner on board *Andromeda II* for the Prime Minister of Singapore.

"Alex?"

"You'd better come and look at this," Alex shouted, over the sound of the shower; his voice sounded strange.

Helen went into the bathroom and saw a shimmering gold and black reptile staring at itself in the mirror. It turned toward her and said, "Well?"

"The color scheme is brilliant, Alex. How did this happen? Can you change back?"

"I think the bite V gave me, way back, remember?"

"Yes. I remember. Gosh, it's you, it's really you." She was running her hand along his arm; she looked down, but where is … ah … where is your …?"

Alex looked down between his legs and gave what Helen took to be a reptilian grin – she knew Sabrina's and Claire's expressions by heart and was very talented, she thought, rightly, at deciphering reptilian moods and expressions. "Well," he said, "that's very interesting – it's got this little protective flap you see, and … if I just look at you or think of you … well, here, you see …"

"Oh, oh, oh – very impressive! Right, I see, darling, I see. You'd better put it away; we have to be ready to go to this dinner in" she glanced at her watch "in about forty minutes. And by the way, V bit me too."

"She did?"

"Yes, just a little tiny scratch, and she poured whiskey on it too. She told me that, whatever happens, I had to be equal to Alex, to you."

"Maybe you should concentrate – try, see if you can do it too."

"Alex, we are supposed to –"

"It won't take a minute."

Helen squeezed her eyes shut and concentrated.

And thus it happened, in an instant.

The dinner for Lee Hsien Loong VI was a smashing success. Sabrina was in great form – dressed in a shimmering clinging creation Claire had designed specifically for her – it transformed her body into an entrancing and fluid replica of a scarlet-and-black reptile with its serpentine sinuousness reflected in myriad iridescent nuances each time she moved.

Helen Guerrera glittered in a diaphanous dress. Using new fabrics, Claire had designed a clinging creation that made the wearer, in this case Helen, look like she was virtually naked but immersed in a continually changing cascade of silvery water or silver mercury depending on the angle of the light, molding in the most suggestive way even the most intimate parts of Helen's body, and revealing, in the end, everything – and nothing. Alex was of course impeccable in a tux and black tie, and all the men, including Henry, had a fine time.

The Prime Minister's wife, who was a millionaire businesswoman, had had forewarning and had insisted on her own CVJ – Claire V Jacobs – "creation" – and she was very glad she had done so: her rippling and diaphanous Josephine meets Napoleon dress was just what was needed and what she had always dreamed of.

Claire herself was dressed in a sober echo of Sabrina's dress and for Aimi Claire had designed a modernist caprice that evoked the classical Geisha kimono and the Samurai warrior tradition all in one swirling yet modest pirouette of elegance which had echoes of an Armani jacket echoing the 1940s wide-shouldered cinematic dresses, spiced up with a touch of Greta Garbo's austere Communist *Ninotchka* look. Aimi's mimimalist makeup had been styled by Claire to give Aimi's face just a faint suggestion of Geisha-like hieratic mystery.

Alex said, "Compared to the women, we look like penguins."

"Admirable animals, penguins," said Henry, "stoic, loyal, and they stand on their own two feet."

"And they don't have great wardrobe problems."

"True, indeed, Alex, true indeed."

During the dinner, Alex and Helen took careful notice of one fact: their appetite for food, and for drink, human food and drink, was absolutely undiminished – no nausea, no nausea at all!

A characteristic they shared, they noted, with Sabrina and Claire.

"Our vampirism is optional, it seems," Alex whispered to Helen.

"Well, I am glad of that, but there are some people …"

"Yes, well, we can ask V if we can join her on the hunt sometimes."

"Just for the sport of it – but, yum, yum, yum," said Helen.

"Just for the sport – and in pursuit of justice, of course." Alex adjusted his tie, and downed a glass of Champagne.

After the dinner, which continued to one in the morning, Alex and Helen returned to their apartment. They kissed and then they undressed, and Alex gazed fondly at Helen and felt a tense trembling in his loins, and he said, "Do it again!"

"Only if you do it too," Helen double-locked the door.

"Okay."

"One, two, three, on your mark, go!"

Helen's reptilian form was pure shimmering silver with a scarlet-and-black embossed design, which made her unique.

"Wow," Alex said, flicking his tongue, and extending his claws so that he could embrace her. "We are complimentary – you are silver, and I am gold."

"Yes, my man, so we are – complimentary in all things. Now, let's see if you, my dear Alex," she hissed, "are a fully functioning demon."

There were, in fact, a few loose ends to tie up. V didn't like loose ends.

It was a dark moonless night and the gravel and clay lane had been rutted by heavy rain and a recent thunderstorm and Jed Baker, the Cambridge criminologist, was worried that the carton of milk and the packet of eggs might spill out of his bicycle carrier – as he wobbled his way home, riding slowly and carefully. Tomorrow was Saturday and he was looking forward to a leisurely, luscious breakfast. He did manage to get home from Cambridge, along the lonely side road that wound between high dark hedges – and past low, rolling, fields and copses of trees – without incident and without spilling the groceries, though the front wheel of the bicycle was squeaking dreadfully, and he scolded himself that he had not remembered to oil the bloody thing.

He stopped in front of his cottage – a picturesque isolated little thatched roof affair that dated from the 17th Century – and thought, Well, what a brave fellow am I, living in this isolated spot, alone, when I am the criminologist who has put some of the most dangerous criminals in the world behind bars, but, since I work behind the scenes, they don't know who I am, not many of them anyway. So …

He wheeled the bicycle into its little garage, placed it in its slot, locked it in, and lifted the carton of milk and the carton of eggs out of the basket and closed the garage door. He went to the front door, fumbled with his keys, and opened the door, and went into the dark house.

It was in the hall, while bending down to take off his bicycle clips, that Jed began to think that – something was not normal. He took a deep breath and tried not to betray any nervousness. He adjusted his glasses on the end of his nose and he went into his studio-living room, which was like darkness itself.

"Hello, Jed." Sitting in a chair in the corner of his studio was a dark shape, and Jed said, "I'm going to put on the light," and the shape said, "Go ahead!" Jed put on the light, and there was a very beautiful woman sitting in the chair; she had very dark eyes and jet-black hair and skin that seemed flawless and was only lightly tanned, or so it seemed to Jed.

Jed was frightened, but he felt that it was a good sign that she had revealed herself, and not just sprung on him from the dark.

"Who are you?" he asked.

"My name is V," she said, and smiled.

"Oh," Jed said, "V."

And she said, "You took something that was mine, a number of years ago, Jed, you took some of my DNA."

"Oh," said Jed, thinking now I am going to be killed; now I am going to be a victim of my own damned cleverness, now I'm going to see the end of days.

V stood up. She was dressed in a very fine classic Armani suit, with a short skirt, and black stockings, and moderately high heels.

Jed said, "Whatever you are going to do, I'm very curious, I'd like to ask you some questions."

"Jed, don't worry, I'm not going to kill you, a friend of yours is with me, and she'd like to talk to you, and there's somebody else who would like to meet you, since what has happened, well, it's all because of what you did, Jed Baker."

Out of the hall came a strange and awesomely frightening creature, an overly-voluptuous female scarlet-and-black demon. It was wearing a collar, and the collar blinked on and off, "*Doctor Sabrina Jacobs! Doctor Sabrina Jacobs! Doctor Sabrina Jacobs!*"

"Sabrina?"

And Sabrina spoke into his mind, "Yes, it's me, Jed, it's me transformed by the DNA you gave me."

"Oh, my God," Jed could hardly breathe. *What had he done?*

"And," Sabrina added, as she came up close and kissed him, running her reptilian tongue along his cheek. "I want to meet someone else."

A stunning young person stepped out of the shadows. She was holding a bottle of wine. "My name is Claire," she said, "both I and Sabrina are a result of that night in the fens when V rescued the two little girls and put an end to the career of a serial killer and left a few strands of hair on a sweater that you were able to analyze and that you and that chap from the Home Office gave to Sabrina. So to celebrate our birth or rebirth, I brought a bottle of wine."

"My God," said Jed, and he sat down.

At the end of the evening – an evening full of memories and laughter and deep discussions of genetics and criminology – it was decided that Jed would cooperate with V and with V's criminologist, Maria, in helping V track down fodder, and that Jed would not offer any of V's DNA to anyone else. He had not yet done so, so no extra damage, so far, had been done.

In fact, the copies of V's DNA stored in Cambridge were given to Claire and to Sabrina for safekeeping, and Claire carried them away in a little portable freezer. They would be stored, in high security, aboard *Andromeda II*.

A few days later, V had a drink in an exclusive bar in Mayfair with Sir Geoffrey James, the smooth Home Office official who had engineered the original Clone deal with Sabrina. V briefed Sir Geoffrey on the events that had led to the birth of Claire, to Sabrina's – now reversible – transformation – and to the destruction of *Andromeda* and to its rebirth in the form of *Andromeda II*.

"Though only two or three people know of this, V, I can tell you that His Majesty's Government is very grateful that you contained the dangers posed by Dmitry Pavlov and his terrorist projects," said Geoffrey, "Perhaps there is hope for the human race after all." He raised his glass. Sparkling in the light from the fireplace, their glasses clinked together, and they drank. V did have, Sir Geoffrey thought, the most beautiful, the most beatific, smile.

CODA

A year or two later …

Just outside Rome, Italy, the road was rutted, and it was raining and dark and the wind, a warm wind from the sea, had come up, making old papers and fliers and a few autumn leaves swirl around in small wet tornadoes.

The girl put more charcoal on the brazier and the fire flared up. The road was lined with women standing beside little fires. The glow from each fire lit up each girl's face, her legs, and her flimsy costume.

A few trucks and cars were cruising along the road, gawking, stopping, and bargaining. Farther down, closer to the ruins and to the film and video studios were the transsexuals and transvestites.

The fire lit up the girl's features – she was exceptionally beautiful and very young, you could tell that she was top rate merchandise, thought Guido; he pulled over.

"How much," he asked.

"How much for what?" she bent over close to the car, her nostrils quivered, and her mind-radar focused on Guido's thoughts and appetites. *No, he's not the one.*

"Five hundred euros," she said.

"Are you crazy? What a bitch!" And he gunned his engine and speeded away, splashing her with the ribbon of muddy water raised in his wake.

She fumed but then went back to waiting. It was her third night on the job. The first night the pimp who controlled the three prostitutes next to her had come to pay a friendly little threatening visit – she had shown him her false police documents – documents provided by friends in the Rome vice squad – so, in fact, her cover story was, in a way, legitimate, her detective contacts wanted her to "take out" a particularly vicious killer of prostitutes – and so she said she was looking for the guy who had been killing prostitutes and as soon as she found him she would be gone.

"Well, I hope you find him quick," the pimp said, "these killings are bad for business. It makes the customers nervous."

"Yeah, bad for business," V said, thinking, Maybe this pimp – he was pretty skinny and bony – should be next on her menu, even if he was not particularly appetizing.

That was three nights ago, and V was beginning to wonder if this little gambit was going to pay off. Her friends at the Rome vice squad would be disappointed. *And I am very hungry!* It was just at that moment, when a gust of wind raised some leaves and rustled its way through the scrub behind her, that a black Mercedes appeared, slowly coming down the road, and V felt a rush of excitement, just as a lioness feels a rush of adrenaline, V supposed, when a browsing and unaware wildebeest, munching on grass, comes into view.

Here I go again, she thought. She struck a provocative pose, one leg angled out, the short skirt hitched up, and when the car slowed, she puckered up, giving the man a slight pout, her lips crimson, her eyeliner shining black satin, her eyelashes flapping.

"Hop in," the man said.

V's radar clicked, locked. *This is him!*

"Hop in," he repeated; he had a very nice smile, warm and welcoming and strong. "Yes, of course," said V. She slid into the car, smelling the rich leather of the seats, letting her nostrils quiver, and leaning back. "Buckle up," he said, smiling at her, and he signaled and pulled out, off the shoulder, and onto the road. The road led up into the hills and the man didn't say anything for a long time. V monitored his thoughts and was patient. For her own purposes, in order to feed, it would have been best to seize him now, on a side road, and feed, and just leave him, but she was trying to find out if any of his latest victims were still alive, and where he had buried the remains of those he had killed. Relatives and friends of the victims and the chief of the vice squad wanted *closure*. "Where are we going?" she asked, "I mean, the more time we spend together, the more it costs you, you know that."

"Money is no object," he said.

"That sounds good," she said.

He turned on the radio.

"Hello, my name is Sabrina Jacobs, and I work at Andromeda Corporation."
"Hello, my name is Alex Wolf" "Together, working with all of you, we at Andromeda Corporation, are pushing the frontiers of scientific research – to make life better for all the peoples of our planet. Today and together – we are creating tomorrow."

"They think they are so great – so-called Masters of the Universe! I hate those people!" He turned off the radio.

V said nothing. She looked down at her hands and then up through the windshield at the rain. She wiped away a tear.

He drove up a narrow, winding road and then stopped and turned into an even narrower laneway. It led to an old farmhouse, a group of buildings around a courtyard.

"Classy," V said.

"Wait until you see," he said. He braked the car. The wheels crunched on the pebbles of the courtyard. None of the farm buildings were lit.

"Get out," he said. It was a very lonely and isolated place.

"Sure." V unbuckled and got out of the car.

The man got out of the other side of the car, and he locked the doors; the doors went click. "Now," he said, "follow me."

"Okay," V said, feeling that docile and a bit stupid was the best role to play here. Her stilettos made it difficult to walk on the coarse gravel, big and small pebbles, all mixed together.

"Let's have a few drinks first," he said, over his shoulder.

And V thought, Oh, Oh, this is the danger point, drinks may have drugs or poisons, and some of those are effective even against me.

He took V into a long hallway that led to a big living room sort of space. He put on a few low table lamps. It was a luxuriously appointed space, modern, minimalist furniture, black leather, polished wood, a large fireplace, and, by the fireplace, standing in a metal holder, what looked to V's practiced eye like branding irons.

He poured drinks and handed one to her.

V sniffed at the drink, and her mind said, *Yes, it is drugged!*

When his back was turned, V tossed the drink into a potted plant. He didn't notice; he was lighting a fire in the fireplace.

V was perky for a few minutes and then she pretended to be drowsy, and her head fell on her chest, and she collapsed off the divan and rolled onto the Persian rug, lying on her back, ready to spring upward if he did anything particularly dangerous – like trying to drive a stake through her heart.

He leaned over her, and he said, talking to himself, "You are a true beauty, the best yet perhaps, why a girl like you is out on that road plying such a degrading filthy trade is beyond me, but then I guess that's my good luck, isn't it."

He picked her up and carried her. V kept all her muscles limp. She was slung over his shoulder. He is strong, she thought, really strong; he's carrying me like I was a piece of fluff, a feather doll.

When he lowered her down, she was in a room where the images of cruelty and slaughter were so vivid and baroque that even V was thunderstruck. Her eyes were wide open, staring and expressionless, like the eyes of a doll. On the walls were photographs of slaughter, fragments of bodies, faces torn from their skulls, eyes without faces, faces without eyes; hanging from hooks and chains were instruments of slaughter.

He took a knife from a hook on the wall and held it over V. It was a large butcher's knife. "I'm sorry," he said, "but I can't help myself."

Her eyes stared at him.

"Yes, I really am – I am sorry – but I cannot help myself." He lifted the knife higher, his muscles tensing, ready to bring it swinging down. The overhead lamp reflected in silver iridescent ribbons of light on the razor-sharp edge of the blade.

The wind rose. Rain pattered in sudden gusts against the tiled roof – it was a strangely comforting sound – V took a deep breath, tensed her muscles, and she thought that, Yes, yes, this time she would …

Looking into her wide-open eyes, the man said, once again, "I'm so sorry." And the glittering knife, sparkling from the light of the lamp, came slashing down.

NEXT: VOLUME 3 IN THE
ADVENTURES OF V

PANDEMIC

BOOK 1
PARTY BALLOONS

by
GILBERT REID

TWIN RIVERS
PRODUCTIONS

PANDEMIC BOOK 1:

PARTY BALLOONS

NIGHT – AUGUST 2046

Beaded with sweat, coated in slime, the president of the United States lay sprawled on her back, semiconscious, naked, on a muddy sandbar in the Atlantic Ocean, just off Florida.

A former Miss Universe, charismatic television star, media billionaire, Katherine du Bois Hughes, 43, was the first black female president of the United States of America.

Forty miles away, on the mainland, Miami and Fort Lauderdale were going up in flames. Vast explosions echoed across the water.

America was dying.

The president's eyes opened. They stared at the night sky, at the low, fast-running clouds that glowed, mottled red and black, reflecting raging fires and towering explosions. The flames of Hell had been unleashed. All the demons were running free.

"Where am I? Who am I?" Katherine shook herself. Groggily, she sat up., Dazed, feeling strange, she looked down at herself. Naked! She ran her hand over her shaved head. She remembered …

She remembered where she was, who she was, and – what she had become. So much had changed – and so fast!

Six hours earlier, acknowledging a cheering crowd, Katherine raised her arms overhead, hands clasped in triumph, *Hail to the Chief,* ringing in her ears. She was the president of the United States of America, acclaimed, beloved, even worshiped.

In an instant, all that changed …

Now … The United States was under massive attack.

And she, Katherine du Bois Hughes, was a marked fugitive, head and pubis shaved, her bruised, naked body beaded with pearls of sweat, dripping with steamy clay. And, even worse, much worse, she was a … She had been transformed into … a … into … an unclean thing! She had forfeited her immortal soul.

She had become what she most despised. Never would she be able to undo what had been done … She refused to finish the thought.

She would not even think it. She *couldn't* think it.

Would God ever forgive her?

CHAPTER 1 – A SCHOOL BUS

Texas – ten months earlier …

November; it was a sweltering winter day.

Twelve dead …

Teenagers: all but one of them.

Yellow ribbons of thin plastic – "Police Investigation: Do Not Cross" – fluttered in the dust-filled wind blowing across flat fields where a crop of something people used to eat – misshapen brown clumps and leafless stalks – had died, a long time ago.

Other ribbons flickered in the wind: "Homeland Security: Do Not Cross."

The sun, veiled by brown streams of sand and ripples of low, leaden, muggy, slow-moving cloud, was a vast, oyster-gray splotch, radiating sizzling heat and sticky humidity. The air dripped oily sweat.

Yellow dust devils zigzagged, miniature tornadoes, across the fractured, melting asphalt, the pebbly, broken hardtop of rural road 25-B.

A loose end of one of the yellow "Do Not Cross" ribbons snapped back and forth, a wicked, whipping, slapping – *slap, slap, slap* …

Slewed sideways across the road was a yellow-and-black school bus. Its windows were shattered. Jagged edges of glass reflected the dull shimmering light of the sun. Its door and part of its side had been torn off, peeled away. Its insides had been painted – in blood.

Scrawled in capital letters, also in blood, on the side of the bus, just next to the emergency exit, was one word: "APOCALYPSE."

Sheriff Lloyd W. Huston, sixty-four years old, unshaven, sweating heavily, seriously overweight – he never had been able to bring that paunch under control – and longing for a cool beer and – the Lord be praised – for his retirement, coming up at the end of this, his last term, tilted back his tan cowboy hat and wiped the sweat from his forehead with a big soiled white handkerchief. "Dust gets in the pores out here, weather like this, the wind drives people crazy."

He glanced at the word – "APOCALYPSE" – and then at the young woman standing beside him. She was a cool character alright, just flown in from London, England, an expert, he'd been told, on bioterrorism, on hybrids and Synthetic Individuals – those dangerous, mysterious newfangled SINs. Homeland had told him: "Let the woman see everything."

"Grit gets in everywhere," he said, "Rarely gets so hot in November – 115 degrees – My God, is it hot!"

The woman nodded. But in truth this woman – Laura Giordano was the name they'd given him – looked like the heat didn't bother her one bit, not a trace of sweat. She had black hair, cut stylishly short, and chalk-white, flawless skin, and she was wearing an Andromeda Corporation baseball cap, wraparound dark glasses, paratrooper type boots, black jeans, a black T-shirt with the Andromeda Corporation Logo, a yellow dragon breathing fire, and a black military-style vest, and, hitched over her shoulders, she had what looked like a cutting-edge, high-tech backpack.

"To tell the truth, I sort of expected a guy wearing tweeds and with horn-rimmed glasses and maybe test tubes in his pockets, maybe with a mustache." The Sheriff pushed the sweat-soaked handkerchief into the side pocket of his pants, "I mean, when they said somebody was coming all the way from Europe."

He was hoping she'd take off her glasses; he wanted to see her eyes.

As if she'd heard his wish, she lifted off the glasses, hooked them into a pocket of her armored vest, tilted her face up to him, and smiled – a marvelous smile, dazzling, and it was aimed straight at him. Goddamn, he thought, she is beautiful; she is just about the most beautiful woman I have ever laid eyes on, and I've seen some beauties in my time. And then it struck him: She had the darkest eyes he'd ever seen – almost pure black; it was as if there was nobody in there.

"Yes, I guess I don't exactly fit the image," she said.

"But you know about these creatures – these so-called hybrids, and these bio-creatures, BIOCs, and the *Synthetic Individuals*, the SINs," the sheriff said, thinking she looked too young to be an expert on anything so complex or on anything at all, maybe: What was she, twenty-two or twenty-three, somewhere in there, ten years younger than his youngest, Fran, and he thought, with a sigh. How time passes! You are young. Then you are old.

"I've been following them from, well, really, from the beginning," she said, and, crinkling her eyes, she smiled again. "Well, Sheriff, I guess we'd better go and have a look."

The school bus was sitting all alone, slewed across the road, one wheel twisted and trapped in the ditch, its broken windows reflecting the vast sickly glare of the sun.

"Yes, indeed," Sheriff Huston wiped his forehead and squinted. The bus was all alone – forensics had been through it several times already. Now it was as if nobody wanted to go near the thing.

The word in red shimmered: APOCALYPSE.

A few hundred feet away, FBI SUVs and County Sheriff cars blocked the road, and just beyond them, there was a laboratory truck from HLS – Homeland Security – and another from the FBI. Aside from a few military guards, and FBI and HLS men, posted down the road, and some of the sheriff's own men, there was nobody in sight. The whole area, circumference three miles, had been sealed off. Every damned level of authority was here, thought the sheriff, and nobody was here.

It was a dead zone.

"DNA analysis confirmed the thing was a hybrid," said the sheriff, "human and ... and alien, whatever that means."

"Yes, I read the reports." She gazed at him again, with that smile, the perfect teeth, those dark eyes.

"Not happy reading," he said, thinking, with a touch of unease, she's too good to be true, too cool, too perfect ...

"No," she said, "Not happy."

As they walked toward the bus, yellow-brown dust swirled around their feet, and a helicopter flew over the field to the left, its rotors making a fluttering whap-whap-whap sound that V, even after so many decades, still associated with war, with side-mounted Gatling guns, with napalm, with Agent Orange, with burning palm trees, veterans without eyes or limbs, heaps of Vietnamese civilian dead piled up to rot in ditches, and with children's fire-scarred bodies. She glanced toward the helicopter, narrowing her eyes – a pale dark shadow moving over the dusty flatness – and then looked away.

The front door of the bus had been torn off its hinges, and part of the side of the bus had been ripped away, the raw metal left hanging, like a silver lip of melted steel; the driver's seat had been twisted off its frame; it lay cantilevered sideways, and was dark with dust-coated blood.

The sheriff stood back to let the woman go first.

"Thank you," she said. Her nostrils quivered as she stepped up, entered the hot stinking shadowy ruin, and took in the scene, breathing the metallic smell of blood, drinking in the blood lust, the caked, clotted remains of slaughter. She half closed her eyes. I could have done this! I could have torn the bus apart, decapitated the driver, and ripped those kids limb from limb – but I don't do such things, no, I don't, I don't, I never have, and I never will kill such innocence – except … except in self-defense. She bit her lip. She fought back the hunger, the desire, the yearning. She could sense the presence of the hybrid, clearly a product of her DNA. Yes, he was her brother, her double, her mirror, but created and nurtured by an evil genius. This alien-human *hybrid* had become – well, he was – a monster, an unrestrained killer; my brother, my son, my love, and – myself … The male version of me, designed to kill.

Why was he doing what he was doing?

Why kill like this?

Who created him and why?

She sensed that, behind the hybrid, there was something much deeper, more powerful: a dark vortex, a transcendent malignant presence, brooding, waiting, and, again, behind that – there was true darkness, a dark god, *the* Dark God, infinite darkness: evil, something evil: Supreme Evil.

Usually, she could decipher mental currents – this she could not decipher. It was mindless, a barrier.

ACKNOWLEDGMENTS

Thanks to the many people who made the *Adventures of V: Return of the Goddess* possible: Adrienne Clarkson, Andra Sheffer, André Kirchberger, Anna Porter, Bernice Landry, Bernie Lucht, Beverly Topping, Bob Ramsay, Chuck Shamata, Claudia Neri, Denise Jacques, Diana Leblanc, Diane Shamata, Dianne Rinehart, Dorothy Vreeker, Duncan Derry, Ed Cowan, Elena Solari, Florence Treadwell, Heather Reid, Irene Spampinato, Irene Tudisco, Jacqueline Baker, Jacqueline Park, Jacqueline Swartz, Janie Yoon, Jennifer Hambleton, Jennifer Puncher, Jim Downs, John McGreevy, John Pearce, John Ralston Saul, Josephine Khu, Jules Cashford, Julia Belluz, Julia Hambleton, Marie-Christine Dunham-Pratt, Mark Fenwick, Martine Matus Siebert, Norm Barber, Norm Christie, Nuala Fitzgerald, Paola Pugliatti, Peter Williamson, Ramsay Derry, Sandra Martin, Simona Barabesi, Susan Mahoney, Susan S. Senstad, Tony Robinow, Trisha Jackson, Wendy Trueman, and many others too numerous to name. I owe an infinite number of literary debts, too, but in particular to Joyce Carol Oates, Justin Cronin, and Stephen King.

TITLES IN THE
ADVENTURES OF V

WORKS BY
GILBERT REID

SHORT STORIES
So This is Love: Lollipop and Other Stories
Lava and Other stories

GRAZIA SERIES
Son of Two Fathers (with Jacqueline Park)

ADVENTURES OF V
Vampire vs Vatican
Vampire Clone
Pandemic Book 1: Party Balloons
Pandemic Book 2: The Gateway
Extinction Book 1: Girl with the Golden Eyes
Extinction Book 2: Revolt of the Angels
Extinction Book 3: Elysium

GWENDOLINE SERIES
By Gwendoline
The Shaming of Gwendoline C
Gwendoline Goes to School
Gwendoline Goes Underground

To receive a free book or novella
And to learn more about V and get notes on writing and other topics:

Sign up at

https://gilbertreid.com

Please write a short review!
Just two or three lines.
And post it to Goodreads or Amazon
or any other book group you may belong to.

Or send it to me!
At: gilbert@gilbertreid.com

GILBERT REID is the author of two short story collections: *So This is Love: Lollipop and Other Stories* (2004, 2019) and *Lava and Other Stories* (2019). He also co-authored, with Jacqueline Park, the historical novel *Son of Two Fathers* (2019). He has written extensively for television and radio. Most notably he researched, wrote, and narrated two five-hour radio series: *Gilbert Reid's Italy* and *Gilbert Reid's France* for CBC's flagship radio program IDEAS. His many television series include *Paths of the Gods*, *For King and Empire*, *For King and Country*, and *Sir Peter Ustinov in Burma: Road to Mandalay*. After thirty years in Europe working as an economist, university lecturer, diplomat, script doctor, journalist, and adventure travel guide, Gilbert now lives in Toronto.